I0736361

Glass Owl

Glass Owl

**A Serialized Novel by
Wesley Adams and Daphne McGee**

**Book 1 of the Soap Opera Inspired Story Collection
Series Created by Gary Brin**

Episodes 1-25

Part 1

Standish Press

The serialized story in this novel is fiction. Real persons, geographical locations, books, television shows, films, music, and specific events mentioned or which appears as part of the multi-character ensemble in this story were dramatized for entertainment purposes only and have no actual connection to fictional characters and created storylines in this book or reflects upon actual reality of things that may have happened previously or of which seems somewhat similar to real-life situations.

Names of real people mentioned in this book are in bold letters.

Comments about true crime cases involving real people mentioned by fictional characters within the pages of this novel are based on fact and additional information about these events can be found online and in published books.

Additional comments made by fictional characters about historical figures or pop culture icons are based on fact and more info can be found on select Internet sites as well as books and magazines published by reputable publishing companies.

Cover photograph courtesy of Wikimedia Commons.
Cover photograph was digitally enhanced and visually altered for this edition.
Cover design and book layout © 2020 by Standish Press

FIRST EDITION

Copyright © 2020 by Standish Press

All rights reserved. No part of this book may be reproduced by any means whatsoever without written permission from the publisher.

For more information about reprint rights please visit
www.standishpress.com

ISBN—978-1-945510-00-7

MANUFACTURED IN THE UNITED STATES OF AMERICA

To the dedicated writers who wrote scripts for daytime soap
operas from the 1950s to the 1990s.

____

Writing is hard work.

Contents

Intro

In the tradition of popular daytime soap opera classics such as *All My Children, Another World, As the World Turns, Capitol, Days of Our Lives, Doctors, Edge of Night, General Hospital, Guiding Light, Love of Life, Loving, One Life to Live, Passions, Santa Barbara, Search for Tomorrow, Secret Storm* and the *Young and the Restless* as well as such memorable prime time soap classics as *Bare Essence, Berrenger's, Colbys, Dallas, Deception, Dynasty, Emerald Point NAS, Falcon Crest, Flamingo Road, For Love and Honor, Grand Hotel, Knots Landing, Pacific Palisades, Paper Dolls, Pasadena, Peyton Place, Savannah* and *Yellow Rose* comes *Glass Owl*—an original, modern episodic serialized novel (published in two parts in script format) set in a small, sleepy southern Maine town where nothing is what it seems to the unsuspecting daily visitor—but where every lurid secret has an unpleasant price for those directly involved.

Glass Owl was originally conceived in late 2012 as an extended serialized novel that would focus on the lives of citizens in a small town in New England. The real-life picturesque village of Camden, Maine was used as the inspiration for Marble Hills but the drama and people populating the storyline in *Glass Owl* bears no resemblance to anyone who lives in Camden or who has lived there previous. Initially the idea for this novel was to create a dramatic saga using similar storylines of beloved long-ago soaps, but present-day events from local news and pop culture scandals were instead used to make the serialized writing more realistic. And while silly plotlines of long-cancelled soap operas which relied on outlandish storylines in order to hold their audience for decades were avoided, several references are made in *Glass Owl* about serials such as *Passions*—which aired on NBC and went as far as daytime dramas were allowed to go—as a way to poke fun at how ridiculous its storylines actually got during its initial run before it was cancelled. But that said—despite its connection with daytime soap operas and prime time dramas such as *Knots Landing* which aired for fourteen seasons on CBS—*Glass Owl* was specifically written to resemble a filmed YouTube web drama series and though it occasionally imitates traditional classic soap operas to a certain extent—it was written with the intention that it is playing to a visual audience and therefore will emulate a scripted format (without camera angle directions) rather than the usual storytelling methods displayed in such popular full-length novels as *Gone with the Wind* and *Scruples*. It should also be noted that each episode of this series were written in a relative brief span of 6-12 days or less and therefore shouldn't be confused with being great literature by any means. The goal of this upcoming series of serialized books from Standish Press was simply to mimic the episode style of modern-day soap operas that remain popular decades after they were cancelled—or the filmed YouTube web series episodic dramas created by upcoming filmmakers—by creating visual entertainment on a printed page instead and not to create a definitive literary masterpiece.

Glass Owl was initially written as a standalone novel but was later reimagined as the pilot episode for a collection of serialized novels featuring characters that would move from book to book, continuing unfinished storylines from previous novels in the series—and while this novel does have some elements of a filmed soap opera it ignores many of the tired plotlines that have been a staple of daytime television for more than half a century such as long-dead characters coming back to life with lame explanations as to their supposed demise years previous in order to justify a unnecessary rehiring of a popular soap opera actor—or having established characters travel through time where fantasy replaces reality as credible actors seemed to be held captive against their will as they spout bad dialogue written by people who actually thought time travel was a good story idea despite the fact of its unrealistic plausibility. In steering clear of such foolish missteps undertaken by below average soap opera writers from the past—the serialized stories in this book were not only created to hopefully entertain an audience familiar with soap opera storytelling but also to tell a story of people everyone knows or have known at some point in their lives by melding as much real life situations as possible into a fictional tapestry.

Gary Brin
Series Creator

In an effort to have an accurate portrayal of the dialogue used for the *Soap Opera Inspired Story Collection Series* people were anonymously observed in shopping malls, schools, places of employment, and on public streets in order to capture a definitive portrayal of how people of various ages and cultures interacted and talked to each other when they thought no one was listening. While some select dialogue was exaggerated for dramatic purposes when needed—the manner and tone of which people were observed speaking to each other in casual and private conversations is accurate. Exact wording was not copied verbatim for the most part, but the way certain types of topics and conversations are addressed by characters in this serialized series is based on actual situations that were observed over a period of several dozen years.

A Look at the 1st Episode

Alden Washington returns to his hometown after a successful career in Hollywood believing the long-forgotten tragedy that devastated his life—and the lives of so many others years before was no longer an issue for everyone involved. But he couldn't be more wrong as even more devastating secrets from the past and present threaten to destroy the seemingly perfect lives of every single resident and visitor in this scenic New England village.

Mind Games

The Return

Alden Washington looks up at the huge mansion that looms majestically in front of him from the estate gates a short distance away. It hadn't changed one bit. It had been eighteen years, yet it was almost as if time stood still when it came to the appearance of the stately Victorian building. He smiles. He'd had some good times playing on the estate grounds when he was young. But then—then came the "event." It changed everything for him and so many others of which he was sure probably hadn't gotten over what happened that fateful night in June following his graduation from high school. He turns to walk away just as a silver-colored car drives up. He recognizes the driver instantly. It is his childhood friend—Kyle Madison—eldest son of the richest man in town and resident of Glass Owl—the magnificent mansion of which he was admiring only a few brief minutes before.

"What the fuck are you doing back here?"

Alden slowly turns to face Kyle. He notices a teenage boy sitting in the passenger seat of Kyle's car. Alden turns away.

"How dare you show your face here again?"

Kyle stops the car at the entrance of the winding driveway. He seems to be in shock as he sees Alden standing a few feet away. He hops out and charges toward Alden with his fists ready—almost as if to settle an old score from the past.

"I asked you a question motherfucker—what are you doing back in Marble Hills—after what you did to my sister?"

Alden glances at the mansion at the end of the driveway again. Suddenly Kyle violently grabs Alden by the neck and spins him around. He doesn't react which upsets Kyle even more.

"I ought to break your neck."

They look at each other coldly but say nothing. Kyle seems irritated by Alden's stubborn stare and looks away.

"You should have stayed gone."

The door to Kyle's car opens and the teenage boy jumps out. Alden watches as he pulls something shiny from the front pocket of his Levi's. He comes toward them in a frenzied rush.

"Want me to work him over, dad? Got the knuckles with me—could easily crack his head open—and spill his brains."

Kyle glances at Alden and then at his son.

"No—I got this under control."

Alden watches as Kyle's son casually shoves the pair of brass knuckles back into the front pocket of his Levi's. Kyle faces Alden again—glaring at him silently for a few seconds with confused anger. Alden looks away for a moment and sighs.

"I want you gone—you have ten minutes to get into your car and disappear like you did eighteen years ago after you killed Marah. Go away and never come back here—or I swear."

Alden glances at the mansion again.

"Who died and made you God? Last time I checked this town was still part—part of the state of Maine—so deal."

Kyle sighs loudly and looks back at where his son is standing with his hands in the front pockets of his jeans.

"Why *are* you here? It's not like you have any family left to visit—they left long ago—so why are you back in town?"

Alden glances again at the teenage boy.

"That's for me to know—and you to find out."

Kyle watches as Alden silently turns to walk toward where his rented car is parked several yards away. Kyle continues to glare at Alden angrily as his son watches his odd reaction.

"Get out of Marble Hills or else."

Alden turns and flips his middle finger at Kyle as he gets into his car. Kyle angrily turns to look at his son who seems slightly confused at the situation playing out in front of him.

"Who *was* that guy?"

"He—*he* was my best friend."

Wesley Madison runs his fingers through his hair.

"*That* was Alden Washington?"

"Yep—exactly—son of a bitch is back."

They look at each other.

"Why didn't you let me beat the crap out of him?"

Kyle shakes his head.

"You've already had two brushes with the law because of your aggressive behavior from here to Boston. Want a third?"

Wesley glares at his father and then turns to face the majestic mansion at the end of the long tree-lined driveway.

Pete's Cafe

Several customers move about the narrow aisles among several rows of chairs and tables of a small diner as Alden enters through the front door. He notices the crowd carefully as he walks toward a woman standing behind the counter at the far right of the front door. A few people look up at him but say nothing. As he approaches, the woman looks up and smiles.

"Oh my God—I can't believe it."

She seems frozen in shock.

"It's you—*it's really you*—I can't believe it."

Alden seems confused as he looks at the woman who seems to know him from somewhere. He becomes uneasy.

"*Channing Harwick.*"

Alden manages a slight smile.

"Guilty as charged."

"Those idiot network people shouldn't have killed you off *Larkspur Lane* last year. Seriously—having your character fall off a cliff and simply disappear in a thick fog—it was *so* 1980s."

Alden laughs.

"Budget cuts—at least that's what they told me."

He waves his hand in the air.

"I was on quite a long time—I guess it was time to move on to other roles. There's just so much you can do with the same character over a period of several years—a decade can really push the limits to what storylines will still seem believable."

The woman sighs loudly.

"Doesn't matter—they're still idiots. I swear these fools have the business sense of a dead squid. I still haven't forgiven them for canceling *As the World Turns* and *One Life to Life*. I mean, like seriously, those shows had the best writing up to when they were cancelled. What were they thinking? Daytime soaps are dead to me now—since you left *Larkspur Lane* last year I've tuned out completely. I watch reruns on YouTube whenever I can—but nothing new like I once did previous. I'm done."

Alden notices as the woman smiles slyly and leans closer to him—she looks around briefly and whispers in his ear.

"I miss seeing how your character would get into trouble and then lie his way out of whatever situation he had gotten himself into that week—but you were such a dog—you always seemed to end up in bed with your sister-in-law who was obviously a whore with no class—an unfaithful wife that brought so much shame to her family. Sleeping with her husband's twin brother had to be the lowest. How could she? Especially in the limo on the way to her own wedding—minutes before she took her vows—excuse me—but there's nothing lower a woman like that can do—it was just despicable. What was she thinking? By the way I *never* bought the story that she didn't know which twin she was sleeping with. The two of you were nothing alike. Your twin brother was a shy geek and you were a sly, promiscuous stud. Like hello, you bedded her again right after the wedding as well as her two trampy friends. You even trolled the local high school and nearby colleges looking for easy conquests. I swear you couldn't keep it in your pants long enough. You just had to have every woman in town, didn't you? Bragging that you could only know a woman after you've slept with her—of whom once you had your way with you'd drop them like an old shoe and immediately bed someone else. And then of course there was that really messy baby situation a few months later with your sister-in-law—seriously, how could you do that to your own brother who had helped you get through college and looked up to you—to this day no one knows who's the actual daddy—you or your geeky twin brother? That was when stories were really written well and had bite to them—storylines now are dull."

Alden grins broadly and gestures with his hand.

"It was a good ride—but it's over. I'm just an unemployed actor hoping I don't end up homeless by the end of next year."

Alden watches curiously as a broad grin slowly spreads across the face of the excited woman he just met seconds ago.

"Do you need a place to stay?"

He nods.

"It depends."

Suddenly a massive gust of wind whistles through the front door as several fishermen lazily stroll toward where Alden is standing at the front counter. The distinct smell of dead fish immediately permeates the small restaurant completely as the door closes shut. Several people quickly get up and walk out.

<u>Port Clyde</u>

"You're definitely not a boy anymore."

Corey Bentley laughs.

"Glad we hooked up today, aren't you?"

Denise Madison smiles and kisses Corey as her finger slides across his lips. She kisses him again several more times.

"Your persistence paid off nicely."

Corey reaches out and pulls Denise toward him and kisses her passionately again. He grins as they look at each other.

"Should I tell my girlfriend about us?"
Denise slides her fingers across Corey's erection.
"Not a good idea by any means."
Corey smirks.
"I don't see why though—she knows I've been cheating on her—knows I'm not boyfriend material—knows I'm a dog."
Corey sits up in bed.
"The way I see it if I want to have sex with someone I should be able to. It's my dick—if I want to stick—I should."
Denise sits up in bed and seems worried.
"Wesley wouldn't understand."
Corey laughs slyly.
"He'd kill me if he found out I was doing his mother on the sly—kill me and not think twice about it either—uh-huh."
Denise looks at the wedding ring on her finger.
"More importantly what would Kyle do if he found out I was sleeping with his son's best friend behind his back?"
She looks at her wedding ring again.

<u>Bradford Beach</u>

Abby Marshall slowly walks toward her best friend Gina Bentley as she lazily kicks sand with her feet while she stands at the edge of the surf. The beach is narrow with a large row of jagged rocks on the right side bordering dense woods nearby.
"Do you think your brother is still cheating on me—even though he says he's been faithful for over a month now?"
Gina turns to face Abby and shrugs.
"I warned you about Corey."
She sighs loudly.
"My brother is a slug—plain and simple."
Abby seems upset at Gina's comment and turns away.
"I like him. I can't help how I feel."
"Have you forgotten already about Genie and Shirley—or about Lana, Natalie, Daphne, Corinne and Elizabeth?"
Gina makes a lewd gesture with her finger and sighs.

Page 20

"With my brother it's not who he's slept with, it's who he hasn't slept with. Let's face it he's banged a lot of girls."

Abby sits down on a nearby sand dune.

"But he promised?"

Gina shakes her head several times.

"And you believed him? Come on, my brother lies all the time—endlessly. Believe me I know—lying is his best game."

Gina sits down next to Abby.

"Once he told my parents that he was going to Brad McKinley's house to study for an exam. Guess what? They found him in bed with Corinne Massey less than one hour later."

Gina waves her hand in the air and sighs loudly.

"Do you know what his excuse was Abby? He said that he accidentally fell on top of her—and then blamed her for what happened—said she seduced him—like really—such lies."

Gina wags her finger knowingly.

"Does that sound like someone who you should trust when it comes to whether or not he's sleeping with half the town? I mean, don't get me wrong with what I'm saying, I love my brother dearly—but he's sleazy—a total toad—garbage."

Abby stares at the ocean as tears come to her eyes.

"But he said this time was different?"

Gina puts her arms around Abby.

"You're not the first and you certainly won't be the last to fall for his charms—my brother has a way about him when it comes to women. It all started with our babysitter. Corey lost his virginity to her. He was twelve at the time. My parents came back from dinner and found him in their bed having sex with our twenty-one year old babysitter. But that's not the worst part of this story—seems the whore wasn't smart enough to be on the pill—and of course Corey wasn't using a condom that night."

Gina suddenly seems upset and shrugs.

"Anyway, to make a long story short—she got pregnant and our parents freaked out. Neither of them knew what to do. Luckily the problem went away quickly when they found out the babysitter had a quickie abortion—or so we thought at first."

Abby seems upset and sighs loudly.

"She had the baby?"

Gina nods.

"He's four. He lives in St. Thomas with his mother."

Abby seems stunned by the news.

"Corey never told me about any of this?"

Gina laughs loudly.

"It's not exactly the kind of thing he'd want to talk about with his virginal girlfriend. That—and, well, our parents insisted this unfortunate mess never be mentioned publicly again."

They look at each other.

"That's why I never told you before."

Abby seems confused.

"Didn't your family own a villa on St. Thomas?"

"We did—but we haven't been back there since on account that filthy whore lives at the villa now. My father paid off the babysitter to keep her mouth shut about Corey and what happened between them. She threatened to go public if my father didn't do what she wanted. She played us like fools."

They look at each other. Abby twirls the edges of her hair for a few seconds. She faces Gina again and sighs loudly.

"I just don't know if I can stop seeing your brother. He's got—he's got this hold over me—he told me I'm special."

Gina rolls her eyes in disgust and looks around. Abby seems uneasy at Gina's behavior. She sighs loudly again.

"You can do better."

"Do you really think so?"

Gina stands up.

"I do—I do."

She pulls Abby to her feet and glances at her car in a distance. Gina points at the car and snaps her fingers.

"I think you need a break from Corey."

She snaps her fingers again.

"Come on—let's go to the mall—I hear there's a really cute guy working at the new ice cream kiosk as of last week."

Abby follows Gina toward her car.

<u>Pete's Cafe</u>

Alden watches as the group of fishermen sit down at the adjacent counter. One of the men glances at him curiously for a few seconds. He begins grinning broadly soon afterwards.

"I can't believe it. I really can't believe it."

Alden looks blankly at the fisherman.

"Alden Washington you've got some nerve showing your face back in Marble Hills—but hell, I always liked you. Screw those scummy Madisons and all their ill-gotten money."

Alden looks at the fisherman somewhat confused as the man takes his cap off and moves closer to him. He blinks a few times trying desperately to remember the smelly fisherman.

"It's me Alden—*Todd*—Todd Spencer."

Alden shakes his head.

<u>Police Station</u>

The front door suddenly swings open loudly as police chief Daryl Anderson looks up from his desk situated in the corner of a large one-room station. He seems annoyed and sighs loudly.

"Ever heard of knocking Madison?"

"We have a problem Anderson—a very big problem."

Daryl seems bored and yawns loudly.

"If this is about Wesley's parking ticket from last week I'm tuning you out as of this second—your rebel son is a menace."

Kyle shuts the door.

"Forget about Wesley—try Alden Washington."

Daryl seems confused.

"Doesn't he live somewhere in Southern California—Los Angeles I think—in Pasadena I believe? Last I heard he was an actor or something—on some soap opera if I got it right?"

"He's back. The bastard who killed my sister and got away with it all those years ago—is back—back in Marble Hills."

Silence spreads across the room.

Page **23**

<u>Port Clyde</u>

Denise walks over to Corey as he grabs his boxer briefs and slides her fingers across his exposed penis and winks. He grins broadly as she slowly licks her fingers seductively.

"Tomorrow—same time—same place—OK?"

Denise kisses him lightly.

"Don't forget to bring plenty of condoms."

She kisses him again passionately. He laughs.

"I swear if Wesley knew I was sticking his mother for the second time—he'd blow my brains out for sure—yeah."

Denise grins broadly.

"Can I help it if I find his handsome best friend absolutely intoxicating? There's just something about you—no doubt."

Corey makes a lewd gesture with his finger.

"You're on the pill, right?"

Denise smirks.

"*Of course*—like really—condoms aren't a sure thing by any means—do you think I would ever risk becoming pregnant by my son's best friend—imagine how scandalous the talk."

Corey laughs and kisses Denise again.

"Good—wouldn't want to have to explain myself."

"You and me both—Kyle would kill me."

Denise and Corey kiss passionately once more.

<u>Mall</u>

Abby and Gina enter and look around. Mall groupies are scattered throughout the enclosed shopping area. Gina grins broadly as she sees an ice cream kiosk several yards away.

"God, he's hot—so, so hot."

Abby turns to look where Gina's attention suddenly seems to be focused. She notices a teenage boy standing at the kiosk nearby. Gina begins walking toward the kiosk in a mad rush.

"I wonder if he's experienced."

Page 24

She licks her lips and faces Abby.

"Don't matter much anyway as far as I'm concerned if he isn't—he won't be for long—I'll make sure of it—guaranteed."

Gina laughs again as Abby rolls her eyes.

"*What?*"

Abby stops.

"You're planning to sleep with him aren't you?"

Gina rolls her eyes.

"Uh-huh—unless if he's gay and digs banging buff dudes."

Gina gestures with her hand.

"Then—I'll introduce him to Tyler Van Pelt."

"Tyler's gay?"

Gina nods. Abby seems confused.

"I guess that would explain the comment he made to the science teacher last month—complimenting his tight pants."

"Took you that long to figure it out?"

They stop a few yards away from the kiosk.

"I wonder if he's circumcised."

Abby rolls her eyes.

"Is his dick all you can think about?"

Gina grins broadly.

"Pretty much—yeah—you bet."

They slowly approach the kiosk. The teenage boy stops wiping the counter as he notices them and smiles shyly.

"Hi. Can I help you?"

Abby watches as Gina moves closer to the kiosk making sure her breasts are clearly visible under her tight designer lace sweater. She smiles knowingly as the teenage boy notices right away. Abby turns away with a disgusted look on her face.

"You're new in town, aren't you?"

Abby watches as the teenage boy nods.

"Just moved here from Augusta a week ago—my dad got a job with the local paper—he's the new associate editor."

Gina glances at Abby briefly and then turns around again in disgust at Gina's bold behavior toward Kelly Nelson.

"Do you have a girlfriend?"

Abby slowly turns around to see the teenage boy give Gina a weird look. He seems nervous and sighs loudly.

"Why are you asking?"

"Like why do you think I'm asking? I want to ask you out."

Abby watches as a grin spreads across the teenage boy's face. He seems to really be enjoying the sudden attention.

"I don't have a girlfriend at the moment."

Kelly gives Gina a knowing look.

"I've been flying solo since I moved to Marble Hills."

Abby glances at the teenage boy. He appears to be waiting for another question from Gina. Gina glances at Abby and grins. She faces the teenage boy again—her attention focusing on his snug-fitting pants at this point. A few seconds later he offers his hand nervously as he looks at Abby. She sighs.

"Kelly Nelson."

"Gina Bentley."

Gina turns to face Abby again.

"This is my best friend Abby Marshall. We've been friends like forever. She's dating my toady twin brother by the way."

Kelly offers Abby his hand. They shake.

"It's nice to meet you Abby."

Kelly continues looking at Abby as Gina notices.

"Likewise—welcome to Marble Hills."

Gina suddenly pushes Abby out of the way and focuses her attention on Kelly again. She grins slyly and winks at Kelly.

"So, how about it—do you want to go out with me or not? Marble Hills is a small town—not much choices out there."

Kelly seems uneasy.

"I guess."

Kelly glances at Abby.

"I've never had a girl ask me out before."

Gina grins slyly again.

"There's a first time for everything—especially in Marble Hills. I'll meet you in front of the mall in three hours—OK?"

Gina pretends to kiss Kelly on the lips then pulls away. He grins broadly. Abby notices his behavior. Gina rolls her eyes.

"Bring a package of condoms with you. I don't do guys that think condoms are too much trouble. I like the ribbed ones in case you were wondering. They slide much better if you must know—allows the guy to stay harder much longer—I'm all about stamina—so deal already. I don't find limp dicks appealing."

Gina licks her lips several times.

"If you're really good in bed I'll blow you as well."

Abby reacts as Kelly looks at her curiously.

Boston

Loud screeching of tires can be heard as a man spins around to face a car approaching him in a deserted parking lot. Seconds later two well-dressed men immediately step out. He nervously looks around for a place to hide. But there's none.

"Madison—where *is* our money?"

"I—I—I'll have it tomorrow. I've just got to call a few friends that owe me money—I promise I'll have it. I swear."

They edge closer.

"Seems we heard that one before?"

One of them glances back at the parked car.

"So have Whitney."

The frightened man's eyes dart around nervously.

"I'll have it tomorrow. No more excuses."

"Talk is cheap—time to pay up."

"But I just said?"

"We want it now—or else."

Greg Madison looks at the two men nervously.

"What are you going to do to me? I mean?"

Greg watches as the men laugh.

"I think you already know exactly how Whitney deals with problems like you—I hope you have your affairs in order."

"I'll pay Whitney back—really I will."

Greg glances nervously at the car parked a few feet away and then at the stairwell nearby. Without warning he dashes to the stairwell and leaps down the narrow stairs in a panic.

"Get him already—kill the bastard."

The two men follow closely but soon lose him halfway down. He makes it to the street and looks back at the stairwell behind him. He sighs loudly and mingles into the pedestrian traffic on the sidewalk within a few seconds and disappears.

Pete's Cafe

Alden seems confused. Todd grins.

"Todd Spencer?"

He looks closely at the fisherman dressed in overalls.

"Is it really you? But I assumed?"

"I guess I wasn't what you expected after all these years. I bragged to everyone I was going to be a big shot lawyer."

He laughs.

"I had a crisis of character in New York City a few years after my college years were a distant memory—so I decided to let it all go and came back here to Marble Hills for a simpler life with the wife and kid—been here ever since. I love it. It's great."

Todd glances around the cafe.

"Yep, came back and bought a fishing boat. It may not seem the best career choice to most people but I enjoy it. Got ten boats and one hundred employees—life is sweet—charmed."

"Cool."

Todd looks around.

"Hey, I'm off for the day—how about you come by my place later to catch up—say, in about an hour or so? If you want to come by now that's OK as well—the wife will just love it and you and I can catch up on old times like I mentioned—definitely want to know about you bedding chicks all over Hollywood."

Alden seems embarrassed at the comment and laughs nervously. He runs his fingers through his hair and sighs.

"It was nothing really—most of it was just tabloid fodder."

Todd gestures with his hand.

"*I bet*—once you scored a tight piece what else was there to stick around for—time to move on and hit another mark."

Page **28**

Todd winks slyly.

"I know how it works buddy—every guy in Hollywood is a player—he's got to be in order to keep interest—or else."

Todd casually makes a slashing gesture across his neck.

"If you begin to bore the tabloids you're done."

Alden notices more and more people nearby seem to be listening to their conversation. He seems slightly uneasy.

"Where do you live?"

"101 North Maple—it's right behind."

Alden smirks.

"Right behind the orphanage where Eddie Kane used to live—had bright red hair—and a nasty temper to match."

"Exactly—by the way Kane is now the owner of a mall here in town—seems he made good regardless despite the odds. He was a street fighter—took no crap from anyone. Who would've ever thought Eddie Kane would end up being almost as filthy rich as frigging Kyle Madison and his miserable stuck-up family?"

Alden reacts slightly to the mentioning of Kyle Madison's name of which Todd notices briefly but says nothing as he continues talking about Kyle and his dysfunctional family.

"Madison may have all the money in the world, but I swear—I swear he has more problems than God. His son, well, he's trouble with a capital T. The kid can't seem to avoid getting himself into one huge mess after another. My own kid seems to think he's cool. I can't remember how many times I've had to tell Simon to stay away from Wesley Madison. But does he ever listen—absolutely not. Does what he wants, whenever he feels like it. I'm not sure where I went wrong in my deal with him."

Todd notices Alden's reaction and sighs loudly.

"Being a dad is hard work. I never know when I'm making a mistake until it's too late—then I catch serious hell for it. Simon is really tough on me when I let him down. He holds grudges."

He shakes his head several times.

"But enough of me—come over later and we'll catch up on when we both had zero problems except remembering to wear condoms when we banged our way through high school."

Alden seems uneasy and sighs.

"I'll be there."

Todd slaps Alden gently on the back.

"I don't have a mansion but it's cozy—nice."

At that moment Daryl walks into the diner. He slowly heads toward Alden quietly without saying a word as people begin whispering to each other as he silently passes them by.

Mall

Abby and Gina are sitting at one of the open cafe booths situated inside the mall. Abby seems oddly quiet as she stares at people walking by. Gina notices and grabs Abby's hand.

"What's up with you?"

"I can't believe you talked that way to a total stranger? Did you see the way he looked at you? He was royally shocked."

Gina grins broadly.

"Big deal—guys like it when girls take the lead and make a pass at them like I did—poor guy—just needs to get laid."

"I bet."

Gina rolls her eyes.

"You don't have to take my word for it."

Gina makes a lewd gesture with her finger and winks.

"I know what guys like."

Abby glances at Kelly standing at the kiosk tending to several female customers. She seems upset and sighs.

"He probably thinks you're a whore."

"I have been with a lot of guys as you know—one of which was your hot cousin Jarod Keller—who is a stud by the way—he should pose nude online if truth be known. He's gorgeous."

Abby seems disgusted by Gina's comment.

"Like I could forget—I'm the one who was unlucky enough to find the two of you together in the backseat of his girlfriend's car having extremely noisy sex the afternoon before last year's prom—seeing the two of you do it like a couple of animals in heat gave me serious nightmares for weeks—ugh, like so gross."

Page **30**

"He's a looker—just deal with it already. He's magic in the sack by the way—pure magic. I give him five stars easily."

Abby rolls her eyes and then makes a gagging gesture.

"As you recall his girlfriend was none too pleased when she found out Jarod had fucked you in the backseat of her car and then tried to pretend it wasn't what it seemed. I remember she threatened to kill you with her bare hands that night—and tried twice. If it wasn't for Daryl Anderson you'd be at Crestview."

Gina laughs again.

"That's why she's at Marshland right now. She completely lost it—like total wacko. Serves her right—sick freak."

Gina grins slyly and licks her lips.

"Jarod called me last week by the way—said when he comes back in a week or so from Edwards College he and I are definitely going to hook-up a lot while he's here in town."

Abby seems uneasy.

"What about Kelly Nelson?"

"What about him?"

Abby glances at Kelly again.

"Are you really going to make a play for him?"

"Why not—he's a really good-looking guy—but probably inexperienced—he seems like it actually—but no worries—I'm determined. I'll add him to my list just because he's a serious challenge—experienced or not—I've just got to have him."

Abby notices Kelly talking to a teenage girl.

"Apparently, you're not the only one in Marble Hills who has her eye on Kelly. Seems he's quite the magnet. Look."

Gina turns to look at Kelly. She seems upset.

"How dare her."

She clenches her fists.

"*That bitch*. The nerve of her—I hate that slut. I really hate her. I swear Tiffany Johnson is always trying to crash my party. She thinks every guy I'm interested in is fair game for her slutty motives. Ugh—she's really trying to get on my bad side—make me do something she'll regret in the worst way. If I had a gun I'd shoot that trashy whore dead—bang—end her right now."

Abby smiles as she sees Kelly writing Tiffany's number down on a piece of paper. Gina seems livid with anger.

Boston

Eldon Whitney turns away from the huge window that looks down on the enormous city below and faces the two men nervously entering his office slowly. He seems visibly upset.

"Well? What the fuck happened in the parking lot?"

The two men look at each other.

"He got away."

"You dopes let him go?"

Eldon wipes his face with a washcloth and shrugs.

"What the fuck do I pay you idiots for?"

They look at each other again.

"He got the slip on us and pulled a disappearing act. It wasn't our fault—dude is slippery—seemed to be expecting us."

Eldon angrily slams his fist down on the desk nearby in a rage. He walks over to Carlo Rogers and Duane Pyle.

"Find him or else—do you hear me—I want that lying backstabbing weasel dead—or else I'll be forced to call Juan."

Carlo and Duane look at each other nervously.

"We know that loser has family in southern Maine—he probably went back to—went back there to hide out."

"Don't care. Find him and put a damn bullet in his head."

Eldon glances at the two men closely.

"Do you idiots hear me loud and clear—I want that worthless piece of trash on a slab in the morgue like yesterday or I guarantee both of you that your empty skulls will be used for target practice by your dear friend Sabrillo from Santiago."

Eldon smiles as he sees their panicked looks at the specific mentioning of Juan Sabrillo's name. He grins slyly.

"Yeah—that's right. If he has to come all the way from Santiago to clean up your mess—I guess I don't have to tell you what that would mean for you two moronic clowns. Dear Juan still had it out for you guys after what happened in Miami."

"We'll take care of Madison. He's as good as dead—we know where he's hiding—it'll be easy as pie to get to him."

Eldon smiles knowingly and wags his finger at Carlo and Duane as he makes a threatening gesture with his finger.

"Good—just so we understand each other when it comes to Madison and his impending fate. Nevertheless, to make the deal sweeter, if you two queens want to have some *extra fun and games* with Madison before you rub out that lousy son of a bitch once and for all—feel free to play—I won't ask and I won't tell."

Eldon laughs loudly.

"Beat him up first—then fuck him—whatever—but kill the bastard—I won't ask for details and I certainly won't tell anyone what you two do for thrills—I just want Madison on a slab."

Carlo smiles slyly and faces Duane.

"It's as good as done."

Eldon seems pleased and sighs.

<u>Stanley Pier</u>

Wesley sits down on a wooden bench at the wharf and looks out toward the sea. He glances at his watch briefly and then notices Corey walking toward him from the parking lot.

"What's up?"

Wesley stands up.

"I've got a favor to ask."

He digs his hands into the front pockets of his Levi's and smirks. Wesley slowly takes a step forward and grins.

"How would you like to help me beat somebody up?"

Corey looks at Wesley curiously.

"I thought we both decided to leave Ashton Markway alone for the time being—especially since his dad said?"

"This isn't about that loser Markway."

Wesley seems enraged.

"Markway will get what's coming to him soon enough. I have someone else in mind. Someone who needs to be taught a lesson that he won't forget anytime soon—hardcore justice."

Page 33

Corey grins slyly.

"Oh really—do tell? I'm intrigued."

"It's about the man who killed my aunt years ago."

"I thought he was in Los Angeles?"

"He was—*until today*."

"What do you have in mind?"

Wesley grins broadly.

"I was hoping you'd ask me that."

Corey watches as Wesley pulls out his cell phone.

<u>Mall</u>

Abby watches as Gina angrily walks up to where Tiffany is standing as she flirts with Kelly at the ice cream kiosk.

"*You bitch*—you'd think that taking Caleb Winthrop away from me was enough for you—you've got some nerve."

Tiffany turns to look at Gina.

"Excuse me?"

Abby watches the confused reaction on Kelly's face as Gina and Tiffany glare at each other for several seconds.

"You knew I liked him."

Tiffany rolls her eyes and turns away.

"I didn't take Caleb away from you. He said he was done with you when we hooked up last year before the prom at Lake Smythe. How was I supposed to know he was lying to me?"

Tiffany gestures with her hand.

"How was I supposed to know he was really horny and just wanted to get laid that day? I mean, let's face it, if you were any kind of a girlfriend to him he wouldn't have been looking in my direction for an extra slice of entertainment, would he?"

Tiffany watches Gina's reaction and smirks.

"Oh—oh my—such wonderful memories—Caleb Winthrop couldn't keep his hands off me that day in case you were wondering—and if you hadn't interrupted us we would've done it a fourth time—he was still so hard even after three—oh my."

Tiffany slides her tongue across her lips.

Page 34

"Did I tell you I also gave him a blowjob that day?"

Gina slaps Tiffany. Tiffany reacts in shock.

"Caleb told me you seduced him that day and not the other way around. He said you wouldn't leave him alone."

Tiffany waves her hand in the air.

"Believe what you like."

She licks her lips again and smirks.

"Caleb and I are still quite close if you must know."

Gina seems about to slap Tiffany again as a few people walk by with stern looks on their faces. Abby rolls her eyes.

"People are gonna talk no doubt."

Kelly seems mildly amused by the heated argument between the two teenage girls in front of him. Abby sighs.

"This is terrible—people are listening—people will think I'm—I'm like Gina and Tiffany—and I'm not—not at all."

Abby turns away suddenly.

"Why don't you face it Gina—your ex-boyfriend played you for a complete fool and everyone in town knows it."

Tiffany laughs loudly.

"Not that that's hard to do as far as you're concerned sweetie—I mean, seriously look at you—look at what you have to work with—I've seen fat, balding bulldogs that look better than you on their worst day Gina—and I'm being really kind."

Gina slaps Tiffany again.

"*You disgusting bitch—I'm going to kill you.*"

Tiffany raises her hand to hit Gina when they notice that both Kelly and Gina are gone. They look at each other.

"Where did they go?"

Gina pushes Tiffany against the kiosk.

"If I had a gun I'd shoot you dead."

Tiffany glares at Gina.

"That goes double for me—why don't you leave town? Go to some ritzy school? There are plenty of boarding schools in New England. No one likes you anyway. Everyone talks about you behind your back—even Abby can't stand you. You're your own worst enemy as far as I'm concerned—Caleb thinks so too."

Gina reacts to the slight.

"Get away from me this instant or else."

Tiffany takes a step forward.

"What are you going to do if I don't?"

Gina stares at Tiffany for a few seconds and heads to the elevator. Tiffany follows in hot pursuit as people watch.

<u>Pete's Cafe</u>

Daryl walks up to Alden and Todd. The diner remains silent. The two men look at each other. Daryl seems uneasy as he glances at Todd briefly and slowly faces Alden again. He nervously digs his hands into the front pocket of his Levi's.

"Washington—I—I think you know why I'm here when I'd rather be somewhere else in town—like a frigging bar."

Alden and Daryl look at each other silently.

"Kyle Madison is calling for your head."

Todd grabs Daryl's arm.

"So what—you, as well as I know Washington had nothing to do with Marah Madison's death all those years ago."

They look at each other. Todd lets go of Daryl's arm.

"Alden Washington was officially cleared as a suspect eighteen years ago in case it slipped your mind Anderson. Your pop made the call the morning they found her dead in the library at Glass Owl. So what gives, huh? What's your deal now?"

Daryl turns to face Alden again.

"Washington—I came here to warn you to stay clear of Kyle and his family. You know they have this town under their thumbs—and—well, Kyle isn't—isn't the forgiving type."

Todd shakes his head.

"So what else is new? Kyle is a prick and has always been one—some things never change in Marble Hills. Plenty could be said about you too Daryl—especially when it comes to Lori."

"Spencer, I don't need to hear your mouth right now—this is only between Washington and me—get out of my face."

Daryl gestures with his hand.

Page 36

"Look—we both know the kind of guy Kyle Madison is. He blames you for what happened even though my dad cleared you way back when. That said—no one was ever brought to justice for his sister's death all those years ago—so—as you can guess he's not ready to let it go just yet—so if I were you I'd lay low."

"I understand—I'll keep a low profile as much as possible while I'm here—wasn't planning to hang with Kyle anyway."

Daryl looks at Alden curiously.

"How long are you planning to stay in town?"

Alden glances at Todd, and then Daryl for a few seconds as he runs his fingers through his hair nervously. He shrugs.

<u>Boston</u>

"Look, I know the deal with those two losers. I got it covered quite nicely. Nothing can go wrong. Sabrillo knows what he has to do. He'll take out those two fools and Madison too."

Eldon grins broadly as he walks back and forth.

"Of course I'm aware you've been trying to find your daughter and don't need more drama in the mix right about now with those two idiots. That's why Sabrillo is coming all the way from Chile—he knows his stuff. Chill dear brother—relax."

Eldon stops and sighs.

"Keep me updated on when you find your daughter in Philadelphia—I know you've searched for her a long time."

He sighs loudly and looks at his cell phone.

"I never understood why you let her mother dictate the terms of when you could and couldn't see your own child—as you know I never was a fan of that woman—she had attitude."

Eldon rolls his eyes knowingly.

"Of course I know most women have attitude—some more than others if truth be known—but it would've been much easier if you'd simply bought her a nice plot in a cemetery and never looked back—there would be no issues at the moment with your daughter—things would've turned out so much better."

Eldon looks out at the Boston skyline.

Page 37

"Say what you like, but I'd never let a woman run my life like you did dear brother. I deal with such problems directly."

He laughs loudly and makes a lewd gesture.

"There are plenty of headstones in Boston of women who defied me and paid dearly for it. I'm not the type of guy that puts up with crap from the women in my life. If they insult me I take action—many of which led to nice plots surrounded by grassy hills overlooking beautiful ponds. If only you'd played by my rules your daughter would have grown up in Miami surrounded by the finest things instead of a rundown apartment building in Philly."

Loud yelling can be heard coming from the cell phone.

"Uh-huh—keep telling yourself that."

He faces the office again.

<u>Los Angeles</u>

"What do you mean he left town?"

The woman turns to look at the old man and seems enraged. She looks at the empty apartment and shrugs.

"Where did he go?"

She watches as the old man shrugs.

"How could you not know?"

She seems about to explode.

"Oh, that sneaky bastard thinks he pulled a fast one on me. Well, he had better think again—damn him—I'll get my money one way or the other. He'll pay for this—pay dearly."

Faye Washington storms out of the empty apartment and begins walking down the shrub-lined walk out to the driveway of the small boutique apartment building. She stops and looks back at the building for a few seconds. Faye pulls out her cell phone and begins furiously dialing. She sighs loudly as she waits.

"Damn him—how dare he thinks he can get away with not paying me my fair share. Oh, he's gonna pay all right. Make no doubt about it, he's going to pay me every red cent I'm owed."

She clenches her fists several times as her cell phone rings endlessly. She finally shuts it off and faces the sidewalk.

Page 38

"I think it's time I called Jeffrey and see what's going on with my cheating ex—and God help that man if he lies to me."

She walks toward her car parked nearby.

<u>Glass Owl</u>

Greg slowly steps out of his car onto the driveway and silently looks up at the mansion in front of him. He sighs.

"It's been a long time—such a long time."

He pauses briefly to stare at the huge, ornate hand painted stained glass door with an owl at the centerpiece of the elaborate design. Greg walks slowly toward the entrance and stops briefly at the front steps and sighs loudly once more.

"Never thought I'd come back."

He wipes sweat away from his brow.

"Not after what happened."

Greg slowly walks up to the front door and opens it nervously. He seems somewhat surprised it opens. He pushes the door inward and enters his childhood home. He closes the door behind him and takes a few seconds to look around the huge lobby-like area of the Victorian mansion. He glances at the mahogany banister to his right—remembering the endless times he'd slid down it as a young boy—incurring his mother's fierce wrath every time she caught him disobeying her orders.

"My foolish prodigal son finally returns."

Greg hastily spins around to see his father Howard Madison glaring at him—standing about fifteen feet away.

TO BE CONTINUED

A Look at the 2nd Episode

Alden's estranged ex-wife heads to Marble Hills intent on making her ex-husband's life miserable—Gina and Tiffany search for Kelly and Abby without success—Todd and Alden catch up on old times and deal with harsh realities concerning the past—Greg's arrival home isn't welcomed warmly—a marriage is on the brink of collapse as a desperate family seek a new start in Marble Hills—Wesley hatches a sinister plot of revenge against Alden for the unsolved murder of his aunt with the help of his nervous friends—Shirley struggles to keep troubling secrets about her past from Jeremy—as Kyle attempts to force a childhood friend to do his dirty work which threatens their shaky friendship.

Marble Hills

<u>Los Angeles</u>

A beautiful woman paces back on forth in a kitchen erratically. She becomes angrier and angrier as she talks on her cell phone to someone. She then begins yelling at the phone.

"I know you know where that creep ex of mine is hiding."

She pauses for a few seconds.

"I *know* he left town—where did he go?"

There is another pause as she seems to become more irritated as the seconds stick by. She clenches her fist.

"What do you mean you can't tell me? I'm his wife."

The woman rolls her eyes.

"OK—ex-wife—whatever. That cheap bastard stiffed me and unless I get what I'm entitled to—those trashy supermarket tabloids will become my best friend as of the minute I get off the phone with you Jeffrey—so, do we understand each other?"

She smiles broadly.

"That's more like it—thank you."

She shuts off her cell phone and glances at the open doorway leading to a garden outside. She smiles knowingly.

"Well, well, well, you may have thought what you did to me was over and done with—but I wouldn't count on that if I were you Alden—there is nothing worse than a woman scorned."

Faye Washington takes a breath of fresh air and slowly pulls the heavy wooden doors shut. She grins broadly.

Pete's Cafe

Todd Spencer watches as Daryl Anderson closes the front door behind him. He turns to face Alden Washington again.

"Maybe he's right. *You* should stay clear of Kyle Madison."

Alden runs his fingers through his hair.

"I'm not afraid of Madison. *Or* his uber rich family for that matter—as far as I am concerned Kyle can kiss my ass."

Todd shakes his head.

"But I thought you just said?"

"I know what I just said to Anderson but I haven't done anything wrong. I didn't kill Marah Madison—end of story."

"Daryl Anderson is still close friends with Kyle."

"Doesn't surprise me one bit Todd—they've always been really tight—tight from the time they were in junior high."

Todd sighs knowingly.

"Anderson got held back in seventh grade—and he and Madison—well, they became instant partners in crime."

Alden gestures with his hand.

"I remember it well—they practically became permanent residents in Principle Hingle's office—every afternoon."

Todd grins and turns to look at the woman who's been listening to the conversation. They exchange looks briefly.

"Pity how Anderson is such a suck-up now."

She nods in agreement.

"Alden, this is Julia Winthrop. Her mother married Anderson's old man a year after you left town. Julia is originally from Boston by way of Portland—been here ever since."

Todd glances at Julia and grins.

"Julia is a big soap fan actually."

Page **42**

Alden and Julia exchange knowing looks. Todd seems confused as Julia grins broadly. Alden shakes his head.

<u>Boothbay Harbor</u>

Denise Madison opens the door and sees Brad McKinley standing there. She smiles as she stares at the teenage boy. Her eyes immediately fall to his unzipped pants. He leers at her.

"Did you ditch your girlfriend like I asked?"

He grins and enters the hotel room. She closes the door and turns to look at him. She watches as if mesmerized as he begins to unzip the zippers of his faded jeans further.

"She bought my story—I told her I was going to pick up my grandmother from the airport in Portland and wouldn't be back for hours—I was *so* believable. I should be an actor."

Denise seems confused.

"Doesn't your grandmother live in Rockport?"

"Uh-huh—so what—what's your deal?"

Brad grabs Denise and pulls her toward him. He kisses her passionately. Denise glances down at Brad's erection. It strains against the confines of his tight jeans. She seductively slides her fingers over it and grins. She tugs at the buckle on the belt.

"Before coming over here to see me did you fuck your clueless girlfriend in the backseat of your car? Did you?"

Brad shakes his head.

"She's not putting out yet."

Brad kisses Denise passionately again as he watches her reaction. He grins and makes a lewd gesture with his finger.

"Not that I haven't tried to score—I have—but she's just not willing to give it up to me despite my very best efforts."

Denise slides her hand into Brad's boxer briefs as he grins slyly and kisses her passionately yet again. He sighs.

"But I can wait—at least until I work my magic—seducing her with my exceptional charms—convincing her I actually want to have a serious monogamous relationship—yeah, right."

He laughs loudly as he kisses Denise again.

Page **43**

"Ugh—like that could ever be true—then of course I'll plow her mercilessly without an ounce of guilt once she gives it up. Of course immediately after I pull out of her I'll kick the worthless bitch to the curb for making me wait so damn long to stick my dick into her—yep, that's my plan to bag that frigid whore."

Denise looks at Brad and laughs.

"Wow—that's seriously twisted thinking for a young guy like you. Remind me never to get on your bad side."

Brad pushes Denise onto the bed a few feet away. She watches as he pulls off his jeans. Denise glances at his underwear and the stiff outline of his penis as he yanks off his T-shirt. He notices and grins broadly. He walks toward the bed as he pulls off his boxer briefs and stands before her proudly. He laughs.

"If only Wesley knew I was doing his mom—been doing her for months now—he'd really flip out—like totally."

Denise suddenly seems worried.

"I know men talk as much as women do about sex—please don't ever forget and say anything about the two of us?"

"Like I actually would—don't worry—our escapades is no one's business but ours—I assume that's why we're hooking up in a hotel room in Boothbay Harbor under assumed names and not in Marble Hills? Marble Hills is a hotbed of nasty gossip as you know all too well—being a Madison and all—people there have nothing better to do than talk about other people's personal business—like it's their right to invade the privacy of others."

He laughs again.

"How do you think I got the rep of town stud?"

Brad continues standing in front of Denise. As he continues talking, her eyes never leave his stiff erection.

"Even got a few girls pregnant too—man, was that a wild trip for sure—but it—I wasn't about to get snared by anyone."

Denise smiles as she reaches out to stroke Brad's stiff penis with her fingers. She looks up at him seconds later.

"What about their parents?"

Brad rolls his eyes and laughs.

"They think I'm a virgin."

Brad smirks and watches as Denise begins giving him a blowjob. He grins broadly as her tongue works its magic.

Glass Owl

Greg Madison stares at his father in shock. The old man hadn't changed one bit—he hadn't missed a beat—he even looked the same—ageless. Howard Madison stands there glaring at his youngest son with contempt. Greg notices the coldness in his father's haughty demeanor. Howard takes a step forward.

"What are you doing here?"

Greg continues staring at his father.

"I asked you a question?"

Greg sighs.

"I—I—I thought you might be."

"Thought I was dead huh? You thought wrong boy. I'm stronger than ever. So, if you thought things had changed?"

Greg slowly walks toward his father.

"I—I thought you might be glad to see me?"

Howard laughs sarcastically.

"Seems when you took off that November day right after Thanksgiving, what, ten years ago give or take, I remember hearing the words 'I'd rather be dead than live here another second under your thumb.' So, what happened? Oh, let me guess your story—you're flat broke with nowhere else to go?"

Greg sighs again.

"I—I—I thought maybe."

"Well?"

Outside a car can be heard pulling up—then silence. Greg seems unsure of what to do next. He hesitates and sighs.

"I can leave if you don't want me to stay?"

Howard takes another step forward.

"What did you do?"

Greg shakes his head at his father knowingly and turns to leave. He stares at the door for a few seconds and then slowly reaches out to grab the doorknob as if waiting for a reply.

"Wait."

Greg stops.

"Exactly what kind of trouble did you get yourself into?"

Greg nervously turns to look at his father. The old man stares at him intently. His cold glare cuts through Greg.

"What makes you think I'm in trouble?"

"Why else would you have come back here?"

Howard walks over to where Greg is standing.

"This is your father you're talking to boy—not one of your dumb and idiotic loser friends that you place so much value upon though they can't help you—I know you're in way over your head in something huge—must be really bad too—it's the only reason you'd dare show your cowardly face here again after the way you left acting like you owned the world all those years ago—telling me off like your did—so what is it? What did you do?"

Greg looks away for a second. He feels his father's cold eyes on him, watching, accusing, and rigid. He seems nervous as he shuffles his feet. His voice cracks as he looks up suddenly.

"What if I am—what then?"

Howard stands there for a few seconds looking at the worried look on his son's face. He shows no emotion at all.

"Exactly who's after you—and why—or do I even want to know what sort of stupid mess you've gotten yourself into?"

Greg is about to answer as Kyle Madison walks through the front door and stares blankly at his younger brother in a shocked way. They look at each other for a few seconds.

Boston

Eldon Whitney picks up his cell phone as it continues ringing. He smiles broadly and sits on the edge of the desk.

"Sabrillo—so glad you called back."

Eldon glances out the window at the city below.

"I have a job for you."

He pauses.

"Yes—exactly."

Page 46

He grins.

"I want Greg Madison dead."

He sighs.

"Not a problem Sabrillo—it'll be taken care of when you get to the airport—I've left nothing to chance as always."

Eldon laughs.

"Yes—yes—first class—only the best for you."

Eldon smiles broadly.

"Yep—yeah—you get to use both their heads for target practice just as you demanded when we last spoke about the Madison situation at the Hilton in Mexico City. I won't stand in your way if that's what you demand from me in return."

Eldon grins.

"Don't worry Juan—I'm fully aware of your recent history with Rogers and Pyle and of your need for sweet revenge."

Eldon leans against the desk.

"Uh-huh—and I'm aware why you personally want to put a bullet in their heads in retaliation for the messy fiasco that took place at the airport in Miami last year which cost your brother his life and which they never bothered apologizing for causing."

Eldon laughs again.

"Not a problem—you can make the call on what exactly you want to do with them once you guys meet up in Marble Hills later. And no, they have no idea you're coming or that you plan to take them both out once you get there. It'll be a surprise."

Eldon does a little dance around his desk.

"Good—so it's all set then—Rogers and Pyle and then Madison—call me when you arrive in Boston later so we can talk further about how I want Madison dealt with. I expect you to come up with something special for his demise—uh-huh."

He smiles and shuts the cell phone off.

<u>Los Angeles</u>

Faye slams the door to her car shut and smirks broadly as she turns to look at the street. She seems lost in thought.

Page 47

"You thought you'd finally gotten rid of me when you filed for divorce last year—well, think again you selfish creep."

She glances at herself in the rearview mirror.

"No one makes a fool of Faye McAllister and gets away with it—*no one*—especially not a two-timing sleaze bag."

She starts the engine and sighs loudly.

Santiago

Juan Sabrillo glances briefly at a photograph of a man about his age hanging on the wall as he snaps the locks shut on four pieces of luggage nearby. He sighs loudly several times and in broken English begins talking to the photograph hanging on the wall. He wipes a tear from his eye and turns around.

"The time has come for vengeance brother—I will avenge your death—they will die at my hands without mercy."

He picks up one of the pieces of luggage and slings it over his shoulder. He looks at the photo on the wall once more.

"Their blood will quench my grief."

He angrily clenches his fist.

Stanley Pier

Wesley Madison shuts his cell phone off and turns around to look at Corey Bentley who's standing a few feet away.

"It's done."

Corey smiles broadly.

"I can't believe you got Simon Spencer to dance to your tune—his dad is such a prick—such a frigging loser."

"Exactly why he's game now—his dad won't let him hang with us—and of course I played that card to sway him."

Corey laughs and slaps Wesley on the shoulder.

"Trust me—Simon Spencer is ripe for the picking. It won't take too much to push him further—to do our bidding."

"What about Jason Anderson? Do you think he'll play along with us? He's high up there on the loser list too."

Wesley grins and shakes his head.

"Actually—he's already on board with this deal."

Corey turns to look at Wesley curiously.

<u>Pete's Cafe</u>

Todd glances at Alden and Julia several times. Alden looks at Julia again and they share another grin which appears to totally confuse Todd. Alden gestures with his hand and smirks.

"We've already met actually—though I didn't know her name. She's quite the devoted fan of *Larkspur Lane*."

Julia blushes.

"This is *so* embarrassing."

Alden laughs. She looks at Todd.

"I had no idea he was from Marble Hills. The fan magazines I read never mentioned it. I always thought he was from the Boston area. I can't believe they got it totally wrong."

"They didn't—I'm actually from Boston—my folks and I moved here when I was six—looking for a safe place to live."

"So, you're like me—a stranger?"

Alden nods. Todd pats Alden on the back.

"Julia married Peter Winthrop right after he came back from college with a business degree. Then they opened *this* wonderful diner together—they were opened only about four or five years before—then it happened—so terrible—tragic."

Alden looks at Todd and Julia.

"Peter was killed in an explosion in Bangor. He flew planes on the side. Anyway, he must have tripped and sparked the gasoline on the runway at the airport—he was killed instantly according to eyewitnesses—and so was Cassie Winthrop."

Julia sheds a tear as Todd continues talking.

"Cassie Winthrop was Peter's and Julia's daughter. She was only two. Such a terrible tragedy—left a lasting mark."

Alden turns to face Julia.

"I'm sorry."

Julia wipes a tear from her eye.

Page **49**

"It's OK. They're both in a better place now."

Todd looks at Julia and sighs.

"How are things with you and Anderson? I mean—well—I noticed there was some—serious friction between you two?"

Julia shrugs.

"We're still not speaking."

Alden seems confused as Todd and Julia look at each other again and appear to be bothered by something else. Todd waves his hand in the air and glances at the front door again.

"Apparently Anderson is still upset over the fact that Julia called him out for cheating on his wife over a year ago."

Julia waves her hand around.

"If he wants to play that game—let him—I'm not sorry that I told the truth—I couldn't keep quiet about what I saw."

She sighs again.

"Lori Anderson is a friend of mine and I think she had a right to know what my double-dealing stepbrother was up to."

Alden looks at Todd as he shakes his head several times in disbelief. Todd glances at Julia. She rolls her eyes.

<u>Boothbay Harbor</u>

Sounds of loud moaning and joyful laughter echo throughout a hotel room during a bout of passionate lovemaking. Seconds later Brad pulls out of Denise and rolls over—he grins as he looks at her—then winks slyly. She sighs loudly and smiles as she seductively slides her fingers across his chest. He laughs.

"Want to go again?"

Denise nods and they begin kissing.

<u>Los Angeles</u>

The airport terminal is crowded with people as Faye runs up toward the podium which reads BOSTON in yellow lettering. She seems out of breath as she pulls out her ticket and fumbles with her purse looking for her ID as people seem annoyed.

Page **50**

Todd and Julia give each other a strange look as they glance at the front door once again. Todd rolls his eyes.

"Daryl Anderson isn't the troubled but generally nice guy you remember Washington. He's become a total jerk."

Alden runs his fingers through his hair.

"I can't throw stones. I knowingly destroyed both of my marriages because of stupidity—paid a really steep price."

Todd and Alden look at each other.

"Was that actress one of your stupid mistakes?"

Alden shakes his head.

"She wasn't one of my proudest moments."

He gestures with his hands.

"Believe me if I could go back in time and fix the colossal mistakes I made with both of my marriages I would."

"No chance the recent ex will ever forgive you?"

Alden laughs loudly.

"Not a chance—she wants my head on a platter."

Todd smiles and glances at Julia.

"I guess you've been getting an earful—more than you'd actually like to know about—a real-life soap opera."

Julia pretends to slap Todd.

"I've learned to stop judging others as a rule. I'm far from perfect myself—made so many mistakes after Peter."

Alden looks around at the diner again.

"I guess not all is what it seems on the surface."

Alden's cell phone rings but he ignores it.

"Well, at least I won't have to worry that I'm perceived as being perfect—at least not after knowing about my past."

Todd laughs.

"You perfect? Like no way bro—I haven't forgotten about you and Sabrina Belknap. She was royally pissed for years."

Alden seems stunned by the mentioning of the familiar name and reacts. He sighs loudly and looks at Todd.

Page 51

"Is she still here in Marble Hills?"
Todd laughs again.
"I'd say—she *is* now Sabrina Kane."
Alden sighs.
"She married Eddie Kane?"
"Fifteen years now."
Todd glances at Julia.
"Two kids—both daughters."
Todd smiles broadly.
"And yeah—they're as beautiful as their mother. Neither took after Eddie. Bet he's pleased about that fact for sure."
"No red hair like their dad?"
Todd grins.
"Nope—they're both blonde."
Alden looks at Julia again and grins.
"I guess that's what I get for being away so long—I know absolutely nothing about anyone's life in Marble Hills."
Julia nods knowingly.

<u>Maple Avenue</u>

Gina Bentley and Tiffany Johnson slowly exit the mall entrance and look at each other with contempt. Gina sighs.
"Where did they go?"
Gina rolls her eyes at Tiffany. She dials Abby's number on her cell phone. No answer. She faces Tiffany once more.
"Why isn't she picking up? What's going on?"
Tiffany smirks. Gina notices and scowls at her.
"This is your fault Tiffany—if you hadn't been acting like your body was for sale to every guy in town—so shameless."
Tiffany rolls her eyes and sighs.
"The pot calling the kettle black—like really."
"I saw him first."
"Likely story from a pathetic loser—deal already."
Tiffany makes a gesture with her hand.
"Talk to the hand."

Page **52**

Gina ignores the remark.

"Where could they have gone?"

Tiffany turns to go back into the mall seconds later as Gina frantically dials Abby's number on her cell phone once more.

<u>Philadelphia</u>

Lindsay Bennington sighs as she looks at the staircase leading upstairs. All the furniture—including a huge grandfather clock—is covered with thick white sheets. She sighs again.

"OK people—I called our cab already."

She seems angry as she looks at her watch.

"They should be here in ten minutes."

Robert Bennington comes toward her from the kitchen.

"Are you sure you want to leave Philly?"

Lindsay looks at her husband. She seems upset.

"What do you think?"

Robert glances at the covered furniture.

"I don't see the reasoning behind it?"

"Robert, listen, I'm not going to discuss it any further with you—either *we* leave Philadelphia today as planned—or else I swear our sham of a marriage is over—you make the call."

Robert sighs.

"It only happened once."

"So you said."

"I'm telling the truth."

Lindsay walks past Robert and stops suddenly. She turns around to face him. Her eyes blaze with anger. He notices.

"I think we both know as long as you and Chandra Stevenson are in the same city, the possibility that the both of you will continue having a relationship goes up considerably—and you and I both know it's only a matter of time until the line of what is acceptable and what isn't is crossed yet again."

Robert folds his hands across his chest and sighs. He looks at Lindsay silently for a few seconds. He seems defiant.

"It's time to let go what happened."

Page **53**

He sighs loudly once more.

"Exactly how many times do I have to apologize for what happened—I said I was sorry more than ten times already."

"We're not discussing this topic further."

Robert watches as Lindsay leaves.

<u>Stanley Pier</u>

"Exactly what are you planning to do in order to avenge what happened to your late aunt eighteen years ago?"

Wesley grins slyly and winks at Corey before he turns around to face Jason Anderson who seems a bit confused.

"Something that bastard won't forget."

Corey smirks.

"Like what exactly?"

Wesley watches as Jason sits down next to Corey.

"You, Corey, Simon and I will grab that son of a bitch at his hotel room. I just need to find out exactly where he's staying."

Jason seems worried.

"Aren't Brad and Jeremy coming with us?"

Wesley shakes his head.

"I couldn't reach Brad when I tried calling him. He must be in a dingy hotel room with some chick he met and decided to bang at the last minute. That's Brad's type of deal anyways."

Wesley wrings his hands and seems angry. He turns to look at the parking lot for a few seconds. He sighs loudly.

"Jeremy blew me off earlier today as well when we spoke because—because his worthless tramp of a clingy girlfriend doesn't approve of him hanging out with me anymore."

Wesley laughs knowingly.

"Ever since I fucked her last week at Lana's party she's been scared to death that Jeremy will find out she's a slut."

Corey laughs loudly.

"Shirley Moses is a frigging whore. Seriously, who hasn't she slept with since she moved here two years ago? Spreads her legs for old dudes too—caught her a few times in the act."

Page **54**

Corey makes a lewd gesture with his finger.

"I did her last month when Jeremy got drunk at Daphne's party and had to be driven home like a pathetic dweeb."

"You banged her that night?"

Corey laughs and glances at Jason.

"So? She's just a whore. She's been giving it up to every guy that makes a pass—can't turn down a stiff dick."

Corey looks at Jason curiously and sighs loudly.

"Has she given it up to you yet?"

Jason shakes his head.

"She's a skank—I don't do skanks."

Wesley winks at Corey.

"Uh-huh—you're a virgin most definitely."

Jason rolls his eyes.

"*I'm* not a virgin—I've been around."

"Oh yeah—prove it already—like tell us who you've fucked that we know from Lincoln High smart guy—tell us—spill."

Jason seems uneasy as eyes fall upon him. He attempts to change the subject as his behavior is noticed by Corey.

"*So*—Wesley—what are we going to do to the guy you said killed your aunt—is it anything that could get us in trouble?"

Jason seems nervous as he glances at Wesley.

"We're not going to kill the guy—are we—I'm just not into stuff like that. I don't want to end up in the pen for murder."

Corey grins broadly.

"You're not into a lot of things, aren't you Jason—one of which is banging whores here in town like the rest of us."

"*Fuck you*. I don't have to tell you anything."

Wesley seems annoyed.

"Did I say we're going to kill the jerk? No, we're just going to beat him up—bust his jaw—make a point—that's all."

Corey grins broadly.

"I'm down with that idea."

Jason sighs.

"I—I—I don't know."

Wesley seems about to explode.

"Look, are you going to wimp out on me like you always do Jason? I really think you should stop being such a pathetic loser because your pop is the police chief—and not a very good one at that. So, what will it be *loser*—are you game or not?"

"Fuck off. I don't owe you anything."

Wesley suddenly grabs Jason by the neck. Jason tries to jerk free of Wesley's grip. Wesley grins broadly and laughs.

"I could kill you right now—break your neck."

Jason manages to free himself but Wesley grabs him again with a headlock and violently twists his head to one side.

"You had better not piss me off further."

"Whether or not my pop is police chief has nothing to do with anything—especially me—he doesn't tell me what to do. I do whatever I want—whenever I want. I'm my own man."

Wesley lets go of Jason. He shrugs.

"Really—is that so?"

He glances at Corey.

"Prove it *loser*."

Jason turns to look at Corey again.

<u>Boothbay Harbor</u>

Brad comes out of the bathroom of the hotel room zipping up his Levi's as Denise smiles approvingly. She sighs.

"When can I see you next?"

Brad grins and comes toward her.

"I'll have some free time after lunch on Saturday."

Denise slides her fingers between his legs as she pushes him up against the wall. They kiss passionately. She laughs.

"Who'd think with such a nerdy-looking father like yours you'd be so good in bed and not a loser with zero game?"

"Hey, for the record—I'm nothing like my wallflower of a father—he and I are definitely not cut from the same cloth."

Denise laughs.

"I'd say—four times in a row today. Your stamina is absolutely incredible Brad. Your father could barely go twice."

Page **56**

Brad kisses Denise passionately.

"What can I say—my dick likes a lot of play."

They kiss again.

"Speaking of which—loved that thing you did with your tongue earlier—drove me absolutely wild with passion."

"Like I said, I have my own game."

Brad smiles broadly and kisses Denise.

<u>Pete's Cafe</u>

Julia glances nervously at Alden as he and Todd look at her curiously. She leans against the counter and faces Alden.

"Earlier you mentioned you might need a place to stay while you were here in Marble Hills for a couple of weeks?"

Alden turns to look at Julia.

"Yeah—a place that won't drain my bank account and turn me into a pauper—got to watch the pennies unfortunately."

Todd laughs and slaps Alden on the back.

"*You, a pauper*—with all your money from your Hollywood soap opera career—come on—you must be like really loaded with plenty dough—right up there with the likes of **Susan Lucci**."

Alden seems uneasy.

"I was on *Larkspur Lane* for eleven years. I never made movies during that time. I didn't make *that* much money."

Todd smirks and rolls his eyes.

"Sure—whatever—uh-huh—I believe you. Bet you have a beach house in California—one of those Malibu deals."

"No, really—I'm just like anyone else now—I have to pinch my pennies as I mentioned earlier—got to be careful."

Todd slaps Alden on the back again and winks slyly.

"Uh-huh—if you say so rich guy—keep telling that story and eventually it might be believed—by sad sack types."

"I'm serious—I'm not fooling with you."

Alden turns to look at Julia.

"Is the Spring Pine Inn still around?"

Todd gestures with his hand.

"Gone—ten years now—Eddie took over the area for his mall. Tore the whole block down actually—gone—poof."

He winks at Julia.

"But it just so happens that your new best friend owns a small boardinghouse on Peabody Avenue—very popular."

Alden grins.

"I'm game."

"It used to be the Wayside Inn."

She pauses.

"But if you don't mind really small rooms—I do have several available at the moment—completely furnished."

Alden looks at Julia curiously.

"Beggars can't be choosers—how much?"

Todd grins broadly.

<u>Shelby Park</u>

Jeremy Weissmann and Shirley Moses sit down at a picnic table. He seems somewhat uneasy as she looks around.

"If it makes you happy I'll stay clear of Wesley Madison and Corey Bentley—though I don't see the big deal."

Shirley smiles and nervously reaches out to gently touch Jeremy's hand. They look at each other briefly. He shrugs.

"Those two lowlifes are nothing but trouble as you know. I just don't want you messing around with your future."

Jeremy wipes sweat from his brow.

"Understood—but they're not *that* bad. I've known them all my life—they're just not the way you think they are."

Shirley seems annoyed.

"And what—I've only known them for two years since I moved to Marble Hills from Bangor so I'm simply mistaken?"

Jeremy shakes his head.

"I didn't mean it like that—only that they're just regular guys—like me and my brother—they just play hard. Deep down they're all talk and no action—nothing more than that."

Shirley sighs loudly and shrugs.

Page 58

"Yeah—regular guys who both have criminal records already. Wesley Madison has been in trouble twice—and don't get me started on Corey Bentley. I mean—he has a terrible rep when it comes to him using women like tissue paper."

Jeremy pulls his hand away.

"I know all about Corey's rep. I'm no saint myself in case you were wondering. I'm not a virgin—I've been with a lot of girls too. Obviously not as much as Wesley and Corey—but I can't throw stones since my rep is less than respectable given my history with some of the girls I've been with previously."

Shirley seems upset and looks away.

<u>Stanley Pier</u>

"Fine—whatever—count me in too—I'm game."

Wesley and Corey look at each other. Corey grins slyly.

"That's more like it."

Jason seems upset as he glances at the parking lot a few yards away. He turns to look at Wesley and Corey again.

"What if we get caught?"

Wesley laughs.

"So?"

Corey grins again.

"Your father will let it slide like he always does—have you forgotten Wesley's family owns Marble Hills—owns your pop?"

Jason turns to face Wesley.

"Your family doesn't own anything anymore in Marble Hills but Glass Owl—your great-grandpa sold his real estate holdings to some developers from Boston years ago. Everyone in town knows that deal—really old news for decades now."

Wesley smirks.

"Want to bet."

Wesley pushes Jason.

"Ask your pop who pays his bills and he'll tell you what's obvious to everyone else in Marble Hills—facts don't lie."

Wesley glances at Corey.

"Yeah—that's right—my family makes things happen in this town—your pop has no say except to do what he's told like a good little soldier and skip to my grandfather's orders."

Wesley pushes Jason again.

"Don't believe me Jason—whatever—but it won't change anything regardless—facts are facts—deal with it already."

"That's not what I heard."

Corey glances at Jason and smirks.

"It's true, loser—rich people can do anything they want and get away with it after the fact no matter what—seriously, like were you born yesterday or what—this shouldn't be news to average folks like you? It's a way of life here and elsewhere."

Wesley pushes Jason up against the iron gates at the edge of the pier. His eyes flash with anger. Jason seems afraid.

"So, getting back to what we were talking about earlier concerning our plans. We won't get in trouble for busting the jaw of the jerk that killed my aunt. We're just paying him back for what he did all those years ago—he's had it coming for a long time now—what goes around comes around—end of story."

Jason watches as Wesley winks slyly at Corey and turns away. He stops and faces Jason once more with a sneer—making a threatening gesture with his fist. Jason sighs loudly.

"If you tell anybody about what we just talked about—you and I will come to blows—like serious blows—deadly."

Jason nods as Wesley smiles triumphantly.

"*Good*—so, it's agreed. You will help me with my plans to get even with the jerk that killed my aunt all those years ago."

He grins seeing the panicked look on Jason's face.

"If you defy me I swear they'll find your lifeless body in the harbor with a bullet hole in your head and a whiny suicide note saying you couldn't take it anymore and decided to go out with a bang—it's your choice Jason—you decide what you want to do but if you try to screw me I won't be responsible for what happens to you—that I promise. I have a rep for a reason. Be afraid."

Wesley slides his finger across Jason's neck.

"I'll kill you—I swear I will."

Page 60

Jason sighs loudly as Wesley and Corey slowly walk away. He looks at the harbor as loud laughter echoes in his ear.

"When did my life become so complicated?"

He leans against the iron gates.

<u>Police Station</u>

Daryl closes the door behind him as he enters the police station. Seconds later Kyle barges into the office with a scowl on his face. They look at each other. Kyle takes a step forward.

"Well?"

Daryl seems annoyed.

"Well, what?"

"Is he gone?"

Daryl turns away.

"No."

Kyle grabs him by the arm.

"Why not—I thought I made myself clear."

Daryl jerks free of Kyle's grip.

"Do I look like a miracle worker—huh—I can only do so much—you're just going to have to deal with Washington."

"Seems you didn't do anything at all Anderson?"

"Think what you like Kyle—but I did what I could within the law—he knows to stay clear of you and your family."

"That's not what I asked you to do—I expected results."

Daryl sits down at his desk and sighs loudly.

"If you don't like how I handled it—why don't you try handling it yourself—no, wait—you might end up in jail."

Kyle grimaces.

"I can easily have you removed from duty—seems like that's what I should have done years ago—would've solved a lot of problems for me and my family. But it's never too late."

Daryl laughs.

"And replace me with who—no one wants this crummy job or the lousy pay I get—face it Kyle, there's not much you can do at the moment but sit on your damn ass—and fuck off."

Page **61**

Kyle looks around at the office.

"You know he's only here in town to stir up trouble for my family—to throw it in our faces about Marah's death."

Daryl sighs.

"And why would he do that?"

Kyle rolls his eyes.

"Do I look like I know what goes through the mind of a killer on any given day? He should be rotting away in jail."

Daryl sighs again.

"Look, despite what you think or believe to be true, it was never proven that Washington had anything to do with your sister's death all those years ago. The case remains open."

"The case is still open because your pop didn't have the guts to see what was obviously in front of him. Exactly the same deal with what happened to **Natalie Wood** in 1981. LAPD knew who did it from the getgo—it was that bastard gay husband of hers. **Robert Wagner** got away with murder. But they never had the balls to press charges against him—and the case was never solved and remains open to this day with question marks everywhere. Sounds familiar, doesn't it? Uh-huh it does."

Kyle walks over to where Daryl is sitting and looks at him with an accusing look—as Daryl appears slightly annoyed.

"But we all know my sister died at Washington's hands and your old man let him get away with murder despite the fact he had no alibi and was guilty as sin. It's just not fair."

Kyle gestures erratically with his hand.

"He was the last person to see her alive that night—*even* he admitted to it when he was questioned by your old man immediately after my sister's body was found. Who else in town had reason to kill Marah but my so-called best friend?"

Daryl gives Kyle a cautious look.

"On what motive Madison—then and now there's still that question you can't answer that makes a bit of sense—why?"

Kyle wipes sweat from his brow.

"My sister was pregnant—and Washington didn't want to be tied to a baby—so he killed her—and then played dumb."

Daryl stands up.

"As you recall Washington didn't know at the time Marah was pregnant. She never had the chance to tell him she was expecting his baby before she was murdered on prom night."

"So he said—but what if he knew—seems to me that's a really good motive for murder? People have killed for less."

"My dad didn't think so—and neither do I—the reason you keep harping on is just too flimsy an excuse to pursue."

"I bet if Marah was your sister you wouldn't have been so cavalier about the whole thing—you'd have cared more."

Kyle leans closer to Daryl.

"But what do you care Anderson—so what if she gave you her virginity—gave it to you because she loved you."

Daryl turns away from Kyle.

"And—*and* so what if you fucked my sister like she was a common whore for two months—while you were hooking up on the sly behind her back with the likes of Carmen Pendleton."

Kyle sighs loudly as Daryl looks at the front door.

"You turned her into a slut—of which afterwards she gave it up to every horny guy in town—including Washington."

Daryl grimaces at the comment and stands up.

"*OK*—so you're actually going to throw that back in my face—especially with your rep concerning Serena Glick?"

"We're not talking about me—this is about you and my sister—and how you used her like she didn't matter at all."

Daryl walks to the door and turns to face Kyle.

"Get out—get the hell out of my office."

"Can't take it, can you, Anderson. The truth hurts, doesn't it? Well, deal with it—no one has forgotten what you did."

"You're a piece of work Madison. Yeah, I took your sister's virginity. Yeah, I slept around on her. Yeah, I got Carmen pregnant. Yeah, I slept with Carmen's mother too. Yeah, I was a dog. Yeah, I admit it. I'm guilty of that and more. But guess what—I've never claimed to be a pillar of virtue—never even tried to pretend like I was Prince Charming—but what about you?"

Kyle continues standing by Daryl's desk.

Page 63

"I did a lot of crummy things back in the day—but it wasn't my dad that covered up a brutal murder—it was yours."

Kyle and Daryl stare at each other harshly.

"Uh-huh—you on the other hand shouldn't even open your mouth to talk. Look at your record—you fucked so many girls in high school you admitted on more than one occasion you couldn't even remember most of their names. And let's not forget how many made multiple trips to abortion clinics in Portland and Boston. Some more than once if memory serves me right. You played hard—telling lies endlessly to get out of trouble. I clearly recall what your nickname in high school was Madison."

Daryl makes a gesture with his hand for Kyle to leave as he glares at him. He looks at the front door again and sighs.

"Backseat Madison."

Kyle walks to the door and stops.

"You know something Anderson—I never realized how much of a fucking asshole you always were. Freak nutjob."

Daryl watches as Kyle leaves and slams the door shut. He turns to look at the office. He seems upset and sighs loudly.

<u>Boothbay Harbor</u>

Denise watches as Brad walks down the hallway and exits through the stairwell at the left end of the small hotel. She smiles broadly as she watches him leave. She slowly licks her lips.

"So gorgeous—so damn gorgeous—young men and their bodies—oh—I can't help myself even if I could or wanted to."

She licks her lips again and is about to close the door when she notices Lance Weissmann coming toward her from the stairwell at the right end of the hotel. He grins broadly as he sees her standing there waiting for him just as they planned earlier.

"Oh yeah—I'm *so* in the mood."

She glances at his Lycra shorts. It's clearly obvious he's not wearing underwear underneath. Her eyes focus on the outline of his erect penis straining against the confines of the tight-fitting fabric. Lance notices her looking at his legs and laughs.

Page **64**

"Yeah, that's right—I was just at the gym—and yeah—*I'm pumped*—you and I are definitely going to make the earth move this afternoon in a big way—no question about it—I'm ready."

As Lance reaches the entrance to the hotel room Denise pulls him toward her and kisses him aggressively. He kisses her back passionately. They look at each other and laugh.

"Do you have a problem with aggressive women?"

Lance smiles broadly.

"Nope—no problem at all—I like a woman who makes it easy for me to score—even if she's my friend's mother."

They begin kissing passionately. Outside a man takes pictures as they go at it by the open window. Marc Ryerson grins broadly as he watches Denise hastily pull off Lance's T-shirt.

TO BE CONTINUED

A Look at the 3rd Episode

Greg is unable to hide from his sordid past as he's hunted by two killers intent on murdering him in order to preserve their own lives while they become targets themselves of a sadistic stranger bent on exacting revenge for the death of his brother—Gina and Tiffany are stunned to discover that Kelly and Abby possibly hooked up after they left the mall—Alden's ex-wife from Los Angeles who isn't shy about airing their dirty laundry in public heads to Marble Hills with a score to settle—Wesley's anger over his aunt's murder escalates toward Alden—Denise continues to stray from the restraints of her unhappy marriage, involving herself with yet another teenage boy as well as the husband of one of her closest friends—as Kyle begins to see his supposedly charmed picture-perfect world coming apart at the seams.

Dangerous Liaisons

Clark Street

Wesley Madison and Corey Bentley slowly walk toward a parking lot. Corey suddenly stops and nervously looks back at the pier several times. He seems worried about something. He roughly grabs Wesley by the arm. They look at each other.

"Are you sure Anderson won't spill our plan?"

"That loser values his life too much. He knows I don't play. If he fucks with me he knows I'll make good on my threat—he's only too aware of the merciless teasing I've inflicted on that dweeb Ashton Markway over the last couple of years."

"Anderson has his father to back him up."

Wesley becomes annoyed.

"Fuck Daryl Anderson. He's nobody—my family owns his soul—and *we* own this whole damned town too—and everyone in it to do with as we please—no asshole loser like Jason Anderson or his pathetic pop will tell me what I can and can't do."

Corey glances at the pier again.

"But what if—what if he decides to blab?"

Wesley slides one of his fingers across his throat twice.

"Simple—I'll put a bullet in his head."
They look at each other.

Police Station

Daryl Anderson is sitting at his desk shuffling through paperwork with his back facing the front door as it opens.

"I thought I told you to get out already."

"It's me."

Daryl slowly turns around to see his teenage son nervously standing at the entrance unsure if he should enter.

"Oh, sure—yeah—it's OK Jason. Just thought you were someone else I've already had enough of today—that's all."

Jason Anderson walks toward the desk where his father is sitting amid a stack of paperwork. They look at each other.

"What's up?"

Jason slowly sits down on one of the chairs positioned in front of his father's desk. He twitches a little. Daryl notices.

"I was just wondering if you needed help with anything today—since Clay's been away—I could help if you?"

Daryl looks at his son oddly.

"You're actually volunteering to help with—boring—very boring work—well, that's a serious switch—what gives?"

Jason seems uneasy.

"No reason—I just have some free time I guess."

Daryl stands up.

"Now I know something is up for sure. OK—this is highly unusual behavior even for you—worrisome actually. *So*—so what have you done with my son and where can I find his body?"

Jason rolls his eyes.

"Real funny—you're a funny guy."

Daryl walks over to where Jason is sitting. He notices Jason's behavior and seems concerned. He sighs loudly.

"Is something bothering you?"

Jason looks away.

"No—nothing's wrong. I just felt like helping out."

"Really—just offered to help me with work—definitely not normal behavior for you being a teenager—the last time you offered to do anything was when you broke the garage door."

"Broke the garage door—swinging from it trying to be *Tarzan*—really stupid move on my part if I recall correctly."

"Have you done something that I should know about?"

Jason shrugs.

"No—I just."

"Girl trouble—is that it Jason—huh—got yourself in way over your head yet again—you got some girl pregnant?"

Jason laughs.

"Yeah, like that's possible—I'd have to have a girlfriend first—which at the moment I'm in short supply of in case you haven't noticed lately. I'm not a popular guy in Marble Hills."

"What about Corinne Massey? She seems like a nice girl and she's pretty too. What about asking her out on a date?"

"She said no."

"Tiffany Johnson?"

"She said no twice."

"Lana Jefferson?"

"She totally ignores me."

"Elizabeth Pendleton?"

"I won't even bother with her."

Daryl seems confused.

"They can't all be off limits—I haven't heard."

Jason stands up.

"They are—trust me. Everyone is going on dates but me. I'm the lone wolf in this rotten deal, but not by choice, believe me. I definitely don't have any friends with benefits deal."

"Jason?"

Daryl reaches out to put his arms around his son.

"Are you a virgin?"

Jason pulls away.

"You didn't know? That's a surprise. Everyone in Marble Hills knows I've never done the nasty—total loser no doubt."

He walks to the door and stops.

Page **69**

"Girls want guys with experience. Guys like Wesley, Corey, Brad, Caleb, Jeremy, Lance and Jarod have experience. They get laid all the time—like every night with a different girl."

Daryl watches as Jason gives him a curious look and leaves. He stands silently for a few seconds and sighs loudly.

Shelby Park

Jeremy Weissmann watches as Shirley Moses gets into her car. She looks up at him and smiles. He seems uneasy.

"I'll see you later—OK?"

"Sure."

He watches as she drives off.

Glass Owl

Greg Madison is sitting in the den with his father as he finishes his story. Howard Madison has a stern look on his face and leans forward—looking at his son directly in the eye.

"So, that's the whole story?"

Greg nods.

"Nothing else you might have left out?"

"No."

Howard stands up and sighs.

"Who is this Eldon Whitney person anyway?"

Greg turns to face his father.

"I thought I just told you."

Howard folds his hands across his chest and sighs loudly.

"I know what you just told me Greg—but exactly who is he businesswise? What's his bottom line? Can he be paid off?"

Greg shrugs.

"How should I know—I didn't really know him that well other than—his friends are like him I guess—mobsters."

Howard waves his hand in the air as he looks at his son in contempt. His cold exterior toward his youngest son is clear.

"You've really outdone yourself this time."

Howard slowly walks over to the large window facing the well-landscaped garden outside. He turns around suddenly.

"This is what happens when you don't listen to those who know better than you—you make careless mistakes."

Greg nervously turns to face his father.

Philadelphia

Robert Bennington paces back and forth at the airport terminal. He glances at the cell phone in his hand. It rings. He looks around and shrugs. He sighs loudly several times.

"I told you to stop calling me—it's—it's over."

He sighs.

"I know—but it's over. Lindsay made it quite clear."

He sighs again.

"It doesn't matter—it's over between us. I'm really sorry but that's just the way it has to be right now—*have a nice life.*"

He glances around as people walk by.

"No—no—listen to me Chandra—it happened—OK—it happened—but that was then and this is now—and—sorry."

He seems about to shut his cell phone off but stops and continues listening as he becomes more upset. He groans.

"What do you want from me Chandra—my marriage is at stake—my family has to come first—deal with it already."

He sighs loudly again.

"If you want to hate me for ending what we—go right ahead—I've got to go now—it's been real OK—sorry—bye."

He shuts off the cell phone and sighs.

Boothbay Harbor

Denise Madison slowly pulls on her skirt and glances slyly at Lance Weissmann as he grabs his Lycra shorts. They look at each other for a few seconds. He grins broadly and winks.

"You're not mad at me—are you? You know for insisting on another round—got a lot of pent-up energy lately."

Denise walks over to Lance and slides her fingers across his naked chest. His erection immediately begins to swell.

"Mad? No. You had every right to insist—I couldn't say no to you even if I wanted—I love a strong guy in bed."

Lance laughs.

"I just couldn't control myself—had to—too horny."

Denise watches as he slides his hands under her blouse and cups her breasts. She reacts with a sigh. He smirks.

"I like a man who takes what he wants."

"Even if that man happens to be one of your son's friends from school—a friend who enjoys fucking older women?"

Denise kisses Lance.

"You're quite special to me."

They look at each other.

"Wesley would be pissed if he found out we've been hooking up in a hotel room—bet he'd order my death."

Denise seductively slides her fingers across Lance's lips as he kisses her fingers several times and grins broadly.

"What my son doesn't know he doesn't need to know."

Denise kisses Lance again and smiles slyly.

"I live for myself not for my son."

Lance grins.

"I got no problem with that—besides—I don't want your family coming after me with guns blazing—especially Wesley."

Denise glances at Lance's swelling erection under his Lycra shorts and licks her lips. He gestures with his hand.

"I could go another round if you?"

Lance glances at the bed and gestures slyly.

<u>Portland</u>

Carlo Rogers and Duane Pyle casually walk across the airport terminal carrying two suitcases each. Carlo stops.

"I hope this dinky town has a few good bars."

Duane sighs loudly and seems somewhat annoyed.

"Already on the prowl—aren't you?"

Page **72**

"Not everyone is as selective like you—I like to play the field—I thrive on the hunt—seeing what's possibly out there."

"I remember when we were together you had this thing for having multiple boyfriends round the clock in your bed servicing your needs—apparently you still haven't changed."

"I like men—what's the big deal anyway—it's not like you and I were ever exclusive. We just dated—like maybe four times if I recall before we decided we needed space between us."

"Especially not after I came home and found you in bed with Yakov Stajinsky. Imagine how I felt seeing you with your dick up his ass—hearing you laugh while you fucked him repeatedly like he was a paid escort—telling him that you and I were "just friends" and that being in a committed relationship wasn't your thing—and we were not a couple and we would never be."

"I told you I was sorry, didn't I? But you knew I liked playing the field when you met me. As I recall you found me in bed with your ex initially—while we were experiencing quite an intense moment—and I remember you clearly saying it didn't really matter—that the two of you were done ages ago."

Carlo sighs and seems annoyed.

"Nevertheless—before we hooked up you knew I'd been with a lot of guys. I was very promiscuous back in my college days—I just wanted to have as much sex as possible—you knew I had a rep with having casual flings—so, yeah—I apologize again for cheating on you—but hey—it's just who I am—so deal."

Duane glances at the entrance of the terminal.

"Whatever—it's just water under the bridge between us now anyway—I moved on years ago—done—no worries. You can fuck whoever you choose to—even if the guy is a cheap thrill with no redeeming value whatsoever. It's all on you not me."

"Good—we're better as friends anyway."

Duane turns to look at Carlo oddly and sighs. Ahead they see a taxi stand. Carlo smiles broadly as he looks at Duane.

"Think we can get a cab to take us all the way to Marble Hills? You know—travel in style—before we kill Madison."

Duane shakes his head.

"Better to rent a car—besides Whitney will expect us to keep our budget low—very low in fact—he hates to waste money on anything extra—especially on his lowly employees."

They continue walking a few yards further toward a rental budget car agency kiosk. Carlo seems upset as he walks.

<u>Glass Owl</u>

Greg watches as his father shuts his cell phone off. He turns to look at his son nervously. He seems very upset.

"This Whitney person is pond scum without a doubt."

Howard sits down opposite Greg.

"Why would you ever associate with trash like that? The man is seriously shady—uses people—he's a horrible person."

Greg sighs loudly.

"Don't you think I know I messed up royally?"

Greg stands up.

"What can I say? I'm a loser just like you said I always was—a total failure—a royal screw-up—a nobody—zero."

Howard watches as Greg walks toward the window.

"Things were said—harsh things."

Greg turns around.

"Like what? Are you saying you never meant it?"

Howard glances at his cell phone.

"Oh, I meant it without a doubt. You fucked up royally."

Greg reacts to Howard's harsh words.

<u>Boothbay Harbor</u>

Denise kisses Lance passionately and closes the door as he leaves. She leans against the door and smiles—licking her lips several times and glances at the bed a few feet away.

"Oh yeah—he's special—perfect."

She sighs loudly.

"One of the best I've ever had actually."

She licks her lips again and faces the bed again.

Page 74

<u>Spencer Driveway</u>

"Are you sure it's OK?"

Todd Spencer turns to look at Alden Washington standing nearby with a nervous look on his face. He grins broadly.

"Yes—I'm sure. Heather won't mind."

Todd glances at his house.

"Besides, she really loved watching *Larkspur Lane*. Still do actually. Women and their soaps—there's just something."

Alden laughs.

"OK. But for the record I think it would've been better if your wife knew I was coming for an impromptu visit?"

Todd grabs Alden by the arm.

"Come on—enough stalling already."

They walk up to the back porch. Todd opens the door and shoves Alden through without warning. Alden sighs loudly.

<u>Police Station</u>

Daryl glances at the clock on the wall. He sighs loudly. Seconds later he casually grabs a red leather briefcase on his desk and heads to the door—slamming it shut behind him.

<u>Standish Road</u>

Carlo and Duane head to Marble Hills in a rental car. Duane is looking out the window admiring the scenery. Carlo nudges Duane a little with his hand. He seems annoyed.

"Do you know where Madison lives? For some reason Whitney didn't have any info on Madison's filthy rich family."

Duane turns to look at Carlo.

"No—but it can't be that hard. According to Madison his family owns a huge estate. I'm sure everyone in town knows where it is—should be easy to get directions from the locals."

Carlo laughs and snaps his fingers.

<u>Page **75**</u>

"I guess the locals will be forthcoming with personal info about that loser Madison because we asked nicely, right?"

Duane gives Carlo a dirty look.

"I see you haven't lost your sarcastic edge."

Carlo ignores the jab and glances at the briefcase lying on the dashboard. He makes a lewd gesture with his hand.

"Madison will put up a fight I'm sure—he won't give up easily—but it might make for a fun encounter actually."

Carlo makes a sucking sound and grins.

"I've always had a thing for him actually—he's quite the looker—hot actually if you must know—turned me down plenty of times over the years—but I definitely intend to get some ass before I put a bullet in his empty head in the next day or so."

Duane rolls his eyes.

"You're planning to make him beg for his pathetic life while you're fucking him as you hold a gun to his head?"

Carlo grins again and nods.

"Yep—it's just how I roll. I've fucked every hot guy I blew away—might as well get myself a piece of Madison's gorgeous ass while I can—before he becomes a stiff in the morgue."

Duane looks away.

"This is a small town—behavior like that might arouse suspicion. Make for a lot of unnecessary heat—bad press."

Carlo laughs loudly.

"So what—by the time they find his body—we'll be long gone—it'll be assumed his death was attributed to something in his personal life—tongues will wag that he and a unknown lover had a messy tiff—there was a struggle and he was shot accidentally—a crime of passion—no big deal—end of story."

He laughs again and licks his lips several times. Duane looks at the briefcase and seems nervous. Carlo notices.

"There'll be no ties to Whitney after the fact except for a dead dude that was fucked before he got iced. Things like this happen every day—it's no big deal anymore—old news."

"I hope you plan to use a condom."

Carlo laughs loudly again.

"Heather?"

Todd looks at Alden and grins.

"This is so cool."

A scream interrupts the silence. Alden turns to see a woman standing in a doorway leading to the living room with a shocked look on her face. Todd begins laughing loudly.

"See, I told you we grew up together—Alden Washington and I—knew each other from way—should've believed."

Todd watches as Heather Spencer continues standing in the doorway as if in a trance. Todd turns to look at Alden.

"Heather Rollins *meet* Alden Washington."

She turns to look at Todd. He grins.

"Well, I have to get cleaned up. The two of you can chat meanwhile—that is—if my wife can stop acting so freaked."

Alden grins and watches as Todd disappears down a hallway. He walks over to where Todd's wife is still standing in a trance-like state. Alden sticks his hand out nervously.

"Hi, I'm Alden Washington."

She continues standing in front of Alden for a few seconds before nervously taking a few steps forward. She sighs.

"I—I'm sorry."

She takes his hand.

"I just always thought Todd was making it up. I'd heard rumors you'd lived here—but—well—Todd tells tall tales."

"No—it's true—Todd and I were friends—the stories I could tell—he and I got into a lot of scrapes—so many."

Heather glances back at the hallway.

"Yeah—Todd said he was pretty wild back in the day."

Alden runs his fingers through his hair.

"We made plenty of mistakes."

"No one is perfect—I've made plenty too."

A teenage boy comes out of a side bedroom at that moment. He looks at Alden oddly. Heather faces her son.

<u>Movie Theater</u>

Abby Marshall and Kelly Nelson walk out of the movie theater. He turns to look at her with a sly glance and grins.

"Movie was OK—but the company was better."

Abby smiles and holds Kelly's hand.

"You're so sweet."

Kelly grins. From the entrance Gina Bentley rushes up to them out of breath. She seems really upset about something.

"I'll never forgive you—I swear."

Abby and Kelly look at each other.

"Forgive me for what?"

Gina glares angrily at Abby.

"I saw him first—and—how could you?"

Abby looks at Kelly—they both seem confused.

"What are you talking about?"

Gina angrily grabs Abby and spins her around.

"He's mine—you of all people know."

Kelly quickly steps between them as Gina seems about to hit Abby. He gives her a harsh look which she ignores.

"First of all—I'm not a piece of property. Second—I make my own decisions. Third—I convinced Abby to see a movie together while you and your friend were arguing—calling each other all sorts of terrible names I won't bother repeating."

Gina turns to look at Kelly.

"Tiffany Johnson *is* no friend of mine—I hate her. She's a whore—everyone knows it—spreads her legs all the time."

"Whatever."

Kelly glances at Abby. Gina seems irritated.

"Well, you can forget about hooking up with me. I don't do leftovers—especially not after how rudely you treated me."

Kelly seems annoyed.

"No one asked you."

Gina looks at Kelly and then at Abby.

"You'll pay for this Abby—I swear you will."

She mutters something and leaves. Abby shrugs off Gina's behavior with a loud sigh. Kelly slowly turns to face Abby.

"Think I should be worried for your safety?"

Abby seems confused and shakes her head.

"Gina is harmless. She's just accustomed to getting her way no matter what. She'll get over it. Give or take a day."

Abby shrugs several times.

"Or maybe a week—I've seen this movie before."

Kelly reaches out to hold Abby's hand.

"What about the boyfriend you mentioned earlier that you had doubts about—I think—well—do I have a shot with you?"

Abby seems unsure how to reply.

<u>Boston</u>

Faye Washington looks around the terminal nervously. She heads for a small cafe nearby. In her haste she doesn't see a man coming toward her from behind until they collide against a large potted plant at the entrance of the small garden-style restaurant. They fall to the floor as the potted plant rolls off the metal stand it was perched upon and quickly breaks apart.

"Excuse me."

Faye glances at the man as he helps her to her feet. She smiles. His broken English and handsome features immediately attract her attention. Faye brushes herself off quickly.

"I'm OK."

"Are you sure? I'm really sorry. I really should have been watching where I was going. I should know better. It's just."

Faye grins.

"So should I."

They look at each other. Juan Sabrillo sighs.

"Can I buy you something to eat?"

Faye smiles coyly and nods.

"Great. I'll be with you in a few minutes."

He looks at his cell phone.

"This won't take long—got a few things to wrap up."

Page 79

Faye nods again. She watches the man walk to a deserted corner of the terminal nearby. She smiles broadly. She continues watching his muscular body and tight pants. She notices he isn't wearing underwear underneath either—or a wedding ring. She sits down at a table nearby and sighs loudly several times.

<u>Spencer Kitchen</u>

Simon Spencer stares at Alden curiously and seems somewhat bored. Alden runs his fingers through his hair.

"Yeah—your dad and I were good friends in high school."

Simon turns to look at his mother.

"I guess dad wasn't lying after all when he bragged to us that he and this dude knew each other way back when."

Alden reacts to Simon's statement.

"No—he wasn't. I used to live here a long time ago."

Simon looks at his watch.

"Fine, whatever—if you don't mind I have stuff to do."

Alden watches as Simon heads back to his room without another word. Heather shakes her head disapprovingly.

"Acts that way all the time I'm afraid—blame it on being a teenager—can't seem to shake the mood swings."

Alden smiles and runs his fingers through his hair again.

"I was worse when I was his age. I considered anyone over twenty-five to be old—positively ancient and decrepit."

Heather laughs and gestures with her hand.

"Me too—I guess not much has changed—we just hate to admit that it has—especially now that we're no longer."

Alden laughs. A few seconds later Todd emerges dressed in T-shirt and shorts. He grins as he notices their glances.

"What did I miss?"

Heather and Alden look at each other.

"Alden and Simon were just getting to know each other."

Todd seems worried.

"Oh-oh—what did he say?"

Alden glances at the hallway and grins.

Page 80

"Not much actually."
Alden shakes his head.
"Quite the silent type actually—monosyllabic."
"Uh-huh—yep—sounds like Simon all right. Can't seem to form a decent conversation long enough to save his life."
Alden shrugs knowingly.

<u>Nickerson's Bar</u>

Daryl sits alone at the bar and swallows a mug of beer in one gulp. He nervously looks at his watch and seems upset.
"I really need a break."
"Funny, I was thinking the same thing."
He turns around and sees Denise standing directly behind him with a look of disdain. He rolls his eyes. She smiles.
"Come here often?"
Daryl sighs.
"Probably more than I should actually."
Denise strokes Daryl's shoulder.
"I heard about your encounter with Kyle earlier today."
They look at each other as Daryl rolls his eyes.

<u>Pine Street</u>

Tiffany Johnson glances at her cell phone several times as she walks along the street. As she turns the corner in front of a movie theater she spots Gina at the entrance. She seems upset about something. Tiffany smiles broadly and walks up to her.
"So, is it true?"
Gina gives Tiffany a nasty look. Tiffany grins.
"I'll take that as a yes."
She laughs. Gina stops and turns around to face her.
"You knew—didn't you?"
Tiffany laughs.
"Lana Jefferson told me. Apparently she saw them leaving the mall in Kelly's car earlier—quite the cute couple."

Page **81**

Gina angrily glares at Tiffany.

"Enjoy it while you can you ugly cow—but know this about me—when I'm through with you—you'll seriously regret it."

Tiffany stops laughing and watches as Gina heads toward a nearby parking lot without saying another word.

Boston

A couple on a stairwell is going at it with extreme intensity. The woman moans loudly as the man continues to ram into her repeatedly. Finally their passionate lovemaking comes to an end as he pulls out and they look at each other briefly. He laughs in triumph knowing she's at his mercy. She sighs.

"Any doubts?"

Faye smiles and glances at Juan's exposed penis—still lazily sticking out of his pants covered with seminal fluid.

"You were right—I *so* needed something to relax me—*and* you were it—my God—where did you learn to fuck?"

Juan looks at his watch and smirks slyly.

"I think I can safely say we missed our flight?"

"No worries—we can always get the next one headed to Portland. In the meantime we can—oh—fuck again."

She sighs loudly.

"I still can't believe we're both headed to Marble Hills—it's as if what just—we were destined to meet like we did?"

"I take it that you're not upset that I was so forward with you earlier—took you the way I did—never bothered asking."

Faye leans over and kisses Juan.

"Actually—when we get to Marble Hills I'd like to pick up exactly where we just left off—and maybe—we could do."

Juan grins and pulls Faye toward him.

Anderson Kitchen

Jason walks to the refrigerator and opens it. He peers inside for a few seconds. He seems annoyed—and sighs.

"Dinner will be ready shortly."

He spins around to see his mother standing in the doorway. He rolls his eyes and shuts the door of the fridge.

"Thanks."

Lori Anderson watches as he walks over to the sink.

"Is something wrong?"

"Why?"

Lori walks over to where Jason is standing.

"You tell me—you've been acting moody all afternoon?"

Jason sighs.

"I'm a moody guy—deal with it."

He walks away.

<u>Shelby Park</u>

Tiffany is lying on her back in the backseat of an antique convertible as Brad McKinley plows into her repeatedly. He grins broadly as he kisses her again several times. He stops.

"You're on the pill, right?"

"Isn't it a little late to be asking me about that now—with you dick inside me already—like really Brad—did you?"

Brad laughs.

"Hey—at least I'm asking you—being sensitive and all that crap—trying to act like I care about you—which I don't."

"What about Donna?"

Brad slams into Tiffany again and laughs loudly.

"What she doesn't know."

Tiffany grins.

"Don't worry—I won't tell her that her boyfriend has been banging me for over a year—she's so—sort of a prude."

Brad slams into Tiffany yet again.

"Thanks, I appreciate that."

He pulls out. They look at each other.

"I can't believe Donna Markway thinks you've been faithful to her all this time—with your rep the way—oh."

Brad laughs loudly.

Page 83

"Why shouldn't she? No one will dare tell."

"It's her fault anyway."

"I agree. But she won't give it up to me. So, what am I supposed to do—wait patiently? I don't think so—no way—I'm a guy—a very healthy guy who likes living really dangerously."

Tiffany sits up.

"I'm not faulting you. I know you have needs—and if your girlfriend won't play—then—I'm certainly available to you."

Tiffany aggressively pulls Brad toward her. She kisses him passionately as they go at it again amid loud laughter.

<u>Standish Road</u>

Faye and Juan are driving toward Marble Hills in a rented car. Faye seductively slides her fingers between Juan's legs. He grins as her fingers glide over the expanse of his erection.

"You keep that up—and things will happen."

"What sort of things?"

Juan pulls over by the side of the road. He grabs Faye and they kiss passionately. He smiles and kisses her again.

"I intend to teach you a lesson."

He glances at the backseat and smirks.

<u>Marshall Driveway</u>

Kelly watches as Abby walks toward the front door of her home. She stops and turns around to wave. He waves back several times. As Kelly turns away from the entrance of Abby's home he sees Gina driving towards him. She slows down and looks at him coldly as she sticks her head out the car window.

"I hope it was worth it."

Kelly looks at Gina confused.

"My brother won't be pleased when he finds out."

"Like I care about your brother?"

"Oh, you will—believe me—you *will* be sorry. He's not the kind of guy you want to cross—just ask anyone in town."

Page **84**

Kelly watches as Gina drives off. He walks over to his car and glances once more at Abby's house before he opens the door. He shrugs and sighs loudly as he gets into his car.

<u>Nickerson's Alley</u>

A couple is having sex. The man angrily pushes the woman up against the wall and rams into her with intense passion. Her moans echo loudly in the deserted alley. She smiles broadly and looks at him again as he enters her repeatedly with careless recklessness. Denise kisses Daryl several times.

"You haven't lost you edge—if anything you've gained a adventurous streak as well—*like* the new you—wild guy."

Daryl laughs and looks at Denise.

"What can I say—it's been a while since I've really been able to let loose—have a good time—without baggage."

He plows into Denise again.

"You and me—*oh yeah*—it's just like high school all over again—except now we both have problems to get around."

Denise rolls her eyes.

"Don't remind me—Kyle and I—well—we both just have other things that interest us—and nothing has changed."

Daryl laughs.

"I know exactly what you're saying."

He makes a lewd gesture with his finger.

"Lori—Lori's even worse—believe me. She actually seems to think I exist to make her happy every day—*like really*."

He slams into Denise again.

"But surprise—I'm my own man. I do what I want—when I want—Lori doesn't have final say about what I do or who."

At that moment Denise realizes he's coming inside her as her body experiences a jolt. She looks at him and grins.

"Don't worry—I'm on the pill—not like those slutty college girls I've seen you with around Portland. I come prepared."

He makes a lewd gesture with his finger.

Page **85**

Howard nervously turns to face Kyle Madison. He seems worried. They silently look at each other for a few seconds.

"We have trouble."

Kyle seems annoyed.

"Don't you mean *Greg* has trouble?"

Howard looks away.

"Same thing—one Madison or all Madisons—this mess isn't going to go away—thanks to your stupid brother."

Kyle folds his arms across his chest.

"Exactly what had Greg done?"

Howard sighs.

"Your brother apparently fell in with the wrong crowd."

"Tell me something I don't know."

Howard slowly walks over to a large stained glass window and looks out at the sprawling lawn. He seems angry.

"This time it's different—apparently Greg has made some powerful enemies in the Boston mob—and they expect."

Kyle sighs loudly.

"The mob as in *Sopranos* type of mob?"

Howard turns around and nods.

"Yes."

"What are we going to do?"

Howard seems unsure of what to say next.

"I—I'm not sure."

Kyle nervously walks over to where Howard is standing and leans against the window. They look at each other.

"Is there a hit out on Greg?"

"I don't know. I assume there is—that's how those types work—they end their business arrangements with a bang."

Kyle seems upset.

"Is there anything we can do?"

Howard looks outside again and shrugs.

"Pay them off—it might be the only way out."

Kyle looks out the window.

Page **86**

"What if they want him dead—they usually don't take kindly to being slighted—revenge is the name of their game."

"Money speaks everywhere—I'll just pay them off to let the whole thing go—and then I'll deal with Greg's problem."

"What if they won't play ball?"

Kyle looks at the door.

"What if they won't be paid off—then Greg is in serious trouble isn't he? Could affect us all in a really bad way?"

Howard shrugs.

"I've got a lot of strings to pull."

"What about Greg—does he understand?"

Kyle glances at the door nervously—acting almost as if someone might be listening. He leans closer to his father.

"Understand that his stupidity has made us all a target?"

Howard rolls his eyes knowingly.

<u>Tolling Bell Inn</u>

Carlo pulls up in front of a hotel and looks at Duane.

"We're here."

Duane glances up at the bed and breakfast inn.

"Think Whitney already left us directions?"

Carlo nods.

"Is the earth round?"

Duane rolls his eyes and steps out slowly. He watches as Carlo locks the car and looks around. He grins broadly.

"I wonder if they have room service."

Carlo laughs.

"Wouldn't mind a hot bellboy if truth be known?"

"Don't you think maybe just this time you can restrain yourself when it comes to scoping out a potential conquest?"

Carlo smirks.

"Yeah—right—like I actually will."

Duane grabs Carlo by the arm.

"Must you whore yourself out everywhere we go?"

Carlo jerks free of Duane's grip.

Page 87

"I'm OK with who I am—a healthy young man who likes life—loves having uninhibited sex with total strangers. Life is too short to worry about—fuck and be merry is the way to go."

Duane seems upset.

"What about the fact of catching?"

Carlo laughs loudly.

"Never happen to someone like me—I'm too hot."

"You don't really believe that, do you?"

"Of course I do—I'm all that and then some—no chance I'll catch anything—hot guys are lucky—it's part of our deal."

Duane rolls his eyes.

"If you say so—but tell it to an actor named **Timothy Patrick Murphy** who was on *Dallas*—I bet he thought so too."

Carlo rolls his eyes again.

"I see the next few days will be heaven for sure."

Duane ignores Carlo's remark and quickly heads toward the front door of the inn. Carlo glances at the car briefly and then slowly follows Duane inside the small inn reluctantly.

<u>Plymouth Street</u>

Ashton Markway is walking down the street as he sees Wesley coming toward him. He seems in a rush of sorts. He looks around nervously and stops briefly as Wesley approaches.

"Hi Wesley—is everything OK?"

"Fuck off."

Ashton seems upset at the slight but shrugs it off seconds later. He turns to look at Wesley as he walks down the street.

"What a prick—hope he catches an STD."

He shakes his head several times.

<u>Farmington Villa</u>

Faye and Juan pull into a valet-attended parking lot of an expensive-looking hotel. Faye turns to Juan and smiles.

"You're staying here?"

Page 88

Juan laughs.
"No—*we're* staying here."
Faye grins.
"Really—who said?"
Juan nods.
"I did."
She smiles approvingly.
"Pretty sure of yourself—aren't you?"
Juan laughs again.
"I can be very persuasive when I want to be."
Faye looks at the hotel again.
"Is your boss paying for your splendid accommodations?"
Juan nods several times.
"Yep—he knows I expect only the best."
Faye looks at Juan curiously but says nothing more as he confidently pulls up to the valet stand a few yards away.

<u>Harbor Grill</u>

Kelly pulls into a parking lot in front of a popular local restaurant. As he slowly gets out of his car Ashton almost knocks him over as he walks by. Ashton immediately turns around.
"I'm sorry—I didn't see you."
Kelly makes a gesture with his hand.
"Perfectly OK dude—I wasn't watching where I was going either—got to be less clumsy in public I guess—my bad."
Ashton smiles nervously.
"You're the guy who works at the new ice cream kiosk at the mall—aren't you—took the job that nobody wanted?"
Kelly grins.
"Guilty."
They look at each other. Kelly extends his hand.
"Kelly Nelson."
"Ashton Markway."
Ashton glances at the restaurant.
"I was just about to—grab a quick bite."

Page **89**

"So was I."

They look at each other again and slowly head toward the entrance. As they are about to enter, two teenage girls comes out and sighs. One of them glances at Ashton and Kelly. She rolls her eyes at Ashton and continues walking without saying anything to him. Kelly notices her rude behavior and looks at Ashton.

"What's her problem?"

Ashton looks at Kelly.

"Her name is Carrie Spaulding. She's moody. The other one is OK—name's Lana Jefferson—she's a bit of a gossip."

"Good to know."

Kelly laughs.

"I've met a few troublesome types already myself—didn't think a small town like this could have had so much drama?"

Ashton rolls his eyes.

"You have no idea—*no idea at all.*"

He smirks.

"*Knots Landing* has nothing on Marble Hills."

He looks around.

"This town has way too much problems—sick and tired of it actually—not much here to look forward to—if anything."

They enter the restaurant.

<u>Boardinghouse</u>

Alden opens the door to his room and is about to close it when the door is forcibly pushed inward toward him. He slowly turns around to see Wesley angrily standing in the doorway.

"You killed my aunt—killed her and got away with it for years—but now you're going to pay for what you did—I swear you'll pay for what you did to Marah all those years ago—I'm going to crucify you—you'll wish you were never born."

"Wesley Madison I presume?"

Alden notices Wesley is wearing brass knuckles.

"Does Kyle know you're here?"

He glances at Wesley's odd reaction.

Page **90**

"Did your dad send you? I bet he did. Still holding on to the past I see. I think you'd better get your foolish ass out of here before things go from bad to worse between the two of us."

Wesley laughs loudly.

"Bad for whom—bad for whom you fucking prick?"

He takes a step forward.

"You killed my aunt all those years ago and thought you got away with it because no one saw you that night—but guess what you sick freak—it's time to pay the piper regardless. And I swear when I'm finished with you in a few minutes you'll wish you were dead already—dead like my aunt. My dad said she was the sweetest person he ever knew—and told me you killed her because you got her pregnant. Treated her like trash. Oh, I swear—I'm going to royally fuck you over—make you bleed."

He takes a swing at Alden. Alden falls and Wesley quickly jumps on top of him—continuing his ferocious assault.

TO BE CONTINUED

A Look at the 4th Episode

Wesley's assault on Alden is interrupted by Julia's unplanned visit—Robert and Lindsay continue to struggle in their unhappy marriage—Kyle is unable to prevent Wesley from being arrested as tables are turned—Howard tries to save Greg but is forced to realize sometimes money can't buy everything—Denise and Daryl make future plans to relive their past glory—Tyler and Ross make a show of their new relationship—Faye and Juan continue their highly-charged sexual encounters while he secretly pursues his victims and she plans her attack on Alden—Ashton makes a new friend and potential ally—Carrie and Brad reach an impasse about a specific incident—Carlo makes time for a friendly hook-up with a total stranger while unknowingly being stalked by a murderer bent on revenge no matter the risks involved—as Lindsay and Robert arrive in town for a visit with their troubled children.

Episode 4
Rewind the Clock

<u>Boardinghouse</u>

Julia Winthrop is almost at the top of the stairs when she hears sounds coming from the room at the end of the hallway as Wesley Madison and Alden Washington go at it. She rushes over and opens the door with a scream. Wesley turns around to look at her as Alden clocks him over the head without warning. Alden watches as Wesley topples over. Alden stands up and looks at Julia with a smile. His nose is bleeding. His face and neck has multiple abrasions. He glances back at Wesley and sighs.

<u>Standish Road</u>

Robert Bennington sits in the passenger side of a car as he looks out the window staring at nothing. He seems upset.

"I'm going to hate it—like really."

He turns to look at his daughter Susan Bennington. She's a typical teenager with attitude. She rolls her eyes and sighs.

"This stupid town only has one mall."

"Not another word from either of you."

Lindsay Bennington glances at her daughter briefly and then faces the road again as she focuses on keeping her hands on the steering wheel amid her rising anger. Susan sighs loudly.

"I really don't like—let's go back."

Lindsay shoots Susan a nasty look. Her twin brother Hart Bennington laughs. He rolls his eyes mockingly at his sister.

"Are we going to live with grandpa?"

Hart sighs loudly.

"What if he doesn't want us staying—I mean—it's not like we really—when was the last time we visited the old man?"

"It's already decided—besides, it's time you get to know my side of the family—you'll like living at Glass Owl."

Hart grins slyly.

"Uh-huh—grandpa's loaded—so I guess I can have him buy me a new car—maybe a huge yacht too—with perks."

Lindsay sighs.

"You'll *do* no such thing."

"It's not really up to you—is it—I want a car."

"No car—no yacht—*and* that's final. If you guys keep up this attitude I'll be forced to—to send you both away."

"*What*—send us to a boarding school in Europe? Go ahead—I'm sick of the States anyway—I wouldn't care."

Robert turns to look at Susan.

"I've had enough with your whining."

Hart and Susan look at Robert.

"I wonder if there are any hot girls in Marble Hills that would—if there are—I'll bag a few—shouldn't be too hard."

Susan laughs.

"Like you'd know what to do?"

Hart grins.

"I know what to do—just ask Maria Zegrelli."

Susan smirks.

"Oh, I did—and she said you totally struck out—*loser*."

"I pinned her—not just once either—plenty."

Lindsay turns to look at Robert angrily.

"Well, just don't sit there Robert, say something."

Robert looks out the window. Susan rolls her eyes again.

"I can't believe this is my life—I'm bored."

Hart laughs.

"Yeah—deal with it Susan. We're being forced to live in a **Norman Rockwell** painting—talk about a child abuse case."

Lindsay pulls over at the side of the road. She turns to look at Hart and Susan. Her rage seems about to explode.

<u>Harbor Grill</u>

Kelly Nelson and Ashton Markway are sitting in a booth at the far side of the restaurant. Ashton looks at Kelly.

"So, how do you like living in Marble Hills so far?"

"It's OK. Though it seems everybody has issues with each other—way too much anger if you asked me—soap opera."

Ashton laughs.

"You're not imagining it—believe me. This town has more crazy drama than one of those ridiculous old daytime soaps like *Passions* that my mom still watches religiously. The things I could tell you that I've seen happening—way bad—crazy stuff."

Kelly grins broadly.

"So, what's your deal with Carrie Spaulding—what did you do to her that she acted so rudely toward you earlier?"

"I'm just not in her circle."

He sighs.

"Well, you'll find out sooner or later anyway—so I might as well tell you—since it's not going to be a secret for too long."

He sighs again and waves his hand.

"I'm not exactly popular—if you know what I mean."

Kelly nods knowingly.

"Doesn't matter to me—I don't do cliques."

"Good—there's enough problems in the world as it is anyway—doesn't need more petty types—or more haters."

Kelly looks around and shrugs.

"*So*, what's the deal on Corey Bentley?"

Ashton glances at Kelly curiously with a worried look.

Page 95

"Why?"

Kelly smiles broadly.

"I met Abby Marshall earlier—and she and I talked."

"Oh-oh—Abby is a nice girl—but too bad she's like seriously hung up on Corey. He's bad news—like totally."

Ashton looks at the door.

"Corey Bentley is a dog. He's slept with so many girls I don't think he even remembers how many—he's trash—plain and simple—doesn't even try to be discreet with letting people see how sleazy he is—sleeps around with every girl in town."

He glances at Kelly.

"You're not—you know?"

"What—interested in her? I might be."

"Oh—not good."

"Corey Bentley doesn't scare me—I can belt him easily."

Ashton drops his voice to a low whisper.

"Rumor has it he's responsible for the "accidental" death of one of his father's "girlfriends" but it was hushed up."

Kelly looks at Ashton curiously.

<u>Boardinghouse</u>

Julia takes her cell phone out as Alden angrily grabs Wesley by the collar and forces him to stand up. He sighs.

"You've made a big mistake today."

Wesley looks at Alden.

"No—it's you who've made a mistake. My family is going to make you pay—pay for what you did to my aunt."

Alden laughs.

"What? Like have me arrested?"

He rams his fist against Wesley's throat.

"No—I don't think so. But if I were you—I'd definitely be worried—seems you've gotten yourself into a bit of a jam."

Wesley laughs loudly.

"I'm a Madison—or have you forgotten that fact—I own this town—I can do anything I want and not pay for it."

Page 96

"We'll see about that—you little prick—we'll see how smug you are when the State Police get here shortly."

Wesley suddenly seems afraid at the mentioning of the State Police. Alden notices and grins broadly. He points.

"What—cat got your tongue—you didn't think I'd call Daryl Anderson did you? That's right, you're fucked buddy."

Alden glances at Julia.

"Got through yet?"

She turns to face Alden and Wesley. She nods.

"They're on their way."

Alden turns to look at Wesley again.

<u>Harbor Grill</u>

Ashton waves his hand in the air as Tyler Van Pelt walks past them with his college-age boyfriend Ross Harrison. He immediately pulls Tyler toward him and they kiss passionately. Ross glances at Kelly and smirks. He licks his lips in a sexually suggestive way several times as they walk by. Kelly seems stunned by Ross's bold behavior but ignores his rudeness.

"The one in the pink Lycra shorts is Tyler Van Pelt and the other in the bright orange bike shorts is Ross Harrison."

Ashton points at them.

"I gather that it doesn't take being a rocket scientist to see they're seriously involved with each other at the moment."

"To each his own I guess—if they're doing it—that's their deal—not mine—the less I know the better—no worries."

"Tyler is OK. But Ross, well, he's enjoys being in people's faces—acts like everyone in town needs to know his scene."

Kelly nods as he looks at Ross and Tyler again.

"Yeah—I got that impression from him very clearly."

"As you can see Marble Hills isn't a picture-perfect postcard town by any means. Trust me when I say this—it has more in common with the TV series *Peyton Place* than a sleepy hamlet with weird townspeople as portrayed in the 1980s television series *Newhart*—like I said before—imperfect."

Page **97**

Kelly laughs.

"I believe you. I've met a few people already—and a warm welcome I didn't get. More like a really frosty reception."

Ashton sighs.

"I can't wait until next year. College can't come soon enough for me. Once I'm out of here—I'm never setting foot in this town again—no matter what—once I leave I'm gone."

"What about your folks?"

Ashton laughs.

"*They* can visit me."

Kelly laughs.

"What college are you going to?"

Ashton sighs again.

"I'm not sure yet."

"If I get into Emerson College I'll be a happy guy."

Ashton seems confused. He notices Tyler and Ross going at it a few feet away at their booth. He looks away.

"Why Emerson—I mean?"

Ashton glances at his cell phone.

"My grandparents live in a small town called Castle Beach just outside of Boston. My folks moved here for my dad's job."

Kelly nods several times.

"Oh."

They look at each other.

"So, what do people in Marble Hills do for fun?"

Ashton grins.

"Have sex."

Kelly turns to look at Tyler and Ross kissing passionately while a waiter seems irritated at the scene. Ashton nods.

<u>Farmington Villa</u>

Juan Sabrillo and Faye Washington are making love in Juan's hotel room. They finally part and look at each other as Faye grins broadly. Juan pulls her toward him again.

"There's no stopping you—is there?"

Page 98

Juan looks at his exposed penis and laughs.

"What do you want me to say?"

"I'm not complaining—I like a man who can rise to the occasion—over and over—and you certainly have risen."

He smirks.

"Speaking of which—I can go again."

His cell phone rings. They look at each other.

"It can wait—my boss is crazy."

Juan kisses Faye.

<u>Nickerson's Alley</u>

Denise Madison watches as Daryl Anderson slowly zips up his Levi's. She smiles as he looks at her with a sly grin.

"You haven't lost your touch Daryl—nope—not at all."

Daryl laughs loudly.

"You can force a man to marry but you can't tame the dog that dwells inside him—especially if that dog is me."

Denise grins.

"I'll say—Lori Barton just doesn't know the real you."

Daryl smiles slyly.

"And you do?"

Denise slides her fingers over Daryl's erection as it strains against the confines of his jeans. She licks her lips.

"What do you think—need another go round to know for sure—I'm aware you could use the play—and I like to play."

Daryl reaches out and pulls Denise to him.

"You and I together—most definitely—can do."

"I missed how aggressive you used to be when we'd fuck inside the locker room of the gym after Coach Messick went home. You always had to have your way—never could stop."

Daryl kisses Denise.

"What about Kyle and old man Madison?"

"What about them?"

Daryl looks at Denise in disgust.

"Old man Madison knows everybody's business."

Page 99

Denise slides her fingers over his erection once more. He grins again as she seductively continues stroking him.

"Marble Hills *is* a small town."

Denise laughs.

"So?"

She kneels down in front of Daryl.

"I always get what I want."

"That I know."

She kisses his erection and stands up.

"How about you and I meet in Rockport tomorrow?"

Daryl grins broadly.

"Perfect—it's a date."

She glances at the cell phone sticking out of his pocket.

"It seems you have a call?"

Daryl glances at the phone.

"I guess I do."

He flips it open and looks at the number.

<u>Boardinghouse</u>

Alden and Julia continue to look at Wesley who sits on the bed with a smirk on his face as he watches them. Julia sighs.

"*See*—no one's coming."

Julia looks at her watch again. Alden glances at the door for a few seconds. He seems worried. He looks at Wesley.

"We'll see."

Wesley smirks.

"You'll pay for this—I'll make sure you get what's coming to you for what you did to my aunt—I swear you'll pay."

"It's you who's going to pay."

Seconds later there is a knock on the door. Julia opens the door to see two State Police officers staring back at her. She turns to look at Alden. He grins broadly and glances at Wesley.

"Hi—my name is Colin Hartley. Someone called earlier about some kind of assault or possible attempt at murder?"

Alden turns to face Colin.

Page 100

"That would be me."

He glances at Colin and the second State Police officer. He watches as the man steps forward. Julia seems nervous.

"Will McColl."

Alden and Julia turn and point at Wesley.

"This is the person who attacked you earlier?"

Alden nods.

"Yes—I want him arrested."

They look at Wesley. He grins.

"I'm Wesley Madison—*as* in the grandson of Howard Madison. I'm sure the name rings a bell—very loudly."

Colin and Will look at each other.

<u>Harbor Grill Parking Lot</u>

Tyler and Ross are having sex in the backseat of Tyler's car. Loud laughter erupts during passionate lovemaking. Ross kisses Tyler again and smirks as he looks at the stained fabric.

"Still think I should've worn a condom?"

"No, you were right—it's more intense this way."

Ross pulls out of Tyler and they look at each other as Tyler sits up with a dazed look on his face. He sighs loudly.

"This weekend is definitely open."

Ross grins.

"What about the folks?"

Tyler laughs.

"They'll be away."

Ross pulls Tyler to him and they kiss.

"I think we should do it in your parents bed—to send a message—make it clear they know you and I are a couple."

"I think they already know."

"I'm not convinced."

Ross pulls Tyler toward him again.

"You know us college guys only have one thing on our minds every day—and it isn't academics by any means."

Ross kisses Tyler again. He smiles.

Page **101**

"Think your parents suspect you're gay?"

Tyler shakes his head.

"I assume they do—they think I have a girlfriend—a wonderful girlfriend who never calls me—and never visits."

"Me, well I lost my virginity four years ago to my hot neighbor. He was older than me—twenty-five actually. He invited me into his house one afternoon after I'd gotten home from school—and one thing led to another and before I knew it he had pulled my jeans down—and was giving me an incredible blowjob, then he took me in the shower where I gave it up to him easily, carelessly, almost recklessly—never once thought twice about giving him my virginity—I knew he had a bad rep where boyfriends were concerned. I knew he'd been with a lot of guys and was very promiscuous—from all the boyfriends he'd had over to his house the year previously—I knew he played the field pretty hard. But that was what I needed actually—I had to be with someone who'd been around—been with hundreds of guys. We fucked every day after I got home from school for weeks afterwards—until—*until* he met Matt Brewster—you know, the famous cyclist that came in second in the last Olympics—at a gym a month later and dumped me right after without saying anything to me other than thanks for the great ride—and to have a nice life—admitting he'd already slept with Brewster earlier in the day and that was just the way it had to be between us. He dumped me like it didn't matter—ignored me afterwards."

Ross seems upset and shrugs.

"Brewster sleeps around a lot too from what I hear—likes picking guys up in gay bars and taking them to his condo."

"Is Brewster and your neighbor still together currently?"

Ross shakes his head several times.

<u>Glass Owl</u>

Kyle Madison looks at his father as he shuts his cell phone off. Howard Madison shakes his head and seems annoyed.

"Eldon Whitney isn't taking my calls."

Page 102

Kyle sighs and looks around.

"What now?"

Howard shrugs.

"I don't know."

"Are you going to tell Greg the bad news?"

Howard looks around.

"What choice do I have—where is your little brother anyway—haven't heard a peep out of him for hours now?"

"He's probably getting himself into more trouble like he always does. What else is new when it comes to Greg?"

Howard glances at the door.

<u>Boston</u>

Eldon Whitney leans back in his chair as he talks on his cell phone. He grins as he looks at Greg Madison's photo.

"Yeah—they're worried. But so what—Greg Madison is a dead man—family money or not. He'll be a stiff shortly."

He laughs and gestures with his hand.

"His father has been calling. But I see no point in discussing the matter further. I want that fucker Madison dead ASAP. He slighted me *and* no one slights me and lives to tell about it—no one—I fully intend to dance a jig on his grave."

Eldon glances out the window.

"Of course I haven't forgotten your deal with Rogers and Pyle. Do what you must if you see fit—good riddance."

He grins broadly.

"Perfect. I love it—cause pain before you kill them both."

Eldon nods several times.

"They won't see it coming. No better way than going out with a bang—especially if it's from a gun in your hand."

Eldon laughs loudly.

"Just make sure there's no mess to clean up."

He grins again.

"Oops sorry—I forgot—you've been there—done that."

Eldon smiles broadly.

"OK. Call me tomorrow right after you've taken them both out. *Then* we can concentrate on finally eliminating Madison and resuming our lives as if nothing else matters in the world."

He shuts off his cell phone and glances at paperwork lying on his desk. He grabs Greg Madison's photo in a rage.

"With those two clowns out of the way Madison is as good as dead. That bastard will be on a slab by this time tomorrow."

He crumples the photo and laughs joyfully.

<u>Farmington Villa</u>

Faye looks up as Juan comes from the balcony toward the sofa. He smiles as he throws his cell phone on a table.

"Sorry about that—had to take that call."

Faye stands up.

"No need to explain anything to me—your boss shouldn't be ignored—would be rude—and you wouldn't want."

She sighs.

"Especially given the fact he's paying for this wonderfully perfect room—of which is something out of a fairy tale."

Juan grins as he walks toward her.

"I agree."

Juan grabs Faye and pulls her toward him.

"But—since I'm done with him—*now* I'm going to do you once more. I can't seem to get enough today—so horny all of a sudden with tired talk about boring movie location shoots."

Faye laughs.

"I have no objections."

Juan pushes Faye down onto the sofa.

"I'm glad we met."

"I agree—we barely know each other—yet here we are having sex for the umpteenth time—like a pair of teenagers."

Juan laughs loudly.

"Strangers make the best partners."

Faye watches as his hands slowly slides under her blouse and cups her breasts. He reaches out to lick her fingers.

Page **104**

"I can't be stopped when I'm in the mood."
Faye reacts as he kisses her again.

<u>Standish Road</u>

Robert glances at his wife as her eyes stare straight at Susan and Hart. He sighs. Lindsay seems to become angrier as the seconds tick by. He sighs again as Hart rolls his eyes.
"I'm bored."
Hart leans forward from the backseat and grins slyly.
"This blows chunks."
Lindsay shoots him a look.
"Keep dancing on the minefield."
Susan grins.
"Like you'd ever make good on one of your threats?"
Lindsay glances at her watch. Hart and Susan look at each other nervously as Lindsay faces them with a harsh look.
"I'm waiting."
She looks at her watch again. They both ignore her.
"Get out—both of you."
They look at each other and laugh.
"You're joking right?"
"Do I look like I'm joking?"
Hart and Susan nervously turn to look at Robert.
"Don't look at me—I can't help you now."
Lindsay steps out of the car.
"I'm not kidding—get out or I'll drag you out."
Susan gestures with her hand.
"No—you can't—you wouldn't dare."
Lindsay looks at Susan angrily. She walks over to the right side of the car and opens the door, dragging Susan out. Lindsay turns to look at Hart. He quickly jumps out of the car. She shuts the door and walks over to the left side of the car. Hart and Susan seem shocked at the sudden turn of unprepared events that unfolds before their eyes. They turn and look around the area.
"You can't leave us here—you wouldn't?"

Page 105

Lindsay smiles as she quickly gets into the car.

"Watch me."

They watch as she drives away.

"How far is Marble Hills from here?"

"How should I know?"

Hart glances at some houses in a distance.

"There are some houses over there—it can't be that far a walk—come on—let's go—before a pack of wolves get us."

Hart suddenly grabs Susan by the arm without warning and they slowly begin walking toward Marble Hills.

<u>Pike's Bar</u>

Carlo Rogers walks into the crowded bar and immediately begins scoping out possible conquests. He notices a man in faded Levi's at the end of the bar seemingly alone. He grins and walks over to him intent on furthering his interest for a partner.

"Mind some company?"

The man turns to look at Carlo. His eyes carefully look over Carlo's tight-fitting corduroy pants as he grins slyly.

"Nope—sit down."

Carlo sits down and smiles broadly.

"Carlo Rogers."

"Matt Brewster."

They look directly into each other's eyes for a few seconds as Matt licks his lips and grins broadly. He sighs loudly as his fingers casually tug at Carlo's belt. They look at each other.

"Hey, let's blow this stand—my condo is not far from here. It's much more private—you know—for maybe some action?"

Carlo winks at Matt.

"I'm down with that—love your directness."

Matt smirks.

"It's part of my charm. I don't believe in wasting time when I see something or someone I like—and want to know."

They leave the bar together.

Page **106**

<u>Boardinghouse</u>

Wesley sits silently on the sofa in handcuffs as Colin reads him his rights. Will turns to look at Alden and Julia briefly as he casually opens his laptop and begins typing. He shrugs.

"Are you sure you want to go this route—I don't have to tell you what probably will happen from here with his family?"

"Don't care. That piece of garbage needs a lesson taught to him—and I'm just the guy to do it. He needs a reality check."

Will shakes his head in a confused way.

"OK—just thought I'd let you know what could?"

"No prob—but this is my deal now."

The door opens suddenly and they see Daryl standing there with a shocked look on his face. He takes a step forward.

"Alden? You and Wesley—how did?"

Alden nods and turns to look at Wesley.

"Punk thought he could best me but fucked up."

Daryl sighs loudly and seems upset.

"What happened?"

"Kyle's brat tried to kill me."

"*I did no such thing.*"

Daryl and Alden turn to look at Wesley.

"Tell it to a judge."

Daryl pulls Alden aside and whispers.

"Come on, don't do this—it'll just make things?"

"It's done—or haven't you noticed that's why the State Police got here before you did. This punk is screwed."

Daryl sighs again.

"Please—don't—let's talk."

"Get the fuck out of my face Anderson. I'm doing it—and there's nothing you or your friend Kyle can do about it."

They watch as Colin forces Wesley to his feet. Wesley looks at Alden and then back at Daryl. He seems frightened.

"Young man, you're in serious trouble. If I were you I'd start taking this very seriously before things really slide."

Wesley glares at Alden and tries to push Colin away.

"You'll both be sorry."

Alden looks at Colin and Will.

"Hope you heard that—I want that added to his charges."

"Duly noted and it will be added."

Colin pushes Wesley toward the door. Daryl grabs Colin by the arm. They look at each other for a few seconds.

"Where are you taking him?"

"Portland."

Daryl seems worried.

"Can't you leave him here in Marble Hills?"

Will shakes his head as he turns to look at Daryl.

"No—I'm sorry."

Daryl watches as they leave with Wesley and then turns to face Julia and Alden. He seems disappointed and shrugs.

"Well, I hope you're happy now."

Alden sighs.

"Not yet—but I will be."

Daryl turns to face Julia. He tries to hold her hand.

"Can't you do anything to help? You know Wesley is a good kid. He just has a hot temper that's all—a bit troubled."

Julia seems irritated at Daryl.

"*Oh*, now you want to talk to me Daryl—but *only* when you need me to help clean up your mess right? Well no."

Daryl seems confused.

"What? Huh?"

"I witnessed Wesley Madison attempting to murder Alden earlier and I will not pretend otherwise. I can't help you."

Daryl glares at Julia for a few seconds and then angrily storms out of the room. Julia and Alden look at each other.

<u>Standish Road</u>

Hart and Susan are slowly making their way toward Marble Hills when they see Lindsay driving toward them a few seconds later. She barely looks at them as the car comes to a stop. They seem confused. Robert doesn't look at them.

<u>Page **108**</u>

"Get in the car."
Hart reaches for the door handle.

Glass Owl

"This mess with Greg—it can only get worse."
The phone rings. Kyle looks at his father.
"Hold that thought."
Kyle looks at his cell phone and seems annoyed at being interrupted. He sighs loudly several times as he answers.
"I'm not in the talking mood Anderson."
Kyle listens and becomes pale. A shocked look spreads across his face. He turns to look at his father seconds later.
"My God—is he serious?"
He sighs loudly again.
"No—I'll go."
Kyle shuts off the phone. He slowly turns to look at his father again who seems confused at Kyle's curious behavior.
"What does Daryl Anderson want?"
Kyle reacts in shock.
"Wesley just attacked Alden Washington. He's being charged with attempted murder. The State Police are involved unfortunately. They've already taken him to Portland."
Howard seems stunned by the sudden turn of events.
"This is a joke *right*?"
"I wish it was a joke—but Wesley."
Kyle leans against the door.
"What else can possibly go wrong today?"
The front door opens. Standing in the doorway are Robert and Lindsay. They both seem to be in a very bad mood.

Boardinghouse

Julia closes the door and nervously turns to face Alden.
"Is there anything I can do for you?"
Alden shakes his head and seems confused.

Page **109**

"No—I'm good."

"Are you sure—Wesley Madison just tried to kill you—if it were me I'd be freaked. That kid is a serious piece of work."

"I'm OK. Trust me—Kyle Madison is more of a mess than I am right now. Not the kind of news he wanted to face."

Julia smiles broadly.

"I would just love to be a fly on that wall."

"So would I."

Julia glances at the door. She seems nervous as she looks at Alden again. He wipes away dried blood from his mouth.

"Do you think they'll come after you?"

Alden shakes his head.

"I didn't do anything—Wesley Madison attacked me—not the other way around. He brought this mess upon himself."

Julia looks at her watch.

"Well, if there's anything you need—just call."

Alden nods several times. Julia slowly walks to the door and opens it. She looks back at Alden once and leaves.

<u>Brewster Condo</u>

Matt and Carlo enter his condo. He shuts the door behind them and turns to look at Carlo with a sly look on his face.

"Want something to drink."

Carlo shakes his head.

"It's no problem—I'm going to make myself a drink—and then you and I can get to know each other a lot better."

Carlo grabs Matt. He kisses him on the lips—shoving his tongue down Matt's throat as Matt reacts with a grin.

"Oh—wow—didn't see that coming. Like a guy who knows what he wants and takes charge. Uh-huh—I like it a lot."

Matt pulls away briefly—grins again—and begins kissing Carlo passionately as they're overcome with intense lust.

"The bedroom—you and I have to—can't hold out another second—got to have you—need you so badly—right now."

"Uh-huh—I know the feeling."

Page 110

He passionately kisses Matt again. Matt grins and guides Carlo toward the hallway leading to his bedroom seconds later.

<u>Harbor Grill</u>

Faye and Juan sit down at an empty booth as Ashton and Kelly walk past them as they head toward the front door.

"So, you never told me what business you had here in Marble Hills? Like what do you do? What's your deal?"

Juan grins.

"I could ask you the same thing."

Faye looks at Juan curiously. He grins broadly and reaches out to stroke her face. She looks away. He rolls his eyes.

"I asked first."

He laughs.

"OK. OK You got me. I'm here to kill two hit men and their target. Satisfied now? Or do you want the grisly details?"

Faye laughs loudly.

"Be serious. Just tell me."

"I'm here in Marble Hills to scout locations for a movie that is set in a tiny hamlet somewhere in Maine—a tawdry drama."

Faye seems confused and shrugs.

"But didn't you say you were from Chile?"

"And what—I can't have a job scouting movie locations because everyone in Chile owns huge cattle ranches?"

"I didn't mean it like that."

Juan reaches out and kisses Faye.

"I'll forgive you this time—but just this once."

Faye kisses him. He pulls away.

"OK—I told you why I'm in town—so why are you here?"

Faye rolls her eyes and laughs.

"My lousy ex-husband—he used to live here."

Juan seems confused.

"He was a soap opera actor. But they canned his ass—and now he's just an unemployed sorry loser—with no game left."

He notices Faye suddenly seems upset.

Page 111

<u>Mall</u>

Carrie Spaulding is sitting alone at an open cafe in a food court as Brad McKinley approaches her. He grins broadly.

"I see you're still in a mood."

Carrie rolls her eyes.

"Wow—I guess you're not as dumb as you look."

He pulls out a chair and sits down.

"Come on—what happened two weeks ago is ancient history. It meant nothing—just two friends having fun."

"To you—but what about me, Brad? As I recall you never asked—asked if I just wanted to be treated like a whore."

Brad laughs.

"You knew I had a girl—you know my deal."

"A what—a girlfriend—really—oh yeah Brad—right—like in name only—everyone in Marble Hills knows your pathetic game except dear Donna Markway—at least for now anyways."

Carrie rolls her eyes.

"But things can change so easily in this town—if you know what I mean—come to think of it I think it's time she knew."

Brad grins.

"OK. OK. I play the field—so shoot me already."

Carrie glances at Brad slyly.

"Don't tempt me—there's nothing better I'd like to do than put a bullet in your head for how you've treated me."

Brad leans toward Carrie.

"I fucked you—nothing more—I didn't rape you—*you* didn't tell me to stop when things got out of hand that night."

Carrie leans backwards and sighs.

"But I thought you really wanted to be with me? You promised me this was real—said I wasn't like the others."

"Of course I wanted to be with you—I never said I didn't want to—but it was only to stick my dick into you—I never said that I wanted to date you—I mean—get serious—get real."

"Just get lost—like now—OK?"

Page 112

"Whatever—but you know where to find me if you change your—you know—for a good time like before—fun only."

"I'd rather eat dirt."

Brad grins broadly and stands up. Carrie notices his grin and seems more irritated than before. He smirks knowingly.

"Be gone—or I swear."

"I'm going—I'm going—but I'm always ready whenever you need a stiff dick inside you. *You* know my moods."

"Tell it to someone who cares."

"No wonder you have trouble getting laid."

Brad looks at Carrie once more and leaves. She sighs loudly and picks up her cell phone. She seems angry.

<u>Johnson Driveway</u>

Tiffany Johnson angrily slams the door to her convertible shut as her cell phone rings unexpectedly. She reaches for it.

"Hello? Oh hi Carrie. What's up with you?"

Her facial expression changes as she listens to Carrie on the other end. She rolls her eyes in dismay several times.

"Of course he's a dog—he'll sleep with anything that moves—Brad McKinley isn't boyfriend material—toad."

Tiffany laughs.

"Believe me I know—been there and done that—he's all about a good time—that's all. His rep is what it is—plays girls."

Tiffany seems annoyed.

"Oh, I know he's been on the prowl—he and every other straight guy in town can't seem to keep it in their pants long enough for more than—except Ashton Markway of course and no girl is willing to give it up to him—no matter what the deal."

Tiffany laughs again.

"Yeah—like I would ever touch that dweeb."

She licks her lips several times.

"Forget about Brad. I met this guy—he's new in town—I had him in my sights but Gina Bentley messed it up—and Abby Marshall of all people scored—I still can't believe it myself."

Page 113

Tiffany slowly begins walking toward the front door of her home. She stops suddenly. Tiffany seems annoyed.

"Of course I'm pissed at her—he would've scored with me without trying—*he* was that hot. But Gina fucked it up."

She sighs.

"What am I planning to do about it—about Abby Marshall and about Gina Bentley messing my plans up? I'm not sure."

Tiffany smiles slyly.

"I haven't decided yet—but they're going to pay."

She gestures with her hand.

"Yep—you know it—it'll be something really awful—like highly unpleasant. But they had it coming—both of them."

Tiffany opens the front door of her home.

"Yeah, I know I have to get even. Gina especially caused me a lot of problems of late—I'm going to do something to her she won't forget. Maybe even release some of those pictures I took of us at Pearl Beach last year—where she stripped."

Tiffany nods several times and smirks.

"Exactly—those photos in the wrong hands would ruin her rep in Marble Hills. People would be talking for years."

She laughs slyly.

"It would serve her right if I did."

She gestures with her hand.

"It's time she realizes I'm not to be trifled with. When those pictures come out she's done—she'll have to leave town."

Tiffany rolls her eyes knowingly.

"Ask me if I care."

She closes the front door behind her.

<u>Brewster Condo</u>

Carlo pulls out of Matt. He grins broadly and kisses Matt several times, sighing loudly as he lies back on the plush bed.

"Oh yeah—I could go for hours."

They look at each other.

"Man, you were seriously on fire earlier."

Page 114

"Hey—it's not every day I fuck a world-famous cyclist in his gorgeous condo. Had to go for broke—couldn't hold."

Matt grins broadly.

"Well, in my defense I have to say I wanted you as much as you did me—wild, uninhibited sex is the sweetest kind."

"Is tomorrow too soon for an encore?"

Carlo looks at Matt curiously.

"Unless you have a friend on the side—could be messy?"

Matt laughs loudly.

"No boyfriend—lots of acquaintances, though."

They embrace each other.

<u>Harbor Grill</u>

Faye watches as the waiter walks away from their booth with their bill. She turns to face Juan and reaches out to touch his hand. He looks at her curiously. She strokes his fingers.

"Thanks for a most illuminating dinner."

Juan grins.

"I should be thanking you."

He glances at his watch.

"Hey, I hope you won't get pissed but I have something to do—then you and I can pick up again where we left off."

Faye looks at Juan curiously.

"What do you have to do right now?"

"Oh, nothing important—I'll be back before you know it."

Faye looks at Juan suspiciously.

"Is it another woman? I don't care much for guys that play games—had enough of that with my ex—he played me."

Juan looks at Faye curiously and smirks.

"I'm not your ex."

He leans over to kiss her.

"Like I said I'll be back shortly—I'll meet you back at the hotel—two hours possibly—got to keep my boss happy."

"It better not be another woman."

Faye watches as Juan suddenly leaves abruptly.

Page **115**

Howard and Kyle seem in shock as Robert and Lindsay nervously stand in the doorway—behind them are Hart and Susan. They both seem bored. Howard takes a step forward.

"Lindsay?"

She glances at her father and Kyle.

"You kept saying for the longest time for us to come for a visit—well—be careful what you wish for dad—you just might get what you claimed you wanted for years now from me."

Howard regains his composure and walks toward his daughter as Robert nervously eyes Howard cautiously.

"Is everything all right?"

Lindsay glances at Robert.

"Possibly—the jury is still out."

Kyle looks at his watch and then at Lindsay.

"Well, I hate to be rude but I have my own problems to deal with at the moment—your nephew is in jail yet again."

Lindsay and Robert look at each other as Kyle exits through the front door, walking past Hart and Susan without saying a word to them of which they seem oblivious anyway.

"Maybe this wasn't such a good time to visit?"

Lindsay shoots Robert a nasty look. Howard notices.

"Of course it's a good time—Kyle is just—just having trouble with being a father of a troubled teenage son."

Lindsay smiles and looks at Hart with a knowing look. He seems annoyed as she looks at her father again. She sighs.

"The stories I could tell you."

Hart sighs.

"I've never been in jail."

Susan rolls her eyes and jabs him.

"Uh-huh—not yet."

She jabs Hart again.

"I give it two weeks tops."

Lindsay shoots Hart and Susan a harsh look.

"One more peep out of you two and your cousin won't be the only member of this family to have problematic jail issues."

Lindsay closes the front door and turns to look at her father. They hug. Howard glances at Robert and sighs.

<u>Tolling Bell Inn</u>

Carlo enters the pitch-black room. His footsteps echo as he closes the door behind him. He listens to the silence in the room and seems frozen for a few seconds. He sighs loudly.

"Duane?"

He is about to turn on the lights when he sees someone slowly walking toward him in the darkness. He calls out.

"Duane? Is that you?"

There is no answer. He sighs again.

"If you're still pissed about what happened earlier?"

Carlo slowly reaches for the light switch and flips it on. Juan stands a few feet away from him. He grins broadly.

"Hello Carlo—it's been a long time—too long."

Carlo notices the gun in Juan's hand. Juan laughs loudly as he takes a step forward. Carlo seems in shock. He reacts.

TO BE CONTINUED

A Look at the 5th Episode

Kyle arrives in Portland to see Wesley but his son isn't exactly pleased to see his father—Carrie ruthlessly schemes to expose Brad's lies to Donna in order to exact revenge on her foe—Denise and Daryl's chance sexual encounter is noticed by a unprincipled stranger with blackmail on his mind—Carlo finds a nasty surprise in his hotel room—Kelly's friendship with Ashton creates social problems for him while Abby deals with her disintegrating friendship with Gina over Kelly—Greg takes the easy way out rather than deal with the mess he caused—Alden rekindles a friendship with a childhood friend—Denise and Kyle play the blame game over Wesley's situation—Robert and Lindsay's failing marriage becomes the subject of family talk amid tragedy—as Matt unexpectedly finds himself involved in a potentially dangerous situation involving two brutal murders.

Murder is Easy

Boardinghouse

Alden Washington is sitting in front of a computer when he hears a knock at the door. He walks to the door and answers it. As he opens the door he sees Eddie Kane staring back at him with a huge grin across his face. Alden seems somewhat in shock.

"Heard you were back in town?"

Alden grins broadly.

"*Eddie Kane*. You haven't changed one bit."

He offers his hand. Eddie shakes it and comes into the room still with a grin on his face. He turns to face Alden.

"So, how was Hollyweird?"

Alden laughs.

"Weird."

"You know, you could have visited us ordinary folks once in a while. Especially after you took off so suddenly?"

Alden closes the door.

"Yeah, right—and Kyle Madison would have been right there with everyone else—welcoming me—with handcuffs."

He laughs again.

"I think not."

Eddie sits down on the sofa.

"Fuck Kyle Madison. Damn him. He and his punk son are ruining this town—thinks everyone owes them something."

"Certainly that doesn't apply to you—I mean—look at your deal—you made good for a local boy—heard your story."

Eddie grins.

"It wasn't easy. Madison and his scumbag of a father did everything they could to block every fucking deal I went after in the beginning—but then I decided to push back and push back hard and—and well—the rest is history—I made a killing."

"I guess this means you two aren't friends?"

Eddie rolls his eyes and shrugs.

<u>Tolling Bell Inn</u>

Carlo Rogers nervously glances at the oak dresser at the far end of the room. Juan Sabrillo notices and laughs.

"Don't even think of it. You won't make it in time to save your miserable life. Vengeance will be mine—I win."

Juan laughs again.

"Yeah—you clowns thought you'd gotten away free and clear without punishment for what happened in Miami."

Juan grins.

"Well, think again. You mess with my family and I take it personally. An eye for a frigging eye—a death for an accidental death—sounds familiar doesn't it—uh-huh, thought so dear sweet Carlo—especially given how you've dealt with anyone who crossed you. But two can play that game though. Time's up."

Carlo looks around.

"Where's Duane?"

Juan shrugs.

"He's out. But don't worry. He's gonna get it just like you will shortly. That I can promise—time to pay the piper."

"Whitney isn't going to like this?"

Juan laughs loudly.

Page 120

"Who do you think ordered your hit? Duh—Whitney is as sick of you guys as I am. Seems you two have messed up just one too many times. Greg Madison should have been taken out in Boston. But as usual you and your boyfriend messed up what should've been an easy job to handle—just like you did last year in Miami—causing my brother to lose his life for your inane stupidity. But don't worry—after I take both of you out—I'll finish off Madison for good and Whitney will be satisfied—finally."

"I don't believe you."

Juan smirks.

"Suit yourself."

Juan moves closer to Carlo.

"I'm so going to enjoy putting a bullet in you—you'll die at my hands exactly as I promised Ernesto you would."

Juan suddenly grabs Carlo and angrily shoves his gun against the back of Carlo's head—pushing him toward one of the beds. Carlo resists briefly as Juan gives him another rough shove and sighs loudly as Carlo trips but regains his balance.

"I won't be taken out like a common mark."

Juan rolls his eyes.

"Maybe you're forgetting that I'm the one with the gun pointed at your head—the one that *will* take your life and avenge my brother's tragic death—which you caused—because if you've suddenly become an idiot I can refresh your feeble mind."

Carlo spins around suddenly and attempts to grab the gun from Juan. Juan regains his grip and then kicks Carlo hard.

"Get on the bed tough guy."

Carlo stands there without moving.

"I'm not going to ask twice."

He looks around nervously.

"I'll—I'll do anything you want—just don't."

Juan laughs loudly again.

"What? Don't kill you? Forget it. No deals."

Juan waves the gun around.

"I've waited too long for this sweet moment. *Ernesto* has waited too long. Your death is necessary for closure."

Page **121**

Juan jams the gun against Carlo's head once more.
"This is just the way things have to be."
He looks at Carlo lying face down on the bed.

<u>Mall</u>

"What was so important you wanted me to come over and talk to you—I have things to do—and I don't think?"
Carrie Spaulding looks up to see Donna Markway looking at her curiously. She rolls her eyes in a disgusted way.
"Sit down."
Carrie watches as Donna sits down.
"You never talk to me and now you want to? What's going on Carrie? Did Genie Van Pelt and her friends say?"
Carrie folds her hands in front of her across the table. She appears upset as Donna looks at her nervously. She sighs.
"Look, I know we're not friends—but so what—I have some information that you need to know—*should* know."
"Like what?"
Carrie sighs.
"Brad McKinley."
Donna leans across the table.
"Brad? What about Brad?"
Carrie looks around, smiles broadly and whispers.
"He's not what he appears to be."
Donna shrugs.
"I know he's not rich. He pretends his dad is loaded."
Carrie sighs again.
"That's not what I mean."
She sighs loudly again and seems stressed.
"Reality check, Brad McKinley is a dog—*there* I said it."
Donna leans backwards.
"I know—I know he's been around. But he said?"
Carrie snaps her fingers several times.
"Said what—that he wasn't playing around on you?"
Donna nods several times.

Page 122

"Well, he's a liar. He and I were—look—he fucked me two weeks ago—told me you weren't giving him anything."

Donna seems shocked.

"No—you're lying."

"Believe what you want—but he took me in his car—in the backseat to be precise—right after he dropped you off at your Key Club meeting. We laughed about how stupid you were not to even suspect he was playing behind your back—when it was so obvious to even the most clueless person in Marble Hills that he wasn't going to be tamed by someone of the likes of you."

Donna reacts.

"*No*—he wouldn't."

Carrie laughs.

"What—he wouldn't fuck another girl other than you—*oh*, that's right he's never fucked you—you've been playing hard to get—well, he's been doing it with everyone else despite the fact you've held out like a frigging prude—too frigid to—cold."

Donna seems about to cry. Carrie grins.

"Face it, Brad McKinley is a lying, two-faced scheming piece of filth—every girl in town has seen him naked."

Carrie smiles slyly.

"Why don't you go ask Elizabeth Pendleton, Tiffany Johnson, Gina Bentley, Natalie Standish, the Bingham sisters, Shirley Moses and Lana Jefferson just for starters—he's slept with all of them too—plenty of times. Go ask them—I dare you."

Donna looks at Carrie suspiciously and jumps up—she seems about to cry—and begins running toward the exit of the mall as tears stream down her face in a rushing flood.

Glass Owl

Howard Madison leads his daughter into the den and shuts the door. He seems upset as he looks at her cautiously.

"OK—so what's going on with you and Robert?"

Lindsay Bennington looks away.

"Nothing—we've just come for a visit."

Page 123

Howard spins Lindsay around. She seems uneasy.

"What did he do?"

Lindsay sighs.

"I—I don't want to talk about it."

Howard appears angry.

"Tell me—tell me what he did to you."

Lindsay seems about to cry.

"Did that bastard—did he fool around with some slut?"

Lindsay stares blankly at her father.

"I swear—I'll make him pay."

Lindsay shakes her head.

"No—just leave it alone—it'll only make things worse."

"How can things be any worse than—*than* they already are? I think he needs to be taught a lesson—harsh and cruel."

"It was just one time—he said he ended it."

"Is that so—or it that what he told you? No one ever just cheats once—I know he's been doing this for quite a while."

Howard clenches his fist.

"Robert Bennington needs to be taught a lesson and I'm just the man for the job—bastard pushed too far this time."

Lindsay grabs her father's arm.

"No—let it go."

She sighs loudly and releases her grip on her father's arm.

"He knows he's on a short leash. If he even thinks of continuing down the path he's been—he and I are over."

Lindsay grimaces.

"He's used up all his chances."

They look at each other as Howard wraps his arms around his daughter. His eyes glow cold with rage. He grimaces.

<u>Tolling Bell Inn</u>

Juan laughs as he jams his gun against Carlo's head even harder. Carlo immediately panics and seems about to cry.

"*Please*—I'll do anything you—*anything you want*—just don't kill me—I don't want to die like—I love my life."

Page **124**

Juan grins broadly.

"Ernesto loved his life too before your stupidity put an end to it. He must be avenged—you must experience exactly what he experienced—it's only just and fair—your time has come."

"I'm begging you—don't—oh please?"

"Shut up fool—you've played your last card."

Juan begins laughing again. His fingers dance on the trigger for a few seconds as Carlo tries to push him away.

"This is for you Ernesto—just like I promised."

Juan laughs joyously as he pulls the trigger. A single bullet rips into Carlo's skull. The bullet partially comes out through the front of his forehead. Juan grins triumphantly as Carlo's body jerks a few times and then becomes still. Juan looks at the gun proudly and kisses it several times. He laughs again.

"Vengeance is mine—sweet vengeance—one down—one to go—oh yeah—life is fucked up but revenge is glorious."

He glances again at Carlo's body lying motionless on the bed and grins. He turns to look at the door and at his gun.

Maple Avenue

Gina Bentley seems angry as she talks on her cell phone while slowly walking around in a circle. She sighs loudly.

"You didn't—tell me you didn't blab."

She looks at the cell phone briefly.

"You told Donna Markway we've all slept with Brad? How could you Carrie—I mean seriously, how dumb was that?"

She sighs again.

"Why would you do something so stupid?"

She sighs loudly.

"I understand he's a jerk—but now Brad is going be on the warpath—against all of us—and you know how cruel."

Gina shakes her head knowingly.

"No—it's you who doesn't understand what you've done wrong—how can you be so foolishly idiotic? Brad isn't going to let this slide if he can't pop Donna—he wants her on his list."

Page 125

She shuts off her cell phone and looks around. She suddenly seems nervous. Gina glances at the cell phone.

Portland

Kyle Madison glances at his son sitting defiantly inside a plain-looking cell looking as stubborn as ever. He sighs.

"Are we going to play this game?"

Wesley Madison continues staring at the wall. Kyle bangs his fist angrily against the metal bars several times in a rage.

"Were you on something Wesley—is that it?"

He hits the metal bars again.

"What were you thinking? Just what was going through you mind earlier? I mean—like were you thinking at all?"

Wesley turns to look at Kyle.

"He killed my aunt—your sister."

Kyle seems uneasy.

"So, you decided to take the law into your own hands? I hope you're proud of yourself now—locked up in jail."

Wesley comes toward Kyle.

"He should be here for what he did."

Kyle sighs loudly.

"Seems to me you're the one who's behind bars right now? I assume by now you realize that you're in way deep."

Wesley looks at the hallway a few feet away.

"So what—I'm a Madison. They have to let me out right away. They can't keep me—I'm rich—and rich people."

Kyle sighs again.

"*They* don't have to do anything they don't want to do as far as—not after what you just—rich or no rich—dumb."

Wesley seems upset.

"What are you saying dad? You can't get me out of here today so I'll be stuck here with all these poor losers?"

Kyle nods.

"I tried—but—they're not budging."

He looks at Wesley nervously.

Page **126**

"You've been denied bail. They won't even consider it until the hearing is over. They think you're a possible flight risk."

Wesley laughs.

"What? Where would I go?"

Kyle rolls his eyes.

"*Oh, I don't know*—how about London, Paris, Geneva, Rome, Amsterdam, Madrid, Copenhagen, Sidney and Auckland for starters. We have homes in every one of those cities. I think it's a good bet that they assumed you might skip town."

"So what—we hardly ever go there."

"Doesn't matter to the judge one bit—it's a done deal."

"No—it's not fair—I'm rich—I have connections."

Kyle watches as Wesley slowly stands up.

<u>Tolling Bell Inn</u>

Duane Pyle inserts the card into the lock on the door of his room and enters. Eerie stillness envelops him immediately as he closes the door. He sighs loudly and waits a few seconds.

"Carlo?"

He is about to snap on the lights when a figure slowly comes toward him from the inky darkness. Duane reacts.

"Hello Duane."

Duane recognizes Juan instantly. Juan grins slyly. Duane notices the gun pointing directly at his chest. He begins to back away from where Juan is standing with a smirk on his face.

"Times up—your nine lives are over."

Juan laughs loudly. Duane seems confused.

"Carlo will be back any second."

Juan shakes his head mockingly.

"Oh, I don't think so."

Juan laughs loudly again.

"Carlo's dead."

He laughs even louder.

"I killed your queen."

Duane looks around nervously.

Page 127

"He wouldn't let you kill him—he wouldn't."

"Is that so?"

Juan makes a lewd gesture with his finger and laughs.

"Who said he had a choice?"

Duane watches as Juan inches closer toward him as their eyes lock. He can't look away. The gun seems to glow.

"Ernesto's death must be avenged. You and your boyfriend cost him his life—now you must die as well to right the wrong that was done in Miami—your blood must be spilled."

Duane takes a step backwards.

Nickerson's Bar

Marc Ryerson smiles while he looks at the cell phone in his hands as he licks his lips and watches the video footage.

"Oh-oh, you've certainly been a bad girl lately Denise Madison—a very bad girl indeed—quite dirty—oh my."

He flips off the camera.

"What do I do?"

He grins broadly.

"So many possibilities to consider—so many indeed—I think it's time I pay Denise Madison a friendly visit to go over exactly how much money it'll take for me to remain quiet."

He smirks as he looks at his cell phone again.

Glass Owl

Howard leads Lindsay toward the stairs. Suddenly there's a scream from upstairs. Lindsay reacts. Howard and Lindsay look at each other. Lindsay runs up the staircase in a panic as another scream echoes loudly while Howard follows right behind.

Tolling Bell Inn

Juan laughs triumphantly as he orders Duane to turn around. Duane nervously turns to look at Juan. He sighs.

"Please—spare me—I know I can serve you—just give me a chance to prove myself. I'll do anything—I'm begging."

Juan laughs loudly.

"No deal—the only thing I care about right now is putting a bullet in your miserable skull to avenge my brother."

Juan flips the lights on. Duane looks in horror as he sees Carlo's body lying on one of the beds in a pool of blood. It's obvious he's dead. Duane turns to face Juan again.

"Yep—he's dead—I told you I killed him didn't I?"

Juan begins laughing loudly again.

"But don't worry your sweet head about dear Carlo—in a few minutes you'll be joining him for an extended dirt nap."

He forces Duane onto the other bed—orders him to lie down and grins as he jams his gun against Duane's head.

"Whitney will have your head for this?"

"I don't think so."

"Of course he will—he'll figure it out."

Juan begins laughing.

"Whitney ordered your hit."

Duane seems shocked as Juan slides his finger into place on the trigger. Juan laughs again as Duane sighs loudly.

"I've waited for this moment for so long."

He smirks.

"You must die so Ernesto can rest in peace."

He begins laughing again.

"It'll just hurt for a minute. I promise."

Juan pulls the trigger and laughs triumphantly.

"Vengeance is mine—mine and Ernesto's."

He smiles and flips off the light. He leaves the room.

<u>McKinley Driveway</u>

Brad McKinley is standing by his car talking on his cell phone as Donna drives up. She jumps out of the car and runs toward him. Tears are streaming down her face. Brad turns to look at her. She stops suddenly. He seems confused.

Page 129

"Donna? What's wrong?"

She stops.

"Have you been cheating on me?"

He shuts off his cell phone abruptly.

"No—why would you ask me something like that? I love you—I thought you knew—I've never lied to you."

Donna wipes tears from her eyes.

"I—I just don't know who to believe anymore?"

"Who have you been talking to?"

Donna seems about to cry again.

"No one—I just."

Brad walks over to where Donna is standing.

"Who said I was cheating on you?"

Donna sighs.

"Is it true?"

Brad pulls Donna toward him. She pulls away.

"Who told you?"

"Please—just tell me—have you been—you know?"

"No—absolutely not—no way—I would never do such a thing to you—I've been faithful to you since we began dating—I know you want to wait—and I can wait too—now tell me."

Donna hugs Brad.

"I'm sorry—forgive me. Please forgive me."

Brad smiles slyly.

"Done—forget it."

They look at each other.

"*So,* who told you?"

Donna looks at Brad curiously.

Boardinghouse

Alden hands Eddie a beer. He sits down and sighs.

"I thought I had it all—but I got stupid. My life is like a bad movie that plays endlessly on YouTube. I screwed up royally in every which way. Two marriages—two divorces. Yeah—I'm a winner for sure—every woman's dream—yep, absolutely."

Eddie grins.

"Ever thought of writing a book?"

Alden smiles broadly.

"No—but I should. I've certainly made so many mistakes in the last ten years I could write several books on the subject."

Eddie laughs.

"Join the club. I made my share too believe me."

Alden seems confused.

"But you married the sweetest girl in town. How could you have made mistakes? Your life should be absolutely perfect."

Eddie laughs again.

"Life wasn't perfect for me in case you forgot. I was the kid from the wrong side of—had nothing and no one."

"No one blames you for being an orphan. Your parents dying was just a fluke—it could have—wasn't your fault."

"I know—but it happened to me."

Eddie sighs.

"It took me years to get over what happened. I still have nightmares about it—about the accident—it still haunts me."

Alden looks at the can of beer in his hand.

"You remember what happened? But you were four?"

Eddie sighs loudly.

"Never been able to forget what happened that day—I can still see the car and the flames—and the look on my mother's face as the car became engulfed—I still don't know exactly why it—it just doesn't make sense—never did. There was always something in the back of my mind—like—maybe there was more."

"I thought it was a drunk driver?"

Eddie nods.

"Yeah—that's what Anderson's father said too—but I can't remember a car hitting us—I just remember hearing a loud noise of some kind—almost as if it was—like a loud explosion."

Alden and Eddie look at each other.

"Like a bomb? You think the car was rigged?"

Eddie nods again and shrugs.

"Yeah—uh-huh—it certainly would explain a lot."

Page 131

"But why—would someone want to do something like that to your parents? They were good people—decent folks."

Eddie shrugs.

"I have no idea. My parents were nobody. My mom was a teacher and my dad was a fisherman—just normal citizens."

Alden nervously runs his fingers through his hair.

"Where would the files from the accident be now? Did you ever—you know—ask where they might be kept presently?"

Eddie looks at Alden curiously.

"Why?"

Alden runs his fingers through his hair again.

"Well, what if there's something the cops missed and you're right about—that someone may have rigged your car?"

"You think I could be right—that maybe someone did something—caused the accident for whatever reasons?"

Alden nods.

"As far as I know all the old police files from Marble Hills are stored in Portland at the—might be worth a look."

Alden pats Eddie on the shoulder.

"How about we check it out tomorrow?"

Eddie grins broadly.

"It'll be like old times. You and I pretending to be the *Hardy Boys* like from that old show from Universal Television."

Alden laughs as Eddie sighs.

"Did you ever meet get a chance to meet **Parker Stevenson** and **Shaun Cassidy** while you were in Hollyweird, you know, the actors who played the *Hardy Boys* on television?"

Alden laughs again.

"Yeah, I did actually—at an Emmy show a while back. Met **Pamela Sue Martin** too—as you recall she played *Nancy Drew* on the same ABC series. They were there for a tribute special."

Eddie jabs Alden playfully.

"Ever made a play for her?"

Alden playfully pokes Eddie back.

"I was way out of her league—that and the fact she was much older—the idea never crossed my mind at the time."

"Since when did that ever stop anyone?"

"I'm not you Eddie—I lack confidence in myself."

Eddie smirks.

"That's not how I remember it."

Alden takes a swig from the can of beer in his hand.

"You've given me way too much credit. I was a dork in high school—missed so many chances to be a player."

Eddie rolls his eyes.

"Tell that to Denise Madison."

Eddie playfully jabs Alden again. They both laugh.

<u>Farmington Villa</u>

Faye Washington is about to go into the kitchen when she hears the front door opening and turns to see Juan closing the door behind him. She smiles broadly. He notices and grins.

"Missed me?"

Faye looks at Juan curiously.

"Where did you go?"

Juan grins again.

"I went to look at a house for the film I told you about earlier—what a huge waste of time—the front yard was an absolute mess—what were they thinking—the only thing that house is good for would be to use in a low-budget horror film."

Faye rolls her eyes knowingly.

"You must be talking about the old McMartin estate out on Standish Road. Alden used to say it—say it was haunted."

Juan walks over to Faye.

"First time you mentioned your ex by name. I'm—I'm not sure my fragile ego can handle you thinking about *him*?"

Faye slides her arms around Juan's waist. He grins.

"Well, I know how to make you forget."

"Is that so? Exactly how would you go about that?"

"I have my ways."

Juan laughs and suddenly lifts Faye into his arms and head to the bedroom. She giggles as she kisses him over and over.

Page 133

<u>Glass Owl</u>

Denise Madison slams the door to her car shut when her cell phone rings. She rolls her eyes and looks at the name on the screen. She sighs loudly and answers it several seconds later.
"Hello?"
Her reaction changes immediately.
"Portland—he's there now?"
She sighs.
"Isn't there anything you can do?"
She sighs again.
"Fine—whatever—I'm on my way."
She shuts her cell phone off and looks at her car.

<u>Red Barn Gym</u>

Kelly Nelson is lifting weights as Corey Bentley comes up to him. He pauses for a few seconds. He seems angry.
"Kelly Nelson?"
Kelly nods.
"I hear you've been making a play for my girlfriend?"
Kelly gives Corey a curious look.
"You must be Corey Bentley?"
"Never mind who I am—just stay away from Abby Marshall—or I swear you'll regret ever coming to Marble Hills."
"What if I don't? What are you going to do?"
Corey seems annoyed.
"Don't push me—I assure you the end results will be quite unpleasant when I get through with you—you'll wish."
Kelly laughs.
"Bring it on—if you're man enough."
Corey looks at Kelly curiously.
"You have no idea who you're dealing with. I've got a terrible rep in this town—with good reason I assure you."
Kelly laughs again in a mocking way.

<u>Page **134**</u>

"Actually, it's you who has no idea who you're dealing with—but trust me—you'll find out if you cross the line."

Corey clenches his fists.

"I'm warning you—don't get on my bad side."

Kelly smiles broadly.

"Don't you have somewhere else to be right now? You know, like trolling Nickerson's Bar? Or looking for more young girls to corrupt? I hear that's your main deal—people talk."

"You little piece of—I'm so going to break."

"Careful, words hurt."

Kelly smirks at Corey. He clenches his fists as he looks at Kelly again and walks away. Kelly waves goodbye and laughs.

<u>Marshall Driveway</u>

Abby Marshall and Gina are talking in front of Gina's car. It is clear Gina is upset as she looks at Abby. Gina sighs loudly.

"Is that all you have to say?"

Abby shrugs.

"What do you want me to say? I like him."

"But you have Corey?"

Abby looks away as Gina appears annoyed.

"I don't want him anymore. Kelly is so much better for me. He's a nice guy and doesn't think he's all that—he likes me."

"But what about me—I wanted him. You knew I intended to make a play for him. I told you—how could you stab me in the back after you knew I wanted to sleep with him. It's not right."

Abby gestures with her hand.

"You only wanted to have sex with him for like ten minutes—nothing more. It isn't like you really cared about."

"I really liked him—and—and I saw him first."

Abby shrugs again.

"Things happen—deal with it."

Gina grabs Abby by the arm in a rage.

"You'll pay for this Abby—I swear I'll make you regret ever crossing me—you and Tiffany Johnson both. I hate you."

Page 135

Abby jerks free of Gina's grip.

"I think you should leave now Gina—we have nothing more to talk about. You're giving me a headache. Bye."

Gina looks at Abby's house.

"This isn't over yet."

"It's over Gina—I'm done talking."

"When I get through with you—I'll tell everyone."

"You'll what—tell everybody in Marble Hills I'm a whore? Go ahead—no one will care—especially from someone with your reputation—you know, for giving it away so easily every day."

"I hate you—*I hate you*."

Abby watches as Gina gets into her car seconds later and drives off in a rage. She shakes her head and seems confused.

<u>Glass Owl</u>

Lindsay is almost up the stairs as Susan Bennington suddenly rushes out of Greg's room in a panic. Lindsay stops.

"He's dead. He's dead."

Lindsay stops. Susan runs into her arms.

"Who's dead?"

Susan wipes tears from her eyes.

"Greg. Uncle Greg."

Lindsay turns to look at her father as Susan sobs loudly still in shock. She notices that Howard seems oddly relaxed as he casually runs toward Greg's room as if in very slow motion.

<u>Farmington Villa</u>

Faye sighs loudly as Juan pulls out of her. He looks at her and grins broadly as he lies back in bed. He smirks slyly.

"Who would've thought you and I would be."

Faye laughs.

"Yeah—it's a surprise for me too. Seriously, you've already banged me nine times—that must be some record for a guy. Even for a guy like you—given with your experience with women."

Page 136

Juan laughs loudly.

"Not for me it isn't—my dick has seen much action—I'm not one of those guys that can be with just one woman."

Faye seems upset at the remark. Juan begins laughing as he makes a lewd gesture with his finger. He winks at her.

"I can be quite charming when I want to."

Faye leans over to gently stroke Juan's penis.

"I'll just bet."

She leans back on the bed.

"Exactly how many sexual partners have you had?"

Juan laughs loudly again.

"Seriously—you're asking a guy a question like that?"

Juan smirks and pulls Faye toward him.

"What does it matter anyway—you know you're hooked on my charms—and I can do as I please if I choose to."

Faye kisses Juan.

"There's just something about you—I can't resist you no matter how much I know I should say no—you've got me."

Juan grins broadly again.

"Good—that's the way it should be—a woman should always be hooked on a man's charms—hopelessly devoted."

He strokes Faye's hair and winks.

"Especially if that man has a big frigging dick—and knows how to use it to its full potential in order to have his way."

Faye kisses Juan again and sighs loudly.

"How long is this going to last between us?"

Juan seems confused.

"That depends."

"On what—I mean—am I just a fling."

Juan pulls Faye closer.

"How about we just play it by ear—there's so much more moments to fully experience—let's not ruin it right now."

Faye glances at Juan's erection as it begins swelling once more—anticipating yet another sexual encounter. He smirks.

"You want to go for a tenth round—don't you?"

Juan nods eagerly and winks.

"Probably an eleventh and twelfth time too before the night is over—with me you never know—it just happens."

Juan's cell phone rings.

Bentley Driveway

Corey looks at his watch again. He seems somewhat impatient and sighs. Seconds later Brad pulls up. They look at each other for a few seconds. Brad rolls down his window.

"OK—what's going on—what was so important you wanted me to—you know I have a life right—don't need?"

Corey rolls his eyes.

"I need your help bro—like seriously—I need help."

Brad seems confused.

"For what exactly—spill it."

Corey pounds his fist against Brad's car.

"What the fuck do you think you're doing to my car?"

"I have a problem—a really annoying problem."

Brad glances at the Bentley mansion a few yards away.

"What sort of a problem?"

"The kind that is six feet two, brown hair, big mouth and a huge ego—and who took my girl from me earlier today."

Brad laughs loudly.

"You must be talking about Kelly Nelson."

Corey seems annoyed. Brad grins.

"It's all over town—your innocent girlfriend stole your sister's boyfriend from her without even trying—drama."

Corey sighs.

"Boyfriend my ass—my sister was just going to use him like she's used every guy she's been friends with since giving it up to you last year—you know, that night you lied to her."

Brad smirks knowingly.

"Doesn't matter—everyone in Marble Hills is saying your sister got played really hard by your girlfriend—fun times."

Corey clenches his fist as he seems to understand exactly what Brad is saying. He angrily shakes his fist in the air.

"I want to bust him good—he needs to be taught a cruel lesson—one that lousy bastard won't soon forget—if ever."

Brad looks around.

"You probably shouldn't talk so loud when you make threats Corey—someone might hear you talking and decide to call the State Police—and you'll end up exactly like Wesley."

Corey looks at Brad curiously.

"What are you talking about Brad—and what does Wesley have to do with busting Kelly Nelson for what he did?"

Brad sighs.

"You haven't heard?"

"Heard what?"

Brad glances at his cell phone.

"Wesley Madison was arrested earlier by the State Police for attempted murder at Julia Winthrop's boardinghouse."

Corey reacts in shock at the news.

<u>Portland</u>

Denise looks at Kyle harshly as he sits down on a wooden chair in the lobby of the police station. He seems upset.

"So, now it's my fault."

"Did I say that? Did I say you were to blame?"

Kyle waves his hand in the air.

"You implied it earlier when we talked."

Denise shoots Kyle a sharp look.

"If it's anyone's fault it's your father's. He let Wesley run wild—and now look at what that's led to today—a jail cell."

Kyle sighs.

"Playing the blame game isn't going to work."

A door slams nearby.

"Enough—OK? Enough—I've had it with you two."

They turn to see Will McColl coming toward them from a side office. He seems visibly annoyed at their behavior.

"No wonder the kid turned out this way. Look at who his parents are. Neither of you have a clue about parenting."

Page 139

Denise glares at Will.

"How dare you speak to me like that—I could have your badge for such talk—for being so incredibly rude to me."

"If the shoe fits wear it."

Will sits down at the desk.

"Maybe the two of you haven't really thought about this like you should—but here's an eye-opener on reality."

Kyle sighs loudly and watches as Will pulls out a stack of paperwork and shoves it toward them. They react in shock.

<u>Farmington Villa</u>

Juan slowly closes the door to the bathroom and answers his cell phone. He grins broadly as he leans against the sink.

"Yeah—it's done. I took care of both of them just as I promised I would—sweetest job I've ever had—thank you."

He laughs.

"Yep—they both begged. But you know me—I must have my way no matter what—and I wanted them dead—dead for what they did—and *so* they are—two cold bloody stiffs."

Juan gestures with his hand.

"Of course I cleaned up any prints that were possibly left behind. I left nothing to chance—why would you even ask?"

He rolls his eyes as his anger seems to build.

"Do I look like a rank amateur? This isn't my first hit in case it slipped your mind. No fingerprints left anywhere. No witnesses either. It was clean and quick—absolutely perfect—no one will ever think of looking for someone like me when they start figuring—especially with no way to connect the dots."

Juan shrugs.

"It's just a matter of time before someone finds the bodies—probably tomorrow morning when the maid comes."

Juan grins broadly.

"Yeah—I know I have to be more careful with the Madison hit—but don't worry about the deal—I'll take him out just like I did Rogers and Pyle—he's as good as dead—worm food."

Page 140

Juan shrugs again.

"How am I spending my free time?"

Juan laughs loudly.

"Fucking a beautiful woman of course—sexual play always adds to the excitement of a righteous kill—especially today."

Juan looks down at his erection.

"Speaking of which—I've got things to attend to."

He shuts off his cell phone.

Tolling Bell Inn

Matt Brewster glances at the door nervously. It is slightly ajar. He hesitates and pushes it forward slowly and stops.

"Carlo?"

There's no answer as he walks into the room and closes the door behind him. He looks around. The room is dark. Drapes are drawn tightly together everywhere—blocking out all light.

"Is anyone here?"

Silence permeates the room.

"Maybe he stepped out for a drink?"

He reaches out and turns on the lights. He looks at the scene in shock. He leans against the wall in disgust.

Glass Owl

Lindsay holds Susan close to her as she closes the front door. She turns to look at her father with a nervous look.

"How could?"

Howard seems oddly unresponsive.

"I can't believe he actually did something like that—he had—had so much to live for—it just doesn't seem possible that he would—doesn't seem like Greg at all. He loved life."

Susan looks at her mother.

"Do you think he suffered before—before he took all those pills—and—realized he was going to die? Do you think he changed his mind at the last minute and wanted to live?"

Lindsay shakes her head.

"I don't know."

Lindsay looks at her father again.

"I'm so glad mom isn't here to see this—it would've just destroyed her—she loved him so much—and now?"

Susan pulls away from her mother.

"Are they sure he's dead?"

Howard nods

"Greg's dead. From what Dr. Wallingford could guess he's been dead about three hours—maybe four—a while."

Lindsay glances at Susan again. Susan wipes a tear from her eye and looks at her mother and then Howard.

"I never even got to know him—it's just—it's not fair—he must have felt so alone—with no one to talk to when he?"

Lindsay hugs Susan and nervously looks at her father again. Howard turns away quickly and sighs. Lindsay notices.

"There's more to this—isn't there?"

Lindsay glances at Susan again and then her father.

"Exactly what happened between you and Greg earlier that would have brought him to such a rash decision?"

"Nothing—he—he seemed OK."

Lindsay gives her father an odd look.

"Did you say something—you know—that might have made him—do something this illogical? Did you say?"

Howard shakes his head.

"No—nothing—he said he was tired."

He looks at the front door again.

"There was absolutely no clue beforehand that he would do something this rash. It never even occurred to me he'd choose to end it like this—seemed ready to make a fresh start."

Howard glances at Susan and turns away when he notices her cold accusatory stare. He waves his hand in the air.

"Maybe he just couldn't handle the thought of having to deal with the mess he brought upon us with his actions?"

Lindsay looks at her father curiously.

"You and Greg—he had problems—but you."

Howard seems annoyed.

"This isn't my fault—your brother was a weak individual who couldn't cope with the real world—facts are facts."

"Are they?"

Lindsay looks at her father as he appears uneasy. She looks at Susan and then back at Howard. She sighs loudly.

"He needed you."

Howard rolls his eyes. He suddenly seems annoyed.

"It's over—he's dead."

Lindsay reacts.

"Is that all you have to say?"

Howard turns away. Lindsay seems upset as she glances at Susan's reaction. She suddenly reaches out to grab his arm.

"You and I need to talk privately."

Howard looks blankly at Lindsay and Susan. He sighs nervously just as Robert Bennington walks into the room.

TO BE CONTINUED

A Look at the 6th Episode

Kyle and Denise argue about what to do about Wesley as a family tragedy has a hit man wondering what to do next—Greg's sudden death offers no answers to his confused family—Jason and Ashton find common ground in their dull imperfect lives—Matt finds himself in trouble with the law after stumbling upon a grisly murder scene—Carrie's vendetta against Brad intensifies into violence—Wesley's arrest sparks careless gossip around Marble Hills—Howard and Daryl come to an uneasy understanding about carefully guarded secrets of the past—Juan continues to lead a double life with an unsuspecting Faye—a mobster thinks his troubles are over but not everything is what it appears—as Denise continues her quest for sexual enjoyment while unwittingly becoming the main target of an unscrupulous blackmailer.

Episode 6
Secret Desires

<u>Tolling Bell Inn</u>

Daryl Anderson rolls his eyes as he looks at the covered bodies as they are wheeled out in a gurney. He turns around to face Matt Brewster again and sighs. He seems annoyed.

"OK—tell me again how you just happened to come upon a murder scene of two men you claim you didn't know?"

Matt sighs loudly.

"I—I met Carlo Rogers earlier at Pike's Bar—we hit it off and I—I stopped by to return his—his watch and then I found."

Daryl seems confused.

"You and him—oh—like seriously?"

Matt rolls his eyes.

"What—you didn't know I was gay?"

Daryl shakes his head.

"Didn't know—don't care—you're not a real athlete anyway. So, you met him a Pike's and then you and him."

Matt sighs again.

"We went back to my condo."

"And then what lover boy?"

Matt rolls his eyes at Daryl again.

"And we fucked—OK. I took him back to my condo and we did each other—twice if you really want to know the details."

Daryl winks.

"Fine—you fucked—and then what happened."

"He left—and about an hour later I realized he'd forgotten his watch in my bed. So I decided to return it when—when I found them—Carlo and—and they were both dead—murdered."

"The other deceased was named Duane Pyle—seems he had some sort of a relationship with Carlo—probably sexual."

Matt seems bothered by the revelation.

<u>Portland</u>

Kyle Madison paces back and forth as he watches Will McColl and Denise Madison talking in hushed tones about Wesley. Denise glances over at him every few seconds until he finally can't take it anymore and walks over to where they are talking. They stop and turn to look at him oddly. He shrugs.

"Is this really necessary?"

Will turns to look at Kyle.

"Like I was trying to explain to your wife—Wesley is going to be charged. Unless Alden Washington decides to drop the charges—it looks like your son will be confined indefinitely."

Kyle sighs.

"Washington is lying. My son would never attempt to murder anyone. He's not a killer—he's just a rebellious kid."

Will looks at Denise and shakes his head knowingly. He glances at the stack of paperwork nearby and sighs loudly.

"If I had a dime for every parent who thought their kid was incapable of murder—but the end results always say otherwise."

"But *he* isn't a killer. Sure he has issues—what kid today doesn't? I—I know this sounds just like some excuse—lame."

Will glances at the paperwork.

"Doesn't matter—this is the deal you guys have right now and—and there's no way getting around it—no way."

Page 146

"But this *is* Wesley Madison we're speaking about?"

Will looks at Denise curiously and then at Kyle.

"It's out of my hands—sorry."

Kyle and Denise look at each other.

"This *is* your fault—yours and your father's."

Kyle gives Denise a harsh look and walks to the door. He slowly opens the door and looks at Will again. He shrugs.

"I'll be back tomorrow."

Will nods in acknowledgement.

<u>Bentley Driveway</u>

Corey Bentley sighs—still reeling from the news Brad McKinley just dumped on him. He wipes sweat from his brow.

"Wait a minute—Wesley actually made good on his threat to off that Washington dude? Like really? Is he totally nuts?"

Brad nods.

"Yep—seems like it. Dude snapped."

He shakes his head.

"Apparently Julia Winthrop interrupted his attack on Washington and the State Police was called immediately."

"Oh-oh—Wesley's fucked for sure."

Brad nods.

"I guess the Madison money isn't going to get him out of this mess—man, things couldn't get any worse for him."

Corey grins.

"I wouldn't want to be Wesley Madison right now—not for anything—that's for sure—think we should slip him pills?"

"Like we could ever get stuff like that through—I bet they'll be watching him like a frigging hawk—and then some."

Brad digs his hand into the front pockets of his jeans.

"Oh man—I just thought about something."

He grins slyly and begins laughing.

"Wesley could be in the big house for years. Man, imagine living that long without sex? I'd rather be dead—a corpse."

Corey laughs and gestures with his hand.

Page **147**

"He won't be missing out believe me—he'll still be getting laid as much as he did before—except he'll be the girl."

Corey laughs again and wags his finger.

"Uh-huh—some ugly dude named Bluto will make Wesley his prized bitch and he'll be putting out every day—probably several times a day for Bluto and his *friends*—and then he."

Brad laughs loudly.

"You're one twisted freak—I thought I was royally messed up—but—you've got the jump on me for sure—so twisted."

"I say it as I see it."

Corey makes a lewd gesture with his finger.

"It would actually be funny if you think about it—I mean like, let's face it—once Madison gets out he might just become best friends with Tyler Van Pelt. Friends with benefits—if you know what I mean—like they'll be screwing each other."

They both roar with laughter.

"Old man Madison is probably like peeing himself right now—I mean—seriously—his precious grandson being charged with attempted murder of some washed-up soap actor—if this wasn't really happening here in Marble Hills I would've thought this was just some episode of an old show from the 1980s called *Falcon Crest* that my grandmother used to watch religiously."

Corey smirks again.

"Wesley is one stupid fucker."

He wags his finger again.

"That dude has always been a few marbles short upstairs. He should've been locked up years ago in a loony bin."

They begin laughing loudly with glee.

"Wouldn't it be really funny if before the trial even starts poor Wesley is killed suspiciously in his jail cell by someone?"

Brad licks his lips and begins laughing.

"Probably by Bluto—because Wesley refused to suck his dick or something—oh man, I can just see the headlines now."

They begin making vulgar sucking sounds.

"Teenager murdered by vicious jailhouse queen."

They erupt in laughter.

<u>Glass Owl</u>

The room has a somber tone as Lindsay Bennington and Howard Madison sit together on the sofa. Across from them on the other sofa is Robert Bennington. He's staring into space as the front door opens and Kyle quietly enters with Denise. They both notice the eerie silence in the living room immediately.

"What's going on?"

Howard looks at Kyle.

"Greg is dead."

Kyle seems shocked and looks at Lindsay.

"*What*—is this some sort of joke?"

Denise seems confused by the presence of Robert and Lindsay but says nothing as she closes the door. Kyle reacts.

<u>Tolling Bell Inn</u>

Daryl grins slyly as he watches Matt stumble over his words. He looks at Matt with a sense of joy and contempt.

"Didn't know about the boyfriend—did you?"

He stifles a smirk.

"So, you came back here to return the watch and found your new "friend" and his boyfriend together in bed and freaked out—freaked out and killed them both after finding them?"

Matt shakes his head several times.

"I didn't kill anybody."

He sighs.

"Carlo was just a fling to me. A good time—*only* a good time—for about an hour—that's all—nothing more than that."

He clears his throat.

"I—I'd just met him earlier today—didn't really know his story or his last name—only interested in a fuck partner for an hour or so—but if you want to behave like you're better than me despite your terribly soiled reputation—then go right ahead."

Daryl licks his lips seductively.

Page 149

"Nothing but a cheap whore, aren't you Brewster—bet you've slept with a lot of guys—given it away a lot—like candy?"

"I don't see what my behavior has to do with anything. I had nothing to do with what happened to Carlo earlier."

Matt looks at the room again then back at Daryl.

"Look, I didn't kill either of them. I didn't know about the other guy and I knew Carlo only briefly. I—he and I had—well, we had other things on our minds—and finding out each other's relationship history wasn't a top priority for either of us at the time—just a casual thing as I said before—nothing more."

"I'll bet."

Daryl smirks.

"I'd like nothing better than to arrest your gay ass for murder—but at the moment the gun that did these two in seems to have vanished. So, until further notice—don't even think of leaving Marble Hills for parts unknown anytime in the next few days—understand—or I swear I'll find you no matter what."

Matt nods.

"And another thing—if I do find out you had anything to do with this mess I'll make you—make you really sorry."

Matt looks away again and sighs. Daryl grabs his arm.

"I'm not kidding—your kind makes me sick. Sticking your dick up each other's asses—nothing but sick freaks—you—you deserve what you get from religious nuts if you ask me."

Daryl and Matt looks at each other.

"Can I go now?"

Daryl glares at Matt briefly and nods. He watches as Matt leaves and rolls his eyes several times in disgust. He sighs.

"Sick—sick piece of garbage."

He glances at the room again and sighs loudly.

"If I had my way I'd forget I ever saw any of this filth today and pretend nothing—certainly wouldn't be the first time. I've let a few "slide" in my day really easily—especially if I got paid."

He laughs and gestures with his hand.

"I've let worst things slip by."

He looks at the bloodstained beds and shrugs.

Page 150

<u>Spaulding Mansion</u>

Carrie Spaulding carefully skims through an Internet site with listings of hundreds of medications that can be purchased online. She stops halfway on the list and grins broadly.

"Perfect. This will do nicely."

She looks at the various prices under bottles of discount tranquilizers and shrugs. A smile spreads across her face.

"He'll never know what hit him."

Carrie grins broadly and shuts off the computer.

<u>Boardinghouse</u>

Alden Washington pats Eddie Kane on the back and closes the door to his room. He stands there for a few seconds.

"Who would ever have guessed?"

He smiles and turns to look at the small room.

<u>Farmington Villa</u>

Faye Washington angrily looks at her divorce agreement in front of her. She flips through the pages slowly and shrugs.

"I'm *so* going to get you—you and I aren't as over as *you* thought. You'll pay for what you put me through Alden."

She flips through the pages again.

"Think your life is complicated now—you just wait. I'll really give you something to think about—oh yeah you'll pay."

She glances at Juan Sabrillo sleeping next to her.

"Uh-huh—and I know how I'm going to make it all happen my way—with help from my new—my new boyfriend."

She smiles and strokes Juan's hair.

"No one plays me for a fool and walks away free and clear without having really bad things happen to them afterwards."

She looks at the papers in front of her again.

"I didn't deserve being pushed aside like trash."

Page **151**

She clenches her fist.

"I'm going to drain his bank account of every red cent he has ever made from that wretched soap opera. He'll have to wash dishes for a living when I'm done with him. Sweep floors."

She begins laughing hysterically.

The Next Day

<u>Bus Terminal</u>

Tiffany Johnson waves as she sees Caleb Winthrop walking toward her after getting off a Greyhound bus. She runs up to him and they embrace. He kisses her passionately.

"Missed me?"

Tiffany grins as she slides her hand around Caleb's waist and hugs him warmly. He looks down at his Levi's as his erection begins to show. He sighs. Caleb grins slyly and nods twice.

"How about you and I make—how about we make use of the backseat in your car? You and I have some catching up."

Tiffany laughs.

"Is that all I'm good for?"

Caleb grins.

"*What do you think?*"

Tiffany begins to unbutton his jeans.

"You're so lucky you're cute."

Caleb smirks as his erection swells further.

"I could always hook-up with Gina Bentley? I'm sure she's up already—like it's already eight o'clock—I know she wouldn't mind impromptu morning sex from her favorite college guy."

Tiffany gestures with her hand.

"Don't get me started on that trashy whore—I wish she was dead—seriously, I wish someone would take Gina out—like permanently already—I'd even offer to pay—damn bitch."

"You two still on the outs?"

Tiffany rolls her eyes and seems annoyed.

"It's all on her—she thinks she owns this town."

Page **152**

"There was this guy named."
Caleb gives Tiffany an odd look.
"I don't really care for high school drama."
Tiffany rolls her eyes and sighs. They walk to where Tiffany's car is parked. Caleb looks at the backseat and motions for her to get into the car. She grins slyly as she unlocks the door and watches while he finishes unbuttoning his jeans and whips out his erect penis. He climbs into the backseat quickly pulling Tiffany under him. He laughs and kisses her several times. A weird look comes over his face suddenly as she watches.
"I just fucked this waitress I know from a greasy spoon in Portland before I got on the bus—I'm still so charged up."
Tiffany seems upset as she looks down at his massive erection jutting out at her. She sighs and kisses him again.
"Like I said, you're just lucky you're so cute. Otherwise I might not be in such a forgiving mood about the waitress."
"Cute nothing—you can't resist having my charming dick inside you. I know it and you know it—deal with it already."
Tiffany strokes Caleb's erection.
"You know me so well—I can't say no to you."
Caleb laughs loudly.
"I should hope so—after all, us getting together caused me plenty of grief—which by the way caused Gina and I to split last year—she's still not over what happened between us."
Tiffany winks at Caleb.
"I'm yours to do with as you please."
"No doubt about it whatsoever."
Caleb grins broadly and penetrates Tiffany.

<u>Glass Owl</u>

Kyle opens the front door and is about to leave when Howard calls out to him from the hallway next to the library.
"Kyle?"
Kyle turns around to face his father.
"Where are you going at this time of the morning?"

Page 153

Kyle sighs.

"Isn't it obvious?"

Howard walks over to where Kyle is standing.

"Want some company?"

Kyle shakes his head.

"No—Wesley is in enough of a bad mood already—better you stay here at and deal with Lindsay and Robert."

Howard rolls his eyes.

"Don't remind me—that bastard needs to be taught a lesson. I won't tolerate anyone hurting my daughter."

Kyle looks at his father curiously.

"Lindsay can handle Robert herself."

Kyle wrings his hands nervously.

"Don't you start anything—there's enough drama in this family as it is. Greg's suicide didn't help matters much."

Howard sighs.

"I'm aware of the mess Greg caused."

He leans against the wall.

"The local press—I bet they're having a field day with the news of—damn vultures—don't they have anything else?"

Kyle looks at his watch.

"Got to go—if there's any change in Wesley's deal it would be helpful if I'm there—might be able to talk to him too."

Howard nods.

"Tell Wesley we're all behind him. OK?"

Kyle nods and leaves. Howard stands at the front door for a few seconds before he closes the door. He seems worried.

<u>Pete's Cafe</u>

Abby Marshall and Kelly Nelson are having breakfast as she carefully folds a newspaper and puts it down on the table in front of her. She looks at Kelly and seems upset. She shrugs.

"I can't believe he did it."

Kelly seems confused at Abby's odd comment.

"Who are you talking about?"

Page 154

"Greg Madison."

Kelly shakes his head. Abby sighs.

"I didn't even know he was back in town—he was sort of the black sheep of the Madison family—troubled actually."

Kelly picks up the paper.

"What did he do?"

"He took his own life yesterday afternoon."

"Oh."

Abby glances at the front door and she sees Gina Bentley coming toward her. She seems angry. Kelly notices.

"This could get nasty."

Gina walks by both of them without saying a word. Abby seems upset as Kelly watches curiously. She sighs loudly.

"She's still mad at you."

Abby turns to look at Kelly.

"Gina is just being Gina—I wouldn't expect anything less from her. She's always been this way—since we were kids."

Kelly leans closer to Abby.

"Think she'll make good on her threat to get even with both of us? She certainly seemed serious yesterday?"

Abby sighs.

"Let her. I didn't do anything wrong. She's always in these types of weird spiteful moods. Frankly, I'm really sick of it."

Kelly watches as Gina sits down alone at the far end of the cafe and begins glaring at them. Abby rolls her eyes.

<u>Shelby Park</u>

Ashton Markway is jogging along a wooded path and almost runs into Jason Anderson who seems lost and confused as he walks aimlessly along the path. Ashton stops and turns around to face Jason. He notices a weird look on Jason's face.

"Jason—is everything OK?"

Jason gives Ashton a strange look and shrugs.

"What's wrong?"

"Leave me alone—OK?"

Page 155

Ashton watches as Jason sits down on a nearby rock.

"Look Jason, I can see something's wrong with you—what happened? What did Corey and his goons do this time?"

Jason wipes his brow.

"It's—it's my deal."

"Is it Wesley? Are you upset because that stupid jerk got arrested yesterday afternoon for trying to kill some actor?"

Jason shakes his head.

"Fuck Wesley. He's a prick. I could care less if that bastard goes to jail for what he did—serves him right—hope he rots."

"If it's not Wesley—who is it?"

Jason sighs loudly.

"I'm a loser—a fucking loser—a total zero."

Ashton seems confused.

<u>Bus Terminal</u>

Caleb winks at Tiffany as he casually shoves his penis into his jeans and zips up. He looks around and smirks slyly.

"Thanks for the ride—love a sweet deal."

Tiffany smiles broadly.

"Glad to be of service—just promise me you won't go after Gina while you're back in town. I don't want you—I hate her."

Caleb laughs.

"Can't promise you that—you know she still has a thing for me—got to explore that—probably today or tomorrow?"

"But we—I just gave myself to you?"

"We're just friends—that's all—nothing more—come on Tiffany—like seriously don't cop an attitude—not after?"

Tiffany seems upset.

"I hate her. I can't help it. She is such a bitch. She's always in my way—making me look bad. She has a bad reputation."

Caleb grins knowingly and winks at her.

"I know—and she's a whore too, right—but hey, she knows how to give a guy a great blowjob—knows techniques."

He pulls Tiffany toward him and kisses her.

Page 156

"If it makes you feel better—she means absolutely nothing to me—absolutely nothing. I just like fucking her—that's it."
Tiffany slides her arms around Caleb's waist.
"OK—as long as you don't have any feelings for her."
Caleb laughs loudly.
"What's up with women and competition?"
He laughs again and kisses Tiffany once more.

<u>Farmington Villa</u>

Juan and Faye are making passionate love while the television blares loudly. Suddenly the morning talk show is interrupted by the announcement of Greg Madison's suicide. Upon hearing the newsflash Juan immediately rolls over and seems shocked at what he's hearing. Faye seems confused as Juan sits up in bed and listens intently to the blaring news.
"Is something wrong?"
He sighs.
"Is it true?"
Faye notices Juan's reaction.
"Juan?"
He turns to look at Faye. She reaches out to touch his chest as he seems in a trance-like state. She looks at his curiously as he finally seems to be aware of her presence. She sighs.
"Did you know Greg Madison?"
He shakes his head.
"No—it's just—well, he was rich—why would a rich guy kill himself? It doesn't make sense if you have everything?"
Faye shrugs.
"I don't know—probably overdosed. My ex actually grew up with his brother. *Or* so he said anyway. He lied a lot."
She kisses Juan's neck. He seems tense.
"Are you sure you didn't know him?"
"No—never met the guy before. It's just weird thinking someone my age would actually take their own lives. I'm just spooked—trying to process the news that's all. End of story."

Page 157

Juan jumps out of bed. Faye watches as he closes the bathroom door behind him. She shakes her head and lies back in bed slightly confused as she looks at the television again.

<u>Rockport</u>

Denise laughs as Lance Weissmann slams into her yet again. He grins broadly as her moans echo loudly in the room.
"I'm so in the mood today—need to relax."
Denise laughs again.
"I'm not complaining about anything."
Lance looks at Denise.
"How's Wesley?"
Denise sighs.
"He's not talking. I tried."
Lance smiles broadly.
"Well, at least now you don't have to worry about Wesley catching us together. Quite sweet if you ask me—nice."
Denise wags her finger at Lance.

<u>Maple Avenue</u>

Carrie is about to get into her car as she sees Elizabeth Pendleton slowly coming toward her. She seems upset.
"I thought you said earlier you weren't feeling well?"
Carrie seems annoyed.
"I took some pills—and perked up."
Elizabeth notices a package in Carrie's hand.
"What that?"
Carrie glances at the package.
"What does it look like?"
"What's inside?"
Carrie hastily opens the back door to her car and then throws the package inside. It lazily rolls onto its side.
"CD's—OK. Satisfied?"
Elizabeth seems confused by Carrie's rudeness.

Page **158**

"I was just asking."

Carrie sighs and faces Elizabeth.

"I'm sorry. I'm still pissed about last night."

Elizabeth looks at Carrie curiously.

"Why do you even care anyway if Brad McKinley is playing Donna Markway? She's a troll. She deserves to get played—and Brad's just the right guy, excuse me, slug for the job. It's obvious he'll sleep with anyone in town—especially if he's sniffing around that certified loser Donna Markway. Like so gross—nasty."

"I know—but just for once I'd like to make him pay—you know, have something really cruel happen to him—something really unpleasant—like a terrible accident or something."

She smiles slyly.

"It would be hilarious actually."

Elizabeth seems confused at Carrie's comment.

Rockport

Marc Ryerson grins as he carefully focuses his video camera on the window of the hotel room where Denise and Lance are going at it like rabbits. He sighs and grins broadly.

"Oh man, this is my lucky day. Denise Madison is making it easy for me—too easy actually. I bet Daryl Anderson sure wouldn't be pleased if he knew she was being banged really hard by one of his freaky teenage son's horny classmates."

He laughs loudly.

"Oh-oh—so much action—look at them go."

He grins again and glances at several prints of photos taken seconds before showing Denise and Lance kissing.

Farmington Villa

Juan erratically paces back and forth talking on his cell phone. He seems nervous. He wipes sweat from his brow.

"Of course I'm sure—it's all over the local news. It said Madison committed suicide yesterday afternoon. He's DOA."

He stops pacing and begins laughing.

"Yeah—I know. I'm sticking around until it's confirmed. But I think you're missing the point about Madison—he knew he was played—knew it was just a matter of time before I put a bullet or two in his empty head—ending his miserable life in the process—so he just decided to do it himself—made it easy."

He smiles broadly.

"Yep—exactly what I was thinking on that loser."

Juan looks out the window.

"The funeral—I'm not sure yet. It's still early—but it should be in a few days at the latest. I assume that much anyway."

Juan smirks.

"No problem—it's your dime—I'll stay as long as you deem necessary to make sure the deadbeat is toast—buried."

Juan laughs loudly.

"Yeah—some local idiot found both stiffs. Seems Carlo banged a celebrity before I blew him away—so the locals think *he* did it—and not anyone else—it's perfect—works for us."

Juan laughs even louder.

"I know—I couldn't have asked for a better distraction to cover our tracks—some stupid gay guy got fucked royally."

There is a knock on door. Faye calls out.

"Got to go—talk to you later. Bye."

Juan shuts off his cell phone and opens the door. He looks at Faye and grins broadly. She stares at him curiously.

"Who were you talking to?"

Juan smiles slyly.

"Heard me laugh—didn't you? Seems my trip here wasn't a waste of time after all—I was just telling my boss about meeting you and how much I really like—and he is totally down with us playing—thinks it's so sweet you and I hooked up like we did."

Faye grins.

"You *really* like me?"

Juan winks.

"I like you—like fucking you—oh yeah no doubt about it. You and I have to get to know each other even better now."

Page **160**

Faye's eyes fall on Juan's erect penis sticking out from between the folds of his bathrobe. They look at each other briefly and at the rumpled bed a few feet away. He grins broadly.

Boardinghouse

Julia Winthrop hugs Caleb warmly. She looks at him for a minute. He grins as they look at the steps leading upstairs.

"Don't worry—I'll be fine. It's just for a few days at the most. A week tops. Then I'm off again—to visit friends."

Julia looks at his luggage lying nearby.

"Are you sure you don't want to stay at my place?"

Caleb laughs.

"No—you know how I like—well, you know, so it's best I have a place of my own—that way you don't have to hear, well you—you know, sounds coming my room late at night."

Julia blushes.

"OK. OK. I get it. You want to be able to bring over girls and not make me think less of you—and your friends."

Caleb grins slyly.

"Hope you don't mind?"

"No—you're a grown man—a senior in college. If you want to have sex with skanky girls from town—it's your right."

Caleb grins. They hug again for a few seconds.

Rockport

Marc watches as Lance leaves after kissing Denise passionately one last time. Marc continues focusing his video camera on the window as Denise seems to be waiting for someone. A few minutes later the door to the hotel room opens and another young man enters and kisses Denise. Marc grins—it's Corey. Marc smirks slyly as he watches them together.

"She's definitely on a roll today no doubt. Oh-oh—I guess the Bentley kid really is as bad as everyone says—playing with fire—what would happen if he got outed in the local press?"

He watches as Corey pulls off his Lycra shorts. His penis sticks out in front of him as he forces Denise down on the bed. Seconds later they go at it. Moans of pleasure echo into the parking lot across from the window of the hotel room.

"I'm rich—no question about it—I'm so filthy rich."

He laughs as he continues filming.

Glass Owl

Several news reporters are hanging out on a nearby street as Howard turns away from the window to face Lindsay. He shakes his head. He seems upset at the scene outside.

"Damn freaks."

Lindsay wrings her hands nervously.

"You still haven't told me why Greg took his own life."

Howard sighs.

"That boy had a mind of his own. He seemed fine when I spoke to him yesterday. I had no clue he was so messed up."

Lindsay stands up.

"Something just doesn't add up. He came back asking for help—you agreed to help—and less than two hours later he takes his own life? Why? This just doesn't make any sense to me."

Howard sighs loudly.

"I'm going for a walk—I'll see you later."

Lindsay looks at her father curiously. As he leaves she notices Hart Bennington looking at her suspiciously.

Stanley Pier

Brad pulls Donna Markway toward him. She resists and pulls away. He seems irritated and grabs her again more forcibly and kisses her roughly. She seems afraid and tries to pull away.

"Come on—give it up to me already. I can't wait any longer—need to—need to have you—must have you now."

He tries to kiss her again as Donna pushes him away.

"No—please—I'm not ready yet."

"If this is about yesterday I already told you."

She seems uneasy.

"I believe you."

Brad grins.

"OK then—give it up to me. You know I want to fuck you more than anything else—my dick expects it—can't wait."

"I want it to be the right time."

"For what Donna—I already told you hundreds of times I love you and I want to be with you—what more do you want from me—just give it up already—I want—I really need you."

Donna notices his erect penis sticking out from his unbuttoned Levi's. He grins as she turns away. She sighs.

"I want to save myself for my husband."

"Like in us being married? I can't wait that long. You know I can't marry you until we're in college next year. But today."

He sighs.

"Come on—it's no big deal. Just give it up."

He kisses her again—forcing her under him. He grins and slides his hand between her legs. He strokes her repeatedly.

"Just just give me what I want right now—you know you want to fuck—show me how much you love me—show me."

Brad laughs.

"I love you. Really I do."

Donna seems confused as she looks at Brad.

"You really love me?"

Brad nods several times as he continues showering her with kisses as he slips his fingers into her vagina again.

"Yes. Yes. I love you."

He grins broadly as he pulls her panty down. She doesn't resist as he moves his body into position and aggressively penetrates her completely within seconds. He laughs loudly.

"Oh yeah—you're a nice deal no doubt."

He begins ejaculating seconds later.

"Hope you're on the pill."

"*What*—did you say something?"

He laughs again.

Page **163**

"I'm just thinking aloud like always."

Brad grins broadly as he comes inside her a second time and watches her shocked reaction. She seems visibly upset.

Police Station

Daryl looks up as Howard enters the office. They look at each other for a few seconds in silence. He rolls his eyes.

"I'm really sorry about Greg."

Howard sighs.

"Thanks. But he made his own bed."

"Any idea what drove him to do such a thing?"

"No—none—doesn't really matter."

He walks closer to where Daryl is sitting.

"If I knew what made my son tick—obviously the coward wouldn't have run away to Boston all those years ago if we thought alike—but of course he didn't—just his sorry deal."

Daryl leans back in his chair.

"I guess it was inevitable."

He glances at the door and shrugs.

"If you're here about Wesley—it's out of my hands. I can't do anything—got cut out of the situation from the getgo."

Howard leans forward.

"I think you can."

He looks at Daryl with a cruel glare.

Maple Avenue

"Brad's not such a bad guy you know—he's actually quite charming—when he wants to be anyway—sweet actually."

Carrie laughs sarcastically at the comment.

"Yeah—sure he is Elizabeth—as long as he can bed you like a cheap prostitute—that's who he is—a worthless toad."

"He's no different from any of the other guys in Marble Hills—they only think with their dicks—it's who they are."

Carrie sighs and seems to become enraged.

"I know—but he made a fool of me—and I can't—I won't let that go—he has to—he will pay for—and pay dearly."

Elizabeth shrugs.

"Whatever—*so*—what do you think will happen to Wesley Madison? Think he'll buy his way—you know out of jail?"

Carrie smirks.

"Serves him well that's he's in jail—if he gets knifed to death I certainly wouldn't shed a tear knowing what I know."

"You *are* seriously harsh—so harsh Carrie."

Carrie laughs.

"Deal with it—I keep grudges."

Elizabeth seems uneasy.

"Well anyway, I heard that old man Madison will get him off without a trial and make that guy who got Wesley in trouble pay. Wouldn't surprise me one bit if he does—from what I heard he's done some awful things to people who crossed him over the years—I bet he'll easily bribe some political bigwig—or he'll try blackmail to get his way—maybe even murder—anything."

Carrie shrugs.

"Old man Madison is a creep—totally."

Elizabeth notices Tiffany walking toward them.

<u>Police Station</u>

Daryl stands up.

"I think you'd better leave."

Howard grabs Daryl and shoves him against the wall.

"Listen, you *will* do as I say or else. If the charges against my grandson aren't dropped ASAP you will feel my wrath in ways you never imagined—I'll turn your life into a hellish nightmare and you know I can do it—no holds barred—I'll gladly do it."

Daryl jerks free of Howard's grip.

"Get out—or I swear I won't be responsible."

"Is that a threat I hear?"

"I'm warning you old man."

Howard smirks knowingly and sighs.

Page 165

"Or what—obviously you've forgotten your place again and what a complete nobody you are—but that can be remedied soon enough and I'm just the man that can make it happen."

He grabs Daryl again and forces him down on the table and laughs loudly as he shows off his strength. Howard smirks.

"Didn't think I had it in me, did you—well, I'm strong as an ox. Something you'd better not forget. If you cross me I swear you'll live to regret it—starting with the many indiscretions you've had with Caroline Bentley. Oh, I think John Bentley would love to know you've been screwing his wife for years behind his back when he's away on business. Oh yeah, I'm certain he would love to know—the question is—what would he—what would he do if he knew about his shameless wife and the police chief—and what if he also knew the awful truth about your bastard brats."

Howard laughs triumphantly.

"How would he handle finding out Gina and Corey Bentley wasn't really his offspring—but yours actually. What would happen if they knew? Things could get really unpleasant."

A look of terror spreads across Daryl's face. Howard grins broadly in triumph. He gives Daryl a knowing look and laughs.

"What do you want me to do?"

Howard releases his grip on Daryl.

"What do you think? Talk to Washington ASAP—get him to drop the charges against Wesley immediately or else."

"I'll get right on it."

"See that you do—it would be a real shame if Gina and Corey Bentley were to accidently find out they weren't really Bentleys. Of course that's nothing compared to what—what John would do when he learns the filthy truth about you and his unfaithful wife—oh, I think if he found out your secret he would possibly come after you with a loaded gun—maybe even take a few shots before he actually knew the disgusting details."

"What about Kyle? Does he know?"

"Not yet. But that could change really quickly."

Daryl seems bothered by the comment. Howard grins.

"Imagine the possibilities."

Howard heads to the door. He turns to look at Daryl one last time and grins. Daryl nervously leans against the desk. He seems about to faint. Howard smiles broadly in triumph.

"You're absolute evil—rotten to the core—right up there with the worst of the worst scumbags—no soul at all."

"I'm a nightmare and don't you ever dare forget it."

He opens the door.

"I'm not playing Anderson—either you make me happy or I'll ruin your life—I guarantee it—bad things will happen."

He leaves. The door slams shut. Daryl continues to stand in the middle of the room motionless as if he's paralyzed.

Rockport

Marc grins as he watches Corey slip on his Lycra shorts and kisses Denise goodbye. He leaves and she closes the door.

"Denise Madison is real piece of work."

He laughs loudly.

"But oh—what's going to happen when the truth comes out about her—about her and all her teenage boy toys?"

He laughs again.

"The question is how much—how much is this worth to her—how much is my silence going to cost that whore?"

He glances at the photographs again.

Boardinghouse

Caleb laughs as he forces Gina onto his bed and enters her. Intense lovemaking follows for almost ten minutes.

"I'm glad you're not mad at me anymore."

Gina kisses Caleb.

"I tried—believe me I tried. But I just can't. You know you've always had a hold on me—could make me do things."

She kisses him again. He laughs loudly.

"I wonder if Tiffany still feels the same way you do about me now—she and I had a lot of good times together."

Gina pushes Caleb away.

"If you go near her—I swear you and I will be over."

Caleb stifles a laugh.

"Oops—too late."

Gina looks at Caleb oddly.

"No—tell me you didn't just come from her."

Caleb gestures with his hand.

"I did—earlier this morning—what can I say—she couldn't wait to sample my wares—had to have me right away."

Gina jumps out of bed.

"You actually fucked that bitch Tiffany Johnson this morning before you and—I'm getting loser seconds?"

Caleb grins as he glances at his penis sticking out like an arrow in front of him. He sits up in bed and seems confused.

"*Seconds*—there's no seconds with my dick—only great moments of which you've got to admit you enjoyed."

Gina glares at Caleb.

"You bastard—I hate you."

Caleb smiles broadly.

"Uh-huh—until you want me to stick you again—of which probably will be tomorrow morning—and then—well, I think."

Gina throws a pillow at Caleb.

"Never—you and I are through—for good. I hate you. I wish you were dead—wish you get hit by a car or something."

Caleb smirks as he pulls on his Levi's.

"We'll see."

Gina rushes over to Caleb and pushes him backwards on the bed. He begins laughing hysterically. She slaps him.

"Don't ever call me again—it's over."

Caleb watches as she runs to the door.

"So, I guess expecting a friendly hook-up tomorrow like we planned initially is out of the question? I still need. You know how I behave when I get horny—can't relax—got to score."

"I swear if you ever come near me again."

Caleb makes a lewd gesture with his finger and laughs.

"You'll what—kill me? Kill your main guy."

Gina nods and leaves—angrily slamming the door. Caleb looks down at his erection still sticking out in front of him.

"I think it's time I give Lana Jefferson a call."

He begins whistling as he picks up his cell phone.

Rockport

"Yeah, that's right. I've got the goods—time to pay up like you promised last week—Denise Madison is a cheater."

Marc sighs as he looks at his cell phone.

"Look—you told me to get evidence—and I've done as you demanded—either you pay what we agreed upon or I'll take my business elsewhere—supermarket tabloids comes to mind."

He rolls his eyes.

"Whatever—OK I'll get more stuff. See what falls out."

He shuts off his cell phone.

Boston

Eldon Whitney leans back in his chair. He grins broadly as he looks at a copy of the *Marble Hills Gazette* in his hand. In bold letters the headlines tell a story. GREGORY MADISON TAKES OWN LIFE AS NEPHEW IS BUSTED FOR ASSAULT.

He begins laughing hysterically.

TO BE CONTINUED

A Look at the 7th Episode

Daryl's chaotic life continues to spin out of control while he continues his reckless behavior with Denise as a blackmailer plots his next move—Carrie and Brad's dislike of each other intensifies even further—Simon and Todd come to blows—Lindsay and Lori rekindle an old friendship amid failing relationships—Marc continues to pursue Denise's sordid escapades—Julia's feelings for Alden continues to grow—Juan and Faye has an unpleasant encounter with Alden—Corey plots diabolical revenge against Abby and Kelly's budding relationship—Ashton draws a positive line in the sand about his dull image and future—Caleb recklessly plays his conquests against each other—Robert and Lindsey's troubled marriage reaches an unpleasant standstill—Gina and Tiffany fight over Celeb—Carrie offers to help to Abby and Kelly in order to thwart Corey's devious plans to wreck havoc in their lives—as a tragic car accident results in an unexpected death.

Bad and the Beautiful

<u>Boardinghouse</u>

Caleb Winthrop grins broadly as he opens the door and sees Lana Jefferson standing in front of him dressed in a tight leather skirt. She smirks. He leers at her for several seconds.

"Oh-oh—what—what are you trying to do to me today being—dressed like that—I swear—so hot—oh yeah."

Lana smiles and walks into the small room. He closes the door and leers at her again. She seems pleased. He laughs.

"You've certainly filled out in all the right places—I certainly approve—uh-huh—high school girls are hot."

Lana slides her arms around Caleb.

"And you—I bet you can't remember how many girls you banged while you were away at college—plenty I bet."

Caleb laughs.

"Guilty as charged."

Lana kisses Caleb.

"Have you seen Gina yet?"

Caleb grins slyly.

"Gina Bentley is pissed at me at the moment."

Lana seems confused.

"Already—what did you do?"

Caleb laughs again.

"I slept with Tiffany."

Lana shrugs.

"So? That's like old news. Everyone in town knows that tale—I can't believe Gina is being such a bitch after the fact."

Caleb smirks.

"I fucked Tiffany earlier."

Lana slides her fingers across the buckle on Caleb's jeans.

"Oh really—*and Gina*—did you?"

Lana seems upset as Caleb laughs loudly and wags his finger at her. She sighs and focuses her eyes on his jeans.

"It's no big deal—besides it's your dick—end of story."

Lana glances at the bed again.

"You know I can't say no to you. From the first time you took me two years ago in my father's car—took me despite my protests that I was only fourteen—told me your dick couldn't and wouldn't wait—and made it clear it was inevitable that you would have me no matter what I said—underage virgin or not."

"It seems like just yesterday I took your virginity without thinking—made you a woman—made you popular."

Lana kisses Caleb again.

"You also gave me an unwanted pregnancy."

Caleb smirks again.

"Yeah—but I paid for you to get it taken care of before anyone found out—didn't I—that should count for something right about now—I could have refused to pay—could've ignored you completely and pretended I had nothing to do with it."

Lana begins unbuttoning Caleb's Levi's.

"I apologize for bringing my pregnancy story up again after all these years—you're a really sensitive guy Caleb—really nice—perfect—*wonderfully charming*—every girl's dream for their first time with an older experienced guy—many thanks."

"I just did what any other guy would do."

He leers at her yet again.

Page **172**

"I fucked you and didn't wear a condom—and after you told me you were pregnant there just was no other way out."

Caleb watches as Lana slides her fingers inside his boxer briefs and strokes his swelling erection. He grins broadly.

"In case you're wondering—I came prepared. I know you hate wearing a condom when you fuck—but I insist."

Caleb laughs loudly.

"Love when a woman takes charge."

He grabs her and they begin kissing passionately.

<u>Rockport</u>

Marc Ryerson grins broadly as he focuses his video camera on Denise Madison and Daryl Anderson walking toward the entrance of a cheap motel. He shakes his head several times as they stop briefly and kiss passionately. He sighs loudly.

"Oh man—this is just too good a deal. The "respected" chief of police banging the wife of the son of the richest man in Marble Hills—oh-oh—*they* do like to play with red-hot fire."

He watches as they enter the main lobby. A few minutes later they come out and head to one of the small bungalows to the right of the main building. Marc grins while he continues to follow them with his camera as they enter the bungalow and shut the door immediately after entering. He looks around.

"I think I need a closer look."

Marc quickly steps out of the car—locks it—and heads toward some bushes by one of the windows facing him.

<u>Pete's Cafe</u>

Julia Winthrop pours a cup of coffee for Todd Spencer. He looks around at the empty diner and sighs several times.

"This sucks—blows chunks by the millions."

Todd and Julia turn around to look at Simon Spencer.

"Seriously, you're going to make me spend the entire day with you on your crummy boat hauling smelly dead fish?"

Page 173

Todd seems annoyed.

"It's either that or you get a summer job."

He looks at Julia.

"I've got to make sure he doesn't have time to hang out with Corey Bentley or his troublemaking gang of idiots."

Simon rolls his eyes.

"Corey's not in a gang. He's cool. Everyone likes him."

Todd shrugs.

"Exactly the way everyone likes Wesley Madison?"

He laughs.

"Oh wait—he's in jail—charged with attempted murder."

Simon glares at his father.

"He wouldn't be if it wasn't for your loser friend."

He sighs loudly.

"*By the way*—I hate him. I wish Wesley had killed him—it would've served him right for what he did—he's a sicko killer."

Todd slams his fist down on the table.

"Keep it up and you'll find yourself at Pine Hill Academy."

Simon glances at Julia. He seems scared as he nervously turns around to face his father who seems about to explode.

"You wouldn't—no way."

"Wouldn't I—keep pushing the envelope and see how fast you end up in Augusta for the next two years—dare me."

Simon looks at Julia again. He shrugs.

"See what I have to deal with—my dad is a total loser."

Todd grabs Simon by the arm.

"We'll see who the loser is later when you have to gut all the fish that we take out of the traps past Camden Point."

Todd forces Simon to his feet and then glances at Julia.

"If you see Alden later tell him I said hi."

Simon tries to jerk free from Todd's grip.

"Dude's a loser."

Julia watches Todd's reaction.

"Tell Heather I have those magazines she asked about."

Todd nods and pushes Simon several times.

<u>Glass Owl</u>

Lindsay Bennington comes out of the library and sees her husband standing in the hallway. Robert Bennington sighs.

"How about you and I go for a walk?"

Lindsay gives him a nasty look.

"You can hide from it all you want but sooner or later we have to talk this thing out—talk about you and Chandra."

Lindsay notices Robert's reaction.

"Talk about how you cheated on me with *her*—and we both know it wasn't just once—or even a few times either."

Robert sighs again.

"I messed up OK—can we just get past it?"

Lindsay looks at her watch.

"I have to see someone in an hour—bye."

Robert watches as she leaves. He turns to look at the empty hallway. He angrily slams his fist against the wall.

<u>Mall</u>

Carrie Spaulding shuts off her cell phone as she sees Brad McKinley coming up to her. He grabs her arm and spins her around to face him. Her cell phone falls to the floor.

"I hear you've been talking trash about me again."

Carrie laughs.

"I don't know what you're rambling about."

"You thought you'd derailed my plans to fuck Donna Markway—didn't you—but guess again bitch—I got her."

Carrie jerks free of his grip. Brad laughs.

"I fucked her earlier—she gave it up to me—but you need to learn a lesson about what happens when you cross me."

"This tedious conversation is over."

Brad grabs Carrie again as his rage builds.

"You're gonna pay for what you did."

He twists her arm backwards and laughs.

"You need to be taught a lesson for messing with me."

Carrie pushes Brad out of the way and is about to walk away when he grabs her and forces her through a nearby exit. He shoves her toward the stairwell and laughs as he quickly shuts the door behind him. He faces her. He seems enraged as he glances at the buttons on his Levi's. Carrie tries to push him away.

"You need to show me respect."

Carrie smirks.

"Is that so—maybe it's slipped your mind how much I hate your guts—how much I wish you were laying in a morgue."

Brad laughs loudly.

"It's not my guts you need to worry about right now—it's my dick—my dick wants revenge for your rudeness."

Carrie glances at Brad's erection as he forces her against the rail in the stairwell. He unbuttons his Levi's and pulls out his penis—laughing loudly. Carrie tries to push him away.

"No—I won't let you do—I hate you."

Brad smirks as he slaps her.

"*Like you have a choice bitch*—seems you've forgotten your place when it comes to how much power I and every guy in town have over a used-up trashy whore like yourself—yeah."

Brad pulls her panty down and brutally rams into Carrie as she tries to push him away again. His strength immediately overpowers her and she grimaces as Brad forcibly penetrates her repeatedly and laughs. He continuously laughs as he slams into her multiple times. Simultaneously Carrie manages to open her purse and pulls out a loaded syringe. She smiles wickedly as she looks at it and without warning she jams it into Brad's back. He looks at her in shocked disbelief with a slightly confused look. She smiles triumphantly seeing the look of fear on his face.

"What did you just do?"

"That's for me to know and you to find out."

Brad pulls out of Carrie.

"Tell me what you just gave me—tell me or else."

Carrie notices semen running down her leg.

"You'll know soon enough—rapist. Oh yeah—and then I'll let Daryl Anderson know what you did to me. You're toast."

Page **176**

Carrie brushes herself off as she wipes away the trail of semen from her legs and watches as Brad pulls the syringe out of his back. Carrie walks to the door and faces him as she reaches for the doorknob. She grins broadly as he seems about to faint.

"You made a big mistake today—and when I'm finished with you—you'll regret what just happened between us."

Brad sighs loudly.

"I need to know what you just—*please?*"

Carrie smiles triumphantly and looks at Brad one last time before opening the door and leaving. The door slams shut.

<u>Rockport</u>

Daryl pulls out of Denise. He grins broadly.

"You're still at the top of your game."

Denise grins.

"Still having problems with the ball and chain?"

Daryl sighs.

"Lori is the least of my problems right now."

Denise leans over and strokes Daryl's exposed penis.

"If she isn't—then who is a thorn in your side?"

Daryl sighs loudly.

"Howard Madison wants me to do something for him."

Denise rolls her eyes.

"What does the old man want now?"

Daryl pulls Denise toward him. He grins.

"How about we fuck again and relieve more pressure."

Denise grins slyly.

"You know I can't resist a man in need."

Denise welcomes a passionate kiss from Daryl.

<u>Philadelphia</u>

Chandra Stevenson sighs loudly as she glances at a framed photo of Robert Bennington on a mantle nearby.

"I know you said we were through—but I can't."

Page 177

Her eyes fall on a single piece of paper lying nearby on a desk. She sighs again as she glances at it for a few seconds.

"But you need to know."

The word PREGNANT is spelled out in bold lettering on the cream-colored stationary. Chandra sighs loudly again.

<u>Pete's Cafe</u>

Julia smiles as Alden Washington sits down at one of the stools. He seems tired. She leans toward him and whispers.

"Are you OK?"

He sighs.

"No—not really—this damn thing with Wesley Madison is making me crazy—too much drama *way* too fast—a circus."

Julia shrugs.

"I feel bad about Kyle's kid—but trust me—he had it coming for some time now—been on the edge for years."

Alden nods.

"I know—but this whole incident just put a target on my head. Old man Madison is probably prepping a hit on me."

Julia leans toward Alden.

"I guess you haven't heard the latest?"

Alden seems confused.

"Heard what?"

"Greg Madison killed himself yesterday."

Alden looks at Julia curiously.

"Kyle's little brother took his own life?"

Julia nods.

"Seems like it from what I heard—apparently he got into serious trouble with some nasty mob types in Boston."

Alden shakes his head.

"Sounds like Greg all right. Man, he and his dad certainly didn't like each other one bit from what I remember."

Alden looks around at the empty diner.

"How's old man Madison taking the news?"

Julia hands Alden a mug of coffee.

Page 178

"I'm not sure. But I can't believe he's too broken up about it—he certainly didn't have much love for Greg—hated him."

Alden takes a sip of coffee.

"Maybe I should drop this thing against Wesley. I just don't think it—think it will help matters much now."

"It's up to you—but you and I both know if the situation was reversed—Kyle has never been the forgiving type."

"I know—I know—but maybe I should just drop it?"

Julia shrugs again.

"I know it seems like this might help—but we both know what we assume and what actually is can be far different."

Alden is about to answer when Faye Washington and Juan Sabrillo enter the diner. He turns to look at them and seems confused at seeing them standing there. He shakes his head and looks at Julia with a weird look on his face. Alden shrugs.

"What is my ex doing here in Marble Hills?"

Julia watches as Alden stands up and walks over to where Faye and Juan are standing. Faye's expression changes seeing Alden coming toward her—she reacts and turns to face Juan.

"*What are you doing here Faye?*"

Alden seems upset.

"Here in Marble Hills of all places?"

Faye turns to look at Juan again and sighs.

"Juan Sabrillo, meet my worthless ex."

Juan and Alden exchange looks. He turns to look at Faye again as Julia glances several times at Faye. Alden sighs.

"I asked you a question Faye. What are you doing here?"

"Why do you think? I want what I'm entitled to."

Alden looks at Julia and then at Faye once more.

"I thought that was already decided."

"For you maybe it was decided—but not for me as far as I'm concerned. Seems you forgot to mention the settlement you received from the production company of your soap opera."

Alden runs his fingers through his hair.

"I received that after we were divorced last year Faye. I owe you nothing—nothing at all—not one red cent more."

Page 179

Faye looks at Juan.

"*Oh really*—have you forgotten California law. I'm entitled to half of everything you made while we were married. Whether or not you received the settlement after we were divorced is irrelevant—I'm still entitled to my share and I plan to collect—no matter what I have to do—even if it means you get hurt."

Alden runs his fingers through his hair again.

"Or else what Faye—you'll have me killed—iced?"

Faye smirks.

"Or else I'll take you to court and sue you until you have nothing left but two pennies to rub together—of which you'll end up a pathetic homeless loser before the frigging year is out."

Alden looks at Juan curiously.

"So—*who is this*—your enforcer? What do you have in mind Faye? Are you going to have your muscle-bound gorilla beat me up like a ragdoll to satisfy your selfish ego for revenge?"

Faye laughs smugly.

"Don't tempt me. But no—Juan is only my friend—I met him coming to Marble Hills—he and I—well, we connected right away—in ways you and I never did if you know what I mean."

Faye slides her hand into Juan's hand.

"He's everything you're not and can never hope to be in this lifetime—starting with being an incredibly phenomenal lover in the sack—he's my knight in shining armor if you must know—a real man unlike—unlike you—a worthless cheater pretending to be a man while you broke our marriage vows for over a year."

Alden rolls his eyes.

"That's because he doesn't know the real you. But, oh he'll find out soon enough no doubt what a bitch you really are—what a hateful person you can be when you don't get what you want or what you think you are owed for whatever sick reasons."

Juan looks at Faye as she glares at Alden.

"Shut up."

Juan and Alden exchange glances.

"Just wait until you piss her off and she goes off the deep end. Trust me that moment isn't far away. Faye has issues."

Page **180**

"How dare you talk to me like that?"

She seems ready to slap Alden but stops herself.

<u>Mall</u>

Corey Bentley notices Carrie coming into the mall from one of the exits. Minutes later Brad comes through from the same exit a bit wobbly. He's about to follow Carrie when Corey calls out to him. Brad looks at Corey slightly confused at hearing his voice and stops. He seems about to fall and yells out.

"*That bitch*—that bitch just stuck me with something."

Corey watches as Carrie disappears in a crowd and then turns to face Brad. He shakes his head several times.

"I told you to stay away from her—she's not playing with a full deck. Bitch is a freaky psycho—should be locked up."

"Tell me about it—she just did something."

He notices as Corey rolls his eyes.

"So, what's up?"

Corey grins.

"I'm going to get that weasel fired."

Brad seems confused.

"Weasel—who—*who* are you talking about?"

Corey smirks.

"Kelly Nelson."

"Your ex's new boyfriend?"

Corey nods.

"Yep—as soon as that piece of trash comes back from his break I'm going to create a scene and get him fired from his job at the kiosk—he'll see that I'm not to be messed with—prick."

Brad laughs.

"That's going to be hard to do—considering."

Corey looks at Brad curiously.

"What are you talking about McKinley?"

Brad laughs again.

"His dad and Eddie Kane were in college together."

"So? Why should I care about that?"

<u>Page **181**</u>

"Eddie Kane owns the ice cream kiosk Bentley. He'll never fire Kelly Nelson—especially if you're somehow involved."

"Eddie Kane barely knows me."

"I guess you forgot the incident with his daughter last year? Kane's got a nasty reputation for keeping grudges."

Corey grins broadly.

"I tried to bed his precious daughter—big deal."

Brad slaps Corey on the back.

"His daughter is twelve—like in seriously young."

Corey laughs loudly.

"Oh yeah—I forgot about that."

He turns to look at the kiosk a few yards away.

"Well, I still want to get Nelson. That fucker took Abby from me and I can't let him beat me—nope, he's got to pay."

"Why do you care anyway Corey? You already fucked that slut—she's just used goods now buddy—a piece of trash—like seriously, forget her already. She's nobody—plain—a zero."

Corey looks at the ice cream kiosk once more.

"I know—but I really want to fuck Nelson up anyway—he needs to suffer my wrath—made me look like a sad chump."

"Well, there is another way—to spite Nelson."

Corey turns to face Brad.

"I'm all ears."

"Think about the worst thing you can do to a person without killing them outright—bet Nelson won't suspect you."

Corey grins broadly again.

"I'm beginning to see your point."

Brad winks at Corey.

"First up Nelson—then Carrie gets her just desserts."

Corey nods in agreement.

Rockport

Marc grins broadly as he watches Daryl and Denise leave the motel. They kiss passionately several times before heading to their own cars. Marc shuts off his video camera and sighs.

Page **182**

"That's three so far—she's quite a busy bee. I've never met a woman who can bed so many guys in such a short time."

He watches as they both drive way.

"I wonder how Howard Madison is going to feel when he finds out his daughter-in-law has been playing his precious son for an absolute fool—oh yeah, he'll be mad—so very mad."

He gestures with his hand several times.

<u>Pete's Cafe</u>

"Is this is how you plan to play your hand Faye—either you get what you think I owe you—or you'll turn my life into a nightmare—using this pathetic **William Levy** wannabe."

Alden turns to look at Julia.

"Still think I lead a charmed life?"

"You had a charmed life Alden—until you cheated on me and then lied about it for over a year despite the obvious."

Faye glances at Juan.

"You know—having you pummel my cheating twerp of an ex-husband might be fun—break a couple of bones."

Alden watches as Juan flexes his arms—showing huge muscles. He smiles broadly as he shoves them into the front pockets of his jeans. Juan gives Alden a mean look and sighs.

"What if I break his neck just because I can?"

Faye shrugs.

"Just make sure not to get any blood on your clothes—it would be such a shame afterwards—jeans are hard to wash."

Julia looks at Faye and Juan.

"OK—I think you both need to leave."

"Excuse me but who died and made you God?"

Julia leans over the counter toward Faye.

"Since I own this cafe—that's who. Now get out before I call the cops—and have your sweet boyfriend **Ignacio Figueras** deported. I barely know you and already I don't like you."

Faye glances at Alden.

"I want my share—or else you'll regret it."

Page **183**

Alden watches as Faye and Juan leave. He turns to look at Julia. He smiles broadly and turns to look at the door again.

"Thanks."

"She had it coming. She's a bitch."

She smirks.

"Think your ex will try to get back at me?"

Alden shrugs.

Mall

Kelly Nelson is busy cleaning the counter of the kiosk as Carrie walks up to him and smiles. He stops and faces her.

"Hello, Kelly."

Kelly seems confused as he looks at her odd behavior for a few seconds. He watches as she sits down at the kiosk.

"Carrie Spaulding—right?"

She nods.

"How much longer is your shift?"

"In about two hours I guess."

Carrie reaches out to touch Kelly's arm.

"Don't worry—I'm not making a play for you. I'm glad you and Abby Marshall hooked up. You're a really cool guy. Trust me—she's certainly better off with you than she ever was with that lame prick Corey Bentley—he's just trash—a toad."

Kelly looks at Carrie curiously.

"Thanks."

"I'll meet you here when your shift ends."

Kelly nods.

Maple Avenue

Caleb is coming out of a drugstore when he sees Denise pulling up in her car. He grins and casually walks over to where she's parked a few feet away. Denise smiles while her eyes fall immediately between his legs as he leans against her car.

"When did you get back in town?"

Page **184**

"Not long—been catching up—but only for a week or so until I split—but still plenty of time to make time for you."

Denise slides her fingers across his chest.

"You and I definitely have to get together for a drink—you know, to get reacquainted especially after a month apart."

Caleb smiles broadly.

"I agree—just say when and where."

Denise licks her lips seductively and lets her fingers slide down to his belt buckle. He watches as her fingers play with the zipper on his Levi's. Denise looks around the parking lot.

"No time like the present—say, Port Clyde—one hour?"

Caleb grins slyly and leers at her for a few seconds.

"What about your hubby?"

Denise smirks and strokes Caleb's bulging erection and sighs loudly twice—almost in dismay. She sighs loudly.

"He's a total bore."

Caleb shrugs.

"Whatever—not that it really matters to me either way as you recall—I'll still fuck you—husband or no husband."

Denise grins broadly.

<u>Pete's Cafe</u>

Julia gives Alden another cup of coffee, pats his hand, and then notices Lindsay entering the diner with Lori Anderson.

"Lindsay Madison—didn't know she was back in town? Man, it's been such a long time. She's all grown up now."

Alden turns to look at Lindsay and Lori.

"I assume she must be here for Greg's funeral?"

Julia nods.

"Oh—I forgot."

"I guess she feels the same way her family does about you on account of her sister's death—thinks she knows the truth?"

Alden shakes his head.

"She and I never had issues—if I remember correctly she didn't believe I had anything to do with her sister's death."

Page **185**

"I heard she married some guy from Philly. Rumor has it their marriage has not been quite a merry-go-round."

Julia turns to look at Lindsay and Lori again. They seem to be having an intense conversation about something.

<u>Stanley Pier</u>

Todd runs after Simon and grabs him by the arm. He spins him around. Simon suddenly takes a swing at Todd.

"I hate you—OK—there I said it."

Todd rubs his jaw as Simon glares at him coldly.

"I hate your guts—you make me sick."

Todd grabs Simon again and shoves him against an iron railing a few feet away. He seems angry as he looks at his son.

"Keep up that attitude—and I swear things will go from bad to worse between us—starting with Pine Hill next week."

Simon charges at Todd.

"I swear if I had a gun I'd take you out."

Todd grabs Simon in a headlock.

"You'd kill your own father?"

Simon pulls free of Todd's grip and glares at him angrily as a few seconds pass by. Simon shakes is fist in the air.

"Damn straight I would—I'd put a bullet in you and never look back. Skip the country right after—go to France."

Todd glances over at his truck parked nearby and as Simon watches he opens a rusty metal box and pulls out a small handgun. He hands Simon the gun and sighs. Simon reacts.

"Go ahead—now is your chance tough guy."

Simon looks at the gun and shrugs.

<u>Mall</u>

Corey grins broadly as he leans over Brad's shoulder while he enters information on the computer lying on his lap.

"Are you sure this is enough?"

"Trust me—all it takes is a few clicks."

Page 186

His fingers whip through the keyboard with intense speed and then he turns around to look at Corey with a sly smirk.

"Done—finished."

They look at each other. Brad grins again.

<u>Pete's Cafe</u>

Lindsay sighs loudly as she looks around the diner while people walk by and stare briefly as they stop to notice her.

"I guess we each have something in common."

Lori nods in agreement.

"I just feel my marriage is going nowhere. Daryl says he's been faithful—but his rep with other women says otherwise."

She glances at the crowd nervously.

"I've heard things. Things that make me feel like he's been lying—telling me tales while he plays around behind my back."

Lindsay takes a sip of coffee from her mug.

"I warned you way back when—I told you Daryl was no good. Slept around on my sister—slept with many of her closest friends behind her back and—he's a dog—really sleazy."

Lindsay shakes her head.

"Men—they're all dogs—pond scum."

Lori nods in agreement as she glances at Lindsay.

"Unfortunately I found out the hard way after the fact—I wish I'd listened to you all those years ago—would have saved me a lot of grief today—and I guess some dignity too—oh."

Lori rolls her eyes.

"Well, speaking of which—one of his whores. I wonder how many times she's been tested for STDs in the last year."

Lindsay turns around to see Caroline Bentley entering the diner. She glances at Lori and coldly ignores her as she walks by their table. Lori rolls her eyes in disgust at her and sighs.

"You'd think she'd at least have the decency to say sorry after what she did—apologize for bedding my husband."

"Never been her style—some people never change."

"I'm sure she's tried every penis in town."

Page 187

Lindsay looks at Caroline briefly as she sits down several tables away almost on purpose. Her stare is cold as ice.

"Bet she's had plenty of abortions too."

Lori continues glaring at Caroline.

"I can't help it—I can't stand her—it's just—she did."

Lindsay reaches out to pat Lori's hand and turns to look at Caroline again with an icy stare. Their eyes meet briefly.

<u>Lighthouse Grill</u>

Faye looks at her mug of coffee intently. Juan notices.

"If you want I can easily break his neck?"

Faye looks up.

"Break his neck?"

Juan laughs.

"Your ex's neck of course."

Faye smirks.

"I'd like nothing better—but no."

Faye slides her fingers along Juan's muscular arms.

"Despite the cheating creep that he is—I don't want him ending up dead with a broken neck—at least not yet."

She laughs slyly.

"Just an empty bank account—cleaned out."

Juan leans over and kisses Faye on the lips—at first just lightly—then more passionately. He grins broadly.

"Well, I offered. Just say the word and I'll work him over in the worst way. Breaking his scrawny neck would be child's play for someone like me—especially if it makes you happy."

Faye blushes.

"You're so sweet to offer—maybe later."

They kiss again.

"Seems he has a new girlfriend too?"

Juan seems confused.

"Girlfriend—I didn't see anyone else there? Who'd want him? He's a pauper since he got canned from *Larkspur Lane*."

Faye takes a sip of coffee.

Page 188

"Oh right, *the cashier*—excuse me—*owner* of that cafe we were at earlier—I bet she's already got her hooks into him."

Juan grins broadly.

"Do you care if they're involved?"

Faye shakes her head.

"No—I just don't want him to be happy so quickly after what he did to me last year—it isn't fair. He needs to pay."

"Like I said earlier—just say the word and I'll break his neck—crack his spine too if needed—make him beg plenty."

Faye looks at Juan oddly.

<u>Port Clyde</u>

Denise laughs as Caleb plows her again. They look at each other. He has a satisfied look on his face and grins slyly.

"I *so* missed being with you—definitely."

Denise smirks.

"I bet you say that to all your conquests."

Caleb grins again.

"Yep—pretty much—I lie a lot too."

He rams her again.

"Who'd think we'd still be hooking up five years after we first hit the sheets? It's been quite a wild ride for us both."

Denise smiles slyly.

"To think it all started when you offered to help me carry groceries from the market to my car—you were so sweet."

Caleb laughs loudly.

"Remember what you asked me?"

Denise pulls Caleb toward her and kisses him.

"I asked if you were a virgin."

Caleb kisses Denise.

"I laughed and told you I wasn't."

He kisses Denise again.

"I told you I'd been around town quite a bit—was very, very experienced with women—especially older women."

Denise runs her fingers through Caleb's hair.

Page **189**

"I told you I'd be the judge of that—and two hours later in the backseat of your car you proved not to be lying when it came how much experience you had—you were addictive."

Caleb leans backwards.

"I swear, like I can't believe that stupid husband of yours ignores you—what a loser. Fucking rich loser—dweeb."

Denise sighs.

"Kyle and I—things just aren't the same anymore. He acts like an old man. He hasn't touched me in years. Ugh."

Denise sighs again.

"When we were in high school back in the day he was horny all the time—but now—well he's, he's just—tired."

Caleb glances at his penis jutting upward.

"I guess his loss is my gain—I'm always in the mood."

Denise smiles broadly at Caleb as he winks.

"How about you and I make the earth move again?"

He pulls Denise toward him.

<u>Mall</u>

Abby Marshall walks up to the kiosk and smiles as she sees Kelly. He pulls his apron off and gives it to his replacement. He turns to face Abby and grins broadly. They hug warmly.

"OK—I'm ready."

They are about to walk away when Kelly sees Carrie coming toward them. He looks at Abby with a nervous look.

"Oh Abby, I forgot—Carrie wanted to talk to me about something earlier—said it was really important—serious."

Abby looks at Kelly suspiciously—he grins.

"No—it's not like that at all. She said it wasn't."

Abby and Carrie look at each other for a few seconds.

"Abby, glad to know you kicked Corey to the curb. I think it's great you and Kelly are together—much better deal."

Carrie sighs knowingly.

"Corey Bentley—ugh—like he's a disgusting creature times two—calling him a troll is an insult to trolls—hate him."

Page 190

Carrie continues looking at Abby as she smiles slyly while she quickly leads them a few feet away from the kiosk.

"I want to help you guys deal with Corey. It seems like your ex has declared war after you dumped his sorry ass."

"Corey said he was OK with us being over—said he was mad at first—but said he had moved past what happened."

"And you believed him? I saw him with Brad McKinley earlier. You know whenever those two get together it can't be good—Brad is bad news—uses everyone—plays people."

Abby shakes her head.

"Anyway, I wanted Kelly to know if you guys need my help I'm game—if Corey gives either of you problems let me know and I'll—well, I'll make sure he's otherwise occupied with issues of his own—which he definitely won't like one bit—guaranteed."

Carrie glances around the mall.

"In case you're wondering what do I get out of causing Corey moments of unhappiness—it's simple—I can't stand Corey Bentley—and I think you already know why I dislike him."

Abby nods. Carrie hugs Abby and Kelly briefly before walking away. Kelly smiles broadly and turns to look at Abby. He sighs loudly as he pulls her toward him. They kiss several times.

"Carrie Spaulding's some piece of work—absolutely lethal. Remind me never to get on her bad side—she's plays hard."

"You don't know the half of it."

Abby grins broadly.

"Trust me, you don't want to know—like ever."

They kiss once more and begin walking across the mall toward the escalators unaware they're being watched.

<u>Red Barn Gym</u>

Ashton Markway is about to walk over to where a receptionist is sitting at a circular podium when Lisa Taylor, Elizabeth Pendleton, Daphne Garfield, Natalie Standish and Genie Van Pelt walk past him in a rush. Daphne laughs loudly.

"Out of our way dweeb—this gym is for winners."

Page 191

She laughs again and joins her friends inside the gym. Ashton turns to see the receptionist staring at him and sighs.

"Forget them—they're not worth it."

He grins broadly and nods.

"Tell me about it—skanks—all of them."

He walks over to the podium.

"I'm here—here to get courage."

"Here to feel better about yourself is how you phrase it."

Amanda Spencer extends her hand to Ashton.

"I'm Amanda Spencer."

"Ashton Markway."

Ashton looks around nervously.

"Aren't you related to Simon Spencer?"

Amanda nods.

"Uh-huh—he's my nephew."

Ashton shoves his hands into the front pockets of his shorts and seems nervous as he glances at Amanda again.

"Oh."

"Todd Spencer is my big brother."

Amanda pulls out a clipboard and hands it to Ashton.

"You've made the right move coming by here today Ashton—it's time for you to make a change—for tomorrow."

As Ashton is filling out the form on the clipboard a muscular man comes toward them. Amanda smiles broadly when Damon Mayo leans against the podium and glances at Ashton briefly. He winks at Ashton and casually extends his hand. He gazes at Ashton oddly for several seconds and sighs loudly.

"Hi, my name is Damon Mayo."

Ashton turns to look at Damon noticing the tight T-shirt and Lycra shorts he's wearing. They look at each other.

"Sorry—I'm not into dudes."

Damon looks at Amanda and laughs.

"I'm not trying to pick you up. I'm the owner of Red Barn Gym. I'm also a trainer. Looks like you need some tips."

Ashton glances at Amanda for a second.

"I'm sorry—I just thought you were hitting on me."

They shake hands.

"That's OK. I get that all the time. Except I'm the one who gets hit on—but what can you do—that's life—people think."

Amanda leans forward.

"Damon is really good at what he does—everything in fact—and I'm not just talking about his training skills either."

Ashton gives Amanda and Damon a weird look.

<u>Hollow Oak Lane</u>

Tiffany Johnson is about to get into her car as Gina Bentley approaches her. She seems quite angry.

"Stay away from Caleb Winthrop or else—or else I won't be responsible for what I may do to you. I'm tired of you always trying to steal every guy I'm friends with—I've sick of you and will do what I have to if you dare cross me again—be warned."

Tiffany turns to face Gina and laughs.

"Last time I checked Caleb and you were through—he's not yours—you don't own him—he can play the field."

Gina grabs Tiffany by the arm.

"I'm warning you bitch."

Tiffany jerks free of Gina's grip.

"Fuck off—no one tells me what to do. Especially someone like you—a washed-up whore who can't keep her man happy—if you could, Caleb and I wouldn't have hooked up so easily on prom night—he was so horny that night—couldn't keep his hands off my body. It's just wrong such a virile guy couldn't get what he needed from you—he was so relaxed after he fucked me just so you know—so polite too—told me thanks when he drove me home later—and from then we kept hooking up."

Gina grabs Tiffany's arm again.

"You are *so* going to pay—you've crossed a line and you must be taught a lesson—one you won't forget—ever."

Tiffany pushes Gina away, laughs loudly, and gets into her car as Gina angrily pounds on the hood of Tiffany's car.

"Don't say I didn't warn you Tiffany."

Page 193

Tiffany gives Gina a strange look as she drives off.
"I hope her parents can afford a funeral."
She begins laughing.

Stanley Pier

Todd puts his arms around his son as they sit on the pier looking out at the sea. Simon sighs loudly and shrugs.
"I'm sorry for what I said earlier."
Todd smiles and hugs his son again. Simon sighs.
"I didn't mean it."
"It's OK—I've not exactly been a model father either."
Simon sighs again as he looks at his father.

Port Clyde

Marc grins as he looks at Denise and Caleb walking across the parking lot holding hands like teenagers. He laughs.
"Oh-oh—she's finally done with another of her toys."
He watches as they kiss passionately.
"I wonder how Kyle Madison would feel knowing his wife is addicted to virile young men—that she's already had three so far today—and Daryl too? Man—if those walls could talk."
He grins broadly.
"I wonder who's next on the menu."
He smirks as he watches Denise get into her car.
"Those celebrities in Hollywood have nothing on Denise Madison—they should be so lucky to get laid so often."
He smirks again.
"Compared to her antics **Gary Cooper** would have been considered a lonely virgin with no game whatsoever."
Marc watches as she drives away.
"I hope she's making her suitors wear condoms. It would truly be scandalous if she got pregnant—Kyle would freak."
He makes a lewd gesture with his finger.
"Howard Madison would kill her without a doubt."

He grins broadly as he relishes the thought.

"I could just imagine the headlines now if he caught her in bed with one of her teenage studs at the wrong moment."

He smirks and drives away.

<u>Standish Road</u>

Tiffany is driving aimlessly listening to loud blaring music as she talks to Caleb on her cell phone. She rolls her eyes.

"Yeah—I told you—no problem—tomorrow morning at the boardinghouse—I'll be there and willing. *Yeah*—Gina Bentley was seriously pissed that you hooked-up with me first—said she would get even with me. She made threats—several in fact."

She nods several times.

"That's perfect—you're so sweet."

Tiffany shuts off her cell phone.

"Bet she'll hate what happens tomorrow—time to ramp up the game—if she wants to bring it—I'm ready to teach her."

She smirks.

"Wonder how she'll handle my game?"

She glances at her cell phone.

"Bye bye bitch."

As she spins the curve Tiffany realizes the brake in her car is jammed. She slams her feet on the brakes several times in a panic to stop the car as it accelerates forward—but to no avail. She screams as the car smashes through a nearby guardrail seconds later and then begins spinning out of control toward the edge of the jagged precipice. Suddenly the car goes airborne.

TO BE CONTINUED

A Look at the 8th Episode

Todd and Simon come to an understanding about their relationship—a figure from Robert and Lindsay's recent past makes her next move—Denise dallies around with yet another virile playmate—Hart and Susan venture into town and attracts the wrong attention—Ross and Tyler have a falling out—Eddie and Alden's trip to Portland is sidelined by an unexpected tragedy—Ashton furthers plans for his new image—Kelly and Abby decide to take their relationship to the next level—Elizabeth and Corey briefly enjoy each other's company—Brad has a potentially embarrassing situation with Susan—Damon and Amanda enjoy quality time together despite ominous dark clouds looming in their "perfect" future—Ross tries to make a move on Hart which doesn't go as planned—as fallout from an accident takes a decidedly interesting twist for more than one person.

Episode 8
All Fall Down

<u>Shelby Park</u>

Juan Sabrillo and Faye Washington sit down under a grove of trees. They look at each other briefly. Faye sighs loudly.

"*I want it all*—everything that I'm entitled to."

Juan leans over to kiss Faye.

"Uh-huh—I think we should seriously start shadowing your cowardly ex tomorrow—and make him really nervous."

Faye grins slyly.

"I agree—he's afraid of you—said as much."

Juan kisses Faye again and laughs.

"I got that feeling too. Hey, how about you and I find a secluded spot somewhere nearby—and spread a blanket."

Faye gives Juan a strange look.

"Is fucking all you ever think about?"

Juan laughs loudly.

"Got a problem with that?"

She shrugs. He pulls her to her feet. They walk back to Juan's car and he hastily grabs a blanket from the trunk.

"Came prepared—didn't you?"

Page **197**

Juan grins broadly.

"Everything but a condom—oops—forgot again."

Faye shrugs and begins rummaging through her purse in a panic as Juan immediately begins unzipping his jeans.

<u>Pete's Cafe</u>

Eddie Kane walks toward Julia Winthrop and Alden Washington sitting at the front counter. He seems upset.

"Hello, Eddie."

Eddie acknowledges Alden as Julia turns to face him with a worried look on her face. Alden smiles broadly.

"Right on time—same old Eddie."

"I am who I am."

Alden faces Julia and grins.

"Eddie and I are headed to Portland—going to look up info on an old case—see if we can shake loose some facts."

Eddie nods in agreement.

<u>Maple Avenue</u>

Gina Bentley steps out of her car as Carrie Spaulding drives by and reverses. Carrie appears annoyed and sighs.

"Gina, have you spoken to Tiffany Johnson lately? I've tried calling her back twice—but she's not returning my calls."

Gina rolls her eyes.

"Why are you asking me?"

Carrie sighs.

"I spoke to her about a half hour ago and she said the two of you had words—said you outright threatened her."

"Yeah—I warned her to stay clear of Caleb Winthrop if she knew what was good for her—told her what I'd do if she dared."

"Why would you care if Caleb and Tiffany were involved? I mean, like he sleeps around all over town—he's a toad."

"I know he's a slug—but I still don't want that whore dallying with him—like ever. I'd rather see her dead first."

Page 198

Carrie tries to suppress a smile but isn't very good at it.

"OK—whatever—I was just asking."

Gina watches as Carrie drives away. She shakes her head and looks at her car once more. She clenches her fist.

<u>Stanley Pier</u>

Todd Spencer stands up and looks out to sea as several fishing boats can be seen in a distance. He sighs.

"How about we go camping next month on Bradford Mountain—just the two of us—would that be OK with you?"

Simon Spencer grins broadly.

"Yeah—I'd like that."

He stands up.

"Hey—I just want to say again how really bad I feel about what I said earlier—I didn't mean any of it. I wouldn't."

Todd pulls his son toward him.

"I know you wouldn't."

Simon extends his hand.

"Start over point?"

"Uh-huh—I'm for that."

They walk toward the parking lot.

<u>Mall</u>

Ross Harrison and Tyler Van Pelt walk into the mall and look around the empty lobby as a few people walk by.

"It must be a slow day."

"I wonder if the stairwell is deserted."

Tyler seems confused and looks around again.

"Why?"

Ross smirks.

"Why do you think?"

Tyler looks around nervously.

"What if someone sees us getting hot and busy—how would we—how would we explain what we—you know?"

Page **199**

"If anyone sees us, they see us—so what—besides as far as I'm concerned there's absolutely nothing more beautiful than a hot guy fucking his friend simply because he's really horny and can't wait one more second to do what comes naturally."

Tyler smiles broadly.

"OK—if you want to fuck me that badly—let's go find a place where we—*where we can be together*—I'm game."

"Trust me—by the time summer's over you'll be so uninhibited—I assure you—you *will* be experienced when it comes to fucking guys—every type of guy—I'll make sure of it."

Tyler reaches out to hold Ross's hand.

<u>Philadelphia</u>

Chandra Stevenson forces her suitcase shut. She looks at the room as she reaches out and hastily grabs the suitcase.

"Well, I tried calling—but you won't answer your phone because—so—I guess this is the only way—to see you."

She sighs loudly and walks to the door.

<u>Bar Harbor</u>

Marc Ryerson watches as Denise Madison looks around and then steps out of her car nervously. He grins broadly.

"Oh-oh—bet she's on the prowl again."

He smirks as he sees a young man walking toward Denise with a grin on his face. Marc rolls his eyes in disgust.

"Oh-oh—she's caught yet another virile young man in her web—and by the looks of him—he's certainly not meeting with her to talk boring academics—maybe biology is his thing?"

He laughs as she watches Denise passionately embrace the young man. Marc grins broadly as they head toward the entrance of a small motel holding hands. Marc snickers.

"She's really likes them young—I'm surprised she hasn't gotten caught yet—arrested for dallying with teenagers."

He smirks as he continues watching.

Page 200

"Dude looks like he lives in a frigging gym. I'm surprised he has any energy left to satisfy that cougar. That woman leaves nothing to the imagination with her taste in young men—ugh."

Marc continues to aim the video camera at them until they disappear inside the motel. He steps out of his car and heads to the rose garden on the other side of the building. He grins broadly as he adjusts the lens on the camera and as they come into view at one of the windows while he makes the sound of a cash register being opened several times. He sits down on a nearby bench and begins whistling. The area is void of people.

<u>Glass Owl</u>

Hart Bennington is walking to the front door when his sister calls out to him. He turns around and faces her.

"Where are you going?"

Hart ignores the question and opens the door and leaves. Instantly Susan Bennington runs after her brother, grabbing his arm before the door closes—she seems visibly annoyed.

"I asked you a question."

Hart rolls his eyes.

"Last time I checked you're not the boss of me."

"I just asked—no need for you to act like a total brother?"

Hart sighs loudly again.

"Look, if you want to hang around this mausoleum the rest of the day—go ahead—but I'm not down with that—I actually want to have a life—you know, meet girls—get laid."

Hart looks at Susan curiously and then leaves. A few seconds later Susan joins him somewhat out of breath.

"Hey, wait up."

Hart turns around.

"Did you leave a note—or anything that—anything that can give me away—like I don't want to be followed by cops."

Susan smirks and jabs Hart several times.

"What kind of a fink do you think I am?"

Hart laughs.

Page 201

"Do you really want to go there? I mean, really."

Susan rolls her eyes.

"OK—OK. I messed up before. But I've learned—I won't play their game again—I know their deal every which way."

Hart grins.

"We'll see about that."

He motions her to come with him. They begin walking toward the street where they are accosted by several reporters. Hart immediately flips his middle finger at them and keeps walking. Susan does the same and follows her brother.

<u>Standish Road</u>

Eddie and Alden are headed toward Portland when they see a crowd gathered in front of a broken guardrail overlooking a nearby cliff. Eddie seems curious as he looks at Alden.

"I wonder what that's about."

He slows down and sees smoke rising from the bottom of the cliff. He reacts and faces Alden. A few people turn away.

"I have to stop—see if help is needed."

Eddie pulls over. He and Alden jump out of the car and head to where the guardrail is broken as more people stop and rush over to look at the car engulfed in a fireball below.

"How could this? I thought."

Alden watches as Eddie grabs his cell phone and begins calling frantically. Alden looks over again at the wreckage.

"Yes—yeah right—on Standish Road—oh, I don't know if there's—just get here quickly, OK? Yes—a car went off at the corner of Pilgrim Hill and—yes like, like Pilgrim Hill—OK?"

He sighs loudly.

"I told you already I don't know."

He sighs loudly again.

"I just got here."

He nods several times and shrugs.

"Didn't I just say I don't know—look, stop playing twenty questions—get here before—before there's no reason to?"

Page 202

Eddie looks at the cell phone.

"My God, how many dumb questions are you going to ask me—just get over here already—like now OK—today?"

He shuts off the cell phone and looks at Alden.

"I swear some people are truly stupid."

They look over the broken guardrail again. Large areas of nearby shrubbery are on fire as people continue to gasp.

"I hope whoever was in that car managed to get out somehow? I wonder who—who the unlucky person could."

He and Alden look around.

"I'm going to ask a few questions."

Eddie mingles with the crowd.

<u>Mall</u>

Ross hastily pushes Tyler up against the stairwell and aggressively penetrates him from behind. He laughs loudly.

"Oh yeah—that's what I'm talking about."

Ross begins kissing Tyler's neck passionately as he recklessly slams into him. Tyler begins moaning loudly as Ross's joyful laughter echoes throughout the stairwell. Ross sighs.

"This is as good as it gets."

Tyler grins.

"Hope I don't get pregnant?"

Ross laughs again.

"You might—I'm not wearing a condom."

Tyler chuckles.

"*You* never wear condoms."

Ross laughs loudly.

"Bite me."

Tyler reacts.

"It's not like you're fucking other guys."

Ross doesn't answer.

"You haven't been with anyone else, right?"

Ross grins broadly.

"What if I have? Does it really make a difference?"

Page **203**

Tyler pushes Ross away from him.

"You've been with other guys?"

Ross grins broadly again.

"Big deal—I never said we were exclusive—we have a good thing—but I'm—but we're not a couple—just good friends."

He smirks as Tyler glances at him with a look of shock and confusion for a few seconds. Ross leers slyly at Tyler.

"I'm a young guy—like, really young, OK—and I like having sex—especially with older guys with experience—deal with it already. Seriously, what do you want from me anyway?"

Tyler wipes sweat from his brow.

"How many has there been so far?"

Ross shoves his penis into his Lycra shorts as Tyler leans against the stairwell with a disgusted look on his face.

"How many guys have you slept with since we started going out together? I want to know an exact number."

Ross laughs slyly.

"Are you for real?"

Tyler glances at the door.

"Just tell me already—how many?"

"I can't. I don't know how many—it's been a lot. I don't keep track of who I fuck—most of whom I never see again."

Tyler seems about to faint.

"You do remember some of their names, right? Like you just didn't hook-up with them without knowing their names, did you? Even you wouldn't be so careless about casual sex?"

Ross laughs slyly again.

"Well, actually, that's pretty much the deal. I go to Pike's a lot—meet up with a hot guy—and we have sex in the parking lot like seconds afterwards—no names, no questions, just really hot fucking. Then, it's over. Most of the times I don't know their first names, much less their last as they stick me repeatedly."

Tyler looks at Ross and seems about to throw up.

"I—I—I'm not like—just leave me alone."

He walks toward the door as Ross grabs his arm and swings him around. He seems confused at Tyler's outburst.

Page **204**

<u>Maple Avenue</u>

Hart and Susan are walking down the sidewalk and they both seem lost. Their behavior is instantly noticed by Brad McKinley as he drives by. He pulls over a few seconds later.

"Hey, you guys seem lost—need help?"

Hart glances at Brad curiously as Susan smiles broadly when she notices Brad's car. She gestures with her hand.

"What if we're sort of lost—what's it to you?"

Brad grins slyly.

"I live here in Marble Hills—I can show you two around a bit? Name's Brad McKinley—I do tour guides on the side."

Susan looks at Hart. He rolls his eyes knowingly at Brad and faces Susan cautiously. He gestures with his hand.

"He's a creeper, OK? Seriously, he's like, what seventeen. He just wants to get in your pants—just wants to get laid."

Susan laughs knowingly.

"So? Maybe I want him to be my first? I can't hold out any longer—I'm getting really old—I'm almost sixteen—it's just a matter of time before I give it up to someone anyway—so why not just give it up to a hot, hunky seventeen-year-old guy?"

Hart shakes his head.

"Go ahead—see if I care?"

Susan turns to face Brad with a smile.

"So, you're one of the locals—like you've lived here all your life—I bet you have the dirt on everyone you know?"

Brad laughs loudly.

"Yeah—but I'll never tell."

She reaches for the doorknob. As she opens it she turns back to face Hart. They look at each other for a second.

"Aren't you coming or not?"

Hart shakes his head.

"Nah—I don't think so—three's a crowd."

Susan hesitates slightly. Brad smirks.

"Come on—I won't bite."

She looks at Brad again and then at Hart. She quickly hops into the front seat and shuts the door as Brad looks at Hart with a sly glance. Hart rolls his eyes in disgust and ignores Brad.

"OK—see you round."

"Whatever."

Hart shrugs and watches Susan wave to him as Brad drives away. He shoves his hands into the front pockets of his Levi's and begins walking down the street toward the mall up ahead.

<u>Bar Harbor</u>

As sounds of intense lovemaking echo throughout the room Jarod Keller laughs loudly as he pulls out of Denise and sighs. She reaches out to kiss him several times. He grins.

"Oh—love the fact you came all the way to Bar Harbor to hook-up with me—really says a lot about my value."

Denise laughs knowingly.

"How else was I going to see my incredibly gorgeous college guy? It's been one very long month and counting."

Jarod gestures with his hand.

"True—but you know I plan to be back in Marble Hills in a couple of days—you know, visiting my sister and all that crap."

"I do—but I couldn't wait another second."

Jarod laughs loudly.

"Yeah, I get your deal—a month is just too long a wait for us to be together. But hey, I have endless classes to deal with since my bitch of a sister gave me an ultimatum—either graduate this year or else—*totally sucks*. She's being so unreasonable."

Denise kisses Jarod passionately.

"Your sister *is* a bitch."

He nods in agreement.

"I hope you still make time for those innocent coeds in your dorm—give them personal lessons in biology?"

Jarod laughs slyly.

"They're not innocent anymore—believe me I know—I've sampled their wares plenty—wasn't hard either—sluts galore."

Page 206

Denise smiles broadly.

"Seeing anyone special—you know, like seriously?"

Jarod grins again.

"If you mean do I have a girlfriend—I do. But I still see other people. I mean, like until there's a ring on my finger I'm going to stray—and stray often—and even after I get hitched I still might—what they don't know certainly can't hurt me—right?"

Denise kisses Jarod passionately again.

"A ring means nothing nowadays anyway."

Jarod laughs again.

"I certainly have no plans to let a little thing like marriage curtail my sexual activities—I'm not that kind of guy."

Denise kisses Jarod again.

"I love the way you think—such an honest guy."

He gives Denise a knowing look.

"Marriage certainly hasn't stopped you—seriously how dumb is your husband—doesn't he have eyes—doesn't he care that I'm poking you—that other guys have poked you?"

Denise smirks.

"Let's not talk about Kyle—OK?"

They resume making love.

Shelby Park

Juan and Faye are packing the last of the picnic supplies into the trunk of Juan's car when they see several fire trucks race by the park in a panicked frenzy. Faye seems worried.

"I wonder what that's all about."

Juan shrugs and turns to face Faye.

Mall

Tyler jerks free of Ross's grip and pulls on the door leading back inside the mall. Ross follows as a few people stare.

"Come on—what's the big deal if I fuck other guys?"

Tyler stops and glares at Ross.

"I'm not like that. I don't think it's cool if you bang every guy you like—trolling isn't who I am—you're disgusting."

Ross smirks.

"It was just sex—like no big deal."

"Whatever."

"Seriously, are you going to act this way with me?"

Tyler sighs.

"I've only slept with two other guys besides you."

Ross smirks again.

"You knew I was popular."

"Yeah, but I didn't know you'd been with just about everybody—I think I might need to go to a clinic for STDs."

"I don't have an STD. I'm clean."

"Uh-huh—says you."

At that moment Ross sees Hart walking over to one of the open area cafes a few yards away. They look at each other. Tyler glances at Ross and notices the outline of his penis under his Lycra shorts immediately beginning to swell. Ross sighs.

"OK—whatever—suit yourself if you're going to be a prude—I think I've just found my next weekend boyfriend."

Ross leers at Tyler briefly and heads over to where Hart is sitting. Tyler seems dismayed at the scene in front of him.

"I should've listened to Carrie Spaulding."

He walks toward the escalator.

<u>Standish Road</u>

As Eddie watches from the edge of the broken guardrail a team of firemen descend to where the wreck is lying. Several ambulance personnel also descend down the hill cautiously.

"This can't be real. How could it?"

Alden walks over to where Eddie is standing at the broken guardrail and look over at the horrific scene unfolding.

"Hey."

Eddie turns to look at Alden. He seems upset.

"I can't believe."

Page 208

Alden puts his hand on Eddie's shoulders as multiple hoses of water sprays the still-raging fire coming from the wreckage lying on the rocks a few feet away from the surf. He shrugs.

"Oh man."

Eddie turns around to face Alden.

"This brings back bad memories about my folks."

Alden nods.

"I know—I'm sorry—I shouldn't have said."

"It's OK."

They watch as the flames are extinguished.

"I tried—but it's probably too late."

Alden nods again.

"How about we leave?"

Eddie shakes his head and glances at the other spectators milling around. Alden turns to look at the crowd and shrugs.

"I'm surprised the local news haven't shown their faces yet—this is just their kind of story—tragedy galore."

"They're probably still out in front of Glass Owl."

Eddie seems confused.

"Greg Madison?"

Alden nods.

"Greg Madison was the only human one in that wretched family—well, him and Lindsay anyway. Kyle is a freak."

Eddie and Alden look at each other.

<u>Red Barn Gym</u>

Ashton Markway closes his locker and turns to face Amanda Spencer. He seems out of place among the lockers.

"I can't believe I actually have a gym locker."

She smiles.

"This is the beginning of the new you."

"I hope I don't fall short."

Amanda grins.

"I won't let you—and neither will Damon."

They look at each other.

Page 209

"Damon is a lucky guy. Like, really lucky."
Amanda blushes.
"I'll remember to remind him of that when I see him."
Ashton looks at the door.
"Thanks again."
He quickly heads to the door as Amanda continues looking at him. As he turns around she waves to him.

<u>Bradford Beach</u>

Kelly Nelson looks at a slice of apple as Abby Marshall slips it into his mouth. He winks at her slyly. Abby notices.
"I think we should go toward the next step."
Abby stares curiously at Kelly as she grabs another piece of apple. She seems confused as he grins broadly and smirks.
"Exactly what do you mean by that?"
Kelly nods.
"You know—get to know each other better."
Abby seems confused.
"You want to have sex?"
Kelly nods.
"Yeah—you know, maybe in a few days—if I can keep my hands off you that long—or you and—uh-huh—us together."
Abby leans over to kiss Kelly.
"What if I say no?"
Kelly sits up.
"Then, I guess I'll have to wait—but it'll probably shorten my lifespan—guys hate to be told no—crushes their ego."
"Really—is that so?"
Kelly nods again and pulls Abby toward him.
"I'm thinking I only have months to live—maybe even less if things get worse—bruised ego and all—tragic—so tragic for a guy to face—makes for quite some sad moments in life."
Abby strokes Kelly's lips.
"Well, I certainly wouldn't want to contribute to your early demise—especially since you're so sweet—and gentle."

Page 210

"I was hoping you'd say that—would've been so bad if you rejected me without a second thought—oh-oh—oh yeah."

They kiss again. Kelly seems pleased.

<u>Pine Street</u>

Donna Markway is about to enter the drugstore just as Gina exits. They look at each other. Gina grins with a malicious glint on her eye as Donna seems uneasy with her behavior.

"If I were you I'd seriously stock up on medication for STDs. Your so-called boyfriend is already on the prowl—seems you weren't that good the first time around—so sad for someone like you—whatever—not that it would've made much of a difference where Brad McKinley is concerned if truth be told. I should know—that bastard can't be trusted—he's a toad."

"What are you talking about?"

Gina grins broadly and walks away.

"Brad swore he was faithful—he wouldn't lie—he just wouldn't—especially not after I—he promised—he and I."

A look of unhappiness comes over Donna suddenly as she stands at the entrance of the drugstore. She seems in shock.

<u>Standish Road</u>

Eddie and Alden watch as the fire is finally put out. They continue watching as several firemen pry the car door loose.

"It's been a while since someone died out here."

As they continue watching the charred body of the passenger is pulled out from the burned-out wreckage.

"My God—this just got real."

Alden puts his hand on Eddie's shoulder's again as the corpse is placed on a stretcher and covered with a sheet. Eddie sighs as they watch the firemen climb the hill to the waiting ambulance. People began to disperse as several local news reporters finally arrive on the scene. Eddie and Alden look at each other briefly. Eddie glances at the charred wreckage again.

Page 211

"I wonder who—whose car is that?"

Eddie turns to look at his car as the sheet-covered corpse is placed into the back of the ambulance and the door is slammed shut. Alden notices several reporters looking at the wreckage from the broken guardrail. He runs his fingers through his hair.

"I—I—can't imagine."

Eddie unlocks his car. Alden turns to face him.

"Still feel like going to Portland?"

Eddie seems somewhat bewildered and shakes his head several times as he gets into his car. He turns to face Alden.

"I guess—there's nothing more I can do here today anyway—what's done is done—but I—oh—it's hard to relive."

Alden gets into Eddie's car and shuts the door.

"Are you OK?"

Eddie shakes his head.

"It's just that it all came flooding back."

"What did?"

"The accident—my parents—the whole thing just—it was buried for so long—and now it's back in front of me—all of it."

"I'm sorry."

Eddie waves his hand.

"Don't be—it's not like it's your fault—it."

He starts the engine.

"It happened and I dealt with it."

He wipes sweat from his brow several times.

"I can't imagine how the family of whoever was killed just now will deal with their loss—but it won't be easy—that—I know from experience—so much pain lies ahead—terrible grief."

"Think it was someone local?"

Eddie nods.

"Uh-huh—I think it was somebody from Marble Hills—for some strange reason I recognize that car—despite it being burned up so much—I—I think—but I can't be sure—not yet."

He leans against the steering wheel.

"OK—OK—OK—enough. Let's go to Portland and find out if your hunch is right—might add a spark to my dreary day."

Alden watches as Eddie sighs once more and begins driving away from the side of the road. He seems in a daze.

Mall

Hart is about to walk toward a nearby counter to pick up his order when Ross casually leans against his chair. He leers.

"You're new in town—aren't you?"

Hart looks at Ross suspiciously and rolls his eyes. Ross grins broadly as he leans even closer toward Hart. They look at each other. Hart backs away slightly from Ross. He sighs.

"Yeah so—want to make something of it."

Ross grins broadly again.

"Nope—just thought you'd like some company—some companionship—I can be a really good friend—really good."

Hart rolls his eyes.

"I'm not gay."

Ross leers at Hart again.

"I'm just trying to be friendly. Seems to me you don't really know anyone in town. I'm really nice—sweet actually."

Hart sighs.

"Yeah right, just trying to pick me up—come on, you assume because I'm new in town I'm stupid too and wouldn't know a pickup line where I hear it—fuck off creep—get lost."

"I never said anything."

"I don't fuck guys—OK—I fuck girls."

Ross grins broadly and leers again.

"Yeah, sure you're straight—I've never met a guy that didn't want to sample my dick for a nice round of specials."

Ross suddenly grabs Hart and tries to kiss him. At that moment he's grabbed from behind by Lance Weissmann.

"Well, well, well, it's Ross Harrison—and he's on the prowl again—seems we meet once again—and not in a good way."

Ross turns to face Lance.

"Don't you have some whore to bang?"

Lance laughs.

"I could say the same for you Ross—oh wait—oops—what happened—oh-oh—don't tell me—you got thrown out of Pike's again for hitting on the staff for the umpteenth time—yuk."

Ross glares at Lance.

"You're just jealous because I get more action than you on any given night—you resent the fact I banged your cousin."

Lance gestures with his hand.

"Yeah, right—that's it. I'm jealous because you take it in the ass like some used-up sicko perv from San Francisco."

Ross turns to look at Hart and then back at Lance. They stare at each other for a few seconds and then Ross storms off swearing loudly. Lance grins and turns to face Hart who still seems confused by what happened. Lance sits down next to Hart seconds later. He gives Hart an odd look and shakes his head.

"Are you OK?"

Hart nods.

"Yeah—I guess so. Thanks for stepping in—dude is a freak for sure—wouldn't leave me alone for anything—just kept."

"No problem. It was actually fun. Man, I can't stand that dude. He never lets up—wants to bang every guy he sees."

Hart stands up.

"Is he a local?"

Lance nods and stands up seconds later.

"Unfortunately—his name is Ross Harrison. Dude is a straight up pervert—he tried to hit on me last year—twice."

He sighs loudly and waves his hand.

"Don't get me wrong—I don't have a problem with gay people—but Ross is the exception. He hits on every guy he sees whether they're gay or not. Thinks every male he comes in contact with is a frigging homo who wants a nasty thrill."

Lance offers his hand.

"Lance Weissmann."

"Hart Bennington—just moved here yesterday afternoon from Philly. Not a fan of small towns if truth be known."

They shake hands.

"Got family here?"

Hart nods.

"Howard Madison is my grandfather."

Lance reacts.

"*Oh*—you're one of *them*."

Hart seems confused at the comment.

<u>Pilgrim Motel</u>

Elizabeth Pendleton is lying motionless underneath Corey Bentley as he pounds into her repeatedly. He laughs loudly.

"Aren't you glad we hooked up today?"

Elizabeth sighs.

"More or less—but I would've liked a little more notice beforehand. Getting a call from you to meet here at Pilgrim Motel to fuck isn't exactly romantic if you know what I mean."

Corey makes a lewd gesture with his hand and laughs.

"You want romance—get a boyfriend."

Elizabeth pushes Corey off her.

"You're such a toad."

Corey smirks.

"And you're a friend with benefits—otherwise known as an unpaid whore—how many times do I have to repeat myself."

Elizabeth looks at the stained sheets.

"I just thought—thought that you and I could?"

Corey rolls his eyes and begins laughing.

"Ugh—you thought what—come on—whenever we fuck it means nothing to me—it meant nothing the first time and it still means nothing now—it's just sex and you're just a trick."

Elizabeth seems upset as she climbs out of bed and pulls on her clothes. She turns to face Corey seconds later.

"I know—but—maybe it could be different between us."

Corey grins broadly.

"No buts. Deal with it Elizabeth—there's no *us*—we don't exist as a couple—never going to happen—never—ever."

Corey grabs his Levi's and pulls them on as he continues to grin while he watches Elizabeth. He leers at her.

Page 215

"If that bothers you—get over it—like today OK."

Corey walks over to Elizabeth. He pulls her to him and kisses her passionately. He smirks as she pulls away.

"Tomorrow—same time as today—don't be late."

He leers at her yet again.

"From now on I don't want to hear about you wondering if we're a couple—because the answer is no—we're not—you and I exist only as friends who fuck every day just because."

Corey laughs slyly.

"Look—you girls know the deal OK—us guys rule Marble Hills—you either put out or you're instantly a zero—you exist to service our needs—until we say otherwise. We call the shots."

Elizabeth glances at Corey's erection.

"I wish—I wish I hadn't."

Corey grins broadly again.

"What? You wish you hadn't given it up initially to Lance Weissmann two years ago? Oh well—seems it's a little too late to be worrying about that now—once you spread your legs."

Corey grabs Elizabeth and pulls her toward him again.

"Every guy wanted a piece after Lance took you. He opened the doors for everyone else. Facts are facts."

He gestures with his hand.

"No doubt in my mind whatsoever."

He makes a lewd gesture with his finger again.

"You gave it away to Lance and then spread your legs for Jeremy, Brad, Jarod, Wesley, Caleb and me that same week. Like I mean, come on, everyone took a shot at you. Seriously, you were fucked by two horny brothers on the same day, hours apart—and now you think somehow we see you differently than what you are—like girlfriend material? I think not—ugh."

Corey kisses Elizabeth again.

"Nope—us guys see you only as a whore—one with endless benefits whenever we get horny and want to fuck."

Elizabeth pushes Corey away. He leers at her once more and heads to the door. He turns to look back at her with an evil grin on his face. She seems about to cry. He laughs loudly.

Page **216**

"By the way—don't even think of trapping any of us by getting pregnant thinking we'll marry you—big mistake."

Corey looks at his erection.

"None of us would ever marry you."

He opens the door and leaves.

Massasoit Terrace

Brad grins as he kisses Susan again. He slyly slides his hand across her blouse and smirks as he cups her breasts.

"I'm so ready to take a shot at you."

Susan leans closer to Brad.

"You want to fuck me, don't you?"

Brad grins broadly.

"Why else would we be in a motel room?"

Susan nods.

"Well?"

Brad seems confused. He watches as Susan glances at him with a coy look. He stares at her for a few more seconds.

"Well, what?"

Susan begins unbuttoning her blouse.

"I'm yours."

Brad grins broadly again.

"I assume you're on the pill."

He begins unzipping his Levi's—then seems to realize something is wrong. He looks at Susan and then at his penis.

"No—it—it—it can't—not me—I've never had."

Susan glances at Brad's exposed penis. It hangs limp. He seems horrified at the sight. Susan shrugs knowingly.

"You can't get hard?"

Brad looks at Susan as he continues touching his penis.

"No—this has never happened—never."

"Oh-oh—you can't get it up—that's not good."

Brad looks at Susan in shock.

"I've already fucked several girls today."

"Well, apparently something is not working now."

Brad shoves his penis back into his jeans and zips up. He jumps out of the bed in panic—and hastily pulls on his sneakers and heads for the door of the hotel room in a frenzied rush.

"*That bitch*—she did this to me—I'll kill her."

He leaves. Susan leans back in bed and seems confused.

"I guess he wasn't the one."

She sighs loudly.

<u>Portland</u>

Eddie and Alden arrive at a police station. They both get out of the car and head toward the garden-like entrance.

"Think we'll find something that could lead to the truth?"

Alden nods several times.

"This is your best bet—this is where all the files should've ended up after seven years give or take a year or two."

Eddie reaches out to open the front door.

<u>Mall</u>

"Exactly what do you mean by that?"

Lance nervously wipes sweat from his brow and sighs.

"Everyone in Marble Hills hates your folks."

Hart nods.

"Is it because we're rich?"

Lance seems confused and shrugs.

"No—not really—it's because they're—they're not nice people—everyone in town hates your family with a passion."

Hart sighs.

"Says who?"

Lance looks around.

"Says everyone that lives here in Marble Hills—especially your grandfather—he has an enemy list several miles long."

Lance lowers his voice slightly.

"Your grandfather has crossed people. Ask anyone."

Hart seems upset.

<u>Page **218**</u>

"Well, I'm not like him. I'm a Philly boy—and everyone likes me because I'm real—never had a problem before."

Lance smiles knowingly.

"Good—maybe there's hope yet."

Hart grins broadly.

"Look—thanks again for getting that sick creep away from me—and for the free info about my family—I mean it."

Lance gestures with his hand.

"No problem."

Hart glances at the people walking by.

"Don't worry—I won't tell my family how everyone in town really feels about them—not that they'd care anyway."

"I'm glad you feel that way."

They shake hands again.

<u>Red Barn Gym</u>

Damon Mayo grins broadly as Amanda slides her arms around his waist. He kisses her lightly on the lips and winks.

"So, are your folks still not on my fan list yet?"

Amanda rolls her eyes.

"Todd is fine with the whole deal—it's my folks that won't play ball with my decision—they think I can do better—like that really makes a difference in the end—it's as if they."

Damon sighs.

"What do they want from me? Seriously, I've bent over backwards to be nice—there's just so much I can do."

Amanda kisses Damon.

"I know—it's not you, it's them—whatever."

Damon pulls away from Amanda and leans against the counter seemingly upset. He sighs loudly several times.

"I've worked so hard to please them."

He sighs loudly.

"So hard to be what they want—it wasn't easy pretending to be what they wanted or expected—but I did it anyway."

Amanda pulls Damon toward her.

"I know it wasn't—your dad—your dad did a lot of bad things—my parents aren't the forgiving type—they think."

Damon sighs again.

"Yeah, I bet they do."

He waves his hand in the air.

"My dad ran gambling rackets all over Boston for years before he got caught. I didn't know until he was arrested."

He seems irritated.

"I shouldn't be blamed for the sins of my father."

He clenches his fist angrily.

"I don't even speak to him anymore."

"When is he getting out of jail?"

Damon shrugs.

"Two years."

Amanda strokes Damon's hair with her fingers.

"They'll come around eventually—just give it some time. I know they will—they'll have to—it'll just take a few."

Damon seems upset.

"I've given so much already—too much actually."

"Love you for that by the way—you're such a generous man—always have—couldn't ask for anyone better."

Matt Brewster silently enters the gym at that moment.

Police Station

Daryl Anderson is standing by the edge of his desk shuffling through papers as his deputy Clay Blankenship calls out to him as he enters the office. Daryl looks up and sighs loudly.

"I see you're still clueless without my help?"

Daryl rolls his eyes mockingly and seems annoyed.

"I thought you had two days left on your vacation? Seems to me you claimed you wanted some time off with Eva."

Clay walks over to where Daryl is standing.

"I did—that was until I heard about the accident out by Standish Road—had to come back—huge mess for sure."

Daryl seems upset and shrugs.

Page **220**

"I'm still waiting for the coroner to ID the stiff found in the wreck—won't be an easy job—body was burned to a crisp—not much left to identify—such a royally messed-up way to go."

"Any ideas—about who it could be?"

Daryl shrugs.

"No—could be anybody at this point—so much traffic out that way on any given day—tourists and locals alike."

He sits down.

"Hopefully it wasn't anyone local—I really don't need to deal with something like that right now especially after."

"What happened—something I should know about?"

Daryl rolls his eyes.

"No—just two frigging queers getting offed at Tolling Bell. Probably some sloppy lovers spat gone bad—led to murder."

He makes a lewd gesture with his hand.

"I'm *so* over that story."

He makes a gesture with his hand.

"Glad you're back regardless."

Clay nods and glances at his desk nearby stacked high with paperwork. He shakes his head and looks at Daryl again.

TO BE CONTINUED

A Look at the 9th Episode

In Portland, Eddie and Alden begin putting the missing pieces together from Eddie's cloudy past—Damon and Amanda enjoy a private moment together—Hart makes a potential new friend with unexpected benefits—Donna deals with fallout from a permanently soiled reputation as gossip spreads about her encounter with Brad—Matt and Ross get to know each other better—Denise finds herself yet another playmate to satisfy her passionate desires for young healthy men—Clay and Eva explore relationship issues—Daryl faces an impossible task as the victim of the tragic accident is positively identified—Howard plans the ultimate revenge for a rival—Jason and Brad have a violent encounter—news of a tragedy and its victim sweep across town and of whom may have caused it and why—Brad and Carrie face off for yet another battle of the wills—as Eldon encounters an unexpected visit from a sworn enemy that isn't welcomed.

Nothing Lasts Forever

Red Barn Gym

Damon Mayo forcibly pushes Amanda Spencer up against the locker and penetrates her within seconds. He smirks as her moans echo through the small room where several lockers are lined up against one side of a wall. Her moans become louder as his thrusts intensify. They look at each other. He laughs.

"I couldn't wait another second."

He grins.

"I have a lot of pent-up frustration on account of the shabby way your parents have treated me since last year."

Amanda sighs.

"I like a man that thinks outside the box—knows what he wants and takes it—on his terms—that was what drew me to you from the moment we met in Boston last year at the art gallery on Beacon Street. It had been a while since I met a smart guy."

Damon laughs again.

"Love the fact you're so open-minded. It makes our sex life that much more interesting—keeps the fires burning."

Amanda kisses Damon several times.

"So what if my folks don't care for you—I like you and that's all that matters—they need to get over it already."

Damon gestures with his hand.

"I like the way you think."

He seems upset and pulls away.

"But—enough is enough—your folks needs to deal with reality—you and I are a couple and no matter what they think of us being together—I demand respect—no matter what."

Amanda seems curious at the brash comment made by Damon. He sighs loudly and nods several times.

<u>Portland</u>

"What makes you think we have the files here?"

Will McColl looks at his computer again as Eddie Kane and Alden Washington hover impatiently over his shoulder.

"Can you just check—I know they exist."

Will seems annoyed.

"OK—but even if they exist it's been over thirty."

Eddie leans against the desk.

"I know."

Will glances at Alden and then resumes looking at file names—slowly scanning the list for Kane multiple times.

Alden turns to Eddie.

"What if you find someone or something was behind what happened to your folks all those years ago—what then?"

Eddie shakes his head.

"I don't know—but I'm a revenge kind of guy."

The door to the office opens suddenly and Alden turns to see Kyle Madison staring suspiciously at them. He sighs.

"What are you doing here Alden—haven't you done enough already—as if murdering my sister wasn't enough?"

At that moment Kyle notices Eddie.

"Oh—I should've known you'd be here too Kane—bet you're pleased at what's happened to Wesley? Damn you."

Eddie shoots Kyle a nasty look.

Page 224

"Seriously, you can ask me that? What nerve. I haven't forgotten what your worthless son did to me last year. Seems to me Wesley is getting exactly what he deserves times two."

Eddie walks over to Kyle.

"Too bad it's not you in the lock-up Kyle. The rotten apple certainly didn't fall far from the tree—not far at all."

Kyle seems about to take a swing at Eddie as Alden steps in between them. He notices Eddie's clenched fists.

"Look—I feel really bad about Wesley—but he did try to kill me—the law is the law—and now it's time to get real."

Kyle shakes his head in frustration.

"He didn't—you know my boy isn't a killer—he wouldn't hurt anyone—he's had problems—he just needs help."

"Yeah—like seriously—psychiatric help."

Kyle turns to face Eddie.

"Shut the fuck up—nobody asked you."

Will stands up.

"Guys, take your soap opera issues outside."

Kyle turns to look at Will harshly.

"I'm here to see my son."

"Then do—and be quick about it."

Kyle turns to walk toward the hallway as Eddie and Alden share a smirk. Kyle turns back a few times and glares.

<u>Mall</u>

Lance Weissmann and Hart Bennington watch as Natalie Standish walks up to them and kisses Lance passionately.

"Still on for tonight—hope you didn't get a better offer than—I know you can do as you please—but I was hoping?"

He grins broadly.

"Nope—you and I are still on for our date at Hope Point tonight—my backseat awaits—expect quite a nice workout."

Natalie grins broadly and looks at Hart briefly.

"Your wish is my command."

Natalie looks at Hart again and smiles.

Page **225**

"Do I know you?"
Lance waves his hand in the air.
"Natalie Standish—this is Hart Bennington."
They look at each other.
"Are you from Marble Hills?"
Hart shakes his head.
"Philly—my folks just moved here."
Lance gives Hart a strange look and turns to look at Natalie who doesn't catch the odd glances between them.
"Think Elizabeth Pendleton has anything to do later?"
Natalie grins broadly again.
"Why? You want a threesome?"
Lance laughs loudly.
"I wouldn't mind that idea actually—fucking two beautiful girls in the back of my van would definitely put a smile on my face that would last a few hours—an idea for later no doubt."
Lance winks at Hart.
"But no—at least not today—think Elizabeth would want to get to know my friend Hart better—you know—for—for a moment—like we—like you and me usually have together?"
Natalie looks at Hart curiously.
"Barely arrived in town and you're already looking to get laid—score a few quick hook-ups with some of us locals?"
Hart seems confused and shrugs.
"Cool—whatever—horny guys make the best friends anyway. After you do Elizabeth—give me a call—we can hang tomorrow—I've got lots of experience at being popular."
Natalie gives Hart a sly glance and kisses Lance again before heading toward the elevator. Hart seems in shock.
"Is she serious?"
Lance turns to look at Hart and laughs.
"Yeah, she's on the level. She's quite a fireball. I like to help my friends—you can thank me later for being generous."
Hart seems somewhat nervous and wrings his hands.
"Thanks but—I've never—never really."
Lance makes a lewd gesture with his hand.

"What? You're a lowly virgin—well, don't worry. When Elizabeth gets done with you later—oh man—she knows."

Lance smirks knowingly.

"Let's just say she's been around the block—I should know—I'm the first one who popped her—made her a trick."

Lance smirks again and begins laughing.

Pine Street

Donna Markway stares at her cell phone.

"Why aren't you returning my calls?"

As she turns to walk toward her car she sees Lana Jefferson and Marilyn Bingham walking past her. They look at her and both make lewd gestures with their hands indicating a sexual encounter. Donna becomes upset by their crude behavior.

"Do they know?"

She looks at the cell phone again.

"Oh my God—he's been telling everyone he fucked me earlier—he said he wouldn't tell anyone—how could he?"

She sighs.

"That's why Carrie said—*she* knew."

She shuts her cell phone off.

"No—he wouldn't have told. He *said* he loved me."

She seems panicked as she rushes over to where her car is parked. She fumbles with the keys and then nervously opens the door. She hops into the car and shuts the door quickly.

"Carrie Spaulding was right. She told me Brad was no good—said he just wanted to score—add a number to his list."

She sits in front of the steering wheel for a few seconds as tears begin forming in her eyes. She wipes the tears away.

Drugstore

Ross Harrison looks through several XXX DVDs in his hand. He smiles broadly as flips through them again.

"Oh yeah—these will do just fine."

He turns to walk away and bumps into Matt Brewster. They look at each other. Ross gives Matt a curious look.

"Did you kill that dude?"

Matt reacts.

"Excuse me?"

Ross rolls his eyes.

"The murder of those two dudes that got offed at Tolling Bell—bet you did it—uh-huh—after what you did to me."

Matt seems irritated.

"No—not that it's any business of yours."

"Must still think you're something—well, you're not—your cycling days are long gone—washed-up nobody—a zero."

"Fuck off asshole."

"Face it—you're just a washed-up old homo looking for an easy hook-up now with whomever while trolling the mall."

Matt angrily grabs Ross by the arm.

<u>Pete's Cafe</u>

Carrie Spaulding grins broadly as she listens to Donna complain about Brad's behavior after their encounter.

"I'm ruined. Completely ruined—I'm just a slut now."

Carrie laughs.

"You're not the only one—many on that list."

Donna seems confused.

"He used me—just like you said he would. I'm *so* done now—everyone is laughing at me—calling me names."

Carrie laughs again and gestures.

"This morning I gave Brad McKinley a *special* present."

Donna looks at Carrie curiously.

"A present—what—why would—why would you give Brad anything—especially after what you said he did to you?"

Carrie smirks.

"I didn't say it was a good present."

She watches as Donna seems to become even more confused. Carrie folds her hands neatly in front of her.

Page 228

"Let's just say Brad McKinley won't be messing around with women for quite a while—maybe a week or more."

"What? What are you saying?"

Carrie laughs several times.

"Dear Brad got what he deserved and more—the next week will be a horrible nightmare for him in every way."

She grins slyly.

"Much worse than death indeed—death might be nicer actually for someone like him with his bad rep—oh the joy."

Donna wrings her hands.

"I want him to pay dearly. He needs to pay for what he did to me even after he said—maybe I should run him down?"

"Like I said, it's been handled."

Carrie and Donna look at each other.

"How—you still haven't said?"

"That's for me to know and you to find out."

Carrie smirks and gestures again.

<u>Boardinghouse</u>

Caleb Winthrop sighs loudly and looks at Marilyn with a sly wink as he pulls out. He looks down at his erect penis.

"Gina is harmless."

Marilyn sighs loudly.

"Whatever—but don't dare tell Gina. I don't want to get on her bad side. That girl is certifiable—capable of hurting me."

Caleb laughs loudly.

"What's this deal with Gina anyway?"

He strokes his erection several times and smirks.

"Gina's not the boss of me—we're over—not that we were ever really together—she doesn't tell me what to do—and she most certainly does not dictate who I fuck or don't fuck."

"I know—but she gets crazy sometimes."

"Gina has moods—we all do—but there's nothing to be afraid of—she knows my rep—knows I sleep around a lot."

Marilyn sighs loudly.

Page 229

"Maybe you should tell that to Tiffany Johnson—Gina has made it clear how she feels—threatened to kill Tiffany."

Caleb looks at Marilyn curiously. He seems bothered.

<u>Bar Harbor</u>

Denise Madison and Jarod Keller kiss passionately and look at each other. Unknown to them several yards away Marc Ryerson is filming their activity. Denise pulls Jarod close to her again and kisses him passionately one last time. She grins.

"I really hate to leave—but I have to."

They look at each other and sigh. Suddenly a blond man grabs Jarod in a friendly headlock. Denise takes instant notice of his ultra tight T-shirt and Levi's corduroys. Jarod wriggles free.

"Denise Madison, meet Miles Dandridge."

They look at each other briefly and shake hands. Denise glances at Miles intently and licks her lips several times.

"Jarod, why didn't you tell me before that you had such good-looking friends—especially one who can fill out a pair of cords so nicely—you know my rule on rude behavior."

Miles grins broadly.

"Yeah, Jarod—what gives?"

Jarod smirks.

"Miles is my scrawny roommate—quite needy—and he has lots of things he has to do right about now—don't you?"

Miles grins slyly.

"I got nothing to do at this moment."

Jarod shoots Miles a nasty look.

"OK. OK. I guess I *do* have something to do."

Denise watches as Miles walks away. Jarod notices her watching Miles. He seems upset over her behavior.

"He has a girlfriend in case you were wondering—they've been pretty serious about each other for several months now in fact—like engaged—he's as faithful as a church boy."

Denise reaches out and strokes Jarod's cheek and winks.

"Is my boy wonder jealous?"

Page 230

Jarod laughs loudly.

"Yeah, right I'm worried about Miles hooking up with you—you and I are only about a good time and nothing more than that. I'm not into real relationships—besides I have plenty to choose from if you think of looking elsewhere for friends."

Denise aggressively pulls Jarod to her again.

"I like jealous men—they make the best lovers."

They begin kissing.

<u>Red Barn Gym</u>

Amanda watches as Damon waves and drives away. She sighs. She closes the door and walks toward the front desk.

"Pretty hot—nice bod—big dick I assume?"

Amanda turns to see Gina Bentley standing in front of her with a curious look. She smiles and nods in agreement.

"Uh-huh—he is quite the deal if I do say so myself."

"I bet he can't get enough."

Amanda rolls her eyes.

"Well, look at him. His body is like a sculpture."

Amanda sighs again.

"Is there something I can help you with today Gina?"

Gina gestures with her hand.

"Like no need to get upset Amanda—I was just making an observation about Damon Mayo—it's not like I plan to make a play for your honey—at least not yet and not today."

Amanda reacts to Gina's comment.

<u>Brewster Condo</u>

Ross and Matt are going at it passionately. They finally relax as Ross slams into Matt one final time and pulls out.

"God—that was good."

Ross laughs.

"Still think I'm inexperienced?"

Matt laughs loudly.

"My bad—I was wrong."
Ross kisses Matt.
"Sorry about earlier—I was a bit of a prick."
Matt smirks.
"Sometimes the best sex is with someone who just pissed you off—and I *was* royally pissed off at you no doubt."
Matt laughs again and grins.
"But look at us now?"
They kiss once again—then more passionately.

Bar Harbor

Marc watches as Jarod drives away. He waits until Denise gets into her own car and leaves before following her.

"This bitch isn't discreet—not at all."

Denise drives slowly along several side streets as if looking for someone or something specific. He sighs loudly and shakes his head several times in disbelief as he continues watching her every move, along the narrow streets. He rolls his eyes.

"She's cruising for guys—I swear this woman obviously doesn't know the meaning of being careful—so tacky."

He notices a blond man standing at the curb, the same man she met earlier with Jarod, talking with several other college students outside a nearby coffee shop. Denise shouts out to him and waves. Marc watches as he grins broadly and comes over to where her car is casually idling on the street. Marc sighs.

Portland

Eddie's fingers flies across the keyboard as he brings up file after file pertaining to the tragic accident that changed everything for him decades before. He sighs loudly.

"Man, there's a lot of general stuff on what happened to my parents that day—think McColl will let us copy it?"

Alden gives Eddie a curious look.

"I don't see why not—these are public files."

He watches as more files appear.

"You're a taxpayer—you have rights. These are technically your files anyway—I'm sure he won't have an issue."

They glance over at Will. He is arguing with Kyle.

"There's never a dull moment with Kyle Madison and his endless issues—pity he never tried to launch a reality show."

Alden nods in agreement.

"He'd make millions."

Eddie stifles a laugh and jabs Alden.

"He's got enough money—he just needs an audience for the drama his family viciously inflicts on us common folks."

Alden glances at Kyle and Will once more.

Police Station

Clay Blankenship watches Daryl Anderson closely as the color drains from his face. He seems in shock and shrugs.

"How will I tell them?"

Clay watches as Daryl shuts off his cell phone.

"What is it?"

Daryl turns to look at Clay.

"I—I—I think I need a breath of fresh air."

Daryl heads to the door as Clay seems confused.

Boardinghouse

Caleb pulls on his Levi's—then slips on his socks and glances at Marilyn with a sly look. He grabs his sneakers.

"I think I'll call Gina."

Marilyn seems upset as she combs her hair.

"Don't you dare call Gina—if she knew what we just did—I don't want to think what she'll do to me for revenge."

Caleb laughs loudly.

"Relax—I was just yanking your chain Marilyn—but seriously—just forget about Gina—she's not a problem."

Marilyn finishes combing her hair.

"Like I told you before, she threatened Tiffany. Gina can be very mean when she feels someone wronged her—please don't tell her we fucked—my life depends on your silence."

Caleb stifles a laugh and grins broadly.

<u>Bar Harbor</u>

"I have a girlfriend."

Denise grins licks her lips sensuously.

"Who said you have to tell her?"

Miles smiles broadly.

"What about Jarod? Aren't you and him—sort of like a couple—or something—at least it looked to me earlier."

Denise motions for Miles to lean closer.

"We're not exclusive."

Denise licks her lips seductively.

"Earlier when we met I wondered what you would be like in bed—there's just something about a guy going commando in corduroys—seriously, you definitely rock the commando look for sure—like totally—and I was wondering if we could—talk."

Denise looks down at his erection.

"I can see you're packing a heavy load—the question I have for you is simple—can you deliver what you're packing?"

Miles glances at his erection and grins broadly as he looks directly at Denise. She licks her lips again and smirks.

"Oh, I can deliver all right. I'm young, I'm strong, I'm healthy, and I'm definitely not the type to back down from a challenge—especially if it involves fucking—fucking a woman who knows what she wants and isn't afraid of going after it."

Miles walks over to the other side of the car and leans close to Denise and whispers in her ear. He winks twice.

"Just say when and where—and I assure you—I will make the earth move—and then some more—you'll beg for mercy."

Denise reaches out and strokes his erection.

"I would hate to be disappointed."

Miles laughs loudly.

Page **234**

"We'll see. There is a little motel on Strand Street—right at the corner by a large oak—do you know where it is?"

Denise nods.

"I know it well—very well—been there several times this week already—I'm a regular actually—not shy to admit it."

Miles makes a lewd gesture with his finger.

"I'm a horny college guy and lots of issues concerning my commitment to one woman—and I have needs—plenty."

Denise grins again.

"I certainly won't tell—what happens between us is no one's business but ours—especially your girlfriend."

Miles impulsively reaches out and pulls Denise to him. He kisses her passionately, shoving his tongue deep inside her mouth. She hungrily kisses him back. He laughs loudly.

"Any questions before we do the deed?"

"Two minutes—I'll be there in two minutes flat."

Denise nods and drives off as Marc follows her some distance away. He begins humming a musical tune—loudly.

<u>Police Station</u>

Clay looks up as his girlfriend Eva Harper comes through the front door with several shopping bags. He grins broadly.

"I thought you were done with shopping today?"

Eva grins as she walks over to him.

"I lied."

Clay laughs.

"Uh-huh—surprise—surprise."

Eva reaches out to stroke Clay's hair.

"Is that fighting words I hear?"

Clay kisses Eva.

"What if it is? What's your deal?"

Eva slides her fingers through Clay's hair again.

"Wait until you come back to our apartment tonight."

They kiss again. He laughs.

"I'm not worried."

Page 235

Clay leans back in his chair.

"In fact I have it on very good authority my girlfriend is hung up on me—likes me so much she can't think straight."

Eva gestures with my hand.

"My mother is totally to blame for your gigantic ego."

Clay nods in agreement.

"It was perfectly righteous of her to tell me."

He makes a gesture with his hand.

"I like knowing."

Eva strokes Clay's cheek.

"I'm just worried that you'll lose interest."

Clay pulls Eva toward him.

"You make it sound like I'm a stud or something—I had one—*one girlfriend*—that's it. I was so nerdy back in the day. I didn't lose my virginity until my last year of college—and then my girlfriend ran off with a rebellious musician who thought he was God's gift to women—yeah, oh, I'm a popular stud all right."

"Should I trust you with that ego?"

Clay nods.

"You should—you should."

Eva glances at the empty room and kisses Clay.

<u>Morgue</u>

Daryl stares blankly at the charred remains and turns away as Grant Monroe pulls the sheet over the corpse and slides the body back inside the locker. He turns to face Daryl.

"The body was destroyed beyond all possibilities of visual ID—but dental records were obtained from the remains."

Daryl sighs.

"Records matched with no chance of error?"

Grant nods.

"There is no doubt in my mind."

He glances back at the locker and shrugs.

"I've been doing this for sixteen years. The results are not questionable—there's no doubt on the identity of the stiff."

Page 236

Daryl sighs again.

"How am I going to tell them that their kid is dead?"

Grant glances at the lockers again.

"Any word on who murdered those two men that were found at Tolling Bell—just wondering. Rumors are flying."

Daryl shakes his head.

"Nope—probably was a mob hit—it's my guess their killer is long gone by now—back to Boston or the Big Apple."

Grant sighs.

"No one has come forward to claim the bodies? Pretended to be a long-lost relative or something—a brother perhaps?"

Daryl shakes his head.

"I'm planning to have the bodies shipped back to Boston tomorrow. Let them deal with it there—no need to keep the stiffs here any longer—they were both from Boston anyways."

Grant nods.

"I'll get right on it."

Grant sighs and watches Daryl leave.

<u>Bar Harbor</u>

Marc smiles slyly while he follows Denise and Miles as they enter a nondescript-looking motel. He shakes his head.

"Definitely a man-eater—no guy is safe."

He watches as they book a room and head upstairs. Marc grins as he sees them enter a room with huge windows facing the parking lot where he's sitting with his camera. He smirks.

"Man, Denise Madison is unstoppable. The woman has more lives than a cat. Just when I think she was done for the day she scores herself yet another virile young man—and by the looks of him—he's definitely the kind of guy who unapologetically thrives on having one-night stands with women of questionable morals—oh-oh—here they go—this is better than a porno."

Marc watches as they kiss passionately.

"I could sell this easily to every Internet outlet that plays this kind of trash. There would be millions of clicks a second."

Page 237

He grins as they strip off their clothes and go at it. He points his video camera at the window and sighs loudly.

Glass Owl

"Bring the car around."

Howard Madison shuts off his cell phone and heads to the front door. He stops and smiles. He looks at his cell phone.

"Whitney is definitely going to wish he hadn't gone to his office today—oops—too late to worry about that now."

He pulls out a small handgun and grins slyly.

"When I get through with him he'll beg for mercy."

He grins broadly and tucks the gun back inside his jacket pocket and hastily opens the front door seconds later. Lindsay Bennington is standing there. She looks at her father oddly.

"Where are you off to in such a rush?"

"I'll tell you later."

He rushes off as Lindsay stands there with a confused look on her face wondering what her father is up to at that moment.

"He's up to something. I wonder what it could be."

She continues looking at him as he walks to the limo in the driveway. Seconds later the limousine slowly drives away.

Johnson Driveway

Daryl slowly steps out of his car and sighs loudly as he shuts the door. He sighs again as he looks at the driveway.

"This is—this isn't going to be easy."

He leans against his car and digs his hands into the front pockets of his Levi's unsure of what to do next. He shrugs.

"I could use a drink right about now. A nice stiff drink to calm my nerves would be welcomed at this very minute."

He sighs once more and begins slowly walking towards the entrance of the huge Victorian house up ahead.

"She was their only daughter."

He stops briefly before he reaches the entrance.

Portland

"OK. OK. OK. Anything to get rid of you guys."
Eddie grins broadly.
"Thanks."
Will sighs and watches as Eddie and Alden begin copying the files onto Eddie's flash drive. He rolls his eyes.

Brewster Condo

Ross zips up his Levi's and pulls on his shirt. He turns to look at Matt still lying on the bed completely naked.
"Who knew that an old homo like you could be so much fun to fuck? Definitely want an encore tomorrow—uh-huh."
Matt strokes his exposed penis and sits up in bed. He grins slyly as he watches Ross comb his hair. He laughs slyly.
"Come by about eight in the morning."
Ross nods and makes a lewd gesture with his finger.

Police Station

Clay and Eva are kissing passionately.
"Do you think about other women when we're together?"
Clay smirks as he strokes her hair.
"Maybe—what's it to you?"
Eva jabs Clay.
"I don't like sharing you. No way. You better not be thinking of anyone else when we're together—or else."
Clays kisses Eva again.
"Or else what Eva—what would you do?"
Clay kisses Eva again. She strokes his cheek gently.
"You're pretty sure of yourself, aren't you?"
Clay nods.
"Yep—deal with it."
Eva kisses Clay and tousles his hair.

Page **239**

"You're the best thing that's ever happened to me."
Clay pulls Eva closer to him.

Portland

Eddie and Alden look at each other as they walk to the parking lot. Eddie suddenly stops and seems worried.
"Think there's enough info in those files?"
Alden stops and shrugs.
"I assume so—I'm not even sure what we're supposed to be looking for exactly. But I think we got it all anyway."
Eddie sighs.
"There just has to be some link as to why the accident that killed my parents occurred in the first place—a reason."
Eddie looks at the flash drive in his hand.
"But why would someone—anyone want to kill my parents at all—it's not like—they had no enemies—none at all."
Alden runs his fingers through his hair.
"But what if there was something—something that could have been going on that someone didn't want to come out?"
Eddie looks at the flash drive again before shoving into his pants pocket. He looks at his watch and seems angry.
"If someone did cause the accident that killed both my parents—made it happen—they'll wish they were dead."
He sighs as he opens the door to his car.
"Dead and buried—like my parents."
Alden looks at Eddie as he gets into his car. He notices Eddie seems angrier than before as he starts the engine.

Mall

Lance and Hart shake hands. Lance grins.
"I've got it all set with Elizabeth Pendleton—all you've got to do is show up—and poof—you're no longer a virgin."
"Does she know I'm a virgin?"
Lance looks at Hart curiously and nods.

Page **240**

"I didn't say it in so many words—mentioned you were horny and needed a thrill. Elizabeth is one of my favorites."

Hart nods in agreement.

<u>Police Station</u>

Clay looks up from his desk as Daryl slams the door shut behind him. He seems visibly upset as he sees Clay.

"How did it go?"

Daryl sighs.

"How do you think? I just had to tell Bill Johnson that his only child is dead—and it was bad—worst part of my job."

Clay stands up.

"If you want to take the rest of the day off I got everything covered here. Nothing else seems to be happening."

Daryl shakes his head.

"No—this mess is not going away. The forensics guys from Portland should be calling shortly—they texted me while I was at the Johnsons saying they'd finished their inquiry. Apparently they must already know what caused Tiffany Johnson's death—though I think the cause is a slam dunk—her death was an accident."

Clay sighs.

"Is there a reason to think otherwise Daryl?"

Daryl sits down at his desk.

"What other reason could there be?"

Daryl sits down at his desk.

"Obviously it was an accident—like who'd want to kill a teenage girl? What enemies could she possibly have?"

Daryl sighs loudly.

"Her folks said everyone liked her. Said she was popular with her classmates. Said she made friends easily. No issues."

He leans back in his chair.

"Her car is being checked now as we speak."

He looks at his cell phone and shrugs.

"I should know within the hour."

He looks at his cell phone again and seems worried.

Page 241

<u>Bar Harbor</u>

Marc grins slyly as he looks at the images on the video camera. Miles is completely naked as he sits on the sofa grinning broadly while Denise kneels between his legs giving him a blowjob. Marc shakes his head several times and sighs.

"This just gets better and better."

Semen spills out of Denise's mouth as Miles laughs.

<u>Stanley Pier</u>

Jason Anderson is sitting on a bench as Brad McKinley comes up to him. They look at each other silently. Jason seems upset at seeing Brad standing there and glares at him coldly.

"Hey, have you seen Carrie Spaulding today?"

Jason rolls his eyes.

"Who do I look like, your social secretary?"

Brad seems annoyed.

"Did you or didn't you—like tell me, you miserable little prick, before I beat—bust you up good—break your nose."

Before Brad can react Jason lunges at him and punches him hard. Brad falls against the bench in shock. Jason laughs loudly as he violently kicks Brad several times in the chest.

"Before what—before you beat me up?"

He laughs.

"Well, like bring it on fucker—I'm tired of you and every other dumbass jerk in Marble Hills thinking you guys rule."

Brad reacts.

"Fucking asshole—I'll kill you."

Jason angrily lashes out at Brad again. Brad looks at Jason with a confused look on his face as he attempts to stand up.

"You're *so* dead Anderson."

Jason kicks Brad again. He clenches his fist.

"I swear, the next time you threaten me like you did just now you'll get more than you can frigging handle—bet on it."

Page 242

Brad watches as Jason walks away. He struggles to sit up several times before sighing loudly and standing up.

"I'm *so* going to make him pay."

He pulls out his cell phone and dials.

Bar Harbor

Denise and Miles are making love again as Marc grins broadly while he observes the images through the lens of his video camera. He glances at the still images nearby.

"That woman is sleeping her way through the entire male population of Maine. I guess it won't be long before she hits on the paperboy—if she hasn't already made a play for him."

He grins as he continues filming.

Boston

Howard smiles broadly as he steps out of a limo and looks around confidently. People walk past him on the sidewalk as ten dubious-looking men step out of three dark blue sedans with tinted windows parked nearby. They walk toward Howard.

"You guys ready?"

They nod.

"Good—let's pay Eldon Whitney a visit."

Howard points—and then confidently walks toward the entrance of a skyscraper a few yards away—they follow.

"Love surprise visits—oh yeah I do."

In the center above the double doors of the building in bold lettering are the words WHITNEY ENTERPRISES.

"It's time I teach this worm who is boss around here."

They enter the building seconds later.

Pete's Cafe

Julia Winthrop looks up to see Eddie and Alden walking toward her from the front door. Alden grins broadly.

"Well?"

They sit down at the counter as Eddie pulls out his flash drive and dangles it in front of her face. He smirks.

"The truth could be in here—or at least some of it."

Julia seems confused.

"Do you know what you're looking for?"

Eddie shakes his head.

"Not exactly—but I assume Alden will help me figure things out if needed—and then I'll deal out justice."

Alden nods and grins broadly as Julia seems concerned about what Eddie and Alden did earlier. Alden briefly looks at the flash drive in his hand. He hands it back to Eddie and sighs.

"It could be a wild goose chase—old man Anderson let it go initially—so maybe—maybe he knew something we don't or he could've been threatened not to do anything about it."

Alden sighs.

"Or maybe he just conveniently looked the other way because—because he just didn't want to be bothered?"

Eddie looks at the flash drive.

"Is it possible this is connected to Madison?"

Alden runs his fingers through his hair several times.

"It would make sense."

Julia leans toward Eddie and Alden curiously.

"But Kyle never said anything?"

Alden nods.

"He probably has no idea."

Eddie clenches his fist angrily.

"But if his father—I swear—there won't be a rock that man can slither under and hide. I'll destroy him. Kill him possibly."

Julia and Alden exchange looks.

<u>Mall</u>

Lana watches as Natalie shuts off her cell phone. Natalie seems in shock—unable to speak—she sighs. Lana notices.

"What—what is it?"

Page 244

"It can't—it just can't be."
Lana seems confused.
"*Tell me*—what happened?"
Natalie sighs loudly and turns to face Lana.
"Tiffany Johnson is dead."
Lana reacts.
"What?"
"She was killed in a car crash."
Natalie sits down.
"Remember earlier when we heard that there was some sort of accident out on Standish Road—it was Tiffany."
Lana seems irritated.
"OK—joke's over. This isn't funny anymore."
Natalie seems about to faint.
"I'm not playing—Tiffany's dead."
Lana sits down next to Natalie at the table.
"No—*wait*—you're serious?"
Natalie nods.
"Apparently it wasn't an accident either."
Lana looks around. Her face pales. She sighs and leans back in the booth. She seems about to faint with shock.
"What do you mean it wasn't an accident—did someone kill Tiffany? Who? She—Tiffany didn't have any enemies."
Natalie nods again.
"The brakes were cut—in six places."
They look at each other.
"Gina."
Natalie turns to look at Lana.
"What did you say?"
Lana breathes heavily.
"Gina Bentley killed Tiffany Johnson."
Natalie shakes her head.
"She wouldn't do something like that?"
"Wouldn't she? How many times did she comment on the fact she disliked Tiffany? Swore how much she hated her."
Lana leans closer to Natalie and whispers.

Page 245

"I myself heard her say several times she wished Tiffany was dead—even detailed how easy it would be to kill her."

"But—she wouldn't?"

Lana pulls out her cell phone.

"I think it's time I call Daryl Anderson."

Natalie grabs the cell phone from Lana.

"You can't do that."

Lana grabs her cell phone from Natalie and sighs.

"Watch me—I'm telling."

"But she's our friend."

Lana begins dialing again.

Lighthouse Rock

Brad gets out of his car and angrily slams the door. He turns to face Carrie a few feet away. He seems enraged.

"You and me have unfinished business."

"Do we?"

Brad grabs Carrie's arm.

"I want you to reverse what you did to me—or else I swear I'll—I'll make you wish you were never born—yeah I will."

Carrie pulls free of Brad's grip and laughs.

"Or what, Brad—you'll rape me again?"

Carrie laughs again.

"Oh wait—you can't—oh-oh—seems you're having a little problem of rising to the occasion. I guess "little Brad" is seriously down for the count until—well, like forever if what I gave you works—oops—oh just how much did I give you earlier?"

Brad grabs Carrie and angrily spins her around. He seems enraged as he looks at her with contempt. He twists her arm backwards and grins slyly at her. He twists her arm again.

"I'm going to kill you."

Carrie smirks as she jerks free of Brad's grip.

"You're half the man you were—more like one of those pathetic plastic dolls that Mattel is known for. Oh—how sad."

Brad grabs Carrie again.

Eldon Whitney turns around as the door to his office opens unexpectedly. He sees Howard standing in the doorway with two rough-looking bodyguards nearby. He notices his secretary lying face down on the floor a few feet behind the two bodyguards. Blood pours from a huge wound in her head.

"What is the meaning of this?"

Howard laughs smugly.

"You of all people should know what a scene like this means—but don't worry—it'll be over soon—in seconds."

Howard walks toward Eldon with a twisted grin on his face. He struts proudly toward the large window and sighs.

"My people will be here in seconds."

Howard laughs loudly and points at the security cameras.

"Oh, I don't think so—look—such wonderful images."

Eldon glances at the security cameras and sees bodies lying everywhere inside his building. He seems panicked.

"What do you want?"

Howard laughs loudly again.

"Quite funny you should ask such an obvious question."

Howard sits down on the edge of Eldon's desk.

TO BE CONTINUED

A Look at the 10th Episode

Howard exacts fatal revenge on his nemesis—Clay and Daryl has different opinions about a potential suspect—Brad confronts Carrie about his "situation" which results in tragedy—Denise and Miles make plans for another rendezvous as a blackmailer revels in his potential at financial success—Lance finds himself a new, much younger playmate—Lana viciously spreads rumors around town about a former friend—Juan gets some shocking news about his employer—Kyle's former friend makes plans for a visit to Marble Hills with blackmail on his mind—Daryl learns his secret may not be secret for much longer despite his best efforts to keep the truth hidden—Gina finds out that her rival is dead—Donna finds a kindred spirit from an unlikely friend—as someone from Robert's past decides its time they meet again in person.

Episode 10
Out of the Past

<u>Boston</u>

Howard Madison laughs as he sees Eldon Whitney nervously looking at the open balcony a few feet away from his chair. Howard nods at two of his men. They walk over to where Eldon is sitting. They glance at each other and grin broadly. As they come closer Eldon panics and looks at Howard coldly.

"You'll never get away with this—my security team will hunt you down—your family will be slaughtered like pigs."

Howard laughs loudly with glee as he circles Eldon and gestures with his hand as he points to the balcony nearby.

"Oh-oh—that'll be hard for them to do being dead from broken necks—gunshot wounds—stabbings—and my personal favorite—death by injection of an unknown yet fatal concoction of arsenic and cyanide. Everyone in your building is DOA. Yep, I never leave witnesses behind who might blab—the chance of someone talking later is too great—and I just can't leave such things to chance—loose lips sink ships—certainly you can understand such musings—of which you know from how you operate your business—unfortunately it'll cost you dearly."

Page **249**

Howard signals the two men to grab Eldon. They force him to his feet. Howard stands up and walks over to Eldon as he's dragged to the sliding doors that lead to the penthouse balcony. They look at each other. Howard's icy stare is filled with joy as he sees Eldon's terror escalating knowing what awaits him.

"You fucked with the wrong man this time you worthless piece of slime. No one fucks with my family and lives to tell about it afterwards—*no one*—time to say goodbye worm—bye."

Howard grins as Eldon tries to free himself.

"This isn't over—you'll pay. My family in Miami will come after you—they'll make you beg for mercy. I guarantee it."

Howard laughs loudly.

"In a few seconds you'll take a flying header off the balcony of your charming penthouse suite and—everyone will think you took your own miserable life—end of story."

Eldon is shoved through the sliding doors.

"Look—let's talk about this—let's make a deal—a real sweet deal—I'll give you anything you want—anything."

Howard rolls his eyes.

"I've got everything and I'm not looking for a business partner right now. But I'm really looking forward to seeing my men throw you off this really high skyscraper knowing you don't want to die by my hand like the worm you are—oh well."

A vicious grin spreads across Howard's face.

"There will be quite a mess on the sidewalk later."

Howard grins slyly.

"I wish you could see it—oh wait—oops, you'll be dead."

He begins laughing hysterically.

"But perhaps just before you hit the pavement you'll imagine what the mess will look like to everyone else still lucky enough to be alive to see it—such warm moments—nice."

Howard smiles and signals the two men to throw Eldon off the balcony. Eldon seems panicked and begins blubbering.

"No—oh *please*—I'll do anything you want—I beg you."

Howard leans against the railing of the balcony. He waves his hand in the air and seems bored by Eldon's behavior.

Page **250**

"Begging just doesn't become you Whitney—it's just so beneath tough guys like you—say hi to the sidewalk OK?"

Eldon turns to look at the two men.

"Yes—I did order a hit on your son—and yes—two of the hit men I sent to Marble Hills to kill your son met an untimely end before they got the chance to follow through with their orders as you well know. But here's something you didn't know—they were killed by another of my men—from Santiago—and he's the relentless type—he enjoys the hunt and the kill like no other man I've ever known. The things he's done to people—his favorite targets are female—he so enjoys killing women after he's had them—especially after he's brutally raped them without mercy multiple times—and on his terms—he always turns them into his personal playthings before he takes them out. Be aware."

Eldon smiles broadly.

"Know this Madison—when word of my death becomes public—he'll stop at nothing to find my killer—and once he makes the connection to you and your family—your family isn't going to know a moment of peace—especially Lindsay and Susan. He will turn everything you hold dear into a blinding nightmare. Right before he kills each and every one of the members of your precious family in front of your eyes. Think your son's suicide was painful to face—just you wait and see what's coming—there will be no peace from this man—not until revenge has been dealt in the most savage way possible to right the wrong being done to me by your trained killers. So—think about that before—before your entire family falls prey and sees their wretched lives end in a pool of blood at Glass Owl—think about that before you act."

"Enough with this drivel already. I'm so tired of listening to the ravings of a dead man—time is money—my money."

He laughs loudly as he glances at the street below. With a wink from Howard the two men carelessly throw Eldon over the balcony railing. His screams echo as he plummets to his death. Seconds later he hits the sidewalk with a thud as Howard looks over the railing at the grisly scene below. People gather around the body immediately. Howard smiles triumphantly.

Page **251**

Clay Blankenship shuts off his cell phone and looks at Daryl Anderson sitting across from him. Daryl seems bored.

"You'll never believe who just called."

Daryl shrugs and waves his hand.

"Unless it's a lead in the Tiffany Johnson situation I don't want to—can't deal with anything else at the moment."

Clay sighs loudly.

"That's just it—we've just gotten a lead."

Daryl shrugs again.

"Blankenship I don't have time for twenty questions—spill already. Did someone come forward with new info or not?"

"Someone named Lana Jefferson apparently thinks we need to question Gina Bentley about what happened."

Daryl sits up.

"Gina Bentley? Why?"

"Seems she made serious threats against Tiffany not too long ago—made several threats about wanting her dead."

Daryl smiles broadly.

"Those two have been going at it for years—there's no story there—constantly at odds over some guy or other."

Clay stands up.

"Maybe—maybe not—but you never know."

Daryl watches as he walks to the door.

"Where are you going?"

Clay stops and looks at Daryl.

"To pay Gina Bentley a visit—and talk to her."

Daryl jumps up from his chair. He seems upset.

"Absolutely not—leave it be—there's no—no story worth looking at—the Bentley girl is no killer. Just let it be."

"I think we should look into it."

"Lana Jefferson is a troublemaker and town gossip."

Clay seems confused at Daryl's behavior.

<u>Mall</u>

Lana Jefferson shuts off her cell phone and looks at Natalie Standish who seems confused. She smiles slyly.

"It's done—Gina Bentley is as good as arrested for Tiffany's murder. That will teach her to talk trash."

"I can't believe you did that."

"Big deal—I never liked Gina anyway."

She notices Elizabeth Pendleton coming toward them from the escalator a few feet away. Lana smiles broadly.

<u>Lighthouse Rock</u>

Brad McKinley grins as his fingers tighten around Carrie Spaulding's neck as she struggles valiantly to free herself.

"Reverse it—or I swear—by God, I'll kill you."

Carrie smiles and kicks Brad in the groin. She jerks free as he doubles over. She smiles triumphantly seeing his pain. He looks up at her—a look of cold hatred masks his features.

"You're *so* dead bitch—so dead."

"Actually—I'd rethink that idea if I were you. I mean—just think about it for a second—think about your future Brad—so sad and pathetic actually—like bleak—like absolutely bleak."

Carrie grins as she taunts Brad.

"Girls don't go for guys with limp dicks."

Brad gives Carrie a harsh stare as she continues to taunt him gleefully seeing the pain he's experiencing presently.

"Seriously, you're the one who is dead sweetie—think of it Bradley dear. No more sex ever—like never, ever again shall you experience an erection. One year from now you'll be a pathetic, shriveled shell of a man—one that is totally sexless and miserable. It's so perfect when you think about it sweetie dear—your dick will probably fall off from lack of action—and no one deserves it more than you Bradley dear—no one. Have a wonderful life."

Brad lunges at Carrie but she backs away.

"I'll kill you—if it's the last thing I do."

Carrie laughs.

"Who do you think I should tell first? Should it be Corey Bentley or Donna Markway? Think she'd enjoy hearing you can't ever get it up again—oh, yeah, I think she should be the first one I tell about, you know, your limp dick situation—especially after what happened between the two of you this morning—yep, she should be the first one I break the news to—uh-huh yeah."

Brad lunges at Carrie again and they fall against the railing overlooking the ocean below. Brad grabs Carrie and tries to throw her over the railing only to lose his balance. Seconds later they both hang precariously from several large rocks beneath the railing. Carrie holds tightly to one of the rocks as Brad tries to grab her leg. He tries several more times but fails to grab her. She smirks as she looks at him. He sighs as he glares at her.

"You're dead, bitch—dead—do you hear me—I'm going to kill you—you will pay for what you did to me—I swear."

Brad tries to grab Carrie's leg again. She laughs loudly as she kicks him several times in the shoulder. He grabs at her leg again as he begins to lose his footing and slips slightly.

"Nothing will give me greater joy than seeing you fall to your death—filthy whore. I hate you—hate you—bitch."

"Right back at you scumbag prince—limp dick loser."

Carrie kicks Brad in his head again as he grabs for her leg once more. She then kicks him in the face with the heel of her shoe. He loses his grip and begins to fall. He yells out in rage.

"I'll get you—I swear I will."

Carrie watches as Brad falls headfirst into the pounding surf below. She grins broadly and then carelessly shrugs.

"Oh well."

Carrie nimbly climbs up to the railing and looks at the waves crashing onto the rocks below for a few seconds.

"Should I go get help?"

She looks over the railing again and shrugs.

"There's no way Brad survived that fall—and if he does somehow, it won't matter much anyway—the waters are filled with sharks—serves him right if he becomes a tasty snack."

Page **254**

Carrie slowly pulls out her cell phone and sighs loudly. She notices several calls waiting from Lana Jefferson. She shrugs.

<u>Bar Harbor</u>

Denise Madison licks her lips as she watches Miles Dandridge pull on his corduroys. He grins broadly as he glances back at her. He slowly walks over to where she's standing.

"Man, that was some experience—I would never have guessed you—you were so aggressive—unstoppable—hot."

Denise smiles slyly.

"I was inspired by you."

Miles laughs loudly as he pulls on his T-shirt.

"I'll say—four times—that's record for me. Most of the girls I fuck pretty much call it quits at two times—but you—you just wanted more and—there was just no stopping you."

Denise slides her arms around Miles.

"I hope this means you and I will meet again?"

"What—hook-up again? Absolutely—no doubt about it from where I stand—got to get myself more of you this week."

Denise pulls Miles toward her.

"Next time I assure you, you'll be seriously tired when I'm finished with you. I'll exploit your youth—your strength."

Miles grins. Denise kisses him passionately.

"But for the record—Jarod doesn't need to know that you and I hooked up—the less he knows about us the better."

Miles nods willingly.

"You don't have to tell me twice—Jarod would kill me if he knew what I just did—thinks his conquests belong to him. Tells me all the time what he'd do if I went behind his back and scored a few for myself. He's quite selfish if you must know."

He grins slyly.

"I'm nobody's fool."

Denise pulls Miles to her and kisses him.

"Exactly the answer I was hoping you'd give me."

Denise kisses Miles again. He smirks.

Page 255

"Besides—I've been sleeping with his girlfriend behind his back for the last three months or so anyway of which she and I decided it's none of his business to know—just like I haven't bothered to tell her what I know about Jarod's many, many sexual adventures. He was otherwise occupied with one of his most recent conquests one night back in March when she came over asking where he was for whatever reasons—and well, one thing led to another and we fucked for over an hour like dogs unable to stop ourselves from doing the nasty. Since then we've hooked up every weekend on the sly. As far as I'm concerned what Jarod doesn't know, he doesn't need to know. That's always been my policy when dealing with his leftovers that may have arisen from an informal meeting initially. By the way his girlfriend is quite the deal in bed—enjoys kinky sexual positions and rough sex."

Denise gestures with her hand.

"You're such a thoughtful young man—so honest and respectful—a friend to be cherished—a total good guy."

Miles grins broadly again.

"I am—aren't I?"

They kiss passionately once more.

<u>Mall</u>

Lance Weissmann stands at the elevator door—snapping his fingers as he waits. Susan Bennington steps out in an angry rush as it suddenly opens. She aggressively pushes him aside.

"Get out of my way."

Lance seems amused by Susan's rudeness.

"Oh-oh—it looks like we might have a spoiled princess in Marble Hills as of today—or are you just a bitch? Do tell?"

Susan glares at Lance.

"What's it to you?"

Lance grins as he steps out of the way and faces her. He wags his finger at her as she looks at him oddly. He sighs.

"Well, for starters no one likes rude people."

Susan sighs loudly.

Page 256

"Give me a break, OK? I just got made a fool of by some guy who couldn't get it up—so pathetic if you ask me."

Lance leans closer to Susan.

"Some dude didn't want to stick you? I agree—that's the worst thing ever—no woman should be insulted like that."

Susan shrugs.

"That's what I said."

She sighs loudly.

"Brad claimed it wasn't his fault."

Lance grins.

"Brad? Brad McKinley jilted you?"

Susan nods.

"Do you know Brad?"

Lance nods.

"Brad and I go way back. Man, I can't believe he left you without getting a piece first—certainly not his usual style."

Lance smirks.

"McKinley must be slipping."

Susan rolls her eyes.

"Whatever—I just think it was so rude for him to treat me like that—swore he'd take my virginity and then fell short."

Lance grins slyly.

"His loss is my gain—I've got no such problem."

Susan seems confused.

"Huh?"

A few people walk by.

"Look, don't let Brad McKinley's rudeness give us guys a bad rep—we're not all like him—I swear, what a loser—some of us actually like poking women—especially innocent virgins."

Susan looks at Lance curiously while her eyes focuses immediately on the swelling bulge between his legs as his erection reveals the full outline of his swollen penis. She sighs.

"Well, I did want to lose my virginity."

Lance smirks again.

"Trust me, I'm no Brad. Everything works."

He glances down at his erection.

"I'm ready if you are. I can take you right now."
Susan hesitates.
"I'm not sure I should?"
Lance leers at Susan.
"What? You're a virgin aren't you? No problem. I specialize in first times—been there often and done that plenty."
They look at each other.
"So? How about it? You and me in a classy motel room getting to know each other really well—and then, like who knows what may happen afterwards—I may add you to my list."
Lance winks at several women as they walk by and acknowledge him with a smile. They notice his erection.
"I promise you—I don't bite—unless you want me to of course—then I'm game. I'll fuck you—nothing more—just sex."
Susan suddenly seems impatient.
"Let's go."
Lance grins broadly and turns to click one of the buttons on the elevator. Susan seems oddly relieved for some reason.

<u>Pete's Cafe</u>

Carrie closes the door behind her as she enters and sees Julia Winthrop curiously looking at her from a few feet away.
"Carrie, are you OK?"
Carrie looks at Julia with a confused look.
"Sure. Why wouldn't I be?"
Carrie realizes her blouse is ripped.
"Oh that—I fell down while I was at Shelby Park earlier today—the steps were slippery from the truckload of water they use to hose down all the homeless campers every day."
Julia pulls some leaves from Carrie's hair and tosses them in the garbage nearby. They look at each other silently.
"I'm thinking of suing the city for negligence."
"Might be a tough sell?"
Carrie grins.
"Yeah, but I'd be able to retire."

Page 258

Julia laughs at the remark.

"How about a burger—with the works—and fries soaked in ketchup? On the house of course—live a little today—OK?"

Carrie nods in agreement.

<u>Police Station</u>

"Why shouldn't I speak to Gina Bentley?"

Daryl sighs loudly as he looks at Clay nervously.

"The Bentley family has a lot of pull in Marble Hills. You don't want to rock that boat—John Bentley is trouble."

Clay glances at the front door.

"So what if they have money—if the Bentley girl had something to do with it—money can't buy off a murderer."

Daryl sighs loudly again.

"Leave it be—at least for right now."

"Is there something going on that you're not telling me about, Anderson? Like maybe there's something I should?"

Daryl seems annoyed.

"No—it's just not smart to accuse anyone until we have all the facts up front—especially when it comes to a Bentley."

"I wasn't going to accuse anyone—just ask a few questions—see if there's any truth to what I was told earlier?"

"I know—I know—but it'll come across like that to the Bentleys. And then they'll immediately crush you like a bug."

Daryl looks back at his desk.

"I'll be out of a job too—there, I said it. There will be a complaint placed by John Bentley and then—then old man Madison will terminate my employment—not because he has to but just because he hates my guts—and wants nothing more than to use his influence to cut me loose at a moment's notice."

Clay looks at Daryl curiously again.

"OK. I'll let it slide for now—but I'll be following up on this accident regardless—and if Gina Bentley had anything to do with what happened to the Johnson girl—there's no pretending."

Daryl shakes his head.

Page 259

<u>Mall</u>

Lana glances at her cell phone as Elizabeth stares at her with a curious look on her face. Elizabeth sighs loudly.

"I don't believe it—Gina is no murderer."

Lana smiles slyly.

"Isn't she? She really hated Tiffany. Hate makes people do strange things—just look at those racists on FOX News."

"But murder? I mean, really—it's just?"

Lana turns to look at Natalie.

"We've all heard her threaten Tiffany endless times. She's made it clear she wished Tiffany were dead—like really."

Lana smirks.

"And now she is—look, she wouldn't be the first woman to kill someone she thought wronged her—a lot of seemingly sweet women turned out to be freaky psycho killers. Remember **Lizzie Borden**? **Aileen Wuornos**? **Susan Smith**? **Casey Anthony**? **Amanda Knox**? And **Jodi Arias** most recently just to name a few of hundreds? Women can kill viciously just as men have done in the past so don't forget that fact for a moment. And sometimes they, *we* go even farther than men have gone when hatred and jealousy plays into the mix. It's just how we get when we feel wronged—spiteful and crazy—capable of really vicious acts of murder in order to justify what went wrong with a relationship of a friend that did the deed with a guy we cared a lot about."

Elizabeth sighs.

"But this is Gina we're talking about? We've all known her since we were kids? She would never knowingly kill anyone."

Lana rolls her eyes in mock contempt.

<u>Standish Road</u>

Howard smiles broadly as he looks at the television screen in front of him as he sits inside his limo. He sighs loudly.

"This will certainly make the evening news."

Page **260**

He begins laughing. Suddenly on the screen is breaking news coverage from CNN—detailing the unfolding Whitney building massacre while police officers swarm the building as onlookers stand around in shocked disbelief. Howard wags his finger at the television screen and rolls his eyes several times.

"I think I'll send flowers to Whitney's family."

Howard laughs loudly again.

"How dare that worm think he could go up against someone like me—and win? How dare Eldon Whitney even have the nerve to consider such a thing—well, let that be a lesson to that stupid fool—a lesson to anyone who dares to cross me."

He looks at the television screen again.

"Those clowns couldn't find their asses even if it was staring them right in the face—what fools—uh-huh morons."

He smirks and reaches for a glass of wine.

<u>Pete's Cafe</u>

Carrie is about to take a bite of her burger as she notices Kelly Nelson and Abby Marshall walking toward her from the front door. They seem upset. She puts the burger down.

"Have you heard?"

Carrie seems confused.

"Heard what?"

Kelly and Abby look at each other. Carrie sighs.

"Well?"

Abby looks at Kelly and faces Carrie again.

"Tiffany Johnson is dead."

Carrie glances curiously at both Kelly and Abby.

"What? How did?"

Abby sits down opposite Carrie.

"She was killed earlier today out by Standish Road."

Abby sighs loudly.

"Apparently she lost control of her car or something from what I heard—flew off the bluff—she was burned to a crisp."

Carrie glances at her cell phone.

Page **261**

"I guess that's why Lana called so many times."
She shrugs.
"Maybe I should've picked it up."
Abby turns to look at Kelly. Carrie notices.
"*What*—what with the looks."
Abby and Kelly look at each other again.
"Everyone is saying Gina did it."
Carrie leans back in the chair and folds her hands across her chest. She seems unimpressed with the statement.
"Well, she hated her—said that enough times to everyone over the last year ever since Tiffany slept with Caleb."
Abby sighs loudly.
"I know—but she wouldn't hurt Tiffany."
"You don't think she did it?"
Abby shakes her head.
"I—I don't know. I don't want to believe she could do something like that—Gina had problems—but murder?"
"Why not—look what Corey's done to people in the past. I mean, seriously, he's as twisted as they come. So, it shouldn't really be a surprise that his twin—his twin could be a killer."
Abby turns to look at Kelly.

<u>Farmington Villa</u>

Juan Sabrillo sits on the sofa watching the news coverage of the massacre in Boston. He seems confused as he looks at images being flashed across the screen in rapid succession.
"It looks—but it can't—how?"
A look of shock spreads across his face as he realizes what he's watching. He grabs for his cell phone seconds later.

<u>Tolling Bell Inn</u>

Lance grins broadly as he pulls off his Levi's while Susan stares helplessly at his exposed penis as it stiffly juts out in front of him like a magic wand. She seems mesmerized and sighs.

Page 262

"Have you really slept with a lot of girls?"

Lance laughs.

"Uh-huh—I have—been around the block a lot—but hey, what young, seriously horny guy hasn't had a lot of casual sexual experiences today—me personally, I've fucked over three maybe four hundred women—some of which I don't even remember their names or even what they looked like—most of which happened this past year courtesy of me getting a fake ID. My favorite thing is sleeping with siblings—and then watching them angrily compare endless notes on my performance and how many times I fucked them before they figured it out—what can I say, I'm a guy—lost my virginity to my eight grade biology teacher—banged her in study hall after she leered at me."

Susan's eyes continue to remain focused on Lance's penis as he struts toward the bed. He notices and grins broadly.

"I'll be gentle—don't worry."

He climbs into the bed besides Susan.

Sydney

"Serves him right—couldn't happen to a nicer guy."

Gary Glick lays the newspaper down and grins broadly.

"I think it's time I pay Kyle Madison a visit."

He stands up.

"His son is in a mess of trouble—but that's the least of Madison's worries. Wait until I show up in Marble Hills."

Her walks to the door of the coffee shop and heads out into the street. He takes a deep breath and begins laughing.

"Marble Hills here I come."

He grins broadly and pulls out his cell phone.

Police Station

Daryl is about to leave as he turns back to look at Clay just as his cell phone rings. He seems worried as he faces Clay.

"Remember what I said about Gina Bentley. Let it go."

Page 263

Clay looks up from the computer.

"I get the distinct impression you're hiding something."

Daryl seems annoyed as the ringing continues.

"I'm not going to ask you again."

Clay watches as Daryl closes the door behind him and then answers his cell phone nervously. He sighs loudly.

"I told you I'd handle it."

Daryl sighs.

"There was an accident earlier by Pilgrim Hill. I had to deal with that first—not everything is about you and yours."

Daryl sighs again.

"I don't care—I have a job to do."

He rolls his eyes.

"I'll take care of it. And yeah, I know you'll make good on your threat if I don't comply—no surprise by any means."

Daryl shrugs.

"Enough already—I said I'll take care of it."

Daryl shuts off his cell phone.

"He's trying my last nerve."

He clenches his fist.

"What I wouldn't give to commit the perfect murder—and free myself of that horrible scourge—damn frigging psycho."

He looks at the cell phone in his hand.

"No one would blame me."

He turns to see Caroline Bentley staring at him.

<u>Mall</u>

Lana, Natalie and Elizabeth are gossiping nonstop about Gina Bentley as they see her coming toward them. She notices their behavior immediately and seems annoyed. Lana reacts as she turns to face Gina. She nervously watches Gina sit down.

"Real cute, Lana—talking about me again—like don't you have enough to worry about already with your mother's rep."

Lana looks at Gina confused.

"Excuse me?"

Page 264

Gina gives Lana a nasty look.

"It is common knowledge that your slut of a mother and the mailman may have done the nasty in his truck last week by Shelby Park—question is how many times—a lot I bet?"

Gina makes a lewd gesture with her finger.

"Who knows—he may give you and Chad a younger brother or sister—certainly wouldn't be unheard of right? Like everyone knows your brother isn't really—even your father knows—and now the possibility of another half-sibling?"

"Ugh, you're worse than Tiffany ever was—I hate you."

Lana runs toward the elevator as Gina smirks.

"Was it something I said?"

Natalie and Elizabeth seem uneasy. Gina notices.

"Why did she refer to Tiffany in past tense?"

Natalie and Elizabeth nervously look at each other again as Gina seems overtly happy despite her confusing question.

<u>Pete's Cafe</u>

Ashton Markway closes the door behind him as he makes his way toward where Kelly, Abby and Carrie are sitting not far away. They acknowledge him as he approaches them. He notices their behavior. They seem in shock over something. He sighs.

"What's wrong? Did someone die?"

Abby turns to look at Ashton.

"You haven't heard?"

Ashton seems confused.

"Heard what?"

Abby and Carrie look at each other curiously.

"Tiffany Johnson is dead."

Ashton reacts.

"What?"

Abby sighs.

"Apparently her car went off the bluff at Pilgrim Hill by Standish Road. She was killed instantly from what I heard."

Ashton leans against the table.

Page 265

"But I saw her this morning? She was fine."
Carrie shakes her head.
"It must have happened right after—there's talk."
Abby shoots Carrie a look but is ignored.
"There's chatter that Gina Bentley."
Ashton sighs loudly.
"Did Gina kill Tiffany Johnson?"
Carrie nods.
"It's possible—it would make a lot of sense."
Footsteps are heard coming towards where they are sitting at one of the tables at the far end of the small diner.
"What's possible?"
Carrie, Kelly, Abby and Ashton turn to see Jeremy Weissmann and Shirley Moses standing behind them. He glances at Carrie. Carrie ignores Jeremy and glares at Shirley. Jeremy glances at Abby and then Kelly and Ashton. There is silence for several seconds which seem like an eternity. He watches their reactions as he looks at Carrie once more. He sighs loudly.
"What happened?"
Carrie seems to be enjoying being the center of attention as Jeremy and Shirley face her. She rolls her eyes knowingly.
"Tiffany Johnson was killed earlier by Standish Road out past Pilgrim Hill and Gina Bentley may have done the deed."
"You guys think Gina did it—killed Tiffany?"
Carrie waves her hand in the air.
"Well, she seriously hated Tiffany and she most certainly threatened her several times in the past—lots of witnesses."
Jeremy shakes his head.
"But Gina wouldn't do something like that?"
He glances at Carrie again.
"Would she?"
He slowly turns to look at Shirley. He seems confused at the shocking turns of events. He shakes his head several times.
"Wouldn't she?"
They face Carrie once again.

<u>Bar Harbor</u>

Marc Ryerson watches as Denise kisses Miles one final time as he gets into his car and drives away. She smiles broadly as she heads over to her own car. Marc continues to watch as she gets into her car and combs her hair. A few minutes slip by as Denise carefully adjusts her makeup before driving away.

"Oh yeah, when I get through with you—it'll be so worth it. You're making my job so easy—so fucking easy indeed."

Marc laughs.

"White trash—plain and simple"

He picks up his cell phone.

<u>Maple Avenue</u>

Jason Anderson is sitting in his car parked parallel to the sidewalk as he notices Donna Markway coming out of a bakery nearby. She seems upset for whatever reason. He calls out to her as she walks by. Their eyes meet briefly for a few seconds.

"Donna—is everything OK?"

She turns away.

"Leave me alone—I just want to be alone."

She turns away. He jumps out of the car and runs after her down the sidewalk and grabs her arm. She faces him.

"Did that son of a bitch Brad do something to you?"

Donna seems about to cry.

"It was my fault."

Jason seems confused.

"Huh?"

Tears stream down her face as she begins to cry.

"I gave him what he wanted."

Jason clenches his fists.

"That bastard raped you?"

Donna shakes her head several times.

"No. But he might as well have."

Jason seems confused as he watches people walk by.

Page **267**

"I swear—life is so fucked up. Tiffany Johnson shouldn't be the one who's dead right now—it should be Brad McKinley."

Donna turns to look at Jason in shock.

"Tiffany's dead?"

Jason nods.

<u>Mall</u>

Natalie sighs loudly as she looks at Gina. She takes a breath of fresh air and finally opens her mouth. She shrugs.

"Tiffany's dead."

Gina seems shocked by the news.

"What?"

Natalie looks at Elizabeth.

"Tiffany was killed earlier today. Her car went off the cliff at Pilgrim Hill on Standish Road—fried like a piece of chicken."

Gina seems about to faint. Natalie notices.

"You didn't know?"

Gina shakes her head still in shock.

"No. It can't be?"

Natalie and Elizabeth look at each other again.

"People are talking."

Gina glances at Natalie. Natalie shrugs.

"They think you did it."

Gina stands up.

"Why? Why would?"

Natalie and Elizabeth watch as Gina bolts toward the elevator. Natalie sighs loudly as she turns to face Elizabeth.

"Well—someone had to tell her—this certainly isn't going to be a secret for long around here—not in Marble Hills."

Elizabeth leans back in her chair.

"I know—but you seemed to enjoy it just a little too much if you ask me Natalie—like you couldn't wait—quite cruel."

Natalie rolls her eyes.

"Shoot me—truth is truth—even for Gina."

They look at each other.

<u>Page **268**</u>

"No wait—on second thought forget what I just said a second ago—I certainly wouldn't want Gina taking me up on my offer because I bet she'd probably do it too—especially after what just happened to Tiffany earlier on Standish Road and all."

Elizabeth grins.

"I won't tell—at least not right away."

Natalie shoots her a look. Elizabeth grins broadly.

"But I could change my mind later."

Natalie suddenly seems nervous and sighs.

<u>Glass Owl</u>

Lindsay Bennington looks up as Howard walks through the front door. He seems extremely happy as he hums a tune.

"Mind telling me where you went just now?"

Howard smirks.

"Who are you—my mother?"

Howard walks by his daughter, ignoring her annoyed stare. She stands up and follows him into the den. She closes the door behind her and turns to face her father. He turns away.

"I'd like to be alone if you don't mind?"

Lindsay walks to where her father is sitting.

"Earlier you tore out of here like you just found the fabled Loch Ness Monster or something. So, exactly where were you going in such a rush? Or do I even want to dare know?"

Howard grins slyly.

"I think it best you don't ask questions you don't want answers to Lindsay—you might not like what you hear."

Lindsay watches as her father pours himself a drink.

"Does this have anything to do with Greg?"

Howard shakes his head.

"Don't you have something to do right about now—like keeping your wayward hubby from straying any further than he already has—or do you just think your marriage will repair itself without you having to make some sort of a serious effort?"

Lindsay glares at her father.

Page 269

"OK—fine—play that game—but whether or not you want to believe this about yourself—we both know whenever you go and do something rash—we all pay the price—rather harshly."

Howard laughs.

"Bite me."

Lindsay is about to reply when she sees Kyle Madison standing in the doorway. He seems confused about something as he enters the room. Kyle notices Lindsay's reaction and sighs.

"What's going on between you two?"

Lindsay instantly shoots her father an odd look.

"Nothing—it was nothing."

Kyle glances at his sister and father.

"Didn't seem like nothing?"

Kyle closes the door behind him.

"Is it about Greg?"

Lindsay looks at her father again.

"He's in one of his moods again apparently."

Lindsay suddenly walks by Kyle, shakes her head, looks at him briefly, and leaves. Kyle turns to face his father.

"More drama—great—just what I need to offset an already perfect day I've had—lay the deal on me—more bad news."

Howard walks over to where Kyle is standing.

"How did the visit with Wesley go?"

Kyle sighs loudly.

<u>Tolling Bell Inn</u>

Lance pulls out of Susan and grins broadly. She seems in shock at what just happened. He laughs triumphantly.

"I think the earth moved several times."

Susan glances at Lance.

"Are you sure I can't get pregnant the first time? Because I heard I could—heard it only takes one time to mess up."

"I'm sure—besides if you become pregnant, getting an abortion is easy in Portland—easiest thing in the world."

He leans over to kiss her and grins.

Page **270**

"Look, there's nothing for you to worry about—I just blew my load that's all—all us guys do it—it'll be fine—no worries."

Susan glances at Lance nervously.

"You're right—you've been with so many girls—I have nothing to worry about—you know what's best—I trust you."

Lance nods in agreement.

"How about we get something to eat?"

Susan nods. Lance climbs out of bed and faces Susan.

"I know a diner not far away."

He pulls on his jeans and reaches for his sneakers as Susan grabs her bra and blouse lying on the floor several feet away.

<u>Police Station</u>

Daryl looks at Caroline nervously. There is a brief moment of silence between them as he seems shocked to see her.

"I guess you're wondering about the comment you just heard—well, I'm sure you know—no secret at all. I hate him."

Caroline nods.

"Howard Madison."

Caroline shakes her head in disgust. She gestures with her hand as she seems lost in thought for a few seconds.

"Say no more."

Daryl looks at his watch and shrugs.

"Is something wrong?"

Caroline seems upset as she glances around to make sure they're alone on the sidewalk. She glances at her purse.

"I got something this morning."

Daryl seems confused.

"What?"

Caroline pulls out a piece of paper. In the middle are words cut out from a magazine. She hands it to Daryl. He stares at it seemingly confused and then immediately reacts angrily.

"This is—oh my God."

He clenches his fist in anger.

"That piece of—I swear—he's gone too far."

Page 271

Caroline wrings her hands nervously as she looks at the piece of paper in Daryl's hand. She slowly looks around.

"Someone knows—and they'll expose us."

Daryl looks at the piece of paper again—focusing his attention on the wording I KNOW spelled out in bold black lettering. He crumbles the piece of paper into a ball. They look at each other silently. Caroline looks at the front door of the station nervously. She slowly turns to look at the sidewalk again.

"If John finds out about us—he'll go crazy. He'll stop at nothing to punish me—and he'll kill you in cold blood."

Daryl clenches his fist again.

"John isn't going to find out anything—not as long as I silence the *only* other witness—this time once and for all."

Caroline looks at Daryl.

"It won't end—he'll never stop."

Daryl wipes sweat from his brow and shrugs.

"He'll stop if I take a stand."

Caroline reaches out to touch Daryl's hand.

"He's got no soul."

Daryl sighs loudly.

"We'll see about that."

"You know he won't let up easily—enjoys making our lives miserable ever since he found out we were friendly again."

"He can't tell if he's dead."

He squeezes the crumpled ball of paper tightly.

<u>Glass Owl</u>

Robert Bennington is walking to his car as he sees his son coming toward him from the winding driveway. He stops.

"Where have you been?"

Hart Bennington seems upset.

"Ask me tomorrow."

Robert reacts.

"What kind of a lame answer is that?"

Without warning Robert angrily grabs Hart by the arm.

Page **272**

"Exactly where did you go earlier?"

Hart rolls his eyes.

"I'll tell you when I feel like it."

Robert watches as his son walks toward the mansion. He shrugs and looks at the keys in his hands for a few seconds as his cell phone begins ringing seconds later. He sighs loudly.

<u>Standish Road</u>

Chandra Stevenson checks her GPS again and smiles confidently as she sees the picture-perfect town of Marble Hills looming majestically in a distance as she zips along a quaint country road. She glances at the folder lying on the passenger seat nearby and pats her stomach lightly. She smiles slyly.

"Bet you didn't think you'd see me again?"

She glances at the GPS screen again as she drives along Standish Road and sighs loudly while a few cars zip past her.

TO BE CONTINUED

A Look at the 11th Episode

Caroline and Daryl talk strategy concerning a secret in their past—Lance and Susan hangs out with her brother but keep him in the dark about their tryst—Juan's concern over recent tragic events in Boston is noticed by Faye—Howard promises Kyle more than he can deliver—Hart meets Elizabeth for a "date" of which Susan takes an instant dislike to—a mysterious person from Kyle's past heads to Marble Hills with an axe to grind—Denise and Robert find themselves experiencing common interests—Caleb and Genie have an encounter in a parking lot—Eddie angrily confronts Howard over a tragic event in Boston and makes threats—Tyler is given advice by a friend—and an unexpected return creates multiple problems for someone in Marble Hills.

Dark Desires

Police Station

Caroline Bentley nervously looks at Daryl Anderson as he opens up the crumpled ball of paper. They look at each other.

"What are you going to do?"

Daryl sighs.

"Something I should've done a long time ago."

"Daryl?"

He clenches his fists several times.

"I've had all I can take—if he thinks he's the only one who can play dirty—it's time for him to see me in a new light."

They look at each other.

"Don't go do anything rash—he's got nothing to lose."

Daryl looks away as he seems to be looking for an answer before he turns to face Caroline again. He sighs loudly.

"We'll see about that."

Caroline watches as Daryl walks toward a police car. She shakes her head seemingly very worried at his reaction.

"I'm coming with you—just in case."

"I can handle this myself—got scores to settle."

Daryl turns away from Caroline. He seems upset. She notices. He faces her again. She notices his clenched fists.

"He's looking for a fight."

He opens the door of the police car.

"This is between me and that lousy piece of filth."

They look at each other again.

Pete's Cafe

Lance Weissmann walks into the diner with a huge grin on his face. Susan Bennington is close behind. As they sit down at an empty booth nearby he notices Carrie Spaulding, Kelly Nelson, Abby Marshall, Ashton Markway, Jeremy Weissmann and Shirley Moses huddled at a nearby booth engrossed in a conversation.

"Wonder what that's about—bet it's probably just more drama about Gina. Oh well, Jeremy will tell me later."

Susan looks at Lance.

"Did you say something?"

Lance shakes his head.

"Not really—just thinking out loud."

He grins as he touches her hand.

"Come on, let's order something to eat—I'm starved."

Susan smiles slyly.

"I'll just bet you are."

Lance laughs.

"I always get really hungry after a bout of sex."

He suddenly seems nervous.

"Listen, you can't tell anyone what happened between us—you being fifteen and all—your parents would go crazy."

Susan smirks.

"I'm almost sixteen—I'm not a child."

Lance sighs and looks around the diner nervously.

"I usually don't go trolling for girls under sixteen."

"Yeah, and I was born yesterday. I'm not fooled by what happened—especially after that incident with Brad McKinley."

He reaches out to hold Susan's hand again.

Page 276

"Fine—if you must know, yeah I've had every girl I ever wanted to bang—but in my defense—I'm always horny."

Susan gives him a knowing look and sighs.

<u>Farmington Villa</u>

Juan Sabrillo turns the television off. He seems in shock. He stands up and looks around almost as if in a daze.

"Eldon Whitney is dead?"

He sighs.

"I can't believe it. It just—who would?"

He looks at the television again.

"Someone took out Eldon Whitney and his entire building. No witnesses to tell anyone anything. How? Why?"

He sighs loudly.

"Who would want to kill Whitney?"

Juan shakes his head.

"Granted the man had a lot of enemies—but—but the entire building? Someone seriously had a lot of balls."

He hears the door slowly opening and turns to see Faye Washington. She smiles broadly as she walks over to Juan.

<u>Maple Avenue</u>

Donna Markway leans against a flagpole. Color drains from her face. She seems like she's about to faint from shock.

"Are you OK?"

Donna slowly turns to look at Jason Anderson. She seems in shock as she appears unable to move. She shrugs.

"I can't believe it. Are you sure? Are you sure Tiffany Johnson is dead? I saw her yesterday—she was fine—alive."

Jason nods several times.

"Uh-huh—no doubt about it Donna—it's all over the news what happened. She's dead—everyone is talking about it."

"But it can't be. There must be some mistake?"

Jason gestures with his hand.

"It happened this morning—apparently she somehow lost control of her car by Standish Road and went off the bluff."

Donna seems troubled.

"This—this isn't real—she was one of us—young."

As she faints Jason catches her.

<u>Glass Owl</u>

Kyle Madison slowly sits down on the sofa. He seems about to explode with rage. He shakes his head several times.

"I don't know how much more of this I can take—I feel like I'm about to snap—absolutely at my wit's end right now."

Kyle sighs loudly.

"And Wesley, well, some things never change—he's bent on revenge—I'm actually worried—worried for his safety."

Howard Madison looks at Kyle curiously.

"It'll be taken care of immediately. That I promise you."

Kyle turns to look at his father.

"What are you going to do?"

Howard smiles slyly.

"Better you don't know the gory details—nevertheless my precious grandson will be a free man really soon—bet on it."

"How are you going to convince Alden Washington to drop the charges against Wesley—he won't be easily swayed."

"Like I said—better you don't know how. I'll make that pest see things my way—or else I'll make him regret it."

Kyle sighs loudly again.

"Just don't make things worse, OK? Washington isn't exactly the type to forgive slights—especially from us."

Howard stands and walks over to the bar and makes himself a stiff drink. He laughs as he turns around to face Kyle.

"Washington will play my game or I'll make public certain secrets he thinks no one knows about which could be potentially embarrassing if anyone were to become aware of what I've kept quiet about for years—secrets he thinks are long buried."

Kyle sits up suddenly.

Page 278

"Are you going to drag what he did to Marah all those years ago up again—no one in Marble Hills cares anymore."

Howard laughs loudly.

"Like I said best you don't know."

"What could be worse than coldly killing my sister—your daughter—did he rape and kill someone else in town?"

Howard walks over to Kyle and hands him a drink. He smiles slyly as he watches the confusion on Kyle's face.

"Trust me—what I have on Washington is much worse than that incident with Marah—oh yeah much worse."

Kyle takes a swig of his drink.

"Well, are you going to enlighten me on what you have on Washington? Did he rape some young girl in Hollywood?"

Howard smirks.

"Nope—don't think I'll tell you at the moment—but trust me on this matter—Washington won't know what hit him."

Howard laughs again.

"Oh yeah, Washington thinks no one knows about this little incident—but he's *so* wrong—and it'll send shocks."

He waves his hand in the air.

"Uh-huh—sweet deal to know what I know."

Kyle watches as his father takes another swig and begins laughing hysterically as if he can see something in front of him that remains invisible to Kyle. He stops laughing suddenly.

Pete's Cafe

Lance and Susan are talking when Hart Bennington walks up to them. He seems a bit confused as he glances at Susan.

"Susan? What are you doing here with Lance?"

Lance gives Hart a strange look.

"You two know each other?"

Hart glances at Susan briefly and shrugs.

"She's my sister."

Lance looks at Susan curiously.

"I'd never have guessed."

Lance glances at Hart once more.
"Are you twins?"
Susan smiles broadly.
"Hart and I are fraternal twins."
Lance looks at Hart.
"There are a couple of twins here in Marble Hills."
Hart looks at Susan curiously.
"What happened to Brad—he dumped you already? Told you he had only one thing on his mind—total loser—freak."
Susan rolls her eyes at Hart.
"He didn't dump me. He had—*problems*."
She laughs.
"I met Lance afterwards."
She gives Hart a strange look.
"How do you and Lance know each other?"
Hart and Lance exchange looks.
"I met him at the mall down the street earlier today."
Hart sighs.
"Oh—OK whatever."
Hart sits down.
"What do you think of my sister?"
"She's great."
Hart rolls his eyes.
"I think you should be warned—my sister is a handful."
Susan pretends to slap Hart.
"Keep it up Hart—and when you go to sleep later tonight I'll be waiting—waiting in the closet with a huge pillow."
Hart looks at Lance. Susan smirks.
"This time will be for real."
She makes a slashing motion with her finger.
"I'll get away with it too."
Hart curiously looks at Susan and sighs loudly. Hart faces Lance again and gives Susan a weird glance seconds later.
"My sister is a crazy."
Susan jabs Hart. He reacts.

Page **280**

<u>Sydney</u>

"Oh yeah, you may have thought I'd forgotten what happened between you and my sister but you'd be wrong—so wrong buddy. And now, oh—now things will happen."

Gary Glick zips up an overstuffed duffel bag and slings it over his shoulder as he heads to the door whistling loudly.

"Marble Hills—here I come."

He slams the door shut to his apartment.

<u>Farmington Villa</u>

"Who were you talking to?"

Juan seems nervous as he looks at Faye.

"No one—I was just watching CNN."

He looks at the television again.

"This building in Boston was just attacked—and everyone got iced—not one soul left alive—the police have no idea."

"Someone bombed a building?"

Juan shakes his head.

"No—they executed everyone."

He sighs loudly.

"Quite the shock—such anger."

Juan walks over to where Faye is standing. He grins slyly as he slowly begins unbuttoning his Levi's in front of her.

"How about you and I visit the bedroom?"

Faye seems annoyed by his behavior.

"You're incorrigible."

Juan laughs loudly as he guides Faye toward the bedroom and closes the door behind them amid louder laughter.

<u>Glass Owl</u>

Denise Madison sighs as she turns off the ignition to her car. She hastily checks herself again in the mirror. She notices small splotch of dried semen on her cheek. She smiles broadly.

Page 281

"Miles—he's so sweet—with such an incredibly gorgeous body—and his stamina—my God it's incredible—so charged."

She sighs again as she looks at Glass Owl through the window of the garage. Her smile fades immediately.

"I thought that was you."

Denise turns to see Robert Bennington grinning at her a few feet away. She steps out of the car and faces him.

"Not looking forward to going back into the mausoleum are you? Well, I can't say I blame you one bit Denise—I've seen better crypts in Philadelphia—with much nicer inhabitants."

Denise grins.

"How'd you guess?"

Robert grins as he shoves his hands into the front pockets of his pants and leans against her car. He sighs loudly.

"Been there and done that—this place is like one of those ancient houses you see in those old spooky 1930s movies that **Carl Laemmle** used to make that was so great to watch on a rainy afternoon when there was nothing to do but just sit there."

Denise grins again.

"Except this place has no ending."

Robert laughs.

"Tell me about it—an unending nightmare."

They look at each other.

"You know—you're still hot—like you haven't aged at all even after all these years—still got the look—and body."

Robert smirks.

"Tell Lindsay that if you dare."

"I just might."

Denise reaches out and slides her hand between Robert's legs. He looks at her curiously. She smiles slyly and winks.

"I know you're a man with needs—so wrong that Lindsay has been denying you—and I think you and me should."

Robert grins broadly as her fingers begin unzipping his pants. He watches as her fingers slip into his boxer briefs. She looks at him with a sly glance. He laughs loudly and smirks.

"I think we should explore all possibilities between us."

Page **282**

Denise pulls Robert to her and kisses him passionately. He responds. Seconds later he's deep inside her as they recklessly go at it unable to stop. Her moans echo in the empty garage during their intense bout of lovemaking. He laughs several times.

<u>Maple Avenue</u>

Jason hands Donna a bottle of water. She takes a few sips. She still seems confused and looks around several times.

"Tiffany is dead?"

Jason nods.

"They're saying Gina Bentley did it."

Her eyes widens in shock.

"Oh, my God—I always knew she was messed up."

Donna sips from the bottle again.

"But I would never have guessed—never thought she'd."

"Just goes to show you never know about some people. They may seem somewhat normal—until—until they snap."

Donna sighs.

"Too bad it wasn't Brad that killed Tiffany. I'd love nothing more than to see him spend the rest of his life in prison for—for what he did to—let him be mauled by—mauled by perverts."

Jason rolls his eyes.

"Dude's a creep without a doubt—better you found that out before he screwed with you and made you one of *them*."

Donna seems upset.

"Do you think I'm a bad girl?"

Jason shakes his head.

"Why would I think that?"

Donna shrugs.

"I let Brad—let him use me—thought he loved me."

Jason waves his hand at the air.

"Don't you worry—that worthless piece of slime is going to get his just desserts—trust me, it's just a matter of time before someone kills the bastard—he has it coming—hateful creep."

"He's not the only one like that in Marble Hills."

Page 283

Jason rolls his eyes again.

"Don't remind me of the others."

Donna slowly takes Jason's hand as he notices.

<u>Glass Owl</u>

Daryl slams the car door shut and heads toward the front door of the massive structure in a rage. He pounds his fists angrily against a stained glass window seconds later. A minute or two later Kyle opens the door. He seems upset to see Daryl standing there and gives him an icy stare. Kyle gestures with his hand.

"What do you want?"

Daryl grabs Kyle roughly.

"Get out of my way motherfucker—no time for games."

He shoves Kyle aside as he sees Howard standing in the doorway of the den. They look at each other. Daryl stops.

"Think you're funny, don't you?"

Kyle looks at Daryl and Howard curiously.

"I've had enough of your crap—enough already."

Howard waves his hand at Kyle.

"No—it's fine. Apparently Daryl has some issues he wants to discuss with me—seems he had one too many earlier."

Kyle looks at his father briefly and turns away. A few seconds later Daryl pulls out the piece of crumpled paper from the back pocket of his Levi's. He waves it at Howard.

"If you think this will make things move faster with Alden Washington—it won't—blackmail doesn't work with me."

Howard smiles slyly and ushers Daryl into the den. He slowly closes the door behind him and feigns shock.

"What are you talking about?"

Daryl shoves the piece of paper in Howard's face.

"*This*—I'm talking about your sick stunt as if you didn't know already—such childish games from someone so old."

Howard looks at the piece of paper. He sighs.

"This isn't—I know nothing about this needless drama."

Daryl grabs the paper from him.

Page 284

"Of course it's yours—who else knows about?"

Howard glances at the door.

"I didn't send you this—not my style in case you didn't notice—I prefer the direct approach—I don't play games."

Daryl seems worried.

"Then who—who else could know?"

Howard smirks.

"Looks like someone out there got the jump on my game for a change—oh-oh—this could get quite interesting."

Daryl gestures with his hand.

"I know you're behind this—there's no way anyone else could have known about—so that only leaves you."

Howard laughs loudly again.

"Oops—someone else found out about you and Caroline Stuyvesant doing the nasty—seems to me there's plenty?"

He makes a lewd gesture with his finger.

"You're a louse Anderson—I guess you and Caroline hit the sheets one too many times and someone—caught."

Daryl edges closer to Howard.

"I know what I've done—I'm no saint—but how about what you've done Madison? How about the *tragic* accident that killed Eddie Kane's parents over thirty years ago—or the mysterious downing of Carla Keller in 1980—of course there's also the disappearance of your lawyer Martin Sawyer in 2005—and let's not pretend what happened to my father was an accident by any means. Oh yeah, seems I'm not the only one who has something to hide old man—I wonder what would happen if someone were to suddenly link all these juicy tidbits to the right person?"

Howard flies into a rage and grabs Daryl by the neck.

"*How dare you threaten me*—who the fuck do you think you are—you worthless piece of trash—I really ought to end your miserable life right here and now and be done with you."

Daryl laughs smugly as he tries to push Howard away. He seems confident as he watches Howard's reaction. He sighs.

"Maybe—but I'm a worthless piece of trash that can easily bring you down—and the entire Madison empire for good."

Page **285**

Howard's hands tighten around Daryl's neck as he forces him down on the floor. Daryl is taken by surprise and seems to be in shock as Howard angrily begins viciously strangling him.

"You don't want to cross me Anderson—the results could be most fatal—for you and for—if you know what I mean—as you are fully aware I always do what I say—and it would be a shame if—if certain things were to suddenly happen to your family."

He stops choking Daryl.

"You will do what I want or else—or next time I won't be so nice when you and I meet again. Things can happen."

Howard smiles slyly.

"Jason—Jason may find the brakes to his car suddenly malfunctioning just—just when he drives by Standish Road."

Daryl looks at Howard with disgust.

"You—you're absolutely evil—no doubt about it—you're definitely a spawn of the—bet your mother wasn't human."

Howard shrugs.

"Flattery will get you nowhere."

He glances at the door.

"I'll expect results soon—or else."

He gestures with his hand.

"My grandson will be out of prison very soon or your son will have a most unfortunate accident—terrible ending."

Howard slides his finger across his neck.

"I hope you have an extra plot ready at Crestview—I hear crypts are all the rage by the way—but quite expensive."

Daryl heads to the door.

"Either my grandson is cleared of those ridiculous charges against him or your son will be a stiff in the morgue—dead."

Howard smirks as Daryl opens the door.

"But then again—at least you'll still have two children left—would be such a shame if someone told John Bentley."

Howard wags his finger at Daryl and seems gleeful as he sees how his behavior is affecting Daryl. He smiles broadly.

"I own you and don't you ever forget it."

Daryl slams the door as he leaves.

Page **286**

<u>Pete's Cafe</u>

Lance, Susan and Hart are sitting together as Daphne Garfield comes up to Lance and kisses him passionately. He kisses her back with equal intensity. She smiles broadly.

"How about my car in three minutes—missed you yesterday—but I was really busy in case you must know—but not today or tomorrow—can play for hours if so needed."

Lance smirks.

"I'm there."

He stands up and watches her leave. He glances at Susan and Hart briefly for a few seconds as he grins broadly.

"I guess I have a date with her backseat."

He gives Hart a knowing look.

"Don't forget about Elizabeth Pendleton—she'll be worth it—believe me—she's had lots of experience—been with just about every guy in town since I made her a woman—knows how to really please a guy between the sheets—guaranteed."

Susan notices Lance's massive erection as he turns to leave seconds later. Hart gives Susan a knowing look.

"I guess you know he's not looking for a girlfriend."

Susan shrugs.

"No big deal—he can screw whomever he wants—I don't own him—he's just really nice—treats me with respect."

Susan seems upset. Hart notices.

<u>Glass Owl</u>

Denise glances at Robert as he zips up. He turns to look at her and grins broadly as he watches her comb her hair.

"This—this was quite an experience—I think we can both agree no one can know about—much too awkward."

Denise pulls Robert to her and kisses him.

"Mum's the word on this subject."

She laughs knowingly.

Page **287**

"But I don't see why this has to be a one-time thing between us—we're both adults—we can pick up where we left off years ago before Lindsay forcibly dragged you off to Philly."

"I was thinking the same thing—definitely."

Denise kisses Robert again.

<u>Lighthouse Grill</u>

Caroline sits down at one of the tables and looks around slightly annoyed. The place seems utterly deserted.

"I guess my uncle won't be in business much longer if this keeps up—maybe I should offer him some money?"

"Hello, Caroline."

She turns around to see Sidney Stuyvesant staring at her curiously. She briefly looks at him with a guilty look.

"So, how long has it been?"

Caroline shakes her head nervously.

"Two weeks—two weeks since my favorite niece paid me a visit—been worried—so many thoughts to—think about."

Caroline sighs.

"I'm your only niece Uncle Sidney."

He pulls up a chair.

"Is it John again—I swear—I'll go over and make that lousy husband of yours pay attention—enough is enough."

Caroline shakes her head again.

"No—it's not John—it's me—I did something dumb and now it's going to come back to bite me royally in the ass."

Sidney rubs his brow. He shoots Caroline a cautious as they look at each other. He notices how nervous she seems.

"Is this about you and Anderson again?"

Caroline seems surprised.

"You knew about that—but how?"

"I'm old, not blind Caroline. There are no secrets in Marble Hills that I don't know of or can't find out about—none."

He sighs loudly and wags his finger.

"This town talks—can't shut people up."

Page **288**

He wipes sweat from his brow.

"Just this morning I heard from a good friend that Marla Jefferson and her new pool boy—you know—the one that looks like he's still in high school, has been doing the nasty behind Kent's back every day for the past month or so. Oh my, when they get caught—Kent probably will be up for murder one—but at least that young punk would've gotten what was coming to him for a month now—and that goes double for our "drop his pants" mailman too—and then of course there's that messy business with Father Jacob. He apparently thinks that no one in town can see what he's been doing behind closed doors with one of his young altar boys at St. Joseph's Church—such tawdry drama."

Caroline waves her hand.

"Uncle Sidney, I really don't want to hear about other people's drama. I've got enough—got some real problems."

Sidney leans closer to Caroline.

"Stay away from Anderson—he's run afoul of Howard Madison over some trivial matter from what I hear—and I don't think I have to draw you a picture on how badly that'll end?"

They look at each other.

"You don't have to warn me about Daryl."

Sidney glances around at the empty diner and sighs.

"Yeah, I know—business is down—not much I can do about it though—times are really slow—no one is spending."

He seems worried as he looks at Caroline again.

<u>Police Station</u>

Clay Blankenship and Eva Harper look at the room once more before Clay turns off the lights. He grins broadly.

"I'm all yours."

Eva smiles seductively.

"No better words in the English language."

They kiss as he opens the front door. Just as they pull the door open Daryl reaches for the doorknob. He seems upset and gruffly walks past Clay without a word. Clay looks at Eva.

Page 289

"Is everything OK? Did something else happen?"

Daryl and Clay exchange looks.

"Madison is the absolute scourge of all humanity—what I wouldn't give right about now to put a bullet—maybe two into that man's skull. No one would deserve it more than him."

Eva seems alarmed. Clay notices.

"Daryl's just having a really bad day—he didn't mean what he just said—he would never kill Howard Madison."

Daryl sighs loudly.

"The hell I wouldn't. That piece of garbage deserves to have someone take him out—end that bastard forever."

Clay seems uneasy.

"Well, OK—whatever—see you tomorrow Daryl."

Daryl waves his hand in acknowledgement as he watches Clay and Eva leave. He turns to face the empty room.

<u>Brewster Condo</u>

The front door swings open as Matt Brewster passionately kisses Trevor Youngblood. He pushes Trevor through the door and grins. They continue kissing for several more seconds. They finally part and sigh loudly. Matt gestures with his hand.

"I bet you didn't think I was serious when I said I wanted to fuck you—made it quite clear what I wanted from you."

Trevor grins broadly.

"Well, usually it takes an hour or so to hook-up with someone I meet at Pike's. But I never question fate."

He laughs slyly.

"I'm game any which way the ball bounces today. I especially like guys that know what they want and take it."

Trevor laughs again.

"Does the fact I'm nineteen make a difference to you?"

Matt shakes his head and pulls Trevor to him.

"I'm always in the mood for something new and exciting."

Trevor grins as Matt strokes his chest.

Page **290**

<u>Mall</u>

Caleb Winthrop is kissing Genie Van Pelt as she notices her brother watching them. She slowly pulls away from Caleb. He seems upset as he turns to look at Tyler Van Pelt. She sighs.

"He's hurting—I should go talk to talk to him."

Caleb seems annoyed and shrugs.

"He'll get over it. That—and I really don't want to hear about your brother's sex life with that creep Ross Harrison."

Genie rolls her eyes.

"Get over it, will you? My brother isn't interested in you for anything—he knows your deal—he knows you're not gay."

Caleb sighs loudly.

"I really don't care about knowing about the gory details of what Ross Harrison did—Harrison is a freak—twisted."

Caleb gestures with his hand.

"Hit on me once—disgusting—like really."

Genie looks over at where Tyler is sitting again.

"I assume you want us to go back to your car don't you?"

Caleb grins broadly.

"How did you guess?"

He glances at the elevators a few feet away. He winks at her. Genie sighs loudly as she notices how eager he seems.

"I should say no but I can't."

Caleb laughs slyly.

"Uh-huh—I know."

They stand up. Genie hesitantly looks at Tyler once more with a worried look on her face. Caleb rolls his eyes.

"I really should go over and see how's he's doing?"

Caleb rolls his eyes again.

"Look, he's OK. I mean, come on, he got dumped by Ross Harrison. It's no big deal. Harrison's a bigger player than I am or could ever hope to be—except I don't do dudes—trust me, you're bro is better off without that pervert in his life—Harrison makes us straight guys look seriously tame—fucks anything."

Genie hesitates again and shrugs.

Page **291**

"I guess you're right—Tyler knew Ross had a rep before he began dating him—and knew he wasn't going to change."

Caleb nods.

"That's what I said—so let's go already."

They look at each other.

"Ross Harrison better hope I don't run into him anytime soon—after what he did to Tyler—or he'll be really sorry."

Caleb presses the button on the elevator.

"Not another word about that punk Harrison today."

Genie gives Caleb a strange look.

<u>Pete's Cafe</u>

Elizabeth Pendleton walks toward where Susan and Hart are sitting at the booth. They look at her curiously.

"Hi, Hart—I'm Elizabeth Pendleton."

Susan rolls her eyes. Elizabeth turns to face her.

"Who are you—his girlfriend?"

Susan laughs.

"Yuk—like no. I'm his sister."

She suddenly stands up.

"I'm outta here."

She rolls her eyes at Hart and leaves without saying anything else to Elizabeth. Elizabeth shrugs several times.

"Your sister's rude—like really."

Hart nods and sighs.

"Uh-huh—and mean and selfish too—*she's a bitch*—no use pretending otherwise—rains on everyone's parade."

Elizabeth sits down.

"I guess we should."

Hart sighs.

"I'm not a loser."

Elizabeth reaches out to touch Hart's hand.

"I never said you were."

Elizabeth leans over to kiss Hart.

"I think you're cute—got a rebellious look to you."

Hart grins. He makes a lewd gesture with his finger.

"I'm trouble. No doubt about it."

Elizabeth looks at him curiously and sighs.

Glass Owl

Eddie Kane rings the doorbell a second time. As he's about to turn away Howard opens the door. They look at each other for a few seconds as Eddie glares at Howard. He sighs.

"What do you want?"

Eddie grins.

"Oh, that depends on exactly what I find."

Howard sighs again.

"I'm not in the mood for twenty questions or any other game you're playing Kane—spit it out already—quickly."

Eddie smirks.

"It seems not everything is what it seemed."

He watches Howard's reaction.

"I've come across some info—info that if proven will link you to the deaths of my parents—and if that turns out to be true Madison—I swear you're as good as dead—*dead*—DOA."

Eddie grins again.

"If I were you I'd make sure there was room in the family crypt for one more. Trust me—Greg won't be the only one being interred there in a few days—better get your will in order ASAP old man—I'd hate to think that your precious Kyle won't have any money to spend—it would be such a shame—imagine a grown man with all that money yet can't touch it because of legal reasons—might be fun actually to watch—uh-huh sweet."

Howard looks at Eddie coldly.

"How dare you threaten me—seems you've forgotten your place—but that—oh that can change rather quickly."

He makes a gesture with his hand and smirks. He seems pleased as he watches Eddie react. He begins laughing.

"I've taken out better men than you."

Eddie laughs and points his finger at Howard.

Page 293

"Oh, I know all about what you've done and—and if I find out you were mixed up in any way in what happened to my parents—I'll kill you with my bare hands—*that* you can count on no doubt and not have to second guess me—guaranteed."

Howard continues to stare at Eddie coldly.

"Men who've made such bold comments to me have paid dearly for—so many accidents—so many unexplained."

Eddie grins broadly.

"Like I said Madison, if I find out you had anything to do with what happened to—I'll turn your lights out for good."

Eddie turns to leave. He stops.

"By the way don't bother going to Anderson about this little incident—I hear he's on the warpath against you as well right about now—seems you've been making a whole slew of friends lately, haven't you Madison—you know, like that notorious mobster guy in Boston—oh, didn't someone kill him earlier—took him out like a lowly dog—threw him from his building."

Eddie smirks again.

"Wouldn't it be a shame if his "friends" found out from someone—you know, someone who knew for a fact that you were mixed up in Eldon Whitney's sudden demise just a few hours ago? Think about it for a minute—you wouldn't be safe one more second—let alone an hour if they knew what I know about what you did—better yet, your family wouldn't be safe either. Wesley is already a sitting duck, being in jail and all—accidents do happen in jail all the time, don't they—and just think what those guys would do to Lindsay and her family afterwards—from what I hear they can be real vicious animals when it comes to women and bedroom activity. What if I were to tell them what I know?"

Howard reacts.

"Get the hell off my property this minute."

Eddie smiles broadly.

"Gladly—but remember what I just said old man."

Howard glares at Eddie.

"I'm not going to tell you again."

Eddie shrugs and points at Howard again.

Page **294**

"You better hope I don't find out you did anything to my parents, or God help you, you'll wish you were never born."

He rolls his eyes knowingly.

"And just in case you get any ideas about coming after my family, I'd rethink those plans if I were you—give me the least amount of reason to call Whitney's people and tell them what you did and I will—I wouldn't even have to think about it."

Eddie leaves. Howard clenches his fist several times in rage as he stands there. He slams the front door shut.

<u>Parking Lot</u>

The car rocks violently back and forth as Caleb and Genie go at it in the backseat. Caleb's laughter can be heard amid passionate moans coming from Genie. He grins broadly.

"You're on the pill, right?"

Genie rolls her eyes.

"You always ask me that when we fuck—and yeah, I'm on the pill—of course I'm on the pill—wouldn't try and trap you."

"I'm just checking OK—got a right to ask—I wouldn't want what happened last year to happen again between us."

Genie kisses Caleb and laughs.

"It only happened once—I was new to this sort of thing if you remember—you were one of the first guys I slept with in case you conveniently forgot—I was only fifteen and had no idea at the time a girl could get pregnant if the guy pulled out right before he blew his load—and in your case—four. I'm over it—deal."

Caleb laughs slyly.

"Well, at least you did the right thing and got rid of it like I asked—your pop would've had my scalp if he knew."

Genie rolls her eyes again.

"He still would if he knew you were doing me even after he warned you to watch your step—he still thinks I'm his little girl—sweet and innocent like a delicate helpless flower."

Caleb laughs and wags his finger at her.

"That ship has sailed quite a long time ago."

Page **295**

Caleb slides his fingers into Genie's vagina, leering at her seductively as he watches her reaction to his probing.

"How about we hook-up tomorrow too—we could spend the day in Belfast—I know a diner there that serves the best grilled onion burgers—they cook it on an outdoor brick oven and it tastes like really old-fashioned burgers from the 1980s."

Caleb grins broadly as his fingers continue to probe Genie's vagina as a moan escapes her lips. He grins.

"And then we can rent a room at a local motel and fuck for hours—and since you're on the pill—no issues to worry."

Genie kisses Caleb again and begins moaning loudly.

"I'd love to—call me when you're ready."

Caleb grins broadly again—pulls Genie under him and penetrates her effortlessly as she begins moaning once more.

<u>Mall</u>

Tyler stares at the bottle of Pepsi in front of him as his reflection creates an odd image against the clear material. He takes another swig and looks at the bottle again. He sighs.

"Good thing that isn't liquor."

Tyler slowly turns around to see one of his teachers looking at him with a curious look. He gestures briefly.

"I wish it was—could use a drink."

Ben Lincoln sits down near Tyler and shakes his head.

"I'll pretend I didn't hear that."

Tyler shakes his head knowingly.

"My life sucks chunks."

Ben reacts to Tyler's reaction.

"Things will get better—it has to—it will—just give it some time and everything will work itself out for the best."

Tyler rolls his eyes and sighs.

"I don't believe that."

He sighs as he takes another swig.

"Nope—no chance of that happening—my boyfriend—oh excuse me, check that—my ex-boyfriend is a manwhore."

Page 296

Ben glances at Tyler curiously.

"Well, if that's so, you're better off without him, aren't you? You can do better—find someone who's nice."

Tyler takes a swig and sighs loudly.

"I guess—but I thought he wanted me for me and wasn't just using my body but I found out otherwise—he's a zero."

Ben laughs.

"Welcome to the real world."

Ben leans toward Tyler and whispers.

"Before I met my wife I was played many times in fact if you must know—thought it was happening only to me—until a few of my friends told me they'd been played too and had played some as well—it's just the way these things go—terrible."

Tyler rolls his eyes once more.

"If this is the way things are I'm swearing off dudes."

Ben laughs again.

"And what—you're going to chase after girls?"

Tyler smiles broadly.

<u>Stanley Pier</u>

Lisa Taylor shuts off her cell phone.

"That jerk has some nerve."

She turns to leave.

"Is that so?"

Lisa spins around to see Damon Mayo staring at her.

"You're threading on thin ice."

He grins broadly.

"A guy's got to keep his main girl guessing—dull guys get forgotten quickly—not enough game to hold interest."

Lisa grins broadly.

"What happened to Amanda Spencer? I thought you two were hot and heavy? Isn't she your main girl? I assumed."

Damon grins slyly.

"Amanda Spencer is nobody to me."

They look at each other.

Page 297

"I don't like sharing you with anyone else—especially Amanda. I'm really greedy that way—and she's a prude."

Damon laughs.

"I told you why I have to play this game—everyone needs to think I'm her boyfriend so I can get my loan approved."

Lisa smirks.

"If anyone knew what we did last night in the women's restroom in Portland they wouldn't confuse you with being a nice boyfriend ever again after having sex with a high school girl."

Damon laughs again.

"A guy has to do what a guy needs to do."

They kiss passionately.

"I'd like to see what else is lurking beneath."

Lisa tugs at the tight Lycra fabric of his shorts. She slides her fingers across his bulging erection. A short distance away on the other side of the pier Simon Spencer and his cousin Harper Youngblood notices them together. They continue watching Damon and Lisa for a few seconds in shock. Both seem quite disgusted at the scene playing out presently a few yards away.

"Pretend I'm a cheap two dollar whore from Vine Street and you—you're a dangerous ex-con with a terrible rep."

Damon laughs loudly.

"I really don't have to pretend."

Lisa reacts.

"Have you been in prison before?"

Damon grins smugly.

"I'll let you think about it for a while."

He pulls her toward him.

"Remember the first time I took you—pinned you in the steam room at my gym—in all of two seconds if I recall. You tried to resist but I made it clear I was going to have my way."

Lisa kisses Damon again.

"You got lucky that day. I was upset."

She makes a lewd gesture with her finger.

"I didn't expect anything—I could've but I didn't—that should count for something—count for a lot actually."

Page **298**

Damon slides his fingers under Lisa's blouse and cups her breasts with his hands. They kiss passionately. Damon grins.

"Just bought a brand new mattress for the back of my van earlier today—think you and I should try it out right now."

Lisa gives Damon a strange look.

"I don't want seconds."

Damon laughs.

"I said it was brand new."

He looks down at his Lycra shorts.

"In case it matters I haven't fucked Amanda in the back of my van yet—I will at some point—you know how I play—but just not yet. So, how about it? Want to join me for some fun?"

He winks at her.

"I know you like me a lot."

Lisa looks at Damon curiously and sighs.

"I want you to end it with Amanda."

Damon shakes his head.

"No."

He pulls Lisa toward him.

"I don't want to hear another word from your mouth on this subject—I make my own decisions about whom I fuck."

They begin kissing passionately. From behind they hear a muffled sound and turn to see Brad McKinley pulling himself up on the wharf nearby. They are shocked by his appearance.

TO BE CONTINUED

A Look at the 12th Episode

Howard keeps dangerous secrets from Kyle—Sidney considers meddling in other people's business despite being cautioned not to—Clay and Eva spend a private moment together—Kyle confronts Eddie—Caleb and Genie deal with Tiffany's death and a possible suspect—Brad comes back with a vengeance—Simon's unhappy behavior is noticed by others as he ponders his next move—Caroline takes a page out of Denise's book—Tiffany's funeral brings out friends and enemies alike—Damon plays both sides—Eddie and Todd discuss revenge plans—Chandra drops a bombshell on Robert with the potential to destroy his fragile world and the world of many others around him—Denise and Miles enjoy each other's company—Gary puts his plan in motion with his younger brother's help—Alden and Wesley come face to face for the first time since their encounter—Will makes hiking plans—as Gina gets an unwelcomed visit from a former rival.

Trouble in Paradise

<u>Glass Owl</u>

Kyle Madison glances at the window and faces his father curiously. Howard Madison turns away looking annoyed.

"What did Eddie Kane want?"

Howard sighs loudly.

"He didn't want anything."

"Sure seemed like something to me—he tore out of the driveway like he owned the world—and owned you too."

Howard seems irritated by the comment.

"I said it was nothing—now let it drop."

Kyle watches as his father walks toward the door.

"Do I have to ask Eddie what transpired between you two just now—or are you going to tell—should I ask Eddie?"

"Ask him whatever you want—it's not like he'll tell you anything anyway—have you forgotten the man hates you."

Kyle notices a smug look on Howard's face as he heads upstairs. He watches his father slowly climbs the staircase.

"He's up to something again."

Kyle rubs his chin lightly.

"I guess if I want answers I'll have to ask Eddie."

He looks at the staircase again.

"He'll tell me what I need to know."

He grabs his coat and heads to the front door just as Robert Bennington reaches for the doorknob. They look at each other briefly but say nothing. Kyle leaves seconds later.

Tolling Bell Inn

Elizabeth Pendleton watches Hart Bennington as he pulls on his clothes. She climbs out of bed and turns to face him.

"I hope it was what you expected."

Hart sits up in bed.

"It was."

Elizabeth nods.

Lighthouse Grill

Sidney Stuyvesant faces the entrance to his diner and sees Grant Monroe about to sit down at one of the empty booths. He sighs and turns to look at Caroline Bentley nervously.

"Some people—ugh."

Caroline rolls her eyes knowingly.

"Let it go. It wasn't his fault. He dumped me after John threatened him. It was good while it lasted. I'm over it."

He sighs loudly.

"I guess you're right. But I still haven't forgiven him for trying to break up your marriage two years ago—ugh."

"Actually it was three years ago. I was in a really bad place with John and he helped quite a bit—made things better."

Sidney glances at Caroline again.

"I know—but still."

Caroline looks at her watch.

"I've got to go. Behave yourself—OK? Leave it alone."

Sidney looks at Grant again and nods.

"Monroe has no shame—ugh—some people."

Caroline kisses Sidney on the cheek and heads to the door. She acknowledges Grant but he doesn't say a word.

Parking Lot

Lance Weissmann laughs as he zips up his Levi's while Daphne Garfield reaches out to kiss him. They lean against the car and kiss passionately. He grins broadly in triumph.

"You didn't miss a beat."

Daphne grins.

"So, when can we—you know, experience the call of the wild again—it's just I can't seem—you have this power."

Lance laughs.

"Can't seem to get enough—can you?"

Lance kisses Daphne again.

"I'll pencil you in sometime tomorrow morning—it's the best I can do—I'm a popular guy. Deal with it already."

Daphne smirks.

"Tell me about it—you have a whole slew of girls whose virginities you took that have fallen under the spell of your penis. I was almost one of them if you recall. But Brad got me first."

Lance makes a lewd gesture with his finger.

"I'll call you tomorrow."

He kisses her again.

Private Driveway

Eddie Kane angrily slams the door to his car shut and slowly walks toward the back door of his mansion. His cell phone rings. He looks at it briefly before flipping it open. He sighs.

"Uh-huh—I knew you would call to check. Yeah, I spoke with the bastard and made him aware that if he was mixed up in the death of my folks he would pay—made it quite clear."

He sighs loudly as he looks at the cell phone.

"I know—I know—it was sort of like tipping him off. But this way he'll get freaked and maybe make a few mistakes."

He sighs again and shakes his fist.

"Nope—didn't spill anything major—but trust me, he's probably wetting his adult diapers right now in fright."

Eddie laughs.

"No problem—tomorrow sounds fine."

He shuts off the cell phone and looks at the house.

"God help you Madison—I swear if you were behind what happened to my parents—I'm going to take you out—as in permanently—about time you learned a lesson anyway."

He begins walking up the stairs.

<u>Blankenship Apartment</u>

Clay Blankenship and Eva Harper are cuddling on the sofa as he lazily runs his fingers through her hair and grins broadly.

"I'm glad you've came to your senses and decided to stay here in Marble Hills for the time being—knowing I need you."

Eva smiles broadly.

"I mean that much to you?"

Clay grins.

"Uh-huh."

They kiss.

"I'm glad we're together."

Eva kisses Clay.

"I like nerdy guys."

Clay smirks.

"Nerdy? I'm not nerdy."

"You remind me of that dark-haired guy from the old NBC series *Grimm*. He was strong but sensitive when needed."

Clay waves his finger in the air.

"That actor from *Grimm* wasn't nerdy by any means. He was a cool guy and an independent thinker—sort of a rebel."

He kisses Eva lightly.

"Do you really think I look like **David Giuntoli**?"

Eva nods several times.

"Uh-huh—and just as sexy I might add."

Page 304

Clay suddenly pulls Eva toward him and begins kissing her passionately. He slyly glances at the bedroom door.

"How about I show you a few of my bedroom moves?"

He pulls her to her feet.

"I really like being in a relationship with you."

Eva leans closer to Clay and whispers.

"My mother was right about you."

He nods in agreement.

Pete's Cafe

Caleb Winthrop seems in shock as he glances at Genie Van Pelt. She shakes her head several times. He sighs loudly.

"I just can't believe it."

Caleb gestures with his finger and shrugs.

"I fucked her this morning at the bus station. This—this just can't be happening—how can she be dead—how?"

Genie hugs Caleb.

"I'm sorry—I know she was special to you—the two of you had a special connection—even Gina Bentley knew it."

"We did—just the thought of us hooking up would send Gina into a crazy tailspin. She hated seeing us together."

"According to Lana it was Gina."

Caleb shakes his head.

"No—it can't be true—I hope not. I know they had their differences when it came to me—but even Gina wouldn't go that far as to kill someone in cold blood—to commit murder?"

Genie gestures with her hand.

"Are you sure? I mean she did threaten Tiffany multiple times from what I heard—and I heard her myself—several."

Caleb seems confused and shrugs.

Stanley Pier

Lisa Taylor and Damon Mayo look in shock at Brad McKinley as he comes toward them. He seems in a rage.

"What happened to you?"

"That worthless whore happened—that's what."

He walks past them.

<u>Private Driveway</u>

Eddie is about to reach for the doorknob of the back door to his home when he notices Kyle pulling up in his driveway. He watches as Kyle comes toward him. He seems upset.

"You and me—we need to talk."

Eddie rolls his eyes.

"Really—is that so—I can't imagine what about."

Kyle reaches where Eddie is standing.

"What were you and my father discussing earlier?"

Eddie sighs loudly.

"That's for me to know and you to find out."

Kyle grabs Eddie's arm.

"I'm not playing—what did you say to him Kane—I want answers or else—if you two are cooking up some scheme?"

Eddie jerks free of Kyle's grip.

"Fuck off."

He glances at Kyle for a few seconds.

"Or else what—you'll beat me up—oops, you tried that already years ago and I cleaned your clock if you recall."

"What did my father do?"

Eddie smirks.

"Get lost Madison."

They look at each other.

"I'm not leaving until you tell me."

Eddie glances at the house.

"Madison, I'm not going to tell you twice. Go away before I really get mad and splinter that scrawny neck of yours."

Eddie reaches for the doorknob. Kyle grabs him again as Eddie lashes out. He punches Kyle in the jaw. Kyle stumbles backwards from the blow and leans awkwardly against a metal mailbox several feet away. He glares angrily at Eddie.

Page 306

"You'll pay for this—I swear you'll pay dearly Kane."

Eddie laughs loudly.

"Yeah—whatever—like I care."

Eddie enters his mansion and slams the door shut behind him as Kyle continues standing there still rubbing his jaw from the attack. He pulls out his cell phone and begins dialing.

<u>Red Barn Gym</u>

Simon Spencer nervously closes the door behind him and looks around. He sees Corinne Massey sitting where Amanda usually sits and greets customers. She notices the dismayed look on his face as he approaches somewhat hesitantly.

"Is something wrong?"

Simon looks around as he digs his hands into the front pockets of his shorts. He looks around the lobby nervously.

"Where's Amanda?"

Corinne shrugs and looks at her watch.

"Not sure—she called earlier and said she had somewhere to go and asked if I could fill in for the rest of her shift."

Corinne leans forward.

"What's going on?"

"I'll tell you later."

Corinne watches him as he walks away.

<u>Blankenship Apartment</u>

Clay and Eva look at each other. He leans over to kiss her once more and smirks as he watches her reaction. He sighs.

"What would happen if I asked you stop being my official girlfriend and maybe be something more down the line?"

Eva grins broadly.

"I'd say yes."

Clay kisses Eva.

"You don't have to think about it?"

Eva laughs.

Page **307**

"Are you serious?"

Eva pulls Clay toward her. They look at each other briefly and then kiss lightly at first and then more passionately.

"Marble Hills isn't much—but trust me it's better than Boston—with a lot less crime to deal with every day."

Eva strokes Clay's hair.

"Nothing left in Boston for you?"

Clay shrugs.

"I like Boston but right now my job is here helping out Daryl Anderson in Marble Hills until I decide what I really want to do with my life—being a deputy has no future—not really."

Eva reaches out to stroke his cheek.

"I thought you wanted to be a writer?"

Clay glances at the door.

"I'm still deciding on that idea."

Eva nods in agreement.

<u>Hollow Oak Lane</u>

Caroline watches as Andy Tinker comes toward her from his parked van a few yards away. She grins broadly.

"I guess this means you're done delivering for today?"

He laughs.

"Not quite—I still one delivery left."

She grins slyly.

"Really—do explain yourself."

He reaches where she is standing and grabs her. They begin kissing passionately. She looks at him and smirks.

"Where is the delivery you promised me?"

She smiles broadly as he grins and slowly unzips his Levi's.

"It's right here between my legs."

She watches as he pulls his penis out. He looks at her for a second before pulling her toward him. They kiss again.

"Seems my delivery demands special attention—and a lot of TLC—to be administered at once—no questions asked."

Caroline kisses Andy.

Page **308**

"I agree."

They kiss again and glance at Andy's parked van a few yards away. Andy slides his hand under Caroline's blouse.

"The back of my van has been quite lonely today—and I think you need to show it some respect—like right away."

Caroline follows Andy toward his van.

<u>Farmington Villa</u>

Juan Sabrillo nervously paces back and forth across his hotel room as he listens intently on his cell phone. He shrugs.

"Look, I know your brother took a header off his balcony. But you and I both know he didn't do it intentionally."

He sighs loudly.

"Yeah, yeah—I know all about the massacre inside the building on Beacon. So what—are you just going to pretend your brother's death isn't—damn it—I know for a fact his enemies are jumping up and down for joy—but not for long. Someone has to be put in the ground for this slight against your brother—and sooner rather than later—he cries out for justice to be dealt."

He shakes his head several times.

"When I find out who ordered your brother's hit—they will beg for death—I will not rest until every last member of their family have been snuffed out by my hand—I will show no mercy. I assure you of this much—I will avenge your brother's death."

He nods and shuts off his cell phone.

<u>Pete's Cafe</u>

Carrie Spaulding is about to leave the diner as Brad angrily confronts her. His clothes are ripped and filthy. Carrie seems shocked to see him standing in front of her in person. His eyes seem to have a crazed look as they stare at each other.

"Damn whore—I'm going to kill you."

He grabs her arm.

"Say your prayers bitch."

Page 309

Kelly Nelson and Jeremy Weissmann suddenly step in front of Carrie. Brad turns to look at them with contempt.

"Out of my way—I have a lesson to teach her."

Kelly and Jeremy look at each other.

"I think you need to leave—seems to me you've had one too many today Brad—so, if you need help to the door."

Brad laughs hysterically.

"I haven't been drinking you fool."

He glances at Carrie.

"That miserable bitch tried to kill me earlier."

Carrie rolls her eyes.

"I don't know what he's talking about. It's obvious he's been on a "bender" or something. I think maybe we should call someone to—you know—from the state hospital—he may need like serious help. I have the number for Marshland with me."

Brad tries to get at Carrie again.

"I'll kill you—you miserable witch—I swear I will."

Kelly and Jeremy look at each other curiously and then at Carrie. Jeremy glances around at the diner nervously.

"Look Brad, I think you'd better leave. Whatever issues you're having right now with Carrie for whatever—take a breather until tomorrow—you'll feel better—OK—I'll drive you home right now OK—before you do something incredibly stupid."

Brad takes a swing at Jeremy.

"Fuck off loser—man, you seriously need to take a look at your own life before you dare point fingers at someone else."

Brad turns to look at Shirley Moses standing a few feet away with Abby Marshall. He stifles a smile and laughs.

"Yeah, that's right Jeremy—deal with your own problems first before you tell me anything—especially given the facts."

He laughs loudly.

"Your life is completely fake—not real at all. Everyone in this town knows what I'm talking about buddy—*everyone*."

Brad grins maliciously at Shirley.

"Tell him Shirley—I dare you."

He makes a lewd gesture with his finger.

Page **310**

"No one is what you think they are in this town. People in Marble Hills pretend to be friends with everyone else as they plot behind each other's backs—and Carrie Spaulding is the worst of them all—telling everyone else how to live their lives when it is she who desperately needs someone to tell her the ways of the world after the way she treats her so-called friends and lies to everyone's faces. Ugh—why don't you tell everyone Carrie?"

Jeremy turns to look at Carrie and shrugs.

"I think Carrie's right about Marshland—I'm sure Jennifer Parker would love some company right about now."

Brad suddenly takes a swing at Jeremy and knocks him to the floor. He jumps on top of him and begins punching.

<u>Hollow Oak Lane</u>

Caroline watches as Andy holds up a damaged condom in front of her. He grins broadly and lazily tosses it aside.

"It must have ripped when we were fucking."

Caroline seems worried.

"This can't be happening."

Andy laughs.

"Well, I told you I had a big dick."

They look at each other.

"What if I get pregnant?"

Andy shakes his head and smirks.

"So? Just get an abortion. No big deal. I've had girlfriends that got pregnant—it happens. Want me to cry about it?"

Caroline looks at the broken condom again.

"If my husband finds out we slept together—he'll want revenge. He hates it when I sneak around behind his back."

Andy grins broadly.

"He'll what—put a bullet in my head?"

Caroline pulls on her skirt.

"Possibly—or something much worse—God knows what he'll do to me if he realizes—he has such a bad temper."

Andy reaches out to kiss Caroline.

Page 311

"Quit freaking—your idiot husband doesn't know his ass from his face—even you said he was a complete dummy."

He kisses Caroline again.

"How about tomorrow—my place OK—lots of privacy."

She nods. Caroline's eyes focuses on his erect penis still sticking out of his jeans as if to let her know he owned her.

<u>Glass Owl</u>

Kyle slams the door as he enters the house. Howard pokes his head out the door of the library and grins broadly.

"I told you so."

Kyle glares at his father.

"Keep up with the secrets—and see if I help you when the chickens come home to roost—one named Eddie Kane."

Howard seems confused.

"Is that supposed to be some kind of allegorical comment about my behavior—because if it is—you know you're not in any position to comment about anything—given the reality your son is spending yet another night in a Portland jail for trying to kill someone. If I were you I'd think about that instead of wondering what I'm up to. Your son is facing serious jail time in the pen."

"No wonder Greg took his own life."

Kyle makes a lewd gesture at his father and heads upstairs without looking back as Howard begins laughing loudly.

<u>Pete's Cafe</u>

Daryl Anderson sighs as he looks at Brad and Jeremy sitting at one of the booths nearby. Both are in handcuffs.

"What the fuck were you idiots thinking?"

Standing several feet away are Kelly, Abby, Shirley, Julia Winthrop and Carrie. Brad angrily glares as Daryl as Carrie has a smug look on her face. Shirley gives Brad a cautious look.

"Screw you."

Daryl leans toward Brad.

Page 312

"Keep up that attitude and I'll ship you off to Portland so fast your head won't have time to spin. Want to bet how long it'll take for you to be *screwed* by some creepy pedophile with a hankering for young, good-looking teenage punks like yourself who think they're something special when they're not? Yeah, I'd zip it if I were you—or I'll lose what little patience I have left and schedule a date with the Portland police before you can blink."

Daryl looks at Jeremy.

"And you—I swear, why would you ever hit this prick—by now you should know better—McKinley's not worth it."

Brad looks at Jeremy with a sneer.

"Wait until you find out what I know."

Daryl suddenly turns around and grabs Brad by his shirt collar, harshly pulling him to his feet and looks at Kelly.

"Hey, can you call the Portland PD. I think they just inherited themselves a stupid rebel with a foolish cause."

Kelly looks at Brad, grins, and begins dialing. Brad looks panicked as he watches Kelly dial and sighs loudly.

"Wait—I'll."

Brad turns to look at Daryl.

"Look, I'm sorry about mouthing off. Things just got—I've been having a bad day—like a really bad day—terrible OK?"

Daryl rolls his eyes knowingly.

"Join the club buddy."

Brad mockingly wags his finger at Daryl.

"Anyway, look, how about we start over and talk?"

Daryl turns to look at Kelly.

<u>Tolling Bell Inn</u>

Chandra Stevenson unpacks the last of her luggage and turns around to look at the room. She smiles broadly.

"Well, I'm here in Marble Hills. Robert can't hide from me anymore like before. There's just too much at stake now."

She sighs loudly and walks to the balcony.

Page 313

Crestview Memorial Park Cemetery

People are gathered in front of an open grave as the casket of Tiffany Johnson is slowly lowered into the ground. Daryl turns to look at Gina Bentley. Her face seems wreathed in a perpetual smile as Caroline seems to notice. A few feet away he notices Kelly, Abby, Carrie, Jeremy, Simon, Elizabeth, Lana Jefferson, Natalie Standish, and Ashton Markway standing together. Lance is standing a few feet away with Caleb, Corey Bentley, and Brad. He notices Donna Markway looking at Brad with a look of hatred he'd never seen before in the shy young girl. Rounding out the teenage mourners are Genie, Lisa, Daphne and Tyler Van Pelt. Daryl turns his attention back to Gina. He shakes his head wondering if she could actually be responsible for her rival's death. He knows everyone is thinking the same thing as he sighs loudly. Gina and Caroline share a glance. Daryl shrugs.

Red Barn Gym

Damon is flipping through some paperwork as he notices Ross Harrison coming toward him. He smiles broadly.
"Come for a workout?"
Ross grins broadly.
"You bet I did."
They look at each other. Ross looks around.
"Where's Amanda?"
Damon shrugs.
"She's shopping in Portland I guess."
Ross smirks slyly.
"Oh, well."
They look at each other again.
"How about you lock the door to the gym?"
Damon grins slyly and glances at the door leading to the steam room nearby. He faces Ross once more with a smile.

"I was thinking the same thing."

Ross watches as Damon walks over to the front door and locks it. He turns to face Ross who makes a lewd gesture.

"Let's go."

They head toward the door of the steam room as Ross reaches out and aggressively pulls Damon closer and kisses him several times. They look at each other once more and sigh.

"You know, you're going to have to tell Amanda sooner or later you've been using her for appearances sake—and that goes for Lisa Taylor as well. I mean, really, how can you waste your time with either of them when I have more to offer you?"

Damon kisses Ross again.

"In due time—there's just something I have to do first and I need to use them as cover—at least for another month."

He shuts the door behind them.

"But for now just shut up and let me have a go at you."

Damon immediately kneels in front of Ross.

<u>Pete's Cafe</u>

Julia glances at the empty diner with a worried look and sighs loudly. A few seconds later she notices Eddie entering.

"Good morning."

Eddie acknowledges her as Todd Spencer follows close behind him. She smiles as they come toward the front counter together and sit down. Eddie seems happy. Julia notices.

"Well, I may finally have the answers I've always wondered about concerning what happened to my parents and I bet you anything that old man Madison knows plenty about it."

"Did he say anything?"

Eddie sighs.

"Of course not—not that I'd expect him to. But he knows something no doubt—I'd bet on it—bet everything I own."

Todd looks around.

"I guess everyone is at Tiffany Johnson's funeral?"

Julia shakes her head.

Page 315

"I didn't know her well—but no one should have to die that way—especially a young person—so absolutely tragic."

"Uh-huh—Simon didn't want to go—but I made him—I think he had flashbacks to his great-grandmother's funeral in Kittery two years ago and the debacle with the casket."

Julia seems confused. Todd sighs.

"The casket fell off the stand at the gravesite—and it opened—and the body fell out—made a scene for sure."

"I'd have an attitude too if I witnessed such a scene."

Todd nods in agreement.

"I try not to think about it—but things happen."

Julia glances at the front door. Todd and Eddie notices.

"Alden is in Portland."

They react to Julia's behavior.

"Seems Washington is a softy—he let Daryl or someone else—talk him into dropping the charges against Wesley."

Julia seems upset.

"But he said Wesley Madison should pay."

"I know. I know. That's what I said. But you know how Washington is—always trying to do the right thing—even if it blows up in his face—and this will—I assure you it will."

Eddie rolls his eyes and clenches his fist.

"Well, I'm not nearly as nice. I threatened old man Madison the other day—and if he thinks I'm kidding."

He pounds his fist on the counter.

"He'll find out otherwise. I swear I'm going to bring him to his knees—he's done too many people wrong in this town."

Todd pats Eddie on the back.

"Easy, Ed—deal OK—I don't want you to have a fatal coronary over that worthless excuse for a human being."

Eddie smirks.

"If anyone is going to bite it—it'll be Madison. I know things that could bring his empire down—really bad things."

Todd looks at Eddie curiously.

"What things?"

Eddie grins slyly.

"Nice try but the script is still being written on this story."
Todd looks at Julia and then at Eddie again.

<u>Portland</u>

Alden Washington sighs loudly as he watches Wesley Madison slowly coming toward him while Will McColl looks at them curiously. Will notices the tense look on Alden's face.

"He has something he wants to say to you."

Wesley looks at Will for a few seconds. Will looks at the two of them again and then walks away. He stops suddenly.

"No fighting—OK?"

Wesley gives Will a strange look and nervously turns to face Alden. He watches as Will joins Kyle in a nearby room.

"I—I—look I've had time to think—a lot of time."

Alden watches as Wesley digs his hands into the front pockets of his Levi's. He seems somewhat confused.

"I'm sorry—I'm sorry for what happened—I—I'm not sure why I did—I just—I just lost control and then it was hard."

He runs his fingers through his hair.

"I made a gigantic mistake."

Alden seems nervous as he continues staring at Wesley for a few seconds. He watches curiously as the teenager comes closer and extends his hand. They look at each other.

"I—I would like to put this behind."

Alden shakes Wesley's hand.

"I didn't mean for things to get out of hand."

He sighs loudly.

"Maybe we can work together and find out the truth."

Alden glances at Kyle and Will looking at them from the nearby room. He slowly runs his fingers through his hair.

"For what it's worth I never wanted any of this to happen either—but you made it impossible to look—look past it."

Wesley shrugs.

"I know what I did."

They look at each other in awkward silence.

Page **317**

Chandra looks at Robert Bennington curiously as she closes the door to her hotel room. She turns to face him.

"Look, you've got to go back to Philadelphia. If Lindsay even suspects—she'll send her crazy father out after you."

Chandra sighs.

"I'm not going anywhere—Lindsay is just going to have to get used to reality—I'm not going to be pushed aside."

Robert sighs loudly.

"Why are you here Chandra? I told you we were over. I made it quite clear—there is no *us* anymore—old news."

Chandra glances at her stomach.

"That was before—before everything changed."

Robert shakes his head.

"What are you talking about—what changed?"

Chandra pulls up her blouse exposing a huge bump. Robert seems shocked as he realizes the truth facing him.

"No—I always wore a condom—it can't be."

Chandra seems annoyed at his reaction.

"What? It can't be yours?"

Chandra picks up a folder. She throws it toward Robert.

"I know you'd deny you were the father—well, DNA tests don't lie. That, and the fact I haven't been with anyone else since we hooked up two years ago. Face it, there's no way out of this mess—you're going to be a proud daddy for the third time."

Robert flips through the paperwork.

"But I always used a condom—how could?"

Chandra wags her finger at him.

"Condoms are not always a hundred percent guaranteed. It probably broke when we were going at it in your bedroom while Lindsay and the kids were away—the timing is right."

Robert puts the folder down.

"OK—whatever you say—what now?"

Chandra seems annoyed.

"Well, it's simple. The next step is obvious. You have to tell Lindsay about us—it's not like this can be kept quiet for much longer—and if you think I'll keep quiet, well I won't."

Chandra grabs Robert's arm.

"Face it—your marriage to Lindsay Madison is over. It has been for a while now—you just can't face it—it's dead."

Robert leans back in the chair. Chandra seems annoyed.

"Wait—are you worried that—people will talk?"

She looks at the bump under her blouse.

"If this is about the fact my mother is black—get over it already—only idiots in the South think it's bad to have black blood flowing through your veins. Besides, pretty much it can be guaranteed our baby will look white—just look at me—I'm very light-skinned—I could almost pass for white if I had to."

Robert stands up.

"I could care less about what people think."

Chandra smirks.

"If not my background—then what is it Robert?"

Chandra rolls her eyes with contempt.

"What? You love Lindsay? Give me a break already. You have a funny way of showing it Robert—by sleeping around with every woman that showed any interest in you, including me."

Chandra smirks again.

"Seriously, did you assume I thought I was the first? I'm a lot of things but a fool I'm not. I've heard all the rumors about your "activities" behind Lindsay's back. Trust me, that sort of gossip doesn't stay in the background for long—it was an open secret at the office—everyone actually placed bets to see how fast you'd hook-up with every new female employee that had the stupidity to walk through the front doors of Patterson Archives. I was just one in a long line—in a long line of "friends with benefits" that fell for your charming bad-boy demeanor. And yeah—I'm sure I wasn't the only one who got snared—but I assure you I have no plans to terminate this pregnancy—so deal with the reality before you—you're going to be a proud daddy—again."

Robert walks to the balcony.

Page **319**

<u>Red Barn Gym</u>

Ross laughs as he watches Damon wipe his lips with a napkin. Damon stands and looks at himself in a huge mirror on the wall. He turns around to face Ross again and smirks slyly.

"There is just something about a college guy."

Ross laughs loudly.

"I knew you had a thing for me."

He laughs even louder.

"From the first day I stepped foot in your gym and you made a pass at me—there was no turning back afterwards."

Damon grabs Ross and they kiss passionately for a few seconds. They finally part and look at each other. Damon grins.

"I remember it well—I caught you leering at me and when Amanda turned her back I had to make my move—and did."

Ross laughs as he strokes Damon's cheek.

"I agreed to meet you at your place—and we fucked all night and into the next morning—such wonderful moments."

Damon kisses Ross again.

"Look, just so you know this situation isn't going to be happening much longer—and then we can be together."

Ross grins slyly.

"I know—I know—Amanda is your cover—but Lisa is a money pit—and you need to play it safe until you can convince her to have her rich pop invest in your gym—and then they."

Damon smiles broadly.

"And then I will kick her to the curb where she and all the other whores belong. Oh yeah—I *so* can't wait for that day."

They kiss again. Damon grins slyly.

"The mattress in my van is incredibly lonely by the way. I think it's time it's put to good use. Create some magic and a few good memories to boot—and make the earth move a bit. "

Ross makes a lewd gesture with his finger.

"I see where this is going."

Damon gleefully leads Ross outside seconds later.

Page 320

Denise Madison sighs loudly as she looks over at Miles Dandridge. He grins as he slips his fingers into her vagina.

"Yeah—I'm still good to go—again."

He pulls her toward him.

"Man, who'd ever think I'd be banging an older woman over and over instead of my usual targets—like who knew."

Denise laughs.

"It's me that should be giving compliments. Six times already this morning and counting—I like a man with drive."

Miles laughs.

"What can I say in my defense—except my dick knows what it wants—it won't be told no—it simply doesn't understand the word "no." It only understands "yes"—so deal already."

Denise gestures with her hand.

"I've never met a young man like you."

She watches as he slyly positions himself between her legs once again. He begins stroking her hair as he kisses her.

"You've got the strength of ten men—twenty maybe."

Miles laughs as he enters Denise.

Boston

Gary Glick glances over at where a young man is sitting. He grins broadly and shoves him lightly. He laughs loudly.

"Relax already—I told you Madison has no clue what I have planned for him—he'll never see this coming—never."

There is a moment of silence and then Patrick Glick turns to face Gary. He sighs loudly and seems nervous.

"I don't like this—so many things could go wrong."

Gary rolls his eyes seemingly annoyed.

"Like what exactly?"

"Like for starters we don't know if Madison will play our game. He could refuse—tell us to take a hike—call the cops."

Gary laughs knowingly.

"Not bloody likely. He'll play—or I go to "Plan B" of our next move—and then things get messy—really unpleasant."

"That's what I'm afraid of Gary."

Gary shoves Patrick again and rolls his eyes.

"Look, rich people deal with this sort of thing on a daily basis—if you have money you expect blackmail schemes to show their ugly heads once in a while—asking for guarantees."

"I don't like playing games."

"Too bad—I've got too much riding on this already."

Patrick gestures with his hand.

"Mom was right about you—she said you'd do anything to get what you wanted even if it meant ruining someone else's life in the process—but even she never guessed how far you were willing to go. I have a bad feeling about this—like a really bad feeling—and whenever I feel like this I—can't do—I won't."

Gary shakes his head and seems enraged.

"Enough—OK—we're going through with my plan and that's final—you can't back out now—I won't let you."

"But what if someone finds out?"

Gary seems irritated.

"No one knows OK—how would they know? We've been in Australia for the past twenty years. Relax OK? Chill out."

"But what if they find out?"

Gary grabs Patrick by the neck.

"This is a sure thing OK? If you fuck this up I swear I'll kill you—and you know I will. It wouldn't be the first time either."

He relaxes his grip on Patrick.

"Do we understand each other or not?"

Patrick glances at Gary nervously. He seems worried.

"What about Serena?"

Gary grins slyly.

"She's not going to be a problem anytime soon."

Patrick rubs his neck.

"What if she escapes from Lockerton?"

Gary waves his hand in the air.

"No one escapes from that place."

He looks at his cell phone as it begins to ring.

"Our dear sister is where she needs to be in order for this plan to work without interruption. Having her committed against her will was the only way to insure my plan couldn't fail."

Gary makes a lewd gesture with his finger.

"Got any more questions?"

Patrick shakes his head and walks away.

<u>Miami</u>

Calvin Whitney watches as a casket is carried toward a waiting hearse. He appears unusually calm as he watches the casket being loaded into the back of the hearse as two of his men wait nearby. The doors are closed and the driver turns to face Calvin. Calvin gestures to the two men to come toward him.

"This isn't the end but the beginning of a nightmare for his murderer. There will be no peace until he's avenged."

He watches as one of the two men nod in agreement.

<u>Portland</u>

Alden shakes hands with Wesley and watches as Kyle leads his son away. Kyle looks back a couple times at Alden. Will comes over a few seconds later and puts his hand on Alden's shoulder. He watches Wesley and Kyle leave. He shrugs.

"I hope you know what you're doing today. That kid has serious problems that only a psychiatric clinic can handle."

Alden nods as he faces Will.

"I hope so too—on a wing and a prayer."

He wrings his hands.

"Well, what do I have to lose? Oh right, he can try again to complete the job he started—and finish me off for good."

Alden nervously sighs again.

"Or maybe he really meant what he said? Wants to turn over a new leaf and be someone different for a change."

Page 323

"I hope so—for your sake—I'd hate to want to tell you 'I told you so' but couldn't because you were on a slab at the morgue with a bullet in your skull—or a knife in your chest."

"Thanks for sharing that image with me."

Will gives Alden a slight push.

"Just trying to do my part—you know—sort of get you in the mood for the worse—a little touch of Hollywood east."

Alden rolls his eyes at Will and sighs loudly.

"I'll remember that—uh-huh I will."

He turns to leave and then faces Will again.

"Hey, a couple of buddies and I are thinking of going hiking next week. Want to come? Might actually be fun?"

Will looks around the office and nods.

"Sure, why not. I can get someone to cover for me here at the precinct—and I can keep an eye on you too—just in case—you know, if someone who shall remain nameless should decide it's hunting season—except they conveniently forget to tell you."

"OK—if that's how you want to play it."

Will and Alden shake hands.

"Call me later this week and I'll let you know if the plans got sidetracked or if I'm in the hospital for some reason."

Will nods as Alden heads to the door. He stops and faces Will yet again with a grin. He runs his hands through his hair.

"You've been hiking before, right?"

Will smirks and waves his hand in the air.

"I may live in the city—but I'm no city boy—good with hiking, fishing and skydiving—I'm a regular **Daniel Boone**."

Alden wags his finger at Will.

"He lived in Kentucky not Maine."

Will gestures with his hand.

"Duh—no fool am I. I know all about American history and the colorful characters that populated the pages of my eight grade history textbook which made learning a little less boring in school as I made eyes at my secret crush. Unfortunately she thought I was a dork and fell hard for the football captain."

"I know that feeling all too well."

Will watches as Alden grins and leaves.

"Ah school—when my life was simple and easy and I didn't have the problems adulthood brings. If only I could go back."

He wipes sweat from his brow.

<u>Bentley Bathroom</u>

Gina walks into the bathroom and sighs loudly. She smiles broadly as she closes the door behind her. She smirks and turns to look at herself briefly in the mirror. Suddenly a look of horror comes over her a few seconds later. On the other side of the mirror she sees Tiffany Johnson staring back at her. Gina blinks twice seeming somewhat confused. Tiffany laughs loudly.

"That's right, bitch. *I'm back.*"

Gina screams. She turns around and sees Tiffany standing a few feet away from her. Gina begins backing away slowly.

TO BE CONTINUED

A Look at the 13th Episode

Miles and Denise continue threading on thin ice—Gary and Patrick arrive in Marble Hills with questionable plans that could possibly affect many lives—Gina gets an unpleasant visit from Tiffany who has revenge on her mind—Chandra and Robert both face their uncertain futures amid scandal—Alden, Eddie and Todd take a walk back on yesterday—Corinne pleads with Caleb not to make public their many sexual adventures—Kelly, Abby, Ashton and Tyler discuss Gina's possible motives in Tiffany's tragic demise—Greg's funeral has unexpected drama for several people in Marble Hills—Corey unexpectedly witnesses some strange behavior from his sister—Jarod and Caroline make the most of their time together—Miles hooks up with someone else's girlfriend on the sly—Corey and Corinne enjoy a moment together—Jason and Simon make plans to trap a killer—Clay and Eva's behavior irritates Daryl—Susan finds solace in Lance's arms—as a confrontation between sworn enemies turn deadly.

Strange World

<u>Bar Harbor</u>

Miles Dandridge grins broadly as he watches Denise Madison seductively licks the last remnants of seminal fluid from his penis as he gears up for yet another shoot. He smirks.

"Yep, I'm coming again."

Denise swallows several times as his dick throbs repeatedly inside her mouth for almost a minute. He laughs.

"Man, if my girlfriend ever found out—she would lose it and grab a knife—and pin my head in the town square."

Denise looks up at Miles with a sly grin. She sits down next to him on the sofa and strokes his chest for a few seconds.

"From what you told me she doesn't understand you—I don't see why you tolerate her at all—dump her. You could do so much better—you deserve a girlfriend that appreciates you and the fact you're so good between the sheets—a gem."

Miles makes a lewd gesture with his finger.

"You certainly know what you want from a guy like me. Since we met you haven't let up yet with your demands."

Denise rolls her eyes knowingly.

"My life is really drab—I'd be suicidal if I didn't have outside interests—the country club scene isn't my thing."

Denise sighs.

"Well, just let's say that I would rather spend my time in bed with a gorgeous hunk like yourself—than hanging out all day at the country club with a bunch of frigid old biddies."

Miles laughs loudly.

"What you really mean is that you'd rather spend your time being fucked by a healthy young man rather than being around a bunch of boring women more concerned about their upcoming golden years once their rich old hubby kicks off."

Denise nods.

"I couldn't have said it better myself."

Miles looks at Denise slyly.

"So, how do I compare to Jarod? He bags so many women every week—even I can't compare with him and trust me, I've fucked my share of babes—been around a lot—everywhere."

Denise leans over to kiss Miles. He kisses her back.

"Little insecure today—aren't we?"

Miles shrugs.

"Me? Nope. I'm just curious."

Denise pulls Miles roughly toward her and kisses him passionately as she slides her fingers over his exposed penis.

"Let's put it this way—I certainly wouldn't waste time with someone who was ill-equipped to service me thoroughly."

She kisses him again.

"That day we met I wanted you from the start. Nothing mattered to me except bedding you. From the minute I noticed the outline of your dick under your corduroys you had me."

Miles grins broadly.

"I had no intentions of denying you."

"I bet you're going to make some woman a wonderful husband one day—the best kind of husband—experienced."

Miles watches as Denise notices his erection becoming stiff again. He grins and glances at the bed nearby.

Page 328

<u>Standish Road</u>

Gary Glick glances over at his younger brother who seems to be ignoring him. He notices Marble Hills up ahead.

"We're here—the gameplay we discussed begins now."

Patrick Glick sighs.

"I don't think we should go through."

Gary grabs Patrick's arm.

"No one cares what you think. You'll do what I say or else I swear I'll—I have come too far to turn—no options left."

Patrick reacts.

"I have a bad feeling about your plan."

Without warning Gary punches Patrick in the jaw. They look at each other for a few seconds as Patrick rubs his chin.

"Don't make me angry—you wouldn't like me when I'm angry—things can happen—really bad things—deadly."

Patrick continues to rub his jaw.

"Look, I said I'll do it—I won't like it—but I'll do it."

Gary grins broadly.

<u>Bentley Bathroom</u>

Gina Bentley screams as she sees Tiffany Johnson staring back at her from the mirror. She looks around and turns to face the mirror again. Tiffany begins laughing mockingly at Gina.

"You killed me. But now I intend to make you pay dearly Gina—oh, you're *so* going to wish this was a bad dream."

Gina seems freaked as she stares directly at Tiffany. The apparition smirks slyly and quickly moves toward her.

"Thought you'd seen the last of me—but I wouldn't plan just yet for the happy ending you thought awaited you."

Gina sighs loudly.

"If this is about what happened to you?"

Tiffany leans forward and presses against the mirror and disappears suddenly. Gina sighs loudly seemingly relieved.

<u>Page **329**</u>

Chandra Stevenson sighs loudly as she watches Robert Bennington pace back and forth. She seems annoyed.

"Look, nothing is going to change. You and I are going to be parents shortly so just handle it—it's a done deal."

Robert stops and faces Chandra.

"But—this isn't—I can't."

Chandra seems annoyed.

"What? It's not part of the plan? You should have thought about that before you stuck your dick into me—and spilled."

Robert sighs.

"I—I—think this is a really bad—bad idea."

Chandra glances at the door.

"For you or for me—which is it?"

Robert shoves his hands into the front pocket of his Levi's as Chandra sighs loudly and looks down at her stomach.

"Look, why don't you just leave? I've had enough of your whining for one day—we have nothing more to talk about."

Robert turns to look at the door.

"Lindsay—she definitely won't give me another chance if she finds out you and I made a baby—she'll snap for sure."

Chandra walks to the door and opens it.

"So what—Lindsay is going to find out what a dog you really are anyway—like really soon—so if I were you I'd start looking for a hotel room—either that or a cardboard box."

Robert rolls his eyes.

"Think about Hart and Susan—they'll freak."

"I could say the same for you."

Chandra laughs.

"Oh—wait—was that before or after you stuck me with your dick—telling me how much Lindsay didn't really understand who you were—while you fucked me in your office and promised me you'd leave your frigid wife and marry me within a year."

Chandra sighs loudly and points to the door.

"Get out—I can't stand your whining one more second."

"Fine—if that's how you feel."

Robert walks toward the door. They look at each other silently for a few seconds. She angrily slams the door shut.

<u>Glass Owl</u>

Wesley Madison walks through the front door and stops suddenly. He turns to look around and sighs loudly.

"Well, you're home—finally."

Wesley ignores his father and heads towards the stairs without a word. Kyle Madison closes the front door.

"Home sweet home—huh?"

Howard Madison steps out from the entrance to the den and gives Kyle a nasty look. Kyle seems surprised and shrugs.

"Not now—it's been a hard day."

"I see Wesley is still as sullen as ever—maybe a longer stay in jail might have changed his fucked-up attitude."

Kyle seems irritated at the comment.

"I really don't need your two cents worth of advice right about now OK? Especially after—get off my back already."

Howard walks over to where Kyle is standing.

"Yeah—I get that—but like that has ever mattered to someone like me—this frigging mess is not going away."

He grabs Kyle by the shoulder.

"Greg's funeral is in one hour. Afterwards you and I have to talk—and yeah—I know you don't want to but so what."

Howard laughs.

"Time you grew a backbone—act like a man."

Kyle angrily jerks free of his father's grip and heads up the stairs. Howard slams his fist against the wall nearby.

"That stupid boy of mine really needs a strong hand to guide him—made a mess of everything—just like Greg."

He looks at a painting of his late wife nearby.

"This is your fault—all of it."

He turns and walks down the hallway.

Page 331

<u>Van</u>

Damon Mayo aggressively slams into Ross Harrison for a second time as Ross moans loudly and seems a bit annoyed.

"Harder—harder—you know I like it rough."

Damon grins broadly and slams into Ross with even more aggression than before as even louder moans of pleasure escapes from Ross's mouth. Damon smiles as he shoots his load.

"Still fucking that bratty kid Tyler Van Pelt?"

Ross shakes his head.

"No. He seemed to think we were a couple and didn't take kindly to me playing the field—told me to take a hike."

Damon laughs again.

"A righteous homo—just what the world needs."

Ross grins as Damon's penis begins throbbing violently.

"My thoughts exactly—I don't want a nice boyfriend."

Damon pulls out and leers at Ross.

"His loss is my gain."

Ross turns over to look at Damon and smiles.

<u>Pete's Cafe</u>

Todd Spencer, Eddie Kane and Julia Winthrop are at the counter talking. Todd glances at Eddie with a curious look.

"Well? Are you going to spill or not?"

Eddie smirks.

"I'll keep the mystery in play a bit longer."

Todd shoves Eddie gently.

"I'll remember that slight one day dear buddy."

Eddie laughs.

"*I'm so scared*—oh save me already."

Julia glances up to see Alden Washington entering the diner. She smiles broadly as he walks over to the counter.

"How did it go with Kyle's kid?"

Alden shrugs.

"Good—I guess. He and I had a talk."

Page 332

Todd and Eddie roll their eyes.

"Really—I didn't think the kid knew anything other than using his fists to insure his rep in town—*damn punk.*"

Alden grins.

"Is that the pot calling the kettle black?"

They look at each other for a few seconds. Alden turns to look at Julia and then glances curiously at the empty diner.

"Business is kind of slow—isn't it?"

Julia sighs.

"Everyone is still at Tiffany Johnson's funeral."

"Oh, that's right."

"There's nothing worse than losing a kid."

He notices Julia's reaction.

"Hey, I'm sorry. Wasn't thinking as usual—I'm such an idiot for sure—forgot about your daughter and husband."

Julia waves her hand.

"It's OK—it just made me think."

"Again I'm—I'm so sorry."

He sighs loudly.

"I can be really stupid sometimes."

Julia reaches out to pat Alden's hand as Todd and Eddie both notice but say nothing. The front door opens seconds later as a few people trickle into the diner. Eddie turns to look as Ashton Markway, Abby Marshall and Kelly Nelson enter and sit down at an empty booth. Shortly afterwards Tyler Van Pelt enters and joins them. Eddie turns back to face the others.

<u>Bar Harbor</u>

Marc Ryerson watches as Miles and Denise walk toward Denise's car. He grins as he watches them embrace and kiss.

"OK—first one down today—who's next?"

Miles waves as Denise drives away. He briefly notices Marc sitting in his car talking on his cell phone seemingly excited about something. Marc drives away shortly afterwards.

Page **333**

<u>Boardinghouse</u>

Corrine Massey impulsively wraps her arms around Caleb Winthrop and grins. He kisses her. They look at each other.

"I'm glad you finally decided to work me into your schedule. I was beginning to—to think I was old news."

Caleb laughs.

"My dick is in demand—what can I say."

He glances toward the bed.

"I've been quite busy if you must know the truth."

Corinne nods in agreement.

"I should be mad—but I know all too well how powerful a lure you are with us local girls—we can't tell you no."

Caleb pushes Corinne down on the bed.

"I like the way you think."

They kiss again.

<u>Pete's Cafe</u>

Tyler sighs loudly as he looks at the others. He seems upset and taps his fingers nervously. He glances at the door.

"It's unreal—I can't believe Tiffany's gone."

Kelly shrugs.

"I try not to think about death."

Tyler looks at the entrance of the diner again as if he's looking for someone. Abby notices as their eyes lock briefly.

"I know what you mean—when my grandpa died I realized only weeks afterwards he wasn't coming back—like ever—even after everyone told me he was gone I refused to face it."

He seems nervous.

"Do you think Gina killed Tiffany?"

Abby and Ashton look at each other upon hearing Tyler's remark. He watches as Kelly gives Abby an odd look.

"Well? Do you think she did it?"

Abby shrugs knowingly.

"I don't know."

Page 334

Tyler glances at the door again.

"But you're thinking it."

Ashton sighs.

"Well, she certainly is capable of it. Come on—just look what she did to Jennifer Parker—fucked her up royally."

Kelly seems confused.

"Who's Jennifer Parker?"

Tyler looks at Kelly. He sighs loudly.

"She was Jarod Keller's "girlfriend" or at least she thought so anyway. That was until Gina slept with Jarod. Jarod is a real toad. He's slept with just every girl in town. Uses women like disposable napkins—thinks he's all that and then some."

He rolls his eyes.

"Anyway—Jennifer like seriously lost it completely and tried to kill Gina. They had to send her to Marshland."

"What's Marshland?"

"A hospital for the criminally insane—a loony bin."

Abby sighs again.

"Jennifer swore as they put her in a straightjacket at the police station that she'd get Gina—but if Gina killed—oh."

Tyler smirks again.

"Wouldn't it be funny if they end up being roomies at Marshland after Gina is sent away for killing Tiffany?"

Ashton looks at Tyler.

"Hey, you seem to be enjoying what happened to Tiffany a little too much. This doesn't sound like you Tyler."

Tyler shrugs.

"Whatever—maybe I'm enjoying it—but Gina's always been really nasty to me—so it's not like there's any love lost."

He wipes sweat from his brow.

"Why should I feel bad for her?"

He looks at the door again.

"A person can get tired of being called names every day by people who are supposed to know better. Deal already."

Ashton turns to face the others.

Gary and Patrick look up at the building in front of them for a few seconds. Gary grabs his brother by the arm.

"So, you got the plan down perfectly? There's no room for careless mistakes—not even one—do you understand?"

Patrick shrugs.

"I got it—OK. I still think this won't work."

Gary sighs.

"For the last time—listen—Kyle Madison is loaded OK? He has more money than he will ever know what to do with."

Gary looks at the entrance of the inn again.

"As far as everyone is concerned you're the illegitimate son of my sister. And yeah—we'll play it up that my sister is dead and buried. Died from cancer in Sydney last year—went very quickly—and now you want to get to know your dear old dad before—who is all you have left now besides me of course."

Patrick nods in agreement.

"I know what I have to do—I just don't like it. Serena isn't my mother—she's my sister—and living in Sydney. Like really, come on Gary, this is too much like an old daytime soap opera from the 1980s where the writing was so overdone with all sorts of gimmicks and stunts to attract loyal viewers daily."

He sighs.

"Those old shows were all favorites of grandmother, but even she would admit they had nothing on what you're planning at the moment. And we both know she never missed an episode no matter what was going on around her. So, seriously, you actually think they'll believe I'm your nephew and not younger brother? The timing is off too if you forget. I'm a 26-year-old man not an 18-year-old kid. Who'll believe I'm a frigging teenager?"

Gary grabs Patrick roughly by the arm and spins him around. His eyes have a crazy look to them as he grimaces.

"I'm losing patience with your whining and your constant sermonizing—enough already. I'm sick of your attitude."

He seems ready to hit Patrick.

"I'm not going to say it again—this is the deal. You'll go along with it—or you'll live to regret it—in a bad way."

Patrick sighs loudly.

"What about DNA tests Gary? Kyle and his old man will ask for those—you can bet on that fact I guarantee you."

Gary grins slyly.

"Not a problem—I already had my buddy hack into several computer databases for DNA records. The minute your tests gets filed—he'll fix it so it reads like you're really the bastard relative of one of the richest families in America—and then we'll begin the second phase of my master plan to score Madison bucks."

He laughs slyly as they head to the entrance.

<u>Crestview Memorial Park Cemetery</u>

Howard, Kyle, Robert, and Lindsay Bennington are standing at the entrance of a private family crypt. Kyle glances up at the inscribed name on the entrance. In bold lettering it reads MADISON. He sighs. Behind him he notices Wesley seemingly lost as he appears focused on the iron gates a few feet away. Hart Bennington seems out of place too as he shuffles his feet on the marble floor—not really seeming to care that he should be showing respect or pretending to be respectful regardless.

"Fuck it."

Lindsay shoots Hart a nasty look as the casket comes into view. They all watch as it's slid into an empty crypt a few feet away. Susan Bennington turns to look at her mother as the door is sealed. She seems upset as she stares blankly ahead.

"Why can't I just see him one last time?"

Howard turns to look at Susan with a harsh glare. Susan glances briefly at her mother and then at Howard. She sighs.

"Well, when *he* kicks it—you don't have to worry. I don't want to see him before they shove his shriveled body into a concrete box like they just did Uncle Greg—count me out."

Lindsay reacts and gives Susan a sharp look.

"This isn't the time or the place."

Page 337

Howard's eyes meet Lindsay's briefly and from experience she knows he's not about to forget it. Lindsay sighs loudly and watches as her daughter disappears down the corridor past hundreds of other crypts that adorn the marble-lined walls and almost collides with Denise. They look at each other for a few seconds as Susan runs off. Kyle gives Denise an odd look as she comes toward where the others are still standing by Greg's sealed crypt. She ignores everyone's harsh stares and looks away.

<u>Boardinghouse</u>

Corinne watches as Caleb slowly pulls on his Levi's. She smiles approvingly as he notices. He grins broadly and winks.

"Uh-huh—you're not the last one today in case you're wondering—got to keep busy with all my adoring fans."

She laughs.

"Actually I was wondering about Tiffany Johnson."

Caleb seems slightly upset at the mentioning of Tiffany's name. He stops and looks at Corinne for a few seconds.

"I still can't believe she's gone. It seems unreal that I'll never see her again—like ever—and that Gina may have been responsible—never thought Gina was whacked—but now?"

Corinne seems suddenly upset.

"Don't you tell *that* girl we slept together? I don't want her coming after me—not after what happened with Tiffany."

"Come on, we don't know that Gina Bentley did anything to Tiffany Johnson—maybe it was just—just a lot of talk?"

Corinne walks to the door.

"Yeah right—and I'm related to **Jackie Onassis**."

Caleb smirks.

"Hasn't she been dead for like a thousand years or so?"

He notices her reaction.

"OK. OK. I won't tell anyone that I screwed you today."

He grins slyly.

"Unless they ask directly—then I have to spill."

Corinne looks at Caleb nervously.

Page **338**

"Promise me—please."

Caleb walks over to Corinne and hugs her.

"I won't say a thing Corinne. I promise. But I still think you're making nothing out of this deal with Gina Bentley."

"That's easy for you to say—you're a guy—she's just got it out for girls—specifically the ones who've been with you."

"But I've slept with half of Marble Hills?"

Corinne seems about to cry.

"Fine—make jokes—but if anything happens to me later today courtesy of your ex—you'll know I was right."

Caleb shrugs and sighs loudly.

<u>Pete's Cafe</u>

Eddie glances over where Kelly, Abby, Tyler, and Ashton are sitting. They seem embroiled in a heavy conversation.

"I wouldn't want to be a teenager again for anything—just look at that bunch over there—so much messy drama."

Alden laughs.

"In case you forgot we all had plenty of drama too."

Eddie nods.

"I know—that's why I'm so glad to be past that part of my life—being a kid is rough—even more now than previous."

Todd grins broadly.

"Yeah—but being a parent is no picnic either—and it's just a matter of time before your teenage daughters start attracting attention from every horny teenage boy in Marble Hills."

Eddie smirks.

"The first dude that's stupid enough to come sniffing round my precious daughters gets a free ticket to Crestview."

Todd laughs and jabs Eddie.

"Uh-huh—like you could ever kill anyone."

Eddie points his finger at Todd and winks.

"Keep thinking that way buddy. Just keep thinking you know everything about me. I've got a few secrets."

Todd gives Eddie a strange look as Alden notices.

Page 339

<u>Boardinghouse</u>

Caleb hugs Corinne again and they kiss passionately. He looks at her as they part. He grins broadly and looks away.

"I'm leaving at the end of the week."

He kisses Corinne again.

"You and I have to do this again before—before I go."

Corinne kisses Caleb lightly on the cheek as she slides her fingers over his erection straining against his jeans.

"You know I can't say no to you even if I wanted to."

He grins slyly.

"I figured as much."

She turns to leave. He sighs loudly.

"Look, seriously don't worry about Gina. She and I are just friends. Even when we were together she knew it wasn't serious between us—she knew I strayed—couldn't help myself."

"If you say so—but I still think she's bonkers."

Caleb digs his hands into the front pockets of his Levi's.

"She didn't kill Tiffany. It was just a crazy accident that happened to dear Tiffany—nothing more—things happen."

Corinne seems unconvinced.

<u>Bentley Driveway</u>

Gina stands by her car. She is about to open the door as Tiffany appears in front of her. Gina quickly takes a step back.

"Oh-oh—bet you didn't think I was real earlier?"

Tiffany smirks.

"It would be such a shame if something awful happened to you—you know like what happened to me at Standish Road."

Gina ignores Tiffany and gets into the car.

"Be really careful Gina—you just never know if someone might—someone might have tampered with—oh-oh."

Gina puts the keys in the ignition.

"Shut up—leave me alone already."

Page 340

Gina turns to see Corey Bentley standing a few feet away.

"Gina? Who were you talking to?"

"No one—I wasn't talking to anyone."

"It didn't seem like that just now?"

Gina gives Corey a harsh look and quickly pulls out of the driveway seconds later. He pulls out his cell phone.

<u>Standish Road</u>

Jason Anderson looks at the still-broken guardrail and then at the crash site on the jagged rocks below. He sighs.

"I wonder if what everyone says is true—did Gina Bentley do it—could she—could she have knocked off Tiffany?"

From behind he hears a sound and sees Simon Spencer looking at him. He has a smug look on his face.

"Could she—you bet she could do it. That girl is a loose cannon—and I don't mean that in a good way either."

They look at each other.

<u>Bar Harbor</u>

"Oh-oh—never thought I'd find you here of all places?"

Jarod Keller laughs at the remark.

"Really—seems to me you and I have been meeting a lot lately—dealing with so many issues—starting with how."

He grabs Caroline Bentley aggressively and they begin kissing passionately—only coming up for air after two long minutes. He laughs loudly as they finally part. She sighs and watches as he licks his lips seductively. She seems upset.

"I guess this means we're friends again?"

He makes a lewd gesture with his finger and grins.

"I thought you wanted to end it with me from what you told me not long ago—said you were planning a future with one of your pool boys—what's his name again—oh right I remember now—Adam Westerfeldt—wasn't it—or someone else?"

Caroline kisses Jarod again.

Page **341**

"Shut up already—he and I have agreed to be just friends with benefits—seems he slept with Gina on the sly and then tried to cover it up royally afterwards—saying she seduced him."

Jarod laughs.

"Gina can be quite persuasive if need be."

Caroline gives Jarod a nasty look.

"Don't think I've forgotten what happened between you and my daughter—using her like you did a while back?"

Jarod smirks.

"She had to grow up sooner or later."

Caroline pulls Jarod closer and kisses him.

"Well, you're just lucky you played my daughter exactly the way I told you to—I mean—what's a woman to do after catching her daughter in bed with her virile young lover?"

Jarod pushes her against his car.

"You followed me out to my car and pretended to give me a lecture—instead you told me to meet you later at that little motel just outside of town with the charming windmill."

Caroline grins.

"I thought you might be spent after Gina but you proved me wrong and then went that extra mile that night."

Jarod laughs loudly.

"Is it my fault my stamina knows no bounds?"

Caroline glances at Jarod's swelling erection bulging against his Lycra shorts. They look at each other.

"No—in fact I love your stamina—the times we've had since our first encounter—always making me beg for more."

Jarod smirks again.

"Good thing Gina never found out—it would've been quite a deal if she caught us together—scandalous actually."

Jarod makes a lewd gesture with his finger again.

"Maybe—but probably not—I think she's OK with how sexually active I've been—knows I've lied endlessly to her."

He shrugs again.

"Then she caught me with Tiffany and freaked—told me the idea of Tiffany and I together made her really sick."

Page **342**

Caroline kisses Jarod passionately and for a few seconds they go at it with intense dedication. He grins slyly.

"But I'm just an average guy—the girl I'm with now thinks I've been true to her also—though I'm beginning to think she can see through my lies—my rep is what it is around campus."

Caroline slides her hand inside Jarod's Lycra shorts.

"Enough with the trip down memory lane—how about you and me find a motel and work through our frustrations?"

Jarod grins broadly and nods.

"I like how you think—been a few hours—but a guy has needs—gotta keep busy—can never let up—like ever."

Caroline nods in agreement.

Glass Owl

"Do you mind telling me where you were earlier—not that I care really—but there's bound to be questions—especially given how we've been making the rounds lately with Wesley."

Denise turns to look at Kyle as they enter the mansion.

"I was in Boston if you must know—checking out the latest creations by Edna Malloy. You can call her if you like."

Kyle shrugs.

"If that's your story—stick to it—whatever."

Denise sighs and watches as Kyle heads upstairs.

"I think I need a break."

She reaches for her cell phone.

"This house is stifling."

Denise turns around and sees Wesley standing near the front door. He glances at the stairs with a confused look.

Portland

Miles grins broadly as he pushes Courtney Robson up against a wall. He penetrates her immediately and begins laughing loudly. Her loud moans drown out his laughter.

"If only Jarod knew."

He rams her again as she cries out.
"He actually believes he's besting you."
Miles notices Courtney's reaction.
"Would be pretty awkward if Jarod found us together?"
Courtney shrugs.
"What could he do?"
Miles grins as he begins cupping her breasts.
"Kill me for starters."
Courtney kisses Miles passionately as he slams her again.
"Jarod isn't a killer."
Miles smirks.
"Not that we know of anyway."
He pulls Courtney closer to him and laughs.
"But in my defense of sneaking around behind his back with his girl—if he won't watch what's his I will—oh-oh."
Seconds later he begins ejaculating.

Peabody Avenue

Corey watches as Corinne drives down the street. He begins following her until she stops in front of the entrance to Bradford Beach. He pulls up besides her. He grins casually and leers at her half-open blouse. She immediately notices his leer and gives him a knowing look. He continues leering at her.
"You're a hard one to find today."
Corinne seems confused.
"I don't know what you mean."
Corey shrugs.
"I heard you've been dallying around with my sister's ex since last week—Adam is nothing but trouble—be aware."
Corinne glances at the parking lot.
"Adam and I are just friends."
Corey reacts.
"Likely story no doubt."
He watches as she drives into the lot and parks. He walks over to her car after parking his car a few feet away.

"You're on the pill, right?"

Corinne nods.

"What do you think? You guys don't give us a moment's rest—always on the prowl—always wanting something."

Corey laughs.

"Deal with it—it's how we roll."

Seconds later he pushes her down in the backseat and slides his hand under her skirt right after. He grins slyly.

"You're wet already—perfect."

"I was just with Caleb."

Corey seems enraged by the comment.

<u>Pete's Cafe</u>

"So, you and old man Madison had it out—man he must have pissed himself—must have hated to be outplayed?"

Eddie laughs at Todd's comment.

"No—but just about—you should've seen the look on his face when he realized I knew about—oh man—sweet."

Todd sighs.

"Madison must be freaked with worry—you're the one person I'd assume he'd never think—would play dirty."

Eddie laughs again.

"It was just by chance I got this info to begin with—but I guess it pays to know people in high places—well, that and Clyde Bellingham is a good buddy of mine from my college days."

Alden looks at Eddie curiously.

"So, what are you going to do to Madison with info from your good friend in Castle Beach? Ruin him I assume?"

Eddie shrugs and winks at Julia.

<u>Standish Road</u>

Jason looks over the guardrail again and then slowly turns to face Simon once more. He wipes sweat from his brow.

"Well, is your pop going to look into it?"

Page 345

Jason shrugs.

"Yeah right—the Bentley family has a hold on him just as the Madisons do. It's a no-brainer—the case is *so* closed."

Simon looks down at the crash site.

"That isn't right—not right at all by any means."

Jason turns to face Simon.

"Tell me about it—but we both know if Gina caused Tiffany's accident nothing will be done about it on account—of all that money the Bentleys regularly pump into Marble Hills."

Simon grabs Jason by the arm.

"How about we force her to admit to it?"

Jason gives Simon a strange look.

"How would we get Gina Bentley to spill?"

Simon smirks slyly and shoves Jason.

Police Station

Clay Blankenship looks up as Eva Harper enters the room and silently closes the door behind her. He grins broadly.

"Back so soon?"

Eva stops suddenly.

"I could always leave if you think I'm a bother?"

She turns to leave as Clay seems panicked at her reaction.

"Hey, I was just being a jerk."

He grins broadly.

"Since when do you ever listen to me?"

Eva smiles slyly.

"Good point."

He watches as she walks over to where he is sitting. He stands up and hugs her warmly. He strokes her cheek with his hand. They kiss again as Clay pulls back suddenly.

"I've been thinking about you."

Eva glances at his erection straining against his Levi's.

"Is that so—seems to me you're just?"

Clay gestures with his hand.

"I've been lonely—what do you want from me?"

Eva kisses Clay.

"Tonight, you better not fall short."

Clay pulls Eva towards him once more.

"Bet you'll change your mind when you find out what's going through my mind right now—such filthy thoughts."

Eva runs her fingers through Clay's hair.

"Do tell—a girl needs to know everything that makes her boyfriend tick—especially the filthy thoughts in his brain."

Clay grins and whispers in Eva's ears. She smiles broadly.

"*Oh*—you're bad—like really, really bad."

Clay kisses Eva once more.

"Think you'll be able to handle my demands?"

Eva slides her fingers across Clay's lips.

"I can—the question is will you be able to handle me?"

Clay laughs loudly.

"Uh-huh—seems my girlfriend is making threats."

Eva seductively runs her fingers through Clay's hair again.

"Guilty."

Clay smirks broadly.

"Sounds like a challenge to me as well?"

"Well, you've been deprived of my body for several hours so I expect you to let the animal loose tonight no doubt."

Clay makes a lewd gesture with his finger.

"Not a problem—not a problem at all—will do."

Eva tousles Clay's hair for a few seconds.

"Did I tell you how much I like you?"

They begin kissing passionately as Daryl Anderson enters. He looks at them briefly with disgust and sighs loudly.

"Get a room you two."

They look at him and begin laughing.

"What's eating you?"

Daryl turns to look at Clay.

"Go home OK. Go fuck your girlfriend. It's obvious that's the only thing on your mind—have sex—like really soon."

Clay seems surprised by Daryl's behavior. He turns to look at Eva with a sly grin. They share a glance and laugh.

Page **347**

"Are you sure it's OK if I leave?"

Daryl nods.

"Go—before I change my mind."

Clay looks at Daryl again and then faces Eva.

"I guess I'm all yours."

Eva pulls Clay toward her and whispers in his ear.

"I guarantee when I'm through with you you'll be worn out Clay—won't have a muscle left that will be working."

Clay laughs.

"I'm down with that—love going to sleep completely worn out after a bout of intense sex with my girlfriend."

Eva gives Clay a light kiss and leads him to the door as he glances at Daryl several times without getting a response.

<u>Pirate's Cove</u>

Susan rolls over on the blanket and looks at Lance Weissmann. He smirks as he kisses her. He sits up and grins.

"A guy could get used to this—like really."

Susan sighs.

"I'm just so mad right now."

Lance seems confused.

"At me—huh—what did I do?"

Susan leans over and kisses Lance.

"Nothing—you're so sweet. It's my dumb family—ugh, I hate them. My grandfather is such a troll—truly wicked. I can't stand him if you must know—I wish he'd just drop dead."

Lance pulls Susan close to him and grins slyly.

"Well, I know what can relax you—again."

Susan watches as Lance kisses her ears and neck.

"How about we do it again?"

Susan smirks.

"This will be the second time today?"

Lance laughs loudly.

"I can handle it."

He slides his arms tightly around Susan's body.

Page 348

"Come on—just give it up to me again—you know you want to—and besides, I'm really good at making you relax."

Susan glances at Lance's erect penis. He smirks as he proudly shows it off to her. He grimaces for a few seconds.

"Have some pity on my poor lonely dick—it took your virginity, remember—it needs your respect—a lot of respect if the truth be known to make it feel up to the job yet again."

Susan strokes Lance's penis lightly.

"OK. OK. I guess I do owe you."

Lance laughs loudly and pulls Susan underneath his body within seconds and begins to kiss her passionately.

<u>Tolling Bell Inn</u>

Patrick looks at the computer again as Gary steps out of the bathroom with a towel wrapped around his waist.

"Well, how's it coming?"

Patrick sighs.

"Fine—just fine—but I think there's a glitch?"

Gary becomes irritated.

"Just do it—I'm tired of excuses—enough already."

Patrick turns to look at Gary.

"You do know that if they look closely they'll see I'm not who I pretend to be—and if that happens—it might backfire badly when the truth comes out? We could go to jail for fraud."

Gary rolls his eyes.

"Look, you look like a teenager. Who'll look past the idea that you could actually be Kyle Madison's bastard son?"

"Isn't there any other way to play this game with Kyle Madison? He might be willing if he knew what happened."

Gary shakes his head.

"No—there isn't. So, don't ask me again. This is the only way to get a chunk of that frigging Madison fortune."

He smiles.

"Besides, you'll be rich."

Gary makes a sound like a cash register ringing.

Page **349**

"Plus, every chick in town will want to be on your arm. I'm thinking that alone is worth playing this game—especially since we know you've been through a terrible dry spell lately."

Patrick rolls his eyes at Gary.

"I've never had a problem with bagging babes before. At least then I knew they liked me for me—now the only thing they'll like is my enormous bank account—but me not so much."

Gary rolls his eyes again.

"*Poor baby*—we should all be so unlucky."

Patrick stands up.

"I'm only doing this because you're forcing me."

Gary angrily shoves Patrick against the wall and watches as he stumbles to the floor. His rage is evident. He sighs.

"Who cares—you're nothing without me."

Patrick stands up.

Bradford Woods

Brad McKinley watches as Carrie Spaulding steps out of her car. He grins broadly as he slips his cell phone into his pocket and continues to watch her coming closer as his rage builds.

"She's got to be taught a lesson."

He waits until she begins walking toward some dense foliage and then approaches her from a nearby path.

"Seems like we're all alone—pity isn't it?"

Carrie spins around to face Brad and seems shocked to see him. Her face immediately becomes masked in anger.

"It was you who called earlier, wasn't it? I should've known Kelly Nelson would never stoop to such cowardly levels."

Brad grins and moves closer to Carrie.

"I do make a convincing Kelly Nelson if I do say so myself. Fuck that Prince Charming prick—such a pathetic loser."

Carrie looks at Brad suspiciously.

"What are you up to?"

Brad smirks.

"I think that should be pretty obvious."

She tries to run but he grabs her and wraps his muscular arms around her neck and spins her around violently several times. He laughs loudly as he sees a look of fear in her eyes.

"It seems we have some unfinished business that needs immediate attention—payback is sweet—for me anyways."

Carrie tries to free herself of Brad's grip but to no avail. He laughs loudly again as he slips his hand under her skirt and rips her underwear from her body. She screams in panic as he forces her down among the shrubs as his anger intensifies further.

"You damn filthy whore—thought you'd killed me didn't you—but not everything is what it seems—is it? And now you'll find out what happens when I'm crossed—it's time to pay."

He smirks as he hits her again.

"By the way, that concoction you gave me has worn off just so you know—yeah, that's right bitch—everything is working again—and now you'll come to respect me no doubt."

Carrie feels Brad's erection pressing against her body. He grins and angrily hits her again several times with his fists.

TO BE CONTINUED

A Look at the 14th Episode

Brad and Carrie's encounter takes a tragic turn—Lance and Susan share a peaceful moment together—Eddie tells his friends about his unpleasant encounter at Glass Owl with Howard—Chandra and Pierce plot schemes against her rivals—Gary continues to threaten Patrick over his unwillingness partake in Gary's schemes concerning Kyle—Clay and Eva grow closer—Jarod and Caroline dangerously play with fire in Bar Harbor—Wesley's suspicious behavior makes Jason curious about his true motives—Lindsay and Howard have words about Susan—Corey and Brad both play Elizabeth—Jarod smooth talks Natalie yet again—Alden and Wesley talk truce concerning their recent past—Robert's revelations about Chandra and his unborn child finally puts an end to his failed marriage with Lindsay once and for all—as Caleb has a truly frightening encounter with an unexpected visitor.

Episode 14
Scary Behavior

<u>Bradford Woods</u>

Brad McKinley laughs as he repeatedly rapes Carrie Spaulding over and over for ten minutes. Her screams are drowned out by his laughter. He finally stops and grins.

"I told you everything works."

He smirks as he notices her exposed vagina covered in semen and blood. He shoves his penis into his jeans.

"No whore is going to make a fool of me and get away with it. You brought this on yourself bitch—deal with it."

Carrie eyes cloud over in tears. She seems in shock over what just happened. She slowly tries to get up. Brad angrily pushes her back down on the ground. He laughs loudly.

"You'll tell no one about what just happened between us and if you do—I'll be forced to—I *will* fix you for good."

Carrie wipes tears from her eyes.

"You're going to jail—when I tell Daryl Anderson what you did to me—he'll lock you up and throw away the key."

Brad angrily grabs Carrie by the neck.

"I'm not playing with you bitch—I meant what I said."

Page **353**

He forces her into a chokehold and laughs gleefully.

"If you tell anyone I'll kill you—I swear I will."

Carrie tries to free herself from Brad's grip. But he strengthens his grip on her and begins to choke her while his rage intensifies as she continues to fight him. He grins broadly.

"*You* will not tell anyone—is that clear?"

Carrie continues to struggle.

"Fuck you."

Brad laughs.

"Yeah—this coming from the girl who just got fucked by me less than ten seconds ago—because of her big mouth."

"I'm going to tell—and then—I'll make you pay."

Brad grimaces and tightens his grip around Carrie's neck even further. He smiles as he notices her face turning blue.

"I swear—if I have to kill you—I will—but you won't say a word to anyone about what just happened—not a peep."

Carrie tries to fight Brad off once more but his strength overpowers her valiant efforts as she seems to weaken.

<u>Pirate's Cove</u>

Lance Weissmann smiles broadly as he glances at Susan Bennington lying next to him seemingly very happy.

"Any doubts about losing your virginity to me?"

Susan grins.

"None—but you're sweet to ask though. I'm glad you were my first. You stepped up after Brad failed. He let me down."

Lance smirks.

"I'm that kind of guy—so shoot me already."

Susan leans over and kisses Lance.

"I think I'll just kiss you."

Lance pulls Susan toward him.

"So, what's the deal with your family—what happened that got you into such a mood earlier? I was just wondering."

Susan rolls her eyes and sighs loudly.

"My grandfather disgusts me."

Page **354**

She makes a slashing gesture with her finger.

"Grandpa is a prick—plain and simple. He refused to let us see my uncle Greg one last time before they placed his casket in the crypt. It's like he wanted to hide something from us."

"I thought Greg Madison killed himself? His body wasn't damaged, was it? You know like a gunshot wound?"

Susan shrugs.

"No—he took a bunch of pills. He didn't off himself with a gun or something like that. Grandpa is just a total jerk."

"Maybe he just wanted to spare you?"

"Bull—my grandpa is a mean old man. He doesn't give a frigging damn about anyone's feelings but his own."

Susan sighs.

"I think there's more to my uncle's death than he's telling us—I think maybe—maybe Grandpa's involved somehow?"

"You think he killed your uncle?"

Susan looks away.

<u>Pete's Cafe</u>

"So, old man Madison is mixed up in some seriously badass mobster's death in Boston and now you know?"

Eddie Kane looks at Todd Spencer and nods.

"Uh-huh."

"Oh man, this just gets better and better. I swear I feel like I'm watching an old episode of *Pacific Palisades* or something."

Julia Winthrop sighs loudly.

"Bet he'll pay a pretty penny to keep that under wraps."

Eddie shrugs as he looks blankly at Julia.

"Don't matter to me really—I just want to find out if he messed with my folks—then I'll make the bastard pay."

Todd winks.

"I'll help—no need to ask."

Julia leans toward Alden Washington who suddenly seems somewhat preoccupied. They look at each other silently.

Page 355

Bradford Woods

Brad slowly stands up and looks down at Carrie lying at his feet. Her limp body lies before him in a twisted angle—her neck broken from their violent struggle just seconds earlier.

"It serves you right—filthy whore—death by my hand for what you did to me—I told you I'd get even and I did."

He grins broadly as he realizes his erection strains against the confines of his Levi's. He begins to laugh loudly.

"Well, at least I got one final stick before—before I broke your worthless neck—which you righteously deserved."

He laughs hysterically.

"Hateful bitch actually thought she could outsmart me."

He looks around.

"The question is—exactly what do I do with your frigging body now that I've reduced you to stinky worm food?"

He notices a small pond about twenty feet away.

"Perfect."

Brad picks up Carrie's limp body and carries it to her car nearby. He props her up in the driver's seat and smirks as he shuts the door. He stifles a laugh and looks back at the pond.

"Now, all I have to do is push her car into the pond and she's gone for good—yep, I think the bottom of the pond is a perfect place for that miserable bitch to rest for eternity."

Brad begins pushing the car toward the pond.

Tolling Bell Inn

Chandra Stevenson opens the door to see a stuffy-looking man standing before her dressed in an expensive suit.

"Pierce Colby I presume?"

He nods. She slowly steps aside as he walks into the hotel room. She immediately closes the door and faces him.

"How was the trip from Boston?"

Pierce shakes his head and sighs.

"No big deal—let's chat about why you called."

Chandra looks at him oddly.

"I want what is rightfully mine—if Robert Bennington won't leave his wife—I expect him to pay child support."

Pierce smirks.

"Well, from what you told me your boyfriend's money is tied up with the Madison family—and they have plenty."

Chandra nods in agreement.

"That's right—I need you to untie his part—of which will then go toward my unborn child's future—as should be."

Pierce looks around at the room.

"That shouldn't be a problem—I have special feelings toward the Madison family as I mentioned earlier."

Chandra nods again.

"I remember—something along the line of you not liking them—some deal about them fucking you over royally."

She gestures with her hand.

"That family deserves to be punished."

"What do you have in mind?"

Chandra wags her finger at Pierce.

"I want to crucify them."

"I know the feeling quite well."

Pierce seems angry.

"That family has been a thorn in my side for years."

Chandra grimaces.

"Well, I hope you know I don't care what you do to them as long as I get what's coming to me—I'm not picky."

Pierce looks at Chandra and winks at her.

"I understand."

Chandra looks worriedly at her expanding waistline. She seems upset as she looks at Pierce again and sighs.

"It shouldn't have been this way with Robert. He and I had something real—more real than he and Lindsay ever did."

Pierce opens his briefcase.

"Doesn't matter now—you must think about your baby's future first—sadly money means everything in this world."

Chandra seems upset at the comment.

Page 357

<u>Bradford Woods</u>

Brad watches with a smirk etched in his face as Carrie's car sinks to the bottom of Miller's Pond. He grins broadly.
"Good riddance—*bitch*."
He begins laughing and turns away.

<u>Tolling Bell Inn</u>

Patrick Glick looks at his bruised arm. He sighs as faces himself in the mirror. He brushes away hair from his eyes.
"Why am I doing this at this point in my life?"
He hears a sound from behind him. Gary Glick has a huge grin on his face as he casually walks into the room.
"Still think you have a choice—well, you don't."
Patrick rubs his bruised arm again.
"I—I didn't mean."
"Must we do this again?"
Gary grabs Patrick and spins him around.
"I swear if you fuck me over—I'll make sure you regret it in the worst possible way—and I'll enjoy every minute of it."
Patrick's face cloud over in fear.
"I'll do it—I said I would and I will—but that doesn't mean I have to like it—especially given how morally wrong it is."
Gary smirks.
"Who the fuck cares what you think—no one that's who in case you forgot—so get over it already—before I lose what little patience I have left concerning your sissy-ass behavior."
He walks away suddenly.

<u>Peabody Avenue</u>

Corey Bentley grins broadly as he slyly kisses Corinne Massey one final time before opening the door to his car.
"Thanks for a spectacular ride."

Page **358**

Corinne sighs.

"You and me—we go way back."

Corey smirks.

"Uh-huh."

He gets into his car and shuts the door.

"Talked to Wesley yet?"

Corinne shakes her head.

"I haven't heard from him since he was locked up."

Corey seems bothered. Corinne notices.

"Why?"

"He hasn't called me either."

He puts his keys into the ignition.

<u>Police Station</u>

Daryl Anderson looks up as the front door opens. He sees Denise Madison standing in front of him. He grins broadly.

"Well, aren't you a sight for sore eyes."

Denise grins.

"I was hoping you'd say that."

As he watches she opens her coat to reveal nothing underneath. He stands up—his erection is noticeable as he leads her into one of the back rooms and shuts the door.

<u>Blankenship Apartment</u>

Clay Blankenship sighs as he looks at Eva Harper. He pulls her closer to him. They kiss passionately for a few seconds.

"What are you trying to do? Kill me?"

Eva smirks.

"Kill a healthy guy like you?"

Clay laughs.

"You'll be the death of me one day."

Eva seductively slides her fingers around Clay's erection. He laughs as her fingers dance across his exposed penis.

"Should I be worried about my safety?"

Page 359

Eva kisses Clay several times.

"It depends how you look at it—so many ways to define the word safe nowadays—many ways—wouldn't you say?"

She kisses Clay again as he grins broadly.

"If you mean would I hurt you—no—but if you get injured during a bout of lovemaking—well, these things happen."

Clay laughs loudly.

"Sounds like I should be worried."

"I just want to make sure you know now that we're official from today forward—things could change drastically."

Clay seems confused. Eva grins broadly.

"Let's just say I plan to make sure you go to bed really tired a lot from now on—boyfriend duties will be in play."

Clay smirks knowingly.

"Is that so?"

Eva nods and then her face clouds over.

"Unless you cheat on me—then we'd be through."

Clay seems upset.

"I won't ever cheat on you."

Eva leans over to kiss Clay once again.

"I'm a one woman type of dude—and always have been. I don't mess around—not my style—I have no reason to."

Eva seems about to cry.

"You're so sweet—so sweet indeed."

She quickly wipes away a tear from her eye.

"What did I ever do to deserve someone like you?"

"You bedded me—told me you loved me—made me feel like I was something really special—and the rest is history."

Eva runs her fingers through Clay's hair.

<u>Bar Harbor</u>

Jarod Keller opens the door for Caroline Bentley as they leave the motel together. She turns back to face him.

"Thanks for today."

"You're certainly welcomed."

Caroline pulls Jarod toward her and kisses him.

"Glad you're also the type of guy that has no problem being with a married women—I so enjoyed our romp."

Jarod grins slyly.

"I like living on the edge."

They kiss again.

<u>Pete's Cafe</u>

Jason Anderson and Simon Spencer watch as Wesley Madison slowly comes toward where they are sitting.

"What do you want?"

Wesley sighs as he notices Jason's harsh behavior.

"You and I have to talk."

"I don't think so."

Wesley sighs loudly.

"Simon, do you mind if I speak to Jason privately. It'll only take a few minutes. And, no I'm not going to hit him."

Simon gives Wesley a strange look and stands up.

"I'll be over with my pop."

Jason nods as Wesley sits down opposite him.

"Look, I don't blame you for thinking I'm a prick. I was—I treated you like garbage—and there's no excuse."

"You threatened to kill me—that isn't something I can forget all that easily—and it wasn't just one time either."

Wesley glances around.

"I know what I did—and no words can change that. But I've had—I've had time to think—you know, being in jail—and I realized I've been a fucking asshole—like completely."

"No fucking kidding—you're a regular *Sherlock Holmes* all of a sudden aren't you Wesley Madison—so what gives?"

Jason sighs loudly.

"Why are you telling me all this crap?"

"Well, as I mentioned I had time to think and I know I've been a prick—and while I can't change the things I've said and done previous I'd like to apologize—for my stupid actions."

Page **361**

Jason looks at Wesley with a surprised look.

"*You*—you're apologizing to me for what you did?"

Wesley nods several times.

<u>Blankenship Apartment</u>

Clay walks to the kitchen clad only in a towel wrapped around his waist. Eva suddenly sneaks up behind him.

"Hey?"

The towel falls away.

"What if your mother came by?"

Eva grins as she slides her hand between Clay's legs. She pushes him up against the wall as she kisses him.

"She'd approve."

Clay laughs loudly.

"Somehow I don't think that's the way she'd react—she'd probably want to take a sharp knife to my pride and joy."

Eva kisses Clay passionately again.

"I'd protect you—defend your virile honor."

Clay laughs again.

"I'll just bet—seems right now you're determined to have your way with me regardless of the consequences later."

Eva begins kissing Clay's chest and continues to let her lips slide until it reaches his exposed penis. She grins broadly.

"Girlfriends have rights in case you forgot."

He grins.

"Uh-huh."

Clay watches as Eva kisses his penis again and stands up.

"Boyfriends have rights too."

Eva reaches out to stroke Clay's hair.

"You're everything to me—just so you know. I've never felt this way about anyone before and won't ever again."

"Not even that jerk you liked in high school?"

Eva rolls her eyes in mock anger.

"Especially not him—I may have loved him at one time but what we had was nothing like what you and I have."

Page 362

Clay grins broadly.

"You certainly know how to make a guy feel great about his self-worth—my ego just did some major back flips."

Eva kisses Clay again.

"You're special."

Clay seems confused.

"I hope you mean that in a good way. Not special as in a *Rain Man* type of way—which isn't very special whatsoever."

Eva smirks slyly.

"I meant it in a good way."

She hugs Clay.

<u>Glass Owl</u>

Lindsay Bennington quickly follows her father into the library. She shuts the door behind her. She seems angry.

"You're not to say anything to Susan. Is that clear?"

Howard Madison turns to face his daughter.

"She's a spoiled brat—the nerve she had talking to me like that at Crestview—that girl needs to know her place."

Lindsay rolls her eyes.

"She was upset—can you blame her?"

Howard sighs.

"Greg is dead—OK. I saw no reason to further make anyone relive that fact by seeing his body inside a casket."

Lindsay grabs his arm.

"I meant what I said—if you bother Susan you'll regret it."

Howard laughs and jerks free of his daughter's grip.

"Oh really, is that so Lindsay? Is that a threat dear daughter? Inquiring minds would like to know details."

Lindsay glances at the front door.

"In case you haven't noticed it yet, Susan has the Madison blood running through her veins—and the Madison temper."

Howard rolls his eyes.

"Tell me something I don't know already."

Lindsay smiles slightly.

"Susan not only has the Madison blood and temper—she has the Madison eye for cruel revenge—she can get quite violent if provoked—and you'd be best warned beforehand."

Howard seems confused.

"Wait—are you trying to say in your roundabout way that my granddaughter is actually capable of hurting someone?"

Lindsay gives her father a knowing look.

"You said it—I didn't."

They look at each other.

Bradford Woods

Brad smiles broadly as he surveys the area. No trace of Carrie's car is left. He turns to look at Miller's Pond.

"Damn whore thought she had me—well—bet she doesn't think so now. Imagine her nerve coming up against me."

He laughs loudly with glee.

Tolling Bell Inn

Chandra watches as Pierce packs up several cloth-covered folders casually spread out across the coffee table nearby.

"Bennington is going to regret his actions—when I get through with him he'll beg for mercy and then some."

Chandra seems nervous.

"What do you think the Madisons will do?"

Pierce shrugs.

"What can they do? Robert Bennington will have to deal immediately with the dissolution of his failing marriage."

Pierce grins as he looks at the folders. He slowly walks over to where Chandra is standing. He extends his hand.

"Lindsay Bennington will not want to save her pitiful marriage after her husband's infidelities are exposed."

They look at each other.

"Bennington should've kept it in his pants—as should Kyle Madison before him. Hate those wretched Madisons—I do."

Page **364**

He turns away.

"It's time he learned the hard way."

He grabs his briefcases and smiles broadly.

"There's a price to pay."

He walks to the door and faces Chandra again.

"Trust me Chandra, I don't get the big bucks because I'm a nice guy—I will get you what you want—count on it—and if Bennington loses everything he loves—well, so damn what."

He opens the door and leaves.

<u>Parking Lot</u>

As the car rocks back and forth, joyful laughter can be heard coming from inside amid sounds of loud moaning.

"I forgot to take it today—sorry."

Corey looks at Elizabeth Pendleton angrily.

"You stupid whore—you waited until I was inside you to tell me that? Of all the stupid things you women do."

Elizabeth seems upset.

"I—I didn't want to make you mad."

Corey pulls out and rolls over.

"You better not let me hear you're late. I swear if you even think of trapping me with a bastard—I'll beat you up."

"I'm not trying to trap you—I'm sorry."

Corey zips up his Levi's.

"Just make sure—damn it—of all the stupid moves."

Elizabeth pulls the blanket up around her.

"I said I was sorry—OK?"

"So what—is that supposed to make everything all right despite you being so careless? You women are all alike."

He pushes reaches out to slap her.

"I swear you women all read the same manual—always working some devious angle—hoping one day you'll cleverly snare us with a brat—snare some guy into marrying you."

Elizabeth begins to cry.

"I didn't—I swear—please believe me?"

Page 365

Corey looks at Elizabeth.

"Tell it to someone who cares—I don't."

He climbs out of the backseat.

"You're just a filthy whore like everyone said."

He slams the door shut.

<u>Pete's Cafe</u>

Simon, Todd, Eddie, Alden, and Julia watch from the front counter as Wesley and Jason shake hands. Simon seems confused at the scene taking place several feet away.

"I wonder what that's about."

Eddie sighs.

"Uh-huh."

They watch as Wesley comes toward them while Jason follows right behind. Julia seems nervous. Alden sighs loudly.

"Hey."

Alden shrugs as Wesley looks directly at him.

"Look, I'm not here to cause trouble—you and I need to talk—like seriously right now—it's important—like really."

Alden glances at the others briefly and motions Wesley to follow him outside. Todd grabs Alden by the arm.

"Are you sure about this?"

Alden turns to face Todd and nods.

"I'm good."

Alden follows Wesley outside. Todd turns to Jason who still seems somewhat in a state of shock. Todd sighs loudly.

"What just happened between you two?"

Jason shrugs several times.

"I think Wesley had some sort of epiphany in the slammer. I can't explain it any other way—not right now anyway."

Todd seems speechless and sighs.

"Are you for real?"

Jason turns to look at Eddie. He nods.

"Wesley just apologized for every nasty thing he ever did to me and believe me there was plenty he did that was bad."

Page 366

"So, you're telling me that Kyle Madison's rotten spoiled punk kid actually learned something for a change?"

Jason nods. Eddie shakes his head.

"Well, I don't buy it. The kid is evil—like bad news in every way the word can be used—serious no good piece of trash."

"Or, he realized the truth about life?"

Eddie turns to look at Julia.

<u>Blankenship Apartment</u>

Clay sighs heavily and looks over at Eva. She grins broadly and slides her fingers across his chest and grins slyly.

"Up for a fourth round?"

Clay laughs.

<u>Bar Harbor</u>

Jarod grins as he looks at Natalie Standish coming toward him from the bathroom. She's completely naked. She notices the look on his face as she climbs into bed next to him.

"What are you thinking?"

Jarod grins.

"How I can't wait to fuck you again."

"You're incorrigible."

Jarod laughs.

"What's it to you?"

He pulls her toward him.

"Just so you know I really appreciate you coming all this way today just so we could hook-up again like old times."

Natalie kisses Jarod.

"Like I'd dare deny you anything?"

She kisses him again.

"I can't ever say no to my first—I owe you."

He grins broadly.

"Well, it was your own fault if I recall—telling me you wouldn't have sex until I married you—big mistake."

Page **367**

Natalie gives Jarod an odd look.

"You took me out to Bradford Woods the very next day and seduced me anyway—telling me later you had no intentions of ever getting married as I hoped but every intention of fucking me. It was such a sweet thing to say to a girl like me—so sweet indeed to know you felt that strongly about us having sex."

Jarod smirks.

"I was really horny that afternoon. You were a tease and there's so much a guy like me could take. I had no choice."

He laughs.

"But you knew I had a rep—I was the biggest player in Marble Hills—and to say you wouldn't put out was very insulting to me—it was a challenge no doubt. I had to have you."

Natalie smiles slyly.

"How is Courtney doing?"

Jarod shrugs.

"We understand each other."

Natalie looks at Jarod curiously and grins.

"I bet she doesn't know about you and your outside interests—like me and all my friends—like Lana's mother?"

Jarod kisses Natalie again.

"Nope—she foolishly thinks we're in a committed adult relationship. Well, she is anyway I assume—me, not so much."

Natalie sighs.

"Does she think the two of you will get married?"

Jarod makes a lewd gesture with his finger.

"I'm not the marrying type—I thought I made that clear when I popped you last year—say no to marriage—blah."

Natalie seems amused at the statement.

"You did—I just thought—she might turn you. Make you want to walk down the aisle and start a family with her."

Jarod pulls Natalie under him.

"I'm a fuck them and leave them type of guy—no need for me to commit—if Courtney assumes I will—then whatever."

He begins kissing Natalie passionately.

<u>Maple Avenue</u>

Brad sees Elizabeth standing by the corner of the street. He grins broadly and leers at her as he pulls over. He laughs.

"How much is your going rate?"

Elizabeth looks at Brad and seems about to cry. He laughs loudly as she turns away. He calls out to her again.

"Was it something I said?"

Elizabeth looks at Brad.

"I hate you."

Brad reacts.

"What did I do?"

Elizabeth wipes a tear away.

"Did something happen earlier?"

He watches as she looks down at her skirt.

"No."

Brad smirks.

"How about we get a bite to eat?"

Elizabeth sighs.

"Where do you want to go?"

Brad grins broadly as she gets into his car. He continues leering at her for several seconds. She notices his behavior.

"How about we stop by Lighthouse Grill?"

Elizabeth nods and looks away.

<u>Pete's Cafe</u>

Alden glances at Wesley curiously. Wesley runs his hands through his hair as he paces back and forth nervously.

"Look man, I'm on the level. I'm sorry for the ass I made of myself and for what I did to you—I seriously—it was my bad."

Alden sighs.

"I'm willing to forget what happened—but just so you know—I didn't kill your aunt. Marah and I were not having problems when she turned up dead—and I didn't know she was pregnant. I'm a lot of things but I'm no killer—no way."

Page 369

Wesley looks at Alden sharply.

"I believe you—had plenty of time to think about everything I'd heard over the years—and if you killed her it wouldn't have made sense for you to be stupid enough to subject yourself to a polygraph test when those things are not always accurate knowing results can be skewed or manipulated."

Alden sighs again.

"I only left town because everyone thought I did it."

Wesley looks around.

"If you didn't do it then someone else did. She just didn't end up dead at Glass Owl the morning after the prom. The question is who did it if it wasn't you that killed her? Someone knows what happened to my aunt that night. I'd bet on it."

Alden seems uneasy.

"She didn't have any enemies. She was a senior in high school for God's sakes—who'd want to kill her—a kid?"

Wesley rolls his eyes.

"Some dude who was pissed she hooked up with you and not him—or maybe he thought he was the father?"

Alden digs his hands into the front pockets of his Levi's.

"I was the only other guy she ever slept with besides Daryl Anderson after he dumped her for Carmen Pendleton."

Wesley glances inside the diner.

"What about Carmen Pendleton?"

Alden shrugs.

"No—she didn't have a reason. She took Daryl away from Marah. Why kill her after insulting her the way she did?"

Wesley leans against the wall.

"OK—well, what about someone else in town who didn't like her—because she was a Madison and filthy rich."

Alden gestures with his hand.

"In that case everyone in Marble Hills would be suspect to murder—no one likes you guys—which you already know."

Wesley looks at Alden curiously.

"Look man, I'm really trying to see past our—our issues OK—the least you can do is to try to work with me on this?"

"And I appreciate that—but Daryl Anderson's pop pretty much closed the case once I was cleared. I've always wondered why your grandpa didn't go crazy for justice—but in those days I was just happy not to be in jail facing the death penalty."

Wesley glances inside the diner again.

"Well, what about your friends—think they might know something—know of someone who might have a motive?"

Alden glances inside the diner.

"They might—maybe—I never asked."

Wesley opens the door.

"No time like the present."

Alden looks at Wesley oddly and follows him back into the diner. As they enter a few curious patrons look up and seem somewhat confused at seeing them together but say nothing.

Glass Owl

The front door opens and as Susan closes the door she sees Howard and Lindsay looking at her curiously. She sighs.

"I'm not speaking to *him*—drop dead."

Howard watches as Susan walks past him and heads upstairs. Lindsay turns to look at her father angrily.

"Not one word—or else."

Howard grabs Lindsay by the arm.

"That child of yours needs to learn some manners—like really soon before she—she's getting on my nerves."

Lindsay jerks free of her father's grip.

"You don't want to go there daddy—not after how you made a mess of being a parent yourself or did you forget."

Howard seems upset.

"How dare you talk to me like this? I won't stand for such talk from my children—after everything I've done."

Lindsay smiles slyly.

"Seriously, you can say that with a straight face—or have you forgotten Greg already—and what happened?"

Howard reacts.

Page 371

"That boy had problems."

"Keep telling yourself that—but no one believes those lies but you. Face it daddy—*you* and only *you* are to blame for Greg's tragic problems—all of them—and if you think I'll let you tell me how to raise my daughter—you'd better think again."

Howard grabs Lindsay again.

"Is that how you really feel about?"

Lindsay jerks free again.

"Yes—that's how I feel—deal with it."

Howard looks at Lindsay harshly.

"This isn't over yet."

He storms off toward the den as Lindsay seems glad that she forced him to face hard facts. She smiles triumphantly.

"Well, he had that coming for quite some time."

She glances at the stairs.

"Now to deal with Susan—and her attitude."

As she's about to head up the stairs she hears the front door opening and turns to see Robert Bennington entering.

"We have to talk."

Lindsay sighs.

"Not now—I have to deal with something."

Robert slowly walks over to where Lindsay is standing.

"It can't wait."

Lindsay sighs again.

"What is it now—you want to lecture me on ignoring our marriage again—don't bother—I'm otherwise occupied."

Robert looks at the front door.

"It's Chandra."

Lindsay rolls her eyes.

"What is it now? Oh, let me guess. She's mad that you're no longer in Philly to explore the bed in her apartment?"

Robert reacts.

"She's here. Chandra is here in Marble Hills."

Lindsay spins around to face Robert.

"That *bitch* is here in town? Seems I underestimated that whore. That worthless slut just doesn't give up, does she?"

Page **372**

Robert sighs loudly.

"She's pregnant."

Lindsay seems in shock.

"What did you say?"

Robert sighs loudly again.

"Chandra Stevenson is carrying my child."

Lindsay seems about to faint.

"My God—just when I think things can't get worse."

Robert reaches out to touch Lindsay. She pulls away and looks at him in disgust. She leans against the door frame.

"Don't touch me—don't you ever touch me again."

Lindsay heads toward the stairs and stops—then faces Robert with an angry look on her face. She looks at the stairs.

"We're through."

Robert seems shocked.

"I want you out of this house in one hour—no later."

Lindsay seems to be holding back tears as she turns and heads up the stairs in a rush. Robert shakes his head.

<u>Parking Lot</u>

Brad laughs as he pulls out of Elizabeth. She looks up at him slightly stunned. He grins as he sees her expression.

"Oh yeah—I've got my mojo back."

Elizabeth smiles broadly.

"I'm glad I could be of service."

Brad smirks.

"Well, I did buy you a cheeseburger—and in my book that constitutes payment—so, you know what that makes you."

Elizabeth seems upset.

"You guys are all the same. All you care about is slamming us girls—treating us like pieces of meat to be traded."

Brad laughs loudly.

"And this only now occurred to you? Come on, you've been passed around endlessly to every guy in Marble Hills."

Brad smirks slyly.

Page 373

"Not that you or any of the other whores in town have a choice in this matter. It's just the way things are—face it."

Elizabeth sits up.

"You're a toad."

Brad pulls Elizabeth under him.

"It is what it is—just deal with it already."

He begins kissing her.

"I'm definitely up for another round."

Seconds later he effortlessly penetrates her again and begins laughing as she falls for his charms once more.

"Come on—what the big deal—it's not like we don't show you girls a good time for putting out as often as you do?"

Elizabeth turns her face away from Brad.

"You disgust me."

At that moment Brad ejaculates.

Blankenship Apartment

Clay sighs as he tries to catch his breath. He is pinned under Eva. He sighs again and grins as he takes a deep breath.

"I'm spent."

She begins to trace her finger across his chest.

"But you said?"

Clay gestures with his hand.

"I'm at death's door. I've got nothing left to give. I'm seriously drained—tired and sleepy without a doubt."

Eva leans over and kisses Clay.

"I guess four times is enough for one day."

Clay smiles broadly.

"You think."

Eva runs her fingers through his hair.

"Well, now that I know you're weak and helpless—maybe it's time you and I—reorganize our plans for the future?"

Clay reacts.

"No one said I was helpless."

Eva kisses Clay on the cheek and smirks.

"I'm on top of you—you can't move—I'd say you're pretty much helpless Clay—unless you can say differently?"

Clay shakes his head.

"Good point—I'm beat and should know it."

He looks around.

"Well, now that you've made it quite clear that you've incapacitated me—what now? I'm not good for anything."

Eva kisses Clay on the cheek again.

"Well, what if I asked you something you've never been asked before—something that I feel is important?"

Clay rolls his eyes.

"That might be pretty hard—I've been around the block a few times—played the field and saw a lot of the good life."

Eva slides her fingers around Clay's neck and kisses him passionately. He returns her affections immediately.

"I think by now it's no secret how I feel about you."

Clay nods several times.

"Well, what if I asked you a question—a very personal question that could change everything between us from today onward—what would you say if I asked a specific question."

Clay looks at Eva curiously.

"Are you asking me to marry you?"

Eva nods as she tousles Clay's hair repeatedly.

"What if I was—would you say yes?"

Clay looks at Eva curiously.

"You want me that much—even with all my faults?"

Eva grins broadly and nods.

"I do—I do."

Clay sighs loudly and winks.

"I have to think about it."

Eva leans over and kisses Clay once more.

"Will you marry me or not?"

Clay sits up in bed.

"I said I'll have to think about it a bit."

Eva pushes him down on the bed as he begins laughing.

"I want to know this instant."

Page 375

Clay laughs loudly.

"Hey, it's your funeral if you think I'm a catch. But since you're asking—yes—I say yes. I know a good deal no doubt."

Eva throws her arms around Clay and hugs him.

"Hey—hey—be careful with the merchandise—I'm still quite weak from our encounter earlier—lots of TLC needed."

Eva looks at Clay and seems about to cry.

"I'll be the best wife."

Clay slyly looks at the door.

"What if I want to have a mistress on the side?"

Eva looks at Clay oddly. He winks.

"I think I'll be good with two or three."

Eva runs her fingers through Clay's hair again.

"No mistress—I won't allow it."

Clay grins slyly.

"Who said I was asking."

Eva pretends to slap Clay.

"I won't allow it—no mistresses—end of story."

Clay slides his fingers across Eva's cheek.

"What about babies?"

Eva nods several times.

"I'm game for motherhood."

Clay sits up in bed again and reaches for his cell phone.

"I think you should tell your mother the good news on account she likes me—been hinting for months now."

Eva grabs Clay's outstretched arm.

"You'll do no such thing."

He laughs as she pulls him toward her.

"But she likes me?"

Eva grabs the cell phone from Clay's hand.

"I'll tell her later."

Clay glances at the cell phone again and grins.

"Your mother and I are really tight."

Eva runs her fingers through Clay's hair and smiles as he seems pleased by the comment. She tousles his hair.

"Uh-huh—I know. She thinks you're good for me."

Page **376**

"From the moment I saw you spill that huge cup of soda all over yourself at that baseball game in Boston two years ago I fell in love with you—there's just something about a man that's terribly clumsy—something special through and through."

"I'm not clumsy. I can easily handle my own if need be."

Eva slowly slides her finger across Clay's lips.

"I say differently."

She leans over to kiss him again.

<u>Boardinghouse</u>

Caleb Winthrop grins broadly as he walks to the door and opens it. He's clad only boxer briefs as the door swings open.

"You're late—*huh*."

He suddenly seems in shock.

"*You*—what the hell are you doing here?"

Without warning he's stabbed in the heart with a butcher knife several times. He falls backwards and collapses on the sofa as blood gushes from the massive wound in his chest.

TO BE CONTINUED

A Look at the 15th Episode

Clay and Eva spend a quiet moment together—Lindsay and Robert's marriage ends without much fanfare—Brad lays down the law with Elizabeth concerning their casual sexual encounters—Lana finds Caleb—Wesley is confused that his aunt's death seems unsolvable—Daryl deals with yet another death in Marble Hills—Brad encounters hostility from Genie and sets a new plan in motion—Corinne's unaware she's being followed which leads to tragedy—Wesley and Alden discuss strategy—Julia gets an unexpected call from Daryl—Eldon's mobster brother plans a diabolical revenge against his brother's killer—Ashton stumbles upon a murder scene—Kyle and Howard have it out over child rearing issues concerning Wesley—Julia faces the reality over Caleb's tragic death—Juan heads to Miami for a funeral as Faye wonders about his whereabouts—Brad works his sly charms on Natalie—Kyle and Lindsay bond over their failed marriages—as a murderer strikes a third and fourth victim.

Episode 15
Bump in the Night

<u>Blankenship Apartment</u>

Eva Harper kisses Clay Blankenship lightly on the lips and slowly runs her fingers through his hair. He grins broadly.

"So, you have a thing for clumsy men?"

Eva kisses Clay again.

"Do you want to make something of it?"

Clay smirks.

"Me? No. I'm too weak to fight."

Eva runs her fingers through Clay's hair again.

"I meant what I said before—I'll be the best wife—always there for you in times of need—willing to help whenever."

Clay rolls his eyes.

"I'll hold you to that—I'm not a forgetful type of guy—and I do need lots of help—especially being so clumsy and all."

Eva looks around at the apartment and smiles.

"I stand by what I said."

Clay shoots Eva a knowing look. Eva shrugs.

"How does it feel to have your girlfriend want you so much? One who isn't shy to show exactly how she feels?"

Clay gestures with his hand.

"Oh, I'm still not sure—this mistress thing could be deal breaker—a guy like me needs variety—blondes specifically."

Eva kisses Clay and looks into his eyes.

"Like I said I won't allow it."

Clay grins slyly.

"I can't promise I won't play around on you—especially having slept with over a thousand women last year."

"I demand my husband to be faithful."

Clay sits up and pulls Eva to him. He hugs her.

"It's a deal. I'm all yours."

They begin kissing once more.

Glass Owl

Lindsay Bennington watches with a scowl on her face as Robert Bennington walks past her with a suitcase. He slings a garment bag over his shoulder. He stops and faces her.

"Lindsay—can't we talk?"

"Goodbye."

He turns to leave.

Parking Lot

Elizabeth Pendleton sighs as she watches Brad McKinley shove his penis into his Levi's and zips up. She seems upset at his indifferent attitude. He turns to face her with a sly grin.

"It's nice that you don't charge."

He laughs.

"You are definitely one of the easiest whores in town by far. You're always willing to spread your legs—always."

He laughs again.

"Trust me—it's much appreciated by us guys."

He walks over to where she's standing.

"Come on—you knew the minute you gave it up initially you'd be targeted by every horny guy in town for a piece."

Elizabeth rolls her eyes.

"I'm not a whore—stop calling me that."

Brad laughs loudly.

"Whatever."

He makes a lewd gesture with his finger and stops—then faces Elizabeth again. He watches her reaction and smirks.

"You and me—tomorrow morning in the backseat of my car—we've got another dance to attend. Be ready to play."

"I'll think about it."

Brad seems annoyed.

<u>Boardinghouse</u>

Lana Jefferson walks toward the open door. She seems confused that it is wide open. She peeks inside. A few feet away she sees Caleb Winthrop lying on the sofa with a butcher knife sticking out of his chest. Blood is everywhere. She screams and begins running down the hallway in a panicked frenzy.

<u>Pete's Cafe</u>

Wesley Madison looks at the mixed reactions of Simon Spencer, Eddie Kane and Todd Spencer as Julia Winthrop and Alden Washington stands nearby. He gestures with his hand.

"None of you heard anything?"

Eddie stands up and faces Wesley.

"What happened to Marah Madison was really horrendous because we all liked her—but we had no clue—none."

Wesley runs his fingers through his hair.

"No one ever whispered that maybe there was a killer running loose in Marble Hills? Someone everyone knows?"

Eddie and Todd shake their heads in unison.

"Nope—can't say anyone ever did."

Todd looks at the door.

"If someone did kill Marah—they had help."

Wesley turns to face Todd.

Page **381**

"Like an accomplice?"

Todd nods.

"Think about it—getting in and out of Glass Owl isn't the easiest thing to do by any means—seems to me there must have been two killers—not one. Question is—who had a motive?"

Wesley leans against the counter.

"There has to be more to this story."

"If someone didn't sneak into Glass Owl to kill Marah—it was probably one of the staff that did the deed—someone with a grudge who had a score to settle with your grandfather."

Wesley looks at Todd.

"Seems to far-fetched if you ask me."

"Have you been paying attention to the news lately?"

Wesley glances at Alden.

"Whoever killed Marah could be long gone by now—but it might have been one of the staff that did it—with help."

Alden shakes his head.

"Did Kyle ever mention that maybe one of the staff had a grudge against your father—for something he did to them?"

Wesley seems confused.

"Not that I can remember—your name was the only one that ever came up with what happened to my aunt."

Alden seems upset at the comment.

"No surprise there—Kyle still thinks I'm guilty."

He looks at Julia.

"Didn't you tell me your husband worked at Glass Owl briefly to get money for his plane—maybe he heard?"

Julia sits down next to Wesley on the stool.

"Peter wasn't big on gossip as a rule. If someone said anything he never mentioned it—not that I recall anyway."

She sighs and glances at Wesley.

"He didn't like your grandfather or his behavior. Said he was evil to the core. Stated how he treated people who worked at Glass Owl like cattle—never showed any respect for anyone."

Wesley reacts and nods.

"Sounds exactly like my grandfather."

Julia gestures with her hand and sighs loudly.

"But I think it seems plausible that one of the staff at Glass Owl killed your aunt and not some random intruder—look at what happened to **Marilyn Monroe** in 1962. Her creepy maid helped **Robert Kennedy** and **Peter Lawford** administer a lethal overdose in order to silence Marilyn because she knew too much about their dirty deals and threatened to go public just days before she was found dead in the bedroom of her swanky Los Angeles home—was quite the story at the time—took decades for the truth to finally be exposed—so many secrets to play out."

Alden and Todd look at each other.

"My folks talked about that case for years. It took decades for the truth to come out like Julia said and even today people still refuse to believe it really happened the way it did—or that because of what happened that night with the help of the housekeeper later resulted in the Mob offing Robert's brother in Dallas the following year for revenge—and then quickly silencing the supposed shooter before he could talk and tell his story."

"Sometimes fact is stranger than fiction."

Wesley sighs again.

"Fine—OK—whatever—but how does what happened to a movie star decades ago in Los Angeles have anything to do with my aunt's death. That actress was a world famous celebrity—my aunt was nobody—average—just a high school student."

Alden looks at Eddie.

"Regular people get killed every day too—but maybe Marah wasn't killed for anything she did—if someone in the staff did kill Marah—your grandfather would have the answers—he may even know who had reasons to—trust me, if the staff at Glass Owl had reason to hate anyone in your family—your grandpa would be at the top of their list—then and now."

Todd wags his finger at Alden.

"I second that. Old man Madison has a list of haters several miles long. I've never met anyone who liked him."

Wesley runs his fingers through his hair again.

Boardinghouse

Daryl Anderson slowly covers Caleb Winthrop's body with a sheet as Lana stands at the door nervously wringing her hands as tears stream down her face. She seems oddly nervous.

"Is he dead?"

Daryl turns to look at Lana curiously.

"What do you think? There's a butcher knife wedged halfway into his heart. There's enough of his blood spilled to choke a horse—and his body is cold as ice—yeah, I'd say he's no longer alive—but I could be wrong—what do you think?"

"You don't have to be mean about it."

Daryl walks over to where Lana is standing.

"Pay attention, OK—Caleb Winthrop was murdered less than an hour ago—he obviously knew his killer—and you want me to play nice with you while you ask really stupid questions?"

Lana looks at the grisly scene again.

"I came over to visit—to—just to."

Daryl smirks.

"Yeah, I know, I know why."

Daryl winks at Lana.

"What? You think I don't know the deal? Caleb Winthrop slept around—a lot. His exploits wasn't exactly well-kept in Marble Hills—that, and I was his age once too—and that was all I did with my free time during my early twenties, fuck girls for fun because I could—and did—yep, been there and done that."

Lana continues to look at Daryl curiously.

"Like gross—yuk."

"Uh-huh—bet you didn't say that to Caleb when he asked you to spread your frigging legs—and royally entertain him?"

Lana turns away.

Blankenship Apartment

Clay pulls his T-shirt on and zips up his Levi's. Eva wraps her arms around his waist from behind. She grins broadly.

"How do you feel?"
Clay grins.
"You mean after our workout?"
Eva kisses Clay in the back of his neck.
"A guy can get really hungry after a bout of lovemaking."
Clay turns to face her.
"I agree. How about dinner—I'm starved."
Eva gives Clay an odd look.
"You want me to cook dinner for you?"
Clay laughs.
"I wouldn't dare. How about we go to Portland?"
Eva smirks.
"Do you think I can't cook?"
Clay laughs loudly as he backs away from Eva.
"You said it—I didn't."
She grabs him and pulls him to her.
"You'll pay dearly for that crack."
He looks at her curiously.
"What are you going to do to me?"
Eva smirks again and runs her fingers through his hair for several seconds and then kisses him lightly. She sighs.
"Have I told you how much I really love your dry sense of humor—and how much your crooked grin owns my heart?"
She kisses him passionately. He grins broadly.
"Uh-huh—but I don't mind hearing it again and again."
Clay looks around the room.
"Come on, let's go to dinner. Portland's a ways away."
Clay leads Eva out of his apartment.

<u>Peabody Avenue</u>

Brad laughs as he notices Genie Van Pelt looking at him oddly as he rams her in the backseat of his car. He smirks.
"Making up for lost time—deal with it."
Genie sighs.
"A little rough—even for you—don't you think?"

Brad laughs loudly.

"What's up with you damned whores today—do you think you make decisions for us guys now? Like, get real bitch."

"Carrie was right about you."

"Don't mention that bitch's name to me again."

Genie tries to push Brad off her. But he only intensifies his aggressiveness towards her. He whacks her with his fist.

"Have you forgotten who I am—huh?"

He rams into her once more and laughs.

"You're nothing but a cheap pathetic whore—or have you forgotten who made you popular, bitch? I did—yeah I did."

Genie looks up at Brad.

"I'm not a whore."

Brad smirks again.

"Yeah, right—this from the girl who gives it up to every guy in town—spreads her legs no matter what—cheap thrills."

Genie finally manages to push Brad off her.

"If I'm a whore—then what does that make you."

Brad laughs.

"Guys can't be whores you stupid bitch."

He laughs again.

"A guy who sleeps around is a stud."

Genie rolls her eyes.

"Maybe Caleb or Jarod are studs. But you and Corey are losers. You get all their used-up leftovers—like feral cats."

Brad grabs Genie by the neck.

"*Miserable bitch*—I ought to crack your skull open. How dare you insult me like that? Who the hell do you think you are talking to me like I'm nothing? You disgust me. Ugh."

Genie seems frightened. Brad notices her reaction and hesitantly releases her. He looks at her for a few seconds.

"Don't you ever talk that way to me again—do you hear me—you're one of my whores—I own you—period."

He climbs out of the backseat of the car. Genie watches his zips up his Levi's while leering at her. She sighs.

"I didn't mean it—please."

Page 386

Brad looks at Genie curiously.

"What? You're sorry? You should be. How dare you speak that way to me? I'm the guy who took your virginity—I made you popular when no one would look at you much less act like you existed—called you a frigid bitch—made fun of you plenty."

Genie slowly climbs out of the backseat as a thick stream of semen slides down her legs in a gush. She ignores it.

"I'm sorry. God, I'm so sorry Brad. I don't know what got into me—you're right. I should show you more respect."

Brad sighs loudly.

"Well, see it doesn't happen again. You owe me. If it wasn't for the fact I stuck my dick into you—you'd still be hanging out with the pathetic science club girls from Port Clyde—the ones who every cool guy like me avoids like the frigging plague."

He begins to laugh.

"No wonder everyone hates you."

They look at each other. She glances at his erection straining against his jeans. He notices her reactions and grins.

"Let me blow you. You're right. I owe you. I should respect you more than anyone else—if you hadn't taken me the day of the town picnic at Shelby Park last year I'd still be a loser—I wouldn't be popular—and you're right *I am* a whore for the taking. I've put out for every guy that suggested I experience his dick—just like you told me to do in order to be with the "in crowd" in Marble Hills—been with so many guys in the last year."

Brad watches as Genie unzips his Levi's and pulls his penis out. She looks at it briefly and then mouths him. He relaxes and leans against the car as Genie begins to give him a blowjob.

<u>Maple Avenue</u>

Corinne Massey walks along the sidewalk unaware that she's being followed. A car slowly moves with her pace unnoticed as she heads to a parking lot several feet away. A small handgun can be seen on the dashboard of a car as fingers reach for it.

Page **387**

<u>Glass Owl</u>

"I can't believe you did that."

Lindsay turns to look at Hart Bennington standing a few feet away. She sighs loudly as he seems visibly annoyed.

"I had no choice—your father and I are over."

Hart gives his mother a harsh look.

"You already knew dad cheated on you—so what if he and Chandra Stevenson made a baby—big fucking deal."

Lindsay sighs again.

"I'm not having this discussion with you."

"Why not—I think it's cool—I mean, give it up to dad for still being able to get it up—I give him serious props."

Lindsay seems upset.

"*You*—you men are all the same—no respect."

Hart watches as his mother heads toward the stairs. He turns to see his sister coming toward him from the kitchen.

"Is dad really gone?"

Hart nods as Susan Bennington glances at the stairs.

"Not even a goodbye."

"How much more fucked up can this family get?"

He shrugs.

"I mean—like really—we suck chunks."

"Is Chandra's child a boy or girl?"

Hart ignores Susan and heads up the stairs.

<u>Parking Lot</u>

The door to Corinne's car lays open as her hand lies against the steering wheel. Blood gushes from a bullet wound to her head while the horn in her car honks endlessly.

<u>Pete's Cafe</u>

Alden follows Wesley to his car. They look at each other as Wesley opens the door. He stops and sighs loudly.

Page **388**

"I think there may be some credence to the fact that whoever killed my aunt worked for grandfather previous."

Alden runs his fingers through his hair.

"Or at least knew someone who worked at Glass Owl."

Wesley nods in agreement.

Boardinghouse

Lana watches as Caleb's body is slowly wheeled out of the room. She turns to look at Daryl coldly. She sighs loudly.

"Who could've done this?"

Daryl looks around and shrugs.

"Are you sure you didn't see anyone leaving when you got here? Like maybe a chick he just fucked right before?"

Lana shakes her head.

"No."

She wipes a tear from her eye.

"I didn't see anyone leaving his room—no one at all."

Daryl walks over to where Lana is standing.

"Did Caleb have any enemies? You know some whore he screwed and then dumped like he did his usual tricks?"

Lana looks at Daryl with a confused look.

"No—no I don't know—I didn't really know him that well at all—we—we were just—friends—really good friends."

"I'll just bet you were."

Daryl looks at the bloodstained sofa.

"Well, one thing is for sure—Caleb Winthrop is never going to have sex again—just another stiff in the morgue."

He laughs. Lana looks at Daryl.

"Well—it's true, isn't it—why not say it? He'll never bang another girl ever again. He's just nothing now—a corpse."

Lana gestures at Daryl with her hand.

"You're a sick creep."

"Bite me."

Lana leaves. Daryl shakes his head as he looks at the scene and pulls out his cell phone and grins broadly.

Page **389**

"Only thing left to do now is call Julia Winthrop."
Daryl begins dialing.
"Bad news is always terribly received."
He laughs as he looks at the hallway up ahead.

<u>Pete's Cafe</u>

Julia picks up her cell phone. She rolls her eyes as she listens and realizes Daryl is calling. She nods repeatedly.
"I'll be here—probably until five."
She sighs.
"But I still don't know what we have to talk about?"
She sighs loudly.
"OK. OK. Just come over already."
Eddie, Simon and Todd look at her curiously.
"Is something wrong?"
Julia turns to look at Eddie.

<u>Miami</u>

Calvin Whitney stares at his cell phone briefly as he continues talking. He seems upset and stares at the window.
"You think whoever took out Eldon knew him?"
He gestures with his hand.
"Any idea of who would dare do such a thing?"
He clenches his fist.
"Whoever is responsible for my brother's passing will regret the day they were born—I personally guarantee they'll be rubbed out by one of my men. It's just a question of when."
Calvin grins broadly.
"Yes—yes of course. You can help Sabrillo. I know how close you were to my brother—and if you want to bathe in the spilled blood of my brother's killer I obviously do not have a problem with whatever you decide must be done to settle the score and rightfully avenge this most tragic of deaths."
He waves his hand in the air.

Page **390**

"Yes, I know, Eldon most definitely would've approved one hundred percent of such measures to ensure revenge."

He looks at his watch and shakes his fist.

"OK—keep me updated on your progress—and if you find that Eldon was silenced by an acquaintance—show no mercy."

He nods several times.

Parking Lot

Ashton Markway notices Corinne's car in the parking lot as well as the loud honking sound. He walks toward the parked car at the far end of the deserted lot. He approaches slowly.

"Can't she hear that noise?"

As he nears the car he notices blood dripping from the door to the pavement. He stops briefly and realizes.

"Corinne?"

Corinne's lifeless body stares blankly at him. Her eyes are wide open—a look of fright etched on her dead face.

"Who—could do—would do this?"

Ashton begins dialing on his cell phone as he glances at Corinne again. He looks around the parking lot nervously.

Pete's Cafe

Julia watches as Daryl walks toward her. He points to the spare room in the corner off of the kitchen. Eddie, Simon and Todd watches as she follows. They look at each other. Less than a minute later they hear Julia scream. They rush over.

Glass Owl

Wesley shuts the door to his car and heads toward the entrance of the mansion hesitantly. He stops and sighs.

"This isn't going to be easy."

He opens the front door and heads inside. He sees Hart and Susan both looking at Lindsay in a weird way. He shrugs.

Page 391

"What's going on?"

Susan rolls her eyes and faces Lindsay.

"*Mommie Dearest* just destroyed our family."

Lindsay gives Susan a harsh look and sighs loudly.

"Your uncle is going to be a father again."

Lindsay rolls her eyes when she sees Wesley looking at her curiously. She looks at her stomach for a few seconds.

"No—not me—my dear of a husband has been sleeping around for years and apparently one of his many, many whores have finally snared the bastard—with a baby—damn bitch."

Wesley seems bored by the topic and sighs.

"I don't do soap operas as a rule."

He heads toward the den and opens the door. Howard Madison looks up from his desk. He seems confused.

"Wesley?"

Wesley closes the door behind him.

"I need to talk to you."

Howard looks at Wesley curiously.

"Sure—what about?"

Wesley stares at Howard.

"What happened to my aunt?"

Howard's reaction changes abruptly.

"There's nothing to talk about. Alden Washington killed your aunt years ago and that's that—end of the story."

Wesley sighs.

"I'm not so sure."

Howard sits up.

"Is that so—let me guess—you've turned into a frigging detective all of a sudden? Think you know everything."

Wesley rolls his eyes.

"I think there's more to the story than I was told—a lot more if truth be known—seems to me there's plenty that was left out purposely—like who really killed my aunt years ago."

Howard smirks.

"The case is closed. Alden Washington killed my daughter and got away with it—story is old and tired now—over."

Page **392**

"There are some things that were recently brought to light that make sense—I think there might be something to it."

Howard stands up.

"Is that so?"

"Is it possible one of the staff at Glass Owl killed Marah or knew someone who might have? It's no secret that you."

Howard's expression changes instantly.

"No—no one who worked or works currently at Glass Owl would dare try and kill us—they wouldn't dare—no way."

Wesley looks around.

"How can you be so sure they didn't?"

Howard walks toward Wesley.

"I just am—that's why."

He grabs Wesley by the shoulders.

"Get out before I lose my temper boy."

He shoves Wesley toward the door forcibly. Wesley balks and shoves Howard away. He turns to face Howard.

"OK—now I know something is up—what's going on?"

Howard angrily grabs Wesley again.

"Don't make me lose my temper boy—or you'll wish you hadn't—I swear I'll knock that smirk off your face so fast."

He shoves Wesley through the door and quickly shuts the door, slamming it shut behind him in an angry rage. Wesley turns to look at the door briefly and then clenches his fist.

"What is he hiding?"

He turns to see Kyle Madison staring at him.

"What's going on Wesley?"

"Like you'd care?"

He walks past his father. Kyle stands there a few seconds and heads toward the den. He opens the door and looks at his father. There is a brief interlude of silence between them.

"What's up with Wesley?"

"That troubled boy of yours is more trouble than he's worth—mouthed off to me just now like I was a servant."

Kyle seems confused.

"Come again?"

Howard sighs loudly.

"I guess jail didn't put the fear of God in Wesley—but I can and will if I have to—I won't tolerate his attitude—silly punk."

"Last time I checked I was Wesley's father."

Howard slams his fist down on the table.

"Then act like it."

He turns to face the window.

Peabody Avenue

Brad grins as he zips up his Levi's. He looks at Genie still kneeling in front of him—her mouth smeared with semen.

"I'm so sorry for how I behaved earlier—so sorry."

Brad smirks.

"You're just lucky I'm such a nice guy."

He sighs.

"But if you ever—oh man if you ever talk back to me again I'll kill you—take you out like the trash that you are."

They look at each other.

Pete's Cafe

Julia sobs uncontrollably in Eddie's arms as Daryl looks at Simon and Todd with a confused look. He seems upset.

"Despite what you think I didn't enjoy."

Julia turns to face Daryl.

"Do you have any suspects?"

Daryl shakes his head.

"I assume he knew his killer but that's it—no leads."

Daryl's cell phone rings and he answers it.

"This can't be happening."

Eddie looks at Daryl.

"What—what happened?"

Daryl shuts off the phone and looks at Eddie.

"Ashton Markway just found Corinne Massey—dead."

There is silence among everyone.

<u>Farmington Villa</u>

Juan Sabrillo shoves pieces of clothes into his suitcase and is about to head to the door when Faye Washington opens it and looks at him curiously. He seems surprised to see her.
"Where are you going?"
They look at each other.
"Miami."
"What for—I thought?"
Juan sighs.
"To scout a location—I'll be back tomorrow about four."
Faye watches as Juan walks past her and leaves without waiting for an answer. Faye seems upset at his behavior.

<u>Mall</u>

Brad walks over to where Natalie Standish is sitting. He glances at her with a leer. She ignores him and he grins.
"Missed me?"
He sits down.
"You and I have been—like strangers lately."
He leers again.
"Not interested."
Brad leans closer to Natalie.
"And why is that?"
"It just is—like deal with it."
Brad smirks.
"Come on—I'll even buy you dinner."
Natalie rolls her eyes.
"I've already eaten."
"Ouch."
Brad looks down at his erection.
"I'm beginning to take your attitude personally."
Natalie shrugs.
"Why should I care one way or the other?"

Page **395**

Brad slyly unzips his jeans. Natalie looks at his penis jutting out at her. He grins seeing her mesmerizing stare.

"You know you want to say hello."

Natalie hesitates.

"You always do this to me Brad—you treat me like crap and then seduce me with your charms—telling me lies."

Brad smiles broadly.

"I've been busy lately—and then there was that situation that caused me—but I'm OK now—ready for dick action."

He makes a lewd gesture with his finger.

<u>Parking Lot</u>

Daryl, Eddie and Todd look at Corinne's lifeless body while Ashton and Simon silently stand a few feet away in shock.

"First Caleb—and now—oh man."

Ashton faces Daryl.

"Caleb Winthrop is dead?"

Daryl nods.

"Stabbed to death at Julia's boardinghouse—someone turned his lights off with a butcher knife—quite messy."

Ashton seems stunned.

"What if they're connected?"

He sighs.

"Could whoever killed Caleb have killed Corinne?"

Daryl seems confused.

"I don't see a connection between them."

Eddie faces Daryl.

"What are the odds?"

Daryl sighs loudly.

"There is no link between Caleb and Corinne—he had no enemies—and neither did she—who would want to?"

Simon digs his hand into the front pockets of his Levi's and glances at the others with a look of disgust on his face.

"Corinne Massey was one of Caleb's many "friends with benefits" deals—if you know what I mean—like intimately."

Page 396

Daryl laughs.

"So were almost all the women in Marble Hills from what I heard earlier. Caleb Winthrop got around like a bad rash."

Eddie shoots Daryl a sharp look.

<u>Blankenship Apartment</u>

Clay opens the door to his apartment and watches as Eva enters and skips a few times. He grins and closes the door.

"Portland was definitely abuzz tonight with activity."

Eva smirks as she turns to face Clay.

"Blame it on New England being the place to be during a rather dull summer otherwise—lots of drama for CNN."

Clay grabs Eva and pulls her to him.

"I blame it on you."

Eva seems confused.

"Me—what did I do?"

Clay grins broadly.

"Has it slipped your mind already—you pulled a really fast one earlier—slick actually—played a game and got results."

Eva kisses Clay.

"I think I need a refresher course regardless."

Clay pulls Eva even closer to him.

"I don't think I should spill what I know."

He lets go of Eva.

"If you can't remember what you did earlier."

He walks toward the kitchen. Suddenly Eva grabs him from behind and hugs him tightly as he grins broadly.

"Are you referring to my asking you to marry me?"

Clay grins slyly and begins laughing.

"See—that wasn't hard for you to remember, was it? But just for you forgetting—I think you owe me an apology."

Eva seductively kisses Clay's neck.

"Is that so? What sort of an apology do you have in mind? Especially given the fact I made the first move earlier?"

"I think ten kisses should be enough."

Page **397**

Eva slides her hand under Clay's T-shirt.

"Is that all you want?"

Clay watches as Eva's eyes fall on the zipper of his Levi's.

"I can be convinced to ask for more."

Eva begins fumbling with the zipper on Clay's jeans.

"I'll just bet you can—sly fox you are."

He laughs loudly and lifts Eva into his arms and head for the bedroom as she showers him with several more kisses.

Glass Owl

Kyle walks into the garden and notices Lindsay sitting alone at one of the pavilions. He slowly walks over to her.

"How are you holding up?"

Lindsay looks up at Kyle and shrugs.

"Well, all things considered, OK. Nevertheless, having your marriage officially labeled a failure certainly can put a damper on things though. But I guess the writing was on the wall for years now. I just didn't want to face it—or see it for what it was despite my best efforts to play out such a terrible fantasy."

Kyle sits down next to Lindsay and hugs her.

"I'm assuming our dear father is his usual gloating self over this mess? Endlessly telling you he told you so?"

Lindsay nods.

"I'm not in the mood to hear 'I told you so' from him right now—it's just more than I want to deal with after the day I had to endure—but I have only myself to blame for this mess."

Kyle looks around.

"How are the kids handling it?"

"Hart could care less apparently. Seems to think it'll be cool to have a black sibling in the family. Susan is being unusually silent—even for her—and that's saying a lot believe me."

Kyle hugs Lindsay again.

"Well, I'm here if you need me."

They look at each other.

"Thanks—I appreciate that."

He stands up.

"Just so you know—what happened wasn't your fault by any means—Robert was just a creep—plain and simple."

Lindsay nods in agreement.

<u>Mall</u>

Sounds of passionate lovemaking can be heard in the stairwell as Brad and Natalie go at it. Brad laughs loudly.

"Still want to tell me you're not interested?"

Natalie grins.

"Like I said earlier—I can't resist your charms—you always manage to get what you want—no matter what I say."

Brad rams into Natalie again.

"A guy has to do what a guy has to do."

They kiss passionately.

"I can't believe Carrie Spaulding screwed with you."

Brad seems upset.

"Don't mention that damn bitch's name again to me—she almost destroyed me—made me a laughingstock in town."

Brad begins ejaculating.

"Frigging cunt—she's pure evil."

"Exactly how are you going to get even with her after what she did to you—she deserves to pay—and pay dearly."

Brad gives Natalie a curious look.

<u>Parking Lot</u>

Corinne's body is covered with a sheet as Daryl watches it being taken away. He wipes sweat from his brow and sighs.

"OK—here's the deal folks—plenty drama."

He turns to look at the others standing nearby.

"There'll be a news blackout if anyone asks when the word gets out about Corinne. Not one word to anyone in town."

Ashton gives Daryl a strange look.

"Why is that exactly?"

Page 399

"If both Caleb and Corinne were killed by the same person we don't want to tip our hat—let them know we know."

Daryl glances at Eddie briefly.

"That way if someone in town is responsible—and slips info about how both Caleb and Corinne were killed earlier today we'll have our killer—or at least a viable suspect anyway."

Ashton sighs loudly and nods in agreement.

<u>Mall</u>

Brad smirks slyly and zips up. He watches as Natalie continues to stare at his penis straining against his Levi's.

"What about Carrie Spaulding?"

"I'm done with her."

He grins broadly and heads for the door. As he leaves Natalie seems confused. Several minutes later the door opens suddenly. Her expression changes to shocked disbelief.

"You—*but*? How did?"

Before she can react she is shoved toward the stairwell and falls backwards—tumbling down the stairs—finally coming to a stop fifty stairs later at the bottom of the landing. Her eyes look glazed over. It is obvious her neck is broken. Blood drips from her lips seconds later. The door closes and all is silent again.

<u>Blankenship Apartment</u>

Eva lies in Clay's arms after a bout of lovemaking. He laughs as she tickles his neck. He smirks and kisses her again.

"How does it feel to be husband material?"

He grins broadly as he gestures with his hand.

"Is that what I am—husband material?"

Eva rolls over and kisses Clay's chest several times.

"Uh-huh—even my mother thinks so."

He looks at her.

"I'm not sure how it feels yet. You know I've been a player for so long—whored my way through so many women."

Page 400

Eva kisses Clay's chest again.

"Uh-huh—seems to me you told me you'd only had one woman in your life before we hooked up two years ago?"

Clay smirks.

"I lied."

Eva sits up and looks at Clay.

"You lied—is that so?"

Clay nods.

"Yep—actually, I've kept a lot of other things from you—I have been living a double life—one being a serial killer."

Eva looks at Clay curiously.

"Really—how so—inquiring minds want to know?"

Clay pulls Eva toward him and kisses her.

"I'm a really, really bad guy. Been on the lam for over two years now—killed over one hundred people—wicked plays."

He laughs as he sees her reaction.

"I'm a dangerous guy—deal with it—you're stuck with me forevermore—unless I decide to skip town of course."

Eva smiles and kisses Clay.

"Uh-huh—you're a bad boy no doubt."

Clay begins laughing.

"What—you don't believe me? I'm telling the truth—I'm a killer I tell you—I really like killing people—love hearing them scream for mercy right before I snuff them out like a candle."

Eva kisses Clay again. She smiles broadly.

"I don't buy it."

She strokes his cheek.

"You're just too nice. Sweet and caring—gentle too. Nope I don't buy your bad boy act one bit—empty stories—lies."

Clay grins slyly and wags his finger at Eva.

"You need to be afraid—I'm bad to the core—I charm my victims—seduce them with my nice guy act—then I kill them and laugh as they die in my arms while I strangle the life out of them with no remorse whatsoever for my actions—I'm no good—no good I tell you—like a rap song with a really bad singer."

Eva kisses Clay passionately.

Page **401**

"Nope—you can't convince me—no way."

Clay gestures with his hand.

"OK. OK. You win—I'm a nice guy—I've never hurt anyone in my entire life—never even been in a fight—too soft."

Eva pulls Clay toward her and whispers in his ears.

"From the moment I saw you slip and spill that drink all over yourself I knew you were the one for me—perfect."

"My moment of humiliation was when you decided you wanted me—that's the saddest thing I've ever heard."

"It was funny—a grown man in T-shirt and jeans soaking wet from a spill—in a public place no doubt—you looked so helpless—I couldn't help but be charmed—so charmed."

Clay lies back in bed.

"I was humiliated—like totally."

"Remember what happened next?"

Clay kisses Eva's fingers.

"You took me back to your place—told me it was nearby and that I could wash my T-shirt and jeans there."

Eva slides her fingers through Clay's hair again.

"What was I supposed to do—I wanted to get to know you a lot better—it was the only way I could get you alone."

"I couldn't believe it when you told me months after the fact what you'd really wanted to do to me that day."

"I was in love—I had to get you over to my place—tricked you into taking your pants off so I could see what you looked like up close—and then you behaved—so shy—scared almost."

Eva leans over and kisses Clay. She strokes his cheek again as they look at each other briefly. She tousles his hair.

"You were the perfect gentlemen—you didn't even make a pass at me—and you could've had me so easily too."

"I didn't know you wanted me to try anything—I was so embarrassed standing in your apartment in my underwear looking like a total dork—felt so totally embarrassed."

"You know—if you'd made a move back then I would've let you have your way with me—wouldn't have fought."

Clay cracks a sly grin as he kisses Eva.

Page 402

"What about now? Can I have my way?"

Eva nods. They begin kissing passionately for a few minutes. He reaches out to touch her lips with his finger.

<u>Maple Avenue</u>

Ross Harrison watches as Tyler Van Pelt walks past him without saying a word. He rolls his eyes and laughs.

"Why are you making such a big deal about this situation Tyler—I never said it was serious between us? I never did."

As Tyler turns the corner and is out of view, Ross turns back to face the street. At that moment he is hit over the head from behind. He falls backwards against his car like a ragdoll.

<u>Vine Street</u>

Donna Markway screams as she sees Ross fall against his car and watches in horror as a black-clad figure runs away.

TO BE CONTINUED

A Look at the 16th Episode

Donna tries to save Ross's life but is too late—Juan vows to avenge Eldon's death—Ben makes time for Tyler—Brad is back to his old tricks with Daphne—Gary continues to taunt and verbally abuse Patrick—Wesley's talk with Kyle leads nowhere—Gina has another unfriendly visit from Tiffany who vows revenge for what happened—Caroline realizes a persistent blackmailer isn't going away quietly by any means—Matt is confronted with Ross's tragic death—Kelly finds another murder victim in Marble Hills—Julia's grief over her brother-in-law's sudden death overwhelms her as Eddie tries to console her with help from Todd—news of the murders spread across town like wildfire—as a distraught father angrily confronts Daryl about yet another possible murder.

Punish the Sinners

<u>Maple Avenue</u>

Donna Markway frantically runs towards Ross Harrison. Blood pours from the back of his head as she calls for help.

"Help—please—someone help."

Ross slumps to the pavement as Donna pulls out her cell phone and begins dialing in a panic. She seems in shock.

"Help me—please."

Ross passes out.

"Ross?"

Donna shuts the cell phone off. She looks at Ross again as she sees the color drain from his face. Donna begins to sob.

"They're coming."

She looks down at Ross lying on the pavement. Blood is still pouring from the huge wound on the back of his skull.

"This can't be happening."

Seconds later the sound of an ambulance is heard as two white vans pull up. Several attendants rush past Donna and begin to tend to Ross. Several long minutes seem to go by as she waits patiently hoping that Ross isn't dead. She takes deep breath.

"Is he going—is he going to be alright?"

Several more seconds go by and finally two of the attendants sigh. They look at Donna and shake their heads.

<u>Parking Lot</u>

Ashton Markway is about to drive away as Daryl Anderson listens intently on the cell phone. Suddenly he waves to Ashton to come back. Ashton seems confused as he stops and reverses his car slowly. Daryl looks at Ashton curiously and sighs.

"Ross Harrison was just attacked."

Ashton seems shocked.

"What?"

He sighs.

"Your sister is there with him."

Ashton sighs again.

"Donna?"

They look at each other. Daryl runs to his car and yells at Ashton who continues to stare at him oddly. Daryl sighs.

"They're at Maple Avenue and Vine Street."

Ashton nods and drives away as Daryl follows.

<u>Miami</u>

Juan Sabrillo hugs Calvin Whitney warmly. They look at each other for a few seconds. Juan pulls away slowly.

"Eldon was truly something special."

Calvin looks at Juan.

"He liked you too. Loved how you took people out."

Juan grins.

"I like being a hit man—it's what I do best—well, that and banging whores all over the world every chance I get."

He grins broadly.

"And I'm going to love taking out Eldon's killer when I find them. I'm *so* going to love that job more than any other."

Calvin grins and pats Juan on the shoulder.

Page **406**

<u>Mall</u>

Ben Lincoln is sitting at one of the open cafes working on his computer as his wife Grace Zennington sits beside him silently sipping an iced coffee slowly. He looks up and smirks.

"I'm almost finished with these files—I promise—a few more lines and it'll be over—got to check it one final time."

Grace sighs.

"I'm OK. Take your time."

He grins.

"I just had to send off this last report—before the school decides to order my head on a platter for dawdling."

He shuts off the computer.

"OK—I'm done."

They look at each other. Grace looks around.

"So, you're sure you don't mind leaving Marble Hills for San Francisco next month? I know you like it here in Maine."

Ben gestures with his hand.

"Are you kidding—think of the job possibilities for private school teachers in Napa—giving lessons to snobby rich kids and hobnobbing with rich wine people—it's not every day that deal comes across for a small town boy like me—I'll adjust."

Grace sighs loudly.

"I really need to move back to California to look after the folks—Harold's death put a crimp on our plans—unexpected."

They kiss for a few seconds. At that moment Ben notices Tyler Van Pelt entering the mall with a lost look on his face.

<u>Bradford Beach</u>

Brad McKinley grins broadly as he looks down at Daphne Garfield's head nestled between his legs bobbing up and down on his erect penis. He smirks proudly and begins laughing.

"Oh man, you girls really know your stuff without a doubt when it comes to making us guys feel like kings—oh yeah."

Page **407**

She looks up at him just as he ejaculates. Semen sprays in her face seconds later. He laughs loudly. She seems annoyed.

"Uh-huh—I know—it happens."

He licks his lips as she continues letting her tongue slide across the head of his penis as he continues to come.

"Uh-huh—you're quite the thrill."

He shoots again.

"I heard you found yourself a boyfriend?"

Daphne looks up at Brad again. She seems confused.

"I don't have a boyfriend."

Brad smirks.

"If you do—it's cool—I don't care—but it won't change a thing between us regardless. You and I still—well, you know."

Brad smiles broadly.

"You and I will still hook-up in the backseat of my car or wherever I choose—nothing will change whatsoever—got it?"

Daphne nods.

"Good—just so you understand—my dick and your tongue are best friends forever until I say otherwise—and only."

Brad makes a lewd gesture with his finger.

"No question about it—your tongue is too much of a wonder for me to consider ever giving you up—boyfriend or no boyfriend—good whores are hard to find nowadays."

Daphne smirks slyly.

"I wish you'd stop calling me a whore—it's crass."

Brad makes a lewd gesture with his finger once more.

"You are what you are—there's nothing crass in the truth—and the truth is you're a whore—like deal with it."

Brad smirks seeing her reaction. He watches as her tongue continually dances on the head of his penis. He sighs.

"Hey, I always pay attention when one of my girls serves my dick above and beyond—ever since we first did it."

Daphne looks at Brad's exposed penis.

"You were my first—you made me a woman."

Brad grins broadly.

"Uh-huh—no doubt—I popped you."

Page 408

He smirks slyly again.

"Caleb had his eye on you but I bested him."

"I owe you—really I do—I'll never forget that day last year at St. Michael's. I was visiting with my mother and you found out somehow I was going to give it up to Caleb Winthrop later that day and you tricked me—waiting for the moment I was alone when my mother went to talk to Father Steven—telling me Caleb was in the confessional waiting for me and then—then you came in right after and took me without even saying a word. It was so clever of you to come up with that plan—lying about Caleb and then getting me all alone. When you entered the confessional with your dick sticking out of your jeans—I knew you planned to fuck me—to take my virginity—knowing I couldn't say no after you made it clear I wasn't going to come out a virgin no matter what—and then you stuck me without waiting for my reply or even caring if I objected—you just had to have your way with me that day—laughing as you did—telling me you hoped I was on the pill because you most certainly could put a baby inside me—and then you came—it was so sweet of you to care if I got pregnant after—oh—you were such a perfect gentlemen to me that afternoon—of course Caleb was royally pissed afterward when he found out you'd scored with me leaving him out in the cold."

She smiles and resumes giving Brad a blowjob.

<u>Tolling Bell Inn</u>

"So, are you coming or not?"

Gary Glick gives his brother a nasty look.

"I don't have all night."

A few seconds tick by before Patrick Glick joins his brother and heads to the door. He seems oddly quiet.

"Time for us to get to know the dumbass locals—timing is everything in this game—no room for stupid mistakes."

Patrick nods and follows Gary.

"From here on out you are and I are not brothers OK? I'm your uncle and you're my nephew. Is that clear Patrick?"

Page **409**

Patrick nods again.

"I swear if you fuck this up—I'll kill—God help you."

Gary shoves Patrick toward the elevator.

"Madison can never suspect—not even for a second."

Gary looks at Patrick harshly.

"If he does—and I lose my chance to get my hands on his money—there won't be a place you can hide—none at all."

Patrick sighs nervously.

Mall

Tyler walks over to where Ben and Grace are sitting. Tyler looks around—he seems nervous. Ben seems concerned.

"Is everything all right?"

Tyler looks at Ben.

"Not really—I just saw Ross outside."

"Oh."

Grace pulls a chair out for Tyler.

"Forget about Ross. He wasn't good enough for you."

Tyler looks at Grace with a confused look.

Maple Avenue

A sheet covers Ross's body as Daryl and Ashton arrive seconds later of each other. Donna wipes tears from her eyes.

"Is he—did he say anything?"

Donna looks at Daryl.

"Not really."

Daryl looks at Donna curiously.

"Did you see anything?"

Donna glances at her brother for a few seconds.

"I—I'm not sure—but I think it was a woman. Or at least it seemed like a woman running away. Could be—had to be."

Daryl scratches his head.

"You think it was a woman—are you sure?"

Donna nods.

Page **410**

"Yes—I was on Vine Street, but yes, I think it was a woman. It had to be—didn't run like a man would—not really."

Daryl and Ashton look at each other.

"Why would someone want to kill Ross Harrison? He didn't like chicks—he banged dudes—like a lot actually."

Ashton shrugs.

Donna looks at the sheet-covered corpse again as Daryl goes over to talk to the ambulance attendants as they wait for the coroner. Ashton and Donna look at each other.

"First Caleb—then Corinne—and now Ross—all similar but different too—all in the same day—why would someone?"

Donna gives Ashton an odd look.

"What—what are you talking about?"

Ashton sighs loudly.

"Caleb Winthrop is dead. Someone killed him earlier with a butcher knife—from what I heard it was quite messy."

Donna seems in shock.

"But how—why?"

Ashton sighs again.

"Corinne Massey is dead also—she was shot."

Donna seems about to pass out.

"This can't be true."

Ashton nods.

"And now Ross Harrison is dead too—obviously someone in Marble Hills has been awfully busy with offing people."

Donna looks over to where Daryl is standing.

"Do you think—you know—who could've done it?"

Ashton digs his hands into the front pockets of his Levi's corduroys. He seems uneasy with the sudden scrutiny.

"Do I think what?"

Donna leans against the wall.

"Do you think there's a serial killer loose in town?"

A look of horror spreads across Ashton's face as he turns to look at Daryl. They share a knowing look. Donna notices.

"There has to be another explanation."

Donna nervously wrings her hands several times.

<u>Blankenship Apartment</u>

Eva Harper smiles as she glances over at Clay Blankenship peacefully sleeping next to her. His light snoring interrupts the quiet of night. She kisses him lightly on the cheek twice.

<u>Glass Owl</u>

Wesley Madison watches as his father walks through one of the gardens outside the mansion. He waits a few seconds and then follows him. He stops a few times and then calls out.
"Dad—got a minute?"
Kyle Madison turns around to face his son as Wesley walks toward him in the moonlight from the dining room.
"We have to talk."
Kyle seems confused.
"Your behavior earlier was appalling."
"Forget about that—I was upset. Trying to wrap my head around what seems to be coming to light—so much."
"What are you talking about?"
Kyle gives Wesley an odd look. Wesley turns to look back at the house and then faces his father again. He shrugs.

<u>Bentley Mansion</u>

Gina Bentley walks through the house in silence. The wind whistles outside as she stops at one of the windows. She screams loudly as she sees Tiffany Johnson grinning back at her.
"Not really as alone as you thought *bitch*."
Gina slowly looks away from the window. As she turns around Tiffany appears in front of her. She seems angry.
"You and me have unfinished work."
Tiffany snaps her fingers.
"You know you're not going to get away with what you've done—I won't let you. You're going to pay dearly."

Page **412**

Gina looks away.

"I haven't done anything—I don't know what you're talking about. Go away—just leave me alone already."

Tiffany laughs.

"Yeah, right—like when pigs fly."

She smirks.

"Your nightmare is just beginning."

Gina tries to walk past the apparition standing in the hallway but Tiffany stands in front of her. Her eyes twinkle.

"Did you think no one would figure it out?"

Gina stops.

"Figure what out?"

Tiffany smirks again.

"Duh—the walls are closing in around you *bitch*. There's no place to hide. It's only a matter of time before they know."

Gina rubs her eyes.

"You're not real—you're dead—I saw them throw dirt on your coffin. I watched them fill up the grave—really dead."

Tiffany gestures with her hand.

"I'll just bet you did—but sometimes not everything is what it seems—and now you're going to wish you—oh yeah."

At that moment Caroline Bentley enters the house and stops. She hears Gina talking. She seems confused.

"Gina?"

She walks toward the hallway and sees Gina standing alone in the darkness. She seems to be somewhat in shock.

"Who were you talking too?"

Gina looks at Caroline curiously.

"I wasn't talking to anyone."

"But I could have sworn—sounded like."

Gina looks at her mother with a scowl and turns to walk away. She stops and slowly turns around. She shrugs.

"I wasn't talking to anyone just now—end of story."

Caroline watches as Gina heads upstairs. She shakes her head and looks at her cell phone for a few seconds.

Page **413**

<u>Maple Avenue</u>

Ashton looks over at his sister. Donna seems lost as they watch the coroner drive away. He shakes his head and sighs.

"I never liked Ross Harrison—but I didn't want him dead."

"Doesn't matter—somebody offed the sleazeball. I sure won't shed a tear—guy was garbage with a capital G."

Ashton and Donna turn to look at Daryl who is staring at them oddly. They glance at each other for a few seconds.

"No problem—I feel the same as you guys—I'm not sorry Harrison bit it earlier. The creep made a lewd pass at my boy not long ago—sick twisted bastard—good riddance no doubt."

Ashton sighs loudly.

"Harrison's dad probably thinks differently than we do?"

Daryl's facial expression changes suddenly.

"If I wanted your advice I'd ask for it—and until I do—shut the fuck up you pathetic nerd—what a frigging loser."

Ashton rolls his eyes at Daryl.

"And people wonder why Jason has problems?"

Without waiting for a remark both Ashton and Donna begin walking away as Daryl clenches his fists angrily.

<u>Bentley Mansion</u>

Gina slams the door shut to her bedroom loudly. Seconds later Tiffany materializes in front of her once again.

"I'm not going anywhere—you're stuck with me."

"Why—why can't you stay dead—my world is so much better now that you're in a box—peaceful and quiet."

Gina experiences an electric-like shock as Tiffany angrily grabs her and spins her around. They look at each other.

"Yeah—that's right—I *can* touch you."

She laughs.

"You and I still have unfinished business—so get used to me *bitch*—like I'm back for good—and I'm not leaving."

Tiffany shoves Gina toward her bed.

Page **414**

"If you think I was a nasty before—just you wait."

Gina seems afraid.

"I have much more power now—now that I'm no longer alive—sort of anyway—so I guess I should thank you."

Gina seems confused.

"Thank me—I didn't—really I didn't."

Tiffany laughs loudly.

"Keep telling yourself that line *bitch*—maybe someone will believe you—oh right—been there and done that a lot."

Tiffany sits down next to Gina.

"Things are going to change around here."

Gina looks at the mirror. She is alone in the room except for the voice in her head—taunting her. She seems uneasy.

<u>Portland</u>

Caroline nervously watches as Glen Bradstreet comes toward her from the entrance of a diner. His erection under his tight jeans is fully visible leaving nothing to the imagination whatsoever as she seems unable to look away. He notices—grins and sits down quickly noticing her obvious discomfort and pouncing on it. He leans forward suddenly and grins slyly.

"I'm glad you came—I was getting worried."

Caroline seems nervous.

"If anyone knew I was here?"

Glen laughs.

"Last time I checked you didn't have a choice in the matter. I'm the one holding the cards in case you forgot."

He reaches out to stroke her cheek.

"Do you think you're better than me or that I'm so low on the pole I couldn't cause trouble for someone like you? Have you forgotten what I know about a certain night in question that you and I became acquainted because of what I saw you do in Boston with your stupid rich hubby? You and I are on equal footing."

"I didn't mean it like—I'm sorry."

Glen smirks and gives Caroline a knowing look.

Page **415**

"I'm tired of your silly games."

He smirks again and gestures with his hand.

"Trust me when I say it—you don't want to fuck with me Caroline—I play dirty—which I'm sure given our history you know all too well just how far I'll go to get what I want—and on my terms no doubt—always on my terms—you have no say—*I tell you what to do and you do it*—or a certain husband will find out certain things that could and *will* destroy his entire family—forever."

Caroline sighs.

"I'm sorry for being so rude."

"Shut up."

He grabs her by the arm.

"You've been avoiding me."

"I haven't. I've just been busy."

Glen smiles slyly.

"With those committees you act like you care about?"

Caroline looks away. He leans closer.

"Yeah, yeah—we both know the real you—don't we Caroline—you're a cold-hearted whore who only cares about one thing and one thing only—and it's certainly not other people."

"I didn't mean."

Glen looks down at his erection.

"A man like me has needs."

He laughs loudly.

"You and I haven't been friendly lately."

Caroline seems uneasy.

"I told you I've been busy."

Glen leers at her.

"Lately I've been feeling that you've been avoiding me because of the issue we had between us a month ago."

Caroline rolls her eyes.

"That issue as you put it—was an abortion. The fourth I've had since you and me—you and I have been acquainted."

Glen seems bored at Caroline's whining.

"Is it my fault you chose not to use birth control when we fuck? You know my deal—I don't use condoms—no need to."

Page 416

Glen watches Caroline's reaction and smirks.

"Poor baby—tell it to someone who cares—you know from the first time I fucked you at McGill's in Boston I didn't do condoms—and like a dumb whore you got pregnant the night we screwed and thought I should be sympathetic to the fact that one of my spills pinned you? Like seriously? No, it was your fault then as were the three subsequent times you messed up and had to take care of your mistakes. The last time was classic for sure. You actually thought you would leave your husband and I'd marry you? I mean give me a break—marry a whore like you?"

He laughs loudly.

"Man, talk about sad delusional fantasies."

He looks down at his erection again.

"I think before we go back to my place you and I need to get a few facts straight about a few things—or else I."

He makes a lewd gesture with his finger.

"You and I are fused together—period. You will service my naughty dick until I decide I'm bored with you—or if I want to go to your husband and tell him about us—and about that hushed incident in Boston which has so many loose ends even now."

Caroline seems afraid.

"No—please don't tell anyone."

Glen smiles broadly.

"I'll think about it."

He stands up. His erection is straining against his Levi's. Caroline seems mesmerized at the sight. She sighs. He gives her an odd look and she stands up immediately. He pulls her toward him suddenly. She seems afraid. He grins broadly and leers.

"There's no way out of this terrible mess in case you were wondering. You can't save yourself—I own your future."

He twists her head backwards and kisses her.

"As of now this is a new beginning for us and what happened that night long ago. You're my whore. I own you. End of story. If you dare to defy me even once I will destroy your perfect world—and you know I can so don't give me a reason."

Caroline leans against Glen.

Page **417**

"I swear from tonight forward your will is law—I'm your property and I'll do whatever you demand of me whenever you deem the moment necessary—just please don't do what you said you'd do concerning John. I'm begging you to show mercy."

Glen grins broadly again.

"I like a woman who knows her place."

He leads her out of the diner.

Brewster Condo

Matt Brewster kisses his latest conquest goodbye and closes the door. He's naked as he walks to the kitchen.

"Man, strangers make the best lays."

He walks over to the TV in the corner of the room and turns it on. He seems stunned as he sees multiple photos of Corinne Massey flash across the screen and then a photo of Ross Harrison as their gruesome deaths are announced. He reacts.

"My God—Ross is dead? It can't be. It can't."

He turns up the volume and listens.

"This can't be real."

He begins watching the news coverage.

Mall

Kelly Nelson slowly closes the door behind him and looks at his cell phone. He smiles and begins dialing. As he's about to walk toward the stairwell he sees Natalie Standish lying at the bottom of the stairs. He runs down the stairs toward her.

"Natalie?"

He looks closely at her and realizes she's dead—probably dead for several hours. He seems unsure what to do.

"Who could of done this to her?"

He begins dialing again.

"How long has she been lying there?"

He seems frantic as he dials and waits for the line to be picked up. He notices dried blood on Natalie's lips.

<u>Police Station</u>

Daryl is about to leave when his cell phone rings again. He picks it up. Immediately the color drains from his face.

"What? Are you sure?"

He sighs loudly.

"OK. OK. I'll be there in ten."

He shuts off the cell phone and looks around.

"How am I going to tell Ed Standish his precious daughter is dead—what the fuck is happening in Marble Hills?"

He sighs loudly again.

<u>Mall</u>

Kelly continuously wrings his hands as he stands at the top of the stairwell not sure what to do. He looks at Natalie.

"Who—why would someone?"

The door opens and Daryl looks at Kelly.

"The coroner is on his way."

Kelly watches as Daryl walks past him and looks down at Natalie's body lying in the bottom of the stairs. Kelly watches as Daryl seems to be bothered by the sight in front of him.

"This makes four—four tonight."

Kelly seems confused.

"Four?"

Daryl turns to face Kelly.

"You don't know?"

Kelly shakes his head.

"Know what?"

"Someone in Marble Hills has been quite busy—Natalie Standish is the fourth victim today. Caleb Winthrop, Corinne Massey and Ross Harrison were all killed earlier tonight."

Kelly leans against the wall in shock.

"But why would someone?"

Daryl turns to look at Natalie's body again.

Page **419**

"That's the million dollar question at the moment."
They look at each other.

<u>Portland</u>

Denise Madison and Miles Dandridge part after kissing passionately. They look at each other. Miles grins broadly.
"Tomorrow is definitely a date."
Denise kisses Miles again.
"Your stamina is incredible."
They kiss again. Across the street Marc Ryerson is looking at them through his digital camera. His face is wreathed in a sly grin as he watches their passionate exchange from afar.
"Oh man, Denise Madison and I will have so much to talk about really soon—I definitely plan to pay her a visit with what I have—and when she sees what I have she'll flip—like totally."
He continues filming as Denise and Miles part once more and look at each other. Suddenly Denise notices Caroline walking toward a parking lot at the end of the street with an extremely good-looking man she doesn't recognize. She sighs loudly.
"Caroline Bentley has been holding out on me."
"Huh?"
Denise looks at Miles.
"Nothing—oh never mind—I'm just thinking out loud."
Denise continues looking at the man. It's clear he has caught her attention. She smiles slyly. Miles notices.
"Do you know her?"
"No—yeah, I do actually. All this time she's looked down at me and well, isn't this interesting—so very interesting."
She notices the man intently and begins licking her lips.
"Who'd ever think she'd take such chances."
She grins broadly.
"Is that chick your sister?"
Denise glances at Miles as he continues to stare as Caroline and Glen stops in front of her car. Denise sighs.
"I wonder what John would say if he knew?"

Page 420

She licks her lips seductively.

"I could blow up her world with one call."

She gestures with her hand.

"Damn bitch has been messing with me for years and now I finally have something on her. It's time for payback."

Miles curiously looks at Denise.

<u>Jefferson Home</u>

Lana Jefferson is talking to Daphne Garfield on her cell phone. She seems excited as she talks to her friend.

"I heard you had an encounter with Brad earlier?"

She rolls her eyes.

"Oh come on Daph—I know for a fact his dick was in your mouth earlier—secrets come out quickly in Marble Hills."

She rolls her eyes again.

"Whatever—if you want to play that game—but we both know you have a thing for his dick—and you'll do anything."

A second call interrupts their conversation. She seems annoyed and sighs as she looks at the name popping up on the screen. She sighs loudly again and rolls her eyes mockingly.

"I've got a call from Lisa Taylor."

She sighs loudly.

"No—I don't know what she wants—I'll get rid of her."

She answers the other line.

"What do you want Lisa?"

She pauses briefly and her expression changes within seconds. She begins screaming loudly as she hears the news.

"Oh my God—are you joking."

She drops the phone.

<u>Glass Owl</u>

Wesley sighs as he walks through the garden. He stops by a pavilion seconds later. He seems upset as he sits down.

"Exactly what I just said—had nothing to say."

Page 421

He runs his fingers through his hair.

"Uh-huh—I expected it—neither of them was forthcoming with info—played dumb about the facts—denied everything."

He gestures with his hand.

"Of course I won't give up—I think you're right. Somebody in my family knows much more than they're telling."

Wesley runs his fingers through his hair once more and sighs loudly. He seems worried as he faces the mansion.

"The question is who?"

He shrugs and continues talking.

<u>Portland</u>

Glen opens the door to his apartment and motions for Caroline to enter. She looks at him briefly and enters. He shuts the door behind him. He grins broadly and leers at Caroline.

"How is your grubby hubby doing—I'm thinking he'd be shocked to find out what you and I have been—studying."

Caroline rushes over to Glen and kneels in front of him staring directly at his massive erection. She seems somewhat desperate. He smirks as he begins unzipping his jeans.

"I'm begging you—please don't tell John about us. I'll do anything you want—you can fuck me anytime you feel like—I won't try to avoid you again—just please don't tell John."

He laughs slyly.

"I'll think about it—but I reserve the right to change my mind—it's a guy thing—you understand—a man sometimes feels slighted when his penis is rejected by one of his whores."

Caroline notices his penis is sticking out in front of her. The head stares at her with lustful insistence. Glen moves closer to Caroline and grins as the head of his penis presses against her cheek and begins to slide toward her mouth. He laughs.

"But maybe there is a way to change my mind?"

His penis slides into her mouth and as her lips envelop his swollen dick he grins. She begins to passionately blow him.

Page 422

<u>Police Station</u>

Daryl sighs as he turns off the lights and steps outside. He sighs once more as he locks the door and walks away.

<u>Miami</u>

Juan stares at the open casket situated in the middle of a room. He glances at Eldon Whitney lying silently inside the casket. Half his face is badly damaged. Juan seems to be holding back tears as he touches Eldon's stiff hand and grimaces.

"Don't worry—whoever did this to you is going to pay dearly—I swear I won't rest until you are avenged."

He looks around the room.

"I swear—I'm going to turn over every rock and find out who did this injustice to you—starting with—Madison."

He clenches his fist.

"Of anybody, that family had the most to gain—and if I find they had anything to do with what—God help them."

He notices fresh flowers nearby in a glass case.

"I won't rest until the morgue is filled the bodies of those who wronged you—I'll make sure they suffer my wrath."

He sighs again and stands up.

<u>Portland</u>

Caroline's loud, helpless moaning fills the room as Glen continuously rams into her without mercy. He grins.

"That hubby of yours has kept too many secrets as far as I'm concerned. I think it's time he's exposed for what he did."

Caroline looks at Glen in shock and gasps.

"But you said?"

Glen begins laughing as he continues ramming Caroline for several more minutes. He sees her panic and smirks.

"That hubby of yours has done some terrible things."

Caroline seems in shock as Glen laughs.

Page **423**

<u>Glass Owl</u>

Wesley is about to grab for the doorknob when he sees Kyle staring at him oddly from the kitchen. He shrugs.
"Where are you going in such a rush?"
Wesley rolls his eyes but doesn't answer. He leaves.

<u>Pete's Cafe</u>

Brad and Daphne walk by the diner and look at the sign on the door. It reads in huge letters CLOSED. Brad shrugs.
"The nerve—can you imagine that—this place is closed."
Daphne looks at Brad.
"Caleb was Julia's brother-in-law."
Brad shrugs.
"So, do I look like I care? I'm frigging hungry—my stomach is all that matters—not some pathetic stiff in the morgue."
Daphne seems uneasy.
"Some of our friends were killed last night—they were murdered in cold blood—doesn't that even bother you?"
Brad laughs.
"Caleb wasn't really my friend—I just knew him—and Ross certainly wasn't my friend—that freak liked dudes—and as for Corinne and Natalie—well, whatever—I had lots of fun with them in the backseat of my car but did I care about them? No."
Daphne sighs.
"Well, at least you're honest."
Brad grins. Daphne turns away from Brad.
"But you're still a vicious toad."
Brad grabs Daphne's arm.
"Yeah, whatever—nevertheless I'd rather be a toad any day than a whore who gives it up to every guy in town."
Daphne slaps Brad.

Page **424**

"What kind of monster are you Brad?"
He angrily grabs her arm and twists it backwards.
"Keep dancing on the minefield."
Brad laughs as he sees Daphne's discomfort.

Blankenship Apartment

Eva smiles as Clay awakens. He grins as he opens his eyes and sees her looking at him. She kisses him repeatedly.
"Good morning, sweetie."
He smirks.
"How long have you been up?"
Eva shrugs.
"I have some bad news."
Clay sits up in bed.
"What are you talking about?"
Eva shakes her head.
"Daryl called—seemed really upset for some reason—said he wants you in the office ASAP—like right now I assume."
Clay jumps out of bed.
"Did he say why?"
Eva shakes her head.
"No—but it sounded important."
Eva watches as Clay grabs a pair of boxer briefs.

Boardinghouse

Julia Winthrop opens the door to Caleb's room. She looks at the blood-stained sofa. Behind her Eddie Kane seems slightly confused at the whole scene. She tearfully looks at him.
"I—I—it doesn't seem possible."
"I know."
"He was OK yesterday morning—so full of life—had the whole world to enjoy—never even seemed worried."
She begins to cry.
"How did it all go horribly wrong?"

She turns to face Eddie.

"He didn't deserve to have this happen to him."

As she begins sobbing on Eddie's shoulder he turns to look see Todd Spencer standing in the doorway a few feet away.

<u>Stanley Pier</u>

Tyler stares blankly at the gentle waves lazily lapping against the pier as he sits on the edge. He seems in shock.

<u>Bentley Driveway</u>

Gina closes the door behind her and smiles as she begins walking toward her car. From behind her she hears Tiffany's voice. She turns to face her rival nervously. Tiffany smirks.

"Today is a new day."

Gina sighs.

"Leave me alone—I have things to do."

Tiffany laughs.

"I'll just bet—who are you gonna kill next?"

Gina slips the key into the lock.

"Isn't there someone other than me you can bother?"

Tiffany rolls her eyes.

"Frankly no—but the better question to ask is how can you remain so freakishly calm after what you did to me?"

Gina turns to face Tiffany.

"Go away—*please*."

"Nope—I don't think I can."

Gina gets into her car and angrily shuts the door and sighs. Tiffany is gone. She starts the engine and sighs loudly.

"Maybe an exorcist can help me get rid of Tiffany—I don't know how much more of her I can take—it's just not fair."

She rubs her eyes.

"Why does she think I killed her?"

She drives away.

<u>Peabody Avenue</u>

Abby Marshall looks at Kelly curiously. He still seems in shock as he tells her what happened the night before.

"I can't believe someone killed them all last night."

Kelly sighs loudly.

"I don't know how I'll ever get that terrible image of Natalie's body out of my head—it still doesn't seem real."

Abby strokes Kelly's cheek.

"Well, Caleb had it coming, that's for sure. He slept with just about every woman in Marble Hills. Must have made a lot of husbands quite pissed off after they caught him dallying."

She shakes her head.

"But the others—how are they connected to Caleb's murder—it just seems like there must be a connection?"

They look at each other.

"This is a nightmare."

They notice Ashton walking toward them.

<u>Stanley Pier</u>

Tyler is looking down at the water as Jason Anderson approaches him. Tyler seems unaware of his presence.

"Tyler?"

Tyler turns to face Jason.

"Man, you look terrible—don't tell me—Ross made a sick play for you again—told you that freak was no good."

Tyler seems upset.

"How can you make jokes after what happened?"

Jason seems confused.

"What are you talking about?"

Tyler looks at Jason curiously and gestures.

"You don't know?"

Jason shakes his head.

"Know what?"

Tyler looks out to sea and sighs.

Page 427

"Ross is dead."

Jason seems shocked.

"What?"

Tyler watches Jason's reaction.

"You really don't know—but your dad—he?"

"My dad and I aren't exactly on civil speaking terms right now—been avoiding him as much as possible lately."

"Somebody killed Ross last night. They also killed Caleb Winthrop, Corinne Massey, and Natalie Standish too."

Jason seems about to faint.

<u>Boardinghouse</u>

Todd comes toward Julia and Eddie. He shakes his head and reaches out to hug her. Eddie pats Todd on the back.

"I'm really sorry about Caleb."

Julia begins sobbing again. Todd and Eddie look at each other. Eddie sighs and glances at the bloody room.

"Any word from Daryl yet?"

Julia looks at Eddie through teary eyes. She shakes her head. She looks at the room again and turns away.

"No—but from what I've heard it seems three other people were killed last night also—might be connected."

"What?"

Eddie looks at Todd. He nods.

"Corinne Massey, Ross Harrison, and Natalie Standish were also killed last night—maybe by the same person?"

Eddie seems confused.

"I could see the Corinne and Natalie connection—we all know Caleb had a rep with the ladies—but how did Ross?"

He shakes his head.

"How does he fit into this mess?"

Todd looks at the doorway.

"Do you think it was drugs or something? That kid had lots of shady friends from what I've heard. No angel was he according to some of the guys at the docks—kid played really hard."

Page **428**

Julia walks over to the bloodstained sofa and stops.
"What is happening in Marble Hills?"
She begins to cry.

<u>Police Station</u>

Daryl is about to sit down at his desk as the door suddenly flies open and he sees Archie Spaulding standing in the doorway looking angry and disheveled. He strolls into the room.
"Carrie is missing."
Daryl seems confused.
"What do you mean missing?"
Archie comes toward him. He seems frazzled.
"She didn't come home last night. No one has seen her since yesterday morning. She hasn't called—no messages."
Daryl shakes his head.
"So?"
Archie stops.
"Is that all you have to say Anderson? There's a frigging murderer on the loose and now my daughter is missing."
Daryl appears nervous.

TO BE CONTINUED

A Look at the 17th Episode

Daryl deals with Carrie's disappearance in addition to a rash of unexplained murders—Brad continues to use his charms to seduce Daphne—Juan attends Eldon's funeral while making plans for revenge against those who wronged him—Kelly, Abby and Ashton try to figure out who's behind the recent murders as a stranger arrives in town looking for answers—Jason and Tyler deal with the sad events unfolding in town—Todd and Eddie comfort Julia over the tragic loss of Caleb—Daryl and Brad have an unpleasant encounter—Glen gleefully continues to blackmail Caroline despite her pleas for mercy—Gina stumbles upon another murder—Jarod and Denise enjoy more good moments in Portland—Jeremy and Shirley's carefree moment together ends with the news of yet another murder and an arrest of a familiar suspect they are acquainted with and assumed they knew.

Keeping Secrets

Police Station

Daryl Anderson turns around and sighs loudly as he watches Archie Spaulding coming toward him aggressively.

"Anderson, you and I have had our issues in the past but do your job for God sakes—my baby is missing—gone."

Daryl seems annoyed.

"Look Archie, I can't do anything about Carrie right now OK? I've got my hands full—like really full—as you're aware."

Archie pounds his fist on Daryl's desk.

"I swear if anything—if anything has happened to Carrie I'll make you pay—you'll wish you'd done your job—I swear."

Without another word Archie turns and storms out as Clay Blankenship strolls through the door—seemingly confused as he closes the door behind him and turns to face Daryl.

"What was that about?"

Daryl gestures with his hand.

"His precious daughter is missing and he blames me. It's my fault—every damn thing in this town is my fault lately."

Clay seems confused and sighs.

"What do you mean missing? Aren't you going to look for her? Where can she be hiding? This town isn't that big."

Daryl sits down.

"After I let you go early yesterday there was a tragic turn of events in Marble Hills—still seems like a bad dream."

Clay walks toward Daryl's desk.

"Why didn't you call me?"

Daryl sighs loudly.

"I tried—there was no answer. Anyway, apparently there's a serial killer loose in town—been quite busy too."

Clay seems shocked.

"You're kidding, right—like seriously."

Daryl rolls his eyes.

"Do I look like I'm kidding?"

Clay watches as Daryl rubs his forehead.

"Yesterday afternoon Caleb Winthrop was found stabbed with a butcher knife in his room at the boardinghouse on Peabody Avenue. Not long afterwards Corinne Massey was found shot to death in her car on Maple Avenue. While I was dealing with that somebody viciously whacked Ross Harrison over the head with a cinder block further down on Maple Avenue."

Clay leans against the desk.

"Less than an hour later I got a call that Natalie Standish had been found at the bottom of one of the stairwells at the mall with a broken neck. Apparently someone pushed her."

"This isn't some gag—you're not trying to pull my leg?"

Daryl leans back in his chair.

"Do I look like a "gag" type of guy?"

Clay glances at the door.

"This all happened yesterday?"

Daryl nods and looks at his watch briefly.

"Uh-huh—oh—and now Carrie Spaulding is missing also. She just disappeared in plain sight apparently. Damn it."

Clay gestures with his hand.

"Think it's someone from Marble Hills?"

Daryl looks at his watch again.

Page 432

"I hope not but it's looking like a possibility."
They look at each other.

Maple Avenue

Brad McKinley is walking down the street with Daphne Garfield. He grins as he tries to kiss her. She pulls away.

"Come on—are you still pissed I called you a whore?"

Daphne seems confused.

"I can't believe you said that—you told me after you took my virginity I should give it up to all your friends—so I did."

Brad laughs.

"And the problem being—seems perfectly OK."

"I'm being called a whore and you guys think I'm just a piece of choice pussy to pass around—and nothing more."

Brad laughs loudly.

"What do you want from us? We think with our dicks—it's a guy thing—none of us want to commit—we just want to fuck as many girls as we can before we go off to college—where we'll fuck even more girls without a care in the world because we can. Seriously, you knew when I took you in the confessional it meant nothing—I wasn't in love with you then and I'm certainly not now—it was just sex—you know—fun and games—I've never considered you girlfriend material—you were just a trick."

Daphne seems upset.

"I knew you weren't in love with me when you took my virginity—but I thought you cared—at least a little bit."

Brad smirks.

"Yeah, right—like seriously."

He pulls her to him and kisses her lightly.

"Enough talk about caring and feelings—I'm actually quite horny right about now—but it's your own fault actually—trying to get me to tell you I cared—it just made me want to fuck even more—and I think you know how demanding my dick can be when it wants something—and wants it really badly."

He leers at her.

"Uh-huh—yeah, I think a blowjob is absolutely going to happen in about two minutes or so—no doubt about it."

Daphne looks at his swelling erection straining against his Levi's. She seems unable to look away. He smiles broadly.

"It's such a powerful sight isn't it—a man's dick getting stiffer and stiffer—expecting something—right about now you know you're falling—you know can't say no to me—you know you've got a thing for my dick—and you want to please me."

Daphne leans closer to Brad.

"You did something to me that day—I don't know what it was—but you have a hold over me that I can't explain."

Brad kisses Daphne passionately.

"Oh, it can be explained all right. You're in love with my charming personality—face it, I know it and you know it."

"You're right Brad—I hate admitting it but I'm in love with your bad boy behavior. I try and fight it but I can't seem to find the strength to resist—or the intense sexual encounters you've subjected me to since that day in the confessional—you on the other hand I don't care much for—you're just a toady freak."

"Shut your frigging mouth."

He sighs.

"You talk too much."

He angrily gestures with his hand.

"Ugh—you're boring me."

Daphne watches as he begins unzipping his jeans. He motions her to get into the car. Seconds later her head is bobbing up and down furiously on Brad's erection. He grins broadly.

<u>Miami</u>

Juan Sabrillo watches as the casket containing Eldon Whitney's body is carried toward a waiting hearse. He slowly turns around to look at Calvin Whitney. They shake hands.

"Eldon won't be forgotten—left a nice legacy."

Calvin nods.

"I want my brother's killer dead."

Page 434

Juan smiles slyly.

"I understand."

They look at each other.

"I'll leave no stone unturned."

Juan smirks.

"It won't take that long believe me—if Howard Madison had anything to do with this—I'll take his family out one at a time and you have my word that they'll suffer before they die at my hand. I assure you I will revenge Eldon's death the way he'd of wanted—extremely painful for those directly involved."

Calvin smiles broadly.

"One of the Levitov brothers offered his help."

Juan seems upset and sighs loudly.

<u>Peabody Avenue</u>

Kelly Nelson and Abby Marshall watch with blank stares as Ashton Markway approaches them. He seems upset.

"This still seems like a bad dream."

He gestures with his hand.

"Any ideas about who could've killed?"

Abby shakes her head.

"Do you think it's someone from Marble Hills?"

Abby nods.

"I'm hoping it isn't."

She sighs.

"I'm sure there's some sort of a connection between Caleb, Corinne, Ross, and Natalie—but have no idea what it could be besides the fact Caleb slept with both Corinne and Natalie."

Ashton smirks.

"Yeah—he bagged just about every other girl in town and then some—his rep wasn't made up—he was the real deal."

Kelly rolls his eyes at the comment.

"How does Ross fit into—you know—with them?"

"Well, he certainly didn't fuck Ross. Caleb was a lot of things—but gay he wasn't—maybe drugs or something."

Page 435

Abby glances at the parking lot nearby.

"I wonder if what happened to Tiffany Johnson is somehow connected—Daryl Anderson still has no leads from what I heard—it seems like he's come to a dead end."

"Could be—not that he's looking too hard regardless."

Ashton shuffles his feet.

"Could Gina have—you know—killed Caleb?"

Abby shakes her head.

"No—she couldn't. Caleb was a really tall guy—six feet four—and quite strong judging by his biceps. No, whoever killed him yesterday had to have been a guy—and much bigger."

Ashton seems uneasy.

"A jealous boyfriend or husband—wouldn't be surprised given his sordid rep all over Marble Hills and Portland."

Abby nods again.

"But how do the others figure into?"

"Especially Tiffany—and how she died?"

"Could Corey?"

Behind them a man dressed casually in white pants and a blue striped T-shirt comes toward where they are standing.

Stanley Pier

Jason Anderson looks out to sea. Tyler Van Pelt stands a few feet away lost in thought. Jason turns to face Tyler.

"Someone is racking up numbers."

Tyler shrugs.

"Uh-huh—and whoever killed Ross and the others are not going to stop anytime soon—they've tasted blood."

Jason turns to face Tyler.

"What the hell does that mean?"

Tyler sighs.

"There's a serial killer loose in Marble Hills—no one's safe until whoever is doing this is caught—and locked up."

Jason seems confused.

Maple Avenue

Brad is lying on top of Daphne—pounding into her recklessly. A few yards away someone is watching and tapping their fingers on a steering wheel seemingly very angry.

Miami

Juan and Calvin watch as Eldon's casket is slowly slid into a crypt and the entrance sealed. Calvin glances around.

"If you need any help when you get back to Marble Hills to confront Howard Madison—just let me know—call."

Juan smiles broadly.

"No—I can handle it—whole family is about to experience their worst nightmare ever imagined—won't stop until they're all lying in the morgue with multiple bullet holes in their heads."

They turn to look as the marble door is inserted in front of the sealed crypt. Calvin seems about to shed a tear.

Police Station

Clay watches as Daryl shuts off his cell phone. He turns around to face Clay. He glances at his cell phone nervously.

"Well, there's been an interesting development."

Daryl gestures with his hand.

"Apparently Natalie Standish had sex before she was pushed down the stairs—not that it's much of a surprise."

Clay seems surprised and sighs. He stands up and walks over to where Daryl is standing. They look at each other.

"Do they know with whom?"

Daryl nods and seems to enjoy knowing.

"Yep—seems a local resident punk named Brad McKinley has been sowing his wild oats everywhere—apparently."

Clay gestures with his hand.

"Think he did it?"

Daryl shakes his head.

"Not sure—but that boy has quite a reckless streak in him—can't see where he got it from though—his father was quite the dork back in the day—then again his mother—ugh."

Clay rolls his eyes.

"Want me to talk to him?"

Daryl shakes his head again.

"Nope—he and I know each other really well—this isn't going to be the first time he and I had a talk actually."

Clay sighs and sits down. He leans back in his chair.

"What about the others—think they're connected to each other? Bet people are talking about who knew who?"

Daryl shakes his head.

"Could be—but why they're dead is the million dollar question that seems to have no answers at the moment."

He sighs again and heads to the door.

Peabody Avenue

"Ashton Markway and Kelly Nelson I presume?"

Abby turns to see a man standing nearly two feet away.

"Who wants to know?"

"I do, actually, name's Maxwell Pendergraft."

He extends his hand.

"I'm with the Portland unit of the FBI."

Kelly and Ashton look at each other nervously. Abby seems curious but remains silent as Ashton steps forward.

"I'm Ashton Markway."

Maxwell shakes his hand and glances at Kelly.

"Kelly Nelson."

They look at Maxwell curiously and shrug.

"Did we do something wrong?"

Maxwell laughs.

"No."

He sighs.

"I'm actually here about the murders."

Kelly and Ashton look at each other nervously.

"Does the FBI already know about what happened yesterday in Marble Hills—must be a slow day no doubt?"

Maxwell grins.

"Uh-huh—seems someone in town is pretty scared. They think your guy Daryl Anderson just isn't up to the job."

Ashton smirks.

"That's an understatement—seriously."

Maxwell looks around.

"Anyway, I've been sent to make sure this is nipped in the bud before more bodies turn up unexplained around here."

"Got a suspect?"

Maxwell glances at Ashton.

"Trying out for detective school?"

Ashton gives Maxwell an odd look and smirks.

"Maybe—what's it to you?"

Maxwell grins broadly.

"Nothing at the moment—but if this is the work of a serial killer—they won't stop killing until they're caught in the act or they die before being apprehended by law enforcement."

"Yeah, I know the deal—that was the situation with **Jack the Ripper**. Never was punished for his crimes—but I think the bastard died shortly afterwards and that's why the murders stopped—everyone who says otherwise is just clueless."

Maxwell looks at Ashton curiously.

"That's the theory. He wasn't the first and certainly wasn't the last. You guys remember the **Zodiac Killer**? Same deal, he was never caught and is assumed by most to have died shortly after the murders suddenly stopped in the early 1970s."

Ashton nods in agreement.

"That stuff happened way before my time—like way before. Read some of the books though—sick and creepy."

Maxwell shakes his head and grins.

"Uh-huh—but nevertheless these cases were the only two that was more or less known not to have an ending which resulted in an arrest of a viable suspect—even now."

Abby glances at Maxwell.

"Are you going to be hanging out in Marble Hills until whoever is responsible is busted for the murders?"

Maxwell turns around to look at Kelly and Ashton.

<u>Maple Avenue</u>

Daphne watches as Brad shoves his shirt into his Levi's and smirks. He pulls her toward him and French kisses her.

"Oh yeah—nothing like a good fuck in the morning to start the day off right—I assume you're on the pill—right?"

Daphne nods several times.

"Of course—you and your friends warned me about trying to trap you or them whenever you or them fucked me. I wouldn't even consider pulling a stunt like that after—after you told me what would happen to me if I was stupid enough to get pregnant whenever we got together for—so I came prepared."

Brad smiles broadly.

"Good—just checking—wouldn't want a slipup to occur and then have to deal with your irresponsibility—nope."

Daphne rolls her eyes.

"Don't worry—you can continue to fuck me without worry anytime you choose to—I'm here to serve you willingly."

Brad pulls Daphne toward him again and kisses her passionately once more. He grins broadly in triumph.

"Perfect—nothing's better than an obedient whore."

He laughs as he notices her reaction.

"You girls know the deal already."

He smirks and wags his finger at her. She seems angry as he makes a lewd gesture with his tongue and winks. He begins laughing loudly as he sees her reaction—blowing her a kiss.

"It's just the way things are."

He leers at her briefly and then leaves. She watches him walk away and sighs. She looks down at her legs. Semen is clearly visible on her right leg. She pulls out a napkin and begins wiping it away. She seems upset—almost to the point of crying as she looks at the soiled napkin several times and sighs loudly.

Page **440**

<u>Boardinghouse</u>

Eddie Kane watches as Todd Spencer hugs Julia Winthrop warmly. They share a look as Julia wipes a tear away.

"I still can't believe he's dead."

Todd looks at Julia.

"They'll find who did this—this is a small town. There's no way whoever killed Caleb is going to be able to get away."

Julia wipes a tear from her eye.

"This is a nightmare."

Todd glances at Eddie again.

"Bet Daryl isn't really doing much—he said."

Eddie rolls his eyes.

"Sort of figured as much—that's why I called a college buddy of mine in Portland and he recommended his friend—a FBI investigator—he promised his friend would come and look into the case after I told him how incompetent Daryl was."

Todd grins broadly.

"Oh man, Daryl is going to be royally pissed."

"Counting on it—part of the perks."

"Think Caleb was killed because he had a thing for meaningless sex—plenty of pissed off husbands out there?"

Todd looks at Julia and shakes his head.

"It must be some other reason due to the others being killed apparently by the same person—on the same day."

Todd glances at Eddie again.

"I agree that there has to be a connection in some way or the other between Caleb and the others—but what is it?"

"It doesn't make sense."

Todd sighs and leans against the wall.

"Caleb knew both Corinne and Natalie—bet anything that they were his "girls" but Ross? No, he liked guys—and yeah from what Simon told me, Ross was heavy in the gay bar scene and had a thing for older men—so there's nothing linking him to Caleb as far as we know presently—I doubt they even talked."

<u>Page **441**</u>

"I guess I should start making arrangements. When Peter and Cassie died I bought an extra plot. Bought it for me—but Caleb should be with family—Peter would've wanted."

There's a quiet knock on the door. Julia looks up to see Alden Washington silently standing in the doorway.

Maple Avenue

Daphne finishes wiping away the semen on her leg and sighs as she is about to get into her car when she's confronted by a visitor whom she recognizes. She seems a bit surprised.

"I thought—thought you—what are you doing here?"

Suddenly a knife plunges into her chest. She screams and falls against her car as blood explodes from the wound.

Standish Road

Juan drives recklessly along the road as he seems focused on his anger while he clenches and unclenches his fist.

"Oh yeah—they're going to pay—and pay dearly."

He slows down as he heads toward the curve in the road and sighs. He looks out at the ocean and smiles slyly.

"Man, the pain I plan to inflict—oh horrible pain."

He sighs again and begins speeding once more—seeming to be in a mad rush to even the score on behalf of his friend.

Tolling Bell Inn

"This just gets better and better between us."

Lance Weissmann begins laughing as he lies back in bed. He glances at Susan Bennington and smirks broadly.

"Oh yeah—that definitely hit the spot all right."

He makes a lewd gesture with his finger.

"Who'd think you were a virgin less than a week ago?"

Susan blushes.

"Of which you took."

Lance grins broadly.

"Brad McKinley's loss was my gain—man, I can't believe he turned down a piece claiming impotence—he's never turned down a girl before—he's even gone as far as to come after girls while I were making moves on them—he must be slipping—like seriously—guess this whole mess with Carrie rattled him."

He smirks again and pulls Susan toward him. He looks at his exposed penis as he winks at her. He sighs again.

"No one knows about us yet—right? Your grandfather would skin me alive if he figured out what I did to you."

Susan shakes her head.

"No—my parents are splitsville—my dad will probably go back to Philly with his girlfriend—or at least she's hoping they will anyway—since—but I'm not so sure—I think my dad—I think he still likes my mom—but she's definitely through with him."

Lance sits up in bed.

"I think he'd be upset about us if he knew—or the fact I'm a high school senior fucking a barely legal underaged girl."

Susan smiles slyly.

"Well, it's a little late to worry about that now—you've had me already—had me plenty since—like old news actually."

Lance laughs.

"Hey, you wanted to lose your virginity—I was just in the right place at the right time—and took advantage of you."

Susan strokes Lance's hair.

"Uh-huh—you guys are all alike—you pretend to be really concerned but ultimately you'll insist on screwing a girl even if she wants to wait—seducing her with your charms—telling her how much you care—that she's the only one for you ever more while insinuating there might be a future down the line."

Lance laughs loudly.

"Guilty—so guilty—been there and done that—I'm most definitely not the boy next door—I've fucked plenty of girls by saying pretty much those exact words—but in my defense I'm just a guy with who likes to fuck girls. I'm bad and admit it."

Susan kisses Lance.

"Well, at least you're honest—anyway, I wanted my first time with a guy to be memorable—and that meant the guy had to be very experienced—and you certainly were—since you took me I've heard things about you around town and other women."

"What sort of things?"

Susan smirks.

"That you've been with older women?"

Lance laughs.

"I can't lie—played that card too."

Lance glances at his penis again.

"But I offer no apologies for my behavior."

Susan glances at Lance's erection and he grins broadly.

"I'm not asking—just making a point."

He pulls her under him and they begin kissing as they embark on another bout of passionate lovemaking.

<u>Stanley Pier</u>

Tyler turns to look out to sea again as Jason glances at him nervously. His mind seems to be somewhere else.

"Do you think whoever killed the others isn't finished yet with killing folks in town—could we be on the menu?"

Tyler shakes his head.

"Possible—heard rumors already circulating."

Jason leans heavily on the rail as he looks out to sea and seems disturbed by the thoughts running through his head.

"But who—who could be the killer—we know everyone in town and no one wouldn't—wouldn't start killing folks?"

Tyler rolls his eyes knowingly.

"How well do you really know everyone in town? Take me for example—until I told you I was gay last year you thought I was straight like you—but I wasn't—what if whoever killed Ross and the others last night is someone we know and trust?"

Jason shrugs and faces Tyler again.

"But that—it just can't be—we would've seen signs? There would have been something that clued us in before?"

Page 444

"Are you sure about that?"

Tyler looks out at the ocean again.

"I've read a lot of true crime books and no one ever figures out the truth until it's staring them right in the face and by then it's too late to do anything because a whole bunch of people are dead and a nutjob is on the loose with a gun—or a machete."

They look at each other.

<u>Mall</u>

Daryl slowly walks over to where Brad is sitting alone as he munches on a muffin and sips coffee from a paper cup.

"You're a pretty hard guy to get to Brad McKinley—you're quite the busy man about Marble Hills today aren't you?"

Brad looks up.

"Didn't know I was in demand?"

Daryl smirks.

"Yeah—I bet."

Brad seems confused.

"Is there a reason why you're bothering me—or have you suddenly—you know—begun to make an effort at your job?"

Daryl sits down next to Brad.

"I wouldn't be making snarky comments if I were you right about now—especially given what I know about you."

Brad sighs.

"Uh-huh—are you here to arrest me for being smarter than you—or is it—is it that I'm better with your whores?"

Daryl grabs Brad.

"Seems you've been quite popular lately—imagine my surprise when your semen turned up in both Corinne and Natalie's corpses—you know, someone might think you were involved with their sudden demises—and if I were a betting man I'd say you had plenty of reasons to want them dead."

Brad jerks free of Daryl's grip.

"I didn't kill either of them. I was with Daphne when they were killed—you can ask Daphne—I was banging her."

Page **445**

"Oh, don't worry, I will—count on it."

Brad rolls his eyes at Daryl.

"You better not be accusing me of anything—or I'll have your badge—you worthless piece—stupid frigging loser."

Daryl seems about to explode.

"OK—that's it you prick. I've had enough of your lip for one day—I think you need to be taught a fucking lesson."

He grabs Brad by the collar and angrily forces him to his feet. Brad seems surprised at the sudden turn of events.

"Yeah, that's right I'm arresting you."

"I haven't done anything."

Daryl grins.

"Really—how about rape—yep—seems plausible to me given your slimy rep around town with your classmates?"

Brad rolls his eyes.

"I don't have to rape anyone. Chicks love my dick. Ask anyone. I've slept with just about every girl in town."

Daryl laughs.

"So, I've heard. How do you think Gable Markway is going to react when I tell him you raped his innocent daughter not long ago—I'm thinking he won't take too kindly to news of that sort but I could be wrong—how about we put it to a test today?"

Brad suddenly appears frightened.

"You wouldn't—Markway royally hates me."

Daryl laughs loudly.

"Do I look like I care?"

Brad sighs loudly.

"OK. OK. I fucked Corinne and Natalie yesterday—so what. I didn't kill them—I have no beef with any of my girls."

Daryl relaxes his grip on Brad's shoulder.

"And you didn't see anything?"

Brad shakes his head. Daryl seems upset and shrugs.

"Don't leave town—or I swear—I'll find you."

Brad gives Daryl a strange look.

"Don't worry—I'm not going anywhere."

Daryl lets go of Brad.

"I swear if I find out you're mixed up in these murders I'll kill you myself—snap your damn neck like a fucking twig."

Brad appears nervous.

"I don't like being threatened by the likes of you."

Daryl gives Brad a strange look and smirks.

"Tell it to someone who gives a fuck."

Seconds later Daryl's cell phone rings. He glances at Brad briefly and then answers the cell phone and scowls.

"I'll be right there."

Brad watches as the color drains from Daryl's face.

Portland

Sounds of loud moaning are heard echoing from a hotel room as Caroline Bentley looks into the grinning face of Glen Bradstreet as he aggressively enters her yet again. She sighs.

"Oh God—oh God—show some mercy."

Glen laughs loudly.

"Asking God to save you is futile. I own you now—to do with as I please—like the cheap back alley whore you are."

He slams into Caroline again.

"Oh yeah—a guy's gotta live large."

He laughs loudly.

"Hope you didn't forget to pop those pills?"

He slams into Caroline once more.

Farmington Villa

Juan slams the door shut behind him and heads toward the balcony. The sound echoes loudly for a few seconds.

"Damn that family—damn them to hell."

He sighs loudly as he clenches his fists angrily.

"If it's the last thing I do—I'll put them all in the ground."

He pounds his fist against the railing—at that moment Faye Washington comes toward him. She seems happy.

"You're back—I was beginning to wonder."

Juan sighs loudly.

"Wonder about what exactly?"

"Whether or not you were coming back?"

Juan leans against the railing.

"I had some problems—and it took longer than expected."

Faye slides her arms around Juan's waist.

"What sort of problem?"

Juan grins.

"Never mind—right now the only thing I want to do is take you into the bedroom and—and make up for lost time."

He makes a lewd gesture with his hand.

"Fucking you for the next two hours sounds about right."

Without waiting for an answer he lifts her into his arms and carries her toward the bedroom and shuts the door.

<u>Boardinghouse</u>

Julia hugs Alden tightly as he glances at Eddie and Todd with a sigh. They shake their heads several times.

"I'm here for you—especially now."

Julia looks at Alden as tears stream down her face.

"He was so young—had his whole life ahead of him. I knew he wasn't perfect—slept around a lot—but he just didn't deserve to die like this—it was just so—so vicious—like some animal got a hold of him and couldn't help themselves. It was horrible to see his body like that. He must've cried out for help before he finally passed out and bled to death—it's still unreal even now."

Sounds of sirens echo in a distance. Eddie looks at Todd with a nervous glance. Todd shakes his head knowingly.

"I wonder what that's about—hope it's not another."

Eddie and Alden look at each other.

<u>Mall</u>

Brad watches as Daryl shuts off the cell phone. They look at each other. Daryl gives Brad a harsh glare and sighs.

Page 448

"Well—what's happened?"
Daryl glances at Brad with an odd look.
"Like you don't already know?"
"Huh—what is that supposed to mean?"
Without warning Daryl angrily grabs Brad and slaps handcuffs on him. He smiles broadly as he looks at Brad.
"I've got you—you're not going to kill anyone else again."
Brad seems confused. People nearby begin to stare.
"What—what are you talking about?"
Daryl looks at Brad smugly.
"Brad McKinley—you have the right to remain silent."
Brad reacts in shock and sighs loudly.

Maple Avenue

Clay stares at the sheet-covered body. He sighs loudly and turns around to look at Gina Bentley standing nearby.
"So, to recap what happened—you heard a scream as you were about to go into the mall and found the body?"
Gina nods.
"Yes—yes—are you sure Daphne is dead? I mean?"
Clay shakes his head.
"Uh-huh—trust me—she's dead."
They look at each other.
"But it can't be—who would—it wasn't?"
Clay seems confused.
"Why—why can't it be—do you know something?"
Before she can answer he sees Daryl pulling up. In the backseat of Daryl's patrol car is Brad McKinley. Daryl jumps out of the car and heads over to where Clay is standing with Gina.
"Coroner is on his way in about two minutes."
Daryl glances at the sheet-covered body for a few seconds before pulling the sheet away from the body to look at Daphne's face. He sighs loudly as he sees the look of terror still imprinted on her facial features. Clay turns to look at Brad again.
"Why is Brad with you?"

Daryl smirks.

"I got the bastard before he could kill again."

Clay seems confused.

"He confessed?"

Daryl shakes his head.

"Not exactly—but he will—oh—I assure you that bastard will come clean one way or the other. I'll make sure of it."

Clay looks at Daryl oddly. Daryl notices Gina standing a few feet away with a strange look on her face. He shrugs.

"What's she doing here?"

Clay glances at Gina.

"She called me after she heard Daphne screaming."

Daryl looks at Gina again.

"Did you see who?"

Gina shakes her head.

"No. I heard Daphne screaming for help—then came and found her. There was no one else around—really quiet."

She looks at Brad sitting in the patrol car.

"You think Brad killed Daphne?"

Daryl nods.

"Got a better explanation?"

Clay and Gina look at each other.

<u>Portland</u>

Jarod Keller buttons his Levi's as he looks at Denise Madison and grins broadly. He slowly combs his hair.

"Hey, just so you know I'll be back in Marble Hills in two days—just thought you'd like to know—pay me a visit."

Denise smirks.

"Bet you plan to hook-up with all your girlfriends."

"Hope that won't be a problem for you—will it? You and I are just friends right—friends with plenty of privileges?"

Denise smirks again.

"Who you sleep with is your business."

Jarod grins slyly.

Page 450

"Good—wouldn't want there to be problems."

Denise leans over and kisses Jarod.

"I wouldn't think of interfering with your sex life."

"Good to know."

Denise licks her lips seductively.

"Too bad you have to leave so quickly."

Jarod rolls his eyes.

"Meeting Courtney's prissy folks in an hour—got to play the part of the dutiful boyfriend—so boring to be dull."

Denise makes a lewd gesture with her hand.

"Well, I'm glad you called me up—hope I helped with taking away some of your frustration and obvious needs."

Jarod kisses Denise.

"Oh, I'm quite relaxed now—nothing like really good dick action to relax a man with pent-up girlfriend issues."

He smirks slyly.

"But it's all good—come fall I plan to officially break up with Courtney. I'm just not the boyfriend type—can't be."

Denise licks her lips again.

"I agree with you completely."

They begin kissing.

<u>Maple Avenue</u>

Brad watches as Clay drives away. He spins around to face Daryl with a disdainful look as he realizes his reality.

"I didn't kill Daphne or the others. I'm innocent."

Daryl laughs and gestures with his finger.

"Shut up—I'm so sick of your fucking mouth."

"You won't get away with this—my dad will stop."

"Your dad is a loser—just like you—and when he finds out you killed six people—I think he'll see things my way."

"Six?"

Daryl laughs again.

"Yep—I'm going out on a limb and betting you killed Tiffany Johnson also—sick creep—frigging sick bastard."

Page 451

Brad seems in shock.

"You can't do this—no one will believe you."

Daryl turns to face Brad.

"Wouldn't they? You've slept with just about every girl in town—your rep couldn't get any worse Brad—you're not on anybody's list for teenager of the year—oh yeah, it won't be hard for everyone in town to believe you're a nutjob freaky killer."

Brad glares at Daryl.

"Whatever—you're a zero—nobody."

Daryl puts the paperwork down.

"Nothing I would like more than to see you get the chair for this—bet you won't think you're so cool when they flip the switch and fry your worthless ass for six murders—most of all, it'll be fitting revenge for what you did to Donna Markway."

Brad rolls his eyes.

"Donna Markway—is this why you're so sore? You're still pissed because I bagged that whore after taking her away from your dweeb son. How pathetic are you—get a life already."

Daryl glances at Brad with a smug look.

"We'll see who's more pathetic after your trial—at least Jason will still be alive when everything is all said and done."

Daryl laughs.

"But you—not so much if you get the electric chair."

Brad seems frightened for the first time.

<u>Portland</u>

Caroline watches as Glen walks in front of her as he returns from the bathroom. His penis is sticking out in front of him as he grins broadly knowing she's staring intently.

"Yep—there's gonna be a round two for sure. I've got a lot of pent-up energy that needs releasing—quite needy today."

Caroline sighs.

"I guessed as much."

Glen climbs into bed and smirks as he notices Caroline still looking intently at his erection. He looks at his watch.

Page 452

"Uh-huh—I want a blowjob too."

He forces Caroline's head between his legs.

Bentley Driveway

As Clay pulls up behind Gina's car he sees John Bentley waiting in the driveway. Gina runs to her father and they embrace as Clay approaches. John seems nervous and sighs.

"Are you OK?"

Gina nods.

"Yes—but it was horrible."

John looks at Clay curiously.

"I think it's time you guys brought in outside help."

Clay seems irritated.

"We're handling it as best we can given the unusual circumstances of what has happened—lots of strings that are untied at the moment—but there are clues—several."

John sighs.

"Who could be doing this—I mean?"

Clay shrugs.

"I can't make sense of what happened yet."

Clay glances at the house.

Shelby Park

Jeremy Weissmann and Shirley Moses are sitting on one of the park benches kissing when they hear a noise. Shirley whirls around in shock. She seems panicked. Jeremy laughs.

"It's only a raccoon—it can't hurt you—unless you confront them—then all bets are off—not cowards are they."

He gestures with his hand.

"Those things stand their ground if confronted. They're quite nasty and vicious—they only look cute from a distance."

He points toward the nearby bushes as a raccoon sticks his head out of the shrubs and looks at them briefly before disappearing into the brush again. Shirley sighs loudly.

Page **453**

"Well, can you blame me for freaking?"

Jeremy kisses Shirley again.

"Nope—though I think you and I shouldn't be out here much longer—you never know—things can happen."

Shirley looks at Jeremy curiously.

"Like what?"

Jeremy grins.

"You never know—I might be the killer?"

He grabs her and pretends to wrestle her to the table. She pushes him away immediately as he begins laughing loudly.

"That's not funny—weird actually."

Jeremy glances at Shirley.

"It was funny—you should have seen your face."

Jeremy's cell phone rings. He looks at it.

"Why is she calling me?"

Before Shirley can respond, Jeremy rolls his eyes twice as he answers and seems dismayed, sighing several times.

"What do you want Lana?"

He listens and the color drains from his face. Shirley seems upset at hearing Lana's name being mentioned.

"Come on Lana—even for you this is over the top."

He turns away.

"Are you telling me the truth Lana? Did Daryl Anderson just arrest Brad McKinley for killing Caleb and the others?"

Jeremy sighs again.

"Seriously, you expect me to believe this crap—from you of all people—after the lies that you've told everyone?"

Shirley seems nervous and moves closer to Jeremy.

"Fine—whatever—if you say so Lana—I get it."

He shuts his cell phone off and looks at Shirley for a few seconds. He seems in shock as he looks at his cell phone.

"What happened? What did Lana say?"

"Brad McKinley has been arrested for Caleb Winthrop's murder—seems Jason's pop busted him—bet you anything Brad will try to wiggle out of this one too—McKinley is so frigging twisted—I wouldn't put anything past him—so whacked."

Page 454

Shirley seems in shock at the news.

"How did Jason's dad know?"

Jeremy rolls his eyes.

"Not sure—but seriously who's crazy enough to believe anything Lana Jefferson says nowadays? The girl has a problem with the meaning of the word truth—nope—I'll believe it when I see solid proof—that girl lies better than every one of those frigging loser fuck-ups on FOX News. Girl should seriously think of becoming a novelist. **Jackie Collins** would've been so lucky to have known someone as gossipy as Lana for her novels."

Shirley looks at Jeremy's cell phone as it begins ringing nonstop seconds later. This time it's Corey Bentley.

TO BE CONTINUED

A Look at the 18th Episode

News of a suspect in the rash of recent murders makes the rounds around Marble Hills—Denise and Miles enjoy a private moment together—Jarod and Courtney await the visit of her fussy parents—Juan and Faye decide to go their separate ways after an argument—Clay and Eva compare notes—Caroline continues to dance with danger—Julia vows revenge for Caleb's tragic death at the hands of another—Denise makes a bold move against Caroline—Faye plots revenge against Alden—Lana and Gina make a risky bet with unpleasant consequences for both—Denise hooks up with a new lover—Corey blackmails Shirley—Jason and Simon finger a possible new suspect in the recent murders in Marble Hills—Lana plots to destroy Gina once and for all—Clay and Maxwell happily reminiscence about old times—as Hart foolishly makes an unnecessary enemy of a total stranger.

Malice in Wonderland

<u>Shelby Park</u>

Jeremy Weissmann looks at his cell phone again and sighs loudly as he pauses briefly. He seems irritated at the call.

"What's up Corey?"

Shirley Moses watches as his expression changes and seems suddenly agitated by what is transpiring nearby.

"You mean Lana Jefferson was actually telling the truth for a change—it just can't be—McKinley wouldn't."

He sighs loudly again.

"Brad McKinley is a creep—but a killer?"

He looks at Shirley.

"When did Jason's dad slap the cuffs on him?"

He rolls his eyes.

"OK—keep me updated."

He shuts off the cell phone and reacts.

"Apparently Brad lost it and killed Daphne. They think he also killed Caleb, Corinne, Ross, and Natalie as well."

He leans against the picnic table.

"This just can't be real."

He wipes sweat from his brow.

"They're also saying he was possibly responsible for Tiffany Johnson's death—said Brad is acting really weird."

Shirley sighs.

"Oh my God—he—but he's one of us?"

Jeremy nods in agreement.

"That's not all—according to Corey, Carrie Spaulding is missing—and—and Brad could be involved with that too."

Shirley has an odd reaction to the news.

<u>Portland</u>

Denise Madison smiles broadly as Miles Dandridge seductively pulls his penis out of his boxer briefs. He grins.

"Uh-huh—I'm horny—expecting a lot today."

Denise smirks.

"I'm at your mercy—willing to do anything."

He suddenly grabs her by the neck and they begin kissing passionately as they fall back onto the bed and go at it.

"Oh man, from the day we first met—there's never been a moment when I didn't want you so badly—got to fuck you."

"The feeling was mutual I assure you—there's something about a virile young man doing what comes naturally."

Miles laughs.

"Hey, fucking is the best way I know how to relax."

He climbs on top of her.

"Jarod told me you have a son almost my age—man, who would've guessed I'd be banging a woman like you?"

Denise smiles broadly.

"I had Wesley when I was in my last year of high school. But, well, his father is a whole other story—he is—we don't."

She seems upset.

"He and I are through—said I disgusted him."

Miles laughs loudly.

"How could he not want to fuck you—seriously?"

He kisses Denise again.

Page 458

"Guys want to fuck all the time—fuck everything that looks hot—take me for example—this morning I fucked twin sisters in my dorm room—couldn't get enough of me—made plans to have a threesome tomorrow with their cousin."

He smirks.

"Right afterwards, I screwed this cheerleader I wanted to bang for a few weeks now—had to wait until her pathetic dweeb boyfriend went to visit his mother in New York City. But oh, was it worth it—came like less than a minute after I stuck her in the library archive room—we went at it like rabbits for an hour."

Denise strokes his hair.

"Then I fucked this waitress who I've been banging for months now—she's had a thing for me like forever—and I rammed her hard in my car—begged me not to stop."

He grins slyly.

"Last but not least I fucked this whore that hangs around the gym like every day. The first time she met me she told me I looked like **Nick Thoman**—you know, the Olympic swimmer—of which I used to my advantage and took her in the sauna—from that day forward we've fucked every time I drop by the gym for a hit—and now I'm here with you. I'm on a roll today no doubt."

Miles watches as Denise strokes his hair again.

<u>Bar Harbor</u>

Jarod Keller kisses Courtney Robson passionately and grins as his hand slides under her skirt and into her panty.

"My parents will be here soon—and they won't like?"

He laughs slyly.

"That's fine—but we still have time for a quickie."

Courtney sighs.

"I can't—what if they arrive early?"

Jarod smirks.

"They'll see me with my dick sticking out."

Courtney pushes him away.

"Ugh—I don't want them to know."

Page **459**

Jarod grabs Courtney and pushes her against the wall.

"I'm your boyfriend."

Seconds later he penetrates her.

"Once they leave you and I are really going to stain those sheets in your bedroom—lots of action on the menu."

He continues thrusting intently for several minutes and finally pulls out as he shoots his load. He laughs again.

"Nice deal—told you I'd be quick."

Courtney grabs a napkin and wipes her legs. Seconds later a knock is heard at the front door. Jarod grins broadly.

<u>Farmington Villa</u>

"Will you stop nagging me already Faye—man, you're worse than a wife—which by the way isn't a compliment."

Juan Sabrillo rolls his eyes at Faye Washington and plops down on the sofa. She sighs loudly as he ignores her.

"I just want to know what happened in Miami—I get the distinct impression you're trying to hide something."

Juan grins slyly and gestures.

"What if I am—huh—is that what you want to hear me say? Yeah, I went to Miami like I said and afterwards fucked these two sluts I met at a club on the beach. Are you satisfied now?"

Faye seems shocked and hurt at the statement.

"You fucked me after you stuck it to two prostitutes in Miami. You should have told me. I don't want an STD."

Juan gestures with his hand.

"Tell you—what the hell for—it's my dick in case it slipped your mind. You're on a need-to-know basis and nothing more—so deal already—I mean—who do you think you are anyway?"

Faye seems about to burst out in tears.

"I thought—you and I were really close to becoming a couple. I thought what we had was leading somewhere."

Juan looks at Faye curiously.

"Is that so?"

Juan begins laughing and stands up.

Page 460

"Why would you assume we were a couple? Come on, I made it clear from the start we were just friends with sweet benefits—nothing more—deal with it or get out already."

Faye looks at Juan for a few seconds and runs to the bedroom. He smirks and stretches out on the sofa. Seconds later she emerges with two pieces of luggage and heads to the door in a rush. He notices and laughs at the overly dramatic scene playing out in front of him. He makes a lewd gesture with his finger.

"Oh-oh—you're like really mad at me—see ya."

Faye seems hurt.

"I never want to see you again—I hate you."

Juan smirks again and waves his hand at her followed by another lewd gesture. Faye sighs and opens the door, slamming it shut as she leaves. Juan rolls his eyes and laughs loudly.

"That damn woman made up a fantasy in her head."

He grins and glances at the door.

<u>Lighthouse Grill</u>

Clay Blankenship and Eva Harper are having lunch. They watch as Sidney Stuyvesant brings over a huge slice of Dutch apple pie. Clay grins broadly as Sidney places it on the table.

"Oh yeah—my tongue is in heaven."

Sidney smirks.

"I remembered how much you liked it from the first time you dropped by—ate four slices nonstop—quite the record."

Clay grabs a fork.

"Best pie I've had in a while—thanks."

Sidney glances at Eva.

"This one here ate six slices last week—thought he was going to explode—topped his four slice record easily."

Eva smiles slyly.

"Yeah—I know how much Clay likes eating—sucks everything down like a power vacuum—and then some."

Sidney nods. Clay looks up from the plate.

"I'll have another."

Page 461

Sidney nods again and smirks as he heads toward the kitchen. Eva looks around the small diner and shrugs.

"Do think this McKinley kid killed all those people?"

Clay nods.

"Daryl thinks he did—and he'd know better than me on these matters—from what he said Brad McKinley is a real piece of work—his rep is no joke—everyone knows his deal—trouble."

Eva sighs.

"But he's a kid?"

"Quite cold-blooded from what I heard—definitely not **Tony Dow** or **Ron Howard** material—innocent he isn't."

Eva watches as Archie Spaulding rushes past her. He angrily runs toward the kitchen nearby. Clay notices also.

"He seems to be in mood?"

Clay nods knowingly.

"Must have real important information to discuss with Sidney—looks to me like he has some major drama to unpack."

Eva looks at her salad.

"You know I'm not really hungry—maybe you should eat this before it goes to waste—good food and all that?"

Clay glances at her for a second or two and gobbles down the salad. He looks up at her a second later. He sighs.

"Are you OK?"

Eva shakes her head.

"Yeah—just the turn of events in Marble Hills I guess."

Clay looks at Eva nervously.

"You're not—you know—well?"

Eva laughs.

"What—no—I'm not pregnant—I'm always on the pill."

Clay looks at Eva oddly.

"Mistakes happen? We've been pretty busy lately in the bedroom—maybe you forgot—it only takes one time."

Eva reaches out to touch Clay's hand.

"Not with me sweetie—really—I'm just not hungry."

Clay looks at Eva again.

"Really, I'm fine. No issues whatsoever."

Clay notices Sidney coming toward him again with another slice of pie. Sidney quickly disappears as he and Archie resumes their conversation. Clay looks at the slice of pie and at the double doors where he can see Sidney and Archie furiously discussing something through the small window in the middle of the wooden doors. He looks at Eva. She glances at the door again as they both seem concerned about Archie's odd behavior.

"You think something else has happened, don't you?"

They look at each other. Clay seems worried.

Portland

Caroline Bentley licks the final remnants of seminal fluid from the head of Glen Bradstreet's penis. He smirks.

"It's a pity you have to leave so soon—would've liked to continue our adventure—so much more traveling needed."

Caroline stands up.

"I'll be back tomorrow—it's not like I have a choice?"

"No—you're definitely right about that—you have no choice in the matter—my dick *will* be serviced or else."

Caroline wipes away dried semen from her lips and combs her hair. Glen pulls on his Levi's and turns to face her.

"Tell John I said hi—he and I really should be friends."

Caroline rolls her eyes and heads for the door.

"Some things are never what they seem."

Glen seems confused as she slams the door shut. He scratches his head as he looks down at his exposed penis.

"What the hell did she mean by that?"

He smirks again.

Boardinghouse

Julia Winthrop slowly places Caleb's belongings into a large cardboard box. She glances for a few seconds at several pairs of Levi's and multiple pairs of boxer briefs. She sighs.

"It just can't be real—he had so much to live for."

Page 463

She places several more items into a box and finally seals it with duct tape. She stands up and looks around.

"He would've wanted these to go to those who are less fortunate—and since he won't need them anymore."

She sighs loudly.

"Brad McKinley is going to pay for what he's done—I'll make sure of it—he won't get away with murdering Caleb."

She looks around at the empty room.

<u>Portland</u>

Denise licks her lips as she watches Caroline exit the building. She smiles broadly and checks her hair again.

"Well, I guess it's time I pay her gorgeous young lover a visit. I bet he's good—like really good if Caroline enjoys."

Denise slowly steps out of her car.

<u>Shelby Park</u>

Shirley watches curiously as Jeremy dials a number on his cell phone. He suddenly stops as she leans over his shoulder.

"Who were you calling just now?"

Jeremy turns to look at Shirley.

"I was calling Corey back—but he's not picking up."

At the edge of the park not far away from where they're standing he notices Jason Anderson and Tyler Van Pelt talking.

"Oh-oh—I wonder what else has happened. Has there been another murder in town that we don't know about?"

Shirley turns to look.

"Tyler seems quite agitated."

Jeremy shrugs.

"Must be about Ross Harrison's death?"

He sighs.

"Though I can't see why—Ross was two-timing Tyler for months—Harrison being dead is no big loss—not really."

Shirley seems upset at the comment.

Page 464

"Ross Harrison wasn't the nicest of people I admit—but no one deserves to be killed the way he was—quite brutal."

"Whatever—he got whacked and I'm supposed to pretend he wasn't such a jerk—no way—he was a scumbag and I don't see why I should fake how I feel now that he's in the morgue."

Shirley seems upset at the comment.

"You're still holding it against him because he made a pass at you a while back—it was no big deal—none at all."

Jeremy sighs loudly.

"Hey, he just didn't make a pass at me like the usual gay guy would—he tried to stick his hand inside my pants."

"So what—it wasn't like anything was going to happen between the two of you—he was just being himself?"

"You didn't know Ross like I did—oh yeah, if he had the opportunity he would have forced the issue all the way."

He looks at Jason and Tyler again briefly.

"I'm glad the bastard is dead—I for one will not feel one shred of grief if Brad McKinley did off that freak—probably a good thing—the only good thing he will ever do in his life."

He looks at his watch and rolls his eyes.

"Look, I've got to go—got an appointment in an hour with a really eager job possibility at a new kiosk in the mall."

Shirley nods knowingly.

"OK. I've got stuff to do also—see you at four?"

He nods and walks away.

<u>Tolling Bell Inn</u>

Faye opens to the door to the room and sighs.

"Men—I hate them—hate them all."

She shuts the door behind her.

"First Alden plays me for a fool—and now Juan."

She clenches her fist.

"Selfish worthless jerk—after everything that happened between us—he didn't seem to care one bit about me or if I left him—made it seem like I was just a whore he paid for—ugh."

Page 465

She walks toward the narrow balcony and opens the sliding glass doors. As air rushes into the room she takes a breath of fresh air and smiles broadly as she looks out at the town.

"Well, at least now I'll have time to make Alden's life a nightmare—couldn't happen to a nicer guy—hate him too."

She smirks and grabs her cell phone.

<u>Mall</u>

Lana Jefferson watches Gina Bentley walking toward the entrance of a small cafe. She grins broadly and walks over to where Gina is standing. They look at each other coldly.

"I guess you're off the hook as a suspect in Tiffany Johnson's recent tragic demise—oh well, maybe next time."

Gina rolls her eyes at Lana.

"Don't you have somewhere to be? You know, like trolling Red Barn Gym for desperate pathetic guys dumb enough to want to sleep with a plain-looking wallflower like yourself?"

Lana reacts to the slight.

"*You bitch.* No wonder Tiffany hated you—*troll.*"

"Uh-huh—I'm proud to be a bitch—beats being plain and forgettable like you. Must seriously be a drag—die already."

Lana notices several other people looking at the two of them. She seems hurt by the comment just made by Gina.

"God, I swear—I would give anything if Natalie was still alive and it was you they found at the bottom of the stairs."

Gina angrily pushes Lana.

"I could say the same for you Lana—woof."

"OK—OK—enough needless drama you two—this isn't the set of *Dynasty*—make nice or take this outside on the street."

Lana and Gina turn to see Drew Brockmeyer looking at them with a thoroughly disgusted look. Gina rolls her eyes.

"Fuck off—go bother someone else Drew."

"And you wonder why Abby Marshall snagged the guy you wanted—bet you this is exactly the reason why. Uh-huh."

Gina clenches her fist.

Page 466

"I swear—I don't know what I ever saw in you?"

Drew laughs and turns to face Lana.

"You know how Eddie Kane feels about fighting in his mall—one wrong move between you two and I'll have to ban you both for six months—do I make myself perfectly clear?"

Lana nods. Gina rolls her eyes. Drew turns to look at Gina again. He grins and proudly fingers his gold-plated badge.

"I love this position—oh man—I do—I do."

They watch as he walks away. Lana smiles broadly.

"Love a man in uniform—even if he's just the junior head of security—men in tight uniforms—bet he's packing plenty."

Gina seems disgusted and sighs.

"Forget it—I couldn't get him to put out—and believe me I tried every trick—told me he didn't like being played."

Lana licks her lips.

"Bet you I'd score—I'd do him in a flash."

She licks her lips again.

"Yep—that's the difference between you and me—I'll get him in the backseat of my car by next week—guaranteed."

Gina grins slyly.

"Care to wage a bet on that?"

Lana turns to face Gina. She nods.

"Yeah—it'll be like that movie *Little Darlings* where **Tatum O'Neal** and **Kristy McNichol** made bets on one of them losing their virginity before the other did. Except of course, neither of us are virgins and I'm the only one competing to bed Prince Charming—otherwise known as Drew Brockmeyer—say, hello to my new boyfriend—I don't lose bets—unlike you of course."

Gina rolls her eyes again.

"So, do we have a bet or not?"

Lana shrugs.

"What is going to be the loser's punishment?"

Gina grins broadly.

"Loser sleeps with Ashton Markway."

Lana reacts.

"Ugh—that's cruel—like seriously—even for you."

"Take it or leave it."

Lana looks around nervously.

"OK—OK—it's a deal. Hope you like dweebs."

Gina glances at Drew in a distance and makes a sucking sound with her lips as she turns to face Lana once more.

"It's you that had better like dweebs—think about it for a second—Ashton loses his virginity to you in the backseat of his car and then makes you a social outcast in Marble Hills like forever—oh yeah, this will be so sweet—so sweet indeed."

Gina laughs with smug indifference.

"But don't despair—you might get a trashy reality show out of it—and end up a bigger loser than you already are."

"I hate you. I wish you were dead."

"Whatever—but a bet's a bet—and I plan to collect."

Lana looks at Gina harshly and walks away as Simon Spencer comes toward both of them. Lana ignores him.

"What's her problem?"

Gina rolls her eyes.

"It's her time of the month."

Simon seems confused at the comment.

<u>Portland</u>

As the doorbell rings several times Glen puts his drink down on a nearby table and walks to the door. He opens it.

"I'm not buying anything—beat it."

Denise grins broadly.

"I'm not asking you to buy anything—I'm giving it away for free—but only to a man like yourself who knows the score."

Glen looks at Denise curiously.

"I don't do hookers—get lost *bitch*."

Denise laughs mockingly.

"I'm no hooker. I'm a friend of Caroline Bentley. Got some info I think you'll definitely like knowing about—juicy."

Glen quickly ushers Denise through the door and closes it. He turns to look at her—his eyes focusing on her breasts.

Page 468

"So, you know Caroline huh—if she told you to come over here and try to beg for mercy—tough luck—no deal."
Denise smirks.
"I would never help that bitch—I hate her."
Glen leers at Denise.
"But you just said you were her friend?"
Denise suddenly grabs Glen and kisses him passionately. He grins broadly as she aggressively kisses him again.
"I lied."
She smirks.
"I do my own thing."
Glen grins as he pins her against the wall.
"No strings attached?"
Denise slides her fingers across Glen's erection slowly as it continues to swell under his snug-fitting Levi's. She sighs.
"There's always strings attached."
She begins to unzip the zipper on his jeans.
"I want the same thing Caroline got."
Glen smirks again.
"Who said she and I are intimate?"
Denise rolls her eyes.
"*Oh please*—what other use for you could she have—she's married to a man who defines the word dull—and you, well, we both know with a body like yours—you get a lot of play."
Glen aggressively grabs Denise lifts her into his arms and heads to his bedroom. Denise seems pleased and smiles.

<u>Pete's Cafe</u>

Julia opens the door to the diner and looks around. As she is about to go inside she sees Alden Washington slowly coming toward her from the adjoining parking lot nearby. He waves.
"Thought you might need some company?"
Julia sighs.
"You're so sweet."
She looks at the keys in her hand.

Page 469

"But I have to do something—sitting around all day isn't going to bring Caleb back—I feel so helpless right now."

Alden looks around.

"Well, at least they nabbed his killer."

Julia nods.

"Should've known he was trouble—ever since I first met Brad McKinley I had a bad feeling about him—really bad."

She follows Alden into the diner.

"He always had to have his way—always working some sly angle—always using someone to get what he wanted."

Alden runs his fingers through his hair.

"He would've fit into Los Angeles perfectly."

Julia and Alden reach the front counter. She turns to look at the entrance—as if looking for someone—anyone.

"I guess after the funeral I'll accept he's really gone."

She leans against the counter.

"I still don't know why Brad would kill Caleb—I thought they were friends—no known bad blood between them."

Alden looks around.

"Is Daryl absolutely sure this Brad McKinley person killed Caleb? I mean—what—what if it was someone else?"

Julia nods several times.

"I guess—if not Brad—who else can it be?"

Alden shakes his head and sighs.

<u>Maple Avenue</u>

Clay kisses Eva lightly on the cheek. She seems upset.

"You really have to go back to work so soon?"

Clay gestures with his hand.

"I've got a ton of work waiting for me at the station."

Eva slides her arms around Clay's waist.

"I can't wait until your shift is over."

Clay laughs.

"Careful—I may get too excited and do something incredibly stupid—like forget to take my gun with me?"

Page **470**

Eva smiles broadly.

"OK. OK. But just remember that when your shift is over I will be waiting at your apartment—ready to pounce."

Eva leans close to Clay and whispers. A grin spreads across his face. Eva slowly runs her fingers through his hair and sighs.

"A girlfriend can only tolerate so much."

They kiss again.

<u>Standish Road</u>

Shirley is driving aimlessly when Corey Bentley pulls up besides her. He makes a lewd gesture with his fingers.

"Do you come here often?"

Shirley gives him a nasty look.

"What do you want?"

He grins broadly.

"Pull over and I'll tell you—just like old times."

Shirley rolls her eyes.

"I don't think so Corey—get lost."

Corey becomes upset.

"How dare you disrespect me *bitch*—I think I should pay sweet Jeremy a visit—and tell him all about our trysts."

Shirley immediately pulls over to the side of the road and steps out of the car to confront Corey a few feet away.

"Enough is enough—I won't be blackmailed anymore by you—I'm done. Can't you be a decent guy for a change?"

Corey grabs Shirley and throws her against his car in a rage. He slides his hand under her skirt despite her attempts to push him away. He hits her hard across her face and laughs.

"Exactly who do you think you are?"

He angrily hits her again.

"I will decide when our arrangement ends."

As she continues to struggle he unzips his Levi's and penetrates her. He laughs as he angrily rams her repeatedly.

"Still think you're in charge—huh—do you?"

He rams her again.

Page **471**

"I'm in charge—not you—frigging mouthy whore."

She tries to slap him as he blocks her hand and pulls her head backwards. He angrily hits her again with his fist.

"Try that again and I swear you'll regret it."

He rams her yet again.

"I own you bitch—or have you forgotten that if I were to tell precious Jeremy all about our—you know, extracurricular activities he'd drop you without even so much as a second thought—sweet Jeremy wouldn't want a used-up whore."

Shirley grimaces.

"Why can't you just let this go?"

Corey laughs loudly.

"Why should I? I'm in the driver's seat baby—I call the shots and right now fucking you like the cheap whore you are turns me on—seriously—the only thing better would be seeing Jeremy's reaction after I tell him I've been screwing his precious girlfriend—sticking her over and over for the past year."

Shirley reacts.

"Please—don't. I love him."

Corey rams Shirley once more.

"I'm not the kind of guy who shows mercy—certainly by now you know my deal—and I think telling Jeremy might just be the right thing to do after how you've been acting lately."

"I love him—please no—God please."

Corey laughs loudly again.

"Yeah, right—if you did, you wouldn't have ever slept with me, Caleb, Brad, Wesley, Jarod, or icky Daryl Anderson."

Shirley grimaces.

"You know about that?"

Corey rolls his eyes.

"Caught wind of his game when the two of you left the police station together last January—then imagine my surprise when I saw the two of you going at it in his van—he was on fire that day—kept slamming you like a pillow—ugh gross."

Shirley seems about to faint as Corey pulls out. They look at each other. Semen slides down Shirley's legs. He grins.

Page **472**

"Oops—oh-oh—was that supposed to be a secret?"

He makes a lewd gesture with his fingers.

"Yep, you've been quite a busy "friend" for months now haven't you—well, I for one, would never tell—unless?"

Corey smirks slyly.

"Unless I had to—and if you think Jeremy would be upset about—oh man, think about the trouble Daryl would be in for banging a high school girl—like even *Peyton Place* never went there—then again, it might be really funny if everyone knew."

Shirley gives Corey an odd look.

"Please Corey, look, just don't say anything about Daryl Anderson and I—you know, doing it—I'm begging you."

Corey grins broadly again.

"As long as you and I continue with this arrangement I'll remain silent—but a guy like me has options—is that clear?"

Shirley nods in agreement.

"If I play along—promise you won't tell?"

"Can't promise—it's a guy thing—we always keep our options open when it comes to getting laid—deal with it."

Shirley watches as he gets into his car. He looks up at her and winks. He glances at his watch for a few seconds.

"Don't fuck with me. I'm not a nice guy."

She watches as he drives off. She seems nervous.

Mall

Simon is about to get onto the elevator when Jason steps out. They glance at each other. Jason looks disheveled.

"I've been trying to call you?"

Simon lowers his voice to a whisper.

"Hey, I think you were right about Gina Bentley. Like the girl is seriously freaky—getting weirder by the minute."

Jason seems confused. He motions for Simon to follow him to a deserted area of the mall a few feet away.

"What happened? What are you talking about?"

"Gina is whacked—like totally."

Page **473**

Simon glances back at the small dining area where people are gathered in small groups. He lowers his voice again.

"If Brad wasn't already in the lock-up I'd be betting that Gina could be our girl—like in killer—totally bloody."

Jason sighs.

"You think Gina possibly—could be killer material?"

Simon rolls his eyes.

"Look, her ex just got whacked with a butcher knife and she's acting like nothing is wrong—it's like really creepy."

Jason shrugs and gestures.

"Gina and Caleb were over ages ago—it's not like she still has a thing for him—they both moved on from last year."

"That depends whom you talk to—from what I heard she was pissed he hooked up with Tiffany Johnson the minute he got back to town—and well—we all know what happened to her—and now Caleb's dead too—it's just too much an odd possibility if you ask me when it comes to this being merely a coincidence."

"You think that Gina whacked Caleb?"

Simon nods.

"Makes perfect sense to me—especially after what I just witnessed between her and Lana just a few minutes ago."

He rolls his eyes knowingly.

"They were making some sort of bet—anyway whatever it was you can be sure it wasn't something pleasant given their history together—what if Brad didn't—didn't whack."

"Suppose Gina knocked Tiffany and Caleb off—what about Corinne, Ross, and Natalie? Who offed those three?"

Simon smiles slyly and winks.

"Caleb slept with Corinne and Natalie. OK—so he slept with a lot of girls—but did it on the sly whenever Gina was out of town or something—always told me he didn't want Gina finding out what he was doing when she wasn't around—but what if Gina knew he screwed both Corinne and Natalie—then what?"

Jason sighs loudly.

"OK—fine. But then what about Ross Harrison—how does he fit into this messed-up episode of *Diagnosis Murder*?"

Page 474

Simon smirks slyly.

"Apparently from what Tyler told me two days ago, Ross made a pass at Caleb and then bragged about it afterwards."

Jason shakes his head.

"And you think crazy Gina found out and then knocked Ross off for trying to put the moves on her man Caleb?"

Simon nods again.

"You know how she was with Caleb—thought he was hers only—and when she found out he was banging her friends behind her back—well, let's face it, she's always had a few screws loose upstairs if you know what I mean—and now five people—five people are sharing premium rental spaces in the morgue."

Jason seems confused.

"Have you told anybody about your theory yet?"

Simon shakes his head several times.

<u>Portland</u>

Loud moans echo throughout the bedroom as Glen slams into Denise again and again. As she cries out loudly he laughs.

"How do you and Caroline know each other?"

Denise grins slyly.

"We went to high school together—same clique."

Glen smirks.

"Two of you no longer close—why?"

Denise gestures with her hand.

"We are—sort of—she and I have history."

Glen laughs loudly.

"Let me guess—both of you shared boyfriends and dicks."

Denise kisses Glen as he leers at her. She sighs.

"More like I shared her boyfriends and their dicks—I never was the sweet and innocent type—I don't ever play fair."

He grins broadly.

"I kind of figured that about you. Married?"

Denise rolls her eyes knowingly.

"In name only—nothing more—husband is a dolt."

Page 475

Glen smirks again.

"Isn't that always the deal?"

Denise shakes her head.

"Kyle—Kyle and I—it's long dead."

Glen looks at Denise.

"Wait—Kyle—as in Kyle Madison—oh-oh—rich boy."

Denise nods.

"He and I lost the magic years ago."

Glen laughs loudly again.

"Oh man—I'm fucking the wife of one of the richest men in New England and he's too much a lame idiot to care."

Denise seems confused.

"Your point being—what's it to you?"

He laughs.

"This is my lucky day—oh yeah—really sweet indeed."

He licks his lips—a huge grin creasing his face.

"What do you mean by that Glen?"

Glen wags his finger at Denise and begins laughing.

<u>Lighthouse Grill</u>

"Ugh—I hate her—I really do."

Elizabeth Pendleton glances at Genie Van Pelt knowingly with a bored look. They smile in unison and face Lana.

"Well, I do—she's such a two-faced bitch—total zero."

Genie rolls her eyes and winks at Elizabeth.

"Why did you even make such a bet with her?"

Genie looks at Lana curiously.

"You know how she plays—she's sneaky."

Lana nods.

"She just makes me so mad sometimes."

She sighs.

"I miss Natalie—I still can't believe she's gone."

Elizabeth and Genie look at each other.

"Think Brad really pushed her down the stairs after he fucked her at the mall—I mean—that's harsh even for him?"

Page 476

Lana gestures with her hand.

"Brad is a sleaze—but I just don't think he would've."

"I think Gina did the deed—she had motive."

Lana looks at the others and smirks.

"Uh-huh—she had motive as good as any—and let's face facts like right now—she hated Tiffany—Tiffany is dead. Caleb treated her like an old shoe—Caleb is dead. Corinne and Natalie slept with Caleb—and they're both dead. Ross made a pass at Caleb—he's dead too—and now—and now we may be next if she's not locked up before she feels the urge to kill us all."

Elizabeth and Genie look at each other.

"We both slept with Caleb too—come on, you knew how insistent he could be—we had to—he demanded it of us."

Lana shakes her head.

"Let's face it—we're all targets now."

Genie seems upset and notices Ashton Markway a few yards away. She makes a gesture like she's about to throw up as Lana seems annoyed. Genie continues rolling her eyes.

"What a dweeb—bet he's still a virgin."

Lana snaps her fingers at Genie.

"Focus OK—stop acting like a total bitch."

"But I—he's such a loser."

Lana rolls her eyes and glances at Elizabeth.

"Enough already—Ashton isn't Gina's target—we are."

Lana sighs loudly as she faces Genie.

"Tiffany was right—she always thought Gina was a sick freak—used to say it all the time—and now she's dead."

"What are we going to do?"

Elizabeth taps her fingers on the table.

<u>Maple Avenue</u>

Alden hugs Julia again and walks away. She watches him until he turns the curb. As he walks toward his car he notices Faye casually walking toward him. She is grinning broadly.

"Talked to you lawyer yet?"

Page 477

He shakes his head.

"He might have some really interesting things to discuss with you—starting with *my* settlement—plenty to get."

Faye smirks.

"I'm going to get you for what you did to me."

Alden watches as she leans toward him.

"You'll have nothing left when I'm done with you—that I promise—I *so* wouldn't want to be you when the dust clears."

Without waiting for a reply Faye heads toward the mall nearby. Alden shrugs and sighs loudly. He mutters a word.

<u>Police Station</u>

Maxwell Pendergraft opens the door and grins broadly as he sees Clay sitting at his desk looking completely bored.

"Such dedication—and they pay you for this?"

Clay looks up and grins broadly.

"You finally decided to show your ugly face."

Maxwell waves his hand around.

"Been here several hours already—doing your job for you—since it's obvious you're totally inept at simple stuff."

Clay rolls his eyes.

"I don't remember asking for your opinion."

Maxwell feigns a heart attack.

"Words hurt buddy."

Clay walks over to where Maxwell is standing and they embrace warmly. They look at each other for a second.

"Hello stranger."

Maxwell sighs and looks around.

"For you maybe—but I still haven't forgotten what you did before—caused all that trouble and then skipped town."

Clay grins slyly.

"I don't know what you're talking about."

Maxwell suddenly grabs Clay in a playful headlock.

"Still sticking with that story I see—well, go right ahead but I'm not a forgetting type of guy—and all that trouble."

<u>Page **478**</u>

Clay laughs and pushes Maxwell away.

"Is that so?"

Maxwell rolls his eyes.

"Seems to me you forgot what happened on New Year's Eve during our senior year in college—you know—those girls."

Maxwell hugs Clay again.

"God, it's good to see you again."

Clay grins broadly.

"Got a place to stay yet?"

"Tolling Bell Inn—nice enough place."

Clay looks around.

"Got plans for dinner later?"

Maxwell nods.

"Nope—nothing planned yet."

Clay looks at his watch.

"Great. Come by at six—give you plenty of time to talk with Eva—and make a pathetic fool of yourself as always."

Maxwell pretends to jab Clay in the chest.

"Wait—you actually found someone dumb enough to put up with you after all the moronic things you're known for?"

Clay shoves Maxwell playfully.

"Keep that up and you'll leave Marble Hills with a black eye—or worse. Not above breaking a few bones too."

Maxwell laughs and wags his finger at Clay.

"From whom—you—now that's funny."

They shadow box for a few seconds and pretend to let their rage show. Maxwell suddenly seems serious at he looks at Clay and the stack of paperwork on top of Clay's desk.

"Think the McKinley kid is guilty?"

Clay shrugs.

"Daryl seems to think so. I think maybe not everything is what it appears to be at the moment—too many questions."

Maxwell seems confused.

"What's that supposed to mean?"

Clay sits down at his desk.

Hart Bennington sighs as he enters the mall. He walks toward the escalators. Corey rushes past and roughly pushes him aside without saying anything. Hart looks at him harshly.

"Loser—zero from the getgo."

Corey hears the comment and spins around to face Hart with an angry look on his face. He seems to be in a rage.

"What did you just call me?"

Hart rolls his eyes.

"Zero—do you want to hear it again freak show. Or are you deaf or something? I said what I said. You heard me."

Corey notices a small crowd gathering. He clenches his fist as he looks around. He faces Hart again ready to strike.

"Do you know who I am?"

Hart shrugs.

"Do I look like I care? Seriously do I look like I care who you think you are? Probably some stuck up brat from Pinecrest."

Corey clenches his fists.

"Maybe I ought to teach you a lesson?"

Hart mockingly yawns and laughs.

"By you—*please*—go back to the country club and drink yourself into tomorrow like all the other idiot dweebs."

"How dare you speak to me like that?"

Corey grabs Hart and shoves him. Hart regains his balance and pushes Corey against the rows of folded chairs nearby.

"Big mistake asshole—I'm from Philly."

Corey falls backwards and as everyone begins laughing the chairs begin to clatter to the floor. He looks up at Hart.

"You're so dead *motherfucker*—do you hear me—I'll crucify you—your life is over as you know it. I'll break you."

Hart gestures with his finger.

"Your threats are as tired as you."

He turns to look at the crowd standing nearby.

"Can someone call this guy a cab?"

Hart begins laughing.

"I think he's had one too many. Thinks he's someone I should pay attention to. Seriously look at him—pathetic."

Corey seems about to explode.

"You're so dead."

Hart makes a lewd gesture with his finger.

"Go tell it to your mother—she's probably on Vine Street giving it up to every homeless guy that needs a thrill."

He grins broadly.

"Oh wait—I'll tell her myself. I fucked the bitch earlier in the backseat of my car—she and I are on a first name basis."

Corey jumps to his feet ready to pummel Hart as Drew steps between them from out of nowhere. He looks at Corey.

"Enough already—get out."

Corey gives Hart a harsh look.

"This isn't over yet."

Hart laughs.

"I hear your mother calling."

Drew glares at Corey for a few seconds and then turns to face Hart. Several people nearby also stop and take notice.

TO BE CONTINUED

A Look at the 19th Episode

Corey meets a new foe named Hart—peer pressure gets the best of Ashton's classmates—Denise makes a deal with Glen to destroy Caroline's family—Faye hooks up with an unlikely partner—Gina confronts Simon and Jason after overhearing their idle gossip about her—Hart makes a new friend and enemy at the same time—Lance and Elizabeth hook-up for a good time—Daryl enjoys his time away from work—Gina is taunted because of her behavior—Lana encounters tragedy—Lance and Elizabeth make a tragic unexpected discovery at Bradford Woods—Corey gets bad news from his father which sends him into a tailspin—Kelly encounters Gina at the worst possible time while Tiffany pays her rival an unfriendly visit and further complicates her life—a few friends plot to destroy a ruthless rival—Denise slyly seduces her latest conquest and sets up plans to take down her arch-nemesis once and for all—as Corey comes to blows with Wesley.

Unfolding Drama

<u>Mall</u>

Corey Bentley glares at Drew Brockmeyer briefly and gestures to Hart Bennington again and grimaces. Hart smirks and watches as he walks away. He turns to face Drew and sighs.

"What a loser—like really pathetic."

Drew watches Corey for a few seconds and faces Hart.

"That one is trouble—with a capital T."

Hart shrugs.

"So what—I can kick his ass any day."

Drew rolls his eyes.

"Got any action to back up that talk?"

Hart grins.

"Back in Philly I taught karate during the summer."

Drew grins broadly.

"You must be Hart Bennington."

Hart seems confused. Drew laughs.

"This *is* a small town—not much ever happens here."

He smirks and gestures with his hand.

"Everyone talks trash about everyone else."

Hart looks around.

"Seems to me there'd be better things to talk about?"

"You'd think—wouldn't you—but no."

He glances at his watch.

"Hey, how about you and I grab a bite to eat—my break is almost upon me and I'd like to know all about Philadelphia."

Hart nods and follows Drew to the escalator.

<u>Lighthouse Grill</u>

Ashton Markway walks by where Lana Jefferson, Genie Van Pelt and Elizabeth Pendleton are sitting. He smirks.

"If I were you guys I'd be watching my back right about now—a killer is on the loose—killing off whores and jerks."

"Get lost dweeb—beat it."

Ashton laughs as he looks at Genie.

"Uh-huh—think you're cool right now—until someone takes aim at you and shoots—then what would you do?"

"Brad McKinley is in jail."

Ashton glances around.

"Who said he did it—what if it was someone else that did the killings? Could be quite the shocker—you'd be on CNN—after the fact of course—when they mention you being dead."

Genie grabs Ashton's arm.

"It's probably you—killers are always dweebs."

Ashton jerks free of Genie's grip and grins.

"If it was me Genie, you'd already be dead—think about it and focus—focus with what little brainpower you have in that empty shell you call your skull—whoever it is—they won't stop until they knock off everyone they have on their hit list."

Genie seems annoyed.

"Be gone dweeb."

He glances at Lana and Elizabeth and walks away. Genie rolls her eyes in disgust. She seems somewhat bothered.

"Ugh. I hate him so much."

Lana seems nervous and looks around.

Page 484

"Ashton Markway does have a point regardless—if Gina's the killer—she will get us all soon enough—one by one."

Elizabeth stands up.

"Whatever—I'm not worried. Everyone knows I slept with Caleb the same as every other girl in town—big deal."

Lana watches as Elizabeth leaves and turns to Genie.

"Bet she's next."

Genie seems upset and sighs loudly.

Portland

"You can't tell him—he'll destroy me."

Glen Bradstreet laughs.

"Don't see how you can stop me—a guy's gotta do what a guy feels is right—and this information is quite potent."

Denise Madison looks at Glen standing in front of her with his erect penis jutting out like a trophy. She sighs.

"Please—I'll do anything—whatever you demand."

Glen glances at his penis.

"You've already done everything needed whore—there's no stopping a woman who knows what she wants in the sack."

He laughs again.

"But—I see potential income—what's your offer?"

Denise smiles broadly as she jumps out of bed and slides her arms around Glen's waist—they look at each other.

"I'm sure that we can come to some sort of a deal."

Glen grins broadly.

"I'm going to expect a lot from you."

"Well, I was thinking that you and I could work."

He pushes her away.

"What? Fuck? Been there and done that."

They look at each other.

"I was actually thinking of Caroline Bentley."

Glen smirks.

"OK—I'm listening—shoot—spill your game."

Denise leans toward Glen.

Page **485**

"It's her son—he killed someone."

Glen grins broadly.

"Uh-huh—and of course no one is privy to this info?"

Denise nods.

"He caught his father fucking a hooker from Chadwick Street in Boston and pushed her off a balcony—killed her."

Denise smirks.

"John and Caroline covered it up royally. They dumped the body in the harbor and it was labeled a drowning."

Glen seems confused.

"But if she fell off a balcony—wouldn't there have been an inquiry of some kind—these things usually lead that way?"

Denise shakes her head.

"The way the story played out later was that she was working the night she disappeared and they chalked it up to her being drunk and falling into the water—case closed."

Glen shrugs.

"Wasn't that how **Natalie Wood** died in 1981? It wasn't until decades later that everyone found out that it was **Robert Wagner** who actually pushed her off the boat while they were fighting over **Christopher Walken** and he made it look like she'd accidentally drowned in the waters off Catalina Island."

Denise nods again.

"Yeah, I guess so. Anyway, John and Caroline silenced the press about what happened—everyone except for Carlos."

She licks her lips.

"Carlos Espana—oh my, could he fuck—didn't know much English—but he knew how to use his dick as a weapon."

Glen rolls his eyes knowingly.

"This Carlos witnessed the murder?"

Denise slides her fingers across Glen's stiff penis. He grins slyly as she kisses the head and strokes him aggressively.

"He was there that night—saw what Corey Bentley did."

Glen looks at Denise and wags his finger.

"Exactly what are we going to do with this info?"

Denise grins broadly.

"I know you'll come up with something."
They begin kissing.

<u>Standish Road</u>

Faye Washington is speeding when she hears sirens behind her. She pounds her fist on the steering wheel.
"Damn—goddamn frigging assholes."
She slows down and pulls over.
"I hope he's cute—hopes he likes women."
Faye turns around and sees Daryl Anderson slowly walking toward her. He looks mad. Faye fakes a smile.
"Thought you'd test our speed limit today, didn't you?"
Faye sighs.
"I'm sorry—I wasn't aware I—oh so sorry."
Daryl rolls his eyes.
"Oh-huh—likely story—not the first time I've heard that tale—bet you knew exactly what the deal is—don't you?"
He sighs loudly.
"It's time to show your license and registration."
"Is this really necessary?"
"What do you think?"
Faye gives Daryl an odd look and begins riffling through her glove compartment. She stops and turns to face him.
"Can't we work something—you know something really sweet—maybe something we can both be happy with?"
Daryl grins.
"What do you have in mind?"
Faye glances between her legs. Daryl grins broadly and leans toward the window to get a better look at Faye.

<u>Mall</u>

"OK, so we both think Gina Bentley just whacked six people and Brad McKinley is taking the fall for her?"
Simon Spencer glances at Jason Anderson. Jason nods.

Page 487

"The question is what do we do about it?"
Jason shrugs.

"Tail the bitch—if she's guilty of whacking six people—it's just a matter of time before she whacks her seventh."

Simon sighs.

"I'd place bets that Lana Jefferson is next on Gina's list for a dirt nap—though with Brad in jail it could be dicey to try and whack someone else—and still expect people to—not put the pieces together right away—then again this is Gina we're talking about—she's not exactly a candidate for Mensa testing."

They hear a sound and look around to see Gina Bentley staring at them. She seems upset. They both sigh nervously.

<u>Lighthouse Grill</u>

Hart quickly finishes off the last remnants of his burger as Drew takes a sip from a cup of soda and smirks broadly.

"So, Philadelphia is a really happening city I gather?"

Hart nods.

"Yeah, much more than Marble Hills ever will be."

He sighs.

"If it wasn't for my mother's family I wouldn't have to be living in this postcard-sad excuse for a town—so dull."

Drew smirks.

"How's the family?"

Hart rolls his eyes.

"I think you already know my deal."

He watches as the color drains from Drew's face.

"I've heard plenty."

Hart laughs.

"Yeah, yeah—I know everyone hates them—probably can't blame anyone either. I heard about the awful things my grandpa has done to people—he's a piece of work all right."

Drew seems about to choke.

"You don't like your grandpa much do you?"

Hart rolls his eyes again.

Page 488

"Don't really know him—don't care to—he's cold and indifferent—a terrible father—worse than **Bing Crosby**."

Drew looks at the entrance.

"Does Corey Bentley know who you are?"

Hart shrugs.

"Don't care."

Drew makes a gesture with his hand.

"I think when he finds out you're Wesley's cousin, he'll positively have a coronary—I'd give anything to see it."

Drew grins broadly.

"Wesley and Corey were best buds—but lately not much."

Hart seems bored by the conversation.

"Wesley hardly says anything to me—not that it matters much—I do my own thing—don't need to be a follower."

"Good thinking—best that way."

Drew looks at the entrance again as Hart notices.

"Well, I have to get back to work—it was nice talking to you. How about we hang out sometime this week—OK?"

Hart nods.

"Cool—I'll be around."

Hart watches as Drew heads to the door.

<u>Bradford Woods</u>

Lance Weissmann looks at Elizabeth with a sly grin and laughs as he begins to unbutton her blouse. He sighs.

"Hey, you're acting like this is the first time we've—you know—fucked. What's the matter? Did I do something?"

Elizabeth sighs as she looks up at Lance.

"I could be the next one to get shafted."

Lance laughs.

"What brought on this piece of soapy melodrama?"

Elizabeth sighs loudly.

"I know she's coming after me soon—she's a nutjob no doubt as you know—has it out for me. Gina *is* the killer."

Lance grimaces.

Page 489

"Gina Bentley didn't kill anybody, Elizabeth. It was Brad McKinley—and he's in jail—he's the killer. Relax already."

Elizabeth rolls her eyes.

"That's what everybody thinks—but—she?"

Lance slides his hand inside her blouse and grins. He leans over and kisses her as she seems oblivious to his actions.

"But Lana said."

Lance seems annoyed.

"Lana Jefferson—that girl is going to get herself in trouble one day for trying to be **Grace Metalious**—ugh—enough."

"It's not lies—everyone is talking—it's true."

Lance smirks again.

"Yeah—of course they are—they're talking about all the sleazy gossip that Lana is spreading around Marble Hills."

He kisses her neck.

"No wonder she and I don't hang anymore—I got tired of all the baggage she brings—plus she's not very good in bed."

"That's not what she said—said you were boring."

Lance pulls Elizabeth's panty down between her legs.

"Frankly, I don't care what she says about me—I'm done with her for good—to think I actually treated Lana Jefferson like she was someone special—not that she ever thanked me."

He laughs and penetrates Elizabeth.

<u>Standish Road</u>

Daryl slams into Faye as her loud moans echo from the backseat of his patrol car—she smiles broadly and sighs.

"Who'd think a cop could be so intense?"

Daryl laughs.

"Love the perks of this job."

"Still going to bust me—for speeding?"

Daryl slams Faye again.

"Nope—I think you've learned your lesson when it comes to breaking the law—that and seducing an officer."

He grins broadly and gestures.

Page **490**

"I—I on the other hand definitely want to get to know you better—how about we hook-up again later at your place for a few more rounds—and I can show you the finer points—really let you see what I'm capable of doing with big my cop dick."

"What about your place?"

Daryl smirks.

"Can't—I'm married man."

Faye seems upset.

"Oh—that's too bad—married men—boring."

Daryl laughs loudly again.

"Don't worry—I've never let it get in my way."

Faye grins slyly.

"Glad to hear it—because I think you have potential—a lot of potential if you know what I mean—like especially."

Daryl nods.

"Oh yeah—I know exactly what you mean."

He pounds Faye yet again.

"Say, you're on the pill right?"

"Of course—what do you take me for—a virgin?"

They both laugh.

<u>Mall</u>

Simon and Jason watch nervously as Gina circles them for several seconds. Her eyes seem to blaze with anger.

"You two better shut your mouths—if I hear anyone telling me that you two are spreading—I'll make you both sorry."

Simon gestures with his hand and laughs.

"Spread what Gina—the truth? Seriously, everyone knows you hated Tiffany Johnson enough to kill her. Let's just face facts—truth telling moment—Caleb Winthrop dumped you last year like yesterday's newspaper and hooked up with Tiffany on the sly because she knew how to service a guy—popular."

Gina glares at Simon.

"How dare you—that's not how it happened."

Simon laughs and points at Gina.

"Face it Gina—they were doing it nonstop—the whole town knew what was happening—everyone but you of course."

Gina sighs.

"No—he and I were in love. He said."

Simon laughs.

"What about William Crenshaw?"

He smirks.

"No one believes he just fell off Stanley Pier and hit his head on the pilings and drowned—right after you started dating Caleb—seems to me something may have happened."

Gina watches as Simon circles her.

"He fell."

Simon wags his finger at her.

"No one else has forgotten how rich your parents are in case you were wondering—now six people are dead."

"I didn't kill him."

"Likely story—sell that lie to Lifetime Television."

Gina glares at Simon for a few seconds—gives Jason a harsh stare and storms off. Simon looks at Jason and smirks.

"Was it something I said?"

Jason shrugs.

<u>Parking Lot</u>

Lana is slowly walking to her car. She smiles and texts the last of her messages and shuts off her cell phone.

"Today is turning out exactly the way I planned."

There is a sound behind her. She turns around as a glint of steel catches her eye—seconds later a large carving knife rips through her blouse and plunges into her heart. She falls to the ground and looks up in shock at her attacker inches away.

"I thought Brad was the killer?"

Lana continues looking up at her assailant as her eyes slowly close and her body goes limp. Blood continues pouring from the wound. Footsteps can be heard walking away.

Page 492

<u>Bradford Woods</u>

Lance grins as he buttons his Levi's and watches Elizabeth with a smile who seems slightly dazed from their encounter.

"Oh yeah—nice ride—I'll call you tomorrow."

Elizabeth seems upset.

"How about we take a walk and talk?"

Lance seems confused and sighs.

"Talk—talk about what?"

Elizabeth rolls her eyes and looks around.

"I don't want to be alone right now—OK—come on—I'm just asking you to be nice for a change—be compassionate."

Lance laughs.

"OK—OK—I guess I can take a quick walk with you—even though I don't see why I should—it's not like we're a couple."

Elizabeth smiles and they walk toward the wooded path leading to Miller's Pond a few yards away. Lance shrugs.

<u>Parking Lot</u>

Gina walks toward her car in a mad rush. She seems uneasy. Suddenly Tiffany Johnson appears in front of her.

"Killer—killer—uh-huh that's right—you."

Gina blinks a few times in anger.

"Oh-oh—they're on to you Gina dear—it's only a matter of time now—and then they'll lock you up once and for all."

Gina sighs loudly and seems annoyed.

"Go away—leave me alone—you're not real Tiffany—I don't—be gone already—stop bothering me—you're dead."

Tiffany laughs.

"Not real? Are you sure about that?"

Without warning Gina is viciously pushed against the wall by Tiffany. She stumbles twice but regains her balance.

"Still think I'm not real?"

She laughs loudly.

"This is only the beginning dear."

Page **493**

Tiffany smirks knowingly.

"Freak—murderer—admit your guilt already."

Gina begins to run toward her car and stops dead in her tracks as she sees a trail of blood a few feet away.

"Oh my God—this isn't happening."

Her eyes fall to where Lana's body is slumped against her car. She's dead. Gina screams as Tiffany circles her.

"Killer—you killed Lana."

Tiffany leans closer to Gina and grins.

"Killed me—killed the others."

She whispers in her ear once more.

"Killer—you killed Lana—you killed me and the others."

Gina appears frozen in shock at the sight.

"No—it can't be—it can't."

Gina hears a door slam not far away. Seconds later she sees Kelly Nelson standing there silently. He reacts.

<u>Standish Road</u>

Daryl sighs as he watches Faye apply her makeup. She turns to face him. They glance at the huge rip in her skirt.

"Sorry about that—things happen."

Faye waves her hand at Daryl.

"No problem—you more than made up for it. You certainly know your way around women—very skilled."

She leans over to kiss Daryl and smiles.

"You and the wife headed for splitsville?"

Daryl shakes his head.

"I wish—but no such luck—not going to happen. I'm stuck with her until she kicks it. She made that quite clear to me."

Faye seems disappointed at the statement.

"Sorry to hear that—like really sorry."

She pulls him toward her and they kiss.

"But until I leave town you and I can get—well, you know—get to know each other in all sorts of fun ways."

Daryl looks at Faye curiously.

Page 494

"Leave town? What? Why?"

Faye smirks.

"Yeah, once I teach my ex a lesson I'm heading back to Los Angeles—got so many things happening there to attend to."

Daryl looks at Faye oddly.

"Who's your ex?"

Faye rolls her eyes.

"A loser actor named Alden Washington—perhaps you know him—he used to live here years ago—terrible lover."

Daryl reacts to the news.

Bradford Woods

Lance and Elizabeth are walking toward Miller's Pond when they notice something in the pond. They both run toward the edge in a panic and look in horror at a partly submerged car. In the driver's seat they see Carrie Spaulding's body. Elizabeth screams as Lance reaches out to comfort her as she cries.

Bentley Driveway

Corey slams the door to his car and is about to walk toward the house when he sees his father waiting for him.

"What's up?"

John Bentley seems to be in a terrible mood. He glares at Corey for a few seconds. John glances at Corey's car.

"I could ask you the same thing."

Corey seems confused.

"I have no idea what you're talking about?"

John walks toward Corey.

"Really—is that so? Care to go down memory lane with me a second? Might prove to be quite the bad experience?"

Corey sighs loudly.

"Whatever—got things to do."

John angrily grabs Corey and spins him around. He seems annoyed. They look at each other for several seconds.

"Look dad, I don't have time to play twenty questions or any other game—just spit it out—and be done already."

"Seems I just got a call from Eddie Kane's assistant—and as of right now you've been banned from setting foot inside the mall until further notice—which means the rest of summer."

"What? Why?"

John grabs Corey by the arm again.

"Funny you should ask—seems you were seen threatening someone and there was a complaint—Kane is livid."

Corey sighs loudly again.

"I didn't threaten anybody—there was just this jerk that had a mouth on him—I just made a few things clear."

John begins twisting Corey's arm.

"Is that so—making a few things clear, huh? Well, maybe you should have thought about that a little more—especially given who that "jerk" was—like maybe next time you should have checked first—since now it has become—really messy."

"He was just some punk asshole who thought he was someone really important—he was nobody—nobody at all."

John pushes Corey against his car.

"Is that so—how stupid are you Corey—do you have any idea how foolish a move you made earlier with that "punk" kid you so easily dismissed as a nobody—yeah, that's right, pay attention dumbass—you threatened the grandson of Howard Madison—and I don't have to tell you about the implications."

Corey reacts. He looks at John curiously.

"Grandson—but old man Madison only has one frigging grandson. That would be Wesley by the way. Stupid fucker has been ignoring me since he got out of the pen. Damn him."

John watches Corey's facial expression as it changes back and forth between confusion and determined ignorance.

"Are you sure about that—huh—willing to make bets on exactly how much an immature brat like you really knows?"

Corey seems confused.

"What the fuck are you talking about?"

John glances at his watch.

Page **496**

"That so-called jerk—*is* Hart Bennington—and don't you forget it ever again. He could make trouble for you—of which I wouldn't be able to get you out of if—unlike that messy business last year with Alicia Howe—and oh yeah—the situation with the babysitter in St. Thomas and your *son*—so thread lightly—jail is a mighty unpleasant place to spend twenty years of your life without the benefits of easy money if you fuck up royally."

Corey stands there in shock as his father walks toward the house. His face is a mixture of shock and indifferent anger.

<u>Parking Lot</u>

Kelly and Gina look at each other in shock. Gina looks at Lana's body lying nearby. Kelly pulls out his cell phone.

"I didn't—didn't kill her."

She watches as he begins dialing.

"Please Kelly—it's not—please don't call OK?"

"You're busted."

Gina turns to face Tiffany. She blinks a few times.

"Duh—you dumb bitch. I'm not going anywhere—at least not until they lock—lock you up and throw away the key."

"Leave me alone—please."

Kelly looks at Gina. He seems confused.

"Who are you talking to?"

Gina looks around.

"Tiff—oh nobody—just confused."

"Crazy—crazy is more like it."

Tiffany begins making gestures with her fingers as Gina reacts oddly and draws Kelly's curious attention even more.

"You're so close to a padded cell at Marshland—oops, he thinks you're a wacko—oh-oh—this might be fun to play with for a while—wonder how long before you snap and crash?"

"Shut up."

Kelly looks at Gina curiously and heads back to the safety of the elevator. Gina runs after him as the door closes.

"They'll throw away the key no doubt—oh poor baby."

Page 497

Gina reaches out to slap Tiffany in a rage but there's nothing to hit but air. Tiffany laughs loudly from a distance.

"Killer—nutjob—freak of nature—how many more before they finally put you away forever at Marshland—I can't wait."

She turns to see Tiffany standing about two feet away with a huge smirk on her face. She seems happy.

"Killer—killer—killer—killer—Gina Bentley is a killer."

"Shut up—go away."

Tiffany glances at where Lana is lying.

"Can't—I won't."

"Shut up—shut up Tiffany—just shut up and leave me alone—shut up—I hate you—I wish you were dead—go away."

Tiffany begins laughing.

"Dead—you wish I were dead—oops."

Tiffany points at Gina.

"I'm going to make you pay."

At that moment Gina sees Clay Blankenship pulling up in a patrol car. They look at each other briefly as another man steps out from the patrol car too—he looks around as if looking for someone. Moments later Kelly comes toward them from the elevator. Clay notices Lana's body. He draws his gun as Maxwell Pendergraft turns to face Kelly. Kelly sighs loudly.

<u>Standish Road</u>

"You're Alden Washington's ex-wife?"

Faye nods.

"Uh-huh—sad, but true—bastard cheated on me and ruined my life—but he won't get away with it—I won't let him."

"Small world—who'd think I'd meet you here."

Daryl's cell phone rings. He quickly grabs it and as Faye watches—his reaction changes drastically. He sighs loudly.

"You have her in custody already?"

He shakes his head.

"Are you sure?"

He sighs again.

Page 498

"OK—OK—I'll be right there."

Faye watches as Daryl shuts his cell phone off and turns to look at her. He seems upset a she glances at her car nearby.

"What happened?"

Daryl shrugs.

"I've got to go—crap to deal with in town."

They look at each other for a few seconds before Daryl abruptly heads toward his car and drives off without saying anything further to Faye. As he drives away she sighs.

<u>Bradford Woods</u>

Lance sits with Elizabeth a few yards away from Miller's Pond. He reaches out to stroke her hair—she pulls away.

"Who do you think killed her?"

Lance sighs.

"Brad."

She turns to look at Lance.

<u>Standish Road</u>

Daryl is driving recklessly toward Marble Hills when his cell phone rings again. He slowly picks it up and seems annoyed.

"You're there now with Elizabeth Pendleton?"

He sighs.

"This can't be happening. What the hell is going on in this town? Every frigging minute something else happens."

He sighs loudly.

"OK—OK—I'll be there in a few minutes—don't touch anything—just stay where you are and I'll be right there."

He shuts off the cell phone.

"Gina—what have you done—could it be true? Could that girl be responsible for what's been happening in town?"

He wipes sweat from his brow and looks at the cell phone as it begins to ring yet again. He ignores it and sighs loudly.

Page 499

<u>Bentley Driveway</u>

Corey looks at his cell phone again and sighs.

"Pick up the damn phone Wesley. Why are you ignoring me—think you're better than me—is that it—lousy fucker."

He shuts it off.

"I swear that punk is going to pay—but first I'm going to make Drew Brockmeyer wish he'd never been born."

He slams his fist against his car.

"Oh yeah—that asshole just crossed the wrong guy—and now he needs to be taught a lesson—a very painful lesson."

He grabs his cell phone and begins dialing.

"Brad can't help—he's useless to me now—dumbass."

He throws the cell phone into his car.

"Got to think—got to think of something really nasty I can do to Brockmeyer—make him really sorry he—oh yeah."

He begins laughing hysterically.

<u>Parking Lot</u>

Gina looks bewildered as she glances at the cold stares from Maxwell and Clay while she stands near Lana's car. She looks at Kelly standing a few feet away. Tiffany leans over and whispers in her ear—her face contorted in an ugly grimace.

"Freaky monster you are."

Gina rolls her eyes as she watches Tiffany grin broadly.

"Just tell them you did it—you know you're guilty—admit it—do it already—tell them you offed us all—do it—now."

Gina sighs loudly and reacts oddly.

"I didn't do it—stop it—please stop saying."

Maxwell and Clay look at each other.

"Who are you talking to?"

Kelly takes a step forward.

"Earlier she kept calling Tiffany Johnson's name."

Clay turns to look at Kelly curiously.

"Tiffany Johnson?"

Page **500**

Kelly nods.

"Tiffany Johnson is dead."

Kelly nods again.

"I know—but that's whose name she kept calling—like she were speaking to her or something—it got really weird."

Tiffany begins laughing.

"Crazy—crazy—crazy Gina—crazy—it's time for the loony bin—I hear they have really nice padded rooms—loony."

Gina turns to face Tiffany.

"Stop calling me that—please."

Clay gives Gina a strange look. He sighs.

"Gina, you know that Tiffany Johnson is dead, right? She isn't here—you're not really talking to her—it isn't possible."

Gina seems distraught.

"I know."

Tiffany begins laughing loudly.

"You killed—tell them what you did—like tell them you're a crazy loon—total whack job—a freak—just do it already."

Gina wipes sweat from her brow.

"I didn't kill anyone—it was—it wasn't me—please let Tiffany know I didn't kill anyone—tell her—she's here."

Maxwell turns and looks at Clay. They exchange cautious looks. Gina notices and then becomes further agitated.

"I didn't do it—I didn't."

Clay takes a step toward Gina as she back away.

"I think I've heard enough of this soap opera."

Gina tries to push her way past Clay as Maxwell steps in front of her and without warning slaps a pair of handcuffs on her wrists. She looks at him with a harsh glare of hatred.

"You'll regret treating me like this. Don't you know who I am—I'm rich—and my father will make you pay—dearly."

Maxwell smirks.

"Tell it to the judge."

Gina glares at Maxwell.

"You'll be working at Safeway shortly—my father will ruin you—he'll turn your life inside out—make you beg for mercy."

As Gina is led toward the nearby patrol car she turns back to see Tiffany standing with her hands on her hips grinning broadly in triumph. Tiffany waves. Gina continues looking at her until the image fades as she's forced into the backseat of the patrol car. Kelly continues to look at the scene unfolding as if it's only happening on a filmed TV show and not in real life.

<u>Mall</u>

Ashton walks up the small podium where Drew is standing talking to another employee and grins broadly.

"Hey, kudos for teaching that annoying prick Corey Bentley a lesson he needed taught to him for a while now."

Drew grins.

"I only did what had to be done—don't need any fights breaking out in the mall—bad for business—like totally."

Ashton smirks.

"I'll say."

He looks around.

"Think Bentley will come after you?"

Drew makes a lewd gesture with his finger.

"Let him—we've had it out before—whipped his ass then too—made him wish he'd left well enough alone—fucker."

Ashton shrugs.

"Wished I could've seen it unfold—film worthy. I can't stand that fucker—he and his family have ruined this town."

He grins broadly.

"Whenever you want help—let me know—I'm not much with my fists—but I can work wonders with his bank account—bet he'd really freak if he suddenly had no money to spend."

Drew winks.

"I'll let you know."

At that moment both Jason and Simon comes toward the podium and shake Drew's hand—congratulating him for giving Corey a taste of his own poison medicine for a change.

Page 502

<u>Lighthouse Grill</u>

Faye walks into the small restaurant and sits down. She notices Sidney Stuyvesant chatting with some customers and then she notices Juan Sabrillo walking to the front counter.

"Juan?"

He turns around to face her.

"I've missed you."

Juan smirks.

"I bet you have—especially my bed."

"Don't be like that."

He gives her a knowing look.

"Nice seeing you."

He turns and continues walking casually toward the front counter ignoring her. She seems hurt by his rudeness.

"Oh—this is how you want to play it—use me like a whore and now you don't know me—act like I'm nothing to you."

She wipes away a tear from her eye.

"Well, two can play that game also—and I can get even as well—a woman can always change her mind where a man is concerned and I'm definitely the type to change mine."

She smiles slyly.

<u>Bradford Woods</u>

Daryl jumps out of his patrol car and head toward where Lance and Elizabeth are sitting. They jump to their feet.

"Where's Carrie?"

Elizabeth points to the car lodged halfway inside Miller's Pond. Daryl shakes his head in shock as he sees Carrie's body lying in the driver's seat. He sighs loudly, visibly upset.

<u>Port Clyde</u>

Denise moans loudly as Kevin Myers pins her underneath his body on the narrow bed. He looks at her and grins slyly.

Page **503**

"Man, didn't think this would ever be possible—but here you are doing it with me—in a bed at the Pinewood Arms."

Denise smirks.

"I saw and wanted you—took you back here—not much really to think about it as far as I can see—just a hook-up."

Kevin laughs.

"Yeah but—I'm your lawyer's son."

Denise pulls Kevin toward her.

"Is it wrong for wanting what I saw—besides it's your own fault—standing outside on your front lawn in nothing but a pair of Levi's and no shirt—bad idea when it comes to a woman."

Kevin laughs again.

"I was mowing the lawn like always—I wasn't thinking."

Denise reaches out to stroke Kevin's penis.

"Uh-huh and now you're plowing me for the second time—showing me the way—taking what you want."

He rolls his eyes.

"If my girlfriend found out—oh man she'd kill me."

Denise shrugs.

"So what—tell her you're too young to commit—seriously you're a college guy—you need to explore—have fun."

Kevin laughs loudly.

"I said I had a girlfriend—I never said I'd been faithful."

Denise licks her lips.

"Sweet—I like a man who knows what the deal is when it comes to a relationship with his girlfriend—no strings."

"I've had my share of women on the side."

Kevin lies back in bed.

"Man, think about this for a second—my dad thinks you and I hardly know each other—but oh, we know plenty."

Denise reaches and strokes Kevin's beard as he kisses her several times. She grins and seductively touches his lips.

"Do you think your old man has a clue? Do you think he knows his college-age son has been poking his client?"

"Doubt it—he thinks I'm still a virgin."

Kevin begins laughing.

Page **504**

Wesley Madison shuts the door behind him as he leaves the gym. Corey appears in front of him. He seems angry.

"Avoiding my calls—fucking asshole."

Wesley seems annoyed.

"I've been busy. I don't recall having to answer to you for living my life—so, if you have a problem—fuck yourself."

Corey seems about to snap.

"Of course I have a problem—your prick of a cousin has been trying my patience royally—making my life difficult."

Wesley seems confused.

"Cousin—oh, Hart—haven't really—whatever."

Corey rolls his eyes.

"Yeah, I'm sure, but that fucking asshole has been stirring up trouble for me with Eddie Kane—thinks he's all that."

Wesley grins.

"Really—and this is my problem why?"

"I'm banned from the mall—or didn't I just make that like really clear to you—and I have your loser cousin to thank."

Wesley looks at his watch. Corey notices.

"Well?"

Wesley sighs loudly. Corey seems about to explode.

"Oh—am I keeping you from something? Am I? Like what the frigging hell happened to you in jail anyway Wesley?"

Wesley turns away. Corey sighs loudly.

"That damn asshole Eddie Kane is probably having a field day with this right now—but I swear—your cousin is going to get—he'll regret he ever dared to insult me—I'm crush him."

Wesley shrugs seeming not to care.

"Don't know what you're talking about—and don't care regardless—so what else do you want to talk to me about because I have things to do—got a lot on my plate today."

"This mess is your fault—yours Wesley."

"How do you figure that?"

Corey looks back at the gym.

"You could have told me you had a cousin."

Wesley seems annoyed.

"Seriously, did I miss something? I don't have to answer to you or anyone else in this pathetic town—get off my back or I swear I'll bust you up bad and then you'll know my deal."

Corey grabs Wesley by the arm.

"Want to place bets on that motherfucker?"

Wesley jerks free of Corey's grip and angrily shoves him against the wall nearby. They look at each other briefly.

"You're a dead man, Madison—do you hear me—I'm going to break your fucking neck—and laugh while I'm doing it."

Wesley gestures at Corey with his finger and they go at it as punches begin flying between them. Suddenly from out of nowhere Eddie Kane and Alden Washington grab Corey.

<u>Port Clyde</u>

Denise climbs out of bed and looks back at Kevin. He grins broadly and glances at her naked body. He whistles loudly.

"I can go again if you—I'm so pumped."

Denise grins.

"I'd love to—but I have some things to take care of—but you and I definitely will hook-up tomorrow—I'll call."

Kevin smirks.

"Looking forward to it—and yeah, I'll have that info you need from my father's office about Caroline Bentley."

Denise looks at Kevin nervously.

"Just don't get caught—no one is to ever know you've copied this information for me. Do you understand?"

Kevin nods and glances at Denise slyly.

"I still don't know why you need this information?"

Denise walks over to where Kevin is lying on the bed and reaches out to stroke his penis gently. He grins broadly.

"That's for me to know—enough said."

She bends over further and kisses his penis.

Page **506**

"And most importantly whatever you do—don't mention that we know each other to anyone—it could cause more trouble than you would want—no need to tell anyone OK?"

"Is it because you're a married woman—and we shouldn't be screwing each other—especially since I have a girlfriend?"

Denise walks to the door.

"Uh-huh—exactly—glad you see my point."

She looks at him once more and leaves as he grins broadly again and lies back in bed. He begins whistling once more.

TO BE CONTINUED

A Look at the 20th Episode

Eddie and Alden prevent Corey and Wesley from coming to blows—Daryl deals with the aftermath of the discovery of Carrie's body—Clay and Maxwell try to sort out Gina's motive for murder—Tiffany continues to harass Gina in her cell—Glen and Denise plan out their revenge against Caroline—Genie finds out the hard way that she was played by Hart—Daryl deals with Archie's grief over Carrie's death—news about Lana's tragic murder spreads through town—Juan wastes no time in moving on without Faye—strange behavior is witnessed in public making for interesting conversation later—Carrie's brutal murder becomes the talk of Marble Hills—Kyle is confronted by someone from his past with more than just reminiscing about old times on his mind—Hart scores with yet another pretty girl—Brad and Gina play the blame game over the tragic events which cost their friends their lives—good friends come together to deal with recent events in town—as Kyle encounters his long-lost son.

Twist of the Knife

<u>Red Barn Gym</u>

Eddie Kane and Alden Washington forcibly push Corey Bentley against the wall. He glares at them angrily.

"What the fuck?"

Wesley Madison pulls himself to his feet and looks around—still surprised at the turn of events. He sighs loudly.

"Thanks guys."

Corey struggles to free himself from Eddie's grip.

"Let go of me—stupid frigging pricks."

Eddie gives Corey a knowing look.

"Should I call Daryl? Or how about the State Police—good idea or bad—you decide on an extended slammer visit?"

Corey continues to glare at Eddie.

"You're going to be sorry for banning me from your mall earlier. I swear I'll make you sorry—make you pay plenty."

"Is that right? Care to elaborate further?"

Eddie looks at Alden.

"Sound like a threat to you?"

Alden nods in agreement.

"Uh-huh—it does. Let's call the State Police."
Corey looks at Wesley.
"Are these jerks your new best friends?"
Wesley shrugs.
"What's it to you?"
Corey tries again to free himself from Eddie's grip.
"OK. OK. I'm good."
Eddie releases his grip on Corey.
"You better go home and cool off—like right now."
"Like who suddenly died and made you God?"
Eddie smirks.
"Go home before I lose my patience and help you see the almighty faster than you'd wish—and I don't mean daddy."
Corey glances at Alden and Wesley. He sighs again.
"You'll be hearing from my lawyers."
Eddie laughs.
"Oh, you'll be hearing from mine soon enough—got ten ready to do whatever I say—ain't it great to be filthy rich?"
Corey gives Eddie an odd look and turns to leave.
"Oh, by the way Bentley, if I catch you anywhere on mall property I'm going to bust you for trespassing—and no lawyer is going to be able to get you off no matter what you think you can get away with because your daddy has money—just go ahead and try me—think you got issues now—I'll make you wish you were never born—and that's only the beginning I assure you."
Corey angrily glances at Wesley and begins walking away as Alden, Eddie and Wesley watches him. He turns around.
"This isn't over Wesley—you and your punk cousin are going to pay for this—and you know I always do what I say."
Wesley sighs loudly.
"Bring it on—I'll break you. If I were you I'd be worried about your sister—word is she's got several screws loose."
"Fucking prick—I hate you."
Corey begins walking away as Wesley turns to look at Eddie and Alden standing nearby. He begins laughing.

Page **510**

Police Station

Clay Blankenship and Maxwell Pendergraft look at each other as they slowly flip through paperwork on Clay's desk.

"Think she did it?"

Maxwell looks up from the paperwork at Clay.

"She had motive—plenty."

He sighs.

"From what I can gather from town gossip—the deceased and the Bentley girl had plenty of bad blood between them."

Clay nods.

"I guess—but why such a public place?"

Maxwell shrugs.

"I have no clue about the motives of a teenage girl."

"If Gina Bentley did kill Lana Jefferson it means Brad McKinley isn't our guy—means he's actually innocent?"

"From what I hear—that kid is anything but innocent."

Maxwell looks at the files again.

Bradford Woods

Daryl Anderson turns to look at Lance Weissmann and Elizabeth Pendleton as Grant Monroe escorts covered remains toward a waiting van nearby. He sighs loudly and grimaces.

"Did you see anyone around before you noticed—before you and Elizabeth found Carrie Spaulding's car in the pond?"

Lance shrugs.

"No—we were just—we saw no one out of the ordinary."

Daryl glances at Elizabeth. She shakes her head.

"Keep this under wraps OK?"

Daryl turns to see a car pulling up. Archie Spaulding leaps out of the car and runs toward Daryl. He notices the coroner's van. They look at each other briefly. Archie glances around.

"I heard you found Carrie's car?"

Daryl nods.

"It was pulled from Miller's Pond ten minutes ago."

Archie looks around.

"What about—where is Carrie?"

Daryl looks at Lance and Elizabeth. Archie notices.

"Where is my daughter, Anderson?"

Daryl glances at the coroner's van and sighs loudly.

"I'm sorry."

Archie appears to be in shock.

"No—it can't be—this is some sort of sick joke—it has to be a sick joke—Carrie can't be—not my precious baby."

He begins calling Carrie's name out loud.

"Archie—I'm sorry. Her body was found in her car. She's dead—been dead at least twelve hours—maybe more."

He ignores Daryl and turns to run toward where the coroner's van is parked. He seems unable to accept reality.

"Well, so much for keeping a lid on this mess."

Daryl turns to face Lance and Elizabeth once more. He seems upset as he shakes his head and glances at his watch.

"You both can go—if I have more questions about Carrie Spaulding I know where to find you both—right?"

They nod in agreement and head toward the path leading through Bradford Woods as Daryl slowly turns around to look at the scene once more and shakes his head again in disbelief.

Police Station

Gina Bentley paces back and forth in a tiny cell. She sighs loudly several times in frustration. She hears a noise and turns around to see Tiffany Johnson grinning broadly behind her.

"What a shame—the biggest bitch in Marble Hills is exactly where she belongs—in jail—how sad—so very sad."

Gina sighs.

"Leave me alone—go away. I'm tired of you. Go away and never come back. Let me be happy for a change. Be gone."

Tiffany laughs.

"Nope—don't think I can—you and I have so much to talk about—starting with what you did—oh yeah, let's talk."

Gina blinks several times hoping Tiffany will be gone when she opens her eyes seconds later. Tiffany smirks.

"What do you think we're in—some stupid campy soap opera from the 1980s? This isn't *Flamingo Road* sweetie."

Gina walks toward the iron bars at the other end of the cell and shakes it several times as Tiffany rolls her eyes.

"Please—let me out of here—please help."

Tiffany laughs. Gina turns to face her.

"Go away—leave me alone—please just go away."

Tiffany laughs again. Gina begins to pound on the iron bars as the noise awakens Brad McKinley across the hall. He looks up and sees Gina pounding on the bars seemingly talking to an empty cell. He shakes his head several times and sighs.

"Gina? What are you doing here?"

She turns to look at him.

"I don't know."

Tiffany pushes her from behind against the iron bars.

"Tell him what you did *bitch*—tell him."

Gina turns to face Tiffany.

"Stop it—I didn't kill anyone—please."

Tiffany's face twists into an evil grin.

"Yeah, and I'm like **Mary, Queen of Scots**—tell him you cow—tell him what you did to me—tell him—say it *bitch*."

"Shut up Tiffany."

Tiffany pushes Gina against the iron bars again.

"Make me—go ahead and make me."

Brad looks at the weird scene unfolding in front of him as Gina appears to be talking to someone. But there's no one besides her in the cell. He looks in the next cell. It is empty as well. He watches as she continues arguing with someone he can't see. As he continues watching curiously from his cell Gina turns her back to him and seems highly agitated about something.

"Killer—you're a killer—crazy—crazy."

Gina tries to push Tiffany.

"You're a killer—killer—killer—killer—crazy killer."

"Stop it—just stop it—stop calling me that—please stop."

Tiffany grins broadly.

"What are you going to do about it *bitch*?"

She laughs loudly.

"Huh—what are you going to do about it Gina?"

Tiffany slyly glances at Brad before facing Gina again.

"Are you going to kill me—again?"

They look at each other.

"You're not real—you're not real Tiffany."

Tiffany shakes her head.

"Didn't we already have this talk?"

Gina suddenly tries to grab Tiffany and falls against the iron bars of her cell. Tiffany begins laughing loudly. Brad meanwhile continues to witness the odd scene as Gina continues to grab at something that obviously isn't in the cell with her.

<u>Portland</u>

Glen Bradstreet opens the door and watches as Denise Madison walks past him with a sly grin. He closes the door and turns to face her. She begins unbuttoning her blouse.

"It's a done deal—he's playing our game."

Glen gives Denise a knowing look.

"You actually slept with your lawyer's kid?"

Denise nods.

"I told you I would get him and I did—Kevin Myers is a little inexperienced for a college guy his age though—but I did it."

She watches as Glen walks over to her and slyly slides his hand under her bra and cups her breast. He kisses her.

"But will he get me what I want?"

She nods again.

"Caroline Bentley won't know what hit her—when you drop this bombshell on her she'll flip—and you'll own her."

Denise grins broadly and licks her lips.

"Panic will set in soon after—she'll do anything—hoping you'll spare her son from being—completely unaware."

Glen smirks and gestures.

Page 514

"Unaware you're behind the whole deal—right?"

Denise slides her hand into Glen's jeans and strokes his erection. He smiles broadly as his penis begins to swell.

"The question is once she complies with my wishes do I still let the secret about her precious son come out anyway?"

Denise kisses Glen again.

"Of course—what can she do about it after the fact?"

Glen pushes Denise up against the wall.

"You're a piece of work—like seriously dangerous."

Denise rolls her eyes.

"Uh-huh—and don't you forget it either—there's so many different sides to my mystique—most of them quite dark."

Glen shrugs.

"I never forget anything."

"Good—I like a man with a good memory—someone who knows not to push too far if he knows what's good for him."

He grins broadly.

"That's not the only thing I'm good at—I'm also—quite good at fucking—and blackmailing stupid rich people."

"I knew there was something about you I liked initially."

He begins kissing Denise passionately.

"Does that kid know you're married to Kyle Madison?"

"Of course—he doesn't care."

Glen smirks slyly.

"My kind of kid—really stupid and bad in bed too."

He kisses her again and begins laughing.

<u>Parking Lot</u>

Genie Van Pelt watches as Hart Bennington zips up his Levi's. He looks at her and grins broadly. She seems upset.

"What—want a box of roses?"

Genie turns away.

"Ugh—you're like all the rest—I just thought maybe."

Hart gestures with his hand and grins.

"You thought we could—you know—like date?"

Page 515

He makes a lewd gesture with his finger.

"Seriously—what for—Lance told me the deal on you girls—you're only in it for a good time—you're all whores."

He winks and climbs out of the backseat.

"Look, we just had a nice moment—deal with it. It's not like you're a virgin—and I'm not—at least not anymore."

He laughs loudly.

"Seriously, you thought I'd actually date you?"

He smirks.

"Talk about delusional fantasies—cool guys don't date back alley whores—they fuck them—like I just did you."

He looks at her as she puts on her shoes and laughs.

"Seriously, you thought you and I would—*ugh*."

He rolls his eyes in contempt.

"Look, I have to be somewhere soon—but hey, we're definitely going to do this again—say, tomorrow morning?"

He leaves without saying goodbye.

"Bastard—I hate him."

She notices her panty is soaked with seminal fluid and realizes he didn't wear a condom like he promised. She sighs.

<u>Bradford Woods</u>

Daryl forcibly restrains Archie as he watches Grant slowly drive away. He seems about to fall apart as he looks at Daryl.

"I want whoever did this to my baby brought to justice and punished. I want them on the electric chair pronto."

"I'm working on it—trying."

"Do more than just work—according to Grant Monroe from what he observed she was strangled—and also raped."

Daryl turns away.

"I'm sorry for your loss—just please go home."

Archie grimaces.

"Not more sorry than the bastard who killed her. I swear when I get my hands on Brad McKinley—I'll break his neck."

Daryl looks confused.

Page 516

"You think Brad killed Carrie?"

Archie looks at Miller's Pond again.

"Yeah—that McKinley kid did it all right. Carrie told me he was a sick, frigging bastard—I should've listened to her."

Daryl sighs.

"We don't know if Brad had anything to do."

"I do—and he's going to pay—I promise you that."

Archie watches as the coroner's van slowly disappears from sight and faces Daryl again. Daryl seems worried.

"Archie—don't you go taking the law into your own hands—I've got enough trouble to deal with already."

"That McKinley kid is going to pay—I swear he will."

He heads toward his car.

Police Station

Clay and Maxwell are looking at multiple crime scene photographs of Lana Jefferson when they hear Brad's voice yelling loudly from the holding area on the other side of the small building. They look at each other curiously for a few seconds.

"What the—what's his problem now?"

Brad continues to call for help.

"Think it's serious?"

Clay looks at Maxwell.

"Might be?"

"He could just be playing us again?"

Clay sighs and Maxwell nods in agreement.

"That kid is a handful."

They head for the hallway.

Lighthouse Grill

Kelly Nelson watches as Faye Washington gets up and leaves after she sees Juan Sabrillo flirting with a woman at the front counter. She angrily slams the door behind her.

"Guess they had something going before—so over."

He looks at the burger in front of him. He seems unable to pick it up and glances at it with a disgusted look. He sighs.

"Hey, if you don't want to eat it—I'll gladly take it off your hands—I could eat a horse—or a frigging buffalo."

He looks up to see Jason Anderson, Simon Spencer and Ashton Markway looking at him curiously. He sighs.

"Sure—it's yours."

Jason grabs the burger and looks at Kelly curiously.

"Well?"

Kelly looks upset.

"Well, what?"

Simon and Ashton share a glance.

"Why so bummed out?"

"Like seriously, you seem to be way more distraught than a snotty kid being told there is no Santa Claus and there never was—though I could be slightly wrong about the specific details of how such delicate matters might actually be handled?"

Kelly looks at Simon curiously.

"You haven't heard?"

They shake their heads in unison.

"Heard what?"

Kelly sighs loudly.

"Lana Jefferson is dead—Gina Bentley killed her."

They seem somewhat shocked at the statement—but not totally. Jason and Simon then exchange knowing looks.

"*I knew it*—that whack job finally up and snapped."

Kelly looks at the door and shrugs.

"I ran into her right after she killed Lana."

"The Bentleys are going to freak—like totally."

Ashton rolls his eyes.

"All the money in the world won't help them now—their daughter is *so* going away for a very long time—Tiffany, Caleb, Corinne, Daphne, Ross, Natalie, and now Lana—who would've thought it would be her—and not that punk Brad McKinley."

Kelly looks at Simon and sighs.

"I bet he'll be happy about that—*too bad*."

Page **518**

Ashton makes a lewd gesture with his finger.
"I would've so enjoyed seeing him fry for something."
They look at him. He grins.
"Hey, I hate the guy OK. He's a zero."
They nod in agreement.

<u>Police Station</u>

Clay and Maxwell hastily open the door leading to the holding area where Brad and Gina are in separate cells.

"What's the problem?"

Brad continues to call for help as he watches Gina continue to act like she's talking to someone he can't see. Clay gives Brad a strange look as he enters the room. Maxwell is close behind and seems slightly annoyed at Brad for some reason.

"Well—what's the big idea."

Brad turns to look at Gina. She sighs loudly.

"I don't know what he's talking about."

Brad rolls his eyes.

"She's nuts—she thinks she's talking to Tiffany Johnson."

Clay and Maxwell look at Gina again.

"Don't listen to him—he's just mad he's going down for killing everyone—he's guilty, not me—I didn't kill anyone."

Maxwell gives Gina a curious look.

"Brad McKinley couldn't have killed Lana Jefferson—and from what Kelly Nelson said—it seems that places you at the scene of the crime—quite hard explaining away that fact."

Brad looks at Clay and Maxwell.

"Wait—Lana is dead? Someone killed Lana Jefferson?"

They nod in union and glance at Gina.

"Uh-huh—yep—the Jefferson girl is dead alright."

Maxwell continues looking directly at Gina.

"Seems Gina was the last person to see her alive—and had the murder weapon in her hand—hard to explain away."

Brad reacts to the news.

Page 519

Denise slides her hand across Glen's chest as they lie in bed together. He watches as her fingers slide down toward his exposed penis. He grins broadly. Denise continues until her finger slides over the head. She looks back at Glen and smirks.

"What do you think Caroline Bentley will do when she finds out her precious son could face murder charges?"

Glen gestures with his hand.

"She'll lose it of course—beg for help."

He laughs loudly.

"What can she do after the fact though—I'll be holding all the cards in this deal—either she does as I say or else her son goes down for murdering a hooker—especially given his rep."

Denise giggles several times.

"I know I should feel sorry—but she's been my rival since high school—finally besting her will be so sweet a victory."

Glen kisses Denise's hand.

"Think we should just stop at blackmail? How about outing her for being unfaithful—really stir things up?"

Denise rolls her eyes and suddenly seems frustrated.

"Lot of good that would do when it comes to her so-called husband—John Bentley—he has cheated on her from the day they got engaged. He's a dog—he and I—well, we have a history too—I ended it when he insisted on a threesome with one of his favorite hookers—regardless I know he's been aware of her extramarital adventures—he doesn't care either way as far as I can tell from his demeanor—of course he doesn't know about Daryl Anderson and Caroline. I gather that's a big secret."

Glen sits up in bed.

"Daryl Anderson—who's he?"

She sighs.

"Chief of Police of Marble Hills—let's just put it this way—I know him intimately—so does Caroline—he gets around."

Glen makes a lewd gesture with his finger.

"You and the local police chief—damn you're popular."

Denise smirks.

"Uh-huh—so what—got a problem with me?"

Glen rolls his eyes.

"Been around—haven't you?"

Denise leans over to kiss Glen. They kiss passionately.

"Thought you were the only one—didn't you?"

Glen laughs.

"No—I just can't picture you and some law enforcement dude—especially how you seem to enjoy breaking rules?"

"Daryl and I go way back—he and I have been—since high school. He took me to the junior prom—and then we did it in the backseat of his car—got pregnant and had an abortion before anyone knew—then I hooked up with Kyle a month later."

Glen looks at Denise curiously.

<u>Farmington Villa</u>

Juan opens to the door and lets Sabrina Keller inside his suite before he closes the door behind him. She looks around in awe of the lavishly decorated hotel room. She sighs.

"Nice—it's a really nice pad."

Juan grins.

"I like it a lot actually."

He watches as she walks toward the balcony.

"I can't believe you've been here in Marble Hills this long and I haven't seen you around? Usually I notice everything."

Juan smirks.

"I've been busy."

Sabrina walks back toward Juan.

"You have a girlfriend?"

He gestures with his hand.

"Past tense—we're through."

Sabrina laughs.

"I'm not the sharing type by any means."

Juan watches as she reaches out and strokes his cheek.

"Bet you're quite a bad boy—aren't you?"

Page **521**

"I gather you like bad boys?"
Sabrina kisses Juan.
"My brother Jarod is a bad boy—plays like he's God's gift to women—and they beg for more—frankly it bothers me."
"Where's your brother now?"
"Bar Harbor—it's a little town up the coast."
Sabrina sighs.
"But only for another day or so—then he's coming back for a visit—I think you'll like him—the two of you should."
Juan shrugs and looks away.
"The question is—will he like me?"
Sabrina looks at Juan curiously as she gently reaches out to stroke his cheek a second time. They begin kissing.

<u>Red Barn Gym</u>

Wesley turns to look at Eddie and Alden nervously. He extends his hand cautiously. He seems somewhat uneasy.
"Thanks again for being there—whenever Corey is in one of his moods—he can get really crazy with the fists."
"No problem—that kid has serious issues no doubt."
Eddie looks around.
"Bentley needs to grow up—thinks everyone exists for his enjoyment—but that's not the way real life is nowadays."
Wesley nods.
"I know—seen plenty already."
Alden looks at his watch.
"Hey, do you think we can get together sometime this week—I'd like to pursue the idea we talked earlier about."
Wesley nods again.
"Sure—how about Friday—I've already been working angles with grandpa—I know he knows something about what happened that night. He's been acting really weird lately."
"Better believe that old man knows something—he has a knack for being involved in every damn thing that's bad."
Alden shoots Eddie a cautious look.

Page 522

"What Eddie is saying is your grandpa is no stranger to causing people pain—and he enjoys doing it—no doubt."

Wesley shakes his head.

"There's no love lost between my grandpa and me—he and I have had major differences for a while now—plenty."

He sighs loudly.

<u>Lighthouse Grill</u>

Archie slams the door behind him and walks across the diner as Jason, Simon and Ashton look up from their table.

"Oh-oh—Carrie's dad doesn't look happy."

Simon sighs knowingly.

"Too bad Kelly had to leave early—this might be fun to watch—oh boy, he seems pissed—could kill somebody."

They watch as he goes over to Sidney Stuyvesant and begins yelling loudly. Silence permeates the small diner.

"*That sick bastard killed my daughter*—she said he was dangerous and now she's dead—and I just came—oh God."

They look at each other in shock.

"Carrie Spaulding is dead?"

Archie continues to yell loudly.

"I tell you Sidney—he's going to pay—Brad McKinley is going to pay for what he did—I'm going to make him pay."

Ashton looks at Jason and Simon.

"Brad? Brad killed Carrie?"

Jason nods.

"Seems possible—no one has seen her since yesterday."

They watch as Sidney quickly ushers Archie into the back room as he continues to rant loudly about Brad McKinley.

"Do you think McKinley actually offed Carrie Spaulding like her father said? He had it out for her—that's for sure—made no secret about it. I'd place bets her father is telling the truth."

Jason shakes his head.

"Do you think it's actually true?"

Simon gestures with his hand and shrugs.

Page **523**

"Sure—why not—Brad McKinley is a twisted bastard—a real freak—killing someone isn't a stretch—and given how he and Carrie had issues like you said—bet his father will seriously beg the Bentleys to help with a lawyer—looks like Marble Hills just got real—calling all greedy reality show producers right now."

Ashton laughs mockingly.

"Couldn't be happening to a nicer guy—hope he likes his new pad—a jail cell with a really sadistic cellmate to boot."

They nod in agreement and begin laughing.

<u>Farmington Villa</u>

Juan and Sabrina are going at it as his cell phone begins to ring. He leans over and picks it up. He seems annoyed.

"Faye?"

He sighs.

"Really—what's your deal—we're through—get a life."

He hangs up and looks at Sabrina.

"The ex—she can't deal with the fact we're over."

Sabrina grins.

"Uh-huh—you bad boys are such a lure."

Juan laughs.

"It's a damn curse—being so good-looking and wonderful in bed—she can't seem to live without me—ask me if I care."

Sabrina pulls Juan toward her.

"That ex of yours better know her place—I won't tolerate her barging in on my scene wanting you back in her bed."

She slides her fingers across Juan's lips.

"I've got you now—and I don't plan to share you with some used-up whore. I'm a greedy bitch—and don't you forget the kind of woman I am. I'm certainly not the forgiving type."

Juan laughs loudly.

"So harsh are you—ouch—should I be worried?"

Juan pulls Sabrina under him.

"What if I hooked up with Faye after I'm done with you?"

Sabrina seems upset at Juan's comment.

Page 524

<u>Maple Avenue</u>

Donna Markway locks her car and is about to head across the street when she notices Genie slowly coming toward her looking upset about something. Genie stops suddenly.

"Gina killed Lana earlier."

Donna seems stunned.

"Lana's dead?"

Genie shakes her head.

"Kelly Nelson saw her kill Lana and called Clay. It's all over town—Gina's in jail—got busted right after she killed Lana."

Donna sighs.

"What about Brad?"

At that moment Donna's cell phone rings. She looks at it and her face changes color. She glances at Genie.

"Are you sure?"

She looks at Genie again.

"OK—I'll call you later."

She shuts her cell phone off and sighs loudly.

"What happened?"

"Ashton just heard that Carrie Spaulding is dead—from what he overheard he thinks Brad McKinley killed her."

Genie seems aghast.

"I warned Carrie about Brad."

Donna looks at her cell phone once more.

<u>Standish Road</u>

Jeremy Weissmann is driving toward Marble Hills when his cell phone rings suddenly. He grabs it. Seconds later his facial expression changes drastically. He sighs loudly several times.

"You found Carrie? Oh God—so unreal—her dad is going to lose it for sure—how much can that poor man take?"

He pulls over by the side of the road.

"She was raped?"

Page 525

He glances out the window.

"Brad McKinley—doesn't surprise me one bit—I guess this is one mess he won't be able to get out of like always."

He sighs again.

"How's Elizabeth?"

He watches several cars zoom by.

"I'm out on Standish Road—I'll call you when I get back to Marble Hills—hopefully nothing else will happen before."

He shuts off his cell phone.

<u>Mall</u>

Kyle Madison steps onto the elevator with a cup of coffee in his hand. From behind he hears his name being called.

"Hello Kyle."

He turns around and sees Gary Glick standing there with a smirk on his face. Kyle seems confused. He shrugs.

"Do I know you?"

Gary smirks.

"I'm hurt Kyle—given our history you'd think you'd—you'd at least remember me—especially after what happened."

Kyle seems annoyed.

"I really don't have time for games."

Gary gives Kyle an odd glance and shrugs.

"Does Serena Glick ring a bell?"

Kyle looks at Gary closely.

"Serena Glick?"

Gary smirks again.

"Uh-huh—certainly you couldn't forget what happened in the backseat of your father's limo the night of your fifteenth birthday party—when you fucked my sister—used her."

Kyle stops the elevator. He reacts.

"Gary?"

Gary nods.

"You and I need to talk—like today."

Kyle looks at Gary curiously.

Page 526

"What about exactly—how's Serena?"

"First things first—starting with your son—your flesh and blood—that night with my sister was more memorable than you could ever have imagined—but enough history lessons."

Gary pulls out a snapshot of Patrick Glick and slowly hands it to Kyle. He grins broadly as Kyle stares at the photo.

"His name is Patrick Glick."

Kyle seems confused.

"But—what—how come?"

Gary seems annoyed as he circles Kyle several times with a knowing look as he gestures with his hand and grins.

"When you and my sister did the deed in your father's limo the night of your fifteenth birthday party in Portland—you didn't wear a condom—do I really have to play the rest of this story out before you figure out the happy ending to this storyline?"

Kyle looks at Gary suspiciously.

"He doesn't look anything like me?"

Gary rolls his eyes.

"So what—neither does **Peter Fonda** and **Bridget Fonda** if you recall—big deal—he takes after our side of the family—you are Patrick's daddy whether or not you want to face facts."

Kyle looks at the photo again.

"Where is Patrick now?"

Gary takes the photo from Kyle.

"Funny you should ask—he's here in Marble Hills—just wrapped up his second year in college in Sydney—you and Patrick have so much to catch up on—just say when and where."

Kyle sighs.

"Does he know?"

Gary shakes his head.

"Is Serena here in Marble Hills too?"

Gary sighs loudly.

"Serena is dead—she died of cancer a while back—it was so tragic—such a waste—too young—crushed Patrick."

Kyle reacts.

"I'm sorry."

Page **527**

Gary and Kyle look at each other.

"Patrick has wanted to meet you since he found out his father was still alive two months ago—and now he's here."

Kyle seems confused.

"Why didn't Serena ever tell me about Patrick?"

"Your father told her if she ever came anywhere near Glass Owl he'd take Patrick and she'd never see him again."

"My father knows about Patrick?"

Gary nods again. Kyle seems unconvinced and shakes his head several times. He looks at the small snapshot again.

"No—he wouldn't—even for him this would be too low."

"This is your father we're talking about—not a candidate for father of the year—**Hugh Beaumont** he certainly wasn't."

Kyle rolls his eyes at the comment.

"My father is no saint—but he just wouldn't do something so despicable to me—this is just pure evil—vile behavior."

Gary grabs Kyle by the arm.

"If you don't believe me—ask him—I bet you anything he'll deny ever having known about Patrick—but ask him anyway."

Gary lets go of Kyle's arm.

"I want to meet him—meet my son."

Gary grins broadly.

<u>Plymouth Street</u>

Diana Bingham suppresses a laugh as Hart tells her about Genie's behavior with him earlier after their encounter.

"Genie has always thought she was better than everyone else in Marble Hills—I mean—seriously, the only reason she's even remotely popular with guys is because she copied everything my friends and I did—not that it really helped—such an ugly troll."

Hart laughs.

"Which was what?"

"She slept with every straight guy in Marble Hills and put out for old dudes too. Her legs have been spread far and wide."

Diana starts the engine to her car.

Page **528**

"How about we go to Pirate's Cove and make out. No one ever goes there anymore on account of what happened."

"What happened there?"

"About fifty years ago these two teenagers drowned and since then nobody goes there—some people say it's because they haunt the beach—but who believes in that sort of old garbage today—like for real—there are no such things as ghosts."

Hart smirks and makes a lewd gesture with his finger.

"Whatever—all I want to do is fuck—got to rack up my numbers with every girl in town—like right away."

Diana smiles broadly.

"How about I call my sister Marilyn—we can have a cozy threesome—it'll be so cool to try something really bold."

Hart looks down at his swelling erection.

"Oh yeah—call her already."

Diana grabs her cell phone and begins dialing.

<u>Police Station</u>

"You're a sick freak Gina—you actually killed seven people and then framed me for what you did—so sick—so twisted."

Gina glares at Brad from her cell.

"I didn't kill anyone Brad—I'm being framed."

"Is that so—then explain Kelly Nelson."

"Huh?"

"Kelly found you with Lana's body. From what Clay said she was dead only about ten minutes. You killed her."

Gina shakes her head.

"I didn't do it—I swear—I couldn't kill anyone."

Brad mockingly rolls his eyes.

"This is me you're talking to—not Clay or that other clueless dude Maxwell somebody or other. I know what you're really like—remember what happened after we slept together for the first time—you acted like I was your property—and when you found out I had no intention of ever being your boyfriend you tried to run me over with your car on Standish Road."

Page 529

Gina sighs.

"I was only trying to scare you."

"Uh-huh—tell that to Tiffany Johnson—tell her *you only wanted to scare her* as you cut the brakes to her sports car."

"Yeah—tell me—you bitch."

Gina turns around to see Tiffany standing a few feet away with a cruel grin on her face. Brad notices Gina's behavior.

Lighthouse Grill

"Look Archie, you'd better not do something really stupid where that McKinley boy is concerned—it will end badly."

Archie sighs loudly.

"That punk raped and killed my daughter."

Sidney nods.

"Let the law handle it—he'll get what he deserves."

Archie clenches his fists angrily.

"You better believe he will—I'll make sure of it—law or no law—justice needs to be served the old-fashioned way."

"Listen, I've known you since you were a kid—your pop and I were best friends—just leave it be—let it go—OK?"

Archie looks around the storeroom.

"I don't think I can do that."

Without another word he opens the door and leaves. Sidney looks up at the ceiling and sighs.

"That McKinley kid better watch his back if he knows what's good for him—that punk definitely is in trouble."

He turns off the lights and leaves the room.

Stanley Pier

Lance and Jeremy are sitting with Elizabeth as Shirley Moses walks up to them. They look up. She shrugs.

"I got here as soon as I heard the news—poor Carrie."

Elizabeth wipes her eyes again with a napkin.

"I can't believe—how could Brad—how could he?"

Page **530**

Shirley sighs and glances at Elizabeth.

"Simple—he's a wretched slug—worthless."

She glances at Lance and Jeremy.

"I knew they had problems—but I never thought he'd kill her—and to add insult to injury I heard she was raped."

Lance and Jeremy look at each other.

"Her dad is going to go ballistic."

Shirley nods.

"It would serve Brad right if Carrie's dad took the law into his own hands—and gave an eye for an eye sort of deal."

"That wouldn't bring Carrie back?"

Shirley smirks.

"No—but at least Brad McKinley would be toast—I think we can all agree that no one would miss him if someone blew his brains out—especially if that someone was Carrie's dad."

Lance looks up at Shirley again.

"But then Archie Spaulding would be facing a life sentence for taking Brad out for what happened? How does that work?"

"Two wrongs don't make a right."

Shirley smiles slyly.

"Not necessarily—he could get a good lawyer and get off on a technicality—he certainly has lots of money to burn."

Jeremy looks at Shirley curiously.

"You seem to know a lot about this stuff—why is that?"

Shirley rolls her eyes knowingly.

"I watch a lot of **Nancy Grace** OK?"

Elizabeth sighs loudly.

"Does anyone know if Gina Bentley has confessed yet to Daryl Anderson for killing Tiffany Johnson and the others?"

Jeremy shrugs.

"Not that I've heard. But I wouldn't hold my breath on that issue happening anytime—old man Bentley is definitely going to get her the best lawyer money can buy—believe me."

Lance nods.

"I wouldn't doubt it one bit."

Jeremy stands up.

"Today it doesn't matter what crime you commit—all you have to do is get a really good, extra sleazy lawyer with no morals and you can get away with anything you do—especially murder. Remember that old 1994 case with **O. J. Simpson** where his killed his ex-wife **Nicole Brown** and her friend **Ron Goldman**? Everyone knew he did it—his guilt was so obvious even with scummy cops allegedly planting evidence—yet his lowlife lawyer **Johnnie Cochran** pulled out all the stops and got him off even though he knew he was guilty—talk about lawyers being lower than pond scum. Since then the bar has been lowered so many times it's almost expected in cases today to make the victim look like they deserved to be murdered and the killer is actually the victim."

"I wonder how long it is before **Drew Griffin** from CNN descends on Marble Hills looking for a juicy story?"

Shirley smiles broadly.

"I wouldn't mind if he came to town—I like him."

She notices everyone's reaction.

"Uh-huh—I'm OK with him—he does good work and never takes anyone's crap when he's reporting on a hot story."

Lance rolls his eyes.

"Fuck CNN—they've fallen on hard times since they decided to move away from real news and switched to covering political crap every day—all day long—ugh—blah-blah."

Lance gestures with his hand.

"Seriously, they've gone from covering real news to looking for every salacious political story they can, just to get the *TMZ* audience to watch. It's sick. I've seen better reporting from *Entertainment Tonight* and that's saying a lot. CNN has more in common lately with FOX News and that's not a compliment."

Shirley looks at Jeremy as he rolls his eyes.

Tolling Bell Inn

Gary has a smug look on his face as he walks through the lobby with Kyle. Kyle notices Todd Spencer having a drink at the bar but coldly ignores him. He shuts his cell phone off.

"Is Patrick OK with me paying him a visit?"

Gary nods.

"Don't worry. It's gonna be easier than you think."

They enter an elevator and seconds later they get off and begin walking down the hallway. Gary looks at Kyle.

"Are you nervous Kyle? I bet you are."

Kyle ignores the comment.

"Patrick is a good kid—don't worry. He's got Serena's eyes and her demeanor. He turned out pretty well considering how this all came about initially. Probably even better than you or I turned out. Just don't expect anything other than what you would if you were meeting a total stranger for the first time."

Kyle continues to look straight ahead as if in a daze.

"Technically I'm a total stranger."

Gary shrugs.

"This is the right thing to do Kyle."

Kyle watches as Gary slips his card key into the lock and opens it. He sighs and motions Kyle toward the door. Seconds later he sees Patrick Glick standing in the doorway.

TO BE CONTINUED

A Look at the 21st Episode

Gina and her lawyer painfully work through issues involving her case—news of Carrie's death rapidly filters across town—Hart plays both of the Bingham sisters—Shirley fears Brad might be coming after her once he's released from jail—Robert and Chandra have an unpleasant encounter with Lindsay—Tiffany continues to torment Gina as she tries to make her think she's losing her mind—Sidney chastises Caroline over her lack of motherly concern for her troubled daughter—Juan and Sabrina's passionate encounter intensifies while Faye refuses to let go of the past—Alden gives Julia news about Caleb's real killer—Robert and Chandra figure out their next move—Tyler has harsh words for Matt—Gary threatens Patrick again over their arrangement with Kyle—as Sabrina is surprised by an unexpected visitor.

Suffer the Children

Police Station

Pierce Colby walks towards the cell where Gina Bentley is yelling loudly at someone. She stops suddenly when she notices him slowly coming toward her and rolls her eyes in contempt.

"Well, it's about time you got here."

Pierce gives her a dirty look as he stops just outside the metal bars of her cell. He turns to look around at the other cells and seems unimpressed. He faces Gina again and sighs.

"It's nice to see *you* too."

Gina makes a lewd gesture with her finger.

"Get me the hell out of here now."

He looks at her coldly and sighs.

"If I were you young lady I'd lose the attitude or things will get even worse than they already are—have been already."

Gina rolls her eyes again.

"You work for my dad—he tells you what to do—and so do I—and don't you forget it either—I'm your boss—so deal."

Pierce looks around at the other cells.

"Are you enjoying the accommodations?"

"I want out of here this minute—I'm innocent."

Pierce notices Brad McKinley sitting on his bunk watching the odd scene unfold. Brad begins laughing hysterically.

"Gina thinks she sees dead people."

Gina glares at Brad.

"Shut up."

Brad mouths the word "fuck you" at Gina.

"I swear when I get out of here you're so over."

"You'll what—kill me?"

Pierce gives Gina a weird look.

"Miss Bentley, we have a lot to talk about—and right now it's looking to me like—like you're not the least bit sorry."

"I didn't kill anyone."

Brad snickers.

"Uh-huh—I'll just bet you didn't."

Gina grabs the bars in a rage—angrily shaking them.

"Shut the fuck up—or I'll."

Brad snickers again.

"Or what Gina—you'll bash me over the head with a cinder block—or stab me with a butcher knife—or shoot me?"

Gina looks at Pierce nervously.

"I didn't kill anyone—I swear—it wasn't me."

"Are you sure about that?"

Gina turns to see Tiffany Johnson standing less than ten feet away with her hands on her hips. She grins broadly.

<u>Maple Avenue</u>

Donna Markway gets into her car and drives off in a rush as Genie Van Pelt shakes her head. Her cell phone begins to ring loudly. She looks at the text message on the screen.

"Oh God, it's true—oh well—I never liked Carrie anyway if the truth be known—she was always so unpleasant—so rude."

She sighs loudly.

"I wonder if she screamed before she got shafted by Brad. Those two certainly had history—the bitch and the toad."

Page 536

She shuts off the cell phone and then notices Juan Sabrillo escorting Sabrina Keller toward the entrance of her apartment across the street. She rolls her eyes and shrugs at the scene.

"Oh-oh—Sabrina Keller has gotten herself quite a hunky hottie to play with—wonder what her boyfriend will say."

She shrugs again.

"I'd hate to be Sabrina's new guy when Justin Wellington comes to town for a visit—oh-oh—plenty drama no doubt."

She sighs once more and grins.

Parking Lot

Archie Spaulding looks at the gun in his hands. He sighs and flips it over and over as he glances out into the empty parking lot across from the police station. He sighs again.

"Bastard needs to die—die horribly for what he did to my baby—I can't let him get away with what he did—I won't."

He looks at the gun again.

"One clear shot is all I need—just one and his lights will go out for good—no one will care—except his parents—and who cares what they think—they brought that fucking monster into the world and look what havoc he's brought to Marble Hills."

He runs his fingers along the top of the gun.

"Oh yeah—McKinley is a dead man all right—it's just a matter of when—but he's dead for sure—I must—I will."

He grins slyly as he strokes the gun.

Pirate's Cove

Hart Bennington penetrates Diana Bingham again as her moans echo loudly throughout the secluded beach. Marilyn Bingham slides her hand around Hart's waist and whispers.

"I thought we agreed to share him?"

Hart glances at Marilyn.

"I've got plenty of juice left."

Hart makes a lewd gesture with his tongue.

Page 537

"Best idea ever—screwing two sisters in the middle of nowhere—even better when they're willing to try anything."

Hart pulls out of Diana and smirks as he pulls Marilyn toward him. She seems shocked as he pushes her under him.

"What if we both get pregnant from fooling around with you today—pills don't always work every time you know?"

Hart laughs loudly.

"Get an abortion—what's the big deal?"

Diana reaches out to passionately kiss Hart's neck and looks at her sister in a mock expression of anger. She sighs.

"Come on—he's a guy—he shouldn't have to worry about us being careless—we should know better—it's up to us."

Hart smirks again.

"Uh-huh—I second that."

Seconds later he penetrates Marilyn.

<u>Stanley Pier</u>

Lance Weissmann watches as Elizabeth Pendleton drives off. He sighs loudly as he realizes his erection is noticeable.

"Man, this town sure isn't boring anymore."

Lance turns to look at Jeremy Weissmann with a grin on his face. Shirley Moses begins nervously rummaging through her purse. They notice her odd behavior and look at each other.

"What's wrong?"

Shirley rolls her eyes at Jeremy.

"I think I lost my vial of pepper spray."

Jeremy seems confused.

"Pepper spray?"

"I'm not taking any chances if Brad gets off—no one is safe anymore—Carrie—oh God, he killed her—he—killed."

Jeremy and Lance look at each other.

"There's nothing to worry about—just relax Shirley."

Shirley ignores Lance's comment. He grins.

"Daryl Anderson isn't going to let Brad out of jail anytime soon—McKinley is done for—finished—serves him right."

Page 538

Shirley finally locates the vial of pepper spray and rubs it repeatedly as she looks at Lance and Jeremy curiously.

"Poor Carrie—she was such a good friend."

Jeremy puts his arms around Shirley and smiles.

"It'll be all right—you'll see."

Shirley seems about to cry as Lance notices Susan Bennington walking toward him. He grins broadly.

<u>Blankenship Apartment</u>

Clay Blankenship opens the door to his apartment and slowly walks through the entrance as if in a trance. He sighs as he closes the door behind him. As he turns around Eva Harper wraps her arms lovingly around him and gives him a warm hug.

"I could use plenty of TLC right about now."

Eva hugs Clay again.

"I heard about what happened."

Clay sighs loudly.

"Oh man—things have gone from bad to worse in this town—I still can't believe the Bentley girl killed so many people but evidence says otherwise—if I'd pushed Daryl harder."

Eva kisses Clay lightly on the cheek.

"You aren't responsible for what happened—from what I've been hearing around town the Bentley girl is messed up royally. Her whole family is beyond help—totally screwed."

Clay pulls away from Eva and walks over to the sofa. He sits down and wipes his brow. She looks at him curiously.

"Usually men are pegged as killers—not teenage girls."

Eva rolls her eyes.

"Women can kill just as viciously as men. There are plenty of famous cases about women who were cold blooded killers."

Clay waves his hand.

"I know—I know—but it just seems."

He looks at Eva curiously.

"It's just that she seemed so normal—so harmless."

Eva sits down next to Clay.

"That's how people like her seem—that's not how they are—studies have been done—fact is stranger than fiction."

Eva begins to unzip Clay's Levi's. He stops her. Eva seems confused as she glances at the worried look on Clay's face.

"Is something wrong?"

Clay stretches out on the sofa.

"I'm just not in the mood—not after—I'm sorry."

Eva glances at Clay for several seconds.

"It's OK—totally OK if you don't want to make love."

Eva puts his arms around Clay.

"Do you want to talk about what happened?"

Eva kisses Clay on the cheek again. He shakes his head.

"I wouldn't even know where to begin."

He sighs loudly.

"I'm just really depressed at the moment—probably not really good company right now—so seriously messed up."

Eva runs her fingers through Clay's hair.

"I'm here for you."

Clay grimaces.

"I can't believe this is happening."

Eva strokes Clay's hair.

"How about I order us dinner—and then we'll talk?"

Clay nods and tries to smile.

<u>Mall</u>

Maxwell Pendergraft walks toward where Kelly Nelson is standing at the ice cream kiosk. A few people walk away.

"Got time to spill?"

Kelly nods.

"I can spare a few."

Maxwell nods and leans against the kiosk.

"What can you tell me about Tiffany Johnson?"

Kelly sighs loudly.

"Nothing really—I met her maybe once—maybe two times—before she—well, you know—her car accident."

Page 540

Maxwell shrugs.

"What about Gina Bentley?"

Kelly looks at his watch several times.

"I barely knew her—but my girlfriend Abby knew Tiffany very well and she was best friends with Gina Bentley."

"Was—they're no longer talking?"

"They had a falling out—quite harsh."

Maxwell looks around.

"What about exactly—Tiffany Johnson's death?"

Kelly shakes his head.

"No—they had words because of me."

Maxwell seems confused.

"You—explain?"

"Abby and I—well—we liked each other when we met and this pissed Gina off like seriously—she was royally angry."

"Enough to lose it—and snap—have a bad moment right after—enough for her to kill the Johnson girl afterwards?"

Kelly shakes his head several times.

"I didn't say that."

"But it could have led?"

"I have no idea."

They look at each other.

"I think Abby would be able to help you more than I could—I've only been in Marble Hills just over a month."

"OK—I'll be in touch."

Kelly nods again.

Sea View Terrace

Robert Bennington and Chandra Stevenson are about to leave as he notices Lindsay Bennington looking at him with a cold stare seconds after she enters the small diner. He shrugs.

"I thought you said you were leaving—what—think you're getting money from the deal—well, think again Robert."

"No—I have—unfinished business."

Lindsay glares at Chandra.

"Well, I hope you're happy with yourself Chandra. But trust me this thing you think you have with my husband isn't going to last—he'll cheat on you too—like he did me—wouldn't be the first time and certainly won't be the last—that's for sure."

Lindsay notices Chandra's reaction.

"What—you thought you were the first? Seriously even you can't be that naive. Robert is shameless—he can't keep his dick in his pants—you of all people should know that from experience—especially after how the two of you got together."

Chandra seems annoyed.

"Nothing you say will change how I and Robert."

"Hope you remember that when you find out your beloved has been dipping his wick in one of your friends—but hey, maybe he'll even fuck your mother too—yeah—he's done mothers—a few of them if I recall—never showed any preference for what they looked like either—he'll fuck anything that has a pulse—but what can you expect from a filthy rabid dog like Robert."

Robert grabs Lindsay by the arm. She angrily slaps him.

"I swear—if this wasn't a public place."

Robert sighs.

"Look, I told you I was sorry—but like you said too much has happened—my behavior has caused serious—*damage*."

Lindsay laughs knowingly.

"Is that what you call cheating, Robert—damage? You made a baby with *her* and then tried to act blameless?"

She glances at Chandra.

"Hope you're happy now Robert—but when you get back to Philadelphia you'll really wish you were—like really."

Robert looks at Lindsay curiously.

"What are you talking about Lindsay?"

Lindsay smirks slyly.

"Let's just say I hope you and Chandra like standing in the unemployment line for hours like the pathetic losers you are."

Robert seems confused.

"I have a job—the firm has rehired me."

Lindsay looks at Chandra again with disdain.

Page 542

"Are you sure about that Robert—I mean—have they?"

Robert gives Lindsay an odd look.

"What's that supposed to mean Lindsay?"

Lindsay looks at Chandra again and begins laughing.

"Daddy bought the firm you worked for—first thing he did was order your immediate termination—and Chandra's too."

Robert seemed shocked as he looks at Chandra. He faces Lindsay again. He watches as she relishes the moment.

"You didn't?"

Lindsay nods.

"I didn't—daddy did."

Lindsay smirks as she glances at Chandra.

"I guess the both of you will be collecting food stamps and welfare when you get back to Philadelphia—have a nice life."

Lindsay glances at her watch.

"Oh, by the way—daddy also emailed all your business contacts and made sure they wouldn't hire you either."

Lindsay makes a slashing gesture across her neck.

"And if they do—Madison Industries will destroy their companies—and they know from experience it isn't an idle threat by some sick freak egomaniac. Isn't revenge wonderful?"

"Lindsay—you didn't—say it isn't so?"

Lindsay quickly walks away and heads toward where Lori Anderson is sitting with a curious look on her face.

Police Station

Gina watches as Tiffany glances over at Brad and slowly comes closer to where she and Pierce are standing. Tiffany shakes her head several times in a mocking way. She smirks.

"Sick—sick—such a twisted freak you are—not even a little bit of remorse for what you did—such bad manners."

Gina turns away.

"Ignore me all you like—but facts are facts—you're a killer—everyone knows it—there's no place to hide."

Pierce looks at Gina curiously.

"I get paid whether or not you get off in case you were wondering—it's up to you, not me. If you don't care then I don't either—it's that simple—do you understand how this works or do I need to give you further lessons? It's time to get real."

Gina sighs.

"I'm innocent—innocent I tell you."

Brad laughs loudly.

"Yeah, sure you are—and I'm a virgin."

Brad laughs even louder.

"Oh wait—I'm not—not even close—come to think of it I banged you like a cheap whore before you realized I was just using you—Corey and I had so many laughs about you."

Brad notices Gina's reaction and smirks.

"Want to kill me don't you?"

Pierce looks at Brad and Gina. He shakes his head.

"OK—if this is who you—I'm *so* out of here."

"No—please—I need your help."

Tiffany laughs.

"Yeah—you need help all right. Too bad the guys in the white coats aren't around when you need them—so sad."

Gina sighs loudly and shrugs.

<u>Lighthouse Grill</u>

"My life is such a mess right now."

Sidney Stuyvesant sighs as he looks at Caroline Bentley while she takes a sip of coffee from a mug. He seems annoyed.

"Seems to me it's Gina's life that's a mess right now Caroline—and have—have you visited your daughter yet?"

Caroline mockingly rolls her eyes at Sidney.

"What for—she's made it clear I'm not welcomed."

Sidney reaches out to touch Caroline's hand.

"Go to her—first thing tomorrow morning—even if she says to go away out of anger—got to break this wall."

"I—I don't know if I can?"

Sidney sighs loudly.

Page 544

"I do. Tomorrow—first thing—go talk to her—tell Gina you know she didn't do it—I know it'll mean a lot to her."

Caroline takes a sip from the mug again.

"My whole life is slipping away from me—my daughter is in jail for multiple murders—my son has the morals of an alley cat—and my husband is as cold and indifferent as ever."

Sidney gives Caroline a knowing look.

"Oh, and I suppose none of this was your fault—you've just been the perfect wife and mother—never screwed up?"

Caroline becomes upset.

"I've tried to fix things—I really tried—but—but other things happened before—most of which you're aware."

Sidney nods.

"You should have let me finish that monster off when it happened—I was much younger then and could have broken his neck with one snap—but you—you wouldn't let me kill him."

Caroline stands up.

"I'll go see Gina tomorrow—though I don't see the point."

Sidney looks at his watch.

"Let me know how it goes—maybe I can help?"

Caroline looks at the mug in her hand.

<u>Keller Apartment</u>

Juan laughs as he looks at Sabrina's startled face as he rams her again. He smirks as he enters her once more.

"You bring out the wild animal in me."

He laughs loudly and winks slyly.

"There's never a dull moment with American women."

His cell phone rings.

"That bitch is really trying my last nerve."

He picks it up and listens.

"Stop calling me you crazy whore—I thought I made it clear, I'm done with you—over—what part of that don't you understand—fuck off bitch or I swear I'll—enough."

He hangs up and looks at Sabrina.

Page 545

"I swear—my ex is really beginning to annoy me."
Sabrina seems confused.

Boardinghouse

Julia Winthrop closes the door to Caleb's room and turns to walk down the hallway when she sees Alden Washington walking toward her. They look at each other. She sighs.
"It's done—all of it."
Alden nods.
"I could have helped—it wouldn't have been a big deal."
Julia shrugs.
"I know—but I had to make peace with what happened to Caleb—and now I can let go—now that it all seems real."
Alden seems confused.
"You haven't heard—have you?"
Alden sighs.
"Brad McKinley didn't kill Caleb—Gina Bentley did."
Julia seems about to faint.
"What—Gina Bentley?"
Alden looks around.
"She was found earlier today hovering over the body of one of her classmates—someone named Lana Jefferson."
"Gina—Gina killed Caleb—it doesn't—why?"
Alden shakes his head.
"It's all over town from what I heard—bet the local press is going to have a field day with the sordid details—uh-huh."
Julia looks at Alden curiously.
"Did she say she killed Caleb—did she confess?"
Alden shakes his head.
"Not that I know of—but from what I heard her dad hired some big shot lawyer to defend her—heard he's the best."
Julia seems upset.
"Damn Bentleys—this is just like what happened before with Corey and—they'll cook up some lame excuse."
Alden nods in agreement.

Page **546**

"I guess so—well—but the McKinley kid isn't so innocent regardless of the other murders. Apparently he killed one of his girlfriends—raped her first and then strangled her to death."

Julia gives Alden an odd look.

"Who did Brad rape and murder?"

Alden runs his fingers through his hair several times.

"Carrie Spaulding."

Julia leans against the wall.

"First his wife—and now his daughter—how much more can Archie Spaulding take—and I thought I had problems."

They look at each other.

<u>Sea View Terrace</u>

"Oh, he looks mad."

Lindsay turns to look at Robert and Chandra as they leave. She grins broadly as she faces Lori once more.

"Good—for once daddy did something that really works in my favor—I bet Chandra wishes she'd screwed some other guy who didn't have a rich father-in-law to fuck her over."

Lori smirks.

"You're enjoying this aren't you?"

"Damn right I am—this has been going on for way too long—and it's not just with Chandra either—Robert's slept his way through half of Philadelphia. From the week we were married he began to scout new prospects whenever I wasn't around. I tried—I really tried—but enough is enough."

Lori seems upset.

"I wish I had your nerve—Daryl's been cheating on me round the clock for years—of course he says he hasn't—but I know he has—people in this town talk—and his name comes up quite a bit when it comes to who's screwing who around."

Lindsay rolls her eyes.

"Look, he's a dog—always was and always will be—he trolled his way through high school—used my sister."

Lori reacts to Lindsay's comment.

Page 547

"In his senior year he got four girls pregnant—one of which was Carmen Pendleton—goddamn nasty whore."

Lindsay shakes her head.

"Damn bitch left town soon afterwards—some people said she had the baby—while others say she got rid of it."

Lindsay gestures with her hand.

"Her brother was no better—Steve Pendleton—he hung out with Daryl and John Bentley and they all had bad reps."

She clenches her fists.

"Used all my friends while they worked their way through every girl in Marble Hills—I swear—the guys in this town are worst than anywhere else—they treated us like disposable napkins."

Lindsay makes a lewd gesture with her finger.

Police Station

Pierce snaps the locks on his briefcase shut and glances at Gina for a few seconds. He sighs as she rolls her eyes.

"For what it's worth—I think you've got problems—lots of problems—but you're no killer—which leads to one question."

They look at each other briefly and then Pierce heads down the hallway. Brad smirks as he watches Pierce leave.

"Man, he's a dumbass—like seriously—a tool."

Gina shoots Brad a nasty look.

"Go fuck yourself already."

Brad laughs.

"I'll think about it—God knows I've fucked you plenty of times without ever once promising a return—cheap whore."

Gina grabs the bars of her cell.

"Nothing would please me more than to watch you die a painful death—no one would deserve it more than you Brad McKinley—your death would make everything perfect."

"It seems to me you wished me dead—and then you—you made sure I was *dead*—killed—and now here you are—in *jail*."

Gina spins around just as Tiffany appears in front of her again with a malicious grin spread across her face.

Page **548**

"When Brad turns up dead how are you going to explain it away to Daryl—especially given your terribly sad *situation* being in the slammer presently—for killing me and the others."

Gina clenches her fist.

"I didn't mean anything by it—nothing at all."

Tiffany makes a mock gesture of feigning belief in Gina's innocence. Brad notices Gina's weird behavior and laughs.

"I bet you wish you hadn't said that—oops."

Gina turns to look at Brad with a confused look.

"Huh?"

"I should have this recorded Gina—you threatened my life—said you could kill me—and wouldn't care one bit."

Gina makes a lewd gesture at Brad with her finger.

"Big deal—no one would care if you suddenly disappeared tomorrow—you're just poor white trash anyways—loser."

Brad reacts.

"Uh-huh—but this poor piece of white trash has a big stiff dick which took your virginity—and made you beg plenty that day—promised all sorts of things—lied plenty—didn't care."

Gina rolls her eyes.

"I was ready to give it up anyway—whatever."

Brad laughs loudly as Tiffany begins tapping her finger on one of the iron bars which Gina notices as Brad rambles again.

"Yeah right, you begged me as I was coming inside you to be your boyfriend—of which I did if you recall. But I lied."

He laughs loudly again.

"Of course you realized I'd lied to you when you caught me fucking Lana Jefferson less than two hours after I'd promised you we'd be a couple forever—you were pissed—enraged."

He begins laughing hysterically.

"Man, you should have seen your face when you realized I'd been playing you—it was priceless—so fucking angry."

Tiffany smirks.

"I would've given anything to have seen that—watching you being made a fool of by the biggest cad in town."

Gina looks back at the cell.

Page **549**

"You really hurt me that day Brad—I thought you meant every word you said—and then you fucked Lana Jefferson."

Brad makes a lewd gesture with his finger.

"I did—for like ten seconds—then Lana showed up."

He makes a lewd gesture again and winks. Tiffany smirks again as she sees how unhappy Gina suddenly seems to be.

"Imagine your surprise when you found out it was me who was behind it all—that I'd set you up to be played by Brad."

Tiffany smirks as she leans closer to Gina and whispers.

"I know this hurts—but remember how much fun it was when you found out I'd slept with Brad too—and then you found out that it was me who convinced him to tell everyone you were a whore after you lost your virginity to him. I convinced Caleb to pretend he was into you too—that was something all right—he and I laughed endlessly as he fucked me in the backseat of his car knowing how hard he played you all summer for a fool."

Gina lunges at Tiffany.

"You bitch—I hate you."

Brad watches as Gina grabs at the air. He shakes his head.

"Crazy—loony tunes—next stop—padded room."

Tiffany laughs as Gina falls on the floor.

"Is that the best you've got? Oh my—how the mighty have fallen on hard times. Oh well—jail can do that to you."

Gina grabs for Tiffany again.

"I wish you were—oh God I wish you."

Tiffany looks over at where Brad is watching the unfolding events unaware of what is happening and smirks slyly.

"What—dead—oh, that's right—I'm already."

Gina lunges again and falls against the bed a few feet away. Tiffany grins broadly and steps out of the way.

"Think this is entertaining—wait until the trial—you'll wish you hadn't killed me. ABC News is going to broadcast all day."

Gina sits down on the bed and sighs.

"I didn't kill you—your death was a tragic accident—no one killed you Tiffany. Why can't you just go away?"

Tiffany grimaces.

"Like hell bitch—you—you killed me—admit it."

She looks over at Brad.

"But don't worry dear Gina—by the time I get through with you—you'll wish you were dead too—*dead*—so dead."

Tiffany begins laughing hysterically.

<u>Stanley Pier</u>

Susan looks at Lance oddly. He smirks as he pulls her towards him. He slides his hand under her skirt and gropes her as his fingers slide between her legs. Susan sighs loudly.

"Your brother seemed mad at me?"

Lance laughs.

"He'll get over it. He knows I wanted to fuck you—besides he has Shirley to keep him company—forget him already."

Susan seems annoyed and pushes Lance's hand away.

"Is fucking all you think about?"

"What do you think—come on—what else is there?"

He pushes her toward his car and grins slyly.

"Uh-huh—what else is there?"

He unlatches the door to his car and pushes Susan into the backseat. He grins as he seductively slides his hand under her skirt again. Susan glances at his erection straining against his Levi's as he pushes her down onto the seat. He sighs loudly.

"I'm horny—deal with it—we guys just got to fuck you girls as often as possible—nothing personal—just so horny."

She reaches out to stroke his cheek.

"I think I'm falling in love—just can't stop myself."

Lance makes a lewd gesture with his finger.

"Better be with my dick—not looking for a relationship now—we're just friends—nothing more. It's not serious."

Susan sighs again as Lance positions himself.

"I love you—I do."

Seconds later Lance plunges into Susan with reckless abandon. He rams her repeatedly. As his thrusts intensify she begins to moan. He laughs loudly as he blows his load.

Page **551**

<u>Tolling Bell Inn</u>

Robert slowly closes the door behind him and turns to face Chandra nervously. She seems visibly upset. He sighs.

"Look—Madison is a jerk—I sort of assumed he would pull some sort of stunt like this—but not actually—oh fuck."

Chandra seems worried.

"What are we going to do? Both of us with no job back in Philadelphia. It's not how I expected things to be."

Robert sighs loudly.

"And you think I did—man, who knew that Lindsay would go this far—sure she's cold but to do this—so twisted."

Chandra looks at the balcony.

"We've got to figure something out—I don't relish the idea of being homeless on the streets of Philly with a baby on the way—especially with winter just months ahead—not good."

"What about your mother?"

"No way—listening to my mother telling me over and over 'I told you so' isn't my idea of enjoyable family bonding."

"I'll think of something—I will."

Chandra rolls her eyes. Robert notices.

<u>Blankenship Apartment</u>

Eva is sitting on the sofa slowly stroking Clay's hair as he lies on the sofa with his head on her lap. He seems upset.

"Gina Bentley must have hid it well."

Eva sighs loudly.

"Some people never show it—clever all the way."

She strokes his hair again.

"One day they snap and explode—something must have triggered—caused her to target and execute her plan."

"Well, we'll probably never know now."

Clay looks up at Eva.

"Her family has hired a powerful lawyer."

Page **552**

"Typical—rich people always do that—they pay their way out of trouble—there's something wrong with the law."

Clay nods knowingly.

"Gina Bentley is **Kristin Rossum** and **Michelle Carter** rolled into one—except she's ten times more dangerous than those two psychos ever were—starting with being filthy rich."

"I've been hearing rumors—bad stuff."

"What sort of rumors?"

Eva sighs again.

"Apparently she tried to kill Brad McKinley also."

Clay sits up.

"Is that so? I knew those two had a history based on their verbal sparring at the jail—but did she try to kill him too?"

Eva seems upset.

"Word is he took her virginity and then played her for a fool—of which led to her trying to run him off the road."

Clay shakes his head.

"Which is exactly how Tiffany Johnson supposedly died?"

They look at each other.

"Think that'll come out before the trial?"

Clay wipes sweat from his brow.

"It's probably already circulating around Marble Hills."

He suddenly seems upset and sighs.

"Unless Daryl Anderson hushes people from talking about what they know—he's a sneaky one—got lots of secrets."

He sighs loudly and grimaces.

"He's actually been acting rather odd lately where she's concerned—seems to be protecting her—really weird."

Eva slides her arms around Clay.

"Why—why would he protect her?"

Clay shrugs again.

"I have no idea—it's not like she's related to him—so I gather there must be more there than I know about."

Eva leans back on the sofa.

"Is it possible that Gina Bentley's father has serious dirt on Daryl from the past so he's been doing his bidding?"

Clay shakes his head again.

"I don't know—but I wouldn't put anything past Daryl Anderson. He's not exactly what I would call honest."

"How so—did he do something?"

Clay shakes his head.

"He apparently has quite a rep for sleeping around despite the fact he's a married man and should clearly know better."

"Does his wife know?"

"I assume."

Clay glances at Eva.

"Given these turns of events with Anderson I've been thinking more and more of focusing on a writing career—this law enforcement thing was only supposed to be for a few years anyway. Six months here already and two years back in Boston has pretty much soured me in doing this much longer—too much unnecessary soapy melodrama crap happening all the time."

Eva kisses Clay on the neck.

"I'll support you whatever you decide."

Clay smirks and gestures.

"Good—because when I'm sitting around our apartment week after week with no job I'll remember today clearly."

Eva kisses Clay's neck again.

"I have no problem supporting you."

Clay laughs.

"Uh-huh—bet you'll rethink that idea when I'm sitting around in my underwear eating ice cream bars all day."

Eva grins slyly.

"Boxer briefs?"

Clay pulls Eva toward him.

"Uh-huh."

Eva reaches out to stroke Clay's cheek.

"Well, you look hot in boxer briefs—so I wouldn't mind watching you walk around all day in tight underwear."

Clay pretends to be appalled.

"Guys are more than just abs and underwear."

Eva makes a lewd gesture with her finger and grins.

Page 554

<u>Bentley Enterprises</u>

Pierce looks at John Bentley as he gives him a thick folder. John sighs loudly as he flips through it seemingly upset.

"I'm not going to lie to you—this isn't going to be easy by any means—I think we've got a huge uphill battle."

John clenches his fists.

"I want my daughter cleared—no matter what—how much money is it going to take to make this problem go away?"

Pierce rolls his eyes.

"It's not about how much money you have—it's about if your daughter can make a viable witness—credible."

John seems confused.

"What are you talking about Colby?"

Pierce sighs.

"I think your daughter has bigger problems than being on trial for seven murders—though I think she's innocent."

"Spit it out Colby—I don't play games."

Pierce shrugs.

"I think Gina has been experiencing extreme mental instability—and I think it—it could lead to major problems."

"Mental instability—why—like what—how?"

"Earlier I witnessed certain things—let's just say I think your daughter believes she's been communicating with Tiffany Johnson—so much so that I have doubts about her sanity."

"Tiffany Johnson? She's dead."

Pierce nods.

"Exactly—yet your daughter seems to think she's having encounters with this Johnson girl—weird—and very odd."

John looks at the folder in his hands.

<u>Keller Apartment</u>

Sabrina passionately kisses Juan one last time as he looks again at his Rolex watch nervously. He grins broadly.

Page **555**

"I'll be by tomorrow."
Sabrina nods.
"Uh-huh—about ten—maybe nine?"
Juan smirks.
"Don't worry—I'll silence my ex. I think it's time she knows the limit has been crossed with us—time to get real."
Sabrina giggles.
"Love when you talk tough—especially in bed."
Juan grins broadly.

<u>Marshall Driveway</u>

Maxwell looks at Abby Marshall curiously as she talks about her friendship with Gina. She sighs several times.
"I've known her all my life and she's never exactly been what you'd call sweet—but she—she isn't a killer or a nut."
Maxwell rolls his eyes.
"You don't think she killed anyone?"
Abby seems uneasy and sighs.
"I just can't believe she did what everyone says. I've known her all my life—she just couldn't kill anybody like everyone is saying—there has to be another answer. There has to be."
Maxwell's cell phone begins to ring. They look at each other briefly. He ignores the ringing. Abby seems bothered.
"Aren't you going to answer it—I mean—like it could be important—like someone trying to call you—with info?"
Maxwell shrugs.
"It can wait—no big deal."
He looks around.
"If Gina didn't do it—got any ideas who could?"
Abby shakes her head.
"No. No one I can think of at the moment."
"Well, if you remember anything else that could help with this case let me know—right now I'm drawing a blank."
Abby nods again.

Page 556

Parking Lot

Matt Brewster is walking across the lot when he notices Tyler Van Pelt heading toward the elevator a few feet away and begins running toward him in a frenzied rush. Tyler holds the elevator open briefly as Matt catches up with him. Matt sighs.

"Thanks."

Matt catches his breath. Matt looks at Tyler briefly and recognizes him. He grins broadly and extends his hand.

"You're Ross's ex aren't you?"

Tyler turns away.

"Look, sorry about what happened to Ross—he was a good guy—he'll be missed by everyone who knew."

"Ross Harrison meant nothing to me—not after what he did behind my back—with you—loser whore you are."

Matt seems stung by Tyler's words.

"It was nothing personal—he and I—well—we were both single and it happened—OK—no big deal—just experiences."

"You keep telling yourself that if you believe it."

The elevator opens and Tyler bolts out in a rush past Jason Anderson before Matt can reply. He seems upset and shrugs.

Tolling Bell Inn

Gary Glick watches as the elevator closes and heads back into the hotel room whistling a tune. He laughs loudly.

"He bought it—that dumb fucker bought it. He has no clue he's being played royally by yours truly—serves him right."

Gary grins broadly as he looks at Patrick Glick. He sighs.

"This is *so* wrong—what if he finds out?"

"I swear if you do anything to mess this deal up I'll fucking break your neck Patrick—money is thicker than blood."

Patrick nods.

"Yeah—yeah—I know the deal—you'll break my neck and feed me to the sharks—heard it all before—quite old now."

Gary grabs Patrick by the arm.

"Except you won't be dead when I throw you into the ocean—but—oh yeah—you'll be bleeding—like a lot."

He clenches his fist.

"Don't dare fuck with me Patrick—you wouldn't like the end results after the fact—things will get messy if you push me on this—I'm through playing games—I want my money."

Patrick pulls away.

<u>Blankenship Apartment</u>

Eva looks up at Clay as he enters the bedroom. She smiles approvingly as she notices his boxer briefs. She licks her lips.

"Nice fit—tight and bulging. I like seeing the merchandize up close from my soon-to-be husband—gives me ideas."

He grins nervously as he slides into the bed next to her.

"Think I can get some sleep without you trying—trying to grope me like I was some kind of hot male print model?"

Eva nods and winks at Clay.

"I think I can control myself—maybe—possibly—but it's so much more fun to be bad. It's your fault if you must know."

Clay grins broadly.

"Oh—is that so—well, I'm thinking of ditching this look for old-fashioned baggy boxers again—much easier to wear when you think I'm not just a toy to be played with and groped."

Eva seems horrified. She grabs Clay.

"No way—you'll do no such thing—absolutely not will you wear those grandpa boxers—that just won't do—no way."

Clay smirks and waves his hand in the air as he sees the shocked look on her face. He begins laughing loudly.

"It's not like you have a say—it's up to me. I can wear anything I like—and if I say boxers—then it's boxers."

Before he can reply Eva pushes Clay down on the bed and begins kissing his neck over and over. He begins laughing as she stops and looks at him. She kisses his cheek again. He smirks.

"I won't change my mind."

She continues kissing him as he laughs.

Page **558**

"OK. OK. I'll stick with boxer briefs. You win."

She kisses Clay once more.

"I'm really partial to you in your birthday suit if truth be known. Girlfriends have rights—boyfriends must comply."

She begins tugging at his underwear.

<u>Keller Apartment</u>

Sabrina smiles as she leans against the wall. She slides her hand between her legs and moans loudly thinking about her recent encounter with Juan. She licks her lips tenderly.

"Where were you all my life?"

She hears the front door opening and slowly turns around to see her boyfriend Justin Wellington closing the door behind him. He faces Sabrina. He has a huge grin on his face as he sees her standing there waiting for him. He drops his duffel bag and opens his arms as if to welcome her. Justin seems somewhat confused as Sabrina continues to stand there motionless.

TO BE CONTINUED

A Look at the 22nd Episode

Clay and Eva plan their future amid the chaos of the events playing out in Marble Hills—Gary and Patrick continue to disagree on their plan—Denise meets up with Robert while waiting for Daryl—Faye and Juan realize their passion for each other isn't dead after all—Hart sets a goal to bed as many girls as possible before the summer ends—a chance meeting between Denise and Robert leads to an intimate encounter—Daryl and Caroline use unpleasant events as an excuse to hook-up yet again as their behavior is witnessed by another—a blackmailer sets a date to give Denise bad news—Hart deceives Genie once more—Matt and Damon rekindle their passion for each other—several funerals are held in Marble Hills as Brad is released from prison under suspicious circumstances—Tiffany viciously attacks Gina in her cell—Chandra and Robert face reality about their uncertain futures—as Brad has an unexpected surprise inside his car.

Episode 22
Separate Games

<u>Blankenship Apartment</u>

Eva Harper smiles and kisses Clay Blankenship again as she slowly runs her fingers through his hair several times.

"I think you need to give Daryl Anderson notice that you're through—say about four weeks—that should be."

Clay seems confused.

"I'm—I'm not sure about quitting yet?"

Eva kisses Clay's cheek.

"I'm sure—tell him first thing in the morning."

Clay grins.

"Just like that—quit?"

Eva nods.

"Uh-huh—a month is long enough to find a permanent replacement—and then you'll—you'll be free to write."

Clay laughs.

"Yeah—but I'll be unemployed—a loser—no way."

Eva kisses Clay again on the cheek. He sighs.

"I'm not that kind of person."

He turns to face Eva. He sighs loudly.

Page **561**

"I don't want to live off you—I'm a guy—I'm not supposed to let a woman take care of me—people will talk trash."

Eva seems upset and sighs loudly.

"So what if people talk—you didn't ask. I'm suggesting it. I don't mind. In the end everything will work out."

Clay smirks.

"No way—I won't be kept—terrible for a guy."

Eva leans toward Clay and whispers.

"Enough with your old-fashioned way of thinking—I've made up my mind and that's final. I'm going to support you while you pursue a writing career—end of story—done."

Clay rolls his eyes.

"No. Seriously, I can't. I'll—it's wrong."

Eva strokes his cheek with her finger several times.

"I believe in you Clay—it won't be long at all—and once you're a bestselling novelist you'll—you'll thank me later."

Clay shrugs.

"I don't think I'll be the next **Robin Cook**."

Eva nods again.

"It could happen."

Clay reaches out to touch Eva's hand.

"Are you sure about this—I mean—I could be unemployed for a year—maybe two—maybe four years—a nothing."

Eva climbs on top of Clay.

"I'm rich—don't worry about it—daddy left my mother and me millions to spend—it's decided—you're quitting."

Clay sighs loudly.

"I can't—I won't—not who I am. Not the type."

Eva kisses Clay passionately.

"That's why I love you—you're so sweet—that's what I like about you—you don't care about money—you're just you."

Clay gestures with his hand.

"Who would I be if I wasn't me?"

Eva runs her fingers through Clay's hair once more.

"I know you'll be a wonderful writer. Probably end up getting a Pulitzer or something. I don't have any worries."

Page 562

Eva reaches out to hug Clay.

"I believe in you."

Clay seems confused and sighs loudly.

Tolling Bell Inn

Patrick Glick rubs his jaw and turns to look at his brother. He watches as Gary Glick looks at his fist and laughs.

"I meant what I said—fuck this up and I'll kill you."

Patrick sighs.

"When this is over—you and me are through."

Gary laughs loudly.

"Tell it to someone who cares."

He heads to the door.

Nickerson's Bar

Denise Madison glances around the bar and sighs. Her fingers tap nervously on the table. She seems upset.

"Where are you Daryl?"

She looks at her cell phone again. As she turns around she notices Robert Bennington walking into the bar. She grins broadly and signals him over to her table a few feet away.

"Funny seeing you here—thought you and your girlfriend would be hitting the road already—oops, future wife."

He rolls his eyes.

"Some things came up—and I'm not—problems."

Denise gestures with her hand.

"Let me guess—my dear, sweet father-in-law pulled the usual gameplay as only he can—made trouble did he?"

"Someone really needs to take that bastard out."

Denise laughs.

"That bad huh—what exactly did he do?"

Robert sits down next to Denise.

"Bought the company I used to work for in Philly—made them terminate my employment—frigging asshole."

Denise sighs loudly.

"Ouch—that's right up there—definitely Howard."

Robert smiles broadly.

"Tell me about it—Philly is a big place but oh so small when it comes to knowing people who can't be bought."

He sighs again.

"Or threatened?"

Denise slides her fingers over Robert's hand.

"What are you going to do?"

Robert shrugs.

"Not sure yet—but I'd just like to get my hands around my soon-to-be former father-in-law's throat and squeeze the life out of that wretched old bastard once and for all—snuff him."

Denise smirks knowingly.

"Wouldn't we all—but that creepy old man has more lives than a alley cat—he's been targeted plenty of times—but always manages to outplay whomever attempts to take him down."

Denise looks around.

"Though it was never proven it has been whispered endlessly over the years that he was behind the brutal rape and murder of a man named Jennings McNally from Atlanta."

Robert seems confused.

"Wasn't he the guy who attempted to take over Madison Industries in a hostile buyout about eleven years ago?"

Denise nods.

"Uh-huh—one in the same—poor guy—terrible ending for someone so incredibly brave—lessons had to be taught."

She looks around nervously.

"About a year and a half after McNally was forced to withdraw his claim—he was found murdered in an Atlanta condo. According to the police he ran afoul of some local mob kingpins types—supposedly concerning his refusal to pay a few of his male escorts for their services—and well—was brutally stabbed."

Robert gestures with his hand.

"McNally was gay?"

Denise shakes her head.

"Of course not—straight as an arrow—Howard Madison had him raped by several male prostitutes and then killed—to punish him for trying to buy his company—he got away with the whole thing too—no one bothered to make a connection."

"What did McNally's family have to say?"

Denise shrugs again.

"Nothing—at least nothing publicly—this whole thing mirrors the 1935 demise of **Thelma Todd**. When it initially happened everyone was screaming murder—then they suddenly shut up due to threats from the mob—including her own mother—I bet she was threatened and told she'd be next."

Robert wipes sweat from his brow.

"I think I remember hearing about that when I was in college. My history professor was a big fan of old movies."

Denise gives Robert a cautious look.

"From what I hear McNally's wife left the country—lives in Austria somewhere—married someone in royalty."

Robert suddenly seems nervous.

"Think Lindsay would go that far—I mean—have the father of her children killed—killed to exact her revenge?"

Denise reaches out to stroke Robert's lips with her finger. He grins broadly and passionately kisses her fingers.

"No—not even Lindsay is that cold a bitch—but then again I could be wrong about—she's always been her father's second favorite—especially after what happened to Marah."

Robert seems nervous.

"Well—I'm not going to worry about it."

He leans back in his chair.

"Got to find a job soon—Chandra is pregnant."

Denise grins slyly.

"So, I guess you and me—we can't happen anymore with the precious package coming your way—oh well, too bad."

Robert grins broadly again.

"I never said that fatherhood is a death sentence. My dick still works fine with or without a marriage certificate."

Denise and Robert share a glance.

Page **565**

<u>Stanley Pier</u>

Lance Weissmann leans against the hood of his car as Susan Bennington slowly walks over to where he's standing.
"I've got to go."
Lance nods
"I'll call you tomorrow."
Susan nods.
"Uh-huh—no problem Lance—enjoyed it."
He watches her go.
"Man, if anyone found out I was banging her—things could get really unpleasant for me—like really, really horrible."
He shakes his head and sighs loudly.

<u>Tolling Bell Inn</u>

Faye Washington opens the door and sees Juan Sabrillo standing in the doorway. She sighs. He looks upset.
"What the fuck's your problem *bitch*? I thought I told you we were through—done—finished—just a used whore."
Faye turns around and walks toward the kitchen as Juan slams the door behind him. He follows her in a rage.
"Stay the fuck out of my life—or I swear—I'll."
Faye turns around. She has a smile on her face.
"Or what—I'm calling the shots Juan—and if I want to make you play my game—I can—there's nothing you can do."
Juan lunges at Faye and grabs her violently. He begins shaking her aggressively. She seems to enjoy it and laughs.
"Are you sure about that bitch—are you sure there's nothing I can do about it—what if I killed you right now."
Faye pushes Juan away.
"Oh yeah—you like it really rough—well—there's nothing better than having you show me how strong you are."
She giggles.
"I'll take you anyway you like."

Page **566**

Without warning Faye aggressively grabs Juan and begins kissing him passionately. He resists for a few seconds and then they go at it with a vengeance—falling onto the sofa—knocking a large vase with red roses off the coffee table nearby.

<u>Nickerson's Bar</u>

Daryl Anderson looks around and seems confused as he walks toward the bar. He seems nervous for some reason.

<u>Keller Apartment</u>

Justin Wellington watches as Sabrina Keller continues to stand by the kitchen door with a cold stare. He sighs loudly.
"Hey, a hug would do nicely right about now."
Sabrina seems annoyed.
"We have to talk."
Justin walks over to Sabrina. He tries to put his arms around her but she pushes him away. He seems confused.
"I think it's best if we see other people."
Justin looks at Sabrina in shock.
"What—like seriously?"
She turns away.
"Who is he—who the fuck—tell me—damn him."
Sabrina walks to the door and opens it.
"Doesn't matter—I think you should leave now—I'm sorry but you and I are over. Have a nice life Justin—goodbye."
Justin reacts as his anger builds. He grabs Sabrina and shakes her. She angrily pushes him away. He seems confused.
"What the hell is wrong with you—last time we talked I thought you—thought you wanted to marry and have kids."
Sabrina shrugs.
"That was then—this is now."
"I really thought you were different."
Justin looks at Sabrina coldly and walks to the door. He turns to face her. He seems distraught. She looks away.

Page **567**

"Tell that piece of trash I'll teach him to steal another man's girl—oh yeah I'm so gonna bust his jaw—maybe broke his worthless neck while I'm at it—I guarantee it—he's dead."

Sabrina rolls her eyes and shrugs.

"Just go already—OK."

Justin shakes his head and leaves. As the door slams behind him Sabrina sighs loudly. She touches herself again.

<u>Blankenship Apartment</u>

Clay props himself up on a pillow and looks at Eva curiously. She strokes his hair again. He seems confused.

"Nothing happened between us that day."

Eva grins knowingly.

"I know—you were the perfect gentlemen—standing in front of me in nothing but your boxer briefs as I threw your jeans into the washer. You seemed so vulnerable at that moment."

Clay shakes his head.

"I was humiliated—here you were a total stranger and I was standing around in my underwear—it was pathetic."

Eva kisses Clay.

"Do you remember what happened next?"

"You asked me to have dinner with you later—promised me a home-cooked meal—quite the offer—couldn't refuse."

Eva reaches out to stroke Clay's ears.

"That was just a ruse to get you to come back."

Clay smirks and leans over to kiss Eva.

"Uh-huh—I figured as much—especially later that night when you refused to let me leave your apartment—telling me it wasn't safe on the streets of Boston and that I should spend the night—insisted your bed was big enough for both of us to sleep in together—and later when we were in bed—you asked."

"I asked you out."

Eva slides her fingers through Clay's hair again.

"I told you I liked you a lot—thought you were really cute."

Clay playfully pulls Eva toward him.

Page 568

"Of course I agreed—what else could I say—I was already in your bed—at your mercy on a cold winter's night."

Eva grins as she touches Clay's lips.

"But even then you remained a perfect gentleman—you never made a play—never insisted on us going further."

"Getting rejected isn't exactly a pleasant experience for a guy you know—no way. I didn't know what I should do."

Eva looks at Clay slyly.

"Just so you know I knew you would be respectful. I had a feeling about you—never a worry in my mind that night."

Clay waves his hand in the air.

"I'm glad you took a chance that day."

Eva hugs Clay warmly.

Pirate's Cove

Hart Bennington smiles broadly as both Diana Bingham and her sister kiss him passionately. Marilyn Bingham gets into her car and waves. He watches as she drives away. He shrugs.

"That was some experience."

Diana grins as she guns the engine of her car.

"My sister and I like helping a guy out—especially if that guy is cute—and needs to rack up his numbers with girls."

"Tell that to all the girls back in Philly."

Diana blows him a kiss. He watches her drive away.

"Lance Weissmann was right—every girl in this town is a whore. I'm definitely going to fuck my way through this town by the end of summer—no doubt at all—yep, I'll be popular."

He grins broadly as he looks at the beach.

Tolling Bell Inn

Faye grins as she looks over to where Juan is lying. He smirks slyly as he notices her looking at his exposed penis.

"I like a woman who knows exactly how to handle a man like me—makes for some intense moments—dangerous."

Page **569**

He laughs loudly.

"You know I have a new friend, right?"

Faye shrugs.

"Don't care—I'll have you when I want you."

Juan laughs loudly.

"Quite sure of yourself aren't you?"

Faye pulls Juan toward her and kisses him.

"What do you think?"

He glances at his penis.

"Oh, I like this deal a lot—fucking two women and no responsibility on my part to be true to either—sweet."

He laughs again.

"No need to tell my current friend that I'm fucking my ex because I can do as I please. I'd say I had it made completely."

Faye glances at Juan's penis again.

"I wouldn't mind if you took me again?"

Juan pulls Faye under him and they go at it once more as their intense lovemaking echoes loudly through the room.

<u>Parking Lot</u>

Denise moans loudly as Robert penetrates her yet again in the backseat of her car. He laughs loudly in triumph.

"I told you my current situation wouldn't hamper me when it comes to—taking you to the edge—no way—I do."

Denise smirks.

"I'm so pleased you haven't changed one bit—nice guys are really boring—oh so boring and sadly predictable."

Robert laughs loudly.

"Predictable I'll never be."

He rams her again.

"Any idea how we're going to teach old man Madison a lesson—he's certainly due—would like to see him crushed."

Denise looks at Robert and smiles broadly.

"Oh, he's due all right—that I agree—the question is how to go about it exactly, you know—making him pay dearly."

Page 570

Robert watches as Denise gestures wildly with her hand.

"I may know someone who can help us."

Robert looks at Denise curiously.

Nickerson's Bar

Daryl is about to leave as he spots Caroline Bentley sitting alone at a table near the entrance. He walks over to her.

"How's Gina?"

Caroline shrugs.

"She didn't want to see me earlier."

Daryl sighs knowingly.

"She'll come round eventually."

Caroline rolls her eyes.

"It's up to her—I've tried everything."

Daryl looks around.

"How about you and I go somewhere to talk?"

Caroline nods.

"OK."

They leave. As they walk down the sidewalk Simon Spencer notices them leaving. He shakes his head.

"Yuk, Jason was right. His dad is a total toad—he and Gina's mom are definitely doing it—old people—like gross."

He watches as they head toward Daryl's car.

Parking Lot

"I think I've got enough—but the brother-in-law certainly is the icing on the cake—blackmail was never more fun."

Marc Ryerson laughs.

"There is no shaming those two."

He watches Denise talking with Robert and shrugs.

"Uh-huh—I think it's time I pay Denise Madison a visit and explain a few things to her—concerning some photos I think she'll wish didn't exist—but oh well, you play, you pay—so risky."

He glances at a few photos on his cell phone.

<u>Mall</u>

Hart grins as he notices Genie Van Pelt sitting at the far end of one of the cafe booths. He sighs and walks over.

"Hey, funny finding you here?"

Genie looks up at Hart and turns away.

"Go away—like now—be gone from my sight."

Hart makes a lewd gesture with his hand.

"Is that any way to talk to the guy whom you shared a moment with earlier—you'd think at least you'd be nice—and be really thankful for an adventure with someone like me?"

Genie rolls her eyes.

"You lied to me—you used me like a whore."

Hart laughs.

"How did I use you Genie?"

Genie glares at Hart.

"You said you were going to wear a condom."

Hart laughs.

"Guys lie—deal already—get over it."

He sits down next to her and gently reaches out to stroke her arm. She turns away. He pushes up on her even more.

"You can't stay mad—not possible."

Genie pulls away.

"Get away from me."

Hart smirks again.

"How about you and I go somewhere—for a moment—you know—to get to know each other better—like before."

Genie sighs loudly.

"I'm not in the mood—go away."

Hart laughs again and then grabs her hand.

"We'll just talk OK—promise—I'll be good."

Genie turns around to face Hart. She fakes a smile.

"I'm going to hold you to it—I mean it."

Hart nods as he glances at her with a mixture of scorn and desire. As they walk away he turns to look around briefly.

Page **572**

<u>Pike's Bar</u>

Matt Brewster feels a hand on his shoulder and turns around to see Damon Mayo looking at him with a grin.

"Oh man—it's been a while—thought you'd dropped off the face of the earth—starting thinking strange things."

"I've been busy with a few issues."

Damon laughs.

"What's his name—or is your latest just a distant memory already—some nameless stud you bedded and discarded."

Matt seems upset.

"I'm not that bad—am I?"

"Uh-huh—we hooked-up and then you pretty much left me for dead right afterwards—crushed my ego so bad."

"Thought you had a girlfriend?"

Damon rolls his eyes.

"Sometimes a guy needs variety—especially when that variety happens to be a muscular ex-jock with a big dick."

Matt makes a lewd gesture with his tongue.

"I assume you remember the way to my place."

"Uh-huh—I do indeed."

Matt looks at his drink again.

"Let's go already."

Damon follows Matt out of the bar.

<u>Tolling Bell Inn</u>

Juan zips up his Levi's and turns to face Faye. She walks over to him and slides her arms around his waist. He laughs.

"Thanks for a nice romp—seriously needed it."

Faye gestures with her hand.

"I like you a lot—so shoot me already."

Juan laughs again as he pulls away from Faye.

"Just so you know I'm still going to fuck Sabrina—she and I—well—we—it works nicely between us—like magic."

Page **573**

Faye seems upset.
"But I thought?"
Juan laughs loudly.
"I guess you thought wrong."
He walks to the door.
"I'll see you tomorrow. Sabrina and I have a date."
Faye watches Juan leaves.
"We'll see about that Juan. We shall see just how that bitch feels about sharing you with me. I'll break her."
She sighs loudly.

Parking Lot

Hart plows into Genie again and laughs. She seems angry as she tries to push him off her. He forces himself into her again as her efforts prove futile. Genie seems upset and sighs.
"You promised all we'd do was talk?"
Hart smirks.
"I lied—seriously how dumb are you Genie?"
He plows her again.

Brewster Condo

Matt and Damon lie in bed after a bout of lovemaking. Matt sighs. Damon smiles broadly and winks at Matt.
"Yeah, my girlfriend thinks I'm just doing her—but hey, I like to play both sides. It's who I am—I play around a lot."
Matt rolls his eyes mockingly.
"Come out already—free yourself for good."
Damon smirks.
"I don't see the benefit yet in coming out."
Damon gives Matt a shove.
"Probably thinks I'm a creep huh—whatever."
Matt shrugs.
"I don't judge—I have—never do."
Matt lies back on the bed and glances at Damon.

"I've got enough flaws of my own."

Damon laughs.

"I know—a famous athlete like yourself—you must have quite a lengthy list when it comes to friends with benefits."

Matt nods.

"I do OK—but I'm not getting any younger so pretty much my time is limited—maybe it's time I settle down?"

Damon laughs.

"Yeah, right—you settle down with one guy?"

Matt seems upset at the comment.

<u>Port Clyde</u>

Daryl and Caroline leave the hotel and head to their cars a few feet away. Daryl suddenly grabs Caroline by the arm.

"Quite a moment earlier wasn't it—intense."

"Think anyone saw us leave Marble Hills together?"

Daryl smiles slyly.

"No one noticed anything."

They look at each other.

"Is there anything you can do about Gina?"

Daryl shakes his head.

"It's out of my hands—this FBI dude named Maxwell Pendergraft is handling the case—he just showed up."

"Gina is no killer—there has to be another explanation for the Johnson girl's accident and the others—there must be."

Daryl looks at Caroline curiously.

"Maybe I can pin it on the McKinley kid—certainly no one would be surprised given his behavior with Carrie Spaulding's brutal rape and death in Bradford Woods—perfect suspect."

Caroline leans toward Daryl.

"Do whatever you must Daryl—just clear Gina of these outrageous charges—get her back to us OK? Please help."

Daryl shrugs.

"I'll do my best. But it'll take time."

Caroline nods in agreement.

Page **575**

<u>Parking Lot</u>

Denise looks at Robert as he grasps the doorknob seconds later and motions to him to zip up his fly. He grins.

"Wouldn't want Chandra to know I strayed again. She would blow a gasket if she knew I was stepping out on her."

Denise smirks.

"Uh-huh—I'll just bet—I know the type—Chandra can't understand that you need a few extras—have a right to see what else is out there. I've known plenty like her in my lifetime."

Robert laughs.

"No—I bet she wouldn't—but I *will* play. I don't take orders that well—need to sip extra samples every now and then."

Denise smiles broadly.

"I know the feeling quite well."

Robert steps out of the car.

"I might be forced to stay in Marble Hills until things."

Denise nods and smirks slyly.

"Well, it would give us an opportunity to get to know each other really well—considering the situation the way it is?"

"I agree totally."

He closes the door and leans against the window.

"What's the deal with you and Kyle anyway?"

Denise rolls her eyes.

"He does his thing and I do mine—sort of like the marriage of **Prince Charles** and **Princess Diana** back in the day."

"Enough said on that soap opera."

Denise sighs as Robert quickly heads toward his car.

Two Days Later

<u>Standish Road</u>

Maxwell Pendergraft is driving toward Marble Hills. He nervously checks his watch several times as if in a hurry.

Page **576**

<u>Crestview Memorial Park Cemetery</u>

Donna Markway is standing near Jason Anderson as she glances at the others nearby. Simon appears to be looking around at the mourners as Genie looks like she's about to cry. Lance seems to be wishing he was anywhere else as Jeremy Weissmann and Shirley Moses stare blankly at the four caskets positioned near each other as pallbearers begin to lift them separately to carry toward the open graves situated in various parts of the large cemetery. Donna continues to watch as the casket containing Corinne Massey's body is lifted first to begin its final journey. As the casket of Daphne Garfield is lifted Donna turns to look at Diana and Marilyn standing near each other but with no emotion as their friend's casket passes by. Ashton Markway slowly looks over at where his sister is standing just as Ross Harrison's casket is carried past them and nods as Tyler Van Pelt turns to look at him and sighs. Donna shakes her head as she notices Corey Bentley smirking, oblivious to everyone's pained reactions.

"He's such a disgusting toad—cold as ice."

Jason turns to look at her. Donna sighs.

"Well, he is—selfish too."

She watches as Corey's vision seems to be focused on Drew Brockmeyer standing nearby. Donna shrugs.

"I wonder what that's about."

Jason nods and sees Abby Marshall and Kelly Nelson also shaking their heads at the behavior Corey is displaying.

<u>Police Station</u>

Pierce Colby walks toward the cell where Brad McKinley is sitting on a bunk bed. Brad gives Pierce a suspicious look.

"Looks like you got sprung young man."

Brad sighs.

"What?"

Pierce stares at Brad.

Page **577**

"Are you deaf? I said you got sprung."
Brad laughs.
"Since when are you my lawyer—I thought you were Gina's guy? Like what's the catch bozo? I'm not into dudes."
Pierce rolls his eyes seemingly annoyed.
"That makes two of us."
Gina Bentley is sleeping in her cell and wakes up. She looks at the scene unfolding. She seems visibly upset.
"I was hired to represent you—deal with it already."
Brad seems confused.
"My dad is a pauper—how could he afford?"
Pierce laughs knowingly.
"Who said it was your dad—someone called and offered to hire me and pay your bail so you could be sprung today."
"Someone paid the million?"
Pierce seems annoyed.
"Don't look a gift horse in the mouth jerk."
At that moment Brad sees Daryl coming toward him with a set of keys. Daryl doesn't look happy. He sighs loudly.
"Yeah, yeah—you got lucky—but your luck won't last when you go to trial McKinley—a life sentence awaits you."
Brad grins broadly as the cell door is opened. He turns to look at Daryl with contempt. He waves his hand in the air.
"Fuck off loser."
He walks past Daryl and glances at Gina.
"Isn't life wonderful?"
Gina watches in complete shock as Brad walks down the hallway. She turns to face Pierce. Her anger is noticeable.
"What about me?"
Pierce seems upset and shrugs.
"I'm working on it."
Gina rolls her eyes in anger.
"I'll just bet you are."
Daryl looks at Gina curiously and walks away.
"What happens now?"
Pierce faces Gina.

Page **578**

"I'm not the one that got you into this mess—you have yourself to thank for what is happening—so deal."

"I thought you said you believed I was innocent?"

Pierce shrugs.

"I do—but nevertheless you're here."

Gina seems about to cry.

"I hate it."

She watches Pierce walk down the hallway. Tears flood her eyes as she becomes aware of the fate awaiting her.

"What a shame—you're all alone—then again maybe everything isn't what it seems—oh—not at all—oh no."

Gina turns around to see Tiffany Johnson standing at the other end of her tiny cell. Gina backs away from Tiffany.

"Oh yeah—we're going to have so much fun."

Suddenly Tiffany lunges at Gina—grabs her by the hair and carelessly shoves her against the bars of the cell with intense force. Her laughter can be heard echoing throughout the other cells as Gina picks herself up. Tiffany grabs her again and shakes her hard as Gina seems to be in a daze. Tiffany laughs.

"Do you still think I'm a figment of your imagination?"

Tiffany laughs loudly.

"Still think I don't exist—oops—I do."

She forcibly shoves Gina again.

"If you think things couldn't get any worse—well."

Tiffany laughs loudly once more.

"Please—please leave me alone Tiffany—I'm sorry for how I treated you—please forgive me—please—just go away."

Tiffany's face contorts into a nasty grimace.

"It's a little too late for mercy, *bitch*. You and I are only getting started. Oh yeah—I'm so enjoying messing with you."

Tiffany circles Gina again.

<u>Tolling Bell Inn</u>

Chandra Stevenson looks at herself in the mirror. Her baby bump is beginning to show. She turns to face Robert.

Page **579**

"You've got to talk to Lindsay—get her to call off the attack dogs—this has gone on long enough—too long."

"You don't know her like I do—she's not going to budge one bit—and her evil excuse of a father certainly won't back down—he enjoys making people miserable—loves it actually."

"Maybe I should talk—confront the old man?"

"No way—you stay away from the house—I swear there is something about that mansion—it makes people evil."

"*Please*—like I believe in crap like that—what do you think will happen to me? Do you actually buy into all that stupid garbage about ghosts and goblins in scenic New England?"

"Hey, that stuff is true—it's not a joke."

"Yeah—and I'm **Ingrid Bergman**—walking around in old period costumes and looking damn fine on the movie screen."

Robert grabs Chandra by the arm. He sighs.

"Promise me you won't go and talk to Howard Madison?"

"I can't—someone has to act like an adult here."

Robert watches as Chandra heads to the door. Seconds later the door closes behind her. He sits down on the bed.

<u>Crestview Memorial Park Cemetery</u>

As the casket of Natalie Standish is lifted and carried toward an open grave a few yards away Donna glances at the private funeral procession for Lana Jefferson being held at the far end of the tree-covered cemetery. Donna turns back to look at Corey and angrily glares at him as he continues to smirk.

<u>Police Station</u>

Tiffany slams Gina's head against the bars of her cell and laughs as she watches her former rival fall against the wall. She grabs Gina again and forces her to stand. Tiffany laughs.

"Yeah, that's right bitch—no one can help you now."

Tiffany throws Gina toward the floor.

"Please—no more—please stop."

Page **580**

Tiffany laughs loudly.

"Aw—poor baby—can't take it but you can certainly dish it—yeah—but now the tables are turned and I'm in charge."

Gina pulls herself up by holding onto the cell bars.

"I'm sorry—how many times do I have—I didn't kill you."

Tiffany seems enraged even more.

"Just admit you killed me, *bitch*. Admit it."

Gina leans against the cell bars and sighs loudly.

"I didn't kill you—I didn't do it—it wasn't me—why won't you believe me—someone else did it—someone else."

Tiffany glances at the other cell.

"You forgot—either that or you think I don't know the truth—I was there or have you forgotten—you killed me."

Gina seems confused.

"What are you talking about?"

Tiffany grabs Gina again.

"I'm dead because of you—and I want revenge."

She shoves Gina to the floor again in a rage. At that moment Caroline is heard walking down the hallway.

<u>Parking Lot</u>

Pierce watches as Brad struts toward a car parked nearby. He sighs loudly as he watches Brad's obnoxious behavior.

"Maybe you shouldn't act like such a prick?"

Brad turns to face Pierce with contempt and smirks.

"I'm not going back to jail—I'm not—not ever."

"If I were you I wouldn't think the worst is over—the autopsy didn't make you look innocent by any means."

Brad laughs.

"Carrie Spaulding was a bitch—she deserved to die—and I won't pretend I regret—she got what was coming to her."

Pierce grabs Brad by the arm.

"This isn't a joke—things will only get worse once the trial gets underway—people will not see things—wake up."

Brad laughs loudly.

Page 581

"That whore had it coming—she tried to ruin me."

Pierce looks around nervously.

"Maybe you should think about who paid your bail—and hired me—someone obviously wanted you out of jail today."

"Old man Madison probably paid—who else would spring that kind of money—he knows I'm like him—a winner."

Pierce shakes his head.

"I don't think it was Howard Madison who sprung you."

Brad seems confused.

"Well, if he didn't—who did?"

Pierce shakes his head and looks around at the deserted parking lot. He seems nervous as he faces Brad.

"Good question—maybe you should think about it."

The smile fades from Brad's lips.

<u>Glass Owl</u>

Chandra rings the doorbell a second time. She sighs and rings it again and again. There is no answer. She shrugs.

"Tomorrow is another day—I'll be back."

She looks at her watch.

"That bastard can't hide from me forever. I won't let him best me. He's gonna face me one way or the other way."

She turns to look at her car parked nearby.

"He has no idea who he's dealing with yet—but when he finds out exactly what I bring to the table—he'll wish he had."

She checks her watch again and shrugs.

"I've got a secret he won't like."

She begins laughing as she slowly walks to her car.

<u>Police Station</u>

Maxwell slowly reaches for the doorknob and pushes it forward. He sighs as it doesn't budge. He pushes it again.

"Damn—what the fuck?"

He turns around and looks at his watch.

Page 582

"Of course—that's it—the funerals are today—everyone in town is probably there—life in a small town—yeah."

He turns away minutes later.

<u>Blankenship Apartment</u>

Clay awakens and realizes he's alone in the bed. He pulls on a robe and wraps it tightly around his body and heads to the door. He smiles as he sees Eva in the kitchen preparing coffee in two mugs. She grins as she sees him walking toward her.

"Good morning sweetie."

He wraps his arms around her.

"Slept well?"

Clay nods and takes the mug of coffee from Eva.

"I guess—though this dark cloud is hanging over me like a harbinger of doom now that I told Daryl Anderson I'm leaving at the end of the month to become a full-time writer."

Eva waves her hand in the air.

"I know—I know—and he laid a guilt trip on you about the whole deal—but he needs to get real—*this* is his career—not yours—at least you gave him sufficient notice ahead of time."

Eva kisses Clay. He sighs.

"You and I still have to talk—lots of loose ends."

Eva suddenly pushes Clay against the doorway and smirks. He seems surprised. She kisses him several times.

"Not one more word—it's been decided."

"There's still the issue about money."

Eva puts her hand over Clay's mouth and smiles.

"It's done—I'm going ahead with my plan—I'm going to financially support you while you pursue your dream of being a novelist—and I won't allow—won't tolerate one more word."

Clay looks at Eva's determined look before she slowly removes her hand. He seems nervous. She gives him a sly grin.

"I want to discuss this further."

Eva gives Clay another fierce look.

"I meant what I said."

Page **583**

Eva pulls Clay toward her and hugs him tightly. He laughs.

"OK—OK—I can't fight back—you win."

He laughs again.

"I give up—you win I lose—I should've known you would outplay me with a sly move. I have no choice in the matter."

Eva smirks. Clay notices. He grins.

"But this isn't over yet—later we'll take this up when you're not quite so charged up. You and I will talk—bet on it."

Eva strokes Clay's face.

"Sweetie—it's over—you lost."

Clay grins broadly.

"Love you—but the game isn't over yet."

Eva notices Clay's stiff penis poking through his robe. He notices and grins slyly. He slowly looks down at his penis.

"I'm in the mood suddenly. All this talk of power is having an effect on me—on my dick—some things can't be helped."

Eva leads Clay toward the bedroom.

<u>Parking Lot</u>

Pierce seems worried as he looks at Brad who seems to be totally oblivious to reality as he rolls his eyes with disdain.

"Someone paid a lot of money for a reason."

Brad sticks his finger inside his mouth and gestures.

"Are you never happy—seriously, you're like a real killjoy right about now. Stop acting like a motherfucking pansy."

He laughs loudly.

"I'm on top of the world."

Pierce sighs loudly.

"I hope you like playing Russian roulette with your future."

Brad rolls his eyes. Pierce seems annoyed.

"Oh, forget it—I got paid already."

Brad smirks as he watches Pierce walk to his car. As Pierce drives away without any further acknowledgement Brad rolls his eyes and shrugs. He seems upset at the slight and grimaces.

"What an loser—frigging career paper pusher."

Page 584

He turns around and unlocks the door to his car—gets into the driver's seat—and shuts the door. He begins laughing.

"I love my life."

He turns to look at the empty parking lot up ahead.

"Poor Gina—bitch is going away for a long time."

He begins laughing again.

"Oh well—sad to be her—great to be me."

He wipes sweat from his brow.

"Damn Carrie Spaulding—that miserable whore got what she deserved. To think she tried to best me—damn her."

He laughs loudly.

"I wonder when that damn whore is going to be put in the ground. Oh yeah—so enjoyed making that possible."

He hears a noise in the backseat of his car and turns around in a panic. He stares in shock at the intruder blankly.

"*You*—what the fuck do you want?"

He seems shocked at the unexpected visitor.

TO BE CONTINUED

A Look at the 23rd Episode

Maxwell intrudes on Eva and Clay's personal time—Brad encounters a nasty surprise in a parking lot—Corey and Elizabeth share an intimate moment immediately after several funerals conclude—Kyle boldly confronts his father about Patrick—friends gather at the beach to deal with the aftermath of saying goodbye at the cemetery—Denise and Glen continue to plot Caroline's upcoming downfall—Clay and Maxwell suspect Brad may have skipped town upon his release from jail—a perfect finale for Brad is orchestrated—Lance and Marilyn enjoy each other's company amid chaos in Marble Hills—Clay and Maxwell catch Daryl and Caroline together—Glen pays Kevin a visit—Caroline tries to mend fences with Gina—Lindsay has a confusing talk with Kyle about their father—Sidney gives Archie bad news about Brad's whereabouts after his mysterious release for jail—Tiffany pays Gina another "friendly" visit—Susan has a rude awakening about the pitfalls concerning careless behavior—as Archie pays Daryl a visit over the apparent disappearance of Brad McKinley.

Mystery Play

<u>Blankenship Apartment</u>

Eva Harper and Clay Blankenship look at each other. He grins slyly. He kisses Eva several times and then laughs.

"Uh-huh—I admit it—I was in the mood."

Eva smiles broadly.

"I'd say—you came alive."

Clay laughs again.

"Things happen—deal with it."

Eva smirks.

"Things surely did—didn't they? But if you think I'm done with you—think again—I have plans—really wicked plans."

"Do tell."

"I'd rather show you."

Less than a second later the doorbell rings. Eva turns to look at Clay curiously. He begins looking for his robe.

"Maxwell?"

Clay nods again.

"I bet he wants to talk shop."

Clay reaches out and grabs his robe.

"I'll go see what he wants?"

Eva reaches out and pushes Clay back on the pillow.

"You get dressed and I'll let Maxwell in. It's probably like you said—he's probably here to talk about the Bentley case."

Clay watches as Eva pulls on her robe and heads for the door. He sighs and quickly begins pulling on his Levi's as he hears the door opening. He quickly grabs his shirt and sneakers.

"Hello, Maxwell."

Eva watches as Maxwell Pendergraft acknowledges her and enters the apartment. He quickly walks over to the sofa.

"Go tell your sweetie to get dressed already."

Eva closes the door behind her.

"Already did."

Maxwell turns to face Eva.

"I'm sorry if I interrupted anything."

"You should be sorry—just because you can't score doesn't give you the right to mess up my gameplay."

Clay laughs and grabs Maxwell by the shoulders—playfully shadow boxing with him. Eva winks at Clay approvingly.

<u>Parking Lot</u>

Brad McKinley glances at Archie Spaulding sitting in the backseat of his car. He looks around in anger and points.

"Get out of my car."

Archie appears oddly calm as he leans forward.

"Thought you'd gotten away with raping and killing my precious daughter—well things are never what they seem."

Brad sighs loudly.

"Fuck off old man."

Archie smirks.

"Gladly—after I take care of one last loose end."

Brad rolls his eyes.

"You daughter's dead—get used to it."

Archie seems about to explode.

"She won't be the only one you frigging bastard."

Page 588

Without warning he grabs Brad by the neck and shoves a white cloth soaked with chloroform over his nose. Brad struggles against the attack but ultimately to no avail and quickly loses consciousness. Archie continues holding the cloth over Brad's mouth until his struggling body goes limp and slumps over. An evil triumphant smile immediately comes over Archie's face.

"Thought you'd bested me—well think again."

He jumps out of the car and opens the door were Brad's body is slumped over. Archie drags Brad out of the car and toward his own car a few feet away. He grins broadly.

"It's time to put my final plan in motion—oh yeah."

He seems pleased as he drags Brad's limp body.

<u>Crestview Memorial Park Cemetery</u>

Outside the cemetery gates by a nearby sidewalk a lone car is parked under several trees—it shakes several times.

"Shut up bitch—I'm tired of your whining."

Corey Bentley glares at Elizabeth Pendleton as he rams into her yet again. He laughs loudly amid her startled cries.

"Yeah—I planned it this way whore—you and I doing it right outside Crestview—like you actually have a choice in the matter. One wrong move on your part and I'll ruin you."

Corey penetrates Elizabeth again. She seems disgusted as he continues thrusting for several seconds. He laughs.

"Bet Lance would like to know I'm scoring with one of his whores—uh-huh—I think he needs to know your deal."

He laughs again. Elizabeth tries to push him off her.

"Enough already—please stop."

Corey shoves his fist against her cheek.

"I'll decide when I've had enough of you."

He forces himself inside her again.

"Lance is going to be *so* pissed when he finds out—finding out I fucked you right outside of Crestview like a back alley street walker from Boston will crush him—even he wouldn't dare."

He smirks broadly as her cries fade away.

Page 589

<u>Glass Owl</u>

Kyle Madison walks into the library and sees his father looking out the window at something. He sighs loudly.

"What are you looking at—or should I say whom?"

Howard Madison seems stunned by his son's presence and faces him abruptly. They look at each other silently.

"No one—I was just looking at my rose garden."

He seems annoyed and leans against a mahogany desk as he sees Kyle's expression. He clenches his fist angrily.

"What do you want?"

Kyle looks around and seems uncomfortable as he walks closer to his father. Howard notices his strange behavior.

"You and I have to talk."

Howard waves his hand.

"Not now—go away."

Kyle grimaces.

"I've put this off way too long."

Howard sits down.

"Is that so—like you think waiting would change anything and somehow give you the upper hand with me—fine—whatever you want—just spit it out and be gone from my sight boy."

Kyle wipes a bead of sweat from his brow.

"Patrick Glick."

Howard looks at Kyle seemingly confused.

"I don't know that name."

Kyle looks at his father closely.

"You heard me—so don't pretend."

"Like I said earlier—I'm busy and I want to be left alone."

Kyle looks at the door.

"I met him—and he looks like me—he's got some of the same mannerisms as—like as if that's a surprise to you."

Howard leans back in his chair.

"What a fool you are boy."

He grins broadly as he looks at Kyle's reaction.

"What the hell are you trying to say—because nothing makes a damn bit of sense so far—just tell—just tell me what this has to do with me—and then get the fuck out of this library so I can have some peace and quiet for a change—foolish boy."

Kyle seems about to explode as he circles his father.

"You bastard—Gary Glick said you knew—but I just didn't want to believe you could do something so evil and low."

Kyle begins laughing hysterically.

"My bad—look who I'm talking to—of course you would do something like this—bastard—this is *so* you—monster."

Howard jumps up.

"I have no idea what you're talking about?"

Kyle clenches his fists.

"The Glick kid—Patrick—he's my son—and you—*you* knew about it from the getgo all those years ago—knew the truth."

Howard seems in shock at the news.

Bradford Beach

Kelly Nelson, Abby Marshall, Tyler Van Pelt, Donna Markway, Jason Anderson, and Simon Spencer slowly walk toward the surf in a daze. They seem lost in thought.

"I still can't believe it—not real yet."

Donna turns to look at Jason.

"It's so unreal."

Jason nods.

"Gina Bentley wasn't exactly sane—but murder?"

Simon stops.

"I really don't see the reason they have her locked up—it's just a matter of time—before her dad has her sprung."

He sighs loudly.

"Rich people—damn them."

Tyler nods.

"I heard Brad McKinley got bail earlier."

They turn to look at him.

"Who would let that creep out of the slammer?"

Donna seems upset.

"He'll do it again—kill some other girl."

Jason nods.

"I hate lawyers—sleazy motherfuckers."

He looks at Donna.

"No offense about your dad."

Donna rolls her eyes.

"None taken—my dad isn't greedy—he represents only people he knows are innocent—otherwise my family would be living large in a gigantic mansion right next to Glass Owl."

"How would he know if they're innocent?"

Donna smirks.

"He gives them a damnation speech. Believe me, they always crack if they're guilty of anything—my dad can be—be really annoying when he wants to be—which is quite often."

Tyler rolls his eyes mockingly.

"Too bad he didn't give Brad one of those—I heard he denies knowing anything about what really happened to Carrie Spaulding at Miller's Pond even though we all know he did it."

"That's McKinley for you—nothing but a worthless piece of trash—he won't ever change—scumbag extraordinaire."

Jason seems nervous.

"Hey, do you think that loser will skip town?"

Simon clenches his fists.

"I bet he will—he knows if Carrie's dad has his way he'll fry for killing her—so I bet he's making plans right now to skip."

They look at each other.

"I'd like nothing better than to see him lose his life for what he did to Carrie—see him fry in the electric chair."

Simon notices the others looking at him.

"Well, he treated me like crap—I'm not the religious type in case none of you noticed—McKinley deserves death. I'd be more than willing to pull the switch if he got the chair."

Jason gestures with his hand.

"We know—we know—believe me we know."

Tyler looks at the ocean.

Page **592**

"I would've liked to have been a fly on the wall of the cell where he and Gina were kept—imagine what they know?"

Jason rolls his eyes knowingly.

"Yeah—comparing notes on murdering innocent people."

Abby seems upset at the comment.

"I still don't want to believe it—that she could've done such things—it's just not like her—despite her behavior."

Simon makes a gesture with his hand.

"She's a complete psycho—always was and always will be as far I'm concerned—has everyone forgotten what happened a while back—it wasn't that long ago—of what she did."

Abby sighs loudly.

"It was never proven—it was an accident."

"Tell that to William's parents?"

Kelly looks at Abby.

"Are you OK?"

Abby shakes her head.

"Yeah—it's just that all this seems to be happening rather conveniently—like it was all planned out or something?"

Simon laughs.

"Uh-huh—Gina has been busy alright."

Abby looks at the others oddly and shrugs.

"It seems as if someone wants us to believe Gina is a murderer but what if she isn't—what if someone else did it?"

Jason seems confused.

"If she didn't kill—then who did?"

A hush instantly comes over the group.

<u>Portland</u>

Denise Madison smiles at Glen Bradstreet as he pulls on his Levi's. He grins broadly as he notices her looking at him.

"Blackmail and sex—love it—no better deal."

Denise lies back in bed and sighs.

"When are you going to spring the deal on Caroline Bentley about the secret over her precious freak show son?"

Page **593**

Glen grins and faces Denise.

"I'll probably play it out tomorrow or the day after."

He laughs.

"I'll fuck her first—really work her over and then when she thinks everything between us is fine—I'll drop my bomb."

Denise giggles.

"She deserves to be destroyed after what she did."

She seductively strokes her breasts.

"God, I can't wait to topple that conniving bitch from the ridiculous pedestal she's climbed up upon—can't wait at all."

Glen pulls on his T-shirt.

"Trust me, when I slash the wind from her sails she'll be at my mercy—of which I plan to make it most beneficial to us."

Denise smirks.

"I could contact Carlos Espana. He's in Houston at the moment. But no worries—I could make him an offer he can't refuse—of course there's the issue of his wife to handle."

Denise sighs loudly.

"Damn bitch thinks Carlos is her property—well—if he comes back to Maine—all bets are off—I'll destroy her."

She laughs loudly.

"His dick—oh God—his dick—it's magic."

Glen angrily looks at Denise.

"Ugh—enough already with the dick talk."

Denise seems annoyed.

"Think Caroline will suspect anything?"

Glen seems annoyed.

"No way—she assumes she owns the world."

He grins slyly.

"As long as your lawyer's kid keeps his trap shut it should be smooth sailing—hope he zips it or I'll have to silence him."

"Kevin Myers is good with the plan—he won't say a word—he and I—we've become close lately as you know."

Glen rolls his eyes knowingly.

"I'll bet—by now his experience with women must be quite good given how much your tutoring has educated him."

Denise laughs again.

"He's getting better—quite good actually."

Glen slips on his sneakers.

"Uh-huh—you're a piece of work no doubt."

He heads to the door.

"But I like the way you think regardless—we're cut from the same cloth—nothing is ever enough for our ambitions."

He makes a lewd gesture with his finger.

"Caroline Bentley will serve us well once we broke her spirit and make her our pawn—there's no way out for her."

Glen and Denise share a sly smile.

"I've got a few errands to run—you can let yourself out whenever you like—might be a good idea to call the kid—you know—offer him more incentives not to stray—like *ever*."

Denise nods in agreement as she watches him leave. As the door slams shut she glances at the empty apartment.

"But Glen dear, Caroline isn't the only one who should watch her back. I've got plans of my own—and they don't include you—plans which will change things for several people."

She begins to laugh softly then louder.

<u>Spaulding Mansion</u>

Archie parks his car in front of the open garage and looks around briefly before he reaches for Brad's limp body.

"Oh yeah—you and I have unfinished business to attend to. But not for long—that I promise you—not long at all."

He grins broadly.

"Got to teach you a lesson for raping and killing my daughter—one that won't get me fifty years upstate."

He looks at Brad and sighs.

"You brought this upon yourself. Killing my daughter was a huge mistake. Now it's my time to call the shots."

He glances at the driveway again and sighs loudly.

"Such a perfect ending to this story—I win and you lose."

Archie begins dragging Brad's limp body.

Page **595**

Clay and Maxwell open the front door and are about to enter as they notice Daryl Anderson in a passionate embrace with Caroline Bentley. He seems very irritated at the intrusion as they both give him cautious looks which he ignores as they enter.

"It's not what it seems."

Clay turns away.

"I didn't see anything—not a damn thing."

Maxwell ignores Daryl and sits down on one of the chairs near Clay's desk. Seconds later they watch as Daryl and Caroline head to the door in a panic. Maxwell sighs loudly in dismay.

"I thought you said he was married?"

Clay nods knowingly.

"He is—but apparently marriage means different things to different people—he's perfectly two-faced—a cheater."

Maxwell looks at the front door again.

"She seems oddly familiar—have I met her before?"

Clay shrugs and looks at the front door.

"She's always in those society magazines—you know the ones where everyone thinks being photographed with the right people can erase their pathetic social climbing characters."

Maxwell makes a lewd gesture with his finger.

"That would explain the haughty **Gene Tierney** look. Oh man—someone should tell her the 1940s are long over."

"I guess—but who will accept the job?"

He leans back in his chair.

"What do you think is the deal on Brad McKinley being sprung earlier—exactly who is his mysterious benefactor?"

Maxwell gestures with his hand.

"No clue—but I bet that kid skips town today."

"Do you think we should eyeball him?"

Maxwell nods in agreement.

"Can't hurt—kid has nothing to lose at the moment."

They stand up and head to the door.

Archie grins gleefully as he securely wraps duct tape around Brad's ankles several times. Brad is strapped in a sitting position to a wooden chair. His limp body is held fast by ribbons and ribbons of securely fastened duct tape strapping him to the chair with little chance of escape. Archie looks up and smiles. He notices Brad's belt and the sharp edge of the buckle. He begins pulling it out from the loops in Brad's Levi's. He stands up and carelessly throws the belt in the far corner of the small cellar. He sighs loudly as he proudly surveys his clever handiwork.

"Wouldn't want you getting the idea you can beat me at my own game—not that it would do any good at this point."

Archie looks around.

"Oh yeah—this plan is a keeper."

He laughs.

"Yep—you're so dead."

He notices Brad waking up. He grins again.

"Well, well, well, it's about time Prince Charming decided to wake up—I was beginning to get worried—worried you'd miss the fun I have planned for you—a series finale if you wish."

Archie laughs loudly again.

"I bet you're wondering about—where you are?"

Brad looks around and seems confused.

Archie glances at the tiny room.

"Uh-huh—it's exactly what it looks like—you're not at home—in fact, you're never going home again—like ever."

He clasps his hands together and begins circling Brad as his face wreaths into a huge smile. He gestures briefly.

"Yep—now it's all making sense isn't it—uh-huh—I paid your bail—hired that stupid lawyer too—so fucking easy."

Brad's eyes search the room for the door.

"Look all you like Brad—there's no escape—this is it for you—you're in your own personal mausoleum—so perfect."

He circles Brad with a wicked glint in his eye.

"If you remembered earlier—you commented that you couldn't wait to see my daughter in the ground—well, be careful what you wish for you piece of dirt—because—because it is *you* and not Carrie that will be laid to rest first—today, in fact."

Archie begins laughing hysterically.

"This is my great-grandfather's whacked idea of a bomb shelter—the old coot had it built in the 1950s—thought the world was going to end and didn't want to leave his money behind—but guess what Brad—he never had to worry—but you should."

Archie begins laughing louder.

"No one knew he built it—totally secret—so when you turn up missing no one will think to look—and once I seal the doorway with concrete—it'll just be another nondescript wall under the wood paneling I installed yesterday—oh sweet dreams."

Archie leans toward Brad and smirks as he sees the fear building in Brad's eyes. Archie whispers in Brad's ears.

"Think about it—you're going to go out like that story **Edgar Allan Poe** made famous—*Cask of Amontillado*. You know, the one where one man entombs another for wronging him and then leaves him to die—well, surprise—surprise McKinley, this is your deal too—just eighteen hours—and then you die."

Archie smirks again and leans even closer to Brad as he whispers into his ear—viciously mocking him in triumph.

"Once I seal the doorway you'll have exactly eighteen hours of air left—and then—dead—end of the road—oops."

He looks around again.

"Oh, I almost forgot—got to add an epilogue to this wonderful creepy tale—wouldn't be appropriate if I didn't."

He pulls out a picture of Carrie and stuffs it into one of the pockets of Brad's jeans. He stands back and smirks.

"If they ever find you—and that's a big *if*—they'll also find Carrie's photo and it'll explain all—and what you did."

Archie walks to the door. He turns to face Brad again.

"Uh-huh—putting duct tape over your mouth was the best idea of all—got to tell you how I felt—and didn't have to listen to you begging for your miserable life—even for one second."

Page **598**

Brad watches him leave and tries to struggle free of the tightly wrapped duct tape around his body. But it is in vain. He watches silently as Archie seals up the doorway with cinder blocks—coating it with a thick covering of concrete. Archie grins at Brad one last time—and seals up the final opening. Brad continues to struggle to free himself as darkness blankets the tiny windowless room. His face is wreathed in a look of panic.

<u>Standish Road</u>

Lance Weissmann laughs as he glances at where Marilyn Bingham is lying in the backseat. She seems upset. He grins.

"Come on, it was just sex."

Marilyn sighs.

"I know—but we both just came from a funeral—several actually—don't think we should be fucking so soon after."

Lance makes a lewd gesture with his finger.

"I'm supposed to stop living because of a few funerals?"

He pulls Marilyn toward his naked body and grins.

"Not my style—I live for today."

He kisses her.

"You're one of my girls."

Marilyn slides her fingers across Lance's chest.

"It's just—that you seem so cold about everything so soon afterwards—they were our friends—and it just feels weird."

"Look, I know for a fact Corinne, Daphne, Natalie and Lana would want us to go on living—having sex—enjoying the fact we're alive—and well, Ross, for sure he wouldn't have a problem—except he'd probably want to watch—freak."

Marilyn giggles as she watches his behavior.

"He was a pretty creepy guy—especially how he treated Tyler—he just used him like a cheap prostitute—so sad."

Lance rolls his eyes and grins.

"It is what it is—Tyler will get over it—wasn't the first time and certainly won't be the last—just part of the deal."

Marilyn gives Lance an odd look. He laughs loudly.

Page **599**

"Well, it's true so why not say it?"
Marilyn looks at her watch as Lance grins broadly.
"Uh-huh—definitely time for one more play."
Lance pulls her under him again.
"I love being alive—best feeling in the world."
He penetrates her again within seconds.

<u>Parking Lot</u>

"Damn him—I knew this would happen—he's gone."
Clay turns to look at Maxwell as they stand in front of Brad McKinley's empty car. In Maxwell's hand is a photograph.
"He played us for fools—damn that frigging bastard."
He stares at the photo of Rio de Janeiro again.
"Probably on his way to South America—like who'd think that kid was so clever—made a foolproof escape plan."
Clay shrugs several times.
"If we call Logan—we might be able to stop him?"
Maxwell slams his fist against Brad's car.
"He isn't going to try his luck at the airport—I bet he had help—the question is who—who the fuck helped him?"
Maxwell looks at the photograph again.
"Do you think his folks might be in on the plans to help him escape? Did they know what was going to happen?"
Clay looks at the empty parking lot.
"No—they're good people—there's no way they would have that kind of money to facilitate such a slick getaway."
Maxwell clenches his fists angrily.
"I should've known this would be McKinley's game."
He looks at the photograph again and sighs.
"So, you think whoever helped him escape is loaded—and paid for his bail and then—but why would they help?"
Clay glances at the note and shrugs.
"It's the only thing that makes sense—question is—who would do such a thing—especially given what we know?"
Clay takes the photo from Maxwell's hand.

Page **600**

"Think he'll try and make a run for Canada—the border isn't too far away—he certainly—seems like a plausible idea."

They look at each other.

"I'll call my buddies at the FBI—we need to catch this creep before he skips the country—got to get him back."

Maxwell pulls out his cell phone.

<u>Mall</u>

Elizabeth sits down on the bench and pulls out a compact mirror from her purse. She groans as she looks at herself.

"Oh God—I look hideous. I feel like one of those zombies from those TV shows on cable. Ugh—gross. Can it be real?"

She hears a sound and turns to see Amanda Spencer looking at her curiously. Elizabeth immediately turns away.

"Elizabeth—is everything all right?"

They look at each other.

"That depends on what you mean."

"It can't be that bad?"

Amanda watches as Elizabeth slowly puts the mirror away. She notices the teenage girl seems very upset.

<u>Portland</u>

Glen watches as Kevin Myers leaves the diner and heads to his car in a tree-shaded parking lot. He smirks as he slams the door to his car shut and casually walks over to Kevin. As he approaches, Kevin notices. He faces Glen unaware of the danger facing him at that moment. Glen slowly takes a step closer.

"Glen Bradstreet, right? What's up?"

Without warning Glen pulls out a small handgun with a silencer and coldly shoots Kevin point-blank in the head. He grins broadly as he watches Kevin fall backwards against his car—a look of fright on his face as he dies instantly seconds later.

"Couldn't leave a loose end like you alive—no way—have to make sure you keep your mouth shut—now and forever."

Page **601**

He smirks as he slides the gun back into a pocket of his jacket. He pulls a note out of the back pocket of his Levi's and carelessly drops it near the body. He smirks again.

<u>Police Station</u>

Gina Bentley opens her eyes and looks around as if looking for someone. Immediately she hears laughter.
"Hello, Gina."
She looks up to see Tiffany Johnson standing over her with an evil grin on her face. Gina tries to back away.
"It's that time again killer—time to play."
"*Please*—just leave me alone—I didn't kill you."
Tiffany shrugs and laughs loudly.
"Like seriously? Get real."
Footsteps are heard coming down the hallway. They both look up and as Caroline comes into view. Tiffany vanishes.
"Gina I know—we've got to talk."
Gina turns and realizes she's alone in the cell.
"I didn't do it."
Caroline leans against the iron bars.
"I know you didn't kill anyone."
Gina rolls her eyes.
"What are you doing here, mother?"
Caroline sighs loudly.
"I know I've been a terrible mother but I'm trying."
She sighs again.
"Yesterday you told me to go away and never come back and the day before also—but I—we need to fix things."
Gina looks around and seems confused.
"Things—things are happening—really bad things."
Caroline glances at the empty cell. She seems upset.
"Look—you've got to stop telling people you've been seeing Tiffany Johnson—she's dead OK—gone forever."
Gina rolls her eyes.
"I'm not crazy—she's here."

Page **602**

"I didn't say you were—but this talk isn't helping."

Gina turns away seeming about to cry.

"But you implied it?"

"I'm sorry—I just want you to get out of here as soon as possible and saying that you've been communicating with the Johnson girl will only make people think the worse of you."

Gina glances over at Brad's empty cell.

"He killed Carrie."

She gestures with her hand.

"They let him out—can you believe it—he raped."

"I know—but he's someone else's problem."

"Someone paid his bail in full—and hired Pierce Colby to represent him too—someone really has his back—not fair."

Caroline shakes her head.

"Who would do something like that?"

Gina gestures with her hand.

Glass Owl

Lindsay Bennington notices Kyle sitting out in the garden by himself. She walks over to him. He turns to face her.

"He knew—knew all along."

Lindsay seems confused.

"Who knew—what are you talking about?"

Kyle turns away.

"That worthless bastard knew all this time and said nothing to me—things could've been so different—for me."

Lindsay sits down next to Kyle.

"You're not making any sense Kyle—who knew?"

Kyle slowly stands up and looks back at the mansion.

"But I'll make him pay—oh yeah—I'm going to make him pay dearly for what he did to me—that bastard will pay."

Lindsay watches as Kyle rushes out of the garden. She turns around and glances at the house and sighs loudly.

"Is it—no—it couldn't be—but Kyle said."

She sighs loudly.

<u>Port Clyde</u>

Loud laughter erupts as Denise is chased by Miles Dandridge. He finally catches her and pins her to the bed.

"Think you could outrun me huh—you lose."

Miles grins slyly.

"Think you could outplay a college guy with just one thing in his mind—well, you can't. I'm going to have you."

Denise smiles broadly.

"I surrender."

He penetrates her as loud moans echo throughout the room for several seconds as they go at it like two animals.

<u>Standish Road</u>

Lance grins broadly as he silently closes the door to Marilyn's car while she starts the engine. He sighs.

"I'll call tomorrow—OK?"

Marilyn nods.

"I'll be waiting."

Lance smirks. Marilyn winks at him.

"Oh, by the way please forgive me about earlier—I was sort of out of it—things, well they are just—they got crazy."

Marilyn waves her hand.

"No big deal—I like games. You have been quite good with me and my sister—it's only fair I repay favors—love you."

She leans over and kisses Lance.

"We have a lot of history—two years worth."

He nods as she drives off. Lance pulls out his cell phone and dials. He grins as the line is picked up. He makes a lewd gesture with his finger as he waves his hand in the air. He sighs.

"How about we get together later?"

He nods several times.

"I'll be there—probably ten minutes tops."

He shuts off his cell phone seconds later and whistles.

Page **604**

Police Station

Daryl looks up as Maxwell and Clay enter. They seem upset as Clay closes the door behind them. He leans back in his chair as they slowly come toward him with a defeated look.

"What's wrong?"

Clay turns to face Daryl.

"The McKinley kid skipped—gone—left town in a jiffy."

Daryl seems confused.

"What—that can't be—he agreed—promised?"

Maxwell rolls his eyes.

"Did you think you could trust him Daryl? He raped and killed one of his classmates. I think trust is not one of his strong points at this moment. Suspect slipped away on the sly."

Daryl stands up.

"We've got to find him before anyone finds out."

Maxwell sighs loudly.

"I already called my friends at the FBI and he's as good as captured once they get their hands on him—kid's toast."

Daryl turns to face Clay.

Port Clyde

Denise traces her finger down his chest toward his exposed penis while Miles grins broadly as he watches her.

"I'm glad you called earlier."

Denise smirks knowingly as she turns to face Miles.

"There's no stopping a healthy young guy like you is there—even with a pesky girlfriend calling every ten minutes asking where you are—which is quite irritating by the way."

Miles rolls his eyes.

"Tell me about it—she still believes it's just her and me all these months—but hey, let's get real—it's just not true."

He makes a lewd gesture with his finger.

"By the time she figures it out—we'll be long over."

Page 605

Denise glances at Miles slyly and leans down to kiss his penis. He sighs loudly as her tongue slides across the head.

"I'm so spoiled."

He laughs again.

"It's a curse being so good in bed."

Denise nods in agreement.

"How far down on your list am I at the moment?"

He groans loudly as Denise's tongue slides seductively across his penis. She works her way up to the head again.

"I slept with this chick yesterday I met in Portland. Fucked this other chick I met in an elevator in Bar Harbor. Fucked these two sisters from Marble Hills—they were twins—easy."

Denise looks at Miles curiously.

"What were their names?"

"Marilyn and Diana Bingham—I think. Met them in Boston and we talked about a minute and then I hooked up with both of them in an alley off Beacon Street—gave it up quickly."

He laughs loudly.

"Oh man—they knew their stuff too—pinned them one at a time against the wall in that alley I mentioned and I let loose as I took both of them—told them thank you before parting ways an hour later—inexperienced they were not—love twins."

Denise rolls her eyes.

"I know the Bingham sisters. They've been around."

Miles groans louder and louder as Denise begins to suck on the head of his penis intently. He cries out with joy.

"Oh God—you're quite the treat today."

He groans louder.

"You women really know how to break us guys."

He explodes in her mouth.

<u>Mall</u>

Kelly looks up from the kiosk and sees Donna staring at him with a troubled look on her face as she sits down. He glances at her nervously as she leans across the narrow counter.

Page 606

"I can't believe they let Brad go."
Kelly sighs.
"Think he skipped town? I heard that's the talk."
Donna nods.
"He killed Carrie—it's not like he can beat a rap like that after what—so I think he skipped for sure—damn him."
"Not if Carrie's dad has anything to say."
Donna suddenly seems pleased at the thought.

<u>Lighthouse Grill</u>

Sidney Stuyvesant watches as Archie slowly walks toward him. He seems oddly quiet. Sidney sighs nervously.
"Oh-oh—what's the deal now?"
Archie leans against the counter and looks at Sidney with a weird mixture of scorn and indifference. He sighs loudly.
"What's going on with McKinley?"
Sidney looks at Archie curiously and sighs.
"You haven't heard?"
Archie shakes his head.
"Heard what?"
Sidney leans toward Archie.
"They actually let the McKinley kid go."
Archie feigns surprise and glances around the diner.
"Apparently the punk got someone to bail him out and hired that high-priced lawyer Caroline got for Gina."
Archie turns around and pretends to be enraged.
"That fucking prick—how the hell did he swing money like that—his father is dead broke—not a dime to his name."
Sidney shrugs several times.
"Don't know—but someone out there paid his bail."
Archie glances at the door.
"I think it's time I pay Anderson a visit."
Sidney watches as Archie rushes out of the diner without another word. He sighs loudly again and shakes his head.

Page **607**

Gina grabs the bars of her cell angrily as the news about Brad McKinley becomes clear. She kicks at the bars.

"That bastard—he killed Carrie Spaulding and gets to be let out of this hellhole and I—I'm stuck here until trial."

Caroline sighs knowingly.

"I don't make the rules—someone obviously pulled some strings—paid a lot of money—really wanted him out of jail."

Gina slams her fist against the bars.

"Why didn't you guys do that for me—pay some joker off and let me go—then I could fly to Geneva or something."

Caroline sighs again.

"I wish it were that easy—but it's just not in the cards."

Gina watches her mother with cold eyes.

"Why not mother—we're rich aren't we? I thought?"

"Bail has been refused in your case—seems the judge thinks you might try to flee—end up a flight risk situation."

Gina turns away from Caroline.

"What—skip town—what about Brad McKinley—I bet you anything he'll skip—frigging creep probably already left?"

"Where can he go—his father is poor—he has nowhere to go until the trial—and that probably won't go very well."

Gina faces Caroline again.

"Like that's ever stopped anyone before—Brad is a sleazy piece of dirt—of course he'll skip town and not care—damn."

"It's not up to me dear—I'm really sorry."

Gina seems to become enraged at the comment.

"*Get out*—just get out right now—go."

Caroline stands there motionless.

"I said get out—like now—be gone and don't come back again—you're dead to me as of this moment—die already."

Caroline looks at her daughter for a few seconds and slowly walks away. She seems visibly upset at Gina's rage.

"Well, well, well, seems like you are burning all your bridges—oh, that could prove quite the mistake—uh-huh."

Page **608**

Gina turns around and sees Tiffany standing a few feet away. She begins walking gleefully toward Gina.

"Now, where were we Gina—before we were so rudely interrupted by your former mother—oh yes, I was going to make you even more miserable than you already are—oh, let the games begin again—with no one to rudely interrupt us this time."

Without warning Gina is flung against the wall.

Glass Owl

Susan Bennington nervously looks at a pregnancy test strip again. She seems about to cry as she stares at it.

"No—it can't be true. It's not real."

She wipes a tear from her eye.

"There must be some mistake—there has to be."

She looks at the strip again.

"He promised me I couldn't get pregnant—he said it only happened to one girl in a million—but how—why me?"

She sighs loudly.

"I should've insisted he wore a condom."

She drops the strip into the trash.

"I've got to talk to Lance—I bet he'll be mad."

Susan looks at herself once more in the mirror and leaves the room as tears begin to stream down her cheeks.

Police Station

Daryl looks up as Archie slams the front door shut. He seems angry as he walks toward the desk. Daryl stands.

"I warned you this would—and now it has happened."

Daryl sighs.

"I had no choice—had to play by the law."

"Funny you should say that—well—two can play that game—unemployment can be quite unpleasant too."

At that moment Howard strolls through the door looking quite happy. Daryl turns to look at him with an angry scowl.

"Clean out your desk Anderson—you're fired."

He watches as Howard seems to be hiding a grin.

"Well—what are you waiting for Anderson—time is money—especially when it's my money—get cracking."

Daryl turns to face Archie. He notices Howard and Archie looking triumphant—a smile of victory on their faces.

"You won't get away with this—no way."

Howard grabs Daryl by the arm.

"Is that a threat I hear?"

He tightens his grip on Daryl's arm.

"Sounds like it to me—what about you Archie—sound like a threat to you? Did this lowlife fool dare to threaten me?"

Archie smirks as he looks at Daryl.

"Seems to me you forgot your place—seems you forgot just who you're dealing with—and who pays your check."

"McKinley being sprung wasn't my doing."

Howard rolls his eyes as he looks coldly at Daryl.

"Likely story—but I don't give a fuck—you're done here."

He gives Daryl a harsh stare again.

"From what I heard you and McKinley's pop are quite close aren't you. Bet you anything you cooked this scam up."

Daryl rolls his eyes.

"His cousin is my wife."

Archie seems irritated and sighs loudly.

"Why are you still here Anderson?"

Archie glances at Daryl—his eyes filled with hatred. He glances at Howard briefly and angrily faces Daryl again.

"Hope you can afford yourself a really good lawyer."

Daryl seems confused.

"Why?"

"I'm going to have you charged for aiding and abetting with the escape of a known criminal in the vicious rape and murder of my beloved daughter—you're going to be so sorry when I get through with you Anderson—that I promise."

Daryl faces Howard.

"I did no such thing—I wouldn't."

"Tell it to someone who cares about anything you have to say—I want you gone in five minutes—or else I'll have you arrested for trespassing on private property—*my* property."

"You'll pay for this Madison."

He looks around the room.

"I swear you'll regret fucking with me."

Howard shrugs.

"Oh, that reminds me."

Daryl seems annoyed as Howard grabs his cell phone. Howard turns to face Archie and Daryl with a grin.

"Anderson, say hello to the new police chief of Marble Hills—I think you already know each other—pretty well."

The front door opens as Daryl slowly turns around.

TO BE CONTINUED

A Look at the 24th Episode

Daryl and Howard have it out of which threats are made—Denise encounters an unpleasant visit from a stranger who knows all about her—Susan pays Lance a visit and reveals news he doesn't want to hear—Clay and Maxwell try to figure out how Brad skipped town—Sidney becomes suspicious about Brad's disappearance after a visit with Archie—Caleb's funeral is held with no fanfare—Matt and Damon have another steamy encounter—Daryl breaks the news to Kyle about losing his job because of his father—Juan lays the law down with Faye who refuses to give up without a fight—Denise confides in Glen about her encounter earlier with a blackmailing stranger bent on exposing her secrets—Shirley is threatened by Corey over events from their past—Alden and Wesley uncovers a long ago secret about the Madison family while searching for possible clues about Marah's death—Daryl and Caroline enjoy a private moment—as Howard encounters a nasty surprise visitor at Glass Owl.

Page **612**

Episode 24
Shadows of the Past

<u>Police Station</u>

Daryl Anderson looks at the scene playing out in front of him as the door opens and Will McColl enters. Howard Madison notices his confused behavior and shoots him an evil grin.

"Oh Daryl, I'm not done with you yet."

He snaps his fingers.

"McColl—arrest this man immediately for aiding and abetting with the escape of Brad McKinley from jail."

Daryl seems in a state of shock. Will McColl looks at him and Howard. He seems confused about what to do.

"What—you can't—you fucking snake—I swear I'll break you once this is over—you've gone too far—and I won't let you play this sick game—I'm gonna make you pay for this."

Howard turns to look at Daryl with a snarl.

"OK—you all heard him—Anderson threatened me a second time—in addition to the aiding and abetting charge concerning Brad McKinley I want this man charged also with threatening me—a respectable citizen of Marble Hills."

Daryl rolls his eyes as he looks at Howard.

Page **613**

"*Oh please*—you are as respectable as one of those Fascist Tea Party members who pretended to be sane Republicans."

Howard grabs Daryl by the shoulder.

"You watch your step with me—I can make bad things happen—starting with your family—especially your son."

Daryl jerks free of Howard's grip.

"Uh-huh—and what about *your* family—oh yeah—one word from me and I guarantee Kyle will put a bullet in your head over what you did to that poor Glick girl—and his baby."

Howard shoots Daryl a look of disgust.

"I should've killed you when I had the chance."

Daryl smirks.

"But you didn't—and Kyle—what would he say if he knew the truth—from what I heard he's already asking questions about you—and what happened all those years ago with Serena."

Howard looks at Archie Spaulding.

"Let's go."

Archie looks around.

"I thought you said you had it taken care of already?"

Howard gives Daryl a harsh stare and heads to the door as Archie follows. Will looks at Daryl as the door slams shut.

<u>Port Clyde</u>

Denise Madison kisses Miles Dandridge passionately before she slowly closes the door to the hotel room. He smirks as he walks away. Denise sighs loudly as she glances at the thick blobs of dried semen on the bed sheets. She smiles and is about to leave when she hears a soft knock on the door. She opens it with a huge smile expecting to see Miles standing there.

"I'm still in the mood."

Marc Ryerson grins broadly.

"I'll think about it—after you and I talk."

Denise seems confused.

"I thought you were someone else."

Marc laughs knowingly.

Page 614

"Yeah—I'll just bet you did—definitely."

Marc pushes his way into the room and shuts the door.

"You and I have some financial arrangements that need your immediate attention—especially after today."

Denise gestures with her hand.

"Get out or I'll call the police."

Marc smirks as he pulls out a wad of photographs from his jacket and hands them to her. She seems confused.

"Go ahead—I'm sure they would love to know all about your sexual exploits with underage teenage—young men."

Denise looks in shock at the explicit photographs showing various sexual positions between her and Lance.

"Uh-huh—didn't think anyone was watching—oops."

Marc laughs triumphantly.

"I got more if you're wondering—sweet mother—you've got a thing for handsome teenage boys—it would be such a shame if anyone were to find—find out about you and?"

Denise throws the photographs back at Marc.

"What do you want?"

Marc rolls his eyes.

"Duh—what else—money—lots of money—tons."

Denise looks around the room.

"I don't—I can't."

Marc rolls his eyes.

"What—you don't have any money—please—spare me the sob story whore—you're a Madison—you've got plenty of dough and I want some of it or else. You've got no choice bitch."

Denise glances at the door.

"I—I can't—it would look too suspicious if I did. How would I explain what I was doing? It's just not possible. I'm sorry."

Marc looks at the photographs again.

"You can't—oh what a shame—how sad. So many things can go wrong for someone like you if I were to tell Howard Madison about your sexual exploits with half the town."

Denise watches as he flips through the photographs. He grins slyly as he shows Denise photos of her and Daryl.

"I wonder what your husband will say when he realizes his wife and the police chief have been doing it—and oh, if he finds out his brother—soon to be ex-brother-in-law and you have been quite friendly since he arrived in Marble Hills—oh imagine what your father-in-law will do—and of course when Caroline Bentley finds out about Glen Bradstreet and you—*oh my*—scandal."

Denise seems terrified.

"You can't—please don't go there."

Marc pulls out his cell phone.

"I think I can."

Denise seems about to panic as Marc heads to the door.

"OK—OK—I'll find a way—how much?"

Marc turns around with a huge grin on his face.

<u>Police Station</u>

Gina Bentley wipes blood from her lips and sits down on the bed a few feet away. She sighs loudly and shrugs.

"I didn't do it—I didn't kill you—I swear."

She looks up. There is no one there. She begins to cry.

<u>Weissmann Driveway</u>

Susan Bennington silently watches as Lance Weissmann passionately kisses Genie Van Pelt goodbye. She notices the buttons on his Levi's aren't buttoned. As Genie drives away Susan comes toward Lance. He seems confused to see her and sighs.

"Susan—what are—Genie and I—we?"

He seems nervous as she approaches.

"She and I—we're friends."

Susan sighs loudly.

"It's OK—I know—I know you've been having sex with other girls—people talk—that and your rep—I don't care."

She seems upset.

"I have something to tell you."

Lance seems confused.

Page 616

"What?"
Susan pulls out a pregnancy test from her jacket.
"I'm pregnant."
Lance seems shocked.

Portland

Crowds of police cars surround a covered body lying a few feet away. People are milling around talking to various police officers—most of them shaking their heads as if confused.

Police Station

Will stares at Daryl blankly. He seems unsure about what to do next. He sighs. He turns to look at the door again.
"I had nothing to do with what happened."
"Save it—sneaky worm."
Daryl looks around at the office for a few seconds and leaves—slamming the door behind him as Will sighs.
"I—I—things could—get messy."
He turns to look at the desk in front of him.
"Maybe I should've thought this through much better?"
A few minutes later he hears the door open and sees Kyle Madison standing in the doorway with a confused look.
"McColl—what are you doing here—where's Daryl?"
Kyle closes the door.
"Well—where's Anderson? What's going on? Did he spend too much time at Nickerson's last night? Well, do tell."
They look at each other for a few seconds.
"Where's that lazy loser?"
Will glances at the front door and sighs. He seems uneasy as he looks at Kyle again still unable to speak. He sighs.
"Your dad just fired Daryl Anderson—seems they had a nasty falling out or something. He offered me the job."
Kyle shakes his head and seems in shock at the news.

Page **617**

<u>Portland</u>

Denise slowly turns to face Glen Bradstreet. She appears to be somewhat in a daze. She wrings her hands nervously.

"He knows about us—knows about me."

Glen seems confused.

"Who—who are we talking about?"

"I don't know—some creepy guy—showed me—he had photographs of—oh my God—what can I do to stop him?"

Glen sighs loudly.

"You're not making any sense—just tell me exactly what happened—and don't leave anything out—nothing OK?"

Denise sits down opposite Glen.

<u>Boston</u>

Clay Blankenship stares at the computer screen while Maxwell Pendergraft slowly leans back in his chair.

"Looks like McKinley gave us the slip all right—played us all for chumps without missing a beat—or so it looks."

They look at each other.

"You're telling me that an inexperienced teenage boy outsmarted us and skipped the country—unnoticed?"

"Looks like it—apparently he's not as stupid as most people in Marble Hills seemed to think—quite slick."

Clay shakes his head.

"How the hell could he have gotten out of the country so fast—what about security? I thought they were pros?"

"That was supposed to be a joke, right?"

Maxwell points at the computer screen several times.

"McKinley took a cab to Boston on the sly, hopped on a flight to Atlanta using his father's name and from there flew to San Juan, Puerto Rico—of which he left the country within an hour and, well, he's in Rio de Janeiro as of ten minutes ago—oh man, do we look stupid now not figuring this out earlier."

Clay seems annoyed and shrugs.

Page **618**

<u>Portland</u>

"So, all this time some guy has been trailing you—taking photographs of your—your sexual adventures—and now he says he wants a stash of money or else he plans to reveal all?"

Denise nods several times.

"I had no idea—I mean—how could I know? It's not like I asked for attention—I was not prepared—I'm so screwed."

Glen sighs as looks Denise's anguished face.

"Exactly when is this fucking asshole going to contact you again to see if you've got the money he's demanding?"

Denise waves her hand in the air.

"Tomorrow—I'm not sure—he didn't say."

Glen stands up and walks toward the window. He turns to face Denise again as he clenches his fists. He sighs.

"This fucker is going to have to be dealt with—got to get him before he messes our plans up—there's no other way."

Denise seems confused.

"Like how—what are you suggesting?"

Glen rolls his eyes.

"How do you think?"

Denise leans back on the sofa.

"What if something goes wrong?"

Glen smirks.

"One bullet in his head—all his blackmail plans dies with him and we continue what we've been doing without worrying about some dark cloud hanging over our head like—fuck."

Denise wipes sweat from her brow.

"I—I don't know about murder?"

Glen laughs.

"I wasn't asking you to—I'll do it—no problem."

He gestures with his hand.

"It wouldn't be the first time either."

Denise looks at Glen oddly.

"You've killed someone before?"

Page **619**

Glen laughs loudly.

"Hey, do I look like the boy next door—nope—I'm not a sweet guy—I've lived—lived on the edge and—seriously."

"OK—whatever—just so long as this guy doesn't ruin my life—if Kyle ever found out—or worst yet his horrible father."

"I gather you've been with a lot of young guys—plenty of which would fall under the age of eighteen—jailbait city."

Denise smiles slyly.

"I can't help myself—they were cute."

Glen looks at his erection.

"Where does that place me on your list?"

Denise glances at the bedroom door and winks.

<u>Lighthouse Grill</u>

Sidney Stuyvesant watches as Archie walks into the diner and sits down at the counter. He seems oddly happy.

"Well, I just got Daryl Anderson fired—did what Kyle Madison never had the guts to do—oh—such drama too."

Sidney seems surprised.

"What—why?"

Archie leans across the counter.

"You heard me—that louse deserved it too—let Brad McKinley go free—and guess what happened—that sick creep left town without so much as a goodbye to his pathetic parents."

Sidney looks at Archie curiously.

"McKinley's kid left town—but he had?"

Archie nods.

"Yeah—that piece of dirt is never going to stand trial for what he did to my baby—living it up in South America."

Sidney notices Archie's behavior.

"You seem sure they won't find him—why?"

Archie looks around.

"South America is a big place. How the hell will he be found by the FBI—those guys are boobs—total losers."

He turns to look at Sidney and shrugs.

Page 620

"Howard Madison and me are quite tight—have been for several years now—well, it looks like he knows things."

Sidney sighs loudly.

"Don't remind me—that man is pure evil."

Archie looks around again.

"Anyway, he knows all sorts of people—and from one of his contacts we learned McKinley is in South America."

Sidney wipes sweat off his brow.

"Already—but it's only been a few—how could he?"

Archie leans toward Sidney and whispers.

"Apparently someone paid his bail and arranged his getaway—but no worries—a young man in a foreign country with no money—imagine what he'll have to do to survive once he realizes the situation he's gotten himself into—some things are worse than jail—especially if you're a good-looking kid."

Sidney wipes his brow again.

"It just seems so perfect—too perfect if you ask me."

Archie looks at his watch and shrugs.

"Oh-oh—got to go—have to meet with Madison—he and I have another surprise coming for Anderson later today."

He rushes out the door without another word to Sidney.

<u>Crestview Memorial Park Cemetery</u>

Julia Winthrop watches with tears in her eyes as the casket bearing the body of Caleb Winthrop is slowly lowered into the ground. Next to her is Alden Washington and Todd Spencer. Eddie Kane is standing a few feet away. Alden puts his arms around her. A slight drizzle begins to fall around them.

<u>Weissmann Driveway</u>

Lance paces back and forth as Susan watches him nervously. He turns to face her. He seems visibly upset.

"I'll take you to a clinic right now."

Susan seems upset.

Page 621

"I want to have your baby."

Lance turns around to face Susan.

"You can't have a baby—my baby—no way—this would ruin me—please listen—you can't go through with this?"

Lance looks back at his house.

"I'm eighteen—a high school senior and you are a high school sophomore—fill in the blanks and see the problem."

Susan turns away seconds later. She seems about to faint as Lance runs after her. He grabs her by the arm in a panic.

"Please—if anyone finds out I could go to jail."

Susan looks away.

"I wouldn't let—they wouldn't?"

"You wouldn't have a choice—your evil grandpa would see to it I ended up in jail for thirty years or he'd have me killed."

Lance sighs loudly.

"He'll have me killed in jail—probably with an ice pick or something—is that what you want—for me to be iced?"

Susan seems scared.

"No—I don't want you to get killed—but—this baby."

Lance shakes his head.

"You've got to get an abortion—it's the only way—got to get rid of it already—before old man Madison finds out."

They look at each other.

<u>Boston</u>

Clay and Maxwell slowly walk to the parking lot. Maxwell notices that Clay seems upset. He stops and looks around.

"Look—he gave us the slip—probably had help—but he's gone—no way will Brazilian authorities agree to have him extradited back here—besides he probably isn't going to stay in Brazil long—it's not like there's much of a life there—zero."

Clay clenches is fist angrily.

"Man, the Spaulding girl's father is going to be so pissed he skipped—heads will roll for this no doubt—Daryl's fucked."

Maxwell shakes his head.

Page 622

"Don't I know it—I think Anderson better prepare."
Clay stops and looks at Maxwell.
"Don't know how I would handle something like this myself if it happened to me—it's just so hard to relate."
"Losing someone you love to murder is never easy."
Clay and Maxwell get into their car.

Brewster Condo

Matt Brewster and Damon Mayo are going at it on the sofa. Damon grins broadly as he unbuttons Matt's jeans.
"I want you so badly—can't stop."
Matt laughs.
"If your sweet girlfriend could see us now—she'd freak if she knew you played both sides—using her for show."
Damon laughs loudly.
"I like her and all—but I can't resist the lure of your dick Matt—especially one that has been with so many."
Matt grins broadly.
"I never claimed I was waiting for the right guy."
Damon smirks.
"Uh-huh—you and me both—love is for lonely chumps."
Damon strokes Matt's exposed penis.

Stanley Pier

Daryl turns to look at Kyle. They look at each other for a few seconds without saying anything. Daryl sighs.
"Well, I hope you're happy—you always threatened to fire me and now—I guess your old man finally beat you to it."
Kyle shakes his head.
"I—I didn't know—I wouldn't."
"Yeah, sure—whatever—like I'll believe you."
Kyle looks out at the ocean.
"I'm not on speaking terms right now with my father. Frigging bastard kept that fact I had another son a secret."

Daryl gives Kyle a strange look.

"Son—what—with who—who's the mother?"

Kyle shrugs several times.

"Apparently Serena Glick had my baby after all. My father played us all for complete idiots—he's a miserable wretch."

Daryl stifles a smile.

"You're sure your father knew?"

Kyle shakes his head.

"Uh-huh—he didn't deny it when I confronted him—and pretty much admitted to everything. I'm royally pissed."

Daryl seems upset.

"Doesn't surprise me—let's face it, your father is capable of all things horrible—your old man has many faces."

Daryl glances at the harbor and then at Kyle again.

"Where's the kid now?"

Kyle sighs loudly.

"Here—in Marble Hills—I've met him already."

Daryl and Kyle look at one another.

<u>Boardinghouse</u>

Alden closes the door behind him and faces Julia. She looks around the room and sighs loudly. She sighs again.

"It's hard."

"I know."

They look at each other.

"Are you sure you'll be alright?"

Julia nods.

"Yeah—earlier was really hard—but it's over—Caleb is with Peter and Cassie now—no more pain. Good places."

Alden runs his fingers through his hair.

"Any word on when Gina Bentley goes to trial?"

Julia shakes her head.

"No—I guess they have to decide if they're going to try her as an adult—but given the unusual circumstances?"

Alden shakes his head and sighs.

Page **624**

"I still can't believe one teenage girl caused so much grief in such a short time—how could she have pulled it off?"

Julia wipes a tear from her eye.

"I always thought she was *different*—but not a killer."

Alden sighs loudly.

"Well, whatever they do it won't change what happened already—there's just too much violence in this country and not dealing with it effectively isn't helping anyone—guns are for sale everywhere—like candy—available to anyone with money."

Julia turns to look at Alden.

<u>Tolling Bell Inn</u>

Juan Sabrillo zips up his Levi's as he looks at Faye Washington lying on the bed naked. He smirks as she pulls away the sheet indicating yet another sexual encounter.

"Uh-huh—no way do you try that stunt again—I have somewhere to go—too far behind as it is already."

Faye sighs and seems frustrated.

"Look—I played along with it for as long as it humored you—but I want that whore out of your bed—today."

Juan laughs.

"The answer is no—case closed."

Faye sits up in bed.

"But you can't continue to fuck us both?"

Juan laughs loudly.

"Why not—it's my dick?"

"I don't like sharing you with her."

Juan seems annoyed.

"This conversation is over."

Faye pulls on her robe and comes toward Juan.

"I thought we had something?"

Juan shakes his head.

"Give me a break already."

She watches as he heads to the door.

"I hate you—I frigging hate you."

Page **625**

He rolls his eyes.

"Yeah—yeah—whatever you say."

Faye watches as the door slams.

"Damn him—damn him to hell forever."

She turns to look at the bed.

"I think it's time I pay Sabrina Keller a visit—she and I have some things to straighten out—got to make my point to her."

Faye sighs and heads to the bathroom.

<u>Police Station</u>

Clay and Maxwell appear shocked at seeing Will sitting at Daryl's desk as they enter. Clay walks toward Will and sighs.

"Will? What's going on? Why are you here?"

Maxwell watches as Will stands up.

"Has something else happened in Marble Hills while we were in Boston—plenty of crazy stuff happening of late."

Will nods and looks at Maxwell.

"Not everything is about you Pendergraft."

"Then why are you here?"

"Daryl Anderson was relieved of his duties earlier today because—Howard Madison has decided to make changes."

Clay turns to look at Maxwell.

"Daryl Anderson is no longer police chief of Marble Hills and you—but you're—what about your other job?"

Clay watches as Will nods.

"How did he take it?"

"Not good—to say he's pissed off over the turn of events would be an understatement—in a serious rage actually."

Clay and Maxwell look at each other again.

"Well, here is some more bad news—the McKinley kid definitely skipped town—in South America as we speak."

Will glances at the paperwork on the desk.

"Did he have help?"

"What do you think?"

Clay sighs loudly.

Page 626

"I think he did."

He sighs again.

"But who helped him and why?"

They glance at the paperwork on the desk again.

<u>Portland</u>

Denise watches as Glen pulls out of her for the second time. He grins broadly as he sees her shocked expression.

"I can fuck all afternoon if need be."

Denise smirks.

"You've been on quite a high since earlier—like a huge burden have been lifted off your back—joyful actually."

Glen laughs.

"No truer words have ever been spoken."

Denise flips the remote as a newsflash sprays across the screen about a murder. She recognizes Kevin's car.

"Oh my God—Kevin—oh not Kevin Myers—somebody killed Kevin at the diner where he works—but who would kill?"

Glen grins broadly.

"I'm in the mood again—so ready."

Denise turns to look at Glen in shock. He laughs.

<u>Tolling Bell Inn</u>

Corey Bentley pulls Shirley Moses toward him again and laughs as she resists. She glances at the zipper in his pants.

"You'd better stop acting this way—or I'll have to tell sweet Jeremy all about you and me—and Daryl Anderson."

Shirley appears frightened.

"Why are you doing this to me? I thought—you said you'd never tell about Daryl and me—especially after last week?"

Corey rolls his eyes.

"I lied."

He winks at her and smirks as he sees her reaction. He looks at his erection. He blows her a kiss and whistles.

Page 627

"I'm doing it because I can. I know something that can destroy your perfect life—and you'll do as I say or else—or else Jeremy will find out his girlfriend has been doing every horny guy in town for the past year—and the police chief as well."

Shirley seems annoyed at Corey.

"It only happened twice—it wasn't planned."

Corey smirks broadly.

"Maybe—but what about Wesley, Brad, Caleb and Jarod too—and let's not forget Lance—if Jeremy found out his big brother did you too—talk about awkward family moments that could end in a fistfight. Especially if Jeremy found out you had to pay a visit to the abortion clinic to get rid of Lance's baby. Of course there's that pesky issue with Steve Pendleton at the fair last October—quite a private moment for sure—very sexy."

Shirley looks at Corey with a disgusted look.

"I hate you—you're a toad."

Corey slams into Shirley.

"Like I give a frigging damn if a whore hates me?"

He laughs as he rams her again.

"You know it would be too bad if after all you've done to keep your secret from getting out—it came out anyway."

Shirley tries to push Corey off her. But his behavior only intensifies as he angrily plows her again and again.

"Oh yeah—I'm seriously thinking you need to be taught a lesson when it comes to who owns your happiness."

Shirley seems about to cry.

"Please—I'm so sorry Corey—oh please don't—Jeremy wouldn't understand what happened—I'll lose him forever."

Corey laughs as he ejaculates.

"I'll think about—but I can't guarantee I won't—a guy has the right to change his mind—especially where a whore like yourself is concerned—promises are made to be broken."

He makes a lewd gesture with his finger.

"Like I said earlier—if you don't want dear Jeremy to know exactly what you are—you'll play ball on my terms."

He grins broadly.

"You don't want to make me mad Shirley—if I feel slighted by you all sorts of things can go wrong—really wrong."

He reaches for his pants and grins.

<u>Lighthouse Grill</u>

Wesley Madison looks up as Alden comes toward him. He pulls out the folder from his jacket and shoves it across the table toward Alden as he sits down. Alden slowly picks it up.

"On the phone earlier you said you lifted these from your grandfather's files—I assume that means he doesn't know?"

Wesley shakes his head.

"The old man has no clue—made copies when he went to play golf with his friends—left no evidence behind."

Alden flips through the files.

"Are these Marah's medical records—but what about?"

Alden seems confused and looks at Wesley.

"They didn't do an autopsy?"

Wesley nods.

"Doesn't seem like it."

Wesley slowly runs his fingers through his hair.

"It's quite unusual, isn't it—a daughter of a very rich family is found murdered—and no autopsy is performed?"

Alden glances at Wesley.

"I admit—it's very odd—usually even in extreme cases there's no way to avoid having an autopsy done. I remember when I lived in Los Angeles **Brittany Murphy** died suddenly and though it later turned out to be not intentional they did an autopsy anyway—so someone must have pulled a lot of strings with Marah's death—the question is why—and who?"

Wesley gestures with his hand.

"Bet you anything my grandfather pull strings."

Wesley glances at the folder again.

"Oh yeah—he pulled some strings alright. The question is why—since Marah was murdered at Glass Owl—suspicious."

Wesley and Alden look at each other.

Page 629

"What if he had a reason?"

Alden runs his fingers through his hair.

"Could someone in your family have done it—and then your grandfather covered it—blamed me for the deed?"

Wesley faces Alden.

"Wouldn't be the first time—I heard about grandfather's cousin—now there's a piece of work—messed up royally."

Alden seems confused.

"What cousin?"

Wesley rolls his eyes.

"His name was Blake Madison."

He looks at the door.

"From what I was told, my grandfather's cousin was deranged—killed four people in Miller's Pond by drowning them—did it for fun from what I learned—they locked him up right afterwards in a loony bin somewhere in Florida."

"Is he still alive?"

Wesley shrugs.

"Not sure—no one ever talks about him in my family—it's like he doesn't exist—just totally disappeared years ago."

Alden looks at Wesley curiously.

"Would he have been buried in the Madison family crypt at Crestview if he had passed away years before—decades?"

Wesley shrugs again and sighs.

"How about we check?"

Alden smiles broadly.

"I was hoping you'd say that."

He looks at his watch.

"Oops—too late to do it today—the cemetery closed an hour ago—how about tomorrow—say around nine or ten?"

Wesley nods again. Alden seems worried.

"What if we don't find his crypt? Could he have been buried in Florida—or maybe he's not dead—still alive?"

He seems confused.

"What would my grandfather's cousin have to do with Marah's death? Why would he want to kill my aunt?"

Alden glances at the files again.

"What if he didn't die years ago—what if he was kept hidden away somewhere—out of sight and out of mind?"

Wesley gives Alden an odd look.

"Like at Glass Owl—you think he could be there now?"

Alden nods and gestures with his hand.

Port Clyde

"That fucking asshole actually thinks he's going to win."

Daryl sighs and looks at Caroline Bentley.

"Do you really think Archie Spaulding pushed him to fire you after what happened with Brad McKinley's escape?"

Daryl shakes his head.

"No—old man Madison has been looking for a reason for a long time to fire me—any reason to—and now he has it."

Caroline seems worried.

"Maybe I should go talk to him—explain things."

Daryl angrily slams his fist against the steering wheel.

"No way—that creep has done enough to you—I don't want him using this opportunity to—work his magic on you ever again. Damn filthy creep has done enough already."

Caroline sighs.

"OK—but—but he might listen to me?"

Daryl leans over and kisses Caroline passionately.

"How about—you and I spend time together?"

Caroline seems confused as Daryl kisses her again.

"God, I want you so bad—I can't help it."

He kisses her again.

"We make such beautiful music together."

He tugs at her skirt.

"What about Howard Madison?"

Daryl quickly pulls Caroline under him and they begin kissing passionately. Moans echo from the car as he penetrates her. As they go at it his cell phone rings but he ignores it and continues fucking Caroline passionately as she cries out.

Page 631

Brewster Condo

Damon kisses Matt intently as he reaches for the doorknob. They look at each other. Matt grins broadly.

"Stop by anytime—don't even call first."

Damon laughs.

"I will—love open doors."

He glances at Matt's erect penis straining against the confines of his tight boxer briefs. They kiss again briefly.

"I'll stop by tomorrow—around ten."

Matt nods and closes the door.

Peabody Avenue

Shirley is walking aimlessly along the sidewalk when she hears a honk and sees Lance driving by. He slows down and grins as she turns to look at him. She seems upset and ignores him.

"What's wrong?"

Shirley gives Lance a harsh look.

"Like you didn't know—you men are all the same."

Lance seems confused.

"Did I miss something?"

Shirley reacts.

"You told—told that toad about you and me."

Lance looks at Shirley curiously.

"Told what—who did I tell?"

Shirley sighs.

"You promised you'd never tell?"

She sighs loudly.

"You told Corey about what happened between you and me three months ago at the costume party—and now he's holding it over me—demanding I play by his rules or else."

Lance laughs.

"Oh that."

Shirley stops and faces Lance.

Page **632**

"Corey is no good—he'll tell—he pretty much told me that he plans to tell Jeremy the first chance he feels like it."

Lance sighs loudly.

"I'll talk to him—he'll listen to me."

Shirley rolls her eyes.

"Sure he will—just leave me alone OK—get lost."

She turns away.

<u>Blankenship Apartment</u>

Clay opens the door to his apartment and closes it as Maxwell enters behind him. The apartment is eerily silent.

"Eva's probably out shopping."

Maxwell walks toward the kitchen.

"Man, this town has more drama than that old TV show *Savannah*—no matter where I look something is happening."

Clay laughs nervously.

"Tell me about it—small towns and tawdry drama."

He walks over to the sink.

"I'm not sure when anyone finds time to work—so much time is spent just minding what other people are doing."

Maxwell laughs.

"Do you think Howard Madison knows about Anderson's relationship with Gina Bentley's mother? It would be quite an explosive situation if he had the scoop on that sinking ship."

Clay turns and faces Maxwell.

"Not sure—but from what I've heard that old man knows everything that happens in town—and uses it accordingly."

Maxwell looks at his cell phone briefly.

"What's your read on Madison—is he as bad as everyone else seems to think? Town positively hates his family."

Clay shakes his head.

"There's always truth to every rumor and there's not been one person I've encountered yet in Marble Hills that thinks highly of the Madison family—especially Howard Madison."

Maxwell sighs.

Page 633

"Thinks he's behind McKinley skipping town?"

Clay turns to face Maxwell.

"Could be—but proving it—well, that isn't as easy as it might seem—especially when it comes to who knows what."

They hear the front door opening and see Eva Harper closing the door behind her. Clay smiles broadly.

Port Clyde

Daryl looks over at Caroline's naked body and then at the gun on the dashboard nearby. Caroline sighs loudly.

"Don't you go after Madison—just leave it be OK?"

"The hell I will—that old coot needs to learn a lesson—and I'm just the man for the job—got to snuff his lights out."

Caroline reaches out to touch Daryl's hand.

"No—let it go—*please*?"

Daryl turns to face Caroline.

Portland

Denise sighs as she looks at Glen again as he walks her to the door. He smirks as she looks at him. She seems upset.

"Oh so terrible about Kevin—a random shooting took him out—he had so much to live for and now he's—he's dead."

Glen laughs.

"Worm food—we all got to go sometime."

Denise seems upset.

"It's not funny—he was sweet."

"I didn't say it was—but he's dead—so what—life is for the living—forget about him already and think about us."

Denise sighs loudly.

"Think he knew his killer?"

Glen shrugs.

"Maybe—maybe not—who the fuck cares—he's a stiff in the morgue with a bullet in his head—end of story."

He laughs again.

Eva looks at the curious glances on Clay's and Maxwell's faces as she notices their odd behavior. They grin broadly.

"OK—OK—what are the two of you up to?"

They shrug.

"Uh-huh—yeah—I know those sly looks—but I'm on to both of you just so you know—and I'll be watching closely."

Clay grabs Eva and kisses her.

"You know nothing—nothing at all."

He kisses her again.

"So, where did you go earlier?"

Eva glances at Maxwell.

"Boston—met with the official at the church I told you about—wanted to check things out—before things."

Clay nods.

"Right—so how did it go?"

Eva smiles broadly.

"Great—classic New England look."

Maxwell rolls his eyes.

"Are you sure you want to marry this idiot—I mean—he's high maintenance—can't do much to save his life."

Eva nods.

"Uh-huh—I want to—one hundred percent."

Clay gives Maxwell a knowing look.

"You better watch your step good buddy or else."

Clay turns to look at Eva and smirks.

"He's just jealous because I've got you snookered and he still can't tie his shoes worth a damn—such a total loser."

Maxwell suddenly grabs Clay and shoves him against the sofa and pretends to strangle him as Eva seems amused.

"I see I need to teach you a lesson on being a jerk—I swear on everything you and me will spill blood soon enough."

Clay laughs.

"You can't tie your shoes—total loser."

Maxwell pretends to be upset as he continues to tighten his grip around Clay's neck. Clay continues to laugh.

"I want you dead—do you hear me—dead—and then I won't have to put up with your jabs—say your prayers."

They begin laughing.

"What prayers?"

They look at each and begin laughing louder as Maxwell jerks Clay upright on the sofa and straightens out his shirt.

"He started it—so juvenile."

"It was you and your insults that caused my slip of hand."

Eva looks at Clay and Maxwell sitting on the sofa with grins on their faces. She points a finger at Clay and smirks.

"If this was for real how would I explain your death to the church people—they would be so mad—no wedding."

"They would be upset they weren't getting paid—not that I was no longer among the living. Church people are greedy."

Eva rolls her eyes.

"How did work go today?"

Clay looks over to Maxwell.

"The McKinley kid—the one who offed his girlfriend has skipped town—we think he had help—question is who?"

"Who from Marble Hills would help a teenage murderer skip town—especially after he killed one of their own?"

"That's the question of the day."

Eva seems confused.

"Is his parents in on the deal? Do they know?"

Clay and Maxwell look at each other.

"We think he had help from someone with money."

Maxwell sighs loudly and jabs Clay.

"Howard Madison comes to mind right away."

Eva reacts and sighs. Clay shoots Maxwell a look.

<u>Glass Owl</u>

Howard is sitting in his library talking on his cell phone. He seems irritated more than usual as he yells loudly.

Page 636

"Look, just get it done Ryerson—damn it—how many times do I have to say it—what the hell am I paying you for if you can't get what you promised me you could? I want results or I'll find someone else. I want results by tomorrow—no later."

He looks at the cell phone.

"I swear—if I hear one more excuse from you."

He clenches his fist.

"I'm done with your whining."

He shuts the cell phone off.

"Morons—why do I always seem to hire morons?"

He turns to face the shelves of books behind him and sighs loudly. Howard briefly scans the titles with his eyes.

"If only things weren't always so damn complicated."

He stops suddenly and sighs.

"I'm through with waiting for answers."

Suddenly the door to the library opens. Howard turns to see Daryl standing in the doorway with a gun in his hand.

TO BE CONTINUED

A Look at the 25th Episode

Howard and Daryl's encounter has unexpected results for both men—Lance and Corey argue about Shirley—Damon scores with Carter on the sly—Eva and Maxwell talk about Clay—Kyle confronts his father about Daryl—Justin and Faye plot to destroy Juan's relationship with Sabrina—Lisa casually hooks up with Corey to get over another—Glen plans diabolical revenge against a deadly foe—Carrie Spaulding is laid to rest with her friends in attendance—Alden, Eddie and Todd offer support to Julia at the diner on her first day back to work—Gary's plan to fool Kyle continues to play out successfully in Marble Hills—Ashton has an unexpected encounter with a stranger which could change his life in ways he never imagined—as Wesley, Alden, Eddie, and Todd look for evidence at the cemetery concerning Blake Madison.

Cry for the Strangers

<u>Glass Owl</u>

Howard Madison glances at Daryl Anderson with a look of contempt. Daryl smiles broadly. He shuts the door behind him and confidently walks toward where Howard is standing.

"End of the road old man—today you die—die at my hands—seems fitting don't you think after our history."

"Put down that gun before you hurt yourself."

Daryl grins broadly.

"Seems you should be saying that about yourself—not for me—this is it—there's no place to run—you're finished."

Daryl laughs loudly.

"This town will throw me a parade when all is said and done—your death will be heralded as a yearly holiday."

"You really don't know much."

Before Daryl can blink Howard lunges toward him.

"Oh yeah—I love surprises."

They fall against the desk and as Daryl tries to regain his stance Howard grabs the gun from him and laughs gleefully.

"Uh-huh—who's the fool now?"

Daryl glances at Howard as the old man slyly looks at the gun held firmly in his hands. He turns to face Daryl again.

"How things change—so quickly."

He grins broadly.

"Your father was a fool—caused me problems by the hundreds—but in the end—an accident—oh-oh—maybe it wasn't such an accident after all—took care of itself wonderfully."

Daryl seems confused.

"Nothing is ever what it seems—is it?"

Howard laughs in triumph.

"Uh-huh—things are never what they seem—and when they find your body—well—I'll tell them you came in here threatening to kill me and there was a mad struggle—*and*—then you suffered a fatal gunshot—from your own gun—oops."

Daryl watches as Howard points the gun at him and slowly brings it down against his chest—directly over his heart.

"I wish I could say it's been nice—but I can't."

Howard pulls the trigger as Daryl helplessly stands there for a few seconds—almost as if in a trance refusing to believe his luck has turned so drastically as a single bullet viciously rips through his chest piercing his heart—killing him instantly.

"Like father like son."

Howard begins laughing hysterically.

<u>Bentley Driveway</u>

Corey Bentley watches as Lance Weissmann pulls up in his car. He seems a bit irritated. They look at each other briefly.

"OK—what couldn't wait until tomorrow?"

Lance sighs.

"Shirley Moses is upset."

Corey rolls his eyes.

"So?"

Lance gets out of his car.

"She said you threatened her?"

Corey laughs.

Page 640

"Big deal—she's nothing but a cheap whore—bet she didn't tell you that she and I—you know—had a moment."

He laughs again.

"She was so easy—no objections."

Corey smirks.

"Seriously—she's a nice piece of ass—don't know why you stopped sticking her—everyone in town has banged her."

Lance grabs Corey by the arm.

"She's with my brother now."

Corey pulls away from Lance's grip.

"No—your brother thinks she's with him—but, well, let's face it—once a whore always a whore—seriously she'll do anyone who makes a play—yep, she knows how to blow nicely."

Corey laughs loudly.

"Now—if you don't mind I have a date."

Lance watches as Corey heads up the driveway to his home. He sighs loudly and turns to face his car blankly.

<u>Lighthouse Grill</u>

Faye Washington grins broadly as Justin Wellington sits down opposite her. He seems confused as he tries to figure out what is happening. Justin wrings his hands nervously.

"Who the hell are you and how do you know me?"

Faye rolls her eyes.

"Your girlfriend is in way over her head."

Justin sighs loudly.

"Former girlfriend—she's been seeing some dude—we had a thing going for a while—but now we're finished—over."

Faye rolls her eyes again.

"I get it—she's being banged by another guy—he's using her—she means absolutely nothing to him—nothing at all."

Justin clenches his fists angrily.

"She didn't admit it actually—just made it very clear to me it was none of my business right before she dumped me."

Faye reaches over and touches Justin's hand.

Page 641

"Her new guy is my boyfriend."

Justin pulls his hand away.

"*Oh*—I'm sorry."

Faye makes a lewd gesture with her finger.

"I don't like having my man sticking his dick into some two-bit whore from a zero town—not at all—disgusting."

"Sabrina isn't a whore."

Faye waves her hand in front of Justin's face.

"Please—want me to act like she's a nice girl—your cheap slut ex-girlfriend is sleeping with my boyfriend—shameless."

Justin clenches his fist again.

"I could kill him with my bare hands."

"Uh-huh—I can see that happening—but how about we think up some way to split them up rather than kill. I'm sort of partial to his dick—and want him alive rather than dead."

Justin seems annoyed.

"But he slept with my girl?"

Faye turns away.

<u>Pike's Bar</u>

Damon Mayo scopes out the scene in front of him. His eyes immediately fall upon a man sitting nearby with bulging biceps and tight leather pants. He seductively licks his lips.

"Uh-huh—sweet—love a punctual guy."

He walks over to the young man. He smirks as he clears his throat. Carter Boone looks up and smiles broadly.

"Didn't think you'd actually come?"

Damon makes a lewd gesture with his finger.

"You and I have unfinished business to attend to—you still owe me a ride from last week—a really intense ride actually."

Carter motions for Damon to sit down.

"What about your girlfriend?"

"I don't have a girlfriend—no need for one."

Carter seems confused.

"But she seems to think so?"

Page **642**

"It isn't my fault if she thinks I'm her boyfriend."

He laughs loudly.

"Would you and I have done what we did a week ago in your loft if I had an annoying girlfriend to worry about?"

Carter grins.

"I guess not—my bad."

Damon reaches over to kiss Carter on the lips.

"How about you and I hang at the Tolling Bell Inn—where we can get even better acquainted—say, fifteen minutes? Your loft is—well—just too crowded with your jealous boyfriend giving me a lecture on safe sex—don't need such useless drama."

Carter grins again.

"I'm there—and I agree with you—Lane is a bore—got to break up with him before he drives me totally bonkers."

Damon kisses Carter again.

Blankenship Apartment

Eva Harper looks at Maxwell Pendergraft as he grabs a stick of celery while she prepares a pizza and shoves it into the oven. She turns to look at Maxwell again with a sly grin.

"I'm glad you and Clay are close friends—he needs you in his life. You're the brother he never had but always wanted."

Maxwell smirks.

"He's a good guy—couldn't ask for a better friend—and I do think of him like a brother—especially when we fight."

Eva pulls Maxwell toward her and they hug warmly for a few minutes. They look at each other. Eva smiles broadly.

"Thank you."

They look at each other.

"Well, I'm glad he hooked up with you—I know you love him and he needs that in his life—someone who cares."

Eva squeezes Maxwell's hand.

"I couldn't help myself—from the moment I saw him clumsily tripping over himself I knew he was definitely husband material. I like a guy that has a clumsy side to his character."

They look at each other again and hug warmly. At that moment Clay Blankenship comes out of the bathroom clad only in a towel tied around his waist. He looks at Eva and Maxwell curiously and walks toward them cautiously. He sighs.

"What's going on—what did I miss?"

Maxwell grins and winks at Eva. They embrace again.

"I'm stealing your girl—yep I am."

Clay seems confused.

"Uh-huh—Eva and I are going to skip town together and have a whole bunch of kids—maybe ten or twelve."

Clay begins to laugh.

"Yeah—like that could happen—good try though."

Eva and Maxwell look at each other and begin laughing. Clay watches as Maxwell wags his finger and shoves him.

"Didn't buy it one bit did you?"

Clay smirks.

"No way—you're my bro—you'd never do something like that—you and I—we've got too much history between us."

He pulls Eva toward him.

"Besides I know Eva is seriously hung up on me."

Eva looks at Clay.

"Pretty sure about yourself—aren't you?"

Clay nods as Eva kisses him lightly.

"Well, OK—it's true—I'm totally hung up on you."

Clay grins broadly.

"Your mother confirmed it."

Eva kisses Clay again.

"My mother has a big mouth."

Clay grins and they begin kissing again—this time more passionately as Maxwell rolls his eyes in mock disdain as he pretends to be disgusted by what he's watching. He yawns.

"Oh please—cut it out you two—enough with the mushy stuff—I think I'm going to puke chunks—really disgusting."

Clay reaches out and shoves Maxwell.

"It's terrible that you're such a jealous loser."

Maxwell shakes his fist and smirks.

"I think I liked you better when you were a lonely pathetic dweeb who had no game—or a date for Saturday night."

Clay laughs loudly.

"Things change—deal with it."

He kisses Eva again.

<u>Glass Owl</u>

Kyle Madison pulls into the driveway and sees a coroner's van driving away. He seems shocked as he sees Will McColl about to get into his patrol car. He suddenly stops and faces Kyle.

"What happened?"

Will looks back at the mansion.

"Daryl Anderson is dead."

Kyle seems in shock.

"What?"

Kyle looks up at Glass Owl.

"How the hell did that happen?"

Will shakes his head as he faces Kyle again.

"Don't know for sure—according to your father there was a struggle and—Anderson was fatally shot somehow."

Kyle sighs loudly.

"This isn't making sense at all—what was Anderson doing here in the first place—my father fired him earlier?"

Will shrugs and glances at his watch.

"I think he came by looking to get his job back and then somehow he threatened your dad with a gun and they struggled for it at some point and—and then he was shot and killed soon after—that's all I have now—no witnesses to what happened."

Kyle sighs again.

"So, it's my dad's word all the way?"

They look at each other as Will nods in agreement. He looks back at Glass Owl. He seems bothered by something.

"I guess so—not much there other than what he says happened earlier—but he seemed pretty lucid about it all."

Kyle looks at the house again.

Page 645

"The case is closed?"

Will nods as he looks at his watch again.

"I'd say so—unless someone saw otherwise?"

Kyle gives Will a strange look and then runs toward the entrance of Glass Owl in a rush. He seems panicked.

Standish Road

Denise Madison is driving back toward Marble Hills when the news of Daryl Anderson's tragic death blares out at her from the radio in her car. She seems in shock at hearing the news.

"Daryl—not Daryl—this is all—*his* fault."

She pulls over at the side of the road.

"My God—he did it—he actually did it—killed Daryl in cold blood just like he said he would last year—oh God—it's true."

She begins to sob loudly.

"This—this just can't be real—Daryl can't be dead—he and I had such—oh—I'm going to miss him—oh God—so sweet."

She looks around.

"*He* isn't going to get away with it—this time he's gone too far—and now someone must do—must make it right."

She grabs her cell phone and begins dialing.

Lighthouse Grill

Justin sighs loudly as he stands up. He turns to look at Faye curiously. She seems not to notice his odd stare.

"I don't see why you'd want a guy that sleeps around on the sly—in my book that makes him a dog—garbage."

Faye smirks.

"But he's my dog—one who knows how to fuck. He makes me feel alive—never wants to play by the rules—rebellious."

She stands up and looks at him curiously.

"Now, don't you do anything stupid—wait for my signal and then do what I say—right down to the last minute."

She winks at Justin as he nods.

Page **646**

"I always get what I want—and Juan is mine. He's all mine for the taking—and no bitch whore is going to best me."
Justin seems upset at the comment.
"Sabrina isn't like that—she isn't a whore."
Faye rolls her eyes.
"Yeah—just keep telling yourself that."
They head to the door together.
"I'll call you tomorrow."
He nods several times and turns away.

<u>Weissmann Driveway</u>

Lance jumps out of his car and sees his brother sitting outside their house on a bench. He seems visibly upset.
"What's up?"
Jeremy Weissmann looks up. He sighs.
"It's Shirley."
He wipes sweat from his brow.
"Shirley is really upset about something. Whatever it is she seems ready to snap—but she wouldn't say why."
Lance shrugs.
"So?"
Jeremy stands up.
"Can you talk to her? Find out?"
Lance seems confused.

<u>Sea View Terrace</u>

Lisa Taylor looks at Corey curiously. He smirks as she notices his behavior as he slides closer to her in the booth.
"You're being awfully nice to me?"
Corey grins slyly as he strokes her hair.
"Can't a guy be nice?"
Lisa rolls her eyes.
"Well—given the fact that I dumped you for Damon Mayo last year I thought—you know—you might—still be angry."

Page 647

Corey waves his hand in the air.

"Old news—besides Mayo was all wrong for you—like he has a girlfriend—and seriously, he's old—really ancient."

Lisa laughs.

"He's not old—he's thirty-two."

Corey rolls his eyes.

"Anyone over twenty-five is old—outfit the geezer for a rocking chair—besides like what could he do with his dick that I couldn't—like seriously, like tell me Lisa—I'm all ears."

Lisa seems bored with Corey's comment.

"You wouldn't understand."

Corey laughs.

"Uh-huh—like try me already."

Lisa wipes a tear from her eye as Corey smirks.

"I still can't believe he cut me loose—we had something special—he promised he'd dump Amanda this summer."

Corey winks at Lisa.

"Guys always say that—like how many times did I promise you I'd be faithful after we fucked—and how many times did you find out I lied after the fact—sometimes the same day—like every time—and then some—it's a guy thing—like deal already."

"Not every guy is a pig like you."

Corey grins slyly.

"Tell me who in Marble Hills isn't?"

Lisa looks around.

"Ashton Markway."

Corey makes a lewd gesture with his finger and pretends to vomit. He glances at the entrance of the restaurant.

"Yuk—he's a dweeb—I asked you about a real guy—that loser has never gotten laid—nothing but a pathetic geek."

He makes another lewd gesture with his finger.

<u>Glass Owl</u>

"You killed him in cold blood—didn't you?"

Howard turns to face Kyle.

Page **648**

"He tried to kill me—there was a struggle—the fool got himself shot—it's not like he didn't—his dad and all."

Kyle walks closer to where his father is sitting on the sofa with a drink in his hand. The old man seems quite relaxed.

"I know—OK—I know you did it on purpose—you wanted him out of the way for good—to make sure your secrets never got out—and now you play this game of innocent ignorance?"

Howard throws the glass in his hands toward the fireplace. It instantly smashes into thousands of pieces.

"Look boy—you better know your place here—I won't tolerate you speaking to me like I'm nothing—no way."

Kyle sighs loudly.

"Seems to me Stanley Anderson died at your hands too if I recall—though no one ever figured it out—except me."

Howard stands up.

"Enough already boy—be gone from my sight."

Before Kyle can react Howard lunges at him and grabs Kyle by the throat without warning. He seems enraged.

"I'll break your neck boy—don't think I wouldn't do it."

They look at each other.

"Not one more word—or I swear I'll—end you."

He angrily shoves Kyle against the bookcase and leaves the room—slamming the door behind him. Kyle turns around to look at the shattered glass lying everywhere at the fireplace.

"Has everyone been right about him all along?"

He rubs his neck for several seconds.

<u>Tolling Bell Inn</u>

Carter grins broadly as Damon swallows a swig of beer and winks. He leers at Carter and gestures with his finger.

"I don't like your boyfriend."

Carter shakes his head.

"He asked me to marry him last week—bought a ring and everything—said I was the best thing that ever happened to him since he came out to his family—wants to adopt a baby."

Page 649

Damon gestures with his hand.

"You're not going to—are you? Like he would kill your sex drive in ten seconds flat? He's as much fun as a wet dishrag."

Carter smirks again as Damon leans over and kisses him on the lips. They kiss again more passionately. Damon glances at the bed a few feet away. He winks at Carter and nods.

<u>Portland</u>

Glen Bradstreet walks back and forth as he talks on his cell phone. He sighs several times and seems irritated.

"Yeah—yeah—I think you're right about—the question is how—how to do it and make it look like a tragic accident."

He stops and nods several times.

"Uh-huh—I'll let you know tomorrow."

He shuts off the cell phone.

The Next Day

<u>Crestview Memorial Park Cemetery</u>

Archie Spaulding watches as the casket bearing his daughter's remains is slid into an open crypt. As it is pushed inside he notices Wesley Madison, Kelly Nelson, Abby Marshall, Simon Spencer, Genie Van Pelt, Elizabeth Pendleton, Ashton Markway, and Tyler Van Pelt among the mourners. He sighs loudly as the door to the crypt is placed over the opening and sealed. He turns away and immediately faces everyone.

"Thank you all for coming."

Everyone nods and watches as Archie stops in front of the crypt of his wife a few feet away. His grief is noticeable.

<u>Pete's Cafe</u>

Julia Winthrop unlocks the door to the diner and enters. Eddie Kane and Todd Spencer follow. Julia sighs.

Page **650**

"Guys—I'm OK. Really—I am—I don't need you screwing over your busy plans for today to babysit me—I'm OK."

"I took today off—I answer only to myself."

Eddie jabs Todd in the ribs.

"Who are you fooling—you gave orders to everyone at the docks and then rushed over here. In ten minutes flat."

Todd pushes Eddie.

"And what about you—last I heard your office staff can't remember what you look like? Or if you still exist?"

Julia faces Eddie and Todd with a smile.

"I'm surprised that Alden hasn't stopped by yet with some lame excuse too—the three of you are like peas in a pod."

At that moment Alden Washington slowly pops his head through the front door. He seems unsure if he should enter.

"Just thought I'd come by."

Julia shoots Eddie and Todd a glance.

"I'm fine."

Alden closes the door behind him. He looks at Eddie and Todd curiously. They grin broadly as they look over at Julia.

"Thought you two said you'd be busy?"

"We lied."

Todd pushes Eddie again.

"He lied—I didn't."

Julia rolls her eyes as she looks at each of them.

"Uh-huh—like I believe that line."

She stops suddenly and faces them again.

"I think I can handle it from here."

She looks around.

"Really—I'm fine—no worries."

She gestures at them.

<u>Police Station</u>

Will looks at the photos of Daryl Anderson's body taken by the coroner. He sighs and glances at Clay and Maxwell. They shake their heads in disbelief. Will slowly turns away.

Page 651

"I guess this case is closed."
Clay and Maxwell share a glance.
"It's the word of a dead man against one that is still alive presently—one that is very rich—and quite ruthless to boot."
Clay nods in agreement.
"The rumors have already begun."
Will walks over to the filing cabinet a few feet away.
"I know—life in a small town."
Clay and Maxwell look at each other.

Portland

Denise nervously looks at Glen as he opens the door. She walks past him in a rush. He closes the door behind her.

"I did some checking after you called yesterday afternoon and I don't have to tell you—your father-in-law is not exactly a nice man—even I with my extensive record couldn't compete."

Denise rolls her eyes.

"I want him to pay for what he did."

She sits down.

"I know he viciously killed Daryl in cold blood—he needs to be taught a fucking lesson—preferably with his life."

"So, you want to off the old man—an eye for an eye?"

Denise nods.

"Exactly—lots of pain—but dead in the end."

Glen smiles broadly.

"OK—I just wasn't sure from our previous talk that this route is the one you wanted to pursue with the old man."

Denise wipes a tear from her eye.

"I want him dead—a stiff in the morgue."

She wipes another tear from her eye.

"Look, Daryl wasn't a saint—he whored his way through women without guilt—his played everyone in Marble Hills."

She faces Glen.

"But he didn't deserve to die."

Glen sits down next to Denise and holds her hand.

Page **652**

"I'm game—knocking off Howard Madison won't bother me one bit—especially if the price is right—and it will be."

He grins broadly.

"But how about you and I head to the bedroom—you know—to work some frustrations out before we scheme?"

Denise smirks.

"Thinking with your dick as usual I presume?"

Glen nods and points to the bedroom.

Crestview Memorial Park Cemetery

A long procession of cars follows each other out of the cemetery. At the walled crypts Archie places his hand over the blank marble covering his daughter's crypt. He sighs.

"That bastard took you away from me—but he got what he deserved. No one will ever know what I did to him."

"No one will ever know what?"

Archie turns to see Kyle standing a few yards away at the iron gates that lead into the private area lined with walled crypts. He curiously looks at Kyle for a few seconds and then shakes his head. He slowly walks towards where Kyle is standing.

"No one will ever know how much I loved Carrie."

Kyle nods and looks around at the crypts lining the wall from both sides. He sighs as he turns back to face Archie.

"Archie, we have to talk."

Archie looks at Kyle curiously.

"Can't you see I just buried my daughter?"

Kyle takes a step closer.

"I'm sorry—but this can't wait one minute longer—there are things happening—terrible things. I need advice."

Archie gives Kyle a nasty look.

Tolling Bell Inn

Gary Glick looks at the paperwork in front of him. He smiles broadly as he flips through it again cautiously.

"Flawless."

He closes the folder.

"Kyle will never know the difference between a fake and the real thing—and unless Serena shows up this plan is going to score me millions of Madison dollars—oh yeah—*sweet*."

Patrick Glick closes the door behind him and notices Gary putting a folder in a briefcase. They look at each other.

"So, how is the certificate you had Silas dummy up for you? How is he anyway? Is he in Sydney at the moment?"

Gary turns to face his brother.

"Silas Bell knows his stuff—even I'm fooled by how real it looks to the naked eye—and yeah he's still in Sydney. He and his wife are still on the outs though—reality is terribly harsh."

Patrick seems upset.

<u>Los Angeles</u>

Jeffrey Webber nervously looks at the contract in his hands as he faces his assistant Bruce Mansfield. He sighs.

"Think he'll go for it—you know, come back?"

"Of course—why wouldn't he—it isn't like he's worked since—in fact I hear he recently went back to that dinky little town where he grew up—somewhere in Maine if I recall."

Jeffrey sighs loudly.

"Ratings are down—having him return will create interest and well—this is a soap opera—dead characters come back from the dead all the time—especially when no one expects it."

Bruce smirks.

"Exactly—think *Dallas*."

Jeffrey leans forward.

"Did you talk to Diane Schuster already?"

Bruce nods.

"Uh-huh—she's OK with him coming back to work—they were over long before he left—besides, she just married that producer guy who makes those spy movies for cable."

Jeffrey looks at the contract again.

"OK—sounds like all our ducks are in a row. How are you with flying out tonight from LAX? I could book a seat?"

Bruce reacts.

"You want me to go get him?"

Jeffrey nods.

"If you have a better plan—I'm game."

Bruce sighs.

"What about his manager?"

"Fired—pink slipped two months ago."

They look at each other.

"OK. OK. I guess I can make it through a few days in dullsville in the middle of nowhere—oh God shoot me now."

Jeffrey smiles broadly.

"I'll call the airport."

"You owe me."

Jeffrey nods and wags his finger.

<u>Lighthouse Grill</u>

Genie looks at the can of soda in front of her with a straw sticking out from the opening. She seems really irritated.

"Damn him."

She sighs.

"How dare he call me a whore?"

"If the shoe fits wear it."

She turns to see Corey grinning at her. He smirks.

"Go away."

He laughs.

"Oh-oh—miss high and mighty thinks she's all that—but wait—oops she's not—just someone who thinks more of herself than she really is—but I'm just the right guy to remedy that."

Genie rolls her eyes.

"Leave me alone OK?"

Corey grins.

"Nope—don't think I can—you and I have a date with the backseat of my car—like right now if I recall—and I do."

Page 655

Genie turns away.

"I'm not in the mood."

Corey makes a lewd gesture with his finger.

"And what—do you think I care—like have you forgotten who I am—I'm the guy who makes your life possible—without someone like me you'd be just another unpopular girl wishing she had friends in Marble Hills—which if you recall you didn't."

Genie notices Corey's erection swelling under his faded Levi's as he grins while noticing her obvious discomfort.

"Uh-huh—you and I are going to my car—where I plan to get to know your vagina even better than I already do."

Genie seems upset.

"I hate you."

She notices Corey rolling his eyes.

"Carrie Spaulding was just laid to rest earlier—and then there's what happened to Jason's dad. I'm not in the mood."

Corey rolls his eyes again.

"Like I care about Carrie—she was a bitch—good riddance to her—and as for Jason's pop—he was nothing to me."

Genie looks at the can of soda again.

"Troll."

Corey angrily grabs Genie by the arm.

"I'm losing patience with your pathetic dribble."

They leave the diner together.

<u>Peabody Avenue</u>

Ashton is mindlessly walking along the sidewalk talking on his cell phone when he accidentally bumps into a woman taking photographs of the area a few feet away. He stops suddenly.

"Excuse me."

Joan Martinelli seems in shock as she looks at him curiously for a few seconds. Ashton looks at his cell phone.

"I'll call you back."

He shuts off his cell phone.

"Are you OK?"

Page 656

Joan gives him another strange look and smiles.

"Have you ever done print?"

Ashton gives Joan a curious look.

"Print what?"

Joan laughs.

"Catalog work?"

Ashton looks around as if looking for something.

"OK—game over—where's the hidden camera—tell Corey Bentley to shove it—him and his sick jokes—not funny."

Joan shakes her head.

"I don't know anyone named Corey."

"Uh-huh—whatever—I'm not playing his fucked-up game. Tell that sick freak to go find some other chump to bother."

Joan extends her hand.

"I think we got off on the wrong foot. My name is Joan Martinelli—I'm a freelance fashion photographer. I photograph print models for glamour catalogs all around the world."

"Yeah, right—good one—tell that sick prick he can go screw himself if he thinks I'll fall for one of his hate games."

Joan looks around.

"I have no clue what you're referring to—I'm in town to take a few photos for *People*—seems there's possibly going to be a remake of *Peyton Place* and so I'm here to shoot some street scenes—sort of to get a feeling of small town America."

Ashton looks at Joan oddly.

"Huh? Why would anyone want to remake the old **Lana Turner** version—it's a classic—there's nothing wrong with it."

Joan shrugs.

"I only take photos—I don't make movies."

He watches as she pulls out a business card and hands it to him. He eyes her suspiciously as she continues looking at him as if he reminds her of someone else. He seems uneasy as she circles him again. He turns around as she suddenly stops and smiles.

"Has anyone ever told you that you look a lot like an actor named **David Andrew Gregory** from the old soap opera *One Life to Live*? Uh-huh—with the right haircut you could be his son."

Page **657**

Ashton gestures with his hand.

"I don't watch daytime TV—don't know the dude."

Joan turns around to look at her car.

"Would you mind if I photographed you?"

Ashton seems uneasy.

"Photograph me? Why?"

Joan sighs loudly.

"I think you have a certain look—one that might—might be perfect for what I need for an upcoming university shoot."

Ashton looks around again.

"Are you sure this isn't some sort of joke?"

Joan shakes her head.

"How about you meet me later today at this address on Maple Avenue—I've rented out an office—planning to spend several weeks here in your quaint little town. I'm on the level about this—never been my style to play games. Besides I have an eye for talent—and I think with a haircut and contact lenses you can make for quite a stylish print model all over Europe."

Ashton looks once more at the business card in his hand and faces Joan again. He sighs loudly still confused.

"OK—but I'm not going to take my clothes off. I have a strict rule against getting naked in front of a camera—cell phone or otherwise. Not my style at all—kinda shy if truth be told."

Joan laughs with a knowing look.

"I'm not a perv—got a teenage son myself—he's about your age—and besides I'm happily married—like really."

Ashton grins.

"OK—OK—this might be fun actually."

He flips the card over in his hand.

<u>Mall</u>

Kelly glances at Simon as they sit at one of the benches not far away from the ice cream kiosk. He looks around.

"So, how's Jason taking it?"

Simon shrugs.

Page 658

"I'm not sure—he and his dad weren't close."
Kelly sighs.
"Think it was an accident?"
Simon faces Kelly with a puzzled look.
"No way—old man Madison is one sick puppy—the whole town hates him and his family—with really good reason."
"But if he killed?"
Simon mockingly rolls his eyes.
"Doesn't matter—he's not going down for it—he's got every judge in Maine in his pocket—corrupt bastards."
Kelly glances at his watch.
"He has to pay for what he did?"
Simon turns to face Kelly.
"No one is going to go up against old man Madison if that's what you're asking—the man is a royal whack job."
"But someone needs to do something? He just can't get away with what he did. Justice must be served regardless."
"Doesn't matter—the case is closed already."
They look at each other.
"I've been hearing rumors around town."
Simon laughs.
"In Marble Hills—oh what a shock—like really?"
Kelly rolls his eyes and ignores Simon's caustic jab.
"I'm serious—people are saying that Wesley's grandfather also killed Jason's grandfather years ago—made it look like an accident almost exactly the same way Jason's dad got iced."
"I heard all the stories too—but no one will ever stand up to old man Madison—if they did they know what he'd do."
They look at each other again.

<u>Parking Lot</u>

Corey grins as he slips on his boxer briefs and grabs his Levi's. He zips up and looks at Genie still lying on the backseat of his car. She seems upset as she stares at him. He sighs.
"Well, let's go already."

Page **659**

Genie rolls her eyes as she begins putting her clothes on seemingly upset at Corey's comment. He smirks slyly.

"Stop treating me like I'm a whore."

Corey laughs loudly.

"You *are* a whore—banged by every horny guy in Marble Hills looking for a good time. You've outdone yourself when it comes to making sure the traffic between your legs was more traveled than any other girl in town—you even beat Shirley."

Genie seems about to cry.

"Why are you always so nasty to me?"

She sighs loudly. Corey reacts.

"I've always been nice to you. When have I ever been mean to you? I always treat you fairly. But facts are facts—you're a whore and everyone in town knows that you put out a lot. "

Corey smirks.

"I'm just stating facts."

He laughs again.

"You've been with every guy in town practically—with the exception of Ashton Markway and probably Kelly Nelson."

He rolls his eyes.

"I'm sure Kelly would take a tumble if you ask."

He laughs.

"Of course Abby would freak."

He makes a lewd gesture with his finger.

"She'd probably try to kill you."

He notices Genie wiping a tear from her eye and points at her knowing she's on the verge of crying. Corey smirks.

"Think of it this way—when you go to college next year you'll be quite the favorite around campus—every guy will want a piece—especially the ones with frigid girlfriends. They'll definitely want to get to know you better—learn tricks from you."

He makes a lewd gesture with his finger again.

"Face it Genie—you're nothing more than something to be passed around to every horny guy that needs to get laid."

He laughs as she begins to cry.

<u>Pete's Cafe</u>

Alden is talking to Julia, Eddie and Todd when Wesley enters the diner. They turn around to look at him as he walks toward them with a curious look on his face which they notice and acknowledge immediately. Wesley sighs loudly.

"I guess you guys all heard?"

They nod.

"I think he did it. There's just no other way to think of it except as a murder—Jason's dad was killed in cold blood."

Eddie reacts and shrugs.

"Yeah, we know—your crummy excuse for a grandfather killed Anderson and then made it look like self-defense."

Wesley sighs again.

"He isn't talking to anyone in the family about it right now—complete shutdown on what happened yesterday."

"I bet he's talking to his lawyers though."

Wesley faces Alden.

"I still want to follow through with our plans."

Alden shrugs.

"Do you want to go now—the cemetery is open—we should be able to find Blake Madison's crypt if it exists."

Eddie and Todd look at each other.

"Count us in—we love trouble."

Alden grins broadly.

"I guess I don't have to ask."

They head to the door without saying anything to Julia as they leave. She watches as they go and seems upset.

"Trouble is on its way no doubt."

She shakes her head.

<u>Mall</u>

Kelly is behind the ice cream kiosk as Simon notices Ashton walking toward them. Ashton seems confused.

"I just had the weirdest encounter."

Page 661

Simon wags his finger at Ashton.

"Let me guess—you were driving out past Standish Road and you got kidnapped by a UFO like **Emma Samms** did decades ago in that old ABC series *The Colbys*? Should I call someone from the *Marble Hills Gazette* to cover the story? I could use a laugh right about now—even if it's at your expense Markway."

Ashton mockingly rolls his eyes.

"I said weird—not a stupid stunt to boost sagging ratings as ABC did way back in the day—which failed by the way."

Ashton jabs Simon.

"This is serious—quit making fun of me."

He turns to face the others.

"Earlier I was walking on Peabody Avenue minding my own business and some lady told me I had the right look."

Simon gestures with his finger.

Crestview Memorial Park Cemetery

Wesley, Alden, Eddie and Todd walk along the walled crypts and stop briefly in front of the crypt for Carrie Spaulding which is banked with wreaths of flowers. Wesley sighs loudly.

"Terrible about what Brad McKinley did to her."

Todd gives Wesley a strange look as he quickly leads the group further into an enclosed courtyard of private crypts.

"Must cost a pretty penny to be buried here?"

Wesley nods several times.

"My folks built this entire wing."

The name MADISON and HOUGHTON is emblazoned in gold letters on the expensive-looking wrought iron gates.

"I shouldn't be doing this—but I—oh fuck it."

He unlocks the gates and leads the group inside. Up ahead—Alden notices the names on the doors of each crypt and stops when he comes to Marah's crypt. Wesley notices.

"It's just a little ways up?"

Alden snaps out of his trance and joins Eddie, Todd and Wesley at Greg's crypt a few feet away. Eddie sighs loudly.

"Greg Madison had quite a ride before things went south for him. Mostly unpleasant from what I remember—never seemed to be able to catch a break despite having money."

Eddie and Todd look at each other.

"Yet another casualty of old man Madison."

Everyone turns to look at Todd.

"Why pretend? We all know it's true."

He sighs loudly.

"Greg could never measure up to his father."

He clenches his fist.

"If only things had been different for Greg I bet he would've turned out to be someone we could all admire."

Wesley walks around in a circle.

"I can't seem to find Blake's crypt anywhere?"

"Bet you anything he's not dead?"

Wesley shoots Eddie a look.

"He has to be."

They begin looking at all the names on the crypts going back to the 1860s. Todd looks at Eddie and smirks.

"Think any of these guys knew **Abraham Lincoln**?"

Eddie shakes his head in disbelief.

"Wouldn't make a difference now—they're nothing more than a pile of dried bones inside very expensive marble."

Alden and Wesley search furiously from one end to the other but find nothing. Wesley seems upset and faces the others with a look of complete defeat on his face. He sighs loudly.

TO BE CONTINUED

About the Series Creator

Gary Brin was born in 1965 and has lived in the United States Virgin Islands, Hawaii and California. He has edited numerous original literary works over the years—both new and revised. In 2019 he established Standish Press to bring forth interesting fictional and historical material usually ignored by mainstream publishers because of specific views or content. In addition to publishing books, he also created the Nancy Hanks Lincoln Public Library (named after the mother of Abraham Lincoln) in 2014 to make available hard-to-find books to a worldwide audience.

Production Notes

Written by Wesley Adams and Daphne McGee
Manuscript edited by Gary Brin
Cover photograph from Wikimedia Commons
Front cover design and interior book layout by Gary Brin
Cover layout by Victoria Valentine
Additional help provided by Carlton J. Young
Series created by Gary Brin

Character List

Daryl Anderson
Jason Anderson
Lori Anderson
Hart Bennington
Lindsay Bennington
Robert Bennington
Susan Bennington
Caroline Bentley
Corey Bentley
Gina Bentley
John Bentley
Diana Bingham
Marilyn Bingham
Clay Blankenship
Glen Bradstreet
Matt Brewster
Drew Brockmeyer
Pierce Colby
Miles Dandridge
Daphne Garfield
Gary Glick
Patrick Glick
Eva Harper
Ross Harrison
Colin Hartley
Lana Jefferson
Tiffany Johnson
Eddie Kane
Jarod Keller
Ben Lincoln
Denise Madison
Greg Madison

Howard Madison
Kyle Madison
Wesley Madison
Bruce Mansfield
Ashton Markway
Donna Markway
Abby Marshall
Corinne Massey
Damon Mayo
Will McColl
Brad McKinley
Grant Monroe
Shirley Moses
Kevin Myers
Kelly Nelson
Maxwell Pendergraft
Elizabeth Pendleton
Duane Pyle
Courtney Robson
Carlo Rogers
Marc Ryerson
Juan Sabrillo
Archie Spaulding
Carrie Spaulding
Amanda Spencer
Heather Spencer
Simon Spencer
Todd Spencer
Natalie Standish
Chandra Stevenson
Sidney Stuyvesant
Lisa Taylor
Andy Tinker
Genie Van Pelt
Tyler Van Pelt
Alden Washington
Faye Washington
Jeffrey Webber

Jeremy Weissmann
Lance Weissmann
Calvin Whitney
Eldon Whitney
Caleb Winthrop
Julia Winthrop
Harper Youngblood
Trevor Youngblood
Grace Zennington

Real People Mentioned

Casey Anthony
Jodi Arias
Hugh Beaumont
Ingrid Bergman
Daniel Boone
Lizzie Borden
Nicole Brown
Michelle Carter
Shaun Cassidy
Johnnie Cochran
Jackie Collins
Robin Cook
Gary Cooper
Bing Crosby
Tony Dow
Ignacio Figueras
Bridget Fonda
Peter Fonda
David Giuntoli
Ron Goldman
Nancy Grace
David Andrew Gregory
Drew Griffin
Ron Howard
Jack the Ripper
Robert Kennedy

Amanda Knox
Carl Laemmle
Peter Lawford
William Levy
Abraham Lincoln
Susan Lucci
Mary, Queen of Scots
Pamela Sue Martin
Kristy McNichol
Grace Metalious
Marilyn Monroe
Brittany Murphy
Timothy Patrick Murphy
Tatum O'Neal
Jackie Onassis
Edgar Allan Poe
Prince Charles
Princess Diana
Norman Rockwell
Kristin Rossum
Emma Samms
O. J. Simpson
Susan Smith
Parker Stevenson
Nick Thoman
Gene Tierney
Thelma Todd
Lana Turner
Robert Wagner
Christopher Walken
Natalie Wood
Aileen Wuornas
Zodiac Killer

For free public domain books please visit
www.nancyhankslincolnpubliclibrary.org